GAD'S HALL
and
THE HAUNTING
OF GAD'S HALL

GAD'S HALL
and
THE HAUNTING
OF
GAD'S HALL

by
Norah Lofts

NELSON DOUBLEDAY, INC.

GARDEN CITY, NEW YORK

Contents

GAD'S HALL

part one

"It is Tudor," Bob said as the house came into full view.

His speech was still hesitant, uninflected; the product of much patient effort by speech-therapists, much dogged perseverance on his part.

But better; but steadily improving.

Driving over weed-greened gravel, between shrubberies of laurel and rhododendron, the flowers now faded and falling, I responded with cultivated garrulity. If one person can keep up a kind of monologue, it makes it easier for the one whose speech is impaired.

But better; but steadily improving.

"Yes," I said. "For once at least partially conforming to description." I had no need to refer to the advertisement, clipped from the Baildon *Daily Press*.

I said, "Quote. Tudor farmhouse. Needs modernisation. 1⅓ acre of garden, partly walled. Secluded position. Unquote."

One of the many wise men had told me never, never to do anything for Bob which he could conceivably manage to do, however slowly or badly, for himself. So, having brought the car to a standstill, I waited while he tried with his flaccid left hand to manipulate the handle on the car door. He failed, but, undeterred, reached over with his right hand, swung the door open and went through the pitiable—but admirable—business of getting himself out. Both legs together from a sideways sitting position; then his stout stick, and finally, there he stood, triumphant. His smile said: There you are, you see. I did it.

The wise man had said that the most important thing of all was the restoration of self-confidence. I understood. Fall off a bicycle or a pony and the only thing to do is to get up and remount. That

way you may eventually ride again. Fall out of life, as Bob had
done—sixteen days of deep coma . . . But he had got up, fearfully
injured, but ready to live again.

So here we were.

While he struggled with the car door, the stick, the slow shuffle
to the house, the huge key of which he had taken possession, and
the business of turning it, I stood back a little and looked at the
house critically. It seemed solid enough, and compared with some
of the places we had seen, it was in good condition; no broken
windows, no obviously sagging roof. Why it should be for sale at
such an absurdly low price, and put on the market in such a curious, almost furtive, manner, mystified me completely.

The brief advertisement had given only a box number at the
paper. Four days later I received a brief communication; typewrit-
ten. It informed me that the house in question was called Gad's
Hall and was in Stonham St Paul's. The key could be obtained
from Park Farm, Stonham St Peter's. And the price was £4,000.
And that, as my mother-in-law remarked, wouldn't buy a decent
bungalow, these days. Ella—that is her name—always gives the
impression of belonging to another age, no specific period, just
some pretty, flowery time of her own; and she professes not to
understand decimal coinage; she still translates pence into shillings; but she is sound where pounds are concerned; and it was
true. Four thousand pounds would not buy a bungalow, decent or
indecent. Bob and I had spent some time viewing cottages that
looked like tumbledown haystacks and one tragic stately home,
twenty bedrooms, not one of them waterproof.

Bob unlocked the door, and then, forgetful of his disability,
pushed and almost overbalanced. Naturally, they had told me, I
must not let him fall on to a fire, but to be too ready with the
helping hand would be a mistake, psychologically. And he righted
himself, grabbed the door post and gave me a triumphant look.
His eyes, these days, were far more expressive than the careful,
acquired speech.

We stood in the hall together. Preparing myself as well as him
I said with false lightness, "I fear the worst. Dry rot, damp rot;
even death-watch beetle."

"No smell," Bob said.

It was true; there were none of the warning smells. The hall was well lighted, a deep-set window on either side of the door. Other doors, one to the right, one to the left. A very solid staircase with shallow treads ran up to a half landing and then turned. At the bottom, and at the turn, the bannister rail broke into carved knobs, each bigger than a pineapple.

Bob said, "No sliding . . . down bannisters." He smiled; I smiled. In his mother's elegant little Georgian house, the bannister was one smooth tempting curve. John, who was ten, had negotiated it safely; then Alice, almost two years younger, must copy, fail to brake in time. No actual harm was done, except to Alice's nose, but Ella's big blue and white Chinese bowl, full of pot-pourri, and the frail-legged table on which it stood had escaped catastrophe by a millimetre. Ella had been very nice about it—she is an extremely nice woman—but next day the table and the bowl had been moved, though I had forbidden sliding down bannisters, with fearsome threats, mayhem the mildest punishment.

That was why Bob and I smiled at each other. The fact that we still could smile seemed to confound people. What had happened to Bob shouldn't have happened to any decent man; but it had happened, and what were we supposed to do? Set ourselves on fire? Go about weeping forever? Ella cried very easily. In fact she once told me that she could hardly look at Bob without wanting to cry. And for that, if for no other reason, I was anxious to get away. Did Gad's Hall offer an escape hatch?

It seemed to do. I detected no sign of damp and decay on the ground floor. The room on the left of the hall gave upon a long drawing room, papered, green and gold arabesques, faded in places, the colours repeated in the tiles of the very Victorian fire-place. The room on the other side was papered too, warm crimson once, now darkened to a kind of liver-colour.

"Good workroom," Bob said, and I agreed. Dear Bob, poor Bob, he hung on like a bulldog to the belief that, handicapped as he was, he could begin again, making designs for engines or machinery. It was possible, of course, he'd always had an inventive and inquiring mind.

There was a third room on the ground floor. That had hardly been altered at all except that what had plainly been a wide open fireplace had been closed in and fitted with one of those free-standing—except for the pipe which led into the chimney—all-night-burning stoves. Here the panelling had neither been ripped out nor covered with canvas and wallpaper; it was painted white; and there was a big square-bowed window jutting out and overlooking a strip of lawn and a rosebed and a stretch of water. From the front I had not realised that Gad's was partially moated. The bow window had window seats along its three sides, and somebody had not thought it worth while to take the cushions away. They'd been blue once but had faded to grey.

Bob said, "Nice," and sat down gladly. I dived into one pocket of my jeans and produced cigarettes and a lighter.

I'd never been an addict; I could smoke a cigarette in order to be sociable, nothing more. Bob had been what is idiotically called a *heavy* smoker. I'm inclined to be fussy about the use of words and before I would accept that term I'd want proof that somebody, having smoked a packet, weighed more than he had done when he opened it. But, when Bob was still speechless, reducing to scribbling on pads, he had understood the dramatic change in our financial position and had written—I'll give up smoking.

That struck me as very sad; he'd lost so much. Some losses were natural—he'd given up rugger, officially, when he was thirty, saying it was game for the young—but if by any chance one of the Scunwick team dropped out, there he was in a flash. He'd stuck resolutely to cricket, good for another fifteen years; and to tennis no limit, so long as your eyesight served. Now all that kind of activity was lost forever and I couldn't bear to think that he was voluntarily renouncing one small pleasure. So I took to smoking, and Bob smoked with me, not breaking his vow, just being companionable.

Now, on the window seat, the sun warm on our backs, we smoked together. Bob said, "What . . . do you . . . think?"

I said, "All right so far; but there must be *some* snag."

"Tudor kitchen."

"That wouldn't deter me. I can handle a brick oven. Or rig up a spit if I have to." All the same, I thought, I mustn't sound *too* eager to get away; Ella was Bob's mother and her behaviour couldn't be faulted. Our decision to look for a place of our own had been tacit. I had never said—though I had often felt—that I'd be happier camping out in a tent.

"It's been . . . wired," Bob said, pointing his stick at a light fitment in the ceiling, a power plug in the skirting. I certainly hadn't expected that; not in a house so cheap and advertised as in need of modernisation.

The kitchen gave me a shock, in a pleasant way. It had been completely modernised except for one wall which was almost entirely taken up by a huge dresser, built in, part of the house itself. There was a stainless steel sink and a small electric geyser over it; some of what are called kitchen units, and an electric cooker; not perhaps the very latest model, with an eye-level grill, but not all that old. Who, in his right senses, would leave such a thing behind?

One door in the kitchen opened into an airy larder, the other upon a flight of scrubbed wooden stairs.

"I'll take a look at the bedrooms," I said, leaving Bob an option; he could go back to the window seat if he felt tired.

"Other stairs better for me," he said. I knew he hated being watched on stairs, going up as a child just learning would do; sound leg first, a pull on the bannister, his limp leg pulled up on to the same stair.

By the time he reached the landing from his end I had had time to look into several bedrooms, looking for one thing only, those betraying damp patches on ceilings which betrayed a faulty roof. I found none. At his end Bob opened a door and made a noise which in a man with normal control of speech would have been an exclamation. Then he said, "Jill. Look. Bathroom."

So there was, and again quite modern, except for its size. It was large by present day standards. Basin, bath and loo were all pink, and the bath was served by another electric geyser, bigger than the one in the kitchen.

"Move in . . . tomorrow," Bob said, his voice still expressionless but his eyes eloquent.

"One more river to cross," I said. For snag there must be; and the stairs up from the kitchen, having debouched onto the landing, went up again. There was another floor and there, I imagined, I should find the evidence of roof damage that I dreaded. But actually the top, or attic, floor covered only a small part of the house. There was one room that still smelt of stored apples; one completely empty, and one with a padlocked door. Assuming the room behind it to be about the same size as the others, in total this floor could offer protection from damp to only about a third of the house. And both of the attics into which I could look seemed sound and dry.

It simply was too good to be true.

Had we come to the wrong house?

Anybody to whom the impossible has happened is forever vulnerable; the impossible may happen again.

We had followed instructions and gone to Park Farm, Stonham St Peter's, and been told, by a neat, elderly woman, that Mr and Mrs Thorley were both out, but if our name was Spender and we wanted the key to Gad's, here it was; and she had kindly told us how to find the place; turn left at the church, up the hill, left again and into the lane and there'd we be.

And here we were. But it was just possible that we were not at Gad's. It was possible that Mr Thorley had two houses to sell, and that the kind woman facing me had made a very common error, thinking of her left as my right. Somewhere in the opposite direction there might be a house which was worth so little and did need modernisation.

Of this horrid suspicion I said nothing to Bob; for although he was to be treated as far as possible as a normal person, he was not to be subjected to either physical or mental stress.

I ran down the stairs and said, "Sound as a bell. I'll just look at the garden."

Of what I hoped to do, of how I intended to make a living, I had said nothing to anyone. Not to Bob, it would have sounded as though I distrusted his ability to make a living for us all; and not to Ella, who thought that the solution to our problem was for us to buy a nice little house in Baildon and for me to go back to my job as librarian. And Tony could go to a play-school in the mornings. She or Elsie—her faithful retainer—would fetch him at the end of the morning session, give him lunch, see that he had his afternoon's nap and entertain him as best they could until I collected him. John and Alice posed no problem; they'd both settled down happily in their school, took what was called school dinner. John, as extrovert as his father, had joined a number of ex-classroom activities and sometimes was not home until eight o'clock.

I'm old-fashioned; I still believe that up to the age of five at least a child's best friend is his mother. And I could see other flaws in Ella's neat little plan; the difference between school and library hours, and holidays; I couldn't bear to think of Bob, himself liable to accident, being alone, or in charge of two lively children and a toddler, not perhaps often, but at any time. That was why I had cooked up my scheme and looked only at properties

with gardens. My farming blood informed me that, given a bit of
land and a modicum of luck, I could make a living.

Gad's had more than a bit of land. It had a treasure house.
Against the wall which partially surrounded it fruit trees were
espaliered; there was a rather broken-down greenhouse, and in it a
vine which despite its exposure to the weather through some broken panes had flourished and fruited. There were free-standing
trees of apples and pears; there was a bed of the best asparagus I
have ever seen, thick spears thrusting up through last year's debris.

There was also a lawn, which had been cut not long ago, and
on the pergola which divided the pleasure garden from the utilitarian part, the roses did not sprawl in a neglected way.

I thought of how easily typing errors are made. Perhaps that
piece of paper should have said £40,000.

In my mind I bade it goodbye. Wrong house perhaps; wrong
price perhaps—or, a third possibility struck me as I went back
through the kitchen, somebody else in partial possession. Some
lucky, lucky person who had forestalled us, done a bit of modernisation, tidied the garden. Advertisement departments in papers
are not infallible. There could have been a ghastly mistake somewhere. Bob and I might be in the wrong place, or even in the
wrong time. I noticed for the first time that the whole house was
extremely clean; none of the litter that most people, moving out,
leave behind them, and come to that it didn't *feel* unoccupied. I
am not, I think, an unduly fanciful person, but some of the
houses that Bob and I had seen in the last few weeks had seemed
to appeal for salvation and I'd always felt a bit sad as I turned my
back on them. Gad's—if indeed this were Gad's—had none of
that pathos and as we slammed the heavy door behind us I felt no
sorrow for the place, only self-pity for myself because something,
somewhere had gone badly wrong and I knew perfectly well
nobody, in these days, bought for £4,000 a perfectly sound,
modernised house and one and a third acres of fruitful, reasonably
well-conditioned ground.

We went back to Park Farm, a new boot-box of a house, covered with pink plaster and separated from the road by flowerbeds,
each as rectangular as the house, and planted out in a style
reminiscent of public gardens, pink geraniums and blue salvias.
The windows were wide and without panes, the front door of
ribbed glass. For the second time that afternoon I rang the bell,

and this time a man came to the door. Behind the ribbed glass he looked enormous, and only slightly less so when we stood face to face. Well over six foot, broad, but lean. His face was so tanned that his grey eyes looked very pale.

"Mrs Spender?"

"Yes."

"I'm George Thorley." He held out a hand, the palm hard as wood. And he looked at me, so searchingly that I suddenly felt improperly dressed. Since he was himself in his shirt sleeves and braces, a pair of old corduroy trousers, and his slippers, this was no mean achievement.

"It's about Gad's? Well, how did you like it?"

"Very much." I did not intend to say more until I knew that we were talking about the same house; and the same price.

"We must talk things over. My wife has just made the tea. I'll fetch your husband."

"No. I'd better. Just at the moment he's—rather lame" Despite the searching stare, the man had a kindly expression; he'd be just the type who'd try to help Bob out of the car, hand him his stick, offer his arm.

"We're invited to tea," I said.

"Good. I can . . . do with it," Bob said, beginning his struggle.

Going, this time more slowly, between the flowerbeds I noticed the garage, integral as advertisements say. The lift-at-a-finger-touch door was open and a smart MG and a solid Jaguar stood side by side.

Mr Thorley had the good sense enough not to offer his hand to a man whose right bore heavily on a stick. He said, "Good afternoon, Mr Spender. Come in," and led the way through a rectangular archway, into the dining room.

"My dear," he said, "Mr and Mrs Spender. They're interested in Gad's. I'll get some more crockery."

Mrs Thorley was no longer young, but she was well-made-up. I know some women do have blond hair and brown eyes, but I guessed that her blondness was artificial, a shade too golden, and her eyes were black, not brown; also her throat and the bare arms, which her very fashionable, sleeveless shift frock left exposed, were sallow.

She seemed to find it necessary to apologise for the substantial and very delectable meal.

"Mr Thorley is busy hay-making, and I had an appointment, so we had a very light lunch."

"So did . . . we," Bob said.

One of his doctors had told me that a great point in his favour was that his condition did not embarrass him. He was a very rational person; what had happened to him had happened, there was nothing shameful about it and so far as he could manage, nothing pitiable either.

There was, in fact, I thought, some resemblance between the two men now at this table—the beautiful quality of imperturbability.

Mr Thorley carved ham of a kind seldom found nowadays, we passed green salad and potato salad to and fro.

The inquisition began.

I said, "What we must know, Mr Thorley, is whether the house we saw this afternoon was the house you advertised; and whether it really is for sale for four thousand pounds." A forkful of food got as far down as just behind my collarbone and there stopped, growing red-hot, as I waited for the answer.

"Well," he said, "I've only the one place to sell and old Hattie gave you the key. The price, four thousand, was what I thought reasonable."

Mrs Thorley said, "Mr Thorley is very sentimental about Gad's."

"Maybe I am. My family has been there for a long time. Before Domesday Book. Not in the house, that came later, but in the barn—the Danes called that the hall. To tell you the truth I wouldn't sell it now, for any amount of money, but for the way things are going."

Bob said, "Com . . . Compulsory purchase. Squatters."

"Just so," Mr Thorley said. "Our lords and masters can have two or three houses and no questions asked, but the ordinary man . . ." He paused for a second, mastering what I recognised as violence, and then went on with that deceptively calm manner. "I didn't intend to see Gad's turned into lodgings for lunatics or cosy retreats for bad boys. And I didn't want it to be just a week-end place. I went about it carefully. That box number was a protection. I chucked out most of the letters; townees, speculative builders. I wanted no truck with them."

It was plain that he felt strongly about Gad's—so why did he live in a pink plaster boot-box? Mrs Thorley, as though catching my thought, said:

"Mr Thorley and I lived there ourselves until about five years ago. It was inconvenient for him—his herd is here, on the main road. And it was lonely for me. Nobody will live in nowadays; even *au pair* girls won't take country jobs. And with Mr Thorley so often away on business, or attending some committee . . ."

"Let's face it," he said mildly, "Kitty never liked the place. That's why the modernisation is such a makeshift job. Just enough to get by with, till she was settled—which she never did. Have either of you lived in the country before?"

"Baildon . . . Cambridge . . . Kidder mi—minister," Bob stumbled on the word but pressed on. "Scunwick."

"There's a sugar factory there."

"I was manager."

"Ah," Mr Thorley said. His grammar was faultless, his accent barely perceptible, yet in a way his speech was countrified. Only a countryman—and old-fashioned at that—could put so much into one syllable. His "Ah" said, "Yes, before you had your stroke. I understand. I'm sorry for you."

I said, "Scunwick was almost suburban by the time we left. But I spent a lot of time in the country when I was young. In my grandmother's house—rather like Gad's, but not modernised at all."

"I reckoned you were country-bred the moment I set eyes on you."

"George!" Mrs Thorley said sharply.

"What's wrong with that?"

"So personal!"

"I'm just making sure. Mrs Spender, did you happen to notice the dresser in the kitchen?"

"Who could miss it? It's part of the house, isn't it? In fact I imagined it with crockery." I deliberately used his own, slightly outdated word. "Or better still, pewter, but that is scarce now and expensive."

"It takes all sorts to make a world," Mrs Thorley said. "Frankly, I thought it was a monstrosity. It was impossible to make a proper, streamlined kitchen with that great thing looming. But Mr Thorley said that to remove it would bring the whole wall down."

I'm not—I hope—one of these U and non-U observers, but her constant reference to Mr Thorley did indicate something. I know that the Queen's use of four simple words—my husband and I—is good for a sick giggle any day, but it is correct usage. I thought to myself that Kitty Thorley had come up in the world, learning a lot, but not *quite* enough. Then I said to myself: Snob; you're as bad as Ella!

"So," Mr Thorley said, "you think you'd be happy at Gad's. That's all I ask. Somebody happy there and being fond of it."

Bob gathered his forces and said, "Love at first sight," without any hesitation at all.

"I feel the same," I said.

"All right, then. It's yours. Move in tomorrow, if you like. I know lawyers make a business of it. Something they call searches. Necessary where a property has changed hands. Gad's never did. Straight down from father to son. It's never been in hucksters' hands. Mine to sell; yours to buy. Let's call it a deal."

"It'll be a weight off your mind, George," Mrs Thorley said amiably. "No more running up to Gad's to see if a tile blew off, or sending a man to mow and prune."

Sometimes my mind slips and suddenly I had a ridiculous thought: If her hair weren't dyed and her face coloured, she'd have been exactly like Anne Boleyn, whose hold on Henry VIII had been, while it lasted, absolute. She was the example which sprang immediately to mind, but there were hundreds of others, women who without any specific effort had gained ascendancy. What did they have that the others of us had not? Better in bed? But I could think of several cases where complete infatuation had preceded the bed test, or had never been subjected to it. Just one of life's mysteries. Stop meandering; get back to business.

"We can't move in tomorrow, much as we would like to. At the moment we don't possess so much as an egg-cup."

And why should that confession make Mr Thorley look so pleased.

"In that case," he said. "If I might make a suggestion . . . I brought some stuff away. Just a few things I couldn't bring myself to part with. It's up in a loft here. If you like the dresser, Mrs Spender, you might like some of that."

"I'm afraid we shall have to furnish on a shoestring."

"This wouldn't cost you a penny. I'd be very happy to see the old things back in their proper places."

"I said Mr Thorley was sentimental, didn't I?"

"Lofts not . . . for me . . . just yet," Bob said. "I'll wait in the car."

"Oh no. Come into the lounge. With tea so late, it's time for a glass of sherry."

I waited in the hall while Mr Thorley changed back into his boots. The house was built on the open plan, possible only with very efficient central heating; and the whole thing was singularly like a Show House in an exhibition; all the furniture very expensive, Swedish style, possibly more comfortable than it looked. The only individual touch that I could see in the section of the lounge within my view was a flower piece, delphiniums and peonies and poppies, very formally arranged. I heard Mrs Thorley say:

"You mentioned Baildon. I do know a Mrs Spender who lives there."

"My mother. We're . . . staying with her."

"Oh really!" The surprise was blatant.

"We'll cut through the garden and the orchard," Mr Thorley said. Flower garden, vegetable garden, all immaculate, orchard of young trees, all regimented, then into the past again; an old farmhouse, nothing like Gad's for size or style, but a place I should have been very glad to buy for £4,000 only an hour ago.

"That was the original Park farmhouse. It was derelict when I took over, but I made it into two good houses—for stockmen. Two minutes' walk from the job." He jerked a thumb towards some much more modern-looking buildings across the yard. "Rent free. Now everybody is up in arms about what they call tied cottages. Did you ever hear anything so daft? If Joe Snell went to work for a garage in the village and I asked him to leave, I'd be a villain. Well, here we are."

The place still smelt faintly of horses, though it now housed only a LandRover, a pick-up truck and a lorry. The way to the loft was up an absolutely perpendicular ladder made of stout slats nailed to the wall. I climbed them without thinking, emerged through the square opening in the floor of the loft and stood in near darkness until Mr Thorley, following me, went and flung open the wide doors through which, in the time of horses, fodder and bedding had been forked from high-piled wagons. Long rays of light, full of dust motes, streamed in.

The stored furniture lay under stack tilts, under dust-sheets, under sacking.

A dismantled four-poster bed, definitely Tudor; a long heavy table, probably older, its top one solid plank of oak which under a little surface dust revealed the patina that beeswax and elbow grease and sheer use had given it. A high-backed settle. A round rosewood pedestal table; a long-case clock; an elegant little chiffonier. Too much to take in at a glance. But I did specially notice a framed sampler, only slightly faded. Worked by Mary Thorley and completed in June 1815. Under her name and the date she had stitched "God be thanked." Because the tedious work was done, or because the war had ended? I thought of Mary Webb's most touching poem about a little girl working a sampler through "those leafy Junes, those ancient dark Decembers . . ."

I said, "Mr Thorley, have you any idea what these things are worth?"

"To a museum, you mean? To be gaped at. That I did not intend to have. In fact I mentioned all this stuff in my will. I said it was to be burnt. And it would have been. What a man says while he's alive is easily overridden, but wills are still respected. There's an oddity if you like; people are still afraid of offending the dead. Well, take anything you can use, and welcome."

"I can take it all. And I promise to take good care of it." I even knew where the long-case clock had stood—on the half landing; it had left its ghost there as very solid pieces of furniture do, dusted round.

"There was a time," he said, "when I hoped. I thought any son of mine—or come to that a daughter—would have grown up and taken to Gad's and put these things back in place. But I've no children."

He said it as though he were making a comment on the weather. I wondered why, and how long it had taken him to reach such a resigned, dispassionate attitude towards a situation which to him, so devoted to Gad's and its long tradition, must have been more painful than to men who had no roots.

"What a pity."

"It is that, but it can't be helped. I'll send this and a couple of men to shift it, up to Gad's tomorrow. But you'll need more. I didn't store anything the moths could get at. If you take my advice you'll go to Bidwell's."

Bidwell's was a shop in Baildon High Street; very up-to-the-minute and extremely expensive.

"Beyond our means."

"He has another department. Go down Pump Lane at the side of his big shop, and there's a secondhand department; and he's a good, honest chap."

Abruptly I found myself face to face with what I liked to think was my one phobia.

I'd met it first when I was about ten; living with my grand-mother, and provided with two little playmates. A wet morning, so we sought some sheltered place to play in and found a loft, twin to this one. We'd had a happy morning, then the elder of the two, who had a watch, said it was lunchtime. She and her sister had gone down the vertical ladder as easily as they had mounted it; I tried to follow and just could not. The slats of the ladder extended above the level of the square hole; all there was to do was to take the top rung in one's hand and step off the edge of the square opening, on to one of the rungs; and I just could not do it. My knees turned to jelly at the thought, and my hands were equally useless. My friends came up and down several times to show me how easy it was; and then—their mother was strict about time—they ran off.

My grandmother came. She was nearing seventy, but very spry; she came up, went down, to show me how easy it was. Standing well away from the abyss, I said, "I can't. I can't," and cried. My grandmother said, "You'll come down when you're hungry," and went away.

I was hungry already. I was also deserted—by man, not by God. My grandmother was a very religious woman, not ostentatiously pious but firm in her simple and beautiful faith. I shared it then; so I knelt and prayed for courage and it did not come though I edged towards the abyss again, trying to show God that I did be-lieve . . . At the sight of the emptiness into which I must step, the sight of the top rungs which I must grasp, weakness assailed me again. I couldn't do it. I should have to stay here until I died of hunger.

Some very long hours passed before I realised that there was an-other way down. The floor of the loft stopped short of the wall on its inner side so that hay could be pushed over and into the manger immediately below. Not much of a drop, not much of a drop; no waiting void. I jumped, scrambled out of the manger and made for the house, where my grandmother was just starting her pudding. "I knew you could it," she said placidly. I never told her how I had done it.

Now here I was, thirty-five years old, a married woman with three children, faced with the identical situation: obliged to make a humiliating confession to a man I'd known less than two hours. This time I had no need to jump. He went and stood in the manger and reached me down, as he would have done a doll from a shelf.

"There's no accounting for such irrational fears," he said. "Believe it or not, when I was a boy I was sure there were wolves in Layer Wood. And my fear seemed to communicate itself to my pony. Winter afternoons he'd cut through Layer like a race horse."

Physical contact, there in the manger, as he lifted me from one level and set me down on the other, had meant nothing, but suddenly as we went back to the pink plaster boot-box I found myself telling him what I had told nobody—my plans for making some sort of living at Gad's. "Until," I said, "my husband can get some of his ideas going. He's really a brilliant engineer, you know. And although some of his motor nerves suffered, they're mending. His *mind* is all right."

"Anybody can see that. But it'll be a while before he can dig. And if you go ahead with your plan, there'll be some digging to be done."

"I shall do it." I know that physically I am not impressive; quite tall, but so small boned that even as a fat adolescent I never weighed more than nine stone. Now much less, but all tough. And at the moment I was enjoying such a bout of euphoria that I'd have tackled the Great Pyramid and brought it low with a trowel.

"There's a slack time between hay and harvest," Mr Thorley said. "I'll lend you a man."

"I can't afford hired labour, Mr Thorley."

"Who said anything about hiring? I said lend. And he can bring good load of muck with him; it's starved land up there."

*

"Thorley," Ella said, "the name rings a bell. No, I don't mean this Mrs Thorley whom you met. I have *seen* her, either at the Ladies' Luncheon Club, or the Flower Club. Very smart."

My mother-in-law still made a distinction between having seen somebody, meeting somebody, and knowing somebody. "Wait. My memory is not what it was. So infuriating! Really, I do know that we must all grow old and die to make room for the younger generation, but why we couldn't keep our looks, and our senses and our mobility, I shall never understand. But that is by the way . . . Thorley, Gad's Hall. Oh yes, I remember now. I only heard by hearsay. There was a Thorley at Gad's—quite wild, he squandered his substance. He broke his neck, hunting when he was well into his seventies . . . All long before my time, of course, but your father, Bob, had elderly friends who seemed to admire the old reprobate; though what is admirable about ruining one's family, I fail to see."

"Far from ruined . . . now. House worth forty . . . thousand, at least."

"And two cars," I said. "An MG and a Jaguar."

"And he proposes to sell Gad's Hall for four thousand. It must be in a terrible state."

"It isn't. I went over it thoroughly. I thought it was too good to be true. But Mr. Thorley is sentimental about the place."

"I'm very fond of this house," Ella said, "but were I forced to sell it I should expect a fair price. I really think I had better take a look at it. And I'll ask Mr Gordon to look through the deeds." Mr Gordon was not the only solicitor in Baildon, but he was the only one that people like my mother-in-law would ever dream of consulting. He was one of the bridge circle.

"There aren't any; it's been in the same hands since Domesday."

"Presumably there are wills. Some proof of ownership."

"Man struck me . . . dead honest."

"We shall see."

"I'd like you to see it, Ella. Come with us, tomorrow. Unless it rains, Mr. Thorley expects to have his hay in by mid-day and he's bringing the furniture across at around four o'clock."

"What furniture?"

That took some explaining, too, and Ella said that the only conclusion she could draw was that the man was mad. And, by implication, that Bob and I were, too—or so anxious to get away from the prim little house that we were willing to risk anything.

Bob, admitting to feeling a bit tired, but proudly refusing all offers of help, went to bed early and then Ella tackled me.

"I am well aware, my dear, that you need a place of your own. But if I have ever done or said anything that hinted that you were unwelcome here and that you must rush out and do something silly in order to get a roof over your head, I withdraw it, and I apologise."

"You never did. You've been wonderful. Kinder than God." Not perhaps the most acceptable compliment; absolutely orthodox in all her works and ways, Ella was a good church woman, a regular attendant at morning service, a stout supporter of any fund-raising schemes, coffee mornings, garden fêtes, Christmas bazaars.

"Has Elsie upset you in any way?"

"Of course not."

"Then why must you take on such an impossible place? At least six miles from the school where John and Alice seem happy and settled. That means running a car. And an old house, however well patched up, is going to be costly in maintenance. There'll be rates . . . I've been very careful not to decry Bob's idea that he can, one day, make some sort of living, but my dear Jill, you know as well as I do that he never can. So what will you live on? His miserable little pension?"

Back to her fixed idea; buy one of those reconstructed houses in the slum that had once been Scurvy Lane; four thousand down and the other two thousand and five hundred on mortgage; get myself a regular job in the Public Library, or, failing that, in a school. "Be sensible; be practical."

Ella must have been very pretty when she was young, and she was pretty still; neat little kitten face, blue eyes which the years had not faded, and soft, almost beige-coloured hair; she was short, but not plump, just nicely curved in just the right places, always wearing clothes, not quite old-fashioned, but a bit Old World-romantic, in soft pastel shades. But nobody knew better than I did that inside this very feminine, almost fondant appearance, there was a core of steel. In the terrible crisis which had overtaken

us all she had cried floods and floods of tears, and her attitude towards Bob was all wrong. She thought I was heartless, because,
obeying instructions, I had left him to do things for himself—
things not easily managed, I admit, but once accomplished, a
boost to his self-esteem.

"Be sensible; be practical," Ella said, and I said, "Come with us
tomorrow, and I'll show you how practical and sensible I intend
to be."

I spent the next morning at Bidwell's, in the back street department. Mr Bidwell had such treasures to sell, at such extraordinarily low prices because when he sold new things from his
smart High Street shop he would accept used furniture in part
exchange—but, as the man who served me pointed out, only clean
stuff, in good condition. Looking round, one could only conclude
that some people bought new furniture just for the sake of
change. I bought sparingly: I had no intention of using the big
drawing room until our circumstances underwent a dramatic
change. The room with the bow window would be our living
room and would be adequately furnished with a high-backed settle and three chairs, one rather high one—easy to get out of, for
Bob, two lower ones, less well upholstered. I bought three single
beds, a kitchen table, six kitchen chairs, four matching and two
odd, a pretty little dressing table which I thought would please
Alice, two chests of drawers; a few other bits and pieces and all
for just under fifty pounds. I had a preference for new mattresses,
though those in the used department looked clean enough.

In the new department I bought, not only the mattresses, but,
to show my faith in Bob, a proper swivel chair and one of those
lamps which can be adjusted to any angle. Then nylon sheets, and
pillow-cases; foam rubber pillows, blankets. Carpets I must do
without; Mr Bidwell did not take carpets in part exchange and his
new ones were shockingly expensive, except for some rugs, plainly
marked "cotton" and giving the country of their origin.

As this bill was totted up I felt sick, thinking of all the things I
had sold, at give-away prices, less than a year ago and of the
things I had literally given away as keepsakes.

But now I had a bonus to come. The salesman in this department asked whether I wanted to pay cash or have credit and,
when I said I would pay, said that Bidwell's gave a discount for
cash; not in money, but in goods. I romped through the china and

hardware department; in one choosing the cheapest, in the other the best. Crockery, as Mr Thorley called it, was vulnerable, a good frying-pan, properly used, could last for years. I slightly overran my discount and ended by owing another four pounds, fifteen pence.

Bidwell's delivered free within ten miles. Where did I want my purchases delivered; and when?

"Gad's Hall; Stonham St Paul's. And as soon as possible."

He went to one of those intercom telephones and came back with the good news that a small van was free this afternoon.

Mr Thorley did not come—a pity, I thought, because I wanted Ella to see that he was not mad; simply a man with an obsession. He sent three men, all sturdy, and with the usual admonishments —Bit more to your left, Joe. You silly bugger, only just missed my toe, they manhandled the heavy things into place. Then Bidwell's van arrived, with two men.

It was another hot afternoon and I felt badly about not being able to offer even a cup of tea, but Bob said women set too much store by tea and the men would much sooner have money and he had it ready.

Ella, fully as critical as I had been on the previous afternoon, had admitted that on the ground floor, at least, she could find no fault. Some of my purchases from Bidwell's she criticised. "Jill, there was no need to buy a teapot. I am sure I have at least three, never used."

In the end I got her into the garden and there her innate hostility to the scheme surfaced.

"It is far too big. How can you hope to manage a place this size?"

"I'm going to make it earn its living."

"You mean *sell* things?"

"Ella, we have both sold things, and suffered no ostensible damage."

"That was quite different. And look at that!" She pointed to the one space, not very wide, where the moat which held Gad's in a half embrace was open to the garden. Mostly the garden was shut off from the moat, by the south-facing wall, the old hot-house, trees and shrubs, and the outjutting wing of the house where the attics were. But there was this space.

"What about Tony?" Ella asked.

"I'll rig up some sort of fence A few hurdles would do."

"Very effective, but not in keeping. I will give you, as a house-warming present, a length of that chestnut fencing. Much more suitable." With that she turned abruptly away and went into the house. It was as though she were repudiating Gad's absolutely. I stood there for a moment and then remembered the asparagus bed. I went into the kitchen, found a knife, and, having as yet no basket, a cardboard box in which some of the things had been packed, and then I cut and cut, more asparagus and of far better quality than most people ever see.

When I returned to the house I found Bob and Ella in the living room. Half a glance informed me that it looked very nice; the settle and the round rosewood table looked as though they had never been away, and even the foreign cotton rug, borrowing dignity from its surroundings, looked almost Persian. A second half glance showed me that something had upset Ella. She and I had been through a good deal together, and I could see that although she was not—and had not been—crying, she had suffered some kind of shock and was maintaining composure by a great effort. Whatever it was Bob did not share it. He looked very happy, sitting in the chair I had chosen especially for him and talking about the other chair, the adjustable lamp and the wonderful solidity of the great table at which he would work. So why were the pupils of Ella's eyes so dilated that only a mere rim of blue showed? And why did her discreet, carefully applied make-up seem to stand out, as though behind it her face had grown pallid and shrunken?

Nothing was said on the way home, or in the evening until Bob switched on the nine o'clock news, which Ella often avoided, saying it was too depressing. At the door she turned and gave me a beckoning glance. I followed her up to the bedroom which was hers for the moment. She closed the door with something of a conspiratorial air, indicated that I should take the only chair, and seated herself on the dressing-table stool, her back to the glass.

"Jill, you must on no account go to live in that house."

"Why on earth not?"

"There is such evil there."

"Evil? What do you mean?"

"What I say. Evil. I hesitate to use the word haunted—I know you modern young people make mock of such things; and certainly I saw nothing, heard nothing; but I felt it. I was almost . . . overcome."

"Where?"

"On the attic floor. Perhaps you didn't penetrate so far."

"I did. I was looking for signs of damp. Two attics and a locked door."

"And you felt nothing?"

"Satisfaction that the roof seemed sound."

She gave me a look, half-pity, half-despair, as though I confessed an inability to spell cat.

"Then you must; you really must, my dear, be guided by me. I simply cannot allow you to buy that house."

"But we have."

"Don't be stupid! A few words across a tea-table! People retract from far firmer agreements than that. Now listen; ever since this afternoon I have been thinking of an alternative. As you know I have only my annuity and a few shares which depreciate every day. But I have this house. It is in the best neighbourhood, convenient for shops, church, everything. And it is small, easily run. It could be worth thirty thousand pounds. I'll sell it. Then we can pool our resources and buy a house in the country, with the kind of garden you want. What do you say to that?"

For a second or two, nothing. I was stunned by her offer.

She loved her elegant little house; as she said it was most conveniently situated and most of her friends lived nearby. And she did not really care for the country, except as a place to take a drive through, on a pleasant afternoon; she didn't own, so far as I know, a pair of walking shoes. She could not drive a car; in any country place she would be stranded—except for me—as though on a desert island.

"Ella, it's the noblest offer I ever heard of. But I can't let you make such a sacrifice."

I'm a realist, I know that people who make terrific sacrifices in moments of self-immolation regret it and come to hate those for whom the sacrifice was made. Also I could see myself perpetually trying to make up to Ella and wasting a lot of much-needed time, acting as chauffeur.

"I am not proposing that we would live in one another's pockets. We could find a house big enough to allow separate kitchens. I have Elsie to consider."

Snatching at a straw, I said, "Elsie might not fancy country life."

"When Elsie was my housemaid—we had housemaids then— she fell into a coma. Everybody thought she was dead; I didn't. I could run in those days and I ran for Doctor Taylor. It was a diabetic coma and Elsie, since then, has been kept alive by insulin injections. Which *I* give her. They have a contrivance by which diabetics can inject themselves, but Elsie could never bring herself to do it. So . . . every morning and every evening . . . I think it would take more than a change of house to make Elsie desert me."

I looked at those pretty, milk-white hands, their only sign of age the prominence of the blue veins, no brown blotches, no knobbly knuckles. Day after day, year upon year, performing a slightly disagreeable task. One from which I must admit I should have shuddered.

"That," my astounding mother-in-law said, "is just by the way. We were talking about Gad's Hall. I cannot possibly allow you to take Bob and those dear children to that dreadful place."

I said, "Look, Ella. It's a chance in a million. We can move in tomorrow—without disrupting your whole life. I'd be the last person to deny that *you* felt something. You may be sensitive to such things. I felt nothing. Bob isn't likely to tackle those stairs and if it eases your mind at all I'll put the attics out of bounds for the children." I began to improvise. "In the old days servants slept on that floor; some of them may have been horribly unhappy— homesick; ill-treated by an employer or a fellow servant. I can *just* believe that a very strong emotion can leave an impression which somebody with a kind of extra sense can pick up. And even if Gad's were *known* to be haunted, I don't think it would deter me. I can't think of a case where a ghost ever did anybody a physical harm."

"Oh, can't you? I can. It was in the papers. A Council house. A man was pushed downstairs, and his wife received a heavy blow on the shoulder. The Council rehoused them."

I was silent for a minute, thinking of one story; Lytton's about a haunted house in which a man intended to sit up all night with a manservant and a guard dog; the manservant ran away and the dog's neck was broken. But this was fiction; so probably was the experience of the people in the Council house.

My mother-in-law gave a sigh.

"Very well, if you must be so stubborn . . . Will you do one thing for me, before you move in? Ask your Mr Thorley to open that locked door."

*

I don't think I've ever felt more foolish. Here I was, having been offered, and having accepted, the biggest bargain within living memory and quibbling about one locked door.

"So far as I know, there never was a key to it," Mr Thorley said. "My grandfather, or somebody before him, locked it and so it stayed. I never knew him—he must have been fifty before he married, and my father didn't marry till he was clear of debt, so between my grandfather and me there was a gap. I remember once I asked about that door and my father said mind my own business, he'd never seen inside it and why should I bother? And after that I never gave it a thought. But of course, if you want it opened . . ."

He used a pair of pliers and wrenched one staple free; the bit of chain dangled. The door opened upon nothing but another empty attic. It differed from the others only in one way. Its window was barred, slantwise.

"I'd guess that was done," Mr Thorley said, "to guard against storm damage. This gable is a bit exposed and I seem to remember some talk about a window blowing in. But that was before my time."

"I can't understand why nobody had sufficient curiosity to break in before this. It might have held treasure."

"Treasure!" He laughed. "By all accounts my grandfather had disposed of everything that was disposable long before he died. All he left was debts and just the nucleus of a herd. It took my poor father . . . But you don't want to hear about all that."

"On the contrary, I find it most interesting. My mother-in-law, as soon as I mentioned your name, had some memory—about a hunting accident when he was . . . rather old."

"Very old, nudging eighty, and still wild as the devil. Well, are you satisfied that there are no skeletons in the attic?"

"To be honest, I never thought . . ." I began to move away, and as I turned my angle of sight and the angle of light coming through the barred window met, I saw, as you can see in some old churches, something that the whitewash had been intended to obscure. Not the biblical pictures intended to enlighten people who could not read; not, in fact, anything really recognisable, just some bits of faces with unpleasant expressions, and all partly smudged out by something other than whitewash. And even as I stared they seemed to fade away again.

I was able to report to Ella that there was nothing but an empty attic. I made rather much of the blown-in window. Imagine, I said, a maid sleeping up there on a night of howling wind, and having the window blow in; wouldn't that be terror enough to leave a lasting impression?

"It was not physical fear that I felt. However," she shrugged her slight shoulders, "I have done what I could. I feel that perhaps I should speak to Bob, but he is incapable of believing anything that can't be measured on a slide rule."

That day I spent shopping for food and Elsie unearthed a lot of screw-top jars; she never could bring herself, she said, to throw a good jar away; she'd always known they'd come in useful one day. She made a remark which had significance in its omissions; she'd miss Alice, she said. And certainly Alice, when not in John's company, was a very docile, quiet little girl. Apart from mentioning Alice, Elsie made no secret of her relief; before I had finished packing, she was making Ella's room ready for her again; you'd really have thought that the room had been occupied by squatters of a most unsavoury kind. On the other hand she showed goodwill by serving a very substantial tea, sausages and chips and by adding to what I had bought some jars of home-made jams, marmalade, chutney.

I tried to keep my word to Ella about the children and the attics. "It's a very old house," I explained, "and that top flight of stairs and the floor it leads to won't stand any rollicking about. Quite apart from any damage to you—" I looked straight at my son, "and that might mean a leg in plaster for weeks—it would run us into a lot of unnecessary expense." Poor John, he'd come a bit early to the question of what could and what could not be afforded. He understood. And in any case there was plenty to explore; more space, more funny little holes and corners than anywhere they had ever lived in their lives.

John was indeed a very sensible, logical boy and he immediately spotted the danger of that open space where the garden and the moat met. "Tony could fall in there, Mum."

"I know. Gran noticed it, too. She said she would give us a length of fencing."

"I'll see if I can rig up something in the meantime. Come on, Alice, you can lend me a hand."

When I was called to look at what they had rigged up, I remembered that the words engineer and ingenious were closely related. Out of an old window frame which John said he had found near the greenhouse, some logs and a sawhorse taken from a shed, and two packing cases left by Mr Bidwell's men, John and Alice—directed by him—had made a barrier quite sufficient to keep a toddler away from the water.

So, here we were, survivors from the wreck; Bob and I at last together again in a bed which we could consider in a way to be our own; in the big four-poster with the new mattress called king-size. I did not feel in the least guilty about Mr Thorley's generosity, or his waiving of formalities. His delight in seeing some of his family things restored to their rightful place had been so whole-hearted. And, after all, there were many people who felt so strongly about a family place that they'd hand it over to the National Trust— sometimes with a handsome dowry for its upkeep. There were also people who bequeath lots of money to anybody who will take care of a favourite cat or dog. Ella's remark that Mr Thorley must be mad didn't hold water. What was remarkable was that his need for a kind of perpetuation and our need for a home should have coincided. Just on the verge of sleep, I could look back, with a degree of calmness, on the train of events which had brought us here.

*

Bob, with an engineering degree from Cambridge and some chemical qualification too, could have found a post anywhere, and, given a bit of initial training, in almost any industry. He chose to make sugar from beet. I always said, teasingly, and he always denied it, that his choice was decided by the work hours. Beet sugar factories have a season, roughly from September to January or February, and during that time work never stops. Men work in shifts but technical people are literally on call day and night. Their summers are relatively free; not holiday exactly, there is always some old piece of machinery to be overhauled, something new to be installed, but a man who plans his jobs carefully can play cricket, and golf, go sailing.

We married when he got the managership at Scunwick. There was a house waiting for us, a Sugar Corporation house, quite large and well appointed. A thick belt of trees stood between us and the factory, hiding all but the two tallest chimneys of what everybody admitted was an ugly building. In an emergency Bob could cut through the trees and be on the scene in three minutes.

Scunwick was a pleasant, unspoiled old market town and we had many friends in and around it; it had two good schools, an above-average golf course, a decent library. We had our own hard tennis court. I was completely—perhaps dangerously—contented. So was Bob, except for one thing. He never could hit it off with his area supervisor, the man in charge of six factories of which Scunwick was one. Mr Beckworth was oldish, set in his ways, Bob said, dead stupid and that he had reached his exalted position simply by being there when somebody even older and more stupid dropped dead. Mr Beckworth did not, in fact, trouble us much but he made routine visits and almost every one of them ended with a row. Mr Beckworth had manners so good as to be almost courtly; Bob was, on the whole, an amiable person, but they kept up a long-drawn-out running battle about machinery, about procedure. They were in fact perfect examples of the generation gap.

I always made a point of asking Mr Beckworth to dinner and providing dishes that he liked. And inside the house both men dropped their grievances; Bob became the amiable host, Mr Beckworth the honoured guest. And always, on the next morning, I received a sheaf of carnations. A Beckworth Bunch, Bob called it.

I could not pinpoint exactly when the winter of Bob's discontent set in. It came, as all winters do, step by step. He said he'd run into a cul-de-sac; that he'd managed, despite Mr Beckworth's sabotaging activities, to make Scunwick at least 40 per cent more productive than any other factory within the Corporation. And what thanks did he get? That sort of thing.

Then he went to one of the conferences which punctuated the summer, and met a man, a West Indian, who had shared a staircase with him at Cambridge. I had never been privileged enough to be part of Cambridge, or Oxford, but I had a vague idea that

Humbert Wolfe, whose verse I much admired, had dedicated one volume to somebody who had shared his staircase at Oxford.

When I heard what Bob's staircase-sharer had proposed, I had an attack of schizophrenia—in the literal sense; a split mind.

Santa Barbara sounded, and looked—judging by the brochures and other photographs and literature which Bob had brought home with him—more like the Garden of Eden than anyplace on this earth. It was small, the Spanish and the French had never bothered to dominate it; it had fallen under English influence during the Napoleonic Wars. Nelson had for a time used it as a base and one brochure said that he had called it the pearl of all islands free of that scourge, yellow fever. Its peaceful history had never been interrupted by slave revolts or political coups and it had moved, without incident towards independence within the British Empire.

It had a backward economy which Bob's Cambridge acquaintance had set himself to improve by increasing production, inviting investment, and attracting tourists. It had two very small, very antiquated sugar mills. Bob had been invited to go there and take complete control, at a salary three times as large as what he was earning at the moment. In fact, his friend who now bore the title of Minister for Economics had come to England to conduct a recruitment campaign aimed especially at men like Bob who were ambitious and discontented. He'd netted several doctors and schoolmasters already.

I could see that Bob wanted to go; and although my instinct was against it, I could produce no really valid arguments. I could say, "But you are a *beet*-sugar man." Bob said that meant nothing —the principles were the same—and that if somebody discovered how to make sugar out of old rope, he'd be perfectly capable of running a factory for that purpose. I could not plead the climate, for one of the tourist brochures mentioned a cool current which moderated the tropical heat; the immigrant doctors were to have carte blanche to establish a Health Service; the immigrant schoolmasters were going out to assure education for all.

To say the simple truth: I don't want to leave Scunwick, would have sounded too stick-in-the-mud for words. And if Bob heeded it, I should have a frustrated man on my hands.

There was just one frail hope of reprieve. Mr Beckworth had decided to retire from what he called active service and take his place on the Board of the Corporation. If Bob should be offered

his job, as was indeed, his due . . . That would have satisfied his
ambition, and it would, incidentally, have been extremely beneficial to the industry as a whole; Bob's factory was far and
away the best in the group of six which made up the area, and
with him in charge his area would have been the best in England.
And although we might have to hand over the factory house to
Bob's successor, we need not leave Scunwick; within a given radius, area supervisors could live where they liked and Scunwick
was quite central.

Bob did not get the post; and when he heard to whom it had
been given, he was infuriated. "Of course with Bloody Beckworth
now on the Board, I didn't stand a chance in hell. Withersly got
it because he's a yes man, a lickspittle. And if they think I'm
going to work under *him*, they can think again. Damn it all, I told
Chambers that if I did accept his offer, I'd stay and see this factory open in September. Now I shan't. I'll bloody well leave them
in the lurch."

I saw his point. I thought of those tasty little dinners—all
wasted.

In Santa Barbara, the brochure said, there were no hurricanes;
it lay outside the belt; but in Scunwick there was a hurricane all
right. Either Bob on the phone, or somebody on the phone wanting him. Ella rang several times, sometimes wasted several calls
because she began to cry. She was totally against it; she was inclined to blame me, of all unfair things.

At the centre of a hurricane there is an eye of quiet and so it
was with us, once the decision had been taken. Bob was to fly out
at the end of June. I was to stay and dispose of everything that
didn't seem to be worth the freight charges, give him time to settle in, find a house, and then be there for Christmas.

Until then I should have a roof over my head. The new Works
Manager, a nice man with a nice wife, were already established in
a house which suited them perfectly, and had no desire to move.
They had only one child and did not need more space. Nor, apparently, did anyone else. There was a scheme in the pipeline for
turning the factory house Bob and I had occupied into two flats,
but, pending such development, I was welcome to occupy it at the
minuscule rent of three pounds a week. Such a decision must have
been made at Board level, and perhaps after all, those tasty little
dinners had not been totally wasted.

This is what is so very odd about fate, chance, luck, or—as my grandmother always called it—Providence.

Bob wrote me ecstatic letters; Santa Barbara was all and more than he had hoped for; he'd found a house, midway between the two sugar mills, and he was furnishing it with native-made, wonderful things; and even as he wrote, he said, all the plant, turbines, boilers and such things which he had ordered were being delivered. Everything was wonderful, and busy as he was, he was counting the days . . . So was I.

And but for Ella, we all, John, Alice and Tony, would have been there, in Santa Barbara, just before Christmas.

I had given a whole series of parties, all with a farewell tinge, and several things which I treasured I'd given away as pre-Christmas presents, keepsakes really, to my best friends. A few things, easily crated, and all from my grandmother's house, I had reserved.

And then Ella rang me and weeping copiously said what about Christmas? Hadn't we always spent Christmas together, and now, this which might well be the *last* Christmas . . .

Well it was true; Christmas had always been a time for some kind of reunion. Not always bang on the nose because Christmas came in the middle of Bob's working season; but he'd snatch a day and a night and we'd drive down to Baildon and he'd do a lot of little jobs which she had been saving up and have a sedate dinner party and then race home. With one child, all right, with two, just impossible, with three, a muddle. So after Tony's birth, she had come to us. I'd fetch her—from Scunwick to Baildon was only about sixty-five miles.

In those days we'd got on as well as two fairly civilised people with nothing but the family in common could do. When I was in her house I always felt I was walking on eggshells; when she was in mine, she felt, I knew, as though she were camping out amongst barbarians. When she entertained in her neat little, dainty little, precise little house dinner was served. In mine—except for Mr Beckworth's visits—hospitality was a bit haphazard. I'd offer cold meat and potato salad, green salad in season; or a washbowl of curry and another washbowl of rice—perfectly cooked, though I say it myself; every grain fluffy and separated. I added chutney, sour sauce, sweet sauce. And people helped themselves, wore what they liked, drank gin rather than sherry and plonk more often than vintage wines. I often saw a somewhat pained expression on Ella's face.

Still, here she was, weepy on the phone, begging me to spend Christmas with her; just this one last time; for who could tell where we should all be next Christmas?

I gave in, changed the times of our flight and sent a cable to Bob informing him of the postponement.

When on Christmas Eve I received a cable from him I thought it was just a seasonal message. But it said, Hold everything on my way home.

No alarm then. He plainly now had the kind of job which would enable him to come and escort us, or view some special piece of equipment.

On my way home could well mean that he could be with us for the latter half of Christmas Day. The excitement was enormous, the waiting endless. Finally we decided that if the children were to enjoy their turkey, and plum pudding, they'd better have them before they fell asleep and before both comestibles were totally ruined.

Red candles, holly, crackers containing funny hats and would-be funny jokes—can I ever face them again?

It was Alice, always the most reluctant to go to bed, who switched on the television.

Apologising for the interruption in the programme, somebody told us that violent revolution had broken out in Santa Barbara. As usual their men on the spot had been intrepid, indefatigable and there were some pictures, buildings burning, cars overturned, mobs on the move.

I rang Heathrow; clinging to hope by my fingernails. Bob was no fool; if he'd caught even the faintest whisper of this he'd be on his way home. And that explained the apparent abruptness of his cabled message.

Heathrow was sorry, but Flight 24X or some such, due at 14.50, had not come in. No, so far as Heathrow knew there had been no accident, no fog anywhere, no diversions.

Ella cried and cried and said that from the first she had thought about what had happened in the Congo. And so had I. At least we were together on that. Together, also, in our hope that Bob might have got away.

As a matter of fact he almost did.

What had happened in that peaceful, ideal little island was a late explosion; the ordinary people did not like the new ways or the new people brought in to make new things work. There had been a complete revolution. Bob and every other foreigner had been told to go home, taking nothing more than could be carried in an ordinary suitcase. There was, perhaps, a kind of rough logic in that, but none at all in what happened later. Some fanatic, not content that foreigners should go, threw a bomb into the place where they were gathered, waiting to go.

Thank God for America. It cares for its own, as England once did. There were about forty American citizens on Santa Barbara when the boil burst; they and, as a sideline, all foreigners were rescued by helicopters which flew in and out unmolested, protected by the presence of an American frigate in the harbour, threatening instant reprisal if one shot were fired.

The bomb had killed seventeen people and injured a great many others. Bob was one of those seriously hurt.

We were informed, by cable, from a hospital in Miami.

I went, just as I was.

There was the coma; then the series of delicate, intricate operations, and Bob emerged, unable to speak at all and partially paralysed. But he could write, and what he wrote proved that his mind and his memory had not been impaired. The doctors varied in their prognostications; one told me that Bob's age was in his favour and that a good deal of improvement might be expected, in time. Another warned me to be prepared to see him live on in this maimed state. What mattered to me was that he was alive, and he seemed to have found from somewhere a dogged optimism. One of the first things he wrote was: Don't worry. I shall get well.

Because of its suddenness and ferocity, and because it happened at Christmas, season of peace and goodwill, the incident attracted more attention than one might have expected in a world so ravaged with violence. Somebody got hold of the fact that I had rushed to Bob's bedside, "without so much as a toothbrush," as one reporter put it, and because one of the operations performed upon his brain had been frankly experimental, Bob and I received more than our share of publicity. We were overwhelmed with kindness. People from all over America sent me gifts of clothing—

one woman actually sent me a mink coat. Offers of hospitality poured in. One big store provided me with a complete outfit. The hospital waived its charges, the surgeons repudiated all idea of payment.

One day Bob wrote that he wanted to go home. I said:

"You shall, darling. I'll make arrangements straight away."

What arrangements?

The wolf of financial worry which was to gnaw at my vitals from then on took its first bite. Air tickets cost money and we had none. Ella would have sent it, even if she had been obliged to borrow it, but there were so many hampering restrictions. I could have borrowed it; Miami was full of rich, kindly people. I hated the thought.

My assets were the mink coat, my wedding ring and my engagement ring, pretty but not very valuable. It had been bought before Bob was made manager and I said, truly, that I preferred a sizable topaz to a small diamond; and anyway wasn't the topaz a talisman, guaranteeing marital happiness?

While I was thinking about how and where to dispose of such poor assets, I took counsel with the doctors. The paid-up member of the Optimists' Union said that he was sure Bob would benefit by being in his own country, amidst his own family. The Practising Pessimist appeared to think that an air trip could do no positive harm. Doomed anyway, his manner said.

Then, of all things, I was asked to appear on a television programme. Santa Barbara, now in the hands of a party suspected of Communistic sympathies, was still news.

The last thing I wanted to do, but Bob was all for it. He wrote: Chance to thank everybody. I'll come too. Let people see.

It was a composite programme. There was one American who had escaped unscathed; he was important enough to own his private aeroplane. There was a man who invested some vast sum in the beginnings of a canning factory, and lost the lot. He was angered as well as slightly dazed. There was—Oh, why bother? Yap about the too sudden transition from ancient ways to modern times. Yap about infiltration; about Cuba; about the Monroe Doctrine.

Then Bob and me. He was in his wheel chair. Before the operations his head had been shaved. No bandages—a well-stitched wound needed nothing but stitches, such stitches that they did not even need to be removed. They either sloughed off or were absorbed.

I made a few rather tremulous, but utterly sincere remarks about the kindness which we had met with; then Bob wrote with a pen as thick as a candle, on a great sheet of white cardboard, "Thank you all," and held it up with his good hand.

Within ten minutes of that broadcast we were offered free flights home.

Let me not decry the Health Service. It works, up to a point. But it cannot, cannot be expected to, cope with such an exceptional case as Bob was. But there were people and there was a place . . .

Everton Park had been established originally for servicemen who had suffered damage to their brains or their nervous systems. Few ordinary people had ever heard of it, for although ordinary wounds were regarded as honourable some slight taint still clung to any mental or nervous derangement. I only heard of it through a neurologist in Harley Street.

In the years since the war the number of injured servicemen had naturally decreased—though there were still a few; they, of course, were treated free. In order to lessen the Government's burden, Everton now took private patients; there was even a department known familiarly as the Jug and Bottle, where dipsomaniacs could be treated. The charges were extremely high.

Bob and I had been, perhaps, a little happy-go-lucky about money; nothing very extravagant, we'd lived within our means but we had lived well; there had seemed no reason to scrimp; he had a steady job at Scunwick, and always the hope of promotion. When he left for Santa Barbara, we had about six hundred pounds in a Building Society. Out of that I had paid the rent and our living expenses for six months. Bob, from his fine new salary, could send me nothing even had I been in dire need. The Santa Barbara Government was even stricter about letting money go out of the country than the Bank of England was. So the children and I had lived on our savings; I'd bought our flight tickets and my ticket to Miami; and when Everton, the best possible place for Bob, promising improvement if not cure, was first mentioned we had already consulted and paid various specialists.

We had about three hundred pounds in the bank and a week at

Everton cost a hundred and twenty for residence and some treatments; others were extra.

I sold the mink coat, my grandmother's Rockingham tea set, her elegant old rat-tailed silverware, her carriage clock, a few other bits and pieces that I had intended to take with me.

Ella was marvellous. She had two lovely rings, the diamond that marked her engagement, the deep sapphire which had celebrated Bob's birth; she had a pair of diamond ear-rings. She sold them all and then started on her china, most of which was pretty but not worth much.

About parting with her treasures, and even the prospect of mortgaging her house, she was a stoic. Bob must have the best. The dreadful thing was that after one visit she had no faith in Everton. Bob had been there a month and I could see some improvement—I went every day except Saturday and Sunday; driving like a maniac along roads which were fortunately not too full of lorries.

Ella hated driving fast, she let out little squeaks of apprehension, clutched at the door handle, looked anxiously at the speedometer. So she was in a nervous state when we arrived and seeing, as she thought, Bob no better, she broke down and upset him, so that he was *not* better. All the way home she lamented; about his state, about his circumstances; his room, she said was a bleak cell; had I felt his bed? Hard as a board. Had I seen an absolute gibbering idiot in the corridor? How could Bob hope to recover in such a place? We were being swindled.

Then we arrived home to find that John and Alice, left only to Elsie's supervision, had squabbled over the TV programmes and pushed or pulled so many competetive knobs that they had put the set out of action.

A fine day that was! Culminating in my writing yet another letter to the insurance company.

The Corporation naturally had its own insurance for all its personnel and plant, but Bob had taken out a policy on his own; one which made him, he joked, worth far more dead than alive.

Insurance companies are naturally on the defensive and take rather restricted views; they hadn't a slot into which to drop being struck dumb and partially paralysed. Another bother was that Bob, the insured person, was in his right mind and could write, so he had to do some form filling and from the first made light of his injuries. Even to me he still joked, writing on his pad, "Shall I ask them to cut my left leg off? Then we'd qualify for loss of limb."

The insurance people knew about Everton and had suspicions. They pointed out that no policy covered alcoholism, which was neither an accident nor an Act of God. I had to keep writing covering, explanatory letters.

In the end, I'll give them their due, they admitted that Bob had met with an accident, suffered partial disablement and was entitled to six thousand pounds.

I was also writing to the Corporation. They operated a pension scheme which had always seemed a bit odd to me. From the wages of people below a certain level they deducted a few shillings a week, so that at the end of his working life a man who had stayed with them could count on something to add to his State Retirement Pension. From the salary of managers no such deduction was made; they were expected to provide for their own futures. I could not expect much, since Bob had left them, so suddenly and so early; but before he was made manager he had paid in his shillings and we were rapidly approaching a time when even a few shillings mattered.

One morning at Everton I parked my hard-driven car beside a great gleaming Rolls. Inside, in Bob's cell there was Mr Beckworth, two dozen dark red carnations and a bunch of black grapes.

The effect of the sight of his one-time enemy had not reduced Bob as Ella's had done; in fact I think it had helped.

Mr Beckworth, courtly as ever, greeted me and said:

"I would have come sooner, but news takes time to percolate. I heard only yesterday."

I said, "It was kind of you to come."

Trying his newly learned speech for the first time before a stranger, Bob said, "Very kind." There was no intonation in the words but from the look on his face I guessed that had there been, it would have been sardonic.

Mr Beckworth then tactfully confined himself to asking Bob such questions as needed only yes or no for answers, or inquiring about the children, and congratulating me on my fortunate escape. Then he said:

"I was told not to tire you, Spender. Would it tire you to talk business for a moment, or shall I leave it for a later occasion?"

"Go on," Bob said.

"Well, as I said, I heard only yesterday, just before a meeting of the Board. I was therefore able to raise the question under any other business. You were with the Corporation for three years before you became manager at Scunwick, and during that period you paid your contribution to the pension scheme—a total of a hundred and fifty pounds, I understand."

We were now in such low water that even that small sum sounded like a windfall. It would buy a week at Everton.

"As you know, the conditions for granting a pension in the normal way were not fulfilled, but I took leave to point out to the Board that you served for ten years at Scunwick, with results consistently above average. Taking that—and everything else—into consideration, it was decided to offer you two hundred pounds a year. The decision, I may say was unanimous."

"Mag-nanimous," he said, stumbling over the long word. There was, however, no flicker of gratitude in his expression.

"It is only a minuscule sum." Mr Beckworth sounded apologetic. "But it may provide a few cigarettes." I remembered then that he was a passionate nonsmoker.

I was as certain as though I had been there that we owed the little pension to Mr Beckworth, but I dared not thank him too heartily in Bob's presence. To do so would be to upset Bob, who was, I could see, remembering a few other things for which he had Mr Beckworth to thank. However, I made an opportunity. I said:

"Mr Beckworth, is that shining chariot yours? Then I think I may have parked awkwardly. I'll come down."

I thanked him heartily and then went back to Bob, who had not yet sufficient command of his mended motor-nerves to indulge in the flaming angry speech he would have liked to make. So he wrote: Old vulture. Come to gloat. And sundry other derogatory things. And I played along, saying, "Under any other business?" An expression which was to become a standing joke.

Everton was no swindle. When they thought they had done all they could, they said so, and laden with optimistic assurances and pessimistic warnings, I took Bob back to Baildon and began the hunt for a house within the six thousand range and with a garden by which I could supplement our certain four pounds a week and whatever Bob could earn.

And so we came to Gad's Hall.

*

I found a wonderful outlet for anything I could grow—the shop run by the Women's Institute in Baildon. It was patronised by the most discriminating shoppers, people who preferred local, fresh produce not all shrouded in cellophane. The fruit from the south wall, ripening early, found a ready market. So did such things as thyme and parsley and chives which had survived neglect.

Mr Thorley's Joe Snell, in addition to digging, had mended the greenhouse and now there were several things sharing its shelter. Amongst them a bay tree. So many recipes said take a bay leaf, and the best most people could do was to take a dry one, desiccated and flavourless. I had newly plucked bay leaves to sell. Presently I should have big brown eggs, which could rightly be termed free-range. I had ten beautiful Rhode Island red pullets and one gorgeous cockerel in a run which extended across the whole end of the garden. There would be no eggs until late October or early November, but they'd sell like hotcakes.

Every morning I drove John and Alice to school, delivered whatever I had to offer at the WI shop, did a bit of necessary shopping, and most mornings looked in on Ella, for whom I reserved the choicest of what Gad's had to offer. I repeatedly invited her to visit us. It was such a glorious summer, but she always had some excuse which I accepted without question. We had interrupted the placid stream of her social life and she had a back-log to make up; and she did not like Gad's.

One morning, it was late July, almost the end of the term, as John and Alice scrambled out of the car, one of the teachers, plainly on the watch for me, came up and said, "Mrs Spender, if you could spare a minute . . ."

I knew her. I was a conscientious member of the Teacher-Parent Association; her name was Brewster and she was in charge of Art and Craft. Anything less Arty and Crafty in appearance God never devised; grey all over. Grey hair in an untidy bun at the nape of her neck, grey eyes, grey complexion, grey skirt, grey blouse. Grey voice.

"I felt I must have a word with you," she said. "About Alice. You will remember, she came to us in January. And when we first met I told you that I thought she was one of the most promising pupils I ever had. Definitely gifted."

"Yes, I remember, Miss Brewster. I was pleased. But if she has gone off . . . Children do, as you must know."

God forgive me, I thought the poor woman was apologising; perhaps for the fact that at the end of term exhibition of finished work Alice Spender would figure less prominently than she had done just before Easter.

"It isn't that. It is . . . a change. Quite sudden, and in my opinion disquieting. I wondered. You may think me impertinent, but to me a child's welfare outweighs mere good manners. Has she lately come under the influence of . . . well, let us say an extremist religious organisation?"

"No." I could give that positive answer. Ella went to St Mary's for morning service every Sunday morning and if Alice felt inclined she had gone too. Since we moved into Gad's, Alice had been subject to no religious influence at all. "What has that to do with it?"

Miss Brewster did not answer directly. She said:

"I know that TV is often grotesque; but not macabre in quite this way. Excuse me again, Mrs Spender. Do you supervise your children's reading?"

"Yes." I could give a positive answer to that. At least I didn't supervise, I took interest. I had, after all, worked as a librarian and my own children's reading patterns were absolutely conventional. "I think I could safely say that we have never had a macabre book in our house."

I had encountered Foxe's *Book of Martyrs* when I was too young. It was illustrated, too. I'd been careful about things like that.

"Then I find it difficult to account for," Miss Brewster said.

"What exactly?"

"Her work. Macabre. Done by an older person one might even say Satanic. Demons. Imps. Hobgoblins."

"It's probably a phase, Miss Brewster. Isn't there a theory that we all go through every phase that every one of our ancestors on the long climb out of the sludge, went through? Gills, crawling, rearing up on hind legs. Alice is going through a phase." She looked so worried that I felt she needed reassurance. I seized on the one word which made light of it all. "We all go through the hobgoblin stage, Miss Brewster; but we can't all express it in drawing, as Alice appears to have done. Please don't worry. I'll keep a sharp lookout."

Ella had her birthday in August and she wanted to have a party. There was a woman in the village who would baby-sit, if fetched and returned, provided with a snack meal. Bob wished to go to his mother's party, so I engaged Mrs Snell—no relation, as she was careful to point out to the Joe Snell who, at Mr Thorley's bidding, had dug in the garden.

I put Tony to bed and left orders that John and Alice were to retire at eight o'clock, after sharing Mrs Snell's snack. I promised to be back at half-past ten at the very latest. I thought it might be sooner, for this was Bob's first full scale party, and he might tire easily.

In deference to Bob's lack of festive garments Ella had decreed that men should wear lounge suits but women could get themselves up regardless. That meant that Ella could wear an extremely becoming blue lace frock.

It was a small party, all people known to us, including Colonel Murray-Smith, known as The Boy Friend. He and Ella had had for years that happy, undemanding relationship, completely platonic, I am certain, which can exist between two people, growing old, both vain, both with some lingering attractiveness, and both well content with their own way of life. Even if at any time over the last ten years any thought of setting up house together had occurred to them, they would have come up against an insuperable obstacle. The Colonel's house was run with military precision by his ex-batman, a seasoned martinet; Ella's was run by Elsie. Neither of them would have tolerated the other for half a day. And it was impossible to imagine Ella making a home in that leathery, masculine establishment, or Fred Murray-Smith settling in Ella's ultra-feminine one. It suited Ella to have somebody to drive her about and to spare her the slight inconvenience of always being the extra woman which old-fashioned circles like hers seem to find so bothersome; and it suited him to have a still-pretty woman partially, not wholly, dependent upon him, to listen to him, ask his advice. They fitted perfectly.

Bob bore up bravely, but shortly after dinner I could see that he was tiring. I could also see that without us there would be eight people—just right for bridge; so pleading the children as an excuse, we left; but not before I had invited Ella and The Boy Friend to lunch on the following Sunday week. She had never visited us since we moved in, and I thought perhaps in broad daylight, sustained by the company of a man whose courage had gained him more than one medal, she might overcome her fear of the place, and feel happier about it. And realise that I was right.

On the way home I told Bob what I had done; adding, maybe conceitedly, that the lapse of time would give me time to salt a piece of beef properly, for it is true that this once so-common dish had become a rare luxury. The art of properly salting a joint had been lost. Mr Beckworth had once said, I think sincerely, that even at Simpson's . . .

Now Bob said, "Good. Thorleys, too. Been very kind."

I agreed that that was a splendid idea. I knew enough of them by this time to realise that Kitty Thorley was a raging snob and that George Thorley was such a completely natural person, so inwardly sure of himself, that if, in his shirt sleeves, he had found the Queen of England on his doorstep, he'd have behaved to her exactly as he had done to us.

Mrs Snell was in the living room, knitting something in stripes of purple and bright orange, and finishing off a brew of tea.

I said, cheerfully, because it had been a good party and Bob had stood up to it well,

"Here we are, Mrs Snell, nice and early. Has everything been all right?"

"Once they settled down." I detected the ominous note. In the good old days at Scunwick I had employed baby-sitters from time to time and could recognise an incipient complaint a mile off. "It was all right till they started galloping about and woke the little boy. Then he knew I wasn't his Mummy and carried on like anything."

"I gave them strict orders to go to bed at eight."

"So they did. Then they got rowdy and woke the baby."

I said, "I'll sort them out in the morning." I thought, They always know! Left to Elsie they'd put Ella's TV out of action. Left to Mrs Snell, God knows what prank they might have got up to.

I said, "I am sorry, Mrs Snell. I'll drive you home now."

She speared the two balls of wool. I said to Bob:

"Darling, just look in on Tony and see he's covered."

Tony was usually a very sound sleeper. Anything that would wake him must have been rowdy indeed.

No mother should play favourites, but Nature is a bit of arbitrary, the first-born son, so like the man who had fathered him. . . .

"She started it, silly old cow," John said, giving me his straight blue stare. "I don't know what Alice was doing. I was reading. I was nearly asleep and she came bursting in, accusing us of galloping about. We hadn't moved. But she went into a flap and said we had, and that upset Alice. And she cried, and Tony woke up and yelled. I told you, didn't I, that we'd have managed without that silly old cow, clumping about and saying we'd been on the back stairs." I'd known that he resented my hiring Mrs Snell. He'd always been a responsible, self-reliant child, and during Bob's absences had come to look upon himself as the man of the family.

I didn't insult him by asking was that the truth; so far as I knew he'd always been dead honest.

Alice's story was slightly different.

"Mrs Snell heard the bumps, Mummy, and blamed us."

"What bumps?"

"On the back stairs. I've heard them before but John said I was making it up. But I wasn't. There were bumps. And last night Mrs Snell heard them, too. *She* woke Tony, shouting at us. And then I knew I hadn't made up the bumps; and I got scared."

"What exactly do you mean by bumps, darling?"

Alice considered carefully.

"Dull sort of noises. Like people moving something heavy. On the back stairs."

Fear *is* contagious. Just for a moment I felt the prickle of it between my shoulders. What Ella had said I'd dismissed very lightly; she was an overemotional creature and strictly conventional in all her reactions; a rather bleak landing, a locked door in a house that had not been inhabited for five years had had upon her exactly the expected effect; despair; sheer evil; haunted . . .

A child, not yet nine, was rather a different matter. But while thinking of Ella as conventional, I became conventional myself. Applying the old placebos, I said:

"Old houses do make odd noises, Alice. Boards creak and groan. When I was your age," I said, recalling something I hardly knew I remembered, "I lived in an old house. I'd go upstairs, and then every step would settle back into place; just as though somebody were coming up behind me."

(About that my grandmother had been as Draconian as about the loft. Psychologically sound, however. She stood in the hall and told me to go upstairs and listen, count the noises; then come down. Go up again, two steps at a time, and count the noises. Three at a time and count. She had convinced me.)

I said to Alice, "And there are water pipes in this old house too. But I would like to know why things should go bump. Next time you hear the tiniest bump call me and we'll see why."

My modest luncheon party seemed to be successful. The salted beef, coddled and turned about, had the right, the now rare, iridescent glow and I dished it up with the kind of dumpling that they say only a Norfolk-born woman can make. I'd managed it, though.

Kitty Thorley, whose attitude towards me, towards us, had changed as soon as she realised that we were related to *the* Mrs Spender whose gentle voice carried great weight on so many committees, was absolutely enchanted to meet Ella, face to face over a glass of sherry, over a meal. And old Fred Murray-Smith said the right thing, the wrong thing, something that made a link.

"As soon as I turned off the lane, and saw the chimneys," he said, "I knew where I was. Good God, half a century ago. I was staying with my aunt and somebody lent me a pony. The meet was held here. The first time I'd ever tasted cherry brandy. It'd be your grandfather. Marvellous old man."

"That was my grandfather," George Thorley said with no pleasure in his face. Perhaps that was the hunt which had ended fatally. Or perhaps he grudged, retrospectively, the lavish supply of cherry brandy. He had spoken of his grandfather as a spendthrift. Kitty Thorley, however, did relish this reference to past family glory.

We finished our meal with fruit from the wall; a kind of plum which I had not tasted since I was a child; not as ovoid as a Victoria and of a different colour. Absolutely delicious. Favourable comments were made by everyone except Kitty Thorley, and then her husband said:

"You can't buy such stock these days. When we moved down to Park, I laid out a small orchard. It's prolific enough, but nothing tastes the same as the old stuff."

Ella said, "It may be the soil. Mrs Gordon and I once went to the Chelsea Flower Show together and we both fell in love with a new rose. We both ordered a bush. I can only describe it as a silvery pink, quite entrancing and most unusual. In Mrs Gordon's garden it turned almost orange; in mine, plain salmon pink. No trace of the silvery look at all. It was most disappointing. Yes, Mr Thorley," she went on in her sprightly way, "I know what you are thinking—that we received the wrong bushes. But Mr Gordon took it up with the suppliers. They blamed the soil."

George Thorley made the first move to go; explaining that even on Sunday afternoon cows had to be milked and he had only one man who didn't mind working unsocial hours, being a tiger for overtime pay.

Ella, the most resolute dodger of washing-up that I had ever encountered, offered to help me with the dishes. I said I was not going to bother about them just now.

"I must have a word with you. Alone," she said in a low, urgent voice.

We went into the garden.

"Jill, I did warn you about this place—and about Alice. I know, my dear, that you have a great deal to think about. It may have escaped your notice that Alice lives in a perpetual state of terror. She told me that she simply dared not go up to the bathroom alone—in broad daylight."

I had not noticed. I had told Alice to tell me if she heard a bump and we'd investigate it; but she had never mentioned the matter again. Now I was obliged to say, "No, I have not noticed." I had noticed Alice's enthusiastic greeting to her grandmother, and some long, apparently confidential talk. But Alice, quiet and docile, unless led into mischief by John, had always been Ella's—and Elsie's—favourite.

Human behaviour is a very puzzling thing. Here was Ella, very genuinely concerned for Alice, but also slightly triumphant. She had warned me; and the warning was justified. And in me, something that I had always tried to repress—I would *not* fall for that old mother-in-law, daughter-in-law syndrome—reared up. I said,

"Ella, it's just a phase. Most children go through it. I did my-self." Unbelievable as it may sound to you!

Ella said, "That may well be so. I hope it is. But it is a theory susceptible to proof." For a moment I was startled; she sounded like Bob! "I would like to take Alice back with me. If she is still fearful there, then it is a phase. If not, then there is something here to which Alice is susceptible and the rest of you are not." She made a little pause and added, "Mrs Thorley was."

"Oh!"

"Yes. She was trying to explain why they had moved. She told me that from the very first the place had made her uneasy and that to be alone here was torture . . . She doesn't look particularly sensitive, does she? But she is, apparently. Never mind about that. May I take Alice back with me and see what happens."

"Of course. It will, as you say, be a test." Of what?

I did notice that Alice, asked to go back to St Giles' Square—"Elsie and I miss you all so much," Ella said—looked jubilant and then dismayed.

"I must pack," she said and stood rigid. Dear John said:

"I'll come and help you." His next words, "Rather you than me!" I hoped were not audible to Ella.

The test proved positive, from Ella's point of view. In St Giles' Square Alice ran about happily. No fear at all.

For me one of the most immediate results of Alice's going was John's demand for a bike.

He said, very sensibly, "It'd save you a lot of time, Mum."

That was true: school started at nine, the WI shop did not open its doors until ten. If I had shopping to do, I did it in that interval; otherwise it was a wasted hour. Then there were the afternoons. Collect at four o'clock. And I could no longer leave Bob to take charge of Tony. Something that George Thorley had said about harvesting sugar beet had sparked Bob's inventiveness and, working away on something so new as to be revolutionary, he was often lost to the world; so Tony, often objecting loudly, must go with me, wherever I went.

Having a bicycle made John much more mobile; for the few days that remained of that summer term he could do all the after-school things which he had enjoyed while we lived with Ella; and during the summer holiday he and his special pal, a boy called Terry, roamed far and wide, pursuing their newest hobby—brass-rubbing—in such churches as still boasted brasses. They covered a

considerable territory and found at least two churches said to be
haunted; one where, on the anniversary of the Battle of Edgehill,
a bunch of roses mysteriously appeared on a tomb. "Edgehill,"
said my son who had a good head for figures, "was the twenty-
third of October 1642. A bit late for roses, don't you think? The
old woman who was scrubbing about absolutely swore that watch
had been kept. Nobody could have smuggled them in. Terry and I
are thinking of doing a bit of watching ourselves there, this year."
Another expedition took them to the church at Salle, the place
where some people believe Anne Boleyn to be buried under an
unmarked marble slab; and from there John brought home another ghost story. The old sexton had told them that once he had
kept watch all night, and seen only a hare which came in through
a door he'd have sworn was closed and led him a chase and then
vanished. "We might go there, too, but it isn't until May."

"By which time you and Terry will be train-spotting," Bob said.

"Likely!" That was, like "Ah," a country word capable of meaning a great deal; in this case scorn.

During that holiday I felt cut off from Alice. During term time
John saw her, if not in class, in the dining room; his reports were
laconic—she was there, and she looked all right. At the end of
term I had suggested that Alice might like to come home—just
for a little holiday. Alice threw what I recognised as a look of appeal at her grandmother and Ella said, I am sure on the spur of
the moment, that she and Alice and Elsie were thinking of going
to Bywater, just for a breath of sea air. What could I say against
that?

One evening, towards the end of August, with just that faint
hint of autumn in the air, I was in the kitchen, weighing up
runner beans by the pound and slipping rubber bands over each
bunch. I owed the runner beans and several other things to Mr
Thorley, who had given me some plants he had to spare.

John had been out all day, taking with him a very substantial
picnic lunch, but he came in, as always, hungry and said:

"Bacon and eggs! Goodoh!"

"Eggs, sure. No bacon, I'm afraid." I had in fact given up buying bacon; it was fiendishly expensive, and Bob, now settled and
happily occupied, was having a bit of weight problem. Not good
for a weak leg.

"But I can *smell* it. You and Dad ate it all. Gluttons!"

"What you can smell is wishful thinking. We had a meagre, cold, salad supper."

I had in the larder what was left of a bit of boiling bacon—the cheapest of joints. I'd carved it carefully, giving Bob what lean there was, saving the fat for my hens and the bone to make the basis for a vegetable soup. The fat, carefully cut and frizzled in a frying pan, did smell rather like bacon and John ate contentedly.

Then it was September; apples and pears, the last of the plums, the last of the runner beans; the first of the self-sown artichokes which, judging by the demand for them, everybody wanted, and few people bothered to grow. And presently I should have something very rare to sell—walnuts. At the very end of the garden there was a great old tree, one of the few that had survived the eighteenth-century passion for furniture made of walnut wood. In its shade there were shrubs which seemed not to have fared too badly. One, a magnolia, was just breaking into flower and every bloom would be worth fifty pence. We were surviving. Bob had produced some drawing of a sugar-beet harvester, in which a big engineering firm in Peterborough had said—cautiously—that it was interested.

And even Miss Brewster had contributed to the general feeling of well-being; good, conscientious, grey woman she had sent me a note by John; she said that I had been right, Alice's odd drawings had simply been part of a phase; she was still drawing with exceptional originality and skill, but the macabre element which she had mentioned to me had vanished.

That autumn I had another cause for complacency; I was beginning to acquire a few private customers. My first was the proprietress of The Hawk In Hand, once an old coaching inn on the Market Square, now a flourishing hotel. She did all her own buying, and we frequently encountered one another just inside or outside the WI shop and began to exchange Good-mornings, the way people do. Then one morning she said, "I've been waiting for you, Mrs Spender. They haven't got a decent lettuce in the place this morning." It was drawing towards the end of a hot dry summer, but my garden had not suffered; I had access to the moat. Ella had kept her promise to provide a length of chestnut fencing, part of it a gate which could open and shut, all I had to do was to dip out pailfuls. Bob had promised that as soon as his sugar-beet harvester was off the drawing board, he'd devise a less laborious method of irrigation.

Then one morning Mrs Greenfield watched me deliver, and instead of going straight to the counter and buying what she wanted, followed me out to the car, where Tony sat strapped into his little seat inside the passenger seat. She said she had been thinking, how much more convenient for both of us if we dealt direct with each other; it would save her time, and me money.

Naturally the WI shop charged a commission—they had rent and rates to pay, and one or two full-time helpers were paid, too. The idea of saving their percentage was certainly attractive, but I had a somewhat sentimental feeling towards the shop which had given me my start. So I said I'd think about it, and let her know.

The stately old lady who was in complete charge, checking what was brought in for sale, scrupulously rejecting anything not up to her rather exacting standards; deducting from one's credit any perishable article brought in on a former occasion, working out what was due—and all without, it seemed—taking her eyes off what was going on in the shop itself, sat at a high desk, rather like an old-fashioned school-teacher's. She was said to be well over eighty but she had perfected the art of doing four things at once with complete imperturbability.

Tony, who hated being confined in any way, began to drum his heels and shout, "Mummy," at regular intervals, so I had no time to waste. I asked her whether the Women's Institute would mind if I sold a few things elsewhere.

"Why should we? Excuse me. Ah, honey." She held a jar to the light and approved its clarity. "But you *must* fill in the label, Miss Crawley. Place of origin. Have you a pen? We never pretended to hold a monopoly, Mrs Spender. Of course we should still *hope* to have some of your splendid produce. Miss Wade, those iced cakes are in the *full* sun and beginning to melt. I imagine that Mrs Greenfield approached you. Not to *us* a good customer; she buys everything of the best and so much of it. Short of imposing rationing . . . What *beautiful* chrysanthemums, Mrs Yates; we'll try them at seven p. a head and would you tell Miss Barclay to reserve a dozen for me? All *pink*, please. If I may offer a word of warning, Mrs Spender; we are a nonprofit-making concern; Mrs Greenfield is, so keep your eye on current prices and don't be done down."

Feeling slightly dizzy I felt that at least my conscience need not trouble me; and actually all my dealings with Mrs Greenfield were easy and pleasant. She could tell me what she needed and I could tell her whether or not I could supply it. Through her recommendations I found two other regular private customers, both owners of cafés; and through her I learned just a bit more about the house in which I lived. One day Mrs Greenfield produced a very faded early photograph and told me that her great-grandmother—come to that her great-great-grandmother—was thus commemorated.

It is extraordinary how the most unlikely people cling to some sort of lineage. In my days as a librarian I'd met quite a number—some cranks, of course, but some just plain, sensible people anxious to trace, eager to know something about their families. Mrs Greenfield was an eminently sensible woman, and she was plainly a Londoner, but she, and many women before her, had cherished this fading relic. The house in the background was either Gad's or some very similiar building; grouped in front of it were six people. A family; mother and four daughters, and a boy; he was in Highland dress. I judged by the clothes of the young women the date to be in the mid-eighteen forties; the mother had ceased to be fashionable some decade earlier. Except for one, all the girls were of similar height and since Mrs Greenfield was pretty tall, I expected her to point out the tall one as her ancestor; but she pointed to one of the others. "She, we were always given to understand, was our great-grandmother."

I said, "How very interesting." Devoid of colour and even its brown and buff tones fading, the photograph was not very informative.

"And it is Gad's? I've been meaning, ever since we came down here, to go and take a look, but I never had time." She turned the stiff cardboard over and there in ink, as faded as the picture itself, I could read: June 1848; Gad's Glory. First Prize. Mamma; Diana, Deborah, Caroline, Lavinia, George.

I did some of my rather inexpert mental arithmetic and thought that the boy in the kilt might be George Thorley's grandfather, the squanderer of cherry brandy . . . But, given a time-slip, he was the boy the present George Thorley should have had; indeed there was a likeness.

But for that likeness, and the fact that George Thorley had no child, I think I would have borrowed the photograph; a man so wrapped up in the past would have been interested; but it might inflict a hurt.

Mrs Greenfield then said something which relieved my mind of the fear that she might show the picture to him.

"I was given to understand that there've been Thorley's at Gad's since the day of creation, till about five years ago. But my grandmother's name wasn't Thorley; she was born Osborne, and her married name was Spicer. So perhaps she," she touched the girl who looked the haughtiest, "was just on a visit."

"Very likely," I said.

The year moved on and it was time to gather and store apples and pears that would keep and fetch good prices through the winter. For such a job nobody could have better assistants than two lively eleven-year-old boys. Terry and John scrambled about the trees like monkeys all one Saturday morning. Terry was staying for the week-end. In the afternoon they were going to a football match and on Sunday they proposed to carry the baskets and barrels and buckets of fruit up into the attic to store.

George Thorley had taken Bob to a place called Foxton, where there was to be a display of the various virtues of sugar-beet lifters already on the market. I knew that Bob was in good hands. George Thorley had the dead right touch; he didn't think that a weak arm and leg and a hesitancy of speech justified treating a man like an invalid or an idiot; but I knew that if there were seats to be had, Bob would get one and his full share of what the invitation called a Fork Luncheon; and it would all be done without any ostentation.

As soon as the boys had gone it occurred to me that I could usefully employ myself by carrying fruit up to attic so that they could gather in the morning. I'd come up against the fact that I was not quite as lively as I had once been; I often ended the day with a back-ache; nothing to worry about; it stopped as soon as I lay down; but it made me careful about lifting and carrying things. I gave myself reasonable loads as I went up and down that afternoon.

I had some thoughts about Alice. I felt that I had lost her; she should have been here now, helping to gather and carry apples, giving a little time to Tony. I felt that the way she was living was a bit old-maidish and finicky; on the other hand she was plainly the light and joy of life to Ella and Elsie. And I, after all, had spent a lot of time with *my* grandmother, with no lasting harm done, except perhaps a rather too sensitive conscience—something like a grumbling appendix. Real stoics, true Puritans of whatever sect, have at least the consolation of thinking that they have God's approval and are quietly ticking up good marks in some cosmic conduct book. Somewhere along the road I'd lost that happy assurance, but I still wore the harness while lacking the certainty of green pastures awaiting me at the end of the long pull. I was still capable of feeling guilty about Alice and another thing. I'd let Alice go a bit too casually. The other thing was different . . .

All right; if sex mattered so much—or so little—we'd all have been born hermaphrodites. Nature could easily have devised some self-fertilising, self-propagating species and saved everybody a lot of bother.

Like everybody else, I regard myself as normal; I'd certainly been forunate in that I had never felt much urge to bed with anyone until I met Bob; then the attraction was mutual and our married life had been happier than most—and still was, though sex no longer had a part in it. A flaccid leg and arm was no insuperable barrier, I suppose, but all impulses begin in the mind, that is, in the brain, and that part of Bob's had simply gone. When he said to me once, "My poor dear, I'm afraid you're left with only half a man," he meant just that.

We'd accepted the situation calmly, and, I hope, with dignity.

Up to a point George Thorley's behaviour towards us had been the result of his devotion to Gad's; he wanted it to be in suitable hands; he was delighted to see the old things back in place; even the loan of a man to dig, and the gift of a load of manure may have resulted from his desire to see the garden in good shape again.

When I gave my little luncheon party, I had six chairs, all of the kitchen variety, and Bob sat in his swivel chair; John and Alice shared the sawhorse, which was no longer needed as a Tony-deterrent by the moatside. It looked very makeshift and odd, until everyone was in place and eating heartily.

About ten days later George Thorley, on one of his evening visits to Bob, said with his usual inoffensive directness:

"You're a bit short of chairs. I get around quite a lot, sales and such. Would you like me to keep my eye open for you?"

I said, "Yes—so long as you remember that I'm in the market only for chairs at a pound apiece. And at that price, short of a miracle, you're unlikely to find anything that wouldn't disgrace the table."

Very shortly after that he turned up with six chairs, Chippendale style which, had they been genuine, would have been worth thousands. Their drop-in seats were covered with dark brown leather, a bit scuffed but good for another thirty years.

We hadn't then advanced to Christian name terms—when we did it was at his wife's suggestion—so I said, "But Mr Thorley, I told you a pound apiece was my limit."

"Then I got a bargain; six for five-fifty."

"But at Bidwell's, I saw a set exactly the same and that was eighty pounds."

"Floor space is costly now and every now and then Bidwell has a clear-out, and sends a load of stuff along to one of Staple's auctions. This lot nobody wanted; falling between two stools; not genuine antique and not up-to-date. Besides being a bit big for the houses they're building now. Here you are!" He took out and offered me a smudgy bit of paper; Lot 20, £5.50 and a receipt stamp.

He had the somewhat rare gift of receiving as well as giving gracefully. Down at Park there was always plenty of milk and he had a contract with Amalgamated Dairies; but there was often a surplus, and then one of the stockman's wives tried her hand at butter, at cream cheeses, and milk cheeses, she even ventured upon sage cheese. We could have what milk we could use; "What's over goes to the pigs—and they won't miss a pint or two." And other things he'd bring along, just for us to try. In return I gave what I had to spare: two kinds of apple which for some reason did not flourish at Park Farm, and for Kitty, his wife, some boughs of the extremely late-flowering magnolia which grew under the walnut tree. That was a Greek gift, in a way; I wanted access to the fallen walnuts and hacking the magnolia helped . . .

But the moment of truth came over—of all things—a sack of potatoes.

"I'm beginning to lift my main crop," he said. "And they look like being scarce this year. But I don't want you to go short and

I'll set aside some seed ones—they'll be short too—so that you get a good start off with earlies."

The potato shortage was already making itself felt; humble spuds were ten p. a pound and the WI shop had been driven to rationing—nobody to have more than two pounds; and here was I with at least half a hundredweight. Worth five pounds.

I said, "George, I do wish you'd let me pay. For these anyway. Honestly, I can't see why . . ." I broke off because such a change came over his face. God help me, I thought for a second I'd angered him.

"Can't you?"

I blushed so hotly it felt as though my face would melt. I tried to look away, but his gaze held mine; I could only stare, helplessly, and understand and know that my eyes were betraying me, just as his were him.

He broke the spell, or the circuit or whatever it was.

"Where do you want them? Store room or larder?"

I just managed to say, "Larder, please." He lifted the sack as though it weighed nothing. I doubt whether I could have lifted an egg. But I went through into the room which, except for that one occasion, had been Bob's exclusive domain and I said in such an ordinary way that I was astonished.

"George is here. He has brought us a sack of potatoes."

If I'd let go I could have burst into hysterical laughter. A sack of potatoes! And with two words and a look the man had offered himself to me; without saying a word I'd acknowledged—and responded as far as circumstances allowed.

Well, as somebody said—Love is a many-coloured thing. I did not love Bob one whit less. I'd still have gone through hell and high water to save him from a pang of pain or from a humiliating stumble; but I was in love with George Thorley too. And it was ridiculous to make the obvious, trite distinction between the body and the mind. Much of my feeling for George Thorley *was* physical, but I liked him as a person, too.

I'm inclined to think in generalities. Actually what is called the permissive society, wife-swapping, divorces as plentiful as hot dinners, had never appealed to me; too much squalor about it, too many children either completely abandoned or subject to what the papers playfully called the tug-of-love. In a truly civilised society, I thought, with all the taboos, new and old, done away with,

George Thorley and I could have bedded together, with no hurt either to Bob or Kitty, and I'd have given him the son he wanted. And who would have *lost* anything? But that time was not yet; might never be because it demanded a rational approach and the last thing men and women will ever be is rational. They'll be saintly, or devilish, brave or cowardly, intelligent or stupid, but rational, no.

That afternoon, late in October, I went up and down with apples, thinking my own thoughts, minding my own business; making sure for instance that no stored apple touched another. Tony was in the kitchen, engrossed with a new toy. I'd got a good filling dish of mutton and haricot beans simmering away at the back of the oven, awaiting John and Terry, Bob, and George if he chose to stay. On another shelf in the oven I had some of those potatoes, baking in their jackets.

All was well—so long as George and I didn't look at each other, and we no longer did. Alice was all right. I'd rather have had her at home, part of the family, but she was happy with Ella and Elsie and they were happy to have her.

So what hit me as I closed the apple-room door and stood for a moment to ease my aching back? For one thing, utter despair. I knew that Bob would come home with the news that his invention, still under consideration, had been forestalled; I knew that I was heading for a breakdown; mentally I should go silly and do something daft; and physically my back would so cripple me that I could neither harvest what remained nor sow for next year. I thought: I have done my best and it wasn't good enough. Because from the beginning everything has been against me—against everybody. Better, I thought, never to have been born than this; brought out of nothingness, to labour and strive and back into nothingness again; a bit of fungus on the surface of a splinter of a dying star . . .

Tony yelled, "Mummy! Mumm*ee!*"

Moving like an automaton I went down into the kitchen. His new toy—a gift from George—was an engine. It had a driver who when the thing was in action wagged his head, as though surveying the track; at intervals the thing hooted; it had some kind of almost extrasensory organisation because when it ran into an obstacle it would back away and take another course. It ran on batteries.

"Stopped," Tony said. "Mummy do?"

John had always been fiercely independent; Alice moderately so, but Tony was lazy. "Mummy do," had worked its way into the family's private language. Mummy do. Mummy did, remembering some spare batteries in the dresser drawer; George had even remembered to include a box of spares with his present. My hands were shaking so much that I had difficulty in dropping the little tube into the narrow groove.

As clearly and as separately as though it had been the voice of another person, something said in my mind: What you need is a good stiff whisky!

It had never been my drink, except for a dash of it in hot milk as a cold cure. At Scunwick we'd always kept a bottle in the house, mainly for guests. Now, even if we could have afforded to buy spirits, Bob was not allowed them; half a glass of sherry or a glass of white wine occasionally was his limit. But on this late November afternoon there was a half bottle in the house; Ella had kindly smuggled it in, because The Boy Friend would not drink anything else, holding that sherry was bad for the liver and gin a tipple for old hags. In the emotional and physical hustle of removing Alice, she had forgotten to take it back. I'd forgotten about it, too, and until this minute should have had difficulty in finding it. Now I knew exactly. On the top shelf of the larder with several other things not in everyday use and I felt irresistibly drawn towards it. I actually went to the dresser and took a glass.

Tony said, hopefully, "Time for orange juice?" I poured it for him, the neck of the bottle chattering against the glass. I added water and gave it to him.

"Driver first," he said, and spilled a good mouthful over the little plastic figure. I took another glass and went into the larder. As my arm reached up and my fingers closed on the bottle, I knew, in advance, how steadying, soothing and strengthening a good stiff whisky would be. With its aid I could bear with apparent fortitude any bad news Bob brought back from Foxton, realise that an aching back was a very minor affliction, and that being in love with two men not all that unusual.

And that's how drunks are made!

I'd long ago discarded my grandmother's absolute teetotalism —she was a devoted member of the British Women's Temperance Association and invariably wore the little enamelled bow that was its badge—but I seemed to see her face, sorrowful and disapproving. And then I laughed. A fine chance I had of being an alcoholic with the stuff the price it was!

Still, I didn't lift down the bottle and I had grown steadier, capable of testing the meat in the casserole, and of turning the potatoes.

John and Terry came in jubilant; their team had won. Bob and George came in jubilant; there hadn't been a machine at the demonstration anything like the one Bob's would be. A member of the Peterborough firm had been present, had talked to Bob for a long time, and there was to be a visit to the works next week.

George stayed to supper, Saturday being one of Kitty's regular bridge nights. Nothing seemed demanded of me except the dishing out of huge quantities of food. Bob was sticking to his view that rugger was a vastly superior game to soccer. The boys disagreed. George said he'd never played either game. "No time," he said. "My poor old Dad needed all the help he could get, but he was a tiger for education, too. So it was up and milk early in the morning, ride down to Baildon Grammar, scurry home, milking, feeding, mucking out . . . It was those dark evenings I told you about. A wolf behind every bush."

My logical son said, "But Mr Thorley, the last wolf in England was killed in the reign of Henry VIII."

"I knew that. Mine were imaginary wolves. A sight worse than the genuine article." For some reason that sentence seemed to be directed at me; and for the first time since the potato incident we looked at each other, calmly, giving imagination its due; its bad a sight worse, its good a sight better. It was though we had signed a treaty.

In the kind of peace that comes with convalescence, or that follows physical exhaustion, I thought about that attic floor.

Ella had sensed horror and evil.

Mrs Snell had heard bumps; so had Alice; and Alice had felt fright.

I had experienced despair; and there was a time when despair—monks called it *accidie*—was regarded as the ultimate sin, a sin against the Holy Ghost, that indefinable member of the Holy Trinity. Keep the ten commandments and you were all right with God the Father; observe the clauses of the Sermon on the Mount and in addition love thy neighbour and you should be all right with God the Son; but God the Holy Ghost was less easily pacified and because His claims were so very tenuous they must be all the more strictly enforced and reached out not to what people did, or how they behaved, but to how people thought, how they felt; and over such things who has ever had the slightest control? A thought once thought is thought, by no volition of the thinker; a feeling once felt can never be retracted.

I had felt despair, and should never forget it. Ignore it? I could try. What I could not avoid was wondering why. What had happened here? Once upon a time . . .

part two

When, in late summer 1841, George Thorley remarried, his friends—of whom he had many, being a genial and hospitable man—were delighted. A man still in his prime needed a wife, Gad's needed a mistress, the two little girls were growing up wild. Also, considering that there had been a Thorley at Gad's Hall since time immemorial, George needed a son.

There was a little regret that he had chosen a foreigner. For Suffolk men foreigners began at the Norfolk border and the second Mrs Thorley came from Leicester. A few young women, and their fathers, a decent widow or two were disappointed, but George Thorley had always been a bit of a gadabout. He bred pedigree cattle, Durham shorthorns, and was forever going to shows and sales. He'd go to Leicester, Colchester, even London almost as casually as his friends went to a local market.

The wedding took place in Leicester and was very quiet. Nobody was invited and that was understandable; second marriages—the bride was a widow—were perfectly legal, often desirable, but not matters for much display. It was rumoured that the second Mrs Thorley had two daughters of her own, very near in age of the two Thorley girls.

Her arrival was awaited with great interest and curiosity and her actual presence a matter for speculation—and some dismay. What on earth had good old George gone and done?

At first sight, at a distance she looked rather young and pretty; close to she looked older, and worn, her cheeks rather hollowed under high sharp cheekbones, her nose thin and high arched. Beautiful eyes—if you admired them so dark as to be almost black, which nobody in Suffolk did, and a wealth of hair, so black as to have a blue sheen, like a blackbird's plumage. Her figure, though shapely, was slight.

Her older daughter was nine, her young seven and a half. Their name was Osborne. Diana Osborne. Lavinia Osborne. The Thorley girls, with their more homely names, Deborah and Caroline, fitted in between.

Women, much concerned with breeding, were inclined to think that the new Mrs Thorley might not give George the son he needed. She was not as young as she looked, and her second daughter was not—if they were any judge—healthy. Very pale, and what they called pingling.

A few hard-headed men in George Thorley's circle wondered if money might not be concerned. Cattle breeding and showing was likely to cost more than it brought in. Not one of them would have married the new Mrs Thorley, with all her airs and graces, and two girls into the bargain, without considering the financial side. And she always acted as though she had money; very high-handed. And look what she was doing to Gad's! Wallpaper, a new kitchen range. Unless the woman had money, then old George must be daft! And would he, after all, get the boy he craved?

And what kind of stepmother would she make? With two of her own?

The answer to that was: Unique! Even the sharpest-eyed critic never saw a ha'p'orth of difference in the treatment of the four girls. When one had a new outfit, so did the others; identical in quality, similar in style, differing in colour. The new Mrs Thorley once said that if she had only one apple she would divide it into four as evenly as possible.

You could tell an Osborne girl from a Thorley if you saw them close to and knew what you were looking for. Both the Osborne girls had black hair and dark eyes; the Thorleys were fairer, with light eyes. Most people soon gave up trying to distinguish between them and they were known collectively as the Gad's girls.

They all called Mrs Thorley Mamma, and in that simple word something of the change which was overtaking Gad's was foreshadowed. Ordinary people's children called their parents Mother and Father. George Thorley was subjected to some good-natured teasing from his intimates. "And how is Papa today?" It sounded a bit daft in the Corn Exchange or the market at Baildon, but George bore it good-humouredly until one day when he'd had enough of it and said, "Well enough to give you a clout on the jaw Sam Stamper if you don't lay off." And everybody could see that he meant what he said. He was a giant of a man and although nobody, least of all he, himself, knew anything about it, in his veins ran the blood of the Viking people who had come in along the Wren River a thousand years ago, bent not upon a quick raid and a quick retreat, laden with booty, but upon settlement; the acres to plough; the roof tree to build. Permanence.

And, fortunate fellow, all must admit; within a year, the new Mrs Thorley had given him what he wanted—a great, lusty boy.

Imperceptibly, by this little step and that little step, he gave her what she wanted.

None of George's old friends could honestly say that the new Mrs Thorley had discouraged them, done a thing, said a word which hinted at a severance. All his old friends were made welcome, but they dropped away.

No power on earth could really make an East Anglian farmer feel inferior—it was in the Bible; a man diligent in his business could stand before the King and not be shamed—but even a diligent man, ready to stand up before the King, though it was now Queen, could be made to feel awkward.

Awkward because . . .

Well . . . The doctor was somebody you sent for when all the home remedies had failed. The lawyer was somebody you went to to draw up your will or settle a debateable point about boundaries, fishing rights, or some such; and parsons had their function too. But meeting Mr Gordon, Doctor Taylor, the Reverend Mr Spicer and more of their kind at a table, set with too many knives, spoons and forks, that was different. That was awkward.

And wives were inclined to be bothersome after a visit to Gad's. Why couldn't they have wallpaper, a piano, a necessary house with a contraption above the seat which poured sawdust into the cavity under the seat; why couldn't they have a new range cooker and a yellow chinaware sink instead of the old grey stone one? Why couldn't their girls go to Miss Hardwicke's Female Academy?

Women, in fact, were best kept away from Gad's, and before young George was a year old, his father's *real* hospitality was restricted to all-male gatherings after Wednesday market days, sessions where you could discard your jacket, use earthy expressions, play Blind Hookey and drink all you wanted to, trusting your horse to get you safely home.

Mrs Thorley seldom disturbed these parties; she might indeed not have been there, except that the food, solid, simple and easy to manage, was better than in the days when George lived alone; and now and then she could be heard playing the piano in what she called the drawing room, but which in their homes would have been known as the parlour.

If George Thorley ever noticed that his life was now conducted on two social levels, the fact did not disturb him. His dear Isabel was a woman of education, and naturally she preferred the company of educated people. He adjusted easily; he had the natural dignity of his breed without its prejudice against airs and graces; in fact a submerged liking for airs and graces had drawn him to Isabel in the first place. Now and again one of his new friends proved useful in a practical way. It was from Mr Walford, who owned the Sudbury Brewery that George first heard of a new kind of barley, especially suitable for malting. It was Mr Fallowfield, who owned the recently established, but very flourishing Bacon Factory, who mentioned—over the port—the public's changing taste in bacon. "I don't mean the poor," he said, "they like it fat —and they need it. But they rear their own pigs and get the bacon cured by a hit or miss method. We don't cater for them. Those we do cater for prefer more lean meat. And the way to get that is to let pigs range. Cooped in a filthy stye, a pig, however poorly fed, gains weight, which is what most people aim at. We don't. After all," he said, "what was the wild boar, once considered a kingly dish, but a pig which had had plenty of exercise?"

George Thorley was capable of taking a hint. He had inherited from his father three hundred acres of good arable land up at Gad's, two hundred and fifty acres, mainly pasture, down at Park. And the herd, which had been his father's hobby and pride, but which, as some of his old friends suspected, often proved to be a burden rather than a support. For sentiment's sake, for pride's sake he'd kept the herd together and, when necessary, subsidised it from the profits of ordinary mixed farming, and they would come down with a bump if the people now agitating for a repeal of the Corn Laws had their way.

George Thorley was glad to plant the new kind of barley in his biggest field and to turn another one over to pigs which appeared to revel in their new conditions, giving plain proof that pigs were not necessarily filthy, sluggish animals.

He profited, too, from association with Mr Gordon, the lawyer, who knew everything that was to be known about taxes.

Isabel was helpful in other ways. You'd never think of it to look at her, but she had a good head for figures and was more than handy with a pen.

No marriage—leave alone any second marriage—had ever been more successful.

It lasted for seven years.

In June 1848, George Thorley, in perfect health and high good spirits, went off to London to show his very promising young bull, Gad's Glory. The Cattle Show, which took place in Hyde Park, lasted only three days, but beasts must go well beforehand, to get settled in after the journey; careful owners saw to such things themselves, and also supervised the loading up for the homecoming. And, win or lose, there was some celebrating to be done. And a bit of shopping. All in all, he expected to be away for a week, maybe eight days.

Before he left he said to his wife, "Now, let me see, Diana'll be seventeen next month. Leaving school and putting her hair up. Old enough for ear-rings, eh? I'll have a look round. And you, my dear, what would you like as a fairing?"

She was a woman of sound good sense and she was not greedy. She said:

"Nothing, my dear. You have already given me so much."

So much! He had long ago ceased to distinguish between the girls; they were all his, as they were all hers. His little girls had lacked a mother, her little girls a father; goodwill on all sides, needs dovetailing, had produced that happy family atmosphere.

He came home in a state which his wife diagnosed as due to exhaustion and a bit too much celebrating—Gad's Glory had won a minor award.

In the morning he was worse rather than better and she sent a boy on horseback into Baildon to summon Doctor Taylor, who, a friend, a frequent guest, came immediately and for a while straddled the thorny fence which every physician occasionally faced. To tell or not to tell?

Say cholera and throw everybody into a panic?

Keep silent and put the whole household at risk?

It was some time since there had been a major epidemic of the dreaded disease in Baildon, just sporadic outbreaks in unsanitary districts like Scurvy Lane, and even they were frequently confused with what were called putrid summer fevers. There was no known specific cure, just opium to relieve the pains. There was no certain guard against the spread of infection, except isolation.

"Has George been near his father?"

"No. He was in bed when my husband came home last night. And this morning—as you see."

"Servants?"

"Our stockman, Joe Snell, brought him home, carried up his valise, and helped him off with his boots. I am the only person in the house who has been in contact . . ."

And I, she thought with remorse, attributed even his raging thirst to the effect of too much drinking.

Doctor Taylor hesitated. To ask so dainty-handed a woman to nurse, all unaided, what might be a cholera case did not seem exactly right. Perhaps the stockman, already at risk . . .

Mrs Thorley took the decision.

"I will do all that is necessary, Doctor Taylor. I spent the night with him. I have already been exposed . . . to whatever it is."

The old doctor had always considered her charming, and a good manager; now he was grateful for her quick understanding.

On his way home Doctor Taylor looked in at the other farm. Joe Snell was at work, in his usual good health. He'd spent his nights alongside his charge; Master had put up at a hotel on the edge of the Park, very fine place, like a palace. No, he hadn't seen anybody ailing, nor heard anything about sickness being about, but of course the crowds everywhere were so thick that a man might have been dead and not able to fall down.

Giving her orders from the top of the kitchen stairs, Mrs Thorley began organising. "No, Jenny, don't come near me. Doctor Taylor does not yet know what ails your master, but we are taking precautions." A sheet soaked in vinegar to be hung outside the bedroom door; a constant supply of barley water to supply the moisture lost by the frequent vomiting and the evacuations—both of which had now taken on the appearance of water in which rice had been boiled; every hour a shovelful of red hot embers to be brought to the top of the stairs, with a good bunch of fresh lavender. The best disinfectant known.

Her main concern was for George. Six years old, very precocious and more than a little spoiled. She was, in fact, the only person with the slightest control over him, and that influence could not operate through a third person. He'd scent a mystery, lift the vinegar sheet, open the door. The wonder was that he had not already done so, for he was as inquisitive as a monkey. The explanation was most probably the new pony. George—often called Georgie—was a most fortunate child; absolutely idolised by his father, by his mother—a little less absolutely, but far enough; he was, after all, her justification, her return for all that Gad's had given her, and a living contradiction to the doubt which had shown itself in the eyes of George's old friends—was she young enough? Was she able? So in her way, she had been indulgent, too. And there were the girls; three of them; not Lavinia. Perhaps, of all the people with whom she came in contact, the little half-brother, aged about two, had first sensed something different in Lavinia. The others, incipient mothers, had contributed towards the spoiling.

What to do with a spoiled little boy who must be kept safe? Who would be better out of the house? Mrs Thorley, making her eighth or ninth trip to the head of the kitchen stairs, found the answer.

George loved receiving gifts, but he loved even more giving them. This endearing quality could be exploited.

"Jenny!"

"Yes, Ma'am."

"Now listen carefully. Tell Willy to kill a fowl and make it ready for table."

"Is Master better?"

"I cannot yet tell. The fowl is for Mrs Spicer. Listen. I want Master George to ride down to the Rectory with the fowl and a dozen eggs. And a note. Here it is. Catch."

The folded paper fluttered like a butterfly.

Most fortunately, Mrs Thorley was now on Christian names terms with the Rector and his wife and had been able to scribble: Dear Amelia . . .

The Spicers were very poor; the living of Stonham St Paul's was a meagre one, and Mr Spicer's passion for buying old books would have tried even a better-balanced budget. Mrs Thorley had often thought, half-exasperated, that they did not make the best of their resources; surely, between them, they could have kept a few hens, cultivated some vegetables, let off part of the vast rambling Rectory. She had known poverty herself, and knew that it must be fought. The Spicers just drifted along, he resigned, she rather plaintive. They kept only one general maid-servant and spent little on food. A prime table bird and a dozen eggs would predispose Mrs Spicer to accede to the request: Please try to persuade Georgie to stay with you until tomorrow. My husband returned last evening feeling very unwell, and Doctor Taylor has not yet named his ailment. The boy has not been near him. I am sorry to impose upon you . . .

*

"What is a Garden Fête?" George asked suspiciously.

"A kind of Fair, dear."

"Roundabouts?"

"About that I cannot be quite certain. There will be fireworks."

(In her mind, the Rector's wife defined a Garden Fête exactly —a means of extracting money from people; sometimes, as in her case, ill-spared money. Yet it was for a good cause—missionary work in India—and if the Rector of a parish did not support so worthy an effort, it would look very bad indeed.)

"That'll be after dark, Mrs Spicer?"

"Yes, dear. But in her letter to me your Mamma gave her consent for you to stay here. So that will be quite all right. Put your pony in the stable. Can you unsaddle him?"

"Yes. Deb—that is Deborah, you know—she showed me and made me practise. Deb—Deborah knew I was to have a pony this summer and she said nobody was fit to have a pony if he couldn't look after it."

He had mastered the principle of names used within the family and those used outside it. Diana was Di, Deborah, Deb; Caroline, Caro, just as he was Georgie. Outside was different. And for some reason Lavinia had never been called by a shortened version of her name.

"Deborah was quite right," Mrs Spicer said, forgetting for a moment that of all the Gad's girls, Deborah was the one she liked least. For no particular reason, except that there was something . . . well, call it uncompromising about the rather too tall, slightly angular girl with her clear blue-grey stare.

Because they were all going to a Garden Fête at Stonham St Peter's where refreshments would be on sale, they had what Mrs Spicer called a light lunch which George did not regard as a meal at all. Some kind of milk pudding, but not milky and not sweet, rather peppery, if it tasted of anything at all.

But for this deprivation, George made up at the Fête.

He appeared to have a pocketful of money, and, sadly spoiled as he was, he was a well-mannered little boy. He plied Mrs Spicer with sandwiches, with slices of Victoria sponge, with cups of tea, with glasses of lemonade. He bought raffle tickets, tickets for the enclosure where a pig was bowled for, and another where a little plot of ground had been dug and a treasure buried. There you planted stakes, all numbered. He spent at least two shillings on the Hoop-la, sharing the rings with her. You try, Mrs Spicer. Very little expenditure was required of her.

Mr Spicer, at the last moment, had decided not to accompany them. He pleaded lumbago—everybody knew how suddenly that could strike! He would not have let Amelia go alone, but she would now not be alone, she'd have the company of this exuberant, garrulous six-year-old. Mr Spicer knew that it was a Christian's duty to love children. Suffer little children to come unto me, Christ had said; and there was threat, too, that only those who became as little children could inherit the Kingdom of Heaven. But there it was; just as some people could not bear spiders, or cats, he could not abide children. He would not have hurt one for anything in the world, he would have saved the life of one at the risk of his own; it was their company, perhaps just the pitch of their voices, that set him on edge. Yet he had married, stood in front of an altar and heard a fellow cleric pontificate about the purpose of marriage and known all the time that he was marrying Amelia because a country parson—he had just accepted this poor living—needed a wife. A wife was cheaper than a housekeeper, or a curate. He regarded the childlessness of the marriage as a blessing. But there loomed on the horizon a long-dreaded day: if prices went on rising he would be obliged to take pupils. They would be day boys, he decided, and they would take lessons only in the mornings, five days a week.

Left to himself, George would have gone home immediately after breakfast—one egg, no bacon, two pieces of badly made toast. He would demand a proper breakfast when he reached home. He was also anxious to give his mother the prize which the Hoop-la stall had eventually yielded—a piece of pottery in the form of a cow, crude but lifelike. He'd had his eye on it from the first.

However, Mrs Spicer had several errands to be done in the village. "It is such a long time since I had somebody sensible to do an errand for me, George."

"I'll ride," he said, "then it won't take me long. And then I'll go straight home."

"Not straight home, dear. There will be things to bring back here."

Some of the errands were genuine; some concocted. Mrs Spicer was doing her duty as she saw it, and she imagined that soon some message would come from Gad's. She did not regard it as unethical to send George to ask a question of Mrs Catchpole, in whose garden the Fête had taken place: Did you chance to find a glove yesterday? She asked George to return a book she had borrowed—that was a bit of a sacrifice on her part since she had not finished it and although the Rectory contained many books they were all beyond her understanding. With the book went a little note, asking Miss Riley to detain George as long as possible; she would explain this singular request when next they met. The loaf of bread was needed, in a way, though ordinarily it would not have been bought until tomorrow.

No fewer than five gloves had been found, all left-hand ones; three white, one grey, one lavender mauve.

"I don't suppose you noticed, George, what colour Mrs Spicer's gloves were yesterday." He had not. Mrs Catchpole knew something of Mrs Spicer's circumstances and knew that the loss of a glove could be serious. No lady ever went out without gloves.

"I think it would be as well if you took them all. I'll wrap them."

She then remembered that there was lemonade left over.

Miss Riley detained him even longer. She was not inventive, and when she had spent as long as possible over the choice of book to replace the one just returned, and shown him how her cat could sit up, almost like a dog if a tit-bit were offered, she could think of no further delaying tactic, except to ask him to wait while she wrote a little note in reply to Mrs Spicer's. She took an exceptionally long time about it and George fidgetted. He *must* get home soon. Before he starved to death. Since yesterday morning's breakfast he hadn't had what he called a proper meal at all, and although he had himself taken a good fowl to the Rectory, he distrusted what would be made of it. People who couldn't make decent toast even! Last night, Mrs Spicer had said that after all they had eaten at the Fête, a glass of hot toddy would suffice. And the Rectory hot toddy bore absolutely no relationship to the beverage served at Gad's to anyone suffering from a cold. George was only six but he knew milk and water when he saw it.

Nor was his concern only for himself. His pony, Tom Thumb, was a fellow sufferer. At the Rectory there was a stable and once it had been occupied by an ancient horse which might have lived a little longer and still served had anybody understood that teeth wore down, that hay must be munched and oats champed and that very old horses could only survive and go on being serviceable if fed with pappy stuff.

What that long-dead horse—dying of inanition—had left in his manger, some shreds of desiccated hay, a few mouldering oats, had been as unacceptable to the spoiled pony as the food inside the Rectory had been to his young master. Tom Thumb was at the moment better off than his master because at every stopping place he could snatch mouthfuls of grass, managing, despite the bit in his mouth to get some enjoyment, some sustenance. Once let them get back to Gad's . . .

Mrs Spicer had received the expected message and wondered whether it was her duty to break the sad news. She shrank from the task. Some eighteen, nineteen years ago she had been obliged —since there was nobody else to do it—to break the news of total bereavement to a little boy about a year older than Georgie Thorley now was. It was an experience which she did not wish to repeat. To that other little boy she had had the obligation of relationship, though he was only her nephew by marriage. To this little boy she had no such obligation. His mother was alive and the messenger who had informed her would by this time be in Baildon, telling the girls, calling them home to support their mother. So, seeing George off, Mrs Spicer said no more than, "I fear, my dear, that you will find a sad house. Be good."

*

Queen Victoria had not yet made widowhood a full-time profession, but a year in full mourning and at least six months' seclusion from the world were rules enforced upon all but such unfortunate women as must go out to earn bread. Mourning was not intended to be becoming, and that of Mrs Thorley and the girls did not even fit, having been bought ready-made at the one shop in Baildon which stocked such low-class things. Doctor Taylor, now confirmed in his suspicion, and aware of the hot weather, had advocated early interment. Much mourned by all who had known him, George Thorley went to his grave, to lie peacefully amongst his forebears—one of whom had been killed at Crécy and brought home at a cost which had burdened Gad's with debt for two years.

By his own request his coffin was borne by four of his own employees.

He had made a will, not of the makeshift last-minute affairs which served so many of his kind. He had had the advantage of being on social terms with Mr Gordon, and Mr Gordon knew the value of a will, properly drawn and properly witnessed. George Thorley had made his will when his son was eighteen months old, and when he fully expected to live to see a riotous coming-of-age party. He had not regarded it seriously for more than the time it took to make it. But—after all even lawyers must live—once he'd settled down to it, he did, as he had done most things, very thoroughly.

That he wished to be carried to his grave by his own employees was not the only idiosyncratic thing about his will. He wanted his wife, Isabel, to be his sole executor.

"But that is most unusual, "Mr Gordon protested. "Too heavy a burden for a woman."

"My wife has a head for business."

And there was nothing legal against it. By some curious anomaly, which even Mr Gordon recognised, women were nothing; everything they owned, unless carefully guarded by marriage settlements, belonged to their husbands. Even if they earned money it was not their own. On the other hand, there was something almost sacrosanct about the will of a dead man, reaching out from the grave. A will was a will, and made by a man obviously of sound mind . . .

But, taking note of other details, the lawyer wondered what exactly would be the legal position if a man, as sound in mind as George Thorley was, named a monkey in the Regent's Park Zoo as sole executor? To him it seemed almost as extreme as that, though he liked Mrs Thorley as a person and admired the way she ran her house and what could have been an awkward family.

George Thorley evidently had unlimited faith in his wife's ability. To her and to her alone, he entrusted not only the executing of his will, but, until the coming of age of his son, complete control of his estate and all his business interests. After that she was to have an income of five hundred pounds a year.

He had dealt with his daughters and stepdaughters in identical fashion; each girl was to receive five hundred pounds upon her marriage or her twenty-first birthday.

Just as, seven years earlier, there had been much speculation as to what the new Mrs Thorley would be like, so interest now centred about what she would do. The most sensible course, and the most likely, was to appoint a reliable foreman; the two farms together were too much for one woman to handle, and there were aspects to the breeding business quite unsuitable for such a lady-like creature to know about, let alone deal with.

Most of the old friends, and some of the more recent, could name a suitable candidate for the overseer's post. Almost every family had a younger son. Some fathers by pinching and screwing managed to provide farms for their second or even third sons; holdings smaller in size and generally inferior in quality to the family acres. Other boys must seek employment and the area offered few posts both congenial and suitable for a young man with farming blood in his veins. It was a district of farms rather than large estates and such of the gentry, like Lord Chelsworth and Sir Archibald Hepworth, who had more land than they cared to administer themselves, appointed poor relatives who were called agents and often very grand indeed. A good many farmers' sons, armed with what cash was available, emigrated to Canada or

Australia, where land was to be had for the asking. Others remained at home, helping out and hoping that luck would bring them a bride who had no brother.

Sam Stamper made the first approach and was thus the first to hear the startling news. He began gently, commiserating with the widow and saying how greatly George would be missed by one and all. Then he said:

"I'd like you to know, Mrs Thorley, that if there's anything I can do, in any way to be of help you've only to give the word."

"That is extremely kind of you. I am sincerely grateful."

"I expect it's a bit early days for you to decide what you're going to do. I mean about keeping on the farm and suchlike."

"There is no question of decision. Naturally my husband expected me to keep everything going. Just as before."

"Well, I bin thinking about that. As you know, I got three boys. Sam'll hev the old place and I managed to set Tom up on his own. But times ain't what they were and I doubt if I can give Peter a proper start. He's talking about going abroad and that'd just about break his mother's heart."

Although Mrs Thorley had not spent much time in the company of George's old cronies, she knew how, on any important matter, they'd circle round before closing in. She guessed what was coming and said, pleasantly:

"Yes, I am sure Mrs Stamper would feel it very much. He is her youngest."

"He's the best of the bunch, too," Sam said, recklessly sacrificing the others in Peter's interest. "He's the hardest worker of the lot. More interested in animals, too. Rare stockman Peter is."

There it was, the bait plainly dangled. She had only to take it, and there they'd be, everything nicely arranged and without either one of them feeling under an obligation to the other. And that was a very important part of striking a good bargain.

She sat there, a small, fragile figure in her black which emphasised the pallor of her face and hands.

"There's another thing," something that should appeal to *her*.

"Peter is edjercated. He did so well at the village school, my missus insisted he should hev two years at Baildon Grammar."

(Behind that simple statement lay a history of struggle, a clash of arms. By some unwritten law farmwives like Mrs Stamper were entitled to egg-and-butter money, their own to earn, their own to spend. When Mrs Stamper expressed her wish to spend egg-and-butter money on a bit of further education for Peter, her husband had protested. She had retorted by using the underdog's only weapon: the withdrawal of labour. Very well, if what she earned couldn't be spent as she wished it to be, she'd give up. And you couldn't compel a woman to make the best butter, the best cheese, by clouting her over the head. Peter had had his two years.)

Mrs Thorley, as fully aware as Sam Stamper of the formalities that must be observed, said:

"It was so kind of you to think of it, Mr Stamper. But . . . as a matter of fact, I intend to run Gad's and Park myself."

"What?" Momentarily jerked out of rustic caution, Sam Stamper almost shouted. Park meant the herd, and the herd meant . . . well, a lot of stuff no female should dabble in.

"You are surprised? I am prepared to admit that I may not succeed. But I intend to try. Wish me luck, Mr Stamper. I shall need it."

Nobody could know now, or, if she had her way, would ever know, how she was once again in need of luck, good luck. She had known both kinds.

A stormy past; pretty, pampered daughter of a Westmorland squire, she had married young, the man of her choice, handsome, gay, well connected.

Delighted by the match, her father had given her five thousand pounds as a dowry. What was hers was Stephen's, and he knew how to spend money; he also knew, when the money was spent, how to live lavishly for short periods of time, on credit, and how to vanish when creditors became too demanding. There were bad spells, and good ones; he was not a consistently unlucky gambler and although in the end his immediate family renounced him entirely, he received, from time to time, legacies from old aunts who remembered him as a charming boy. A great deal of the charm remained, and for years Isabel could be completely disillusioned and then reinfatuated and furious with herself for so being.

They spent some time in France; once, as a result of a legacy, in Paris, where old families were desperately trying to bring back the old days and forget that the Revolution had ever occurred, or Napoleon ever existed. France at the time was madly Anglophile; the English had sheltered members of the French royal family and a number of aristocrats. The almost legendary figure of the English milord—free with his guineas—was partially restored. That had been a wonderful time. The second visit to France—to Boulogne, where living was so much cheaper than in England—was less happy.

So life had swung like a see-saw and when Isabel was widowed for the first time—Stephen had shot himself in a moment of despair—she was left with almost nothing, and with two little girls to support.

Why had she chosen to settle in Leicester? Because it was new and growing and there she was unlikely to meet anyone who knew her. That was her main concern; not to be shamed.

She set about earning a living with the poor weapons at her disposal. She could sew, draw, play the piano. All her activities must be home-based, because of Diana and Lavinia, whom she certainly did not intend to hand over to some indifferent, ignorant servant. So everything she did must be done within the confines of the narrow, hired house.

No slave ever worked harder. Anybody could sew, but Mrs Osborne could design dresses as well. Mrs Osborne, on a hired piano, taught unwilling little girls with ten thumbs to hammer out a tune. An enterprising man named Blaker started up a pottery factory and Mrs Osborne drew designs for him.

In the end it was the one asset which she had not considered that brought her good fortune. One spare room.

Just around the corner from St Martin's, an old, respectable street, stood the inn; and for the innkeeper's daughter, Mrs Osborne had designed a wedding dress of such glory that the bride's mother felt that something more than mere cash—which in any case would drift through the dressmaker—was needed. She went herself to say: Thank you . . Mrs Osborne received her, civilly but coolly, and gave her a cup of very weak tea—sure sign of poverty in the eyes of the innkeeper's wife, who liked hers almost black. There were other signs, too. Apart from the piano there was not an article of furniture worth twopence; except for a rag rug in front of a wretched fire the floor was bare; Mrs Osborne and her two little girls wore dresses of the poorest material. Yet the innkeeper's wife knew a lady when she saw one, and Mrs Osborne was certainly a lady, brought low, but, to judge from her bearing, proud.

Praising the bride's dress and sipping her tasteless tea the kindly woman cast about in her mind for some way of helping which would not humiliate, and before her cup was empty had hit upon a possible way.

"I did come, Mrs Osborne, to thank you for helping Miss Ramsey to make that dress—it made Maggie's waist look inches smaller; but I had another reason, too. A favour I wanted to ask of you."

"Oh yes?" I am in no position to do you or anybody else a favour.

"It's like this . . . The town's so busy these days we're often fuller than we can hold. There's men that don't mind sharing a room, and others that do. We've talked about building on, but that'd cramp the yard; and we ain't always crowded. I wondered whether, now and again, you'd let us a bedroom. You're so near, you see. We'd pay two shillings a night, just for the bed. And I promise I'd only send you a nice sort of gentleman; nobody rough or drunk."

"I have a spare room," Mrs Osborne said. No need to mention that it was completely unfurnished. Two shillings was what Mr Blaker, Miss Ramsey and one other dressmaker paid for a design; and the price of a piano lesson was sixpence.

Judging by the furniture of the sitting room the bed wouldn't be up to much. Easily remedied, and again done with the most delicate tact. There were men who, while not objecting to sharing a room, insisted upon separate beds, so there were one or two double beds stored away somewhere; together with other various bits and pieces. If Mrs Osborne could find room . . .

The infinitely experienced eye had no difficulty in selecting the kind of guest who would not wish to share a room and would gladly accept the alternative—just a few steps round the corner. George Thorley, up for a Cattle Show, was such a one.

If he noticed the poor gimcrack quality of the sitting-room furniture—in such sharp contrast to the solidity of the stuff in the bedroom—he attributed it to fashion's whim and to the fact that there was no man in the house to require solid chairs and tables. He was much impressed by the airs and graces of the lady of the house, and equally by the behavior of her two girls—much the same age as his own, who were beginning to grow a bit wild.

On the first evening of his stay he decided to turn in early, and found Mrs Osborne, whom the landlady of the inn had described as a friend who now and then obliged her by putting a spare room at her disposal in crowded times, drinking the cup of tea which constituted her evening meal. She offered him one and over it they sat and talked.

She liked him; the deep instinct which under the pressure of Stephen's charm had failed her, informed her that here was a man, solid, reliable and kindly—and, it emerged, badly in need of a wife. Somebody had mended his shirt, so badly that in places the stitches were breaking away. She mentioned it, offered to make a better job of it, which she did, and he was absurdly grateful because she had noticed and bothered; not because a patched shirt meant much; he had brought four others . . . He also had two farms and some prime stock cattle; he reckoned, he said, that the bull he brought to the show, Gad's Goliath, should sweep the board.

She liked him. Even when he showed very clearly that his feeling for her was far warmer than liking and she knew that she was incapable of reciprocation. She'd known love and had seen it wear out as even the sturdiest fabric could do, subject to friction; she wanted no more of it. And although he offered the one thing that she and Diana and Lavinia needed most—reasonable financial security—she was careful about committing herself. She wondered what he was like when he was drunk; Stephen drunk had been another person entirely.

There was the question of class awareness—quite a different thing from snobbery. She faced it squarely; George Thorley was not a man whom her father would have asked to dine at his table. He had natural good manners. No education. No sophistication. He was not of her world—but then who was? Now? It was all too easy, as she had proved, to move from one world to another.

She was not deliberately acting hard-to-come-by; she was genuinely uncertain; but the delay, through the last weeks of June, all of July, all of August, strengthened her hand enormously. During that time, the busiest in a farmer's year, he had snatched time for visits, and he had written to her, letters quite touching in their naïveté. Like a schoolboy's first letters to his love. Which, in effect they were; George Thorley had married, as most men of his kind did, a neighbour's daughter; an eminently suitable young woman for whom he had felt—as a man should—respect and regard and affection. Romance had never brushed him with its extraordinary wing, until Leicester. Until Isabel.

So it had come about, and it had lasted for seven years, and now it was over and Mrs Thorley was once again facing a financial crisis. Not the acute one; not like knowing where the next rent, the next imposition of rates, the next pair of shoes were to come from, but nonetheless a crisis. She certainly could not afford to hire Peter Stamper or any other likely young man. In fact if the girls were to have their dowries, she must be active, cunning, smart.

They sat at the table, and she looked at them, and thought: *All my pretty ones*. And that was something from *Macbeth*, a play which everybody connected with the stage regarded as unlucky to quote from. She knew such things because her first husband, early in their marriage, had conceived a passion for an actress.

My pretty ones! Two pairs of sisters but with no more in common than the bloom of youth—and Lavinia lacked even that—and their ugly mourning dresses. A stranger would have taken Deborah Thorley for the eldest, she was so much taller, a long-legged, rather angular girl who already wore a look of reliability and responsibility. As she advanced out of childhood her fair hair had darkened to something perilously near sandy and her eyes were a clear blue-grey. She was very much like her father, a typical Thorley.

Diana Osborne was smaller with a figure softly rounded above and below the greatly admired eighteen-inch waist. She was very vain of her appearance and spent most of her pocket money on creams and lotions to preserve her already flawless complexion and her milk white hands. Miss Hardwicke, who believed that girls should be clean and tidy and give their serious attention to their lessons, slightly disapproved of Diana Osborne and mentally referred to her as Young Madam. Diana's conduct seldom warranted reproof, her work sometimes did and on these occasions the rebuke was received with an icy dignity which even the schoolmistress found disconcerting. The ability to look down one's nose when being scolded was rare and not altogether desirable.

Caroline Thorley should have been the beauty of the family by the criterion of colour, her hair had deepened to golden, and was curly and her eyes were deep, almost violet blue; but her nose was snub, her mouth too wide; there was something monkeyish about her face though it lacked entirely the melancholy of the simian face; she was gay, frivolous, mischievous, a bit of a hoyden. From

her a rebuke evoked ready tears and earnest promises of amend-
ment. Then, within ten minutes she'd be laughing, in the centre
of a group of giggling girls; not a care in the world.

Neither Mrs Thorley, that careful mother, nor Miss Hardwicke,
experienced as she was, could make anything of Lavinia. Silent,
withdrawn, absentminded, unpunctual, indifferent. She had been
a thin, pale child, and the years had not changed her much.
George Thorley had said, in his hearty way, "The country air'll
soon put the roses in your cheeks." The country air had been of
no avail, nor had the good food, nor the doctor's advice or the
nostrums, cod-liver oil, iron pills, sure cure for anaemia. Over
fifteen now, Lavinia still had the lost-child, waif-like look.

She had inherited her mother's skill with paint brush and pencil, she drew well, but all her drawings had a touch of fantasy.
Mrs Thorley had occasionally thought that if ever—which God
forbid—Lavinia were reduced to making designs for pottery or for
dresses, there would be no buyers.

For her younger daughter's oddity—her complete inability to
make friends, for instance—Mrs Thorley blamed the circum-
scribed life they had led in Leicester. There they could not afford
to consort with their own kind, and because there was a markedly
rough element in the town she never allowed the girls to go into
the streets without her. The country, George had assured her, was
perfectly safe and after the move Lavinia had taken to long, solitary walks, often missing a meal, and coming home with an armful of wilting flowers and foliage. George had feared, at first, that
not being country-bred, she might eat a poisonous berry, and had
given a little lecture on the subject. To that Lavinia had listened
attentively and at the end had said, "Thank you, P'pa," and
kissed him, voluntarily. "She'll come round," George said.

At his death it was Diana, not his child, had made the most display of grief. And that, in a way, was understandable. He had
been the first man in her life—her own father was only the
dimmest of memories. And she was old enough to be grateful for
all that he had bestowed; not least the complete acceptance of her
as his own. Diana cried and cried, hardest of all when the ear-
bobs, each a cluster of chains weighted down with garnets, were
discovered in his coat pocket.

"Oh, my birthday present! To think that his last thought . . ."

Deborah, crying herself, but less copiously, put her long thin arm around her half-sister and said,

"Di, dear. Don't think that way. He loved buying things and giving presents."

"I shall never wear them."

"But you must. He would have wanted . . ." They leaned together, mingling their tears. One of the nicest things about this reconstructed family was the way in which the two elder girls, so different from one another, and each with good reason for jealousy, had taken to one another from the start.

Now, because of the ear-bobs they thought simultaneously of the birthday.

"We must cancel the party," Diana said, nothing of self-pity, nothing but sorrow in her voice.

"I'll see to it all," Deborah said.

Caroline had cried, of course, on and off for some days, but her spirit was volatile enough to make her complain about the ugliness and ill-fit of the mourning dresses. "We look like a lot of crows," she said; and then, pushing up the loose bodice, "like black pouter pigeons." She made a grimace which, given the slightest encouragement, would have become a smile; half-hearted and shamefaced, but still, a smile.

Lavinia had not, so far as anyone knew, cried at all. Informed of her stepfather's death she had said "Oh!" and looked for a moment quite simple-minded. Then she had gone off on one of her walks.

Mrs Thorley had been almost embarrassed by her own inability to weep. Good, kind man, cut down untimely. She felt grief in her mind, a constriction in her chest, a hard painful lump in her throat; but the relief of tears was denied her; perhaps because she had shed so many for so many reasons, in so many places when she was younger; or perhaps because, later on, she had not dared to cry, telling herself fiercely that if she once gave way she'd be done for.

She felt sorry for the girls, especially Diana, whose seventeenth birthday was to have been celebrated so lavishly; a dance in the smaller of the two of the Assembly Rooms' ballrooms in Baildon, hired caterers, a proper band. Now nothing.

It was not a thing about which she could speak to Diana, who would break down into floods of tears. Without fully realising it, during the years and especially in this time of grief and confusion Mrs Thorley had come to rely upon Deb. With her she discussed Diana's birthday, saying:

"I have been thinking, Deb. Could we not mark the occasion with a small, absolutely private dinner party?"

"Why not, Mamma? It would do us all good. Actually I have been asking myself—What good does it do? All this mourning and crepe and going into purdah. It is the very last thing Papa would have wanted. He was all for life, was he not?"

That was true.

"Whom should we invite, Deb?"

"Susan Walford," Deborah said promptly. "She was Di's very best friend at school; and her brother Richard is home now. The Gordons? Doctor Taylor, and Edward, if they could both be free. Enough, Mamma?"

Enough for the present; after a meal, prepared by Jenny, fully determined to show that she could do as well as, or better than, any upstart catering firm in Baildon, the younger people went into the drawing room for a sing-song around the piano. Played by Deborah.

In Leicester, at odd times, on the hired piano, Mrs Thorley had tried to teach both her daughters, with small success. Diana tried, conscientious, labouring, no ear at all, and Lavinia made no effort. On the really beautiful piano, one of the things which George Thorley had enjoyed buying and giving, Deborah played by ear as naturally as her father whistled.

Over their cards at the gate-legged table in the living room, the bow window open and the scent of roses, stocks, and lilies drifting in, the older people heard first the sweet sentimental songs; and then a change; dance music; not merely the waltz, which in Mrs Thorley's youth had been so daring as to be almost improper, but the polka which, even more daring, far less sedate, was becoming popular.

"They are dancing," Mrs Gordon said with a look of sour disapproval.

"Why not?" her husband asked. "They're young. You're only young once, you know."

"How true," Doctor Taylor said, sorting his cards. "Youth's a stuff will not endure . . ." He liked making an apt quotation and he believed that he had long ago accommodated himself to facts of life. People—even young children—did die, despite all he could do. Some lived to be old, getting hard of hearing, sight failing, joints stiffening, muddle-minded, fumble-fingered. He'd seen it happening, to other people, and, steeled by his training, had never related it to himself. Now, suddenly he did, thinking that the time to retire was when one still had one's faculties, and strength enough left to enjoy oneself. He'd served his time, hadn't he? Built up a good practice which Edward was qualified to run single-handed. Since Edward joined him, four years ago, they had had amiable, but vigorous arguments about newfangled methods. Nonetheless, the boy was sound. Unlike poor old Gordon's son, a rattle-pate if ever there was one; never did a stroke of work, cricket and tennis all summer, hunting, shooting, golf all winter. If Gordon wanted his business to survive his retirement, he'd need to take in a good steady partner.

"That was my ace, partner," Mrs Gordon said with some acerbity. Absentminded, she thought; getting old. Next time medical attention was needed in the Gordon household, she'd be careful to ask for Doctor Edward!

The girls did not return to school for the little that remained of the summer term. Diana was not to go back at all and Mrs Thorley told Deborah that she could leave, too, if she wished. She had a vague feeling that in the coming few months—the testing time—she would find Deborah of more help than her own daughter. Deb at least took an interest in the farm, knew the workmen by name, could tell a bull from a cow.

Caroline and Lavinia, offered a chance to curtail their schooling, would have seized it, the one with delight, the other with relief, but Deb, though she said, dutifully, that of course, if she could be of use to Mamma, betrayed her real feelings in her face. She loved her home, revelled in country life, but she enjoyed school and the coming term was one of exceptional promise. She would be head girl—and therefore Miss Hardwicke's orderly—practically a member of the staff. There was the School Concert in November; the special Carol Service in St Mary's and then the School Play at the end of term.

"Oh no," Mrs Thorley said quickly. "I was only thinking that you and Di have always done things together."

"Di will find plenty to do without me," Deb said. When she

smiled a dimple appeared in one cheek, not in the other. It gave her smile a lop-sided look, not unattractive.

As a matter of fact, they would all leave at Christmas, Mrs Thorley decided. It would save the fees and the provision of a secondary wardrobe. Miss Hardwicke did not insist upon a uniform but the clothes that found favour in her sight were such as no self-respecting girl would wear outside school. With skirts getting wider and wider, she insisted upon narrow skimpy dresses, explaining that nowhere in school, not in the clothes closets, the schoolroom benches or in the dining room, was there room for voluminous skirts or full sleeves. Collars must reach at least an inch above the base of the throat, sleeves over the wristbone. The choice of colour was left to the girls' parents—so long as they were sombre. To the best of her ability Miss Hardwicke waged the fruitless war against the most besetting fault in girls—vanity. Diana Osborne and Caroline Thorley—both as vain as peacocks—had passed unscathed through her hands. So had many others, but upon some she had made a mark and long after she was in her grave there were women who avoided any colour brighter than tan, or olive green, or a blue much brighter than cornflower. And there were others who chose brighter shades and wore them with a faint feeling of guilt.

Caroline made a great fuss about going back to school. Since this was usual, nobody took much notice until she said a rather shocking thing.

"I intended to ask Papa to let me leave. And he *would*, you know."

It was probably true. Despite her monkeyish face, Caroline had a way with men.

"Oh," said Diana, tears and handkerchief ready, "must you remind us of what we have lost?"

Deb said, "Shut up, you clown," and administered a sharp kick on Caro's ankle.

"I know just how Caro feels," said George. For what Mrs Spicer had hoped and Mr Spicer had feared had come about and George was to start lessons at the Rectory; mornings only, five days a week, to begin with. "And even when I do have to stay afternoons, I will *not* have my lunch there," George said firmly. "I've seen better pig food in my day."

"If, after all, you need me—if only for company—just let me know, Mamma, and I'll come home," Deborah said at parting. It was obvious that Diana was going to be of little comfort or support in the trying days ahead. The way she had received the news of her mother's intention to carry on her husband's activities had drawn protests from the Young Madam.

"But Mamma, what will people say? Have you thought of that?"

By people she meant her personal friends; all the nice girls who had gone to school with her; most of them slightly older; girls who should have been at her birthday party; girls with whom she meant to keep in touch now that she was also grown up. She planned a whole round of visits. She could just imagine them saying: Is it true what I hear?

"I know exactly what they will say, Di. And I'll be the first to say it." Deb gave her stepmother a brief hug, a glancing kiss. "You're a damn brave woman!"

Mrs Thorley said, "Thank you, my dear. I accept the tribute . . ." The unspoken words, while deploring the language, hung in the air. When Mrs Thorley first came to Gad's, Deborah and Caroline had used very bad language; words far worse than damn.

"Surely, Mamma," Diana said, "you could be in control but hire a man to do, well, you know what I mean, the—the unsuitable things."

"I could, but I do not intend to." Mrs Thorley looked her elder daughter in the eye and said something that she had never said to George. He'd never guessed how welcome the life-raft offered had been. "I have done unsuitable things before, Diana. In Leicester, you may not remember, but I earned a living for us all. What I have done once, I can do again."

But secretly she admitted to herself that seven years of easy living, of being looked after, had softened her fibre. Ahead of her lay things she dreaded.

It would have been idle to pretend that the wives of even prosperous farmers did not work, but in their own homes, dairies, yards, they did not conduct business in the full view of the public. The news that Mrs Thorley intended to do so caused a sensation, the more so because of her la-di-da manner and the fact that she was not even country-bred. The general opinion was that she would make a fine mess of it, as well as being a laughing-stock.

The Corn Exchange at Baildon was a huge Gothic building, lighted from above, so that samples showed up as clearly as in the open. Regular buyers had their own stands; desks on tall legs with the owner's names painted on their fronts. Corn merchants, maltsters and millers were the élite of the assembly and held themselves a little apart from those who plied subsidiary trades, men selling agricultural implements or insurance, or beer.

It was so strictly a masculine preserve that even legal wives, tired of waiting towards the end of market day, never set a foot inside it. Little boys hung about the door, anxious to carry a message for a ha'penny. Usually politely phrased messages about the lateness of the hour. Sam Stamper's wife had once sent an arbitrary one: Will you go tell my husband—he's up there at the bar, with his hat on the back of his head—that if he doesn't come at once I shall drive home and he can walk.

Not to be endured; if Sam had budged then he'd never live it down. He gave the young messenger a penny: Nip out the back way, boy and tell them at the livery stables not to harness up till I come.

Women should be kept in their place!

Mrs Thorley, stepping out of hers, walked into the Corn Exchange on one of the busiest mornings; the third Wednesday in September. In black from head to toe, to her very finger tips, she looked small, pitiable, and there was hardly a man there who, properly asked, would not have done the bargaining business for her. A hush, beginning at the door, spread like a ripple as, moving as calmly as though she were in her own parlour, she made her way to the stand bearing the name Carver and Son. Son Carver, being of a younger and more flexible generation, would probably have handled the situation more easily; his father was so embarrassed that he stammered, stepped down from the little eminence behind his desk and said:

"Mrs Thorley, there was no need for this. Just a note and either I or my son would most gladly have called upon you."

She said, "Thank you, Mr Carver. I came to you first because my husband often dealt with you. But, you understand, I must sell on a competitive market. Look at it . . ."

From the black velvet reticule she carried she took one of the little sample bags, tipped its contents into her black gloved palm and held it out.

From the rear of the hall a slightly drunken voice said:

"Good for you, lady! Beat the old bugger down."

Visibly sweating, Mr Carver said, "Mrs Thorley, you see to what you are exposing yourself. Allow me, please, to conduct you to the door. I will come, tomorrow . . ."

She said, "Mr Carver, I am quite impervious to bad language." And that, God knew, was true. During the bad times with Stephen; low-class hotels, sleazy boarding-houses. Had she wished, she could, she knew, have outsworn any man in the building—and in two languages.

Amongst certain of the élite there was an inner ring made up of shrewd buyers who realised that it was better to cooperate than to compete. They communicated by signs; like bookmakers on race courses.

Mr Carver, stung by her remark about a competitive market and by her refusal to be conducted to the door, almost automatically made the sign which meant: Don't bid against me; we'll do a deal afterwards.

Mrs Thorley was aware of the hush and of the fact that Mr Carver had not made her an offer, and she thought: So that's it! There is a conspiracy against me! She knew a sinking of the heart, and then a mounting anger. Neither showed in her voice or manner.

"Very well, if nobody here wishes to buy the best barley in Suffolk, I can take it elsewhere."

A loud, somewhat strange voice called:

"Spare yeself the bother, ma'am! Fetch it across to me. I'm from Ireland meself."

He was not in the ring, being the rankest of rank foreigners. Buyers from Burton-on-Trent or from Chelmsford could just be tolerated, business making strange bedfellows, but even they were not admitted to the secret enclave. This pushing fellow did not even hire a stand for the day.

"Mrs Thorley, I have not *refused* your barley," Mr Carver said, mopping his forehead. "I'll give you . . ." He was so demoralised that he named a price, sixpence a bushel above the very highest tacitly agreed upon beforehand by members of the ring. It would have been all right had he not inadvertently made that sign; in theory everybody believed in free trade and an open market; but he had made it, and now he would rank with Judas! Even his fellow Freemasons, sworn as they were to brotherly love, would be cool towards him. It was not just as though he had bid against that damned Irish fellow, that would have been permissible, laudable. He would appear to have taken advantage of a privilege; just as Mrs Thorley had—he now saw it—taken advantage of her sex. Had he not been so concerned about her he would have kept his head better and had she been a man that damned Irishman would not have interfered so swiftly. Everybody knew the Irish weakness for the underdog, and momentarily, so small and black-clad, she had seemed to be one. But she was not; she was a damned shrewd woman and his brief encounter with her had cost him money, and, what mattered more, his reputation. She was a brazen bitch, and George Thorley, decent man, must be turning in his grave.

A woman might conceivably be—had indeed proved herself to be—brazen enough to walk into the Corn Exchange, but no woman with a shred of decency, leave alone pretensions to gentility, would go near the Cattle Market, which thronged with drovers, renowned for their drunkenness, rough manners and foul tongues. Even poor old women who had managed to fatten a pig or a couple of geese for sale in October would get some man, relative, friend or neighbour, to deputise for her in the Bedlam of noise and stench.

George Thorley had kept what he called a Cattle Book. A rough record which bore about as much relevance to the real state of the Gad's herd as a record of royal weddings might bear to the state of the countries concerned. It was with this which Mrs Thorley, who could write more quickly and in a smaller, neater hand, had helped him most. Stud fees were proudly recorded— any bull which did well at a show was desirable as a sire. But the truth was that a stud bull—in the hands of a man like George Thorley—cost more than he earned. Horses were different, a good pedigree stallion could be led about, keeping appointments with mares ready for mating. Bulls were more dangerous and the cows must come to them. And then George would offer hospitality . . . supper, bed, breakfast. A loss.

There was also the question of the calves born to the pedigree cows. Nobody knew exactly how they might turn out; no breed was absolutely stable; no calf immediately showed promise. It all took time. A true Durham shorthorn developed a colour called roan, red and white hairs blending into a kind of shimmer. That took time and some never attained it; so there were other pages in the Cattle Book, headed Ordinary Sales, which contained lists of what were virtually failures—butcher's meat.

When it came to this culling of the herd, Mrs Thorley was willing to take her stockman's advice.

"That'n," he said, pointing with his thumb, "should've gone three months ago. We ain't in the fattening business. He never did shape up right. Now that'n," he indicated another and shook his head, "Master had hopes of but look at him; white as a white-washed wall. Good lines to him, but we ain't breeding Ayrshires, are we, ma'am?"

He was whole-heartedly with her now, having had doubts at first. There was a breed of man that didn't mind taking orders from a woman, footmen, butlers, dancing jackanapes. A good, experienced stockman was not of that kind. And there'd been the teasing—coarse to say the least of it. Most of Joe's kind recognized only two forms of humour: something ridiculous happening to somebody else, like slipping in a cow pat and falling face downwards into a neighbouring one; or something randy, meaning sexual. And a breeding herd was very closely related to sex. Joe had borne quite a lot. Questions beginning: What'll you do boy, if she arst you what that owd bull is up to, clambering about on top on that pore little cow?

The idea of working for a woman had been repugnant, but he couldn't let her down all of a sudden while she was in sorrow, could he now? He was a recognised good stockman and attempts had been made to coax him away from Gad's. One such offer had included a new, brick-built house and a rise of two shillings a week. And that had been in Master's day. But there were arguments against any move. He'd liked Mr Thorley, who'd always treated him well and handed over any money prize; always been, in fact, fair and square. There was also the fact that in Stonham St Peter's, and come to that, Stonham St Paul's, there was a close network of relationship; nearly everybody was at least a second cousin or aunt by marriage to everybody else. So he had stayed, helped carry the Master to his grave; lived on edge for fear that a woman, most unaccountably left in full charge, might sell out. Or put somebody else—a hired fellow—in charge.

Instead she had said, "Joe, my husband depended upon you, I

know. I shall depend even more. So you must be remunerated."
She had then upped his wages by two shillings a week; and he was
her man, life and limb.

Now she was relying upon him to cull the herd, and she took
his say-so about the two animals doomed for butchery. But when
he said:

"That'll be all right then. I'll take them into Corby's, come
Wednesday," and she said, "I'll see you there," he was shocked.
He knew that she had ventured into the Corn Exchange, but a
cattle sale . . . Leave alone everything else, think of the filth!
Frightened animals lost all control of their bowels and bladders
and since there was so much to be swilled down at the end of the
day, a lot of men weren't too particular either.

"You can't do that, ma'am. And why should you, with me
ready to stand in? I'll take the creatures in, see 'em sold, collect
the money. You can trust me. Surely?"

"I trust you absolutely, Joe. But—well, I made a kind of promise to myself—to take my husband's place as far as possible. And
that includes the market."

"But Mamma, I do beg you think again. Would Papa have
wished it? Why, even two streets away one can hear the noise.
And the smell! Ugh! Let Joe go for you."

"Joe is an excellent stockman, dear, but I doubt whether he'd
be a match for those who might take advantage of his ignorance."

"You are inexperienced yourself, Mamma."

"True. True. But I am capable of learning."

"What is there to be learned from an auction?"

"That I don't know. Maybe nothing. But I propose to find
out."

The delicate wild-rose colour in Diana's cheeks deepened to
scarlet. She took a long breath.

"I will come with you."

"That is very sweet of you, dear. But it would be most unsuitable. And it would disappoint poor Susan."

The adjective, coupled so often with Susan's name, bore no
relation to money. Mr Walford had taken over the Sudbury Brewery and by sheer hard work and attention to business made it
into a flourishing place. His wife—the pampered only child of the
former owner—had felt herself neglected; her father had always

found time for his family. She then convinced herself that Mr Walford had married her simply to get his hands on the brewery. To gain the attention she craved, and also to retaliate, she took to invalidism. Nerves; impossible to define exactly; impossible to cure. Hired attendants could be afforded, but she never felt happy without one of her family within call. Mr Walford, though less busy than in the early years of his marriage, was busy still; Richard must go to school; so the burden fell upon poor Susan, who for years took lessons with a visiting governess, in Mr Walford's dressing room. It was not until Doctor Taylor detected symptoms of a genuine nervous breakdown in the daughter that she was allowed to go to school. By that time Richard was back from school, and supposed to be learning the brewery business, but his lessons were as often interfered with as poor Susan's had been and finally Mr Walford saw that the boy's only hope was to get away; so he sent him to Burton-on-Trent. And that meant recalling poor Susan from Miss Hardwicke's.

Amongst the many things which made Mrs Walford's nerves much worse, brought her in fact to the verge of collapse, was noise of any kind; so hospitality was impossible in the big brick house, built and furnished with lavish entertainment in mind. People went about on tiptoe, spoke in muted voices. Mrs Walford was not bed-ridden, except on occasion; the further end of the big bedroom had been made into a kind of sitting room, a wide, comfortable sofa, one easy chair, one not so comfortable and a Pembroke table. And of course any of dear Susan's friends were welcome to take tea there; always provided that they were quiet and allowed Mrs Walford to do the talking, in her weak, I-am-about-to-die voice.

Very few visited a second time and Diana Osborne was one of the few. Under the vanity and the strong self-preservative sense, Diana was capable of pity; she was genuinely sorry for poor Susan. (Miss Hardwicke had often noticed that girls paired off in pattern; every pretty girl's *best* friend was a plain one; lively girls seemed to prefer dull ones, and so on, through all the combinations and permutations which a limited community allowed.)

The mention of poor Susan settled the argument; Mrs Thorley set off for Baildon driving the tall horse in the trap, leaving the sedate pony and governess cart for Diana.

The noise and the stench were terrible; and just at the entry of Mr Corby's saleyard, a man stood relieving himself against the wall.

"Button up," another man said. "Ladies present."

"You drunk this early? Ladies?" With a short, rude word the man with the unbuttoned breeches described what should be done to all ladies.

"S'Missus Thorley, you fool." Buttoning himself the man said what should be done to Mrs Thorley, who passed by, seeing nothing, hearing nothing. Against stench she had taken the precaution of sprinkling her handkerchief with lavender water. Holding it to her nose she took her place in the ring of people, gathered about the space where terrified animals were harried about.

Mr Corby sat on a platform, much higher than the ones in the Corn Exchange; his clerk sat beside him.

Mr Corby was a man with two distinct personalities. The private Mr Corby lived in a nice house, with a nice wife, and was devoted to his nice garden. He was a churchwarden at St Mary's, a past master of his Masonic Lodge, a member of the Board of Guardians. That Mr Corby was precise of speech and fussy of manner. He could not have sold an ice-cold drink in a desert. The other Mr Corby was quite another man, loud-voiced, aggressive; a mixture of clown and entrepreneur who could have made Satan put in a derisory bid for hell. He never missed a bid, his eyes flicked about and in a voice that penetrated to the very edge of his saleyard he kept up a constant patter.

Somewhere in her checkered past Mrs Thorley had seen and enjoyed a ventriloquist's act and she was reminded of it now, but had no time to examine the thought.

The first of her calves trotted in, frightened, wild-eyed, and Mr Corby rattled off his pedigree. Somebody said, "Ten bob."

Mr Corby said, "You want me to die laughing? Ten shillings; eleven? Yes, I see you. At the back there? Thirteen. Fourteen. Shillings not guineas you there in the corner. Fifteen. Sixteen. Are you all dead on your feet? All wearing blinkers? All got cotton wool in your ears. Yes, sir, twenty. Against you. You'll regret it. Thank you. To my right; twenty bob . . ."

Mrs Thorley admitted to herself that this was all too quick for her. By comparison the Corn Exchange was a garden party. But she was rallying herself and had noticed you-there-in-the-corner, a man who bid just by raising his hand. Something, the stubborn streak in her which had refused to admit that her first marriage was a dead failure, and that she had been left, very poor, practically destitute, now sprang up again.

Ordinarily, like Mr Corby, she had a quiet voice, but it had a carrying quality.

"Twenty-one," she said. A few people laughed.

Mr Corby had noticed her and been less surprised than he might have been, for the news of her performance in the Corn Exchange had spread. He now perceived how she could be made use of. One of a good auctioneer's aims was to keep—and if possible maintain—the goodwill of the crowd, and there was no surer unifying factor with any crowd than a common hostility. He deliberately paused, feigning astonishment too deep for words, and then looking at the roof of a nearby shed, said:

"We appear to have with us somebody ignorant of the rules. In this saleyard, bids over one pound advance by half a crown; those above three pounds by five shillings. With that understood, we will resume. One pound I'm bid, gentleman in the corner. Any advance on one pound?"

"Twenty-two and sixpence," Mrs Thorley said.

"Twenty-two and a half," Mr Corby corrected her.

"Twenty-five."

"Twenty-seven and a half."

Joe, greatly agitated elbowed his way to her side. He saw and approved her intention, but at sales inexperienced people tended to get carried away.

"Don't go above thirty bob, ma'am. He ain't worth more." He had told her yesterday that with luck they might get thirty bob for each calf.

"Thirty bob."

"Thirty bob, I'm bid. Gentleman over there," Mr Corby said, and made a joke about the high price of veal. Joe was jubilant. Home and dry—and all thanks to her. But for her intervention the too white calf would have been knocked down for a pound. Then, foolish woman, she said:

"Thirty-two and a half." There was no further bid and here they were, landed with their own calf, an animal with no future—except appetite.

Mrs Thorley realised the same thing; a little pang of dismay; on her own thirty-two-and-a-half bid, for her own calf, she'd have to pay Mr Corby's ten per cent charge. She'd be out of pocket. But that feeling lasted no longer than a second; it was money well expended, for it had bought experience. She'd had to be informed, in a nasty sarcastic way, about the stages by which bids rose; she'd learned that; but also another thing. More important. Up to a pound the bidding had been brisk; then Mr Corby, who, after all, made his living by extracting the maximum possible price, had seemed willing to sell for twenty shillings to the gentleman in the corner. After that, she and that finger-raising man had been the sole bidders; and her eyes, anxious, yet curious, and not nearly so able as Mr Corby's at flicking about, had seen Mr Corby finger his neat little greying mustache and the gentleman in the corner had turned away after bidding thirty shillings for a calf which, had she not been there, would have sold for twenty. Another conspiracy?

She stood, thinking things over, and making no bid while her other calf, the one that never had shaped up to standard, was sold for eighteen shillings. To the Baildon butcher from whom she bought her meat. No veal, she thought, for a fortnight; I should feel like a cannibal!

She turned away, but near the entry of the yard was intercepted by a man with a broad red face.

"Mizz Thorley," he said, shifting his hat a fraction of an inch. "If you and me could hev a word . . . That whitey calf. Did you buy him back to set the pace like?"

"No, Mr . . . Mr . . ."

"Hopper," he said.

"No, Mr Hopper. I am, as perhaps you understand, not very experienced. But as that calf went round I saw a kind of glint on his coat. He may well be roan after all. I saw my mistake—and bought him back."

"You take three pound for him?"

Something—and it was difficult to say exactly what—made her say, "No. I think that as a potential breeder—not in the show class, of course, but a good sire to an ordinary herd, he is worth . . . five at least."

"Four's my limit."

"Very well, Mr Hopper. Five is mine."

Another man, and he might have been twin to the other, strolled up and said, "Getting yourself a bargain, Tom?"

Mr Hopper spat in a very uncouth manner indeed, hardly

bothering to turn his head. Then speaking as though she were not present, he said:

"Offered her four. She's sticking out for five."

"I'll go four five," said the newcomer.

"Four ten."

"Four fifteen."

"Five. And sod you, John Borley!"

Mr Corby's ability to hear and see everything at once had reached such a peak of perfection that without missing a bid or hesitating a second in his patter, he was fully aware of what was going on. The damned woman, in addition to her other misdemeanour, was now conducting a private transaction in his saleyard, a place he owned and upon which he paid high rates.

Her other fault had been to take up the bidding just as he was about to knock down the white calf for a pound to his own henchman. All the habitués of the market knew that when Mr Corby's man bid and Mr Corby paused in just that way, it was best to keep silent; for he had a way of getting back at those who broke the unwritten rule. He could refuse to accept your animals at all, saying that his pens and his lists were full. Then you had no choice but to go along to Larkin's, an inferior place in every way. Or he would accept your entry and then conduct the sale in a half-hearted way, making it seem that the beast wasn't worth selling, leave alone bidding for. Both these punitive measures would seem to be against Mr Corby's own interest, but buying in, at practically his own price, through his own agent more than compensated him for such trivial losses. For what he bought in, dirt cheap, Mr Corby had outlets unknown to the ordinary fellow; places far away where money was plentiful and prices high. Nobody really approved of the practice; he should have been content with his ten per cent without extorting a form of blackmail as well. But in this world you had to take the rough with the smooth and Mr Corby, when he tried—which was most of the time—couldn't be matched.

Mr Corby went home to his nice house and his nice wife in what she called a mood; a state she attributed to his digestion. On busy days like this, market day in October and everybody wanting to get rid of surplus stock, he paused only for the most necessary purpose; a dash across to the back of the public house, the Market Tavern, whose back wall was part of his boundary. There he

visited the necessary house, decently screened off, and had a sandwich. New bread. That was the trouble. Ninety-nine of the Market Tavern's customers liked sandwiches cut from new almost
spongy white bread; Mr Corby liked them, too, but they did not
always agree with him. This was one such time. Good, accommodating wife that she was, she changed the supper menu from steak
and onions to coddled egg. A change which did little to restore
his temper. Having eaten his egg without appreciation or enjoyment, he said, "I have a letter to write, my dear."

He was handy with words. He could afford to forfeit the Gad's
Hall trade; it did not amount to much; pedigree stock was almost
always sold privately; and he did not mind if no animal from that
place, belonging to that woman, ever came under his hammer
again. He must vent his spleen.

> Madam,
>   I am aware that you are ignorant of market eti-
> quette. I feel it my duty to enlighten you. There is, of
> course, no law against any seller buying back stock
> offered, but it is a waste of time and money.
>   I must also point out to you that it is unethical, if
> not positively illegal, to conduct, as you did this morn-
> ing, a *private* sale, on the premises of a *public* auc-
> tioneer. A few steps would have taken you and the men
> who were bidding against one another, out of *my* yard
> and into Woolhall Street where any activities in which
> you cared to indulge, would have been acceptable.

There, he thought, signing his letter with a flourish, that should
take her down a peg or two; arrogant bitch!

Having written it, stamped it, hitting the stamp as though he
were smiting Mrs Thorley, he felt a great deal better and emerging from the little room in which he did his writing and kept accounts asked jovially, "What's for supper Bella?"

*

The year ran downhill. For some reason Mrs Thorley always
saw the year in her mind, as an ascent, beginning with snowdrops,
mounting steadily to June with its roses. Then a little plateau;
summer; June, July, much of August, and then the decline into
the trough, with Christmas the only bright spot. This year, so extraordinary in many ways, followed the pattern. The girls came

home. And Joe Snell, who by this time not only accepted Mrs Thorley, but downright admired her, mentioned the Christmas party which had been part of the Gad's Hall routine for as long as he could remember, and his father, his grandfather, before him.

"I reckon, ma'am, you 'on't want to be heving the Barn Party this year?"

"But of course, Joe. Didn't I always say that things should be as usual? You see to the decoration and I will see to the food."

She thought on the periphery of her mind that now the girls were home for good and approaching marriageable age they should all learn the fundamentals of cookery; one never knew what the future held and when hard times had struck her her ignorance had been a great handicap. The trouble was that Jenny disliked having anyone—even Mrs Thorley herself—in the kitchen and made no secret of her feelings.

In former years the Rector and his wife had always been present at the Gad's Hall party for employees on Christmas Eve, but this year like Joe Snell, they had assumed that there would be no such jollification and had engaged themselves elsewhere. When Mrs Thorley came to proffer, in person, her invitation, Mrs Spicer said, with the utmost sincerity:

"Isabel, dear, I am so extremely sorry. Arthur will be too, I am sure." The Rector, on such occasions, said grace, ate heartily and then retreated to the quietude of the house and a glass or two of good sherry. "Miss Riley's brother, his wife and family are spending Christmas with her this year, and on Christmas Eve she has asked us to join them for tea. And that in a way is awkward for me, since I have guest arriving sometime in the afternoon and I can hardly suggest taking him with us; Miss Riley's accommodation is so limited. You will excuse me if I go on with my knitting? Christmas always seems to catch me unawares."

If only her circumstances had been easier Mrs Spicer would have been delighted to go about the parish distributing tea and sugar, tins of biscuits, yards of flannel; as it was, the best she could do was to take advantage of a firm in Bradford who early each year advertised four-shilling bundles of assorted wool, colours which had proved unpopular, odds and ends, discontinued lines as they called them. She was always pleased with her bargain and derived some pleasure in sorting and assigning the many colours, thinking a contrast better than an ill-match. She knitted shawls and scarves, stockings, mittens, and this year had ventured upon a garment known as a hug-me-tight, far more practical than a shawl for women who wanted the full use of their arms. It was not unlike a half-sleeved waistcoat with tapering fronts which crossed over and fastened behind the wearer's back. Such a garment took less wool than a shawl, but it demanded more attention.

As she resumed knitting, Mrs Spicer thought: After all, I obliged you by taking George last summer when his father was dying . . .

"If your afternoon guest would care to come to Gad's . . ."

"Oh, I am sure he would. How very kind. A little lively company . . . Poor Everard, he's had rather a sad life. He's Arthur's nephew. Arthur's brother and his wife were both missionaries, in India, and when he was six he had to come away. He was to go to a school intended for the children of those who labour in the foreign field. Poor little boy, he was actually here when we were informed that both his parents had died in some dreadful epidemic. I was obliged to break the news to him." Mrs Spicer, tapering off the hug-me-tight, recalled the scene which had made her averse from informing Georgie that his father was dead, began on a new line of stitches and a new part of the story.

"Arthur and I could never quite understand why Everard's parents chose Mr Everard as his godfather. He was a merchant, in India, and very rich, but not an educated man. He was still in India then, but he chose the school to which Everard should go, and for which of course he paid, and for a while Everard spent his holidays here. Then Mr Everard retired and came home and bought himself an estate in Buckinghamshire. Naturally after that, Everard spent his holidays there. He was at Eton." She turned the knitting about and began on another decreasing line.

"So far as anyone knew Mr Everard had no children. To speak of expectations . . . I always think it rather squalid, but it certainly looked as though Everard . . . However, it was not to be. When Mr Everard died he left his estate and quite a considerable fortune to his illegitimate son and to Everard just enough to see him through Cambridge and to qualify as a lawyer. Nothing more."

Mrs Thorley said, "That must have been a great disappointment. But a good education is always a sound investment."

"I trust it may prove so. At the moment Everard is with Mr

Gordon, and I must confess that I find it significant that he invited himself *here* for Christmas. The Gordons have a big house and three maids. I have a suspicion that they regard Everard as a kind of office boy."

"She could hardly do that," Mrs Thorley said soothingly. "Not with such qualifications. I expect she thought that having you so near . . ."

"That is possible," Mrs Spicer conceded. Then she sighed. "What makes it the more awkward is that Arthur was hurt and angered when Everard chose law instead of the Church. For one thing the Spicers have always been a clerical family and for another he regards all lawyers with some suspicion. He has never told me why, and naturally I have never asked, but I think he must at some time have had an unhappy experience . . . You may have observed that when they are both guests under your roof, Arthur's manner towards Mr Gordon is somewhat . . . reserved." She turned her knitting again. "Of course what you say, dear Isabel, about a good education never being wasted *is* true to some extent. Poor Everard was finding things very difficult; it is hard to get established when one is without money or influence, when he met James Gordon at some kind of reunion. I think it was to do with their preparatory school. That is how Everard happened to come to Baildon. I think he was offered some hope of a partnership, eventually, but to be honest, judging from Mrs Gordon's behaviour, I have doubts. Everard has looks and manners that would grace any dinner table."

"Well," Mrs Thorley said, feeling that she had wasted enough time, and getting to her feet, "he will be very welcome to our rather rustic festivity. I have things to do."

The idea of match-making was the farthest thing from her mind. Diana was only seventeen and a half, the others ran down the scale of age in a manner impossible with four girls borne of the same mother. And, moulded by her own experience, Mrs Thorley was opposed to early marriages. Girls simply did not know their own minds—she had known hers, been given her head and suffered from it. She wanted all her girls to be about twenty before forming a permanent attachment.

She had told Joe Snell that all should be as before; that he should see to the decoration and she would see to the food. The holly and the ivy, evergreens which symbolised survival through the darkest time of the year. And there was the tree, a custom introduced by Prince Albert.

The barn, into which so much greenery and presently so much food were to be dragged, was very old; far older than the house. It had been the first hall, reared by one of the successful invaders, Creek men, Vikings, so long ago that nothing remained of them even in memory except a few beams carved with Thor's hammer, and his name. Thursday was Thor's day, and Thorley, Thorsby, Thorson were all well-known names. In this place the winter solstice had been ceremonially observed for a very long time before Mrs Thorley came in to assure herself that this, her first Christmas Eve of full responsibility, was in order.

All was as before; and she spared a thought for George, who had so greatly enjoyed this kind of thing.

All along one side of the barn, trestle tables set end to end, and covered with glistening white table-cloths, overlapping. At one end an urn ready to dispense tea, milk jugs, sugar basins, tea-cups. At the other end a cask of ale. In between mountains of food, all prepared by Jenny, helped by Katie, who could be ordered about as the young Misses could not—which was why Jenny did not welcome them in the kitchen. Sausage rolls, sandwiches, salt beef or ham, take your pick; mince pies—made in the old way, with real minced beef amongst the fruit and spices—fruit cake cut into wedges, sponges cut into triangles, buns, biscuits.

All as in former years.

"Mamma, may I light the candles now? It is getting dark."

"Yes, darling. Be careful of the tree."

Christmas trees must be illuminated; tiny candles in little candlesticks which clipped on to the boughs. There had been accidents, but not here, and Mrs Thorley intended that there should not be. Willy, the odd-job boy, stood ready with a bucket of water and a long-handled mop.

The girls came in—Di, Deb, Caro and took their places behind the long table.

Lavinia was not with them. Late as usual, Mrs Thorley thought; and then, with a flash of impatience: She might have made an effort for once.

They looked very pretty, for Mrs Thorley, while intending to remain in mourning for a full year—but not forever, as some widows did, since it was so unbecoming—had decided that for girls so young, six months was sufficient. Diana wore the muted pink, known as old rose; Deborah a soft green, and Caroline a silvery blue, all dresses which had hung unworn since the disaster, and only Deborah's had needed any alteration; it had been lengthened by the addition of a deep hem of velvet, and in order to avoid the contrived look, bands of the same stuff had been let into the sleeves and around the neckline. No doubt about it, Deb was going to be taller than average, which was rather a pity. Men did not like very tall girls.

Mrs Thorley did not think of herself as an ordinary matchmaking mamma, and certainly she did not wish any of her girls to marry before the age of twenty; but marriage must be the ultimate aim since there was no alternative except miserable spinsterhood. Deb was clever and bookish, she might conceivably become a governess, a most unenviable fate. And it was difficult to imagine Deb, so forthright and outspoken, in a subordinate position . . .

How stupid to worry about that now! Dear Deb had only just had her seventeenth birthday.

Lavinia drifted in, wearing her old black dress. For once she volunteered an explanation, not an apology. "I had no time to change. I was busy."

Then Everard Spicer arrived. He was an extremely handsome young man, with bright brown curly hair and eyes of almost the same colour. His manners were polished and his voice exceptionally pleasing, deep and resonant. Mrs Spicer had said that her husband had hoped that Everard would become a parson, and certainly the voice would have been an asset in a pulpit— but equally so in a law court.

She introduced her daughters in order to seniority. Then she said, of Jenny, in place by the tea-urn, "And this is Jenny, who is responsible for all these good things—helped by Katie, of course."

And then she knew, by the way the young man eyed the food, that he was hungry. In bad days the windows of English cookshops and French *patisseries* had reflected her own face with just that look.

"Let us make the most of our opportunity," she said. "Help yourself, Mr Spicer."

"As a matter of fact," he said, "I missed my lunch. I was offered a lift and could not choose my time."

He chose a good solid sausage roll and Mrs Thorley reflected that on a farm whatever economies must be made, one need not stint on food. She took a biscuit and gave Deborah a look which she—far and away the most perceptive of them—instantly understood. Diana and Caroline looked at her as she took a substantial sandwich and felt identical pangs of envy. Deb's figure, of course, was not ideal; her waist was twenty inches, her bosom and hips rather small by comparison, but she could eat anything, anywhere, at any time.

George, a smouldering taper in his hand, hurried up, indignant.

"Mamma, you told me not to *touch* anything. And here you are, *guzzling!*"

"This is my son, George," Mrs Thorley said with justifiable pride. George was handsome, too, and looked very well in the sailor suit—that echo of Trafalgar which formed part of the wardrobe of every boy who was not actually poor—and it had infiltrated to even lower levels, since kindly people often gave outgrown clothes away. "And this is Mr Spicer." At the name George recoiled a little; it stood for everything he disliked; long lessons in a room that smelt of musty old books; long dreary sermons. But this Mr Spicer was different, he said genially:

"It's not too late, George. You come and guzzle, too."

And while George ate a wedge of the fruit cake, and Mrs Thorley nibbled her biscuit and Deborah munched her sandwich, Mr Spicer disposed of two more sausage rolls and a mince pie. George thought: Greedy.

Then Joe Snell, master of ceremonies, came in and said:

"Ma'am, we're ready."

The women with few exceptions wore black. With families so intermarried and so numerous, everybody had to go into mourning once or twice a year, so the best dress might as well be black; and degraded to everyday wear, black had the advantage of not showing the dirt. Just a few young women wore lighter, brighter colours. The women clustered about the tea-urn, the men about the cask of beer, manned by Joe. The children ate, staring at the lighted tree. Ready, presently, to sing carols.

There had been a little argument about one of the old carols.

"We can't sing God bless the master of this house, Joe. Not with him laying down in the churchyard."

"There's the young master."

"Wouldn't be right, would it, to put him afore his mother—and she taking such trouble to keep everything as it was."

"Then how about God bless the mistress of this house, likewise the master, too?"

"Don't sound right, somehow."

"Leave it out then. There's others."

"But that'd be different; and she been very particular to keep everything as it was."

"Then let's keep it like always . . ."

Everard Spicer, standing between Diana's end of the long table and the beer barrel, said, as the carols ended and the gifts from the foot of the tree were distributed, "How delightfully feudal!"

For the first time in her life she regretted not having paid a little more attention to lessons. Feudal? She had the vaguest memory of somebody talking about the feudal system, but for the life of her she could not remember what it was. However, he had called it delightful, so she felt safe in saying, "Yes, is it not?" which seemed to be a completely satisfactory reply.

And this year, although the aim was to keep everything the same, there was a difference. When Mrs Thorley had distributed the gifts—all good useful things which had cost money—Joe Snell stepped from behind the now empty beer barrel and said:

"Ma'am, this year we got a little token for you. We hope you'll accept of it, with best wishes from us all."

Many men, she knew, were handy at what they called whittling —using knives and skill on wood, making spoons and bowls and clogs and buckets, handles for axes, spades, forks—but the thing which Joe handed to her was out of this utilitarian class. It was a small wooden model of a Durham shorthorn bull; horns, genitals. It was not painted, somebody had chosen exactly the right wood, the real roan colour. And it was not Gad's Goliath, getting a bit old and thick now. It was one of his progeny, Gad's Glory, a young bull of which George had had high hopes.

A few tears now, she felt, would be appropriate, but their source was still dammed. She had that old, known lump in the throat, but it did not affect her voice. As clearly as it had sounded through the Corn Exchange and the Cattle Market, it said, "How very beautiful! I thank you all. I shall treasure it forever. And so will my son. And now—Happy Christmas."

"And to you, ma'am. Now—God Save the Queen," Joe said.

Every public gathering ended with the National Anthem, at

least where decent people were concerned; for the goings-on in France had been simply shocking again this year . . .

The long table in the dining room was already set for tomorrows Christmas dinner, so the family and their guest ate what was called a simple supper at the gate-legged table in the living room. A huge log fire burned on the hearth and the simple meal consisted of thick ox-tail soup, the same ham and salt beef from which the sandwiches had been cut, some of Jenny's green chutney and an excellent cheese.

It was the first really *family* meal Everard Spicer had ever shared. There had been India, very vaguely remembered, his parents always busy; he'd had an ayah, of course; ostensibly a Christian, otherwise she would not have been employed, but she would not eat meat. He had never really shared a meal with her. Then England and school. Terribly cold. He could remember his first chilblains—he thought he had leprosy! Holidays at the Rectory, where a whole egg was presented as a favour. Another school. Holidays with Uncle Everard; good food there but no family feeling between him and an aging man, often a little drunk. Cambridge. Baildon, where the only thing that could be said of his lodging was that it was cheap.

Here he was in the very heart of a family and he revelled in it.

Caroline was the lively one; very sure of herself.

She said, "Mamma, I think they are all slightly confused between you and Her Majesty! I thought to myself while they sang:

> "*God save our gracious ma'am,*
> *Giver of cakes and ham,*
> *God save our ma'am.*
> *Thy richest gift in store,*
> *On her be pleased to pour,*
> *So she can give us more.*
> *God save our ma'am.*"

Mrs Thorley showed no sign of being offended, she said, "You have a gift for parody, Caro."

"If only you could carry a tune," the tall one, Deborah, said.

Diana said, "Really, Caro, you are *awful!*"

George came to the defence of his favourite sister. His preference was quite irrational. He should, he knew, have liked Deb best—he'd inherited her pony and she had taught how to ride it, how to care for it. He loved her, and Di—and Lavinia, of course, but Caro was *funny*.

"I don't think Caro is awful, Di. I think she's deuced clever."

Deuced he had discovered—feeling his way about the world—was an acceptable word; he knew about twelve that were not.

Mrs Thorley had brought the model bull and set him, on his solid plinth, in the centre of the table. Now as the meal ended, Lavinia, generally so silent, leaned forward and touched the broad head between the short horns. She said:

"For well-wishing a name should be given." The family were all accustomed to such apparently irrelevant remarks.

"It's Gad's Glory, I think," Mrs Thorley said.

"Wait until tomorrow and you can baptise him, Lavinia. In good red wine," Deborah said.

It was true. Possibly because Gad's Hall was largely surrounded by the moat, it had no cellar. Just across the passage it had a good store room, and although George Thorley had left far less in the way of money than could have been expected, he had left, in that store room, a very respectable cellar.

"What a dry stick," Caro said on the landing. "He never cracked a whole-hearted smile."

"It may be," Diana said, "that you are not quite as funny as you think you are."

"Spare me! You sound like Miss Hardwicke. And I've done with her, thanks be to God."

"That'll do, Caro," Deborah said, opening the door of the room which she and Diana had always shared, just as Caroline and Lavinia had shared the one next door. Mrs Thorley, being tactful, tentatively feeling her way, had thought that perhaps the sisters—two pairs—might have held together, but age seemed to count more than blood kinship; Diana and Deborah had linked up; Caroline and Lavinia, more or less thrown together.

"What I do think," Deborah said, inside the bedroom, "is that he's *greedy*."

"He had no lunch, Deb. He said so."

"So he ate four sausage rolls and three mince pies and two slabs of cake. Then he came in and had two helpings of everything."

"He was hungry."

"Not after all he ate in the barn. Nobody could be. What would you bet me that he is now gorging one of the Rectory rock buns?"

Mrs Spicer's tea-time offering, more rock than bun as Caro had once said, was a long-standing family joke, and when now it failed to elicit even the shadow of a smile, Deborah looked at Diana sharply.

"I do believe you're sweet on him." Every nice girl believed in love at first sight as firmly as she believed in the Creed; yet, in case the attraction should not be mutual, it was wise to conceal one's feelings until some sign of favor had been shown since nothing made a girl look more ridiculous than seeming to be sweet on a man who was not sweet on her. However, with one's best friend—or one's half-sister, one could be frank.

"Well, I do think he's the nicest young man we know."

Two remarks: We know very few; and: We don't really know him, must be resolutely repressed. Any kind of dissension within the family must be avoided.

"You may be right. Anyway you'll see him tomorrow. That reminds me, we shall need an extra place at table. And I intend to put up my hair tomorrow. Christmas dinner has always been more or less my birthday party."

"Yes," Diana said momentarily diverted. "Not high, Deb, you're tall enough already." Not: Too tall, which would have been offensive. "I think drawn back, and dressed low, Deb. A chignon. Oh, if only we had some chenille . . . But net would do. Let me see."

Anniversaries are absolute *hell*, Mrs Thorley thought, remembering how, last Christmas, George had been here. She had decided that everything must be as it had been, but there were times when even routine procedure, apart from a hitch now and then, soon overcome, tended in a way to decry the dead. Take a bucket of water out of a pond, and no hole shows. Not a nice thought. We are all expendable.

Christmas Day was following its usual pattern. Presents.

Bracelets for the girls; gold; no pinchbeck stuff or fake stones. Mrs Thorley, in one of the hard times, had learned what a life-buoy something genuine could be. She hoped with all her heart that none of her girls would ever be reduced to selling a trinket; but just in case, she bought gold.

They gave her presents, too. Deborah and Caroline, working away during the time which Miss Hardwicke allocated to free activities, had made her a petticoat with so many tucks and insertions of lace that it could practically stand up on its own. Diana had made a matching corset cover. Lavinia had given her a picture; slightly more odd than those which Mrs Thorley had received in the past. It portrayed a field of poppies; quite beautiful until one saw in the centre of each flower, a face, ugly, unfriendly. How could Lavinia *know* that the men in the Corn Exchange, in Mr Corby's saleyard and various other places, had appeared just like that; red, alien? Then look again, at a slightly different angle, and it was just a field of poppies.

George was still at an age where he gave what he would wish to receive and hoped eventually to share; chocolates; peppermints and a delicious new sweet called brandy-and-butterballs. For his mother he presented something he could not share—a little flask of lavender water. And from her and from his sisters he had received a number of very acceptable gifts; best of all a clockwork toy; a miniature railway engine.

The railway had not yet reached Baildon, but it was coming; it was almost at Sudbury and should be through to Bywater next year. Everything about it was new and exciting and George was so pleased with his little model that he could not resist smuggling it into church where presently, when Mamma, Di and Deb had gone to the altar rail, he found himself alone with Caro, who had not yet been confirmed. Lavinia had excused herself from church; her back ached from standing at the Barn Party, she said.

Only with Caro would George have dared to do it. With a mischievous, conspiratorial glance, he took the toy from his pocket and pushed it gently along the pew towards her. She made a face of mock reproof, but pushed it back towards him. It was not wound up and he was not yet familiar enough with it to know that the hooter on it was worked, not by the winding mechanism but by the revolution of the wheels. The noise sounded much louder than it had done at home. Mr Spicer almost dropped the silver cup and Caro laughed! Quite as unseemly a noise as the hoot in the hushed church.

"That was extremely naughty of you, George," Mamma said as soon as they were outside. "Give the thing to me. You will not be allowed to play with it until tomorrow." Occasionally she had to make a show of strictness; widows' sons were notorious, and George had in addition four—no, three, for in this as in everything else, Lavinia must be discounted—doting young females around him. Even now Diana was saying:

"I blame *you*, Caro, more than George. To let him do it. And then to laugh!"

"Caro didn't know, nor did I that it would hoot without being wound up."

Mrs Thorley pushed the toy into her sealskin muff; and even that tiny friction was enough to make it hoot again; a muffled, derisory hoot at which even Mrs Thorley smiled. Diana preserved her look of offended dignity. Deb knew why. Diana had always been oversensitive to what-will-people-think; and Everard Spicer had been one of that startled congregation. Without actually sharing Di's feeling that the Thorley family had disgraced itself, she understood. And the immediately comforting words, A good dinner will put us right in his sight, must not be spoken. She had already almost imperilled a long friendship by using the word greedy last night.

Christmas dinner at Gad's had been much the same for six years—it had taken Mrs Thorley a year to organise her campaign. The Rector and his wife, for whom Christmas was such a busy season; Doctor Taylor, and presently his son, for whom it was anything but a busy season; unaccountably, few people felt like dying on Christmas Day. Susan and Richard Walford—their father always did duty on such occasions.

They'd always had turkey, the biggest available; and George had always carved, lavishly but untidily. This year Doctor Taylor said, "May I." and carved with a surgeon's skill. And that was not the only difference. Everybody had aged by a year. Or more . . . or more. Once, really looking at herself in the glass, Mrs Thorley had been ridiculously startled to see silver streaks in her hair. Had they appeared overnight? And once, looking into a shop window, as in the past she had sometimes looked and seen a hungry face, she had seen another and had time to ask herself; Who is that ferocious-looking old woman? in the blink of time that it took to realise that she was confronting herself.

Now the young were beginning to pair up; and doing it badly, as the young always did. As she had herself done.

Take Edward Taylor, that serious, dedicated young man, where in the world could he find a more suitable mate than Deb, so sensible herself, so ready to be dedicated, and so practical. Mrs Thorley was reasonably confident that if Deb were alone, except for a servant, in the big old house in St Giles' Square and somebody rang the bell and showed a thumb hanging by a thread of flesh, Deb would have dealt with it, undismayed. But the silly young man had eyes for nobody but Caroline, who was frivolous, amusing and quite useless in an emergency; once, sharpening a pencil, she'd nicked her own finger and thrown a hysterical fit.

Richard Walford was just as silly, wanting Diana, the last person to settle down to a household geared to the requirements of an invalid. There was in Diana what her mother recognised as a good healthy streak of selfishness. Richard Walford, too, would have done better to direct his attention to Deb.

In any case Richard had lost Diana, at least for a time. Mrs Thorley, having been through the process herself, and suffered thereby, knew love at first sight, recognisable as measles. Diana was offering to drive Everard Spicer back into Baildon on the day after tomorrow.

Driving home to Baildon, Edward Taylor said:

"You know, it's time we did something to return Mrs Thorley's hospitality."

"We mustn't upset Hattie, dear boy."

Hattie was their Treasure; a member of the firm as it were. Be late for a meal, as doctors so often were, and there it was, ready, waiting and never spoiled. Be called out in the night—and for some inexplicable reason all babies who came reluctantly and needed more than the ordinary midwife's attention were born between three and seven o'clock in the morning; and more people died then—come back at some unearthly hour and there was Hattie, in her red flannel dressing gown with a good, heartening hot drink. Never a grumble.

"I shouldn't dream of upsetting Hattie. The Angel does a bit of outside catering. And the rooms just need a good going over."

Dining room, drawing room, all shrouded in dust sheets for the last ten years; ever since Mrs Taylor died of influenza.

"That would mean work for Hattie."

"She needn't lift a finger. I can find a dozen women in Scurvy Lane who'd be only too glad of a day's work."

"Hmm," Doctor Taylor said, expressing his disapproval without saying a word. The younger man thought: He's got into a rut, medically and in every other way; it's time he was shaken out of it. Taking his father's consent for granted, he said, "The piano will need tuning."

Driving home to Sudbury, Richard Walford said:

"Really, you know, Sue, we can't go on accepting invitations, and never asking anybody back."

"I don't see what can be done about it," Susan said gloomily. "You know how Mamma is . . ."

Mrs Walford's hearing was almost uncanny. Her bed-sitting-room was at the front of the house, the kitchen at the back, but let so much as a saucer drop and she heard it. Both Richard and his father had, on very rare occasions, tried to offer the merely token hospitality of a drink and a cigar in the snuggery, also at the back. Entering stealthily as burglars, by the side door, muting their own voices, hoping visitors would imitate, somehow they were always discovered and sent for.

Richard felt sorry for Susan—it was worse for her; he and his father did get out and about, they saw people all day long. Poor old Sue was beginning to look dim and miserable and old. Compare her with Diana Osborne, only a few months younger.

"I know what we could do. And I'll do it. Hire the Victoria Rooms. The whole place, restaurant and all, for an evening. Ask everybody. Have a proper dinner and dance afterwards."

"I'm not sure about dancing—if you're thinking of Diana. And Deb and Caro, of course." She knew that his thoughts were with Diana. "I mean, they're still in mourning."

"They didn't look like it today. Besides, we danced on Diana's birthday."

"That was different. Both times they were in a private house."

"The Victoria Rooms will be private; *our* house, just for one evening. Don't *you* begin waving wet blankets. There're enough of them about."

"I wasn't. I was just thinking. When would it be?"

"How about St Valentine's? That'll give you time to get a new dress. A nice cheerful colour, eh?"

"I know. I have been letting myself go. Everything is so difficult. I do sometimes feel that nothing's worth the effort."

"A lovely poppy red," Richard said, following his own line of thought and naming the colour which was most men's favorite; a fact recognised by bad women, and in a negative way, by good ones, too, in that they tended to avoid it. But poor Susan did need livening up; her hair was fair, but a dim kind of fair, no sheen to it. There were things that could be done to liven up that kind of hair; and also that kind of complexion, the unhealthy pallor that came from too much confinement to stuffy rooms.

As a young man, with plenty of money, serving a purely nominal apprenticeship, Richard Walford, during his time at Burton-on-Trent, had acquired a good deal of knowledge about women who did things to their hair and their faces, wore dresses brighter even than poppy red and did not demand to be called Miss Whatever-it-was for more than five minutes after the introduction. But he had settled, in his mind, for a good girl, dignified, pure, possessor of every virtue, every grace—Diana Osborne.

Diana, who was saying to Everard Spicer:

"Mr Spicer, did I hear you say on Christmas Eve that you had been given a lift. Have you been offered one back?"

"Unfortunately not. But I think that once I am on the main road . . ."

"I will drive you. With pleasure."

Mrs Thorley, infinitely the most experienced person at this, or any other local gathering, recognised, in her own daughter, her young self; infatuated, head over heels in love; and despite all her sophistication, she was surprised to feel a slight dismay; a hope that this would not come to anything. Why?

A young man with everything to commend him; respectable family connections; good looks; beautiful manners—Eton had stamped its own; an honourable profession which, while not very remunerative at the moment, held propects . . . Mr Gordon must retire at some time and James would shrug off the yoke. Gordon and Spicer, perhaps, and who better fitted than Diana to take on the role of a leading citizens wife?

So, why am I not delighted?

Oh, so silly to think—he has a mousetrap mouth! Yet, in her time, battling against the world, Mrs Thorley had learned that mouths, rather than eyes, were indicative of character.

The fact that the young man was a trifle too solemn was not a disadvantage; Diana, though vain, was far from frivolous.

And in any case, why worry, *now*? Everard Spicer would not be in a position to marry for quite a while yet; Diana's infatuation might not last. Her own had done so, but that was nothing to go by.

*

Plans for both parties went rapidly ahead; Mr Walford co-operating fully; deciding that Mamma should be told nothing until nearer the time and declaring that just for once he'd try to get away himself. Some long-buried streak of convivialty stirred within him. What with having had to work so hard, and then Viola becoming such a sad invalid, he'd had little chance to enjoy himself, but the capacity to do so was still there. The champagne should flow, and although February was a poor month for flowers, there was a man on the outskirts of Sudbury who grew hothouse carnations all the year round. He'd order twelve dozen—all red.

Edward Taylor's preparations went far less smoothly. Hattie, though assured that she need do nothing, absolutely nothing, was affronted. "I know I'm not as spry as I once was, Doctor Edward; and the girls I get to help nowadays ain't much good. But I could've managed a nice little dinner without calling in people from The Angel. You'd only to ask!"

As for the women from Scurvy, words failed her. Dirty, dishonest. Did Doctor Edward imagine that she was going to allow them the run of the house, all amongst his dear dead mothers things? And they so dead ignorant. Why, in all her years she's only once hired a kitchen help from the Lane and believe it or not the girl didn't know what an oven was.

"I can well believe it, Hattie. Only three or four houses in that area have ovens. It's an absolute disgrace."

He also was a rather solemn young man; concerned with social problems, in a wider sense than his father was. Doctor Taylor was *kind* enough; he'd treat the poor free of charge, push a shilling or sixpence into a grimy hand—a little contribution towards the extra nourishment needed; always carried sweets in his pocket. But he accepted the state of affairs, not gladly, but with resignation. Edward was not yet resigned.

Doctor Taylor was not resigned to what was going on in his house. Hattie upset, women from the Lane, glad to snatch at an hour's employment—the children left to the care of a grandmother or a neighbour, rushing about with buckets and mops and dusters and Hattie yapping round them like a sheepdog. His comfortable life was being disrupted and the opening of the disused rooms had disturbed him; the worst disturbance coming on the day of the piano tuner's visit. The piano had not been touched since Emily died . . .

And all this, Edward's father knew, for the sake of Caroline Thorley, the one he liked least of the three—except as a patient and a most unrewarding one—he, like everybody else, discounted Lavinia. Diana, Osborne, not Thorley, was tolerable, a bit vain and what he called set-up-with-herself, but these were the faults of youth. Deborah, less pretty and therefore less vain, had good common sense and—a thing a man should take into account when choosing a mate—bounding good health. Caroline was another cup of tea altogether. Altogether too ready with her tongue.

She offended him—not for the first time, but for the worst time—at the dinner table at Christmas, at Gad's. He'd been saying—not for the first time—that the time had come for him to retire; when a woman had come to the surgery and insisted upon seeing the *old* doctor. He spoke of this is a self-deprecatory way which was entirely false; everybody within hearing should have said: But you are not old; or: What in the world should we do without you? Caroline Thorley had forestalled these tributes to his vanity and, leaning forward, cracked one of her silly jokes. "But surely, that was a compliment! The time to retire will be when somebody demands the Young Doctor."

It was, of course, true and none the more acceptable for being true. And what had made Edward choose Caroline, Doctor Taylor would never understand. Face like a monkey; tongue like a wasp. Still, it was Edward who would have to live with her; he himself would be far away . . .

His little hints about retirement had never been intended seriously. Playfully, in order to evoke dismay and contradiction; or angrily when he and Edward had an argument about medical procedure; now amidst the bustle he found himself thinking more and more often a little village in Hampshire where he had once enjoyed a fishing holiday. He had a friend in the neighbourhood, still in practice in Andover. He could help him a bit, keep his hand in and not there be known as the old doctor, for his friend was at least three years older.

He visualised life in a quiet small house, not quite a cottage, something betwixt and between, big enough to accommodate himself and somebody like Hattie. Why not Hattie? Why not? Now he came to think about it, Edward had never shown a proper appreciation of Hattie. Let him learn. Find a woman from Scurvy Lane.

Yet despite all, willing as he was to disturb Edward's domestic life—as Edward for a fortnight had disturbed his—the professional sphere was another matter. He could not, with a clear conscience, leave Edward single-handed. But that problem was easily solved. Get a well-qualified man installed at the hospital, now, thanks to a legacy, well able to afford such expenditure. He brought the matter up at the meeting of the Hospital Committee, which took place two days before Edward's party. He said they must look ahead, "I am not growing younger." A protest then could have swung the balance, but Lord Stanton said, "Who is?" And Mrs Bosworth, whose annual garden party raised a substantial sum for the hospital's upkeep, asked what the Committee, should *do*. "Hire a young man. Well qualified and strong as a horse," Doctor Taylor said.

Edward—flesh of my flesh, bone of my bone—said the most damaging thing of all.

"Well, in a way, I'm in favour. Nobody should die in harness. But are you sure? It has now and then occurred to me that men around sixty go through something equivalent to the menopause in women."

"Absolute rot!"

"Is it? Think of the men you know who at sixty, give or take a year, change completely. In women the state, admitted it comes earlier, is politely called change of life, and that is an exact description. It is a change. Men alter their wills, marry their housemaids . . . I think this decision to throw in your hand. It's premature. Take a holiday by all means, you've earned it, God knows, and I can manage. But don't make a hasty decision . . . Bear in mind I *am* in favour, but only when you've thought it over."

Edward was content with his party; he had done what he aimed to do—show Caroline the house of which she would be mistress if she married him; the lofty, spacious rooms with their swags of plaster flowers below the cornices, the solid, yet elegant Georgian furniture, now gleaming from the recent polishing. He had even managed to get her to himself for a little time and at the same time show her that he was not a dull dog, though often in her company he felt like one.

In the short passage which led from the house to the surgery there hung some posters which his mother had considered unsuitable for any other part of the house.

"Look at this," he said. "It was an election poster. Less than twenty years ago. It'd be considered libellous now." The candidates' names had invited caricature. Mr Hogg was depicted as a grossly fat man with a pig's face, guzzling in a trough labelled Votes; Mr Nunn, in veil and wimple, was on his knees, hands in prayerful attitude, and eyes raised to the sky across which the word Electorate was scrawled. Another poster advertised a longpast Baildon Midsummer Fair one attraction of which had been a competition—a hat for prize—for the best grin through a horse collar. For the benefit of those who could not read there was a man, apparently with horse's teeth, grinning through a horse collar.

Oddly, Caroline did not break into the merry laughter which he found so attractive. Of the election poster she said "What unfortunate names," and of the toothy grin, "How ugly!" It occurred to him that perhaps his mother had been right in banishing the posters to this obscure passage. That no woman—even Caroline— would find them amusing. That perhaps he had been wrong, a trifle coarse, in showing them to her. While he entertained this thought, Caroline gave an exaggerated shiver. "This is a cold passage," she said. Then because she could never resist the flirtatious gesture, "Feel my hands." He took them in his own warm, competent ones; perhaps a little too closely, with too eager and expectant a look, for almost instantly she pulled away and said:

"Edward, we must go back to the others. Our absence will be noticed."

To the besotted young man this was not at all a discouraging speech. For one thing it placed him and her apart from the others. And it proved that gay and carefree as she might appear, she was properly conventional.

On the way back to the drawing room, he said happily:

"It is the Walfords' party next week. Dancing! Will you dance with me? A lot?"

"But of course."

If twenty personable young men had sprung out of the ground

and made the same request, she would have given each the same answer. She was only just out of the schoolroom, but she knew all the tricks; had been born knowing them. She'd cut her man-handling teeth on her own father. He had been generally indul-gent but if ever he said No to Deb—or later to Di—they had only to say, "Go on, Caro. You ask." Nine times out of ten it had worked.

Any kind of gathering in the area had many constant elements, for the social structure was as neatly striated as a layer cake. Mrs Thorley was the only one to have broken through from one layer to another, and she actually could have gone further, had she wanted to. Her maiden name, and even that of her husband, reprobate as he had been, would have opened doors to her, doors closed to those whom she had chosen as friends. She had taken refuge in being Mrs Thorley of Gad's Hall because the so-called "County" families comprised a closely knit network of people who moved about far more than ordinary people did; they inter-married; they went on visits and exchanged letters and gossipped quite as freely as lesser people did. And she wanted none of it; no faint echo of the calamitous past.

So, having established herself firmly in the middle class, pulling George with her, she was content to remain there and to hope that the girls would make sensible, respectable marriages within the circles which of necessity overlapped a bit. The Walford's circle was naturally wider and based on Sudbury rather than Baildon.

Mrs Walford could not be kept in ignorance forever. Once enlightened, she accepted the revolutionary idea with such amia-bility that Mr Walford wondered what exactly he had feared; and why, in God's name, had he not launched such a venture before. She actually showed some interest in the list of guests invited; in the proposed menu; in Susan's dress. Of that she was critical. She said in her die-away voice:

"Such a harsh colour, my dear, and so unbecoming. You should have consulted me."

"I was reluctant to bother you with such a triviality, Mamma."

"So I suppose you consulted Diana. Now with her black hair

and clear complexion, she would look well in scarlet . . . But it is too late now. What with that, and your hair . . ."

In her own bedroom, preparing for the first proper dance of her life, Susan had been delighted by her own image in the glass; the camomile rinse—how did Richard know about such things?—had brightened her hair, and although the red dress nowhere touched her skin, having a deep creamy lace collar, called a berthe, and falls of the same lace from the elbows, something of the warmth and glow of the colour had been reflected in her face. For once in her life she had looked almost pretty; and here was Mamma, destroying it all! As she would destroy the party!

In a blinding flash, Susan knew what would happen. Mamma was only pretending to acquiesce in the idea of being left alone for some hours with only Nurse Hardy and three servants. As soon as the party got under way somebody would come running. Oh sir, oh Master Richard, oh Miss Susan, the mistress is having one of her attacks . . .

Even if Papa insisted upon bearing the brunt and told her and Richard to stay, the whole thing would be blighted. Who could dance with a light heart while their host's wife was having an attack?

It was over Mrs Walford and her attacks that Edward Taylor and his father had had a dispute. The older man was tolerant. "She *is* frail, Edward; and her heart is flabby."

"Keep a prize-fighter confined to one room and in bed much of the time for how long? Fifteen years. And he'd be frail and have a flabby heart." This was direct criticism of Doctor Taylor's treatment and there was an edge to his voice as he asked:

"And what would *you* advise?"

"A normal life. Not necessarily violent exercise; but walks on fine days; drives in a carriage; cheerful company."

"And what about her attacks?"

"I've never witnessed one. What form do they take?"

"Her heart goes nineteen to the dozen."

"That could be fibrillation—not necessarily a sign of a weak heart. The contrary, in fact. A resistance symptom. It occurs in hysteria, too."

"Text-book jargon, my boy."

One day an opportunity came for Edward to try his hand. Mrs

Walford had an attack and Doctor Taylor had influenza. Even with a good fast horse it took a little time to cover the distance, and when Edward arrived the fibrillation had ceased. He could see, though, that she had been frightened and that her state was not helped by the fussy concern of her family, all pale and stricken around the bed. He drove them away and made a pains-taking examination of the patient.

He had none of his father's bedside manner, but he took pains to assure her that there was nothing to be frightened about; her heart was sound enough. He made ludicrous suggestions about going for drives, and when the weather improved, for walks. He also told her a method—so ridiculous as to be insulting—which *might* curtail an attack. At the first sign press her fingers hard on her neck, just below the ears. He promised nothing, but had, he said, known cases where it had been effective.

He upset her so much that before he was halfway home she had another attack. She did not try the suggested cure; nor would she have him recalled. He was quite useless; worse than no doctor at all. She said much the same, in milder terms, to Doctor Taylor next time she saw him, thus flattering his vanity. And he contin-ued to prescribe nostrums for her; mainly placebos, but two things of proved worth; a mild decoction of digitalis for her heart, and a mixture containing morphine for her insomnia. He also advocated a glass of sherry before a meal to stimulate her appetite.

The pretty bedroom must not be cluttered; so all the medicines stood on a silvery tray in Mr Walford's dressing room. Alongside them stood the sherry and a bottle of apricot brandy of which Mrs Walford was very fond. It rounded off a meal nicely, she said.

"If you cared to drink your sherry now, Mamma, I could sit with you while you drink it. I am early."

"That is thoughtful of you, dear. For me it will be a long, lonely evening."

Not if you are asleep, Susan thought, the red taffeta rustling as she went into the dressing room. She tipped in the opiate with a reckless hand. Let her sleep! Let Papa and me and Richard have just this one evening.

Mrs Hardy, the hireling of the moment, liked to be called Nurse, though she had had no training except that of experience. Many nurses were slatterns and drunkards—but they were not hired by people like Mr Walford, to occupy a post which in some ways was very easy. Mrs Walford didn't really need a nurse at all;

it was just that she demanded constant attention. Nurse Hardy was sober, honest, reliable. Not, Mrs Walford felt, entirely sympathetic; she had once opened one of the windows . . .

This evening, aware of the momentous occasion, she bustled in carrying the imaginary invalid's dinner herself. A tenderly poached salmon steak—the first of the season and small new potatoes, imported at God only knew what cost. Tipsy cake, piled high with whipped cream.

Goodnight, Mamma.

Goodnight, my dear. We'll come in very quietly.

"I shall hear you, my dears. I never sleep when one of you is out. Tonight, all three. . . ."

You'll be asleep, Nurse Hardy thought; I'm not going to have you sending for them; making it look as though I couldn't manage! I'm happy here; I'm Nurse Hardy; I don't eat with servants; and there's nothing messy or unpleasant. When Miss Susan takes over, I'm free, to walk in the woods and pick primroses.

You're going to sleep, my lady, Nurse Hardy thought, tipping, with a hand as reckless as Susan's, a good dose of the opiate into the apricot brandy.

It was a wonderful party. Mr Walford was making up, with a vengeance, for the lack of hospitality he had shown in the past. The atmosphere was so care-free; the company so mixed. Mr Walford had spread his net very wide and even Lavinia. . . .

At first Lavinia had not wished to come. She said so, emerging from her vague ineptitude to make a definite statement. Very well, she need not. She'd be perfectly safe at Gad's with Jenny and Katie. Then, in her awkward, unpredictable way she had decided to come after all and appeared to have fallen in with somebody with whom she was in accord.

"Mr Walford," Mrs Thorley said, catching him by the sleeve and making him jump because he'd known all evening that he was enjoying borrowed time. "So many people were introduced, I did not catch all the names. There, under the palm tree, with my youngest daughter. Who is he?"

"Oh. Virtually a stranger. Mr Fremlin. Old Mr Fremlin died a while back. This Mr Fremlin inherited Abbas Hall. He's a nephew. He's been in India all his life and seemed rather—friendless and as I'd met him in the way of business . . ."

There was no need, Mrs Thorley thought, for the half-apolo-

getic way he spoke. Mr Fremlin appeared to be entirely presentable. He was in fact the most elegantly dressed man in the room,
and although he was old—between forty-five and fifty—one of the
most handsome. His face was tanned—India accounted for that—
and his hair was silvery, thick and glossy. His smile revealed splendid teeth. It struck her as slightly strange that he should seem to
be friendless, for old Mr Fremlin had definitely been "County"
and the county people usually looked after their own.

Still, no matter! Obviously he had the ability—unique in Mrs
Thorley's experience—of getting on with Lavinia. Her eyes were
not looking through him, or beyond him. She was smiling. With
something of a shock Mrs Thorley saw that in an animated mood,
Lavinia was positively pretty; perhaps the prettiest of the four. It
struck her for the first time that some of Lavinia's shyness and
awkwardness was due to her place in the family. She was only
slightly younger than Caroline, but Caroline was old for her age,
poised, socially adequate, whereas Lavinia was immature and shy.
Maybe, Mrs Thorley's mind took an unusual flight of fancy, any
crowd, to a shy girl, looked like that poppy picture with the hint
of unfriendly faces half revealed, half hidden. Lavinia would feel
at ease with a man old enough to be her father. Perhaps he was
telling her about India; she seemed to be engrossed. Or she was
telling him about her drawings; she was now sketching something
on the air. And possibly Mr Fremlin was the first person to show
an appreciative interest in her talent.

Contentedly, Mrs Thorley turned her attention to other people. Poor Susan appeared to be enjoying herself wildly. Like Mrs
Walford, Mrs Thorley thought the colour of the new dress a trifle
too bright. She would have opposed such a choice by any of her
girls. Yet Susan looked pretty tonight; the champagne had coloured her pale face and brightened her eyes. Even her hair looked
different. It might be the lighting. This room was often let for
dancing and the people who ran the place understood the value of
pink shades on the lamps which stood on brackets around the
walls. Far kinder than the overhead lighting from the many-
candled chandeliers in the older and more gracious Assembly
Rooms at Baildon.

Richard Walford had determined that Susan should have the
evening of her life; and since it was an unbroken rule that any
man who could dance must dance at least once with the daughter

of the house, he had invited every young man he could think of, including Everard Spicer, whom Edward Taylor had driven over. Doctor Taylor had not come, for although the Hospital Committee had advertised for a resident doctor and were now comparing the applications, no decision would be reached until next week.

Diana never lacked partners, nor, despite her extra inches, did Deborah, whose musical ear made her a good dancer and who was liked by men, though she was not a girl to inspire romantic feelings, even during the most dreamy-tuned waltz. But, as always, at any kind of gathering, Caroline was the centre of attraction. Close your eyes and you could generally tell whereabouts in the big room Caroline was; she could dance and talk at the same time, and there'd be a boom of delighted masculine laughter, and Caroline's ripple of merriment. Mrs Thorley noticed, with slight disapproval, for despite her unconventional way of taking to business she was conventional over smaller things, that Caroline was dancing rather too often, and in a manner far from sedate, with one of the young men a stranger until this evening.

She had no need to be reminded of his name, for Susan had made that introduction, with a faintly proprietorial air. "My cousin, Mr Frederick Ingram." Shortly afterwards, across the carnation-laden table, Mrs Thorley had heard that young man say, "I'm Freddy to my friends." Innocuous enough in the circumstances, he was with his relatives and their friends; but something jarred; there was a touch of that false bonhomie which she had experienced in the past, in the bad days, when some of Stephen's friends had been, to say the least, dubious. Now she encountered it occasionally in the commercial travellers who sold cattle food.

Once, taking a corner, Freddy-to-my-friends swung Caroline clean off her feet; some petticoat showed, and more of a white lace stockinged leg than was seemly. And not long after, in another dance, Caroline, with that same young man, had stopped to laugh, leaning back against his arm.

Well, he was only a transient. And there, she presently learned from Mrs Gordon, she was wrong—though she had been right about the commercial traveller aura. Frederick Ingram did represent a wine company—a very respectable firm, Hodge and Baker; and because he was some kind of relative and very successful, Mr Walford had commissioned him to sell, at the same time, the product of the Sudbury Brewery.

Edward Taylor drove Everard Spicer home, feeling rather sorry for him, plainly as set on Diana as he himself was set on Caroline. But the poor chap had nothing to offer. No house, no conveyance, and only the most mediocre job. Edward, apart from his feeling for Caroline Thorley, was a hard-headed fellow and could see that the Gordons were not treating Spicer as a putative partner; had they been doing so they would have offered him a lift.

About his own position Edward was being equally rational. He had danced with Caroline several times, and laughed a lot. He saw no serious threat from Freddy Ingram. Caroline attracted men as a candle attracted moths, and she was so gay, so careless. And she was having her fling before marriage—surely the better way.

After some deceptively mild weather, primroses studding the banks, hazel catkins nodding yellow and the birds mating—which was the real, ancient significance of St Valentine's Day—the weather had changed. Frost-sharpened stars sparkled in the sky and the wind blew cold.

"If I might suggest," Mr Fremlin said, "my carriage is here. Miss Lavinia tells me that she feels the cold very much and that Miss Thorley can drive; so if you would allow me to convey Miss Lavinia and yourself it would give me much pleasure."

Lavinia was not susceptible to cold; she spent hours in the unheated attic which she now called her studio; she took her long lonely walks in all weathers.

"A very kind offer, Mr Fremlin, but it would take you at least six miles out of your way."

"Nothing to horses habitually overfed and little exercised."

"I will accompany Lavinia, Mamma," Diana said.

"Very well, my dear. Deborah, what about you? If you fancy a drive in a carriage . . . I am not nervous."

"Thank you, no," Deb said with some emphasis.

A carriage with its own coachman always took precedence over a mere trap and it was some minutes before Mrs Thorley's was brought round.

"Let me drive, Mamma, *please*. We'll show *them!*"

Deb had a way with horses; she'd never struck one in her life, not even the light, half-playful flick of a whip that was so usual.

She talked to them in a peculiar language that they seemed to understand; and since the horse which drew the trap was making for home, and those which drew the carriage were, by their reckoning, going in the wrong direction, at what in Suffolk was called a hill, a slight rise out of the flat land, they overtook the carriage and once it was behind Deborah ceased her chatter to the horse, the Oops there, get along; Ya, best foot forward; hup yup! Now and again glancing over her shoulder, to see that she was well ahead, Deb said:

"Isn't he—Mr Fremlin—a bit odd?"

"I had no opportunity of judging, Deb. In what way, odd?"

"There's something—well, to me—almost repulsive about him. Slimy. The voice. Insinuating. Did you not notice?"

"How could I? He was introduced to me and then I had no speech with him until he offered to drive me—and Lavinia—home."

"Well, I did. As a matter of fact I thought Lavinia had got stuck with him. And she isn't very good at managing, so I took James Gordon across. He's such a good dancer; he could dance with a barrel of beer, and Lavinia must learn sometime. You can't sit out forever . . . James did absolutely the right thing; he asked Lavinia to dance; and Mr Fremlin asked me. And I told a thundering lie. I said I'd ricked my ankle and would like to rest for a bit. So we sat and talked. There was this, oh, I don't know how to explain it, Mamma; something about him that repels. Some people feel that way about cats, or spiders." She did not name the things which she most abominated, went, in fact, quite senseless about.

"It is unlike you, Deb, to be so fanciful."

"Well, we all have our little weaknesses," Deb said. And then, Oops, boy, pick your feet up!

Mr Walford's hiss, *Shussh* as they approached the house, was completely unnecessary; they were all moving like mice. They'd all had a wonderful time—the host, who had just for once broken out of and let himself go; Richard, who had danced five times with Diana, and Susan, who had danced every dance and had a quite dazzling party.

The house was curiously silent. Dead. Separately or in pairs they had absented themselves and always come back, if not to a

welcome, at least a fretful recognition of the fact that they had
been away and were now back. Tonight nothing stirred. Thank-
fully they tiptoed away to their beds. Mamma was asleep.

Mamma was asleep forever, they learned in the morning.

Everything had been absolutely as usual, Nurse Hardy said. Mrs
Walford had enjoyed her dinner, been made comfortable and
dropped off to sleep. A lovely way to go.

"There you are," Doctor Taylor said, triumphantly to his son, "I
knew her heart was weak."

*

A letter for Mrs Thorley, written on very thin paper, with very
black ink and in a hand as plain as print.

> Dear Mrs Thorley,
>   My son had recently the privilege of meeting you
> and your daughters. Were I not so infirm, I would have
> called upon you.

Something slightly wrong there, Mrs Thorley thought; it was
for the earlier resident in a district to call upon the newcomer.
But perhaps living in India explained that.

>   I should, however, be delighted to make your ac-
> quaintance and if you could spare time for a short visit
> on any afternoon convenient to you I should be most
> deeply obliged. I could send the carriage should you wish
> it.
>
>   Yours sincerely,
>   Penelope Fremlin

Mr Walford had spoken of the friendlessness of Mr Fremlin;
and now Mrs Thorley visualised an old woman—she must be old
to be his mother—in some way afflicted, yearning for contact with
her neighbours. Also, she admitted to herself, she was curious, so
she wrote back that she would call, at three o'clock on the following Monday and that she would drive herself.

"Am I not invited, Mamma?" Lavinia asked, showing a natural
emotion—disappointment. "Mr Fremlin mentioned the pictures
at Abbas and promised that I should see them."

"Only I am invited this time, my dear."

Abbas Hall was even more remote than Gad's; it was invisible from the road, standing at the end of a half-mile-long avenue of elms. It had been built on the site of, and partly from the stones of, an old nunnery. Some ruins remained, a line of arches, some piers of stone, rearing up from smooth green lawns. So far as one could see approaching the front of the house, there were no flowerbeds, and Mrs Thorley, who cherished her roses and her herbaceous borders, thought that this lack combined with stone to give the place a cheerless appearance. To look out of any window on this side of the house must be rather like looking out over a graveyard.

She was expected; before she had reined in a man appeared to take charge of her horse and trap. His clothes were those of an ordinary English stable-yard man, but his face was dark. He had not merely been in India, he was Indian. And so was the man who opened the door before she had mounted the three semicircular steps.

The hall was wide and high and very grand. Beautiful rugs lay on the marble floor; stags' heads and other trophies of the chase decorated the walls, interspersed by old weapons, pieces of old armour, and a few dark pictures. She had time only for one glance.

The servant said, "If you plizz, madam, this way."

Certainly Mr Fremlin had pictures; the corridor, as wide as a room, and lighted by several windows, all looking out onto the grass and the ruins, was lined with pictures, brighter and more colourful than the few in the hall. To her, walking past, they were merely flashes of colour, but she thought that if Mr Fremlin kept his promise and invited Lavinia to see them, the girl was in for a treat.

But mainly, as she advanced, Mrs Thorley was conscious of the smell of the place; something heavy and spicy, half attractive, but only half; under the sweetness lay something else which for the moment Mrs Thorley could not find a name for . . .

Another door.

"Mizz Thorley, Mem."

It was almost as though he had opened the door of an oven. An enormous fire blazed on the hearth and there were, in addition three lamps, necessary because heavy curtains were drawn across the windows. The room was no bigger than the general living room at Gad's, and it seemed to be full of flowers, great bowls, not only of the carnations which could—as Mr Walford had proved—be obtained, even in winter, but lilies.

Near the fire two large winged armchairs were placed; and one was occupied.

"It was kind of you to come, Mrs Thorley. Please excuse me that I do not rise. I am somewhat lame."

The lamps were so placed that only the firelight shone on the occupied chair and what sat there might have been a heap of cobwebby lace, for even in this overheated room, Mrs Fremlin was all wrapped about. Out of the bundle a hand was extended; not a hand, a bird's claw, so delicate, so frail. And despite everything, cold.

"It was kind of you to invite me," Mrs Thorley said. Except for the suddenly oppressive weight of her sealskin coat, she was perfectly at ease. She had been born into a class absolutely sure of itself, married well; been dragged down, survived. Many another woman, she knew, passing through that impressive hall and the picture gallery, ushered into this inner sanctum and invited to sit down—but not to remove her coat—would have sat there, sweltering. She did not. She said, "I will take off my coat," and did so, laying it on another chair. The bundle said:

"You find the room warm? Personally I find the English winter insufferable. I am never warm." It was a firm, positive voice, with a lilt to it. Mrs Thorley remembered the lilt in Mr Fremlin's, almost undetectable, yet there. In his mother it was far more marked.

"Coming to East Anglia from India you must notice the cold very much."

"I am not only from India. I am *of* India. I wished you to see for yourself. Before I requested a favour of you." The two incredibly delicate hands moved, pushed back some of the enshrouding lace, and Mrs Thorley's eyes, now adjusting to the dim light, saw a face, old, but still of cameo clarity, and pale: paler than Lavinia, always suspected of being anaemic, paler than Susan Walford, who until last week so seldom went out-of-doors; but it was a different pallor. Mrs Thorley could find no word for it; but nowhere, not even in the polyglot communities of Continental watering places, could Mrs Fremlin have been mistaken for a woman of purely European origin.

"You are shocked, Mrs Thorley?"

"Of course not."

"Most people are," Mrs Fremlin said drily. "The more so because I am not pure Indian. You know what is said of mongrels—of both breeds the worst qualities and the good ones of neither! Then I compound the fault. I had beauty when I was young, and I married an Englishman. Of good family, but no wealth. No expectations that he knew of. Ah! You will take tea?"

Very pale tea with a faintly floral flavor; jasmine? mock-orange?

Having poured it into cups of the utmost delicacy, the old woman took up her tale, bridging some years in silence.

"I have been truly blessed in my son. Of the dead let no ill be spoken; but had the inheritance fallen to my husband, he would have come alone. And he would have been wise. Johnny refused to do that. Unless I came too, he would not come. And I, wishing him to take his proper place in the world, came. A mistake indeed. There is more prejudice here than in India."

"I am sorry," Mrs Thorley said, shouldering the fault of her countrymen. She was not conscious of feeling any prejudice herself; yet her thoughts slid away to Deborah, whose response to Mr Fremlin had been blindly instinctive; a bit odd; slimy; insinuating; she'd avoided dancing with him; refused to ride in his carriage.

The old woman had spoken of asking a favour and Mrs Thorley decided to grant it if she could and immediately, upon that thought, ran full tilt into the prejudice which she had not recognised with herself.

Not marriage!

What small information she possessed about India had drifted to her through missionary propaganda; if only enough money could be raised, enough missionaries found, the Indians would stop worshipping cows and burning live widows with the bodies of the husbands; Indian men would give up their harems where wretched women lived in purdah. That kind of thing. And if Mr Fremlin had conceived the mad idea of marrying Lavinia, she would oppose him with all her might, without actually understanding why.

"What I wished to ask of you, Mrs Thorley, is that your daughter—the youngest, I think—Lavinia? should be allowed to visit. My son was greatly impressed by her. She has talent. We both feel that it should be fostered. As you see, this house has

many pictures; the ceiling of the drawing room was painted by
Angelica Kauffmann. My son felt that your daughter should see
such things."

"How can he know that she has talent?" A natural question
enough, for he'd never seen any of Lavinia's work.

"From her talk—they spent much time together. Mrs Thorley,
could anyone have spent an evening with William Shakespeare
and not recognised genius—without seeing a word he had written?"

For Mrs Thorley an unanswerable question. She had never
made any pretence at intellectualism; as a child she had been introduced by her governess to the Lamb's *Tales from Shakespeare*
and enjoyed them moderately; in later life she had seen perform-
ances of the plays, and to be truthful, found some of them boring;
of William Shakespeare and his effect upon a person meeting him
casually, she could make no mental image at all.

"Lavinia is very young," she said.

Mrs Fremlin, pulling the lacy wool, the woolly lace closer
about her head, said:

"Mrs Thorley, I understand. Any kind of—alliance is quite out
of the question. So much misery has been caused . . . We intend
to stay here only until the estate is disposed of. We may go to
Brazil. There, my son says, colour is so much in the melting pot,
and wealth so important . . ." She left that sentence unfinished
and stirring a little amongst her wrappings said, "So you see, if
your daughter wishes to see one of the best collections in private
hands we have no time to waste. Also—one's own wishes should
be subsidary, of course—my son is often absent and I should much
welcome the company of a girl young enough to be free of prejudice; and with talent. You, I understand, have four daughters;
imagine having none, and the prospect of a grand-daughter somewhat remote."

Mrs Thorley gave the matter her most serious consideration
and could see nothing against the proposition. Lavinia had always,
by her very nature, been lonely, and here was a woman made
lonely by circumstance. And her one fleeting suspicion—inspired
by missionary talk about the poor little child brides of India—
had been set at rest by Mrs Fremlin's remark about any kind of alliance being out of the question. Besides, Lavinia was so immature; if Mrs Thorley had understood the missionary lectures

aright the child brides of India, young as they sounded, were at least nubile.

And she rather liked Mrs Fremlin, felt sorry for her. She said warmly:

"Of course Lavinia may visit you. It will be most pleasant for her. She will probably wish to bring some of her pictures. I hope you will not be disappointed in them. I find them rather— strange."

"And you are an artist yourself?"

How did she know that?

"I never made such a claim. I drew a little, at one time, in a purely conventional way."

Patterns, she thought; for potters and dressmakers; a commercial exercise which had made her unwilling ever to touch pencil or paint brush again.

"This is Monday," Mrs Fremlin said. "Johnny will not be back here until Thursday at the very earliest. Would you allow her to come tomorrow. I would send the carriage."

They'd all, of course, wearing decent black, attended Mrs Walford's funeral and now Diana was comforting poor Susan, helping her with mourning that was not downright ugly; Deb was occupied in the garden, pruning the roses and Caroline was rearranging the bedroom which she had delightedly seen cleared when Lavinia moved her painting things up to the attic. Caroline, too, was planning some alleviation of the Walfords' mourning. "After all, Mamma, if you remember, we had Diana's small private party. I think to ask the Walfords who could never get out together, and Freddy Ingram—who is after all, related—would be only kind."

They all, except Lavinia, were enmeshed in ordinary life. And when the carriage came, delivering a great wide basketful of carnations and lilies, and collecting Lavinia, who had taken the smallest valise in the house, just enough for night-clothes . . . but under her other arm a bulging portfolio, Mrs Thorley thought: Yes, she will have something, too.

So it began.

For Richard Walford and Edward Taylor that spring would have been a halcyon time but for the existence of Everard Spicer and Freddy Ingram, who kept cropping up. Not unnaturally. So far as possible all good hostesses liked to keep some kind of balance between the sexes, and Susan and Deborah must be provided for; yet inevitably Everard and Diana seemed to pair off, and Freddy and Caroline. Constituting no *real* threat, since neither had much to offer. Richard and Edward were alike in many ways and it was significant that even now, brought into close and frequent contact, each respected the other, while privately thinking him rather a dull dog. Yet, after each faintly unsatisfactory gathering together, both solid young men entertained the same thought. Richard's apparent rival was little more than a lawyer's clerk, and lived in lodgings; Edward's was no more than a commercial traveller, and lived in lodgings.

Susan had once suggested that Freddy should be invited to live in the big house, which, now that Mamma had gone, did seem empty at times; but Mr Walford had repudiated that idea, looking rather slyly at his son.

"I think we should wait a little. Richard may be thinking of marriage, the house would not be too large then."

Mr Walford was one of the men who heartily admired Mrs Thorley and imagined that he saw many of her qualities reflected in her daughter. Little money or none! Knowledgeable men had agreed that George Thorley, for all that he'd lived in style, couldn't have left *much*, otherwise his widow could have sat back and folded her hands; and in any case Diana was only his step-daughter. But that did not matter; Richard had the brewery behind him. And Susan would have two thousand pounds as well as shares in the Light Suffolk Railway, which navvies were already hacking out towards the coast.

Edward Taylor was in an equally sound position; in fact he had the whole beautiful house in St. Giles' Square to himself. If anything, too much to himself, for his father had taken Hattie with him and so far Edward had not been able to replace her. He was cared for, after a fashion, by a series of women from the Lane who could only spare odd hours, and cooked—when they did cook— like the devil. To his own dismay he found himself ceasing to make excuses for them; a woman who had nothing but an open fire, a saucepan and a frying pan to work with should, one might have supposed, be able to boil a dumpling, fry an egg. But they couldn't, and a horrible suspicion was dawning upon him—they lived in the lane because they were unfit for any other place. And proper, competent housekeepers avoided taking service in doctors' households where hours were so irregular. He now realized how right his father had been in calling Hattie a treasure and in persuading her to go with him.

Edward now took his main, mid-day meal at The Angel, and there was trouble if he were late. All this, all that, had been eaten, he'd have to make do . . .

Look on the bright side, he admonished himself. He now had more free time because the hospital doctor, young, strong, eager, was prepared to work, day and night, and take his free time in a block of forty-eight hours. He had a home—his own or his parents' he never revealed—in Bermondsey and liked to catch the up train at four o'clock in the afternoon of Friday. Down trains on Sunday were fewer and slower, but, starting at two o'clock, he was back on duty by seven.

"She's a gonner," Joe Snell said, looking with disgust at what had seemed the most promising heifer of the herd, struggling, painfully and ineffectually, to give birth to a calf which was presenting itself hind legs first. It was a rare, but not unknown condition, and it was always fatal. Any young animal, in the ordinary way, came almost egg-shaped, head first, front legs, or paws, neatly tucked under; they slipped out. The occasional one went wrong, backside and hind legs blocking the passage. And there was nothing anybody could do about it.

Mrs Thorley, dead ignorant, said, "We must do something, Joe."

"What, ma'am?"

"Help her, poor thing," The heifer struggled and moaned; with each pang and thrust the hindquarters and back legs of the calf were made visible. Then there was the retraction.

Mrs Thorley was making her routine visit in the bright morning light. She never failed. She trusted Joe absolutely, he knew that, but if anything she was more conscientious—more often on the spot—than Master had been.

Now she pushed back her sleeves almost to the shoulder and set her face; the calf's hindquarters, awkward legs, presented themselves at the next thrust and she grabbed, pulled firmly but gently, moved her hands inwards towards where the main body lay; and there the calf was, safely delivered on to the clean straw. And a heifer into the bargain.

"You're a masterpiece, ma'am, if I may say so," Joe said. "Now, if you'd just come across to my place, there's always a kettle on the hob."

"I'll manage with a bucket, thank you. You see, Joe, I'd prefer nobody to know about this . . . operation. I have enough nicknames, without being called a cow midwife."

He wondered how she knew the things that were said about her now that the novelty and the faint respect that mourning evoked had worn off. Coarse-minded, coarse-tongued men put the worst possible construction upon her leaving Mr Corby's saleyard for Mr Larkin—Larkin was a notorious womaniser. To some extent, Joe, when he encountered such jibes, had pretended to be in accord: Well, she'd upped his wage and had his cottage rethatched. It didn't do, in a small community, to seem different, or to have any regard for other than things you could touch and handle. Now, seeing her dowse her arms in a bucket of cold water and dry them on a bit of sacking, he thought: Next chap say a disrespectful word about her, I'll knock flat.

All that spring and summer Lavinia came and went between Abbas and Gad's. Sometimes simply to keep Mrs Fremlin company, sometimes to meet people—all with difficult foreign names. Contact with this wider world had done little to change her behaviour at home.

Once, coming back with a portfolio even more bulging than usual, she'd almost dropped it and some pages slipped out. Mrs Thorley caught a glimpse of some very strange drawings; figures with an unnatural number of arms, legs, breasts; but before she could really observe them, Lavinia snatched them away and said that Mrs Fremlin had drawn them. For it seemed that Mrs Fremlin, before age had quenched her, had been an artist, too.

Then, in late May, Mr Fremlin had taken one of Lavinia's pictures to London, and sold it for fifty pounds.

To whom?

Some dealer in Bond Street or somewhere.

Fifty pounds! It seemed a vast sum of money to Diana and Caroline, who never had enough to spend on their wardrobes; and to Deborah, who was slowly and painfully saving up to buy a proper hunter, one day; and to Mrs Thorley, who had sold what she still thought of as proper drawings for such pitiable sums. Lavinia was entirely unimpressed.

"I would like to keep about ten pounds for materials," she said. "You can have the rest, Mamma."

"I shall bank it—your name, my dear." For there was always the possibility that a girl so undeveloped of body, so withdrawn in the company of ordinary people, might not find a husband.

"Oh, Mr Fremlin thinks he can sell others," Lavinia said with the utmost indifference.

That evening Mrs Thorley looked again at the picture of poppies, and at some of Lavinia's earlier gifts to her. All, by her reckoning, a little queer, out of proportion, out of perspective, and some in colours untrue to nature; but the hostile faces which seemed to come and go in the hearts of the poppies were strangest of all—a talent developing rapidly; and one could not, in view of the fifty pounds, say on the wrong lines. Perhaps what Lavinia did was to set the imagination to work. Twice before the poppy picture had seemed to Mrs Thorley to have an inner meaning; once the faces of men in the Corn Exchange and on the Cattle Market; once as all faces appeared to a shy girl; and now they had meaning again, calling to mind the imminence of the South Suffolk Cattle Show, where the young bull, Gad's glory, was to make his debut, and where she would appear, the first woman, the only woman to take her place in the enclosure reserved for exhibitors. A worse ordeal than the Exchange or the Market, because there would be thousands of faces, many of them those of competitors, and if Gad's Glory did what was expected of him, there'd be plenty of hostility . . .

She had done a lot of arithmetic and a good deal of heartsearching about the business of exhibiting cattle and decided upon half-measures. Distant shows she would avoid; they brought renown but little monetary return; she decided to enter and attend only those within easy reach, enough to keep the herd's name alive and George's memory green.

By this time Everard Spicer was almost one of the family. Diana's infatuation had increased rather than lessened. The Gordons, she felt, were most unfair to him, making him keep the office open every Saturday until noon. And his lodgings, found for him by Mrs Gordon, intent upon doing a good turn to an old acquaintance living in much reduced circumstances, were truly deplorable. Diana had forgotten that in Leicester her mother had

sometimes let a room, or even two, and spoke harshly about amateur landladies.

"People who do things just for pin money never do them properly. Everard would be far better off at Mrs Bolton's."

"Is there any reason why he should not move?" Mrs Thorley
asked. Something about the words amateur and pin money stung
a little.

"Only the cost, Mamma. Believe it or not Mrs Bolton now
charges fifteen shillings a week. The railway men have sent prices
soaring. And Everard is trying to *save*."

A sudden hot blush ran up from the base of Diana's neck to her
hair-line. It receded just as quickly, but Mrs Thorley had read the
message.

"Well, my dear," she said, bringing this conversation back to
where it had begun, "by all means fetch him, bring him back and
give him a few good meals. Food, thank God, is one thing we are
not short of."

So, almost every Saturday Diana with the small pony and trap
waited outside the office and transported Everard to another
world. He was not actually short of friends; a young man with the
right clothes, manners, voice had entry to many homes, but he
had never chanced to meet a girl half as attractive as Diana, or
half as fond and undemanding. By June he was as much in love
with her as he could be with anyone and had enough faith in his
love to ignore something which James Gordon let slip. Quite out
of order, unprofessional, unethical. "There's no real money there,
old boy. Five hundred apiece, so the will read; and I rather doubt
whether, if they all got married tomorrow, the ready cash would
be available."

Everard said, "Oh," in a noncommittal voice; but he looked
disgusted and he had a face singularly suited to take on an expression of disgust. The look was provoked, not as James Gordon
imagined, by the small size of the dowry but by the breach of etiquette committed by the mention of such a confidential matter to
one who was not even a member of the firm. Yet!

"Now Susan Walford—I bet her papa would come down with
something handsome," James said.

In Everard anger flared; he longed to say: You and your family
chose to lodge me with an old woman who has forgotten what a
square meal looks like, you and your father choose my work—al-

ways the dullest and dreariest; I'm damned if you shall choose my wife! But he restrained himself and said stiffly:

"I happen to prefer Diana."

"So does somebody else we know of," James said with a mischievous grin.

Everard had been half aware of Richard Walford as a rival and now that he came to think about it he perceived a real threat. Diana was often at Sudbury, sometimes, since Mrs. Walford's death, staying overnight. Ostensibly visiting Susan; but who knew?

He took stock of the whole situation. In July, Diana would be eighteen. She could afford to wait two years; but would she? With Richard able to marry her this year? Mr Walford would approve; he always spoke very highly of Diana, saying how faithfully she had made visits and cheered Susan when she was so tied. And he seemed to expect Richard to marry soon. That had come out in some casual talk—in Mrs Thorley's crimson-papered dining room. Something about having the big old house at Sudbury completely redecorated. Better wait a little and see, Mr Walford said, people had differing tastes and the lady of the house should be able to give her choice full range. And his glance—yes, his glance had slid slyly about, linking his son with Diana. Susan must be taken into account, too. A girl's best friend often had influence . . .

Look into the future; see it at its least promising; by staying in his uncomfortable—but cheap—lodging and saving every possible penny, at the end of two years he would have saved enough to hire a small but decent house and buy the absolutely necessary furniture. Diana would have at the least twenty-five pounds a year, which would buy her clothes. One could not expect her to scrub and scour, but cleaning women could be hired very cheaply.

They could manage.

They would have no need to manage! For before two years were out the half-promise of a partnership would have materialised. He was already doing most of James' work, as well as his own; and he had the queer idea that the Gordons were trying him out, making him serve, as it were, an apprenticeship.

And in a way being engaged would mean not only security, but economy. A girl firmly betrothed and with an engagement ring on her finger was allowed some latitude; she could, for example, attend a concert in the Assembly Rooms, or a matinée at the theatre without a third person in attendance. Mrs Thorley was usually lenient in many ways, strictly conventional in others—rightly so, of course—and never yet had he and Diana appeared in public, *à deux*. Having no home in which to entertain, unable to afford a hired place, he had done his best to make some return for hospitality, and it had invariably meant three, even four seats at any entertainment.

Early on the Monday morning before the South Suffolk Cattle Show, which always took place on the first Thursday in June, Diana, delivering Everard at the office, just as the clock in St Mary's church tower struck nine, said, "Here we are, dead on time. Everard, do try to get away on Thursday afternoon. Nobody will do business that day. And Mamma needs support. Nobody would believe it, but she is nervous about some things. And this is her first show. And if that young bull—Gad's Glory—does any good, we'll have a wonderful party afterwards. I do so want you to be there."

"I will try. You know . . . I'd do anything within my power to please you, Diana. Dear Diana."

Nine o'clock on a Monday morning was not the best time for romantic speeches, but something kindled.

"I know. As I would for you, darling Everard."

All that had lain, suppressed, shrouded, leaped into the full light of morning, unashamed, triumphant. Moved by a mutual impulse they leaned forward, kissed.

Now, fully committed, they could speak of marriage. Would she mind waiting two years? Two years! She was prepared to wait forever; gladly, gladly. And of course, by all the rules that governed such an occasion, he must ask her Mamma's consent. To that Diana could say truly that Mamma, not being blind, knew how things were going and, had she disapproved, would have shown it long before now.

"And if it could be arranged," Diana said, "I mean asking Mamma is only a formality . . . the party after the Show could be our engagement party. Wouldn't that be wonderful?"

Not only wonderful, but fitting, for of her little group Diana was the oldest member—except poor Susan—not to be yet betrothed. Barbara Catchpole, Charlotte Anderson, Margaret Agnew, all engaged, wearing with pride their engagement rings and saying: You next, darling. Now it had happened.

"It would be wonderful. But dearest, I shall not be able to ask your Mamma's consent before Thursday—even if I get away then. And even about that I am not sure, yet."

"You could write."

"Yes, I could do that." And some things were more easily put down on paper than said face to face.

"And even if you can't manage to get to the Show—but oh, I do so hope, you can . . . I'd pick you up here at six o'clock."

Unnoticed, the hands of St Mary's clock had crept forward, reached the end of its first quarter circle; boomed out the time; fifteen minutes past nine; and Mr Gordon, who prided himself on his punctuality, rounded the corner.

He was getting on in years—he'd married late and there had been two little boys before James; one had succumbed to the croup, and one to scarlet fever; James had survived and, merely by surviving, earned more indulgence than many men showed towards the one who was to succeed them. James could be very clever when he chose, but he was a gadabout. Why not? Mr Gordon could afford, and was indeed proud of, a gadabout son. And he had accepted Everard Spicer to do the donkey work. But he did not like him; hadn't from the first. Too superior; too much inclined to look down the nose which was so perfectly shaped for looking down upon. Many people, wishing to make a will, or driven by this or that dispute to seek a lawyer's services, felt strange, a little nervous; they needed the reassurance of the hearty, hail-fellow-well-met manner which Mr Gordon could assume at will, and which came to James as naturally as breathing. Everard was always the lawyer, correct, formal. He was a very good lawyer, and they were lucky to get him so cheaply—the prospect of a possible partnership had been the lure there; but he'd have to wait a long time . . . perhaps forever.

Mr Gordon would have liked young Spicer more had the young man been open to correction or rebuke, but his work was always faultless and if an argument arose over any point, he could always prove himself right.

However, this morning, just for once he'd put himself in the wrong.

Approaching the little trap Mr Gordon raised his hat and said:

"Good morning, Miss Osborne." He was one of the few who could always distinguish Osborne from Thorley. "Morning, Spicer." There was a marked change, a departure from geniality in his manner. He glanced up at St Mary's clock, took out his watch and ostentatiously checked it. Inside the office he said sourly, "Since when has the week-end extended well into Monday morning?"

Everard's manner remained respectful:

"I'm sorry, sir." But his look showed clearly what he thought of such pettiness.

That so small a lapse should have been noticed, let alone rebuked, was very irksome; but he soon forgot about it as he composed in his mind the letter he would write to Mrs Thorley—and thought about the ring. Diana deserved, and must have a ring which she could display with pride; but how could he afford one? He gulped down his luncheon—an egg that had been too old to poach well, on a piece of sodden toast—and went into the High Street, to study the window of the only jeweller in Baildon.

There were rings to suit most purses except very deep ones; Mr Collins did not cater for the rich; in his display there were only two rings priced above twenty pounds, one at twenty-two, one at the twenty-five, and frankly neither of them was worthy, though both were as much, as far out Everard's reach as if they had been a hundred.

He realised that he had been very rash, very premature. He had not given the ring a thought. He had no-one from whom he could borrow. He had a few things which he could sell, or pawn; all presents from his godfather; a gold half hunter; cuff-links and studs and the signet ring he wore on his little finger. People who sold things because they needed money quickly never got a fair price, he knew that; about pawnshops he knew nothing at all. He'd never seen one in Baildon—if one existed it would be in the Lane.

He might gain a little time by saying that Collins hadn't a ring good enough, and ask Diana to wear, as a token, a temporary substitute, the one from his own finger. But the only point in gaining time was to have some attainable object in view. Being poor was the very Devil and he regretted having let his feelings run away with him.

In a dejected state of mind he sat down to write to Mrs Thorley; his disciplined mind came to his aid; well-composed sentences expressing all the correct sentiments, flowed smoothly. It was a model letter.

"I imagine you know what this is about," Mrs Thorley said, having read it with approval.

Blushing, Diana said, "Well, Everard did intimate . . ."

"I consider it very sensible of him to suggest waiting until he is more established."

"That was understood, Mamma. And two years is not long. But if you do approve, I thought it would be pleasant—and an economy—to combine our after-the Show party with the announcement of the engagement."

"We're not yet sure about Gad's Glory, my dear. I was proposing only a spur-of-the-moment celebration, if he won. But you are quite right. We must, in any case, entertain Mr van Haagen."

Mr van Haagen was Dutch, and some weeks earlier had written a letter to a dead man—George Thorley—from whom at some time in the past he had bought a young bull and a cow. He wrote, in perfect if rather stilted English, that his experiements in cross-breeding of Durham and Friesian had been completely successful. He had not come hastily to this conclusion; it had taken some years. He hoped that Mr Thorley remembered him after so long a time. And he was sure that Mr Thorley would be interested in what he had learned about cross-breeding; which was that the dam had more effect upon the offspring than the sire. "Bearing out the truth of an old saying, my dear Mr Thorley; a jackass could sire a race horse should the mare be good enough. So I come to buy cows."

Mrs Thorley had written back, explaining that her husband was dead, but that since she had kept the herd together, she could offer Mr van Haagen a choice of promising young cows. And as his proposed date for the visit coincided with the South Suffolk Cattle Show when accommodation would be difficult to find in Baildon, invited him to stay at Gad's. He might find the Show interesting.

On Tuesday, quite early for him, James Gordon strolled into the wretched cubby-hole which was Everard's office. He perched in a negligent way on the edge of the desk and said:

"I'm taking the day off, old boy. Newmarket. I'd only two fixtures. See to them for me, will you?" He slapped a scribbled paper on to the desk.

"Of course," Everard said, thinking: Oh how enviable; to be going off, care-free, heart-free to Newmarket Heath on a sunny June day.

Swinging a leg, James said, "All right then," and felt a pang of compassion, almost of self-reproach. Not that he was to blame. His father had kept saying things like, "Well enjoy yourself while you can," and "I can't last forever, you know," and, "Honestly, what you'll need, dear boy, is a reliable partner."

So, by chance, he'd met Everard again and seen in him the best possible future partner; and it was not his fault that things had gone a bit awkward.

Trying to make up for all that had gone awkward, James Gordon said:

"Tell you what; I'll put five bob on the favourite for you. Reward for virtue; dealing with old Mrs. Rorke." He tapped the paper.

Something very near to mental derangement fell upon Everard. He said, "Thanks, James, but I'll make my own bet. Have you a list of runners?"

James hauled a piece of printed paper from his pocket.

Like every inexperienced punter Everard went by names. And one struck him. Laurel's Lad. Laurel; Daphne; Daphnis, taught by Diana. The connection was as tenuous as a connection could be, but it was the only one.

He reached into his pocket and took out a precious half sovereign.

"Put this for me on Laurel's Lad."

"Hell's afire, Everard! A rank outsider. Couldn't win a sack race."

"It's the only one I fancy."

It was already as lost as though Everard had thrown it into the river. But James did as he was told, put Everard's ten shillings on Laurel's Lad, and then, keeping his promise, remembering Mrs Rorke, five shillings for Everard, two pounds for himself on the favourite which did win, but odds against so that the gain was minuscule. In a later race Laurel's Lad appeared to stroll home.

"Old boy," James said, scattering sovereigns on the tidy desk. "You must have access to a crystal ball! I'll consult you before I make another bet." He then added a wise and well-meant warning —in Everard's case unnecessary—about not letting beginner's luck go to his head and turn into a real gambler.

Fifty pounds. And the best ring on offer in Baildon was the one at twenty-five pounds which he had despised when it was far out of reach. And tomorrow was Thursday. Well he'd just have to tell Diana that Collins had nothing good enough, but that he was having a selection sent down.

Mr Collins showed no resentment at being told that what he had in the window was not good enough for young Mr Spicer, who though occupying a pretty humble post at Gordon and Son was in every other respect a toff.

"I don't put everything in the window, sir. I only display what I can afford to insure. I have superior articles. If you would just come through." He led the way into a room occupied by a work-bench—for he mended clocks and watches—and a safe.

"May I ask what kind of ring you had in mind? Up to what price?"

"Forty pounds." And that would leave ten towards the house rent, the furniture.

"Umm," the jeweller said, a trifle disappointed. Neither quite one thing nor the other. People who despised a twenty-five-pound ring should, he thought, be prepared to go to fifty and over. Still, forty was something. Indicating that Everard should sit on the stool by the work-table, Mr Collins fiddled about with the door of his safe and then, keeping his body between his potential customer and what was in the safe, he groped about inside it.

There was nothing dishonest in this side of his business. There was in fact, working at the back of the network, great delicacy of feeling. Everywhere, all over the country, there were ladies—like Everard's landlady, come down in the world, anxious to sell a trinket, but not to advertise the fact. So jewellers in quite distant places made exchanges. In addition to the ladies who were feeling the pinch of rising prices, there were the French who time after time had been obliged to flee their native country in what they stood up in—and their jewels.

Living as he did in a quiet, small country town Mr Collins' part of this network was that of collector, rather than distributor; he bought what he could, very cheaply, exchanged for new goods; sold hardly anything directly. He was in fact awaiting the arrival of his London contact.

Burrowing like a mole he came out with three rings.

"Not new of course," he explained, laying them on the work-bench amongst the entrails of clocks and watches. "Secondhand

and with the added value of antiquity. Forty; forty-five; fifty. And every one of them worth ten times as much."

They were all beautiful, a vast improvement of the best in the window; but only one was Diana's, matching the red stones which danced at the end of her ear-bobs. Red stones, and diamonds alternating, a great flashing half-circle.

"That one," he said, so firmly that Mr Collins, who had lain the things out in order of merit, felt justified in saying, adjusting slightly:

"Ah. The fifty-pound one. Rubies are rarer now than diamonds. A very wise choice, if I may say so."

"I'd like it in a case," Everard said.

Some shows shifted about, but the South Suffolk always took place in Lord Stanton's park, a bit up river from the town. The ring was a great oval. At one end, under an awning and on padded benches, sat the very important people, including, on this exceptionally beautiful June day, a minor foreign royalty. At a slightly lower level along one side of the oval was the judges' stand, not much occupied since they moved about, conscientiously studying animals, even touching them. Next in grade came the stand for those exhibiting animals—they must be considered since without them there would be no show; then a stand for those who were willing to pay a shilling for a seat. And at the far end of the oval the gateway through which animals entered and left. The other side of the oval was for those who wished to watch, but could not pay.

There had been a little trouble about Mr van Haagen, who had surprised everybody at Gad's; they'd thought of him, coming up out of the past, as fairly old, Papa's contemporary—and perhaps because of the roundness of Dutch cheeses, they had visualised him as plump and red-faced. In fact he was tall, lean, young-looking, handsome; and although his spoken English was less perfect than his written, he had so much charm that Mrs Thorley was angered by the fact that some blockhead at the gateway of the exhibitors' enclosure had refused him admission. All seats were booked.

Deborah said, "Mr van Haagen can have my seat, Mamma. I'll go and pay my shilling."

"But no, my dear young lady. Easily, I find a seat." With superb self-assurance he walked away, over to the enclosure of the important. And there, because he sounded un-English and might well be in some way connected with the honoured visitor, he was admitted without question. From his privileged position, he called and smiled and waved his programme of events and entries, making, Mrs Thorley felt, her and her family more conspicuous than they were already, which was conspicuous enough, for she had decided that since the thing must be done, it should be done in style. She and all the girls were wearing new dresses. Her own was half-mourning, a dark lavender colour with black velvet bows. It would serve as her best summer dress for several years, purple bows presently replacing the black ones. The girls were all in muslin, in varying shades of rose colour, and George wore the Highland dress which Queen Victoria's fondness for Scotland had made fashionable.

All the preliminary judging had been done earlier in the day; only potential winners were paraded now. Gad's Glory was amongst them, but victory was not yet sure. Lavinia emerged briefly from her self-absorption and said, "There is no need to worry, Mamma. He will win."

(Because I have willed it! I am only a novice yet, barely initiated; but I know the feeling of power. I have touched the ritual.)

"If he should, George, you know what to do."

"Yes, Mamma." But George had his secrets, too.

The animals paraded. Gad's Glory, Mrs Thorley reflected, was not behaving very well. He was going to be one of those bulls that needed two men, each gripping a pole, linked into the nose-ring to control him.

Diana looked about. Everard had not been able to come; Mr Gordon and James were there—at the very front of the shilling stand. They had in their selfish way left Everard to mind the office.

A man to whom Nature had given a good, resonant voice, now amplified by a wide, lily-shaped horn, shouted the judges' final decision. Gad's Glory, for all his restive behaviour, had won the covetted red ribbon and the prize of five pounds.

Every woman present and some of the men had wondered what she would do, how she would look, crossing the space, all dung-spattered, in her dainty shoes and a dress at least twelve yards wide around the hem.

There was a little dutiful clapping; and somebody stood up in the seats of the privileged and shouted, "Goot! Goot!" Then

George Thorley stepped out. He bowed to the flower-decked stand where the important sat. That he had been told to do. But he turned about, bowed to the people in the shilling stand, and then—God bless his little heart—to those pressing against the rails. He took the five shining pounds in one hand, the red rosette in the other. He slipped the money into the pocket of Joe Snell's beautifully laundered smock and then took two sideway steps which made his kilt swing, to face the bull, its great head tossing and turning.

Mrs Thorley said, "Oh God," and put her hand to her mouth. But it was all right, George chose his moment and slipped the red ribbon into the head harness. Then, unharmed, thank God, he turned and made another bow, towards the place where his mother and sisters sat.

It was a perfect performance, and all but the most envious recognised it. Timing, daring style. The crowd rose to him and his course was set for the next sixty-eight years. Be bold, play to the crowd. In that one sunny afternoon was the embryo of a reckless old man who did not feel very well, whose body would have preferred slippered comfort by the fire, whose purse was thin; but who must dispense cherry brandy as freely as water, and ride a young, untried hunter.

The party at Gad's that evening was hilarious. Diana had collected Everard and he had given her the ring. Congratulations all about and Mr van Haagen saying, "Ah yes; goot! In Amsterdam are the best diamonds, so I am knowing. Is a beautiful ring and the finger worthy of it. I am happy to be sharing so happy an occasion."

It was an occasion for champagne. For little backward glances. Poor George, how he would have enjoyed the double celebration; how proud he would have been of his son. Diana thought that Papa would surely have approved of Everard. Deborah thought how Papa had always predicted great things for Gad's Glory and would have been delighted by the victory.

Susan spared a thought for her brother. Diana had confided in her as soon as Mamma had given her consent and to Susan had fallen the duty—doubly distasteful—of breaking the news to Richard. Of all the girls she knew she would best have liked Diana as a sister-in-law, and although Richard pretended not to care, saying: Well, I'm not surprised, are you? she'd seen his hurt and shared it. He was not here this evening. And despite herself Susan's heart lightened, for it meant that Freddy would have to drive her home. Edward Taylor was absent too for the lovely summer weather had produced the usual outbreaks of summer fever in the Lane.

Still, they could have danced a little, had Mr van Haagen been a dancer; but he was not. "Much to be regretted, but an art I never acquired."

Very well, they'd sing. Unfortunately that was another thing Mr van Haagen either could not do, or did not care for. "For me, no. I will sit with Madam. Not for business. That is finished this morning. With much satisfaction."

But he was their guest; something must be done to entertain him.

"Do you play cards?" Mrs Thorley asked.

"The whist? Not goot." He seemed to realise suddenly that he was being a rather unsatisfactory guest. He looked glum. Then he remembered something, and with the radiant smile which displayed his splendid teeth, he said. "With the cards I can tell fortunes."

It was not a skill which he was called upon to use often, for the circles in which he moved were composed mainly of men who were not interested in such things. He had learned to read cards from his grandmother during long winter evenings in a lonely farmhouse within sound of the sea. She had taken the business very seriously, was sometimes consulted by women, both young and old, and had made some surprisingly accurate forecasts. In earlier days she would probably have been accused of witchcraft. To the boy it had been a form of entertainment, rather like learning another, simpler alphabet, but he, too, had occasionally made predictions that had been startlingly fulfilled.

The girls were all agog; the two young men remained aloof, politely sceptical.

"In order of age, please," Mr van Haagen said, happily taking charge. There were strict rules about the whole business; one being that to attempt to read one's own fortune was absolutely forbidden.

"Oh, don't bother about me," Mrs Thorley said. "I've had more than half my future. Besides, I must confess, I have no belief in such things."

"So! But you have not tried me yet. I am goot!" He had a brief, very brief moment of self-doubt; it must be three years since he had read the cards. Very accurate then. He could have lost the knack. No matter; all that most women wanted was something happy. He had never cheated yet because cheating was as forbidden as reading one's own fate.

"It is private," Mr van Haagen said, taking the pack of cards which somebody had produced and shuffling them expertly. "Go and sing! You, Madam, please, cut into three." He took the top card of each pile and laid it away, gathered the pack together and said, "Please, again." She did so; and again until there were nine cards in the smaller heap. Then with a flick he spread the remainder into a wide half-fan.

"Select three further. Anywhere, Madam." She obeyed. He put her twelve cards together, pushed the rest away.

He turned them over, her chosen cards, and studied them, as one might study a page in a book. He made little adjustments to the pattern; four lines of three; three lines of four; a zigzag shape, a cross, a hollow square.

And something seemed to have happened to him. He was a different man from the rather prosaic cattle dealer with whom she had done business earlier in the day, and the cheerful stormer of privileged places in the afternoon.

"Such hard times," he said at last. "And such grief, the little boy dead. Very sad."

It was something to which she had deliberately shut her mind. The first hurt and disillusionment the realisation that Stephen was not only silly about money but unreliable in other ways as well. The shock had ended her lactation and made the baby dependent upon cow's milk; and milk drawn from cows kept in dark, underground byres was known to be bad for children. There were, however, some cows kept in Hyde Park, eating green grass, enjoying the sunshine. A long trudge every day, but she'd made it. Uselessly as it proved. The little boy had sickened and died.

"There is more trouble. You will overcome it, using good sense and moderation . . . That is to be remembered, Madam; moderation in all things, working, eating, drinking, all things." He shifted two cards. "Of money, plenty. Much successes, as today's. Yes, of success plenty." He bore down on that point because he could not see for her the serenity of old age. He shifted the cards again and said, "A thing to decide, Madam. Yes, a decision of the most momentous. Of family, not business." He moved two cards and looked puzzled. "It is with this as with all things, just so much and no more. The decision and a time of," he lifted his hand and made a see-sawing motion in the air. "But all will be well, with moderation. Money, goot. Health—always with moderation—goot. And that is all they say to me, for you, Madam, this evening. Thank you."

"Me next," Susan Walford said. "I'm older than Diana."

Unobtrusively Mrs Thorley moved to another chair, well within hearing distance. Mr van Haagens mention of her lost child had dented her scepticism and if he said anything likely to upset any of the girls she was ready to intercept at once.

Susan went through the preliminary of cutting the cards and Mr van Haagen, a kindly man at heart, was pleased to see that her immediate future was bright.

"Ah, for you a courtship. How am I to say it? Of the whirlwind? Yes. And marriage soon. Most happy." He shifted a card or two and did not like what he saw. But he adhered to his old grandmother's rule—Tell the pleasant, but not the untrue; tell the true, but not the unpleasant. "Of money you will not lack," he said, and then fell back on repetition. "Yes. An early happy marriage. What more can I say?"

"Happy ever after, Mr van Haagen?" Susan spoke with a sprightliness new to her; glanced at Freddy Ingram and wished Caroline Thorley out of the way.

"That is so." Something impelled him to give a hint of a warning. "Have a care for your health."

Susan made a slight grimace. She'd had enough of caring for health—not her own, her Mamma's.

Diana next, slightly disdainful. With Everard's ring on her finger she felt that her fortune was already assured. Still, now that she and Everard were now practically one, Mr van Haagen might tell her something about Everard's prospects. Not that she really believed much in fortune-telling. And Mr van Haagen's first words bolstered her disbelief.

"London," he said, very positively. Diana recoiled from the thought; she hardly ever thought of Leicester, which she had left at the age of ten, but that city had left her with a distaste for life in towns, noisy and smelly and lonely. Also, because they had been poor in Leicester, town life had an association, in her mind, with poverty. Besides, she liked her own little circle, where she was regarded as a belle, a setter of fashion, one whose advice was sought on what to do about unruly hair or freckles.

"Three children," Mr van Haagen said inexorably. "Girl, boy, girl, I think. Of money, well enough. Moderate means is the word, is it not? Health, goot." He hesitated, for here again was the combination which spelt a momentous decision, a little less wrenching than the one he had foreseen for her mother, but still a decision and a little trouble. Hardly worth mentioning. And now he saw something which would surely take that displeased look from her face. "You are to be married, not suddenly, but sooner than you think. Within a year."

And that was palpable nonsense, for she and Everard had agreed to wait two years, until he was established, and earning more.

"Thank you, Mr van Haagen," Diana said, coolly, dismissingly. He had told her nothing that she wished to hear and two things at least which displeased her. He was a charlatan and she did not intend to give his rubbish another thought.

Rising she called to Deborah at the piano.

"Deb, your turn next. Come and hear what horrors the future holds for you."

That young lady is annoyed with me, Mr van Haagen thought; yet I left out what would have displeased.

To Deborah he said as soon as the cards were sorted:

"Horses. So many horses. My dear young lady, with horses you will spend your life."

"Nothing would suit me better." She gave him her one-dimple smile.

"Other things, too. Marriage, soon, and one child, a boy. Much money."

Damn! It sounded like Simon Catchpole, the only man who had ever shown her any serious attention and for whom she had no feeling at all.

"Someone I know, Mr van Haagen?" At least she was taking it seriously.

"No," he said, having moved some cards about. In the process he uncovered another clue. That decision again and with this young lady something alien to her nature. It would change her, which would be a pity, for she was very nice as she was. And how sad, in the four futures so far inspected, so little of positive happiness.

Perhaps with this third of the Gad's girls, Caroline with the merry, rather monkeyish face and the dancing eyes.

Oh no! If anything worse. Many tears! He made some slight re-arrangement. More tears. A calm; a scandal; then two children, boy and girl and many good works. Sort that out into something acceptable.

"I see marriage within a year," he said. "A decision to be made —you will act wisely. You will have a husband of the utmost de-votion. Of money more than enough. You are generous by nature and will be able to afford to be charitable, and charitable you will be. Renowned for good works."

Caroline thought: If only I can be married to Freddy, of course I shall be charitable and do good works. I shall be so happy that I shall wish to share it with everybody. Mr van Haagen was by her standards old, and until he offered his one parlour trick, he had seemed dull; but he was a man and she gave him one of her gay, mischievous, flirtatious glances as she thanked him.

There remained of the young ladies only Lavinia, who, as usual, had retreated to a corner. Diana, Mr van Haagen noticed, took no part in urging her sister forward, but Susan Walford and Deborah and Caroline said, "Lavinia, you must join in." "Lavinia, he's marvellous!" "Lavinia, do for once join in."

In the ordinary pack of cards, half are black, and even in the black suits the court cards have some colour. So the odds against choosing twelve completely black cards were long. But Lavinia's were all black.

Mr van Haagen said, "We will try again." He shuffled the cards with vigour; and although the odds against all the chosen cards being dead black for the second time must be about a million to one, black they all were.

He wished, heartily, that he had never started this bit of fool-ishness. He felt a little shiver run down between his shoulder blades Only one combination of cards said anything ordinary— flowers, but flowers in completely wrong context. He did his best; he said, "Many flowers. You like them, Miss Lavinia?"

"Yes."

"Are you afraid of the dark?"

"No."

He said, almost violently, "Then you *should* be. You should be-ware of the dark, of anything dark. Stay in the sunshine, Miss Lavinia. You make pictures, is it not? In stitching? In paint?"

"I paint."

He had now exhausted any ordinary line which the black cards offered. Of the rest he could not speak.

He always tried when speaking a language not his own to *think* in that language, but now in his native Dutch, he thought: Oh my God, help me! She is so young!

"I am not speaking of the dark of night, or the light of sunshine. Rather the influence of dark things. Such as melancholy . . . You understand?"

He looked at her and saw something flash behind her steady, blank stare. No warning, however plainly, even brutally expressed could help now. She was already lost. He said, and even to himself he sounded fatuous.

"Hold to the bright side, Miss Lavinia. Paint pleasing things. There is in this world much of beauty."

He began to gather the cards together and she did not ask as any ordinary girl would have done: Is that all? No husband? No future? No children?

Mrs Thorley, who had listened, and heard nothing amiss, thought that she understood the omission of all the usual things from Lavinia's future. Nothing more detracted from a girl's chances of marriage than eccentricity. Most spinsters were eccentric and most people attributed their eccentricity to their unmarried state. But that was to put the cart before the horse. Lavinia would, as her mother had long ago felt, remain unmarried and the advice to paint pleasing things was sound.

It was a little difficult to imagine Diana in London, living on limited means with three children. If that should be a true prophecy I must help as far as I can. Caroline doing good deeds, unlikely as it might appear to a superficial observer, did not appear so to Mrs Thorley. Caro was flippant and now and then her wit had a caustic touch, but she was wildly generous. Once, Mrs Thorley remembered, Caro had given all her pocket money to a beggar, purportedly blind, and then cried half a day because she had thus forfeited a pair of real silk stockings.

Abruptly Mrs Thorley resumed her role as hostess.

"I am sure, Mr van Haagen, that after all that you need a drink."

He would have welcomed a heartening draught of schnapps, but accepted whisky as a substitute. And never, if he lived to be hundred, would he try that parlor trick—which was no trick—again.

Mrs Thorley said, "Come to a more comfortable chair, Mr van Haagen." She looked towards two near the wide-open window.

"Thank you, I do well where I am, Madam." But he did not look comfortable on the rather frail upright chair; in fact he seemed to sit with a curious rigidity and his voice had lost some of its friendliness. It occurred to her that he might be offended because of her eavesdropping. She was willing to explain.

"Until this evening I had little faith in such things," she glanced at the cards, "but your mention of my other child half convinced me. I thought I should listen."

"In case I said something amiss?"

"Let us say rather in case there was something for which I should be prepared or could prevent."

"There never is. Of course the cards do not tell everything, but in my experience what they speak is with a true voice."

Deborah was back at the piano. Horses and money for her. The only likely person in the neighbourhood was Simon Catchpole, for whom she had shown no liking; but she might change. Mrs Thorley hoped she would not marry anyone far away, for although she loved all her girls and took great pains to treat them all alike, she knew that Deb was the most dependable and the most capable.

And I really must speak to Caroline, Mrs Thorley thought; she is too old now to behave with so little dignity. She and Freddy Ingram were sharing a joke and Caroline was lolling—there was no other word for it, against him, and he was holding her by the arm.

"I think," she said, coming back to the cards and their veracity, "that in one respect they were mistaken. Marriage in a year. Diana is engaged, but she and Everard agreed to wait for at least two years and I am old-fashioned enough to think that the eldest should be the first to be married."

"It is also my experience," Mr van Haagen said in that same distant way, "that it is unwise to hold—what is your word?—inquest on such things." He stirred and winced and said:

"I beg you to excuse me, Madam. Sitting so long at the Show, on narrow bench, has provoked in me the lumbago."

On the Continent it had another name—the witch strike; and Mr van Haagen knew just when, and why, it had struck him.

Instantly everybody was all concern. Deborah ran to the stable for the liniment, a fiery lotion used indiscriminately on animals and humans alike. There wasn't much to be done for lumbago, with warmth and rest it vanished as suddenly as it came. Everard and Freddy practically carried Mr van Haagen to his bed and Freddy applied the liniment with more vigour than discretion.

When she was alone in her bed and drifting towards sleep, Mrs Thorley jerked into full wakefulness, seeing for the first time, and wondering why she had not seen it before, a connection between Mr van Haagen's warning about the dark and Lavinia's visits to Abbas, where Mrs Fremlin, for all her pallor, was not white, and sat in that dimly lit room, and Mr Fremlin looked tanned, even in winter, and all the servants were very dark indeed. The cards do not tell everything, Mr van Haagen had said, but tonight they could have conveyed a warning. About the carriage? Black as a hearse, drawn by black horses, driven by a black man. An accident!

Oh, what nonsense!

Yet care must be taken. Lavinia must not ride in that carriage again. How to prevent it? Well Lavinia must drive herself in Diana's little pony chaise.

And that would bring about what Mrs Thorley had always most sedulously avoided—dissension in the family; for such an arrangement would lead to trouble if Lavinia and Diana both needed the pony chaise at the same time.

Lavinia's visits to Abbas were always sudden. There'd be a letter from Mrs Fremlin, written in that very black—there you are, that word again—ink, asking that Lavinia could go to Abbas and spend a night, two, three, because Mr Fremlin would be away and Mrs Fremlin needed company, or because there was to be a guest at Abbas, an artist, somebody who knew about pictures, or a writer whom Mrs Fremlin wished Lavinia to meet. And the carriage would call for her. This afternoon. First thing tomorrow morning.

Diana would resent her own far less haphazard programme being interfered with. She made many afternoon visits to her friends and she went, at least three times a week, in to Baildon, taking a picnic meal to share with Everard in some shady, secluded corner of the Abbey ruins. Often on Saturday she stayed on and went with him to a matinée at the theatre and then drove him back to Gad's for the week-end.

No, Mrs Thorley decided, rising up slightly in her bed and giving her pillow a thump, that arrangement could never work. Lavinia must have a conveyance of her own. After all, I always believed in treating them alike and a pony, in the country, costs very little to keep.

Her mind darted off at a tangent. If it came about that Diana did go to London and have only moderate means . . . Even a pony cost a great deal to keep in a city where there was so little space and all fodder must be bought. And then it struck her, there alone in the dark, that to not one of her daughters had Mr van Haagen promised happiness. What a singular omission!

*

Mrs Thorley had delayed what she called in her mind her serious little talk with Caroline about her behaviour in general, and with Freddy Ingram in particular, and when at last she was forced to it she made a rather tentative approach. With Caroline one never knew; she could make a flippant, yet waspish retort, she could collapse into a flood of tears.

"Caro, dear, I know that you are very popular and it is very pleasant for a girl to be so. But I feel forced to say that you are making yourself conspicuous by your behavior with Freddy Ingram. Twice in this last week you have driven home with him—alone in his gig—when other transport was available."

"Dear me! What is Mrs Grundy saying?"

Caro was going to be flippant. Easier to deal with than tears. And it was easier to take a stern line once this mythical arbiter of morals had been mentioned.

"I think you must know, Caro, that I have never paid much attention to Mrs Grundy. In fact I have allowed myself and all you girls, a good deal of freedom from the Mrs Grundys of this world. What concerns me is your happiness. You are doing yourself damage."

"In what way?"

Very well, hit hard.

"By behaving as though you were engaged, which you are not. And by showing such open preference to one young man, you lay yourself open to humiliation later on."

The shot went home. Caroline had known Freddy almost as long as Diana had known Everard, and there was Diana, stiff as a poker, prim as a dish, safely engaged, a ring on her finger. Bloody unfair. Hurt made Caro jaunty.

"Then I must seek safety in numbers. I'll go with Edward on one of his long dreary rounds. I'll coax Simon Catchpole—Deb doesn't want him. I'll ride with Phil Ambrose. If necessary I'll stand in the road and beg lifts from any passing gig. If riding in a gig means so much."

"Caro, you know perfectly well that I was merely referring to one thing. You are being evasive." Hit hard again! "If after all this, Freddy should chose . . . elsewhere, it would leave you . . ."

"I know! Money! Filthy lucre. That's all anybody thinks about nowadays. God be my judge, if I stood in Di's shoes would I wait, ticking two years away? I'd go and live in Scurvy Lane, I'd have a stall on the market, I'd take in washing, or scrub steps . . ."

George Thorley, Caroline's father, had been a very amiable man, but he was capable of losing his temper and now in the vehemence and the language of Caroline's outburst, Caro showed her breed. But, oddly, also something of Mrs Thorley, no blood kin to her. Mrs Thorley thought: That is exactly how I felt about Stephen and look where that landed me!

In her gentler voice she said:

"What I was trying to say, my dear, is that it is not always wise to show preference too obviously. It sometimes defeats its own purpose. There is something in that old saying about not wearing one's heart on one's sleeve."

Caroline took up another evasive position, completely contradictory.

"I wasn't talking about hearts, Mamma. If I appear to prefer Freddy's company it is because he's the only man I know who can tell a joke from an Act of Parliament. He amuses me; I amuse him . . ."

It was true, but it was only a fragment of the truth.

"So long as you don't make yourself conspicuous," Mrs Thorley said, coming back to her starting point.

"In gigs! Perhaps I could persuade Freddy to exchange his for a covered wagon." What a mistaken thing to say. Oh God, oh God, for the privacy, the intimacy of a covered wagon, with Freddy, even in the wilds of America about which there was so much talk these days.

"Just remember, my dear, a little discretion. That is all I ask. After all you are young, and I am responsible for you."

Caroline went away, flung herself on her bed and cried; and Mrs Thorley was left with a sense of failure.

*

"I s'pose, Miss Diana, you forgot the matches again," Jenny said.

"I'm afraid I did, Jenny."

Being in love did make people forgetful, Jenny knew. She'd been in love three or four times herself. And Miss Diana was not only in love, she was very busy with making a table-cloth; linen, with crochet edging about a foot wide and insets.

"Then what'm I gonna to do?"

It was one of those summer evenings, dark purple clouded that held a hint of darkness coming earlier. Mrs Thorley was doing her paper work at the desk in the window embrasure; Diana had just folded her work. Deborah and Caroline and—for once—Lavinia were there, waiting for supper.

"There must be matches somewhere," Mrs Thorley said a trifle crossly, for she too had forgotten the matches.

"There was," Jenny said. "And I've borrered one here, one there, and all out of the spare room. Now there ain't one in the house. And I let the stove out, it being so hot and me counting on Miss Diana."

"I'll go down and borrow a few from Mrs Spicer," Deborah said.

And then Lavinia spoke, tentatively.

"If we all concentrated," she said almost playfully, but testing herself—and them. "Just for a moment, think about, wish for, matches."

They'd all seen it done, but only as a game called Think of a Word. One of the company—or several—went out of a room and these within whispered, choosing a word; then the other, or the others, came in and in perhaps seven out of ten times did hit on the chosen word, or one very like it. Speculate could be spectrum, or accumulate; coffee could be toffee, or coffle. It was a hit-or-miss game and it dealt only with words. Deborah was the one to point out the absurdity. She said:

"So we all think about matches and a box falls from the ceiling."

Lavinia said, "Just think."

Nothing happened. Outside the wide bowed window the sky lightened and the evening bloomed as the dark cloud moved. Light enough to make candles unnecessary on the supper table. Deborah ate hastily, her errand to the village foremost in her mind.

"Better take a box with you," said George, who had noticed his tutor's wife's parsimonious ways. "Mrs Spicer won't have a spare box."

"Wise boy," Deborah said, and went into the kitchen. Jenny and Katie were at the door, outside which stood a little man, a flat cart and a very poor-looking donkey.

"He've got matches," Jenny said. Apart from that the peddlar's cart was disappointing; nothing pretty; no ribbon, no lace, or tawdry ornaments. All plain household stuff.

Deborah viewed the outfit with a different kind of dissatisfaction. To begin with the flat cart was too big for the donkey and it was loaded with rather heavy things.

She said, "Wait!" and hurried up the back stairs and snatched from a drawer the old cigar box in which she kept her small hoard —her savings toward the hunter she wanted.

"I'll have that, and that, and that." She stood by the cart and made a haphazard selection of all the things that looked heaviest; a big iron preserving pan, several saucepans, two flat-irons, some of the coarse thick crocks used in dairies. The little man danced around the cart, ecstatic and garrulous.

"'S'marvellous thing, lady. I bin on this road regular and never thought to turn up your lane afore. Tonight it come to me. Somebody might live along there, I thought to myself. Somebody might be wanting a thing or two." But not this much, he thought, more than he usually shifted in a week.

Jenny and Katie hovered about, taking the purchases. Jenny with surprise and disapproval. "But Miss Deborah, we *got* a preserving pan. Better than this. Real copper." The purchase of several yards of chain and a bundle of iron stakes amazed even the pedlar. Extraordinary things for a young lady to buy; and not, he somehow felt—for he was an experienced man—done out of any kindly feeling for *him*. Every time her glance met his it was cold and hard and unfriendly, though he smiled his most ingratiating smile.

On the kitchen table there was a basket of apples, the first real sweet ones of the year, clear crimson all over and scented.

And if I give him those, he'd eat them himself, Deborah thought.

"How much is all that?"

"Now, let me see." He pretended to check over, though he knew to the last penny. "Three pound, two shillings and sevenpence."

She paid that without a qualm and then said again, "Wait."

She ran across the yard, vanished, and returned with a good armful of hay which she placed on the cart. He can't very well eat that, Deborah thought almost viciously. She darted into the kitchen and brought out two apples—not for him—for the moke!

Well, she was a curious one all right. And despite the unfriendly looks and giving the donkey what a man could have eaten, not ill-disposed.

"You say you make this round regularly? What day?"

"Monday's my day for the Stonhams, lady."

"Then include us in your round. I can't promise to buy this kind of thing regularly, of course. But matches and candles, hairpins . . . That kind of thing."

She disliked him for ignoring the fact that wheels out of alignment, leaning outwards or inwards, and axles ungreased made pulling twice as difficult as it need be. Next week she'd be ready for him. . . A good bran mash for that poor creature and some suggestions about the cart.

"What on earth?" Mrs Thorley asked, drawn towards the kitchen by the noise, feeling guilty, for she has also had forgotten to buy matches and without a candle, in the kitchen which faced away from the sunset, Jenny and Katie might be dropping things or blundering into one another.

"It was a kind of pedlar, Mamma. He had matches." Suddenly Deborah reverted to the angular awkwardness of her early adolescence, all arms and legs. "He also had household things, very cheap and since Di is thinking of setting up house . . ."

Diana, who had followed Mamma into the kitchen, had great difficulty in holding back an exclamation of dismay. All such cheap, horrible things!

She seldom, looking forward, thought much about her kitchen and when she did she visualised it in romantic rather than practical terms. Everard had said that it would be two years: Mr van Haagen, although on the whole he had displeased her, had spoken of a shorter period, which, accepting the pleasant, discarding the rest, she had convinced herself meant that Everard would get his partnership, and she her house. A kitchen with copper pans, all matching, of different sizes; dishes and bowls all pleasantly blue and white; all kept in order by a neat maid who could cook, answer bells in proper fashion, wait at table. All these clumsy, ugly, cheap articles shattered her dream. Only for a moment. And it was impossible to be cross with Deborah, always so well-meaning.

"It was a kind thought, Deb. Thank you."

Then there arose the question of where the things should be stored. On the attic landing, it was decided. From this operation Jenny exempted herself; the stairs, she said, were as much as she could manage when she had to. The others were lively. George deliberately putting off his bedtime; Katie thinking that if Willy would only come to the point, how glad she'd be of such a wedding gift; Caroline teasing, "I bet, Deb, that pedlar was short of a limb, or had a squint." Lavinia, silent and withdrawn again, glad that nobody, in the confusion, had seemed to connect the thinking about matches with the arrival of them. Secret was best and secret she would be, but the sense of power was there, was growing. One day she would be able to . . . able to . . .

*

The corn harvest promised to be heavy and Mrs Thorley decided that she needed another work-horse. It would, naturally, be of the breed known as Suffolk Punch and it would, naturally, come from Mr Bridges'. He bred the best; some for show purposes, some for ordinary sale. He lived at Foxton, just across the Norfolk border; an area of heath and breckland but containing, as a desert was said to contain oases, a few pockets of rich land.

She wrote, explaining what she required, not a show animal, just a young strong working horse. Foxton was only about twenty miles away and she expected to have the creature within a week.

Instead she had a visit from a youngish man who bore a strong resemblance to the animals he bred. Big, strong, mild-mannered, and amber-brown all over, from the tip of his riding boots to the crown of his gleaming head.

He said, after the polite preliminaries:

"The point is, Ma'am, I never sell a horse without being pretty sure it's going to a good home."

"Very admirable," Mrs Thorley said, slightly annoyed. "If you wish, you may look around my stable and you will see that my horses are well cared for."

Deborah, who by chance was present, and, "But Mr Bridges, how can you know? I mean . . . you could sell a horse to what looked like a good home and it could be sold next day—to a bad one."

"Not with one of mine. I don't aim to have one of mine sold into slavery. They weigh around a ton, Miss; and properly treated they can pull their own weight, and be guided on a cotton thread. And they're not going dragging more than they can and work to death and end up at the knacker's."

"But Mr Bridges, how can you prevent it?"

"Easy. Anybody buys a horse from me signs a legal document. No selling, except back to me. See? Condition of sale. It's worked against me a time or two and I've got quite a few old horses ending their days in peace at my place."

Deborah said with great feeling, "How perfectly wonderful."

"No credit to me. I can afford it."

He was very rich; from his father he had inherited a thousand acres and from his mother a prosperous pottery factory.

"As I said, you may inspect my premises, Mr Bridges." Mrs Thorley's voice and manner were cool. For some reason which she could not exactly define she found herself rather disliking him. There was nothing to which one could fairly take objection; manner, clothes, even voice, perfectly ordinary and when he said that he could afford to indulge a whim, he said it without boastfulness. A flat statement of fact.

"I'll just take a look round," he said. Flat; set in his ways; and, yes, a bit arrogant; not taking her word for the fact her horses were well treated.

"I'll show you," Deborah said, eagerly.

"There is no need for that," Mrs Thorley said. "Will is somewhere about the yard."

"But Mamma, I'd like to show Mr Bridges our horses. And see his . . ."

His was a splendid animal; more chestnut than amber-coloured. It stood, untethered in the yard, placidly waiting, but alert. Deborah remarked on this and Mr Bridges said:

"Oh, it'd take a fire to shift Peter if I'd told him to stand." He dived into one of the capacious pockets of his tweed jacket and produced a little irregular lump of white substance.

"Like to give it to him? It's salt, not sugar. A lot of people make that mistake. All right in winter, helps keep 'em warm. But in summer, they sweat and lose salt."

She offered the tit-bit rightly, flat on the palm of her hand. Peter took it with soft, gentle slobbering lips.

"I need a pretty big horse," Tim Bridges remarked. "I'm heavy."

"I outgrew my pony."

And that linked up with that reckless disbursement of savings, and she found herself telling him about the pedlar's donkey. With one part of his mind noting that the Gad's Hall stables, hay stores, water trough, green pasture were all satisfactory, a suitable home, enough of it ran free to make conversation possible.

"It is," he said, "a problem. I've faced often enough. I mean, buy that poor decrepit beast and put it to pasture. The man'd simply buy another and treat it the same way. The money isn't minted that could save 'em all . . ."

"I do think," Deb said when he had gone, "he's one of the very nicest men I've ever met."

Mrs Thorley gave her a sharp look and said with some asperity:

"I hope you are not going to fall in love with him simply because he cares for his horses. Most men do, after all."

"You didn't like him, did you? Why not?"

"I did not dislike him. In fact I had no great feeling about him either way. Except that to come, and actually *inspect* . . . And to make people sign what he calls a legal document. It smacks of presumption."

"I think he's absolutely right," Deborah said. Her voice was mild enough but she looked stubborn. Mrs Thorley thought: Oh dear me; I've made a mistake! I've probably planted the idea in her head. Just because something about the man ruffled my temper.

She hastened to make amends. "Of course, my dear, you are right. And so is he. It was just that I was annoyed at being as it were under suspicion of not treating my animals properly." She restrained herself from adding that she thought there was something slightly uncouth about Mr Bridges; to say that would simply make Deb stick up for him more. In any case, why worry? They were unlikely to meet again. For although any enlightened person would have hotly denied it, the gulf between Norfolk and Suffolk was almost as firmly fixed as it had been a thousand years earlier when two different tribes settled and divided the bulge of East Anglia between them. County families met, mingled, inter-married, but for ordinary people the invisible barrier was there. Mr Gordon, for instance, would not be consulted by any client living North of the border; any Norfolk man needing a lawyer would choose a Norfolker who might live more than twice as far away. Mr Walford found a readier market for his beer in Cam-bridgeshire, or even Bedforshire, than he did in Norfolk. To any-one like Mrs Thorley, coming from a wider world, the dialect of speech of the two counties was identical, but at shows and some markets—events which flung frail bridges over the gulf—the true Suffolk man either did not understand or pretended not to under-stand the one from Norfolk. There was a strongly held belief in Suffolk that nobody in Norfolk could cure a ham properly; a matching belief in Norfolk that no Suffolk woman could make a good dumpling.

So Mrs Thorley could dismiss Mr Bridges.

Who turned up two days later, just as they were sitting down to their mid-day meal. Katie announced his arrival as she brought in the food.

"It's Mr Bridges, Ma'am. With the horse."

"Very well," Mrs Thorley said. "Call Willy. And give the man something to eat. And a glass of beer."

Katie was not very clear-spoken, and the difference between Mr Bridges' man and Mr Bridges, ma'am, was slight. Even Deborah did not imagine that Mr Bridges would deliver, in per-son, a cart-horse.

Katie went out and reappeared, slightly flustered.

"It's Mr Bridges hisself, Ma'am. And he want to talk to Miss Deborah. Important, he said."

"I'll come," Deborah said.

It was himself. And what he had brought was not the carthorse that was expected, but an animal, a mare, of such breathtaking beauty . . . Deborah said, remembering how she had confided to him her grief about the outgrown pony and her hope of a hunter

—one day; the day deferred by the loss of three pounds two shillings and some odd pence, "But Mr Bridges . . . It is kind of you, but I couldn't possibly afford . . ."

"Affording isn't concerned, Miss Thorley. I want you to have her. I mean, she's useless to me. Bred for racing and she failed one of their daft tests. She was dragging a coal cart . . . And useless to me. I'm too heavy to give her exercise. So I thought. You'd fit together. If you'd accept her."

And it was not, Mrs Thorley thought, that, brought in by Deborah, given a place at table, he was awkward with knives and forks. But the word *uncouth* could not be avoided. Any man who knew anything must surely know that for a girl to accept such a present was absolutely unheard of. Stupid? Arrogant because he was rich? And uncouth; for to force upon a woman something too difficult to explain was uncouth.

She said in her light la-di-da manner, "Run away, all of you. Mr Bridges and I must have a little talk."

She was absolutely brutal.

"Are you not aware, Mr Bridges, that no decent, respectable young woman could possibly accept a gift worth at least fifty pounds? A few flowers perhaps. I believe that nowadays a small flask of lavender water or even a fan. But a horse, Mr Bridges. Quite unthinkable!"

He said in that way, something that had angered her before, a practicality impervious to anything but itself:

"Where would be the harm? There's the mare, useless to me, and there's Miss Deborah with nothing to ride. Why not bring them together?"

Even the term, nothing to ride, was subtly offensive. It must be explained.

"My husband had a good saddle horse; not the most easily handled of animals. My daughter was still at school, so who was to exercise him? My stable-lad"—almost unthinkingly she promoted Willy—"was afraid of him. So I sold him. As a matter of fact I have been on the look-out of a suitable mount for my daughter."

His silence, his look asked: And in a year you found nothing? Aloud he said:

"Well, now it's here. Suitable as could be."

"Entirely *un*suitable," she said shortly; irritation swept her again. "Surely you must see that." Suddenly the exact word for him occurred to her. *Thick*. Thick-headed. Thick-skinned.

Outwitting her again, he said:

"You're thinking about how it'd look? Well, for one thing, I'd have thought you of all people wouldn't bother about that. For another, who'd know?"

She saw a solution.

"It could all be settled very easily, Mr Bridges. I believe you satisfied yourself the other day that this was a fit home for a horse. So I hope you will allow me to buy the mare."

"That wasn't what I had in mind. But if you'll feel happier, all right. Thirty shillings."

"Don't be absurd. I haven't seen the animal but my daughter says it is a pedigree race-horse. Tell me the proper price."

"Thirty shillings is what I gave for her. You find that difficult to believe? You shouldn't, being a cattle dealer. Things you breed that don't come up to standard go to the butcher's, don't they? It's the same wih horses—especially race-horses. Some miss their mark and go to the knacker's. Or worse."

"Very well." She went to her desk near the window and wrote the cheque. Let that be the end of that!

It was not.

"While I *am* here," he said, standing tall, solid, stolid, "I might as well mention another thing. I've had no chance to try out how Miss Deborah feels about me, but I'd like your permission to find out. I know how I feel about her. She's the girl I've been waiting for all my life."

She fenced, feebly. "But Mr Bridges, you have only seen my daughter twice."

"Once was enough. I knew that first day." To some women his artlessness would have made an appeal; and to many mothers what he said would have seemed like an answer to prayer.

"I'm thirty-two," he said. "I'm not well known—except for my horses—in this part of the country, but where I am known, my name is good, I hope. I never fooled around. As regards this world's goods I'm well set up. And within ten minutes of our meeting, I took a great fancy . . . I mean I realised that Miss Deborah and I were meant for one another. I thought it only right to speak to you first."

Another case of love at first sight. Like Diana and Everard. Like —but that was lost in the mists of time—herself with Stephen Os-

borne, and then George Thorley and herself. Who could decry it?
Who fight against it?

And why should one?

No answer to that. All she knew was that she had had slight
misgivings about Everard and had even more about this.

Am I one of those possessive mothers, anxious to keep my girls
with me, resentful of all suitors?

No! I am not. I want all my girls to be happy. And I am
resigned to Everard. To this man I don't think I can ever be. And
yet against him—nothing.

"Certainly you should be old enough to know your own mind.
Deborah is very young. I am growing old and am inclined to
think that hasty decisions are often regretted. And choosing a
partner for life on the strength of two meetings seems to me to be
the height of folly."

He said with the patient air of one attempting to explain something to a child, "That was what I was getting around to. I know
my mind, but she can't know hers until we're closer acquainted.
I'm telling you my intentions are honourable and asking permission to see her."

It was her feeling of helplessness, of being up against some
power much stronger than herself, that made Mrs Thorley say:

"And suppose I withhold it?"

"I should be sorry. I prefer things open and above-board. But I
should see her nonetheless. I mean to have her—if she'll have
me."

And Deborah, in so little time as it had taken her to show him
around the stables, had decided that he was the nicest man she
had ever met.

Another weakening was that memory of Mr van Haagen's
prophecy for Deborah. Horses. Wealth. Possibly some things were
inevitable.

"I also prefer things to be above-board, Mr Bridges. Let me
think . . . In a few days' time my eldest daughter will be celebrating her eighteenth birthday. Just a gathering of young people.
If you would care to join us."

"I would indeed. Thank you."

Diana's birthday actually fell on a Thursday, but was kept on
Saturday for the convenience of Everard.

Richard Walford was no longer one of the little group. Only

Susan knew why he had decided to return to Burton-on-Trent almost as soon as Diana became engaged to Everard Spicer. He'd made business his excuse; some process in the making of beer about which he wished to know more.

Edward Taylor must be asked, if only because—poor boy—he never had a decent evening meal these days; Freddy Ingram; James Gordon, who might—just might divert Caroline, being just as much of a wit and flirt as Caroline was; but with far more behind him than Freddy Ingram had. Simon Catchpole towards whom Caroline had threatened to relent.

Mr Bridges in this company looked old and somewhat odd. He said, "I am a teetotaller." Deborah ran and fetched lemonade—and drank it herself. Mrs Thorley, watching, thought: That took courage; he is a strong character; so is Deb and if they ever come into conflict . . .

Freddy-to-my-friends was the catalyst; in no time at all calling Mr Bridges Tim or dear boy.

Tim didn't drink, didn't smoke, didn't dance, but he could play the piano. Surprising considering the size of his hands.

In the little space left before harvest began, Tim Bridges wasted no time. He invited Mrs Thorley and Deborah to visit his home. In size and style it was much like Gad's, but no modernising hand had been laid upon it, and the room in which they took tea was called the parlour. Mrs Thorley, looking around with critical eyes, saw that while there was no ostentatious evidence of wealth, everything was solid and good and well cared for, by presumably, the one servant, a woman of great age who somehow managed to convey, without speaking, her disapproval of the visitors. Mrs Thorley wrongly interpreted this covert hostility as fear of coming change. Actually it was directed at the flounces and bows which mother and daughter revealed when they removed the thin dust coats they had worn in the gig. The old woman—her name was Emma—wanted to see her master married and settled, and if possible a father, before God called her to heaven; but if this was his choice—after all the good, quiet, *homely* girls he could have married—then it was a pity. A thousand pities, for no doubt about it, the master had fallen victim to the lust of the eye. And acting silly!

"It's not much of a garden," he said. "My mother grew flowers. I've had no time. It's got out of hand."

Emma heard this shred of conversation and was more resentful than ever, for the garden, thus spoken of in such derogatory terms, was extremely productive of vegetables, of herbs. It just went to show . . .

Showing off his useful but not very decorative garden, Tim Bridges said, "I've been thinking; twenty miles here and twenty back . . . Suppose you took my gig-horse, Ma'am, and left yours. Then, the day after tomorrow, I'll bring yours back and collect mine. Would that be agreeable to you?"

Another meeting. A further erosion. Something else to think about in the night.

She began to dread the night. Go to bed tired, ready for sleep, and wake as suddenly as though you had been shaken. Reach in the darkness for the matches, light a candle, look at the watch. Always a quarter to three, or three, or a quarter past. Within the half hour it could vary a little. But the roundabout of thought did not vary at all.

All about the girls; her own; and those whom she had made her own.

Curiously, George never walked down the dark corridors of her sleepless hours. His course ran straight and clear. Mr Spicer was drilling him for entry to Biddle's, the school to which money alone could not ensure entry. Biddle's favoured bright boys and Mrs Thorley favoured Biddle's because it was fairly near. The only school nearly approaching its quality was in Felstead—far away in Essex. She wished to do for George what she had done for the girls, deliver, collect, attend any ceremony. And George was so teachable, so observant . . . No need to worry about George.

The girls? Yes.

Diana, who should really be learning to cook, instead of doing so much fancy work. Mrs Thorley herself had never learned to cook until harsh necessity forced her to do so—and sometimes with little to cook with. She wished her daughter to face the world better armed. So she must speak, must insist, and Diana would be daintily, scornfully resentful.

Deborah. And what was wrong *there* even the wakeful mother could never hit upon. Deb and the man who was plainly set upon marrying her had things in common—a love of horses, a love of music. She'd have a house very much like the home she was leaving; a husband who would certainly allow her a free hand in the garden. And Deb's nature was not only practical, it was cheerful —she was the only one of them who had accepted the discipline of school life happily. What was there to worry about?

Caroline. Plenty to cause anxiety there! The little talk had been quite unavailing and Caroline was still making a spectacle of herself with Freddy Ingram. Even worse, perhaps, since some of the young men who had danced attendance on her in the past, enjoying her gaiety, seemed to have been discouraged by her marked preference for Freddy, and had fallen away. And Caroline herself had changed. There seemed to be something a little feverish about her gaiety at times, and some of her quips had more sting.

The tall-case clock on the landing would boom four strokes as Mrs Thorley debated the wisdom of speaking again, not to Caroline this time, to Freddy. Fathers often demanded to know what a young man's intentions were. Surely a widowed mother was entitled to do the same. But Mrs Thorley shrank from the idea; it would seem to be making too much of the matter. Freddy simply hadn't a serious nature and the idea of being taken seriously by a match-making Mamma would vastly amuse him.

Then there was Lavinia. She no longer rode in the black carriage. Mrs Thorley had acquired, at a reasonable price, a quiet skewbald pony and a miniature carriage. Consciously or unconsciously she had heeded Mr van Haagen's words and was pleased that the pony should have so much white about it, and that the little carriage was largely composed of pale canework. Lavinia still came home laden with flowers—and with exotic fruit; there was a pineapple house at Abbas. Except to say that Mr Fremlin had sold another of her pictures—a hundred pounds this time—she seldom volunteered any information about her visits to Abbas. Asked direct questions she gave short answers. Yes, thank you, she had enjoyed herself. No, Mr Fremlin was not there. Yes, Mr Fremlin was there, so was a gentleman from Brazil who wished to sell some property near Rio de Janeiro. Since the child always went so eagerly to Abbas and seemed to enjoy herself there, one would have expected her to mention the prospect of losing her friends with some change of voice or expression, but Lavinia gave no sign.

Because they had asked her to go with them?

Now that I should never *allow!* Never!

There might lie Mr van Haagen's hint of warning. Mrs Thorley's missionary-inculcated ideas of such places were horrifying; all very dark people and the cannibal pot never far away.

Sometimes, when sleep failed to return, and the clock had struck five, Mrs Thorley rose and went softly down to the dining room and poured herself a small measure of whisky. No decent woman drank spirits of any kind except when suffering from a heavy cold; then a tablespoonful of whisky in a glass of hot milk was permissible. And sleep often followed such a dose. Sometimes, but not invariably, it worked for her, and if she did not actually sleep, her thoughts took a more cheerful tinge. At first she felt guilty about such indulgence, but that feeling wore off; it was medicine, wasn't it? And she was at an age where women who had led far more sheltered lives, done less work, had fewer worries, often had little ailments and resorted to doctors. And after all it was her whisky and cost her nothing. George had liked his whisky and laid in a good store; in casks, each plainly dated, since, unlike some beverages, whisky improved as it aged.

Then it struck her that it was foolish to make this almost nightly excursion, soft-footed through the silent house; far more sensible to keep a supply in her wardrobe, on the top shelf, behind the hats.

A golden, beginning-of-harvest morning and a letter from Susan Walford, in whose life Caroline had now replaced Diana. The friendship between Diana and Susan had been understandable; Diana had been sorry for Poor Susan and Poor Susan had been grateful to Diana. Then Diana had become engaged and naturally had less time to spare. Also to be considered was the fact that between the girl with an engagement ring on her finger and the girl who had not there was a little divergence of interest. For Caroline's stepping into Diana's place in Poor Susan's life, Mrs. Thorley could only assume the most unworthy motive—to keep in touch, through Susan, with Freddy. Caroline had no reason to be sorry for Susan and often, indeed, made rather barbed remarks about her. A friendship of convenience.

It was a longish letter and Caroline read it with darkening eyes and whitening face. Then, never one to control or conceal her emotions, she flung it away, folded her arms over her hardly touched breakfast plate, put her head down and began to cry. Not the easy crying to which they were all accustomed, but racking sobs.

George was the first to move, leaving his own breakfast half eaten. Of them all he liked Caro best and to see her in such misery distressed him, though he had no notion of what it was all about. He went round to where she sat and patted her head, her shoulders. "Don't cry, Caro. Please don't cry. Whatever it is, we can put it right."

It was nothing that anybody could put right.

It was a letter from a happy girl—a girl, Mrs Thorley thought, reading it, either blind or insensitive. Susan wished her best friend to be the first to know; she and Freddy were to be married; Papa had missed Richard so much and was now so happy to take Freddy into the business. She and Freddy were prepared to make their home with Papa, and Papa was happy about that. There'd be an engagement party next week and an Easter wedding; would Caroline be her chief bridesmaid?

Diana asked a question with her eyes and Mrs Thorley nodded. Diana then looked smug. Deborah put her arm around her sister and said:

"Freddy? Damn him to hell!"

"Yes," George said, understanding nothing except that somebody, Freddy? had made Caro cry. "Damn him to hell."

"That will do," Mrs Thorley said sharply. She had always known that no good would come of that flirtation, had tried to warn Caro, was slightly surprised that Poor Susan should be Freddy's final choice—and then not surprised. Freddy was in fact doing very well for himself.

She wished she could say to George: Run along, dear, you'll be late for your lessons. But Mr Spicer kept strictly University terms; when students at Cambridge went down for the long vacation, young George Thorley was set free. The best she could do now was to invent an errand for George.

"Caro is all right, George. Run and tell Willy to get the trap ready. I have to go to Baildon. You can come with me. And ask Jenny to fry you another egg . . ."

As soon as the innocent looker-on had gone, Mrs Thorley could say, kindly, but firmly:

"Come along now, Caro. It *is* a blow. We all understand. But you must pull yourself together, my dear, and make light of it. It is the only way."

Caroline lifted her head and showed her stricken face, more monkeyish in its complete despair than it had ever been in sorrow or merriment.

"There's as good fish in the sea as ever came out," Deborah said. "Come and lie down. You'll feel better soon."

Caroline did not feel better soon. She lay on her half of the bed which she shared with Lavinia, and cried and cried; shedding the many tears which Mr van Haagen had foreseen. She wouldn't eat, wouldn't talk, wouldn't listen. The absolutely obligatory letter had to be written by Diana, who had social sense: We all, she wrote, offer our very best wishes to you and congratulations to Freddy; and we look forward . . .

Perfectly in order; Diana was socially adept.

But the day of the party crept on, soft-footed.

"I can't, I can't," Caroline moaned. "Say I'm ill. Say I'm dead. I wish to God I were . . ."

"But you are not," Mrs Thorley said. "And now, just for once, Caro, you must listen to me. Unless you come this evening, to Susan's party and act as though nothing had happened—nothing that you cared about, be as gay as ever you were—there will be talk. Do you want that?"

Mamma had spoken about *talk* before—but talk of the right kind, admiring, envious, spiteful because envious.

Into her sodden pillow, Caroline said, "No. Not that."

"Then you must get up. An egg shampoo and a vinegar rinse for your hair . . . My dear, I know exactly how you feel. I have taken some blows in my time and learned that wounds should not be licked in public. So far only we—your family—know what has happened. And if you rouse yourself and behave as usual, nobody outside this house need never know."

As gay as ever you were. Over a heart, shattered and frozen, curls could dance, mischievous glances flash. Oh, it might as well be Edward—they're all one to me now, Caroline thought, giving Edward Taylor a smile that dazzled him and everyone else within range. When she chose Caroline could always be the centre of attraction, and since Susan had chosen to have her celebration party in the form of a dance, Caroline had a wonderful time. And a horrible time. It was a waltz—one of their favourites; sentimental, slow, and Freddy Ingram, stupid young man that he was, having done his duty with all Susan's friends, and with Susan, thought that this . . . this he might despite everything be allowed, with Caroline, something to remember forever.

She knew that if he touched her the brittle thin surface of gaiety would crack and she would be crying again, helplessly, hopelessly, and forever. So she said, very clearly:

"Freddy, you have a short memory! I told you at Di's party, I'd never waltz with you again. Fallen arches I just dare not risk."

Inside her the wound which must be concealed bled and the tears which she had been fighting off almost had a victory as she danced the waltz, their waltz, with Edward. He was not a bad dancer, a bit heavy, a bit inclined to talk, seriously. She heard her own voice in an empty, echoing cave, saying: Yes. Yes of course. She was halfway home before she realised to what she had committed herself; to become one of the Friends of the Hospital and to help with Mrs Bosworth's garden fête, the proceeds of which went to that good cause.

"My first good deed," she said, some irony mingling with the forced gaiety "will be to suggest roundabouts and swings instead of all those knitted egg cosies."

"I hardly think Mrs Bosworth's garden is large enough."

"Then we'll borrow the meadow next door."

"A splendid idea," Mrs Thorley said. She was pleased with Caroline's show of spirit. She had learned herself that a pretence at confidence could lead to the real thing; and cheerfulness might be the same.

*

Mr Bridges appeared to think that he had been missed, and opened his interview with Mrs Thorley by explaining that he had been busy harvesting. His harvest had been splendid; he hoped hers had.

"Very good. Quite exceptional," she said. Her irrational dislike —no; perhaps that was too harsh a word—distaste, reared itself.

"I wrote to Miss Deborah, though."

He had indeed been a most faithful correspondent, and Deborah had seized upon and read his letters with an eagerness which showed that her feelings for him were never in doubt . . .

"So now," he said, "it's time for a serious talk, Ma'am. I'd like to ask her today and get married any time between now and Christmas." Now was the first week in September, for the good weather which had fostered the wonderful harvest had continued and ensured that the gathering in went forward without interruption.

Not without a flick of pleasure, Mrs Thorley proceeded to put Mr Bridges—she could never think of him as Tim, though everybody else did—in his place.

"That," she said, "is quite impossible I am afraid. You may think me very old-fashioned, but I am one of those who regard it as desirable that the elder sister should marry first—if at all possible." It had once been a rule, broken only when the older girl was so unattractive for this or that reason, that it must be disregarded; it was still desirable.

"I thought Miss Deborah was the oldest."

"Many people make that mistake. Deborah is in fact six months younger than Diana, and since Diana is already engaged . . . And the time for her wedding more or less fixed—a twelve-month next June, I certainly should not wish Deborah's wedding to precede it."

"I call that silly. Mind you, I can understand the need to wait in their case. Not much of a job yet, and no house . . . But why should I wait? Can you tell me that?"

She wanted to snap out: Because I say so! She restrained herself; open hostily must be avoided. Yet it was there, a steady current below the surface ripples.

"It may simply be that I like things done in order."

"With *some* things," he said. "Were you thinking of order when you went into the Corn Exchange here at Baildon, where never any female except a scrub-woman had ever set foot? Or set Corby's saleyard upside down? The last thing in the world I'd want to do is to be offensive, but there it is. You can't very well defy convention, or fashion, or whatever you call it, on the one hand and stick to it on the other. You have to be—consistent."

"I try to be." She recognised the threat he held and the weakness of her own position. Fathers could forbid marriages for their daughters who were under age. Presumably mothers had the same power. But stepmothers? Unsure of her ground, she offered a compromise. A double wedding, next June not the June after next. Bracing her shoulders, she thought: I'll manage it somehow.

The rocky man said:

"You mean in church?"

"Naturally. Where else?"

"I'm Methodist," he said. And then she understood all. Non-conformity explained his abstention from alcohol and tobacco, his plain speech, his invariably dull clothes and even self-assurance. She had come into contact with several of his kind during her time in Leicester and knew that they all regarded themselves as being in direct touch with God, and provided they followed what they regarded as *His* will need fear no man. Very admirable, of course, but it made them intractable to deal with. She thought: Poor Deb. He would, of course, be a good husband, unlikely to fritter away her money or run after other women but . . . But dull, set in his ways, and always sure, in any argument, of God's full support.

The only Methodist Chapel she knew of was a wretched little building on the road to Sudbury and she certainly was not going to have Deb married there.

"We," she said, rather pontifically, "are Church of England and I wish all my girls to be married according to its rites." Not in some place not even licensed for marriages; a place where a wedding, in order to be legal, must be witnessed by the local registrar.

"Well," he said, amiable and unruffled, "we won't quarrel about *that*. Though my mother would turn in her grave." His mother had brought her form of religion, and her money from the Midlands; she had built a chapel at Foxton, and he largely supported it, for most of its members were poor. It was, he understood, different in the North. "Standing up to be married by a parson will do me no damage," he said. "But I wish you'd be a bit more accommodating about time. Next June is a long way off."

"Ten months," she said crisply. "A short engagement by ordinary standards. And I have already been extremely accommodating—bringing Diana's wedding forward by a whole year." And with, as yet, not the slightest notion of how it could be managed.

"Yes," he said, "I realise that. But it's all right if I ask her and give her a ring? I brought it, in case." He felt in his capacious pocket and produced the ring which he had brought in case, not in a case, but carefully wrapped in tissue paper. With a gesture which, now that she understood him, she found rather appealing, he offered it for her inspection.

"Not new," he said—quite unnecessaily. "But precious in its way. My mother's father gave it to her when she settled on a Norfolk man."

It was a curious ring, wide, gold, with an oval of blue enamel, and on the blue, in more gold, a word: *Mizpah*.

"It's a word with meaning," he said. "It means: The Lord watch between thee and me, when we are absent one from another."

"So much in five letters? Very concise," Mrs Thorley said.

On the whole she had, once she understood, relented towards him. What she had always felt—that slight animosity—was fully explained; and Deb wore the extraordinary ring with as much pride as Diana wore hers. Time slipped away, and Mrs Thorley went house-hunting.

"I may have been precipitate, Everard," she said, "but it did seem to me a chance not to be missed. I do a certain amount of business with Mr Larken, as you know, and he drew my attention to it. Houses for rent, especially in such a nice area, are rather rare and when he mentioned it to me, I thought it worth a look. I took a week's option and—wait—I would like to give you the rent for the first year, as a wedding present. That is, of course, if you and Diana approve of it."

As who could not? A lovely little house, one of six, three aside, facing each other across a cul-de-sac which ended in a wall, topped by high trees from the gardens of bigger houses—one of them Edward Taylor's—in St Giles' Square. It was called Friars' Lane; and its open end just turned the grey bulk of St Mary's church. It was near the wide market square and the streets leading off it.

Ideal for a young couple. Perversely, Everard Spicer felt that he was being hustled. So far no sign of a partnership; old Gordon was still remarkably spry for his age, and James was frivolous as ever. Between them they managed well, unloading any job they didn't fancy on to him. He'd been with the firm a full year now; they'd had time to see his worth; to realise that he was conscientious and reliable and knew more law than the pair of them put together, yet there had been no mention even of a rise in salary. And he sensed something distant and cold in Mrs Gordon's attitude towards him; he was, after all, supposedly James' friend, yet Mrs Gordon asked him to the house only when she needed a man to keep the numbers even—and, he greatly suspected, had been let down by somebody. Never casual, never friendly.

His insecure childhood had rendered him oversensitive, and at the same time greedy. Now, looking back, it seemed as though he had always been dependent upon somebody's favour; and now he was going to be dependent upon Mrs Thorley's. If he allowed her to hustle him, and pay a year's rent.

Of course Diana was the dearest, sweetest, most adorable girl in the world; and of course he was anxious to marry her—but in his chosen time. The extra year would have given him time to be certain of Mr Gordon's intentions; or to look around for some more promising opening. With a wife on his hands, and a house he'd be tied down. Perhaps forever.

He set about looking over the little house as moodily as Diana was ecstatic. He said things like: "It's very dark, don't you think?"

"Not in itself. It's the dark paper and so much brown paint. Easily remedied."

"Redecorating costs money. Then there's the furnishing. I have saved very little, you know."

"But dearest, I shall have some money. Five hundred pounds that Papa left me. It isn't a fortune, but it will be enough." She was so busy planning, the nest-making instinct so active, that she was oblivious to his lack of enthusiasm; even when, at the end of the inspection, he said:

"Well, darling, what do you think?" in a voice which almost defied her to give a favourable answer.

"I love it already. Wasn't it clever and kind of Mamma?"

"Lord love us," Deborah said, "we could do most of the work ourselves. I've never yet papered a room, but I'm willing to have a try."

The quiet little house in the quiet cul-de-sac, until lately occupied by a quiet old woman, became a centre of activity. Diana and Deborah drove into Baildon almost every day, taking with them first one of Jenny's picnic meals and then, as the weather grew colder and the kitchen range was back in working order, with materials for a proper meal. All that the range needed was the attention of the chimney sweep—the quiet old woman had for a long time shirked such an upheaval and the flue was blocked; she'd boiled her kettle and her egg on the sitting-room stove.

"I must master cooking," Deborah said. "I don't much like the look of Tim's Emma and I'm sure she loathes me. I may have to cook if she leaves, as I think she will."

It was Deborah who ordered a ton of best household coal, and paid for it, since she now had no reason to save. With something in the oven, or simmering away in one of the pedlar's pots, she soaked and stripped off wallpaper, pasted and hung new paper, splashed paint about. Disasters in the culinary line—they grew fewer—or in the paper-hanging, were greeted with hilarity. Everard came every day when he knew the girls would be there, had a meal and did a little work, though Deborah limited his activities: "You can't do that, Everard. You mustn't go back to the office looking like a whitened sepulchre."

Deborah's mare must be exercised, and as the year ran downhill so that there was no evening, Deborah often rode in, and sometimes Caroline shared the pony carriage. Edward offered the hospitality of his quite extensive stables. Edward fell into the habit of dropping in to share the rather makeshift meal, and if time allowed he would work for an hour or so.

At Christmas Edward asked Caroline to marry him and she agreed, wondering why in the world he had been so slow to read the signals she had been sending out ever since that terrible, terrible time in the summer.

Caroline was the only one of them actually to choose her own engagement ring. Mr Collins, the jeweller, was, perforce, one of Edward's patients and when Edward said, "Get half a dozen down on approval," Mr Collins gladly did so. Caroline, confronted with such richness, chose, not the dark sapphire which almost matched her eyes, but an emerald, with green upon green in its depths. Green was the colour of envy, and she knew that however long she lived, however much she was pampered and favoured, she would envy Poor Susan.

It would be not a double, but a triple wedding, and in the end a saving, Mrs Thorley reflected; since most of the guests would be the same and one wedding feast served for all. And she would design, and largely make, the white satin dresses which would conform to the rule laid down long ago; equal, but not uniform.

It was March, the daffodils dancing; and Mrs Thorley had spent some of her sleepless hours thinking about veils for brides. She had held on, through all vicissitudes, to her own, which had been her mother's and her grandmother's. By every right, Diana's, but that would be to make an invidious distinction, for no such lace, fine as a cobweb, was obtainable now. So each girl must have a third of it; the thing divided and eked out; the sturdier English lace at the top, taking the weight, the filmy less substantial stuff stitched on, under a band of white satin ribbon which would hide the seam.

Happy, practical thoughts which should have induced sleep, but did not. She saw the dawn invade, despite the curtains, in fragmented shafts of light. She heard the clamour of the morning chorus of birds. And from the purely feminine business of bridal veils, so easily settled by a slash of the scissors, her mind moved to money. The girls must have their small dowries . . . Gad's Goliath must go; and not enough! Several cows, some calves. She was arranging these things in her mind when Caroline opened the door and said,

"Mamma—will you come? Lavinia is ill. She's just been dreadfully sick."

Lavinia *had* been dreadfully sick, and there was Caroline, who in three months' time would be a doctor's wife, vulnerable to worse emergencies, looking very sick herself.

"A glass of hot water, with a good pinch of baking soda in it," Mrs Thorley said, struggling into her dressing gown and thinking that they'd all eaten the same food yesterday, and although Lavinia had always been pale and frail, subject to backache, headache now and again, she's never been bilious; possibly because she ate so little.

But sick this morning she had been and now, very pale and exhausted, she lay on the soiled, disordered bed. Mrs Thorley put her hand on her daughter's forehead. And on her neck. Thank God, no fever; on the contrary, rather chilly and clammy.

A curious thought occurred to her. She said:

"You'll be all right, dear. I can't think why you should be sick, unless—did you lick your paint brush or hold it in your mouth yesterday?"

It was the only explanation she could think of; some paints did contain dangerous colouring matter.

"No," Lavinia said, cold; hostile.

Caroline pattered in with the faintly cloudy glass.

"Come along," Mrs Thorley said, slipping her arm under Lavinia's sharp-boned shoulders, "drink this, and if you don't soon feel completely better, we'll send for Edward."

"I'm all right. I don't need Edward. I'll just lie flat for a little while."

"A clean sheet and pillow-case Caro," Mrs Thorley said. "Don't stand there looking as though it were the end of the world."

Two seconds later she faced the end of the world.

The bulge was all the more conspicuous because Lavinia's body was still that of a child.

Mrs Thorley clapped her hand to her mouth, holding back the terrible cry which had almost escaped her. She felt sick; she felt dizzy; she felt faint. Yet she rallied sufficiently to pull the soiled sheet over the bulge as Caro came in with the fresh linen and her voice was astonishingly calm as she said:

"Take your clothes, Caro, and dress in another room."

While Caro, glad to be dismissed, collected her day's wear, Mrs Thorley had time to think: How ridiculous! This is not a thing that can be hidden.

Then she had another thought. Had she jumped to too hasty a conclusion?

There was the remarkable case of Lady Flora Hastings, a lady-in-waiting who had appeared to be pregnant. The Queen's own doctor had declared that she was. Gossip had even named the putative father. Then the poor lady was found to be suffering from a tumour of the liver—and had died of it.

Better something like that in this case?

Yes! To think thus was terrible. But the thought remained. Illness, early death were tragic, but not shameful. Besides, medicine had advanced . . . Diagnosed soon enough . . .

Caro went out, closing the door softly, and before Mrs Thorley could speak, Lavinia said in a cold, remote way:

"There is no need to worry. I am going to have a baby. But not here. Somebody is coming for me on Lady Day."

That was the 25th of March and only five days away.

"Who? The Fremlins?"

"Does it matter? I shall be fetched and nobody need know anything. Just say nothing for five days."

"Don't talk such rubbish, Lavinia. How could I possibly let you go—into the blue—with people who are . . . who have proved . . . so untrustworthy. Do you realise what you are saying. A baby, and no husband."

It struck Mrs Thorley that Lavinia didn't realise; she'd always been odd—some people said a bit dim-witted; living in a world of her own; a dream world. Of her innocence, ignorance, immaturity, somebody had taken most cruel advantage. She asked, as any mother in her place would have done: "Who was it?"

"I am not going to talk about it."

As Mrs Thorley had suppressed her cry of horror, so she repressed an impulse to take the girl by the shoulders and *shake* her, make her come into the open for once and behave as any other girl, caught, disgraced, shamed, would have done. But even had she given way to the impulse, she knew that she could not have performed the action. Another wave of weakness swept over her; she clutched at the bedpost and almost fell into a sitting position at the foot of the bed.

"It should not have happened," Lavinia said. "I meant nobody to know. I have been sick before and always managed to get out. This morning I was caught unawares. But if there is no fuss, no questions . . . Just for five days, everything will be all right, I assure you."

Mrs Thorley wanted to say: How? How can everything be all right? But even the power of speech seemed to have deserted her. Everything of strength, authority and reason was concentrated in the pale girl on the bed.

The door opened. "Anything I can do?" It was Deborah, of course. And it was Lavinia, not Mamma, who said:

"No, Deb. Thank you. I'm all right now."

Something in Mrs Thorley tried to call out: Help me! But it was like a nightmare in which one screamed and made no sound, or tried to run and made no progress.

"Five days," Lavinia repeated, not coaxingly or persuasively, but with an absurd, though unmistakable air of authority. "Then I shall be gone and you can explain it in any way you like. Until then I shall sleep in the studio."

Not one word of apology, or of regret, not even a hint of explanation. Incredible behavior. Mrs Thorley could hardly believe that what was happening was happening. Her own feeling of utter helplessness was understandable, she had had a severe shock.

In a vague way she recognised that the suggestion of Lavinia's sleeping apart was sensible. All the girls dressed and undressed in a modest way, removing and replacing underclothes within the shelter of their night-gowns, but even so it was amazing that Caroline, sharing a bed, hadn't noticed. But no more amazing than that she herself—always a woman to meet an emergency with action—should be sitting here, passive, dumb and seeming to agree to keep the secret for five days. It was though she were under a spell.

"I'll dress now and begin moving my things," Lavinia said.

It was a dismissal and Mrs Thorley accepted it, summoning from somewhere the strength to get to her feet and walk away.

Outside her own bedroom door she became very conscious of the whisky, hidden away there behind the hats; but it was too early, one really must not give way. She went on, down the stairs, and joined the other girls at the breakfast table.

"She said she was all right," Deborah said. "Is she?"

"Oh yes. Just a bilious attack." Odd, she could now speak normally, even with composure. "She realised that it wasn't very pleasant for *you*, Caro, so she's going to move up into the studio."

"Good," Caro said. "So that old chaise-longue of hers will serve some purpose after all."

Five days sounded so short a time, but for Mrs Thorley they were endless, partly because they were aimless. She had plenty to do, but was completely unable to give her mind to anything. Against all the arguments of good sense, she found herself believing that someone would come on the 25th and take Lavinia away. Then what should she say? That Lavinia had gone to Brazil, invited to stay with the Fremlins? That would surprise no one, but it would be entirely unsatisfactory at another level. After all, Lavinia was her daughter; still very young; pregnant and singularly lacking in good sound sense; maternal responsibility could not be shuffled off so easily. But she was incapable of following that line of thought to any conclusion; she was up against something she could not handle. Something for which there was no precedent.

Lavinia reappeared at the family table and seemed to eat heartily. Mrs Thorley found it almost impossible to address her directly, and tried to avoid looking at her.

George once touched on dangerous ground, saying pontifically,

"Anybody who's been bilious shouldn't eat cream, Lavinia. You'll be sick again, and get fat. Once when I was sick I couldn't face cream for a week."

Diana, always so correct, said, "George that is hardly a subject for talk at table."

"And you are wrong," Caro said. "Once after I had been unmentionably indisposed," she shot one of her mocking glances at Diana, "I ate like a horse for three days."

Once, alone with Lavinia, Mrs Thorley did manage to say, "What are you taking with you?"

"Just what I took to Abbas. Enough for the night. And my pictures."

And on the 25th the little overnight valise and the bulging portfolio were there in the hall, inconspicuous, but ready to hand.

That was the longest day of all. One of those warm, premature summer-like days which March occasionally produced.

Diana and Deborah and Caroline had all gone into Baildon; two to work on the little house, and Caro, in the afternoon, to present a handwriting prize at the Ragged School. As she lightly said, one good deed led to another; she was now a member of the Committee of the Friends of the hospital; a patron of the Ragged School, "and unless I am very careful I shall end up in charge of that place for unmarried mothers!"

George had decided to go with them and Gad's settled down into a waiting silence. Nothing happened.

Nothing had happened when they all came back, ready for supper.

"It's as well," Diana said, with just a touch of spite in her voice, "that Caro is marrying a reasonably well-to-do man. What do you think she did today? She gave every child in the school a currant bun and a packet of sweets."

"Well, there were only two prizes, both dreadfully dull. Ten-shilling vouchers for boots! Not that they aren't needed. And I felt sorry for the losers." A loser herself! "I must say, though, that all through the ceremony—that was dreadfully dull, too—I kept asking myself what would Miss Hardwicke say? *Me*, a judge of handwriting."

"I know what she would say," Deborah said. "That one need not be a hen in order to tell a good egg from a bad one."

Through the chatter and the laughter Mrs Thorley was listening, as she had listened all day, for the sound of wheels and hooves on the gravel. One of her furtive glances at Lavinia informed her that the girl showed no agitation. Placid, confident, she sat at the table. The day died in splendour, hyacinth blue, apple green and daffodil yellow in great swaths across the West.

George went to bed. Deb said that she must wash her hair, despite all precautions it was spattered with whitewash. Caro went with her, but Diana moved to a chair near the lamp and took up the now almost-completed table-cloth. Lavinia sat idle, waiting, but without any sign of anxiety or impatience. Mrs Thorley went to her little desk in the window embrasure and stared at pages which conveyed nothing to her mind, which was busy with what she would say to whoever came.

Finally Diana said, "Well, that is finished. Hardly worth starting anything else now. Goodnight, Mamma." The ritual exchange of kisses. "Goodnight, Lavinia."

Presently the clock on the half-landing struck eleven. Mrs Thorley wanted to break this unnatural silence, to say something, anything. She tried to mention the lateness of the hour, to ask if Lavinia were sure of the date.

Lavinia said, "Whoever comes, please, no reproaches! It would be most unwise. Nobody was to know."

Mrs Thorley thought of all the heated exhortations she intended, the promises she meant to extract—knowing all the time how futile it would be because she would not be able to use the ultimate weapon. She could not, in the circumstances, refuse to let Lavinia go . . . Oh God, what did I ever do to deserve this?

On the first stroke of twelve Lavinia stood up, rigidly attentive, poised, ready to go. Mrs Thorley rose too. The clock seemed to take an extraordinarily long time to complete the marking between March 25th and the 26th, and when the last boom had died to nothing, Lavinia fell to the ground.

Mrs Thorley had seen people faint before, but not like this. Lavinia did not crumple at the knees and subside, she fell prone as a sapling would at the final stroke of the axe. She lay on her back with her eyes open, wide and staring.

Dead?

A feeling of relief, of which she was instantly ashamed and which she regretted for a long time, shot through Mrs Thorley. Nothing now to hide. In the same instant she was thinking: Smelling salts, none handy; cold water; wrist slapping; head between the knees. All effective for faints, but this could be a fit. About them she knew nothing at all.

Feel the pulse. Alive, thank God! She pulled Lavinia into a sitting position, her back against a chair, and proceeded as for a faint, pushing the head forward and down.

"Oh, my dear . . ." The first endearment she had used, even in her thoughts, since her discovery of the girl's position. The nearest she had come to tenderness was pity; poor child, poor innocent, poor deluded girl. And even such thoughts could only be entertained when out of Lavinia's presence. Now she could say, "We'll manage . . . somehow," which in the circumstances was gallant. "Come, let me help you into the chair. I'll get you a little brandy."

"I'm all right," Lavinia said, and as though to prove it, stood up. Physically she *seemed* to be all right, strong on her feet anyway. She still looked blank and stunned—and who could wonder? She'd been so confident, had such complete trust in somebody . . . And now there is only me, Mrs Thorley thought. Released from the kind of trance which had held her passive and dumb for five endless days, she was the more aware of the absurdity of it all. Whoever the guilty man was—and the first suspect was Mr Fremlin—was it likely that he would come? On a date so specified that when the day ended, Lavinia had had a kind of fit.

Lavinia went to bed. She moved in a rather curious way, a bit like a clockwork toy well wound up, but still, part of Mrs Thorley's mind noted, not a word of regret, or explanation, and not a tear. Mrs Thorley went with her to the foot of the attic stairs and said, in a muted voice:

"Try to sleep, Lavinia. We'll think about things in the morning."

You will think about things now, Isabel Thorley, and drunk as you may be, you will try to think straight.

A miscarriage. Lavinia has had a shock and a fall. Miscarriages have been brought about by lesser causes. And she was always delicate, the one who had to be coddled along with cod liver oil and iron pills. A miscarriage would be the most desirable solution.

But not to be counted upon. What then? You have the others to think of. Of the three only Caroline might escape from the resultant scandal unscathed. Edward Taylor, a doctor with a trained mind, might not feel that in marrying Caro he was marrying into a family afflicted with leprosy. But Everard, so cool and precise and ambitious, and Mr Bridges, so Puritanical . . . Strange to think that on the rock of an unprecedented scandal, Diana and Deborah, who loved most, would suffer most.

Think of yourself for a moment. Yes, with what zest would those who regarded her business activities as unwomanly pounce upon this, proof that she had neglected her family, failed to exercise the supervision girls needed. And the coarse jokes about letting the wrong bull get at her heifer.

Of course there were places like that to which Caroline had made such light-hearted reference, Lying-in Hospitals, shelters for Fallen Women. But so far as Mrs Thorley knew, they offered only temporary shelter, and what kind of women would be there? Could she possibly consign Lavinia to such a place. And would Lavinia, who seemed to have no sense of guilt, or shame, connive at the only possible alternative—to go away to some distant place and pretend to be married and widowed cruelly young.

Oh, what to do? Where to turn?

Just hope for a miscarriage, after the shock and the fall.

It was almost daylight when the whisky and utter exhaustion threw her into the abyss of unconsciousness.

"It is unlike Mamma to be late," Deborah said as she set the dish of eggs and bacon on the table.

At Christmas, Katie had brought Willy to the sticking point— and not before time. Mrs Thorley had not replaced her; her wage had been small, but there was her keep to be considered; a tiny saving, but it all counted; and while the girls were here they could help; when they went surely Jenny could manage to cook for one woman and a boy. Jenny had accepted the change with resignation, simply saying that running about could not be expected; not at her age, and not with her legs. Most of the resultant running about had been done by Deborah.

"I'd take a tray up," Deborah said, "but honestly I think a bit of extra sleep would do her more good. This last day or two I've felt that she had something on her mind. She's been unlike herself."

"Yes," George agreed. "So quiet." He looked at his half-sister and his two stepsisters with slight reproach. "Three weddings all in one is rather more than most mothers have to deal with."

Halfway through the meal, Deborah said, "By the way, Di, I shan't be coming in this morning. I must prune the roses here."

"Oh, Deb," Diana said, discontent in her voice and on her face. "With so much to do in Friars' Lane! And I thought one pruned in the autumn."

"I did. But with this warm spring they've made a lot of new growth and if I leave them, and a frost comes . . ."

"Oh, well," Diana said with a resigned shrug. "You coming in, Caro?"

"I might as well. Not to whitewash, though."

George saw and seized his opportunity.

"If you like, Deb, I'd exercise Foxy for you."

Why not? The mare, despite her name, which was a contraction of Foxton was anything but foxy by nature, the gentlest thing alive, and every time Deborah thought of her, pulling a coal cart, she felt something like adoration for Tim, who had noticed and saved her from that fate. Also, George, trained by Deborah herself, was a good rider and he was rapidly outgrowing his pony.

"All right," Deborah said. "But no jumps, mind."

Mrs Thorley woke from what was rare for her, a beautiful, happy dream. In it she had been young, very young again, in Westmorland, playing with an assortment of dogs, not a care in the world.

She woke, realised from the way the sun lay across her bed that she had overslept, and that, waking, she was one of the most care-ridden women in the world.

She rose quickly and was immediately aware of last night's excess taking its toll; inside her head a cannon ball rolled about, but she put on her slippers, pulled on her robe and went towards the attic stairs. Had it happened, the thing which would deliver them all?

Apparently not. Lavinia lay on the chaise-longue which was now her bed, sleeping, curled up like a kitten. She looked peaceful and very young. Once again Mrs Thorley's mind cried out in rebellion; Oh God, *why*? How *could* you allow such a thing to befall us all, through such an innocent instrument?

Downstairs, two cups of strong coffee cleared her head a bit and from the other side of the room the papers on her desk reproached her. Forms to be filled in, giving the pedigree of every animal that she intended to enter for various shows. Awards in themselves were of little monetary value, but they promoted sales, and whatever happened within the family one certainty was that she would need money.

She approached the job with reluctance, but it was one which demanded concentration, and although her personal problem was not banished from her mind it receded a little as she filled in space after space with the neat copperplate hand which George Thorley, himself a scrawler, had admired so much.

A commotion in the kitchen disturbed her. Jenny screaming, Willy's voice, some shuffling sounds and above all Deborah's voice, clear and authorative, "I can manage."

Jenny stood with both hands clenched to her chest, a knife in one, a half-peeled potato in the other. Willy stood gaping by the door which opened upon the back stairs, and four or five steps up Deborah was dragging Lavinia, roughly. Water streamed from them both.

"She ain't dead, Ma'am," Willy said. "Miss Deb got . . . " But Mrs Thorley was already on the stairs; in time to see Deborah free a hand and slap Lavinia hard across the face. There was some blood. After that there was less resistance and within a minute they were on the attic landing and into the studio. There Deborah released Lavinia with a push and said, "You bloody fool! Do you want everybody to know?"

Mrs Thorley took charge.

"Deb, go and get into dry clothes. I'll see to Lavinia."

"I don't like leaving you. She's mad! She *bit* me." Deborah held out her hand, blood oozing from punctures on the inside and outside of the thumb.

"I can manage," Mrs Thorley said, secure in the authority which she had exercised for so long. Without being told she knew approximately what had happened. Lavinia's father, faced with a crisis out of which neither charm nor influence could help him, had shot himself. Lavinia had tried to drown herself. It all fitted.

That terrible thought again: If only Deb had let her! Instantly she refuted it, giving as much care to see that Lavinia was not chilled as she had last evening to see that she did not die in a fit.

"Strip," she said; and although Lavinia still looked blank, she obeyed.

An idea, forming like a bubble on an about-to-boil pan, came to the surface of her mind. It might be just possible, with a vast deal of contrivance and connivance.

"Now," she said, "if you try that again—or anything else—you will go into a lunatic asylum. You know what that means? But if you do *exactly* what you are told, you shall have your baby and bring it up, not as a bastard. You understand me? Of course you do. You're not an idiot. You're just trying to hide. I know you are

there, Lavinia, and I am speaking to you. It's this or an asylum—
and I promise you, a strict one."

Most were. The idea that lunatics—at any rate the harmless
ones—should be kindly treated had been promulgated by a few
humane doctors but it had gained little ground. Whippings, starving and violent purging were still in vogue . . . And of course one
could not hand over one's own daughter, flesh of one's flesh, bone
of one's bone, to such a régime, any more than one could consign
her to the company of women—all rough and most of them prostitutes, in places which took in unmarried mothers.

Lavinia looked sullen but she said nothing.

"Mamma, I know it is a shocking thing to say, but you should
know . . . Lavinia deliberately tried to drown herself. I know, I
was there. I was pruning the roses. She couldn't see me, but I
straightened up, just in time to see her *jump* into the moat. And
she resisted me. She looks so frail, but thrashing about in the
water . . . and she bit me. I yelled and Willy . . . But for him we
could both have drowned. I tried to make it sound like an accident. She is so absent-minded, stepping back to get a better view
. . . But it was intentional. You may not believe—wish to believe
it, but it is true. And on the stairs I simply had to hit her, because
of Jenny and Willy. I mean most people, just rescued wouldn't
have been so . . . so awkward."

Mrs Thorley remembered that she had somewhere heard, or
read, that bites from a human being could be more dangerous
than those from an animal. Carbolic soap was supposed to be
good for wounds which might fester, and so was alcohol. Try
both.

Submitting to treatment, protesting that the little punctures
didn't warrant any fuss, it was just the idea of biting which was so
horrifying, Deborah added:

"And she may try again. Mamma, I hate saying this, but she always has been a bit odd. We must admit that. She never had a
friend, except those people at Abbas. Now they're gone and all of
us . . . I mean there is only three months' gap between Caroline
and Lavinia, and Caro is to be married in June . . . Being so left
out . . . I think it turned her brain."

Speaking shortly but with a distinct feeling of sharing her impossible load, Mrs Thorley told Deborah the truth—so far as she
knew it.

"My God!" Deborah said, and clapped her hands to her face and stayed so still that for a moment or two Mrs Thorley feared that she, the most reliable, most sturdy one, was about to give way. But when at last Deborah dropped her hands, the face revealed was calm, determined and older.

"Then she must be locked in. A suicide calls for an inquest. We should have a double scandal."

"I threatened her, very severely. I said . . . I said that if she didn't behave she would go into an asylum."

"I doubt whether she understood. And if it came to the point who would want to marry into a family with insanity in it? Leave it to me. She must be kept safe until we have time to think."

Deborah was handy with tools and knew where to look for what she wanted. It took her very little time to fix two staples, a length of chain and the padlock. Then she stood, hesitant, thinking of Jenny, who slept in the neighbouring attic and must surely notice. She went into Jenny's room and knocked out the window frame, not a difficult thing to do, the wood was old and rotten. There was no crash, for the whole thing fell on to a tough rosemary bush.

Jenny's wardrobe was not extensive, one good armful. Deborah carried the clothes down and laid them on the bed of what was always called The Little Room. Then from her own room she fetched a hat-box, carried it up and placed in it Jenny's rather pitiable collection of treasures—silhouettes of people cut from black paper, pasted on white and held in tin frames, a few fairings of course pottery and some bits of finery, and mainly things which Mamma and the girls had discarded. The room was soon cleared.

"Jenny, something rather awful has happened. The window of your room has blown out. I've brought all your things into The Little Room."

And what was awful about that? Answer to prayer, rather. That top flight of stairs was steep, the final trial for legs at the end of a day.

"You shouldn't hev bothered about my stuff, Miss Deborah." She was the only one of them who would have done. "I could've managed them stairs just that one more time." A way of saying that once settled in The Little Room, Jenny did not intend to be relegated to the attic again.

"S'funny thing. Katie was allus whimpering about noises up

there. And I allus towd her it was winders or doors. So now we know."

"Miss Lavinia will have a tray. I'll take it up, Jenny. The sousing gave her rather a shock."

"She never was very strong, was she? How did it happen, Miss?"

"I can only think that it was the peach tree. She was stepping back to admire it—perhaps planning to paint it; I don't know. She just stepped back and fell into the moat."

That was to be the story—for the time being.

Deborah thought about windows, how easily the one in Jenny's attic had fallen out; how easy it would be for Lavinia, always a bit demented and now with every reason to be more so, to throw herself out.

Over the meal called lunch, substantial when everyone was present, at other times rather skimpy, and one for which neither Mrs Thorley nor Deborah had much appetite, Deborah said:

"I have been thinking about that window, Mamma. Could you bear to come up and keep an eye on her, while I put up some bars. I must work from the inside because otherwise Willy will notice, and I can't lock the door from the inside."

Deborah's reaction had been exactly what might be expected; helpful, practical. What would that of the others be? Cold disgust from Diana? Hysteria from Caroline? Or—with girls one never knew, perhaps the dead opposite.

Lavinia's attic, into which until today no member of the family had set a foot, was, though furnished with odds and ends, better than some bed-sitting rooms which Mrs Thorley had occupied in the worst days. It occupied the centre of this remote gable end and was quite spacious. There was the piece of furniture to which Caroline had referred as that old chaise-longue of hers, now made into a bed so that its upholstery, silk but tattered, was largely hidden. A wickerwork chair, slightly lop-sided, but still comfortable-looking. An oil lamp on one of the high wooden stools used by clerks in offices, but painted bright lacquer red. Near the window was the proper artist's easel which Lavinia had bought when she sold her first picture, and a trestle table laden with the tools of the trade. Into the corner fitted a triangular washstand. The floor was bare, except by the bed where the, oak planks, some of them eighteen inches wide, were covered by a rug, old and faded but still beautiful. And one wide sweep of whitewashed wall Lavinia had used to paint upon. A confusion of brilliant colour and strange shapes.

Lavinia was at the easel when Mrs Thorley and Deborah entered. Deborah had said, "We might as well make one errand of it," and had carried up the tray. "It's cold anyway, so time can't matter." She now set the tray down rather roughly at one end of the trestle-table and went on to deal with the window. Rather more of a problem than the door, because up directly under the roof and in an exposed gable, air would be necessary. It was a casement window and she must arrange it so that one half at least could be opened, but so that the opening would not be wide enough for Lavinia to squeeze through.

As she worked Deborah brooded over her inability to feel really sorry for Lavinia. Naturally she had been annoyed with her for making the rescue so difficult, and nobody enjoyed being bitten, but when she knew the truth, surely her first thought should have been: Poor little Lavinia! Surely any girl seduced and abandoned should be pitied. But all she had felt—after concern for the scandal—had been repulsion. And she could trace its origin. She assumed Mr Fremlin to be the man concerned, and from the moment she had first met him she had been repelled by him. Now something of him was in Lavinia. Loathsome thought! Her instinct had been right—she had refused even to ride in his carriage. He was evil. And look what calamity he had brought upon them all. Lavinia had always been eccentric, but harmless; now here she was, out of her mind and pregnant, being locked in, barred in. And taking no notice at all, working away at one of her silly pictures as though her life depended upon it. And who ever saw a goat with four horns?

Mrs Thorley, standing guard by the door, had addressed Lavinia and said, "Eat your lunch, Lavinia."

Without looking round Lavinia said, "Presently."

Dared one still hope for a miscarriage? The shock of disappointment, a fall, a drenching in the moat—water was cold in March. Any one of those would have ended a *wanted* pregnancy, in a strong girl, Mrs Thorley thought bitterly. But not this one! No. Not this.

"Mamma, I think the girls should be fortified. I'll get some sherry."

Neither Diana nor Caroline was in a good mood. Deborah, who could be relied upon to do some decorating and make a decent meal, had let Diana down. Diana had made no attempt to continue whitewashing the ceiling, she had painted a skirting board and somehow managed to break two of her cherished nails. Then she had gone to the cook-shop and bought a meat pie, which Everard had eaten, hungrily, but without much enthusiasm. And who could wonder at that? He could have bought a meat pie and eaten it in his office. Because she was so much in love she had apologised for the meagre meal, and smiled so sweetly that Everard had thought: Of course she couldn't be expected to slave in the kitchen. But could they afford a cook? In three months' time? Just because Mrs Thorley must be so hasty, and so managing? What he worried about and resented was reflected on his face and Diana had interpreted it as dislike of the pie, and justifiable, the meat tasteless and rubbery, the pastry like cardboard.

Caroline had endured criticism of another kind.

She had gone to lunch with Mrs Bosworth, who was entertaining all the Friends of the Hospital, and of course Edward was there and he'd administered a rebuke, mildly, kindly, but still a rebuke.

"Darling, I heard about yesterday. How generous you were with sweets and buns . . ."

"You should have seen their faces!"

"I know. But I'm not sure that it was wise."

"Why not?"

"Well, old Miss Meadows was there . . ."

"Naturally. She is one of the governors."

"Darling . . . it's just that she is so deadly poor. She would have loved to give buns and sweets, but she hasn't a penny to rub against a key. The best she can do is cadge bones from the butcher in cold weather and make a little soup for the neediest."

"Then wouldn't you think she'd love to see them gobbling buns?"

"Darling, people's minds don't work that way. She would feel . . . diminished."

"God love me! The things you think of!"

"I was only suggesting that it would have been . . . well, a little more tactful to have left the buns and sweets for the master to distribute. Afterwards. And while we are the subject . . ."

"Yes?"

"Well, darling, there are people who don't like to hear God's name taken lightly."

God love me! I'd love to tear off this ring, throw it at him, say: To hell with tact and schools and hospitals and *you*, Edward Taylor, and all the deadly dreary things you stand for.

She knew she could not afford such a gesture. She had just escaped—by Mamma's advice—looking as though she had been jilted by Freddy. Break her engagement to Edward and talk would be virulent. A near engagement, and a proper engagement broken off. Something very wrong with Caroline Thorley . . . No, she must hold on, at least until they were married; then she'd show everybody, including Edward.

The sherry did something to soothe ill-humour, and supper was not noticeably different to Diana and Caroline, and George, all young and self-engrossed; Mrs Thorley and Deborah tried to keep up a front, for George's sake and Caroline introduced a subject of perennial interest by saying that having had a huge lunch at Mrs Bosworth's, she must be careful about supper or she would have trouble with her waist. Eighteen inches was the ideal for girls who wished to be admired and both she and Diana occasionally slipped over the limit. Severe tight lacing helped, even if it hurt. Caroline would sometimes say that her stays were killing her, she could hardly breathe; then within half an hour she could be dancing, talking, laughing, all at the same time. Deborah was enviable; although she was taller than either of them, she was so naturally slim as hardly to need lacing at all.

That subject exhausted, Caroline gave a list of the guests at Mrs Bosworth's. "Lady Norton was there. As usual she looked as though her clothes came from a jumble sale, but I must say she has a sense of humour."

"Which means that she laughed when you cracked a joke," Diana said. She had always thought Caroline too flippant, and now there was envy as well. Diana, the belle of her circle, slaving away painting skirting boards, while Caroline, over lunch, met Lady Norton. There was envy at another level, too—only half recognised. Diana felt that if Caroline had offered Edward a dog biscuit for lunch he'd have eaten it happily and said that it was the best lunch he had ever had. Not that Diana would have exchanged Everard for Edward, never in a thousand years!

What I must do, Diana decided, is to learn to cook, just a few simple dishes, a guard against an emergency such as today's.

Nobody mentioned Lavinia or her absence from the supper table. Her comings and goings had always been unpredictable.

Pushing her food around and making a pretence at eating, Mrs Thorley thought: And now I must tell them, because they must connive.

She said, "George dear, go to bed."

"Mamma! It's so early."

"Well, go and find something to do. We have something to talk over."

"Oh, I see." Women's talk about the wedding to which he was greatly looking forward because for him it meant new clothes and a chance to shine, socially. And he would be host, after all, he was the son of the house.

Mrs Thorley said, "I have something terrible to tell you," and told them, as briefly as possible.

It was Caroline who said, "Oh, poor Lavinia" before beginning to cry.

Diana said the completely conventional thing.

"Whoever he is he must be made to marry her. At once."

"If he could be found. Mr Fremlin—I suspect him most strongly—is now in Brazil; most of the other men she met at Abbas were foreigners and she refused to tell me . . . So what is called a shot-gun marriage is out of the question. But I have a plan. To carry it out I shall need all your help . . ."

She outlined the plan which had begun as a mere bubble in her mind. Lavinia had fallen into the moat and for a few days could stay in bed, suffering from the resultant chill. That would give time for an invitation to arrive, inviting her for a long, long visit. It must involve a long journey too, to give Lavinia time to find a man and be married aboard ship—sea-captains were authorised to perform marriages. Lavinia would then be widowed, have a baby and bring it home. But of course, all the time Lavinia would really be up there in the attic.

"If you see any flaw in this arrangement, say so. You are the ones most intimately involved."

Caroline—the only one to have uttered a word of compassion—mopped her face and took hope.

"Mamma, can we be sure? She never even . . . Well, you know, the curse, the female benefit . . . Lavinia never had it, so how could she be . . . pregnant? Don't you think that Edward should give her a thorough examination?"

"Lavinia herself said that she was going to have a baby. And I promised her that if she did exactly what she was told, she should have it, without any shame or scandal."

Deborah said, "It might work, if we were sure of her co-operation. But she might do anything, at any time. And think of the endless lies. I think she should be put away. After all she is mad."

And bad. She must be, to have anything to do with Mr Fremlin.

Diana, who had cried, but who had turned whiter than the table-cloth, said:

"Will it affect the wedding?"

"Not if we work together."

Deborah said, "While we are here . . ."

And though that had an ominous sound, in the main things worked very smoothly. India must be Lavinia's supposed destination—a great number of girls went to India and found husbands. It must not be a well-known place, not Bombay, Madras or Calcutta, because even in their small circle almost everybody knew somebody, or was related to somebody in those areas. Deborah's atlas contained a patchwork map which showed spheres of influence, English—through the East India Company, some French still, some Portuguese. They chose a seemingly untouched native state—Killapore.

Everybody said, "Oh, what a pity. I cannot even write a letter of introduction."

But everybody accepted the story. Lavinia Thorley—no, Osborne—had never attracted a suitor here where girls were ten a penny, what more natural than that she should accept an invitation to stay with one of her mother's relatives in Killapore, where men were ten a penny. For even into the so-called native states, white men were moving as military or financial advisors, or as bridge builders.

And of course, the invitation coming so suddenly, there was no

time for farewell parties such as usually preceded a departure.
Lavinia simply vanished and even George didn't wonder why she
had not bothered to say goodbye. She'd never behaved as other
people did.

Food was a problem, made a little worse by George in his inno-
cence. Jenny served so much for so many and however Mrs
Thorley and the girls tried to spare—Lavinia must be fed—
George was almost sure to say, "If nobody wants this, I'll eat it."

Mrs Thorley was driven to ask Jenny to cook rather more.

"Ah," Jenny said, "Master George he do eat like a team of
horses, but bless his heart, he's growing."

Since the girls cleared the table anything that chanced to be
left over could be scraped into a bowl and hidden in the chiffonier
until Jenny's whereabouts, and George's, were certain; it would
never do to be caught carrying food towards the attic stairs.

There were times when Mrs Thorley was forced to rely upon
what she called shop food. It was good enough, thousands of people never ate anything else, but she distrusted it as nourishment
for a girl at a time when she needed the very best. She had herself
eaten a good deal of such makeshift stuff when she was carrying
Lavinia and that might account for her poor physique. Almost imperceptibly, Mrs Thorley began to think of the coming baby in a
proper grandmotherly way. It was misbegotten, but it must have
every chance. Poor little thing, it was not to blame. Linked to this
thought came the problem of exercise. Everybody now agreed that
in the early stages a little gentle walking in the fresh air was
beneficial. The only possible time for Lavinia to emerge from the
attic was on Sunday afternoon when Jenny went down to the village and Deborah would take George riding, he on Tom Thumb,
she on Foxy, but with a promise that at some point he should be
allowed to change the saddles and ride the mare. Then it was possible for Lavinia to come down and take a brief airing. But that
meant no week-end visits and that brought a protest form Diana:

"Everard did so enjoy his week-ends. And after all it is not his
fault that we are in this dreadful position."

Caroline could not resist the quip:

"Wouldn't it have simplified everything had he been?"

It took Diana a breath-space to sort that out; then she said:

"Don't be so disgusting!"

The word echoed in Mrs Thorley's mind. For there was a disgusting side to this secret incarceration. A living body had other needs . . .

Like every well-appointed house, Gad's owned a commode which had been housed in The Little Room. It was now upstairs in the attic and Mrs Thorley was obliged to act as a night-soil remover. About this, as about food, she was conscientious and in what had been Jenny's room she kept a bucket, or rather a slop-pail with a lid. Nothing offensive was allowed to stay in the occupied attic for long. Every night, when the house was asleep, she moved softly about carrying her lantern. Water carrier, too, since Lavinia's ewer must be filled. Everybody must *wash*.

And never, for any service, a word of thanks. Lavinia appeared to be entirely oblivious. She seldom spoke; sometimes she lay on her bed, staring at the ceiling; sometimes in her chair, looking into the garden; or she was painting, at the easel, at the table, or on the wall.

She had cut herself entirely and her mother was cut off, too. She dared hardly leave the house. In a moment of the hopelessness she wrote and cancelled all her entries for shows. But the wedding must take place, that triple wedding, planned before all this begun. It sometimes seemed extraordinary to Mrs Thorley to reflect how active and resourceful she had been, so little time ago, and how now there was nothing left but to go round and round, like a blindfolded donkey turning a mill-wheel.

The problem of laundry was solved by Diana. There had opened recently in Baildon an enterprise called the Hand Laundry, most conveniently anonymous. Each new customer paid three-pence down and received a coarse linen bag, stamped with a number. Diana's was 408. This number was then printed in marking ink on ever article sent to be washed. One handed in the bag of soiled stuff, preferably on Monday or Tuesday, and called for it on Thursday or Friday. Nobody there in the steam and heat noticed or cared how the amount of laundry compared with the size of the household as would have been the case with Jenny and the village woman who since Katie's going came up to help with the Gad's washing.

Having seen to the laundry and the shopping for ready-to-eat food, Diana felt that she had done her duty, beyond occasionally asking, rather perfunctorily: How is she? She felt the whole business to be disgusting and degrading, just when the preparations for the wonderful wedding should have been going forward so happily. Caroline was more sympathetic; for her Lavinia had not ceased to exist as a person. She sometimes bought chocolate or fancy cakes—without Di's knowledge—and would then offer to take up the smuggled supper bowl. Alone of the four, she felt how Lavinia must miss all contact with growing things; she'd been so fond of walking in the woods. Caroline sometimes took flowers, too. But she always came down in a state of distress.

"She wouldn't even look, leave alone speak. How terrible it must be to be in such a state of mind. Poor, poor thing!"

She, too, had known despair, the feeling that life was meaningless, that she did not wish to see or speak to anybody, ever again.

On such occasions, Deborah, the kindly one as a rule, showed that she shared Diana's attitude.

"If you must cry for anybody, Caro, cry for Mamma. She is the one to be pitied." Or, "If the sight of her upsets you so much, keep away." Or, "Caro, you're just being sentimental."

Deborah had had what was, literally, an illuminating experience. From the first, when she was certain that Lavinia was mad and bent on self-destruction, she had insisted that Lavinia should have no lamp, no candle. She was quite capable of setting the house on fire. But one evening in April, carrying up the supper bowl in order to spare Mamma one journey, Deborah had found the attic lighted. Lavinia had rearranged things. The finished picture on its easel, had been pulled close to a cleared space on the trestle-table, and on that space, not in sticks, but fixed to the table by their own grease, there were two candles. And they were black. Between them stood a vase containing a posy, wallflowers and a few narcissi. It was, in fact, a travesty of an altar.

For a girl of her time and class, Deborah was, if not perfectly educated, better read than most, for during her last months at school Mrs Hardwicke had given her the run of her library, which had contained many interesting and curious books. She was horrified by what she saw, and half recognised, yet her response was practical. She said:

"Don't you realise that a light in this window can be seen for miles?" She blew out the candles and in the twilight asked:

"Where are the rest? And the matches?"

Lavinia made a little whimpering sound, but that was no answer.

"Then I must search. Sit down in that chair and if you dare move a finger, I'll knock you silly."

Lavinia did not speak. She stood still, and for a moment, in the dusk, her face assumed something of the leering, sneering look of the four-horned, half-human face of the goat in the picture. A battle of wills, of forces, ranged, momentarily, the heavy battalions on Lavinia's side. Deborah, the strong, the logical, practical one, felt something of the slackening of fibre that had made Mrs Thorley almost fall to the bed on that bright March morning. And what came to her rescue was not, oddly enough, her orthodox religion, or anything she had read: it was something remembered from early childhood, when she and Caro had shown every sign of growing up wild, associating with work people and village children. Without thinking she crossed her fingers and said, "Keep away from me, Owd Scrat!"

Lavinia sat down in the chair and Deborah remembered that under the bed was the traditional hiding place. She reached into the shallow space between the chaise-longue and the floor and found several other candles, all black, and a box of matches.

She went down the back stairs, into the garden and flung them all into the moat. She said nothing to anyone, but she spoke with urgency to Mamma.

"There *must* be some place where such people are cared for. It would be expensive, of course, but Mamma, I don't need my legacy. Tim is well-to-do. You must think of yourself. It's bad enough now, you're worn to the bone. And have you *thought* about what it will be like when the . . . the baby comes? We shall be gone. You'll be left with George . . . And you can't tell a baby to keep quiet. Honestly, Mamma, it is an impossible situation and I'm sorry that I ever connived. She must be put away." It sounded terrible, but it must be said.

Mrs Thorley skirted around the main issue.

"Naturally, Deb, I have thought of the future. About George I have already made my decision. We cannot count upon his gaining entry to Biddle's—the examination is *very* competitive. I have applied for a place at Felstead and he will go there at the commencement of the autumn term."

Just what Mamma did not want; George the well-beloved out of driving reach. Poor Mamma! What a bloody, bloody, devilish mess!

"George's going to Felstead may ease things, Mamma, but only for a time. He'll be home for Christmas . . . And there's Jenny. Oh, I know you made this plan on the spur of the moment and we were all shocked out of our senses and agreed. But it isn't feasible. Look, let me go to London. I could ask about there, amongst doctors. Nobody would know me."

"And what of the child? No, Deborah, I must stick to my plan. And you can help me there, as you did about Lavinia's mythical voyage. How soon may we announce her sudden engagement and decision to be married aboard ship?"

"You are the most pig-headed woman. But quite the dearest," Deborah said. "All I hope is that you will never have cause to regret . . ."

Once, on one of those so-carefully-manoeuvred Sunday afternoons, Mrs Thorley had Lavinia in the garden, her hand like a gaoler's on the girl's elbow, and reaching the place where the view across the moat was unblocked, saw two people. Not locals. No country people would trample about in a field of young wheat. She was past being startled, even the knife-edge of apprehension had its limits, but she was angered. She called, in the voice that could carry without shouting, "What do you think you are doing?" She felt the relief which she knew to be idiotic, of letting free the anger that smouldered inside her.

The couple answered her placatingly. They'd come for a drive and let their little dog out for a little run; and he'd run into the field. Even as they spoke, in another part of the field a pheasant whirred into the air and the woman cried, "There he is! Charlee! Charleeeee!" Trampling more wheat they both ran towards the scene of the disturbance. Mrs Thorley found herself shaking; a tremor that began in the marrow of her bones and spread outwards. It just didn't do, she thought, to give way to anger. For a moment her hold on Lavinia was so shaky that if, as Deb said, she would try again, she could not have controlled her. So she hustled her in, away from the sunny, cuckoo-loud out-of-doors and back into prison. Then to make up for it, cooked bacon and eggs and carried the dish up, still almost sizzling.

A good hour later Deborah and George came in from their ride and George sniffed the air, looking puzzled.

"Who's been having fried bacon in the middle of the afternoon?"

"Nobody!" Deb sounded quite snappy. "It's simply your imagination. You think of nothing but food."

Everybody was short-tempered these days. It was the wedding, George supposed. Why marry if it made you so edgy? He gave Deb a reproachful look and she thought: It's not his fault!

"If you're really hungry, I'll cook you some. With eggs?"

Ships bound for India could stop briefly at the Canary Islands to take on fresh fruit and vegetables. And from there passengers could send letters; and the sooner Lavinia's mythical romance began, the sooner it could end. The news must be broken, with simulated surprise and pleasure.

Mrs Spicer, one of the first to be informed, said:

"Oh, but my dear; I hope she has not made a rash choice. She is so very *young*."

"In fact a mere three months younger than Caroline."

"Of course, but the difference always *seemed* much greater. Did you say his name was Harrington? Now, oddly enough it was a Mr Harrington who wrote to inform us of Everard's parents' death. Or it could have been Harrison. I don't know about you, Isabel, but I am growing forgetful. Is this Mr Harrington in the mission field?"

"No." It had been decided, in a family conclave, which, Caroline thought, would have been comic had it not been so serious, that Mr Harrington must not belong to any network which in India linked people over unimaginable spaces. He must not be employed by the East India Company, either in a military or civil capacity; he must not be a missionary or a doctor or an engineer. It was, of course, Deborah who came up with the word anthropologist.

Mrs Spicer accepted Mr Harrington's profession without question, the mention of Caroline Thorley, to be married on the third Saturday of June, caused her mind to go off at a tangent. Wedding presents. Absolute bugbears to a woman of position and not much money. With the humble it was fairly easy; when, for instance Willy Snell, who worked at Gad's, had married Katie Snell, who also worked there, and Arthur had sighed and said that there should be law against in-breeding, Mrs Spicer had been able to buy from the pedlar with a donkey cart a tea-pot, shaped like a beehive, and cheap at sixpence-halfpenny. It would never be used for teamaking, it would be an ornament, a bit of colour in a drab home. But for the Gad's Hall girls more was needed and Mrs Spicer was plying her needle, embroidering pillow-cases for Deborah and Caroline. To Diana and Everard, since Everard was related, Mrs Spicer proposed to give a different present, six silver teaspoons in a case, given her when she married, but seldom used because what domestic help Mrs Spicer could afford was always hasty and heavy-handed and the spoon handles were of filigree, delicate as lace.

Well, Mrs Thorley thought, driving home after a cursory look in on the herd, and Joe Snell, disappointed over the cancellation of the shows, disappointed in fact with Mrs Thorley, who had seemed so different, and was now showing herself to be, after all, just a female, so wrapped up with the coming wedding as to have no time or thought to give to real business—I've told Mrs Spicer and within twenty-four hours everyone will know. As good as hiring the Town Crier.

Diana told Everard. To him the word anthropologist had meaning. It implied an independent income, the most enviable thing in the world. Foot-free in India! Everard's memories of that country were distorted, glamourised. He could hardly remember his parents, but he still had a clear mental vision of his ayah, a silver ring through one nostril, who had spoiled him inordinately. Of the uglier side of life in India he had seen nothing. He knew better now, of course; his godfather had been free with his reminiscences, blind beggars who looked as though their eyes were filled with milk, lepers with no noses and only stumps of fingers, diseases, such as the cholera which killed Everard's parents—and countless, literally countless, nameless other people. Mr Everard, safe with his fortune in Buckinghamshire, had no illusions about the country in which he had made his fortune. "It's the same with West Africa, my boy; there's a jingle, but with truth in it—Beware, beware the Bight of Benin; Few come out, though many go in—and India is boiling up for something. I may not live to see it, I hope I don't, but there's a bloody bloodbath pending."

Nonetheless, Everard had cherished memories of his childhood fairyland and envied Mr Harrington, whoever he might be.

Of Lavinia he had only the faintest recollection. She had never seemed to be part of the family.

Edward was more concerned. When Caroline told him he said:

"She always seemed so immature. Let's hope she hasn't fallen into the hands of some crapulous old man. They have a weakness for young girls."

"Crapulous? Edward, what does that mean?"

"Drunk, darling. Just not temporarily but as a way of life."

He realised that as usual he had said the wrong thing. And been stupid. Except that he himself had always found Lavinia unattractive, there was absolutely no reason why a Mr Harrington —perhaps young and handsome—shouldn't have fallen in love with her. And now he'd gone and put a clumsy foot wrong again and made Caroline serious. He hastened to make amends.

"I have had an idea, Caro. My wall forms the end of the cul-de-sac. If I made a gateway in that bit of wall, you and Diana would be practically next door neighbours. She wouldn't have to go round the church in order to use my stable, and if, say, I knew I had to be away at night, you could slip across to Di's, or she could slip across to you."

So very kind, well-meaning and *dull*. If I had to be away at night . . . Freddy would never have given a contingency a second's thought. He'd have said: We're off to London, Paris, Timbuctoo . . . We!

It could never happen now, and Caroline had made her bargain. Behind her stretched a long line of Thorleys who had made hard bargains, shrewd ones, but never a cheating one. So Caroline mustered a smile and said that Edward's thought about a gateway in the wall was wonderful and so kind.

Edward, much encouraged, said, "And perhaps we should begin to think about our honeymoon. Where would you like to go?"

"Oh, London, of course," Caroline said. Just for once Edward had surprised her. The honeymoon, in the sense of a holiday, of going away to stay somewhere, was not yet common practice among ordinary people.

"London it shall be," Edward said, happy to be able to indulge her.

Tim Bridges, told of Lavinia's engagement, was momentarily at a loss. Lavinia? Lavinia? If he had ever seen her she had made no impression upon him.

"My half-sister," Deborah said, well aware that last year at this time she would have said: My sister.

"Oh yes. A bit sudden, but we know how sudden such things can be, don't we? I hope she'll be happy."

Dear Tim! If you only knew the truth.

For the first time in his life, Timothy Bridges was concerned about what to wear. He'd always been, in his own opinion and in the eye of all beholders, well dressed. His breeches were made for him by a man whose name was known far beyond the bounds of Norfolk; so were his tweed jackets. He had two dark suits for formal wear, Sunday clothes. All a man could want. They'd last a lifetime, unless he grew fat, which was unlikely, leading the life he did. No Methodist went in for what Tim called fancy dress; and if Tim had been allowed to marry in his own time, and in the place of his choice, one of his dark suits and his good real beaver hat would have been adequate. But he, like Everard, felt that Mrs Thorley had imposed her will upon him. He was to stand at the altar with Everard Spicer and Edward Taylor, both men whose professions demanded what was known as a frock coat; dead black, worn with striped, or lighter-coloured trousers and a hat at least five inches higher than Tim's good beaver.

Expense did not come into it. Tim could afford whatever he wanted, but to be dressed up like that, just for one day, went somehow against his principles. On the other hand he did not want to let Deborah down. So now, quickly dismissing Lavinia from his mind, he tested his ground.

"You're all going to be dressed alike, eh?"

"Not really. That is where Mamma is so thoughtful. We all, always, had the same clothes, but different. That sounds a contradiction, doesn't it? But it is true. All our wedding dresses are made from the same roll of white satin, but they are different. And she was marvellous about her wedding veil. She'd kept it all those years and then cut it so that we should each have a piece."

Abruptly Deborah remembered how Mamma had said that if she had only one apple she would cut into fair quarters. She had cut her delicate lace veil into thirds, because Lavinia . . . Oh dear!

In the blunt way which Mrs Thorley considered uncouth, Tim said:

"What do you want me to wear?"

If she had been explicit, the element of resistance in him would have been fortified, but Deborah said, at once understanding and indifferent:

"Oh. Frock coat and topper? Don't bother. It's only for an hour, anyway."

That decided him. And while Deborah was thinking about the hour—God send it would not be longer—an hour while the house and the secret would be left unguarded, and how could Mamma possibly manage when that hour's ceremony had dispersed them and left her single-handed, was thinking that there actually was Biblical justification for his decision to conform; the person not wearing a wedding garment had not been made welcome.

There was another mention of a wedding, the one at which Our Lord had turned water into wine. Total abstainers like himself argued away that discrepancy by saying that times were different then; it was *because* of the evils of the present days, the gin-palaces which were centres of immorality and the public houses from which men reeled home to their starving wives and children, that a Christian must try to set an example by eschewing alcohol altogether. Tim's mother had had a first-hand story of a young man, the rich inheritor of a brewery and a chain of public houses, who had been so shocked by the sight of poor ragged women and children waiting outside one of his public houses, hoping that the bread-winner would emerge with just enough left to buy a loaf, that he had closed—not sold—all his businesses, given away all of what he regarded as tainted money and gone to work in a factory that made buttons. Not surprisingly such virtue had been re-warded. His employer's only child, a daughter, had fallen in love with him, he'd discovered some new way of speeding up the man-ufacture of buttons and ended by becoming rich again. "As it says in the Good Book," Tim's mother had pointed out, "'I have been young and now I am old, but I have never seen the righteous forsaken, nor their seed begging bread.'"

Such stories and homilies had made a great impression upon the boy's mind; an impression deep enough to resist the possible erosion of a reasonably good education—three years at Baildon Grammar School, where he had borne some teasing—weak ale was still then served for breakfast, being cheaper than tea or coffee, and occasionally a little mild persecution. The teasing he had suffered with that deliberate, cultivated indifference which had hardened into stolidity; the persecution he had resisted with his fists. Who is on the Lord's side? Smite the enemy hip and thigh! That obstinate rockiness of character which Mrs Thorley had recognised, without approval, had begun early.

Tim did not approve of Mrs Thorley. She was unwomanly, and she was worldly. And she had foisted this kind of wedding upon him. Not without a certain complacency, he noticed that she was not doing very well. No cattle on show this year! To Timothy Bridges, who exhibited his great amber-coloured horses every year and studied all show catalogues carefully, the omission of any mention of the Gad's animals was eloquent. Various explanations. She hadn't been able to maintain the standard—and what woman could? Or there might be some sickness in the herd. Tim was not very well informed about bovine diseases—Foxton kept only two cows to supply the needs of the house; but he knew that there was something called foot-and-mouth, a form of consumption and a bovine typhus. Any owner of any herd in which a symptom of such diseases had shown did well to keep out of the public eye. For the first disease there was a cure, slow, not completely certain, and Tim, for all his dislike of Mrs Thorley, who had delayed his marriage by a good eight months, was conscientious, willing to do his duty by his neighbour worldly though she might be. So he broke off the discussion about the wedding and the wedding garments by saying with characteristic lack of preliminaries:

"If it's foot-and-mouth, it isn't lethal. Tar on the feet, sulphur and treacle in the mouth can cure seven out of ten."

For a second even Deborah's nimble mind was at a loss. Then she caught up and said:

"Oh, the herd! All in rumbustious health. Mamma withdrew from all the shows this year because she had other things to think of."

"The wedding?" Typical of a woman, frivolling about in business!

"Yes," Deborah said. She was an unwilling liar and it hurt particularly to lie to Tim, who, she was sure, had never told a lie in his life, and who was so kind and anxious to be helpful—as his last remarks showed.

"Dear George, you are too young."

"And that is where you make your mistake, Mamma. Before I spoke I asked Mr Spicer and he said there were no age limits, provided, of course, that the giver-away could stand up and say I do, when he says who gives this woman? And Mr Spicer agreed with me, I am the girls' nearest male relative."

In the case of Deborah and Caroline this was literally true. Their father had been an only son, and so had his father been, so they had no uncles, no cousins. Away up in Westmorland there was—unless he had died—a man who was Mrs Thorley's brother and therefore Diana's uncle. There were cousins, too. But Mrs Thorley had severed herself from her family forever when her brother—fresh come to his inheritance—had refused absolutely to spare a mere two hundred pounds to save Stephen from the threat of gaol for debt.

She had been considering asking Mr Walford to give the brides away but George had forestalled her.

"Well, it is most unusual, but if you are sure that Mr Spicer agrees . . ."

"He did, Mamma. You can ask him yourself, if you can't believe me."

In his own way, George was clever with words, *don't believe* would have implied a passive inability, *can't believe* implied wilful disbelief.

"Of course I believe you, darling. You shall give your sisters away."

She had an irrelevant thought: George would take up less space than Mr Walford, who, since his wife's death, had grown stout. And in a church such as that at Stonham St Peter's space was extremely limited. It wore its history in its structure.

When, comparatively late, the Angles in the area had been converted, they had built a church, somewhat smaller than a hall in which people ate and slept and entertained or a barn in which stuff was stored. Then the Normans had come, replacing wood and thatch with stone, but although they had enlarged the church slightly much of the extra space had been occupied by the solid rounded pillars, so it was still a very small church. And never, Mrs Thorley thought, had skirts been wider than they were this year. A slender, nimble giver-away was all to the good.

Not without some difference of opinion, it had been decided to dispense with bridesmaids.

When the triple marriage had first been suggested all the girls had been pleased; Diana and Deborah because they were in love and wanted to be married, Caroline because to be married so soon after what had been perilously close to a jilting would show Them —Freddy and all the old cats who had criticised her behaviour. However as the great day came nearer, some doubts had crept in. Diana felt that a girl's wedding day should be *her* day and hers alone. She would have preferred to go to the altar in solitary glory, attended by her four best friends. And she would willingly have waited another year. Though she was not markedly percipient, she could hardly fail to notice how often, over quite small things, Everard drew attention to the fact that financially he had been taken unawares. He said things like, "Darling, I have saved so little. I *had* hoped that by next year . . ." When he said such things, Diana could always say that, thanks to dear Papa, she would have five hundred pounds.

Deborah only regretted the triple ceremony because she knew that Mr Spicer would make the most of it. He was inclined to be High Church but he was also inclined to be lazy, and if she and Tim had had a simple, quiet wedding, he would have been unlikely to have taken much trouble over the things which would certainly affront Tim's nonconformist taste. As it was, she suspected—rightly—that Mr Spicer would rise to the occasion and go digging about, or making his wife dig about amongst the mothballs. Deborah was as willing to dispense with bridesmaids—just one more bit of show—as Diana was anxious to have them. And when the matter was under discussion, Caroline discovered, with a jolt of surprise, that she had no *best* girl friends. At any gathering she'd always been surrounded by a laughing crowd, but the girls were there only because the young men were. Truth must be faced.

The best-man problem had been settled neatly—largely due to Edward's good nature. Everard had chosen, for reasons of policy, James Gordon to stand by him and produce the ring at the right moment. Edward had intended to ask the new young doctor at the hospital to perform the same office for him; and that left Tim odd man out. All his close friends were Methodists and would think he had gone off his head, dressed up like a shop-walker and being married in such style, to say nothing of the reception afterwards with all the spirituous liquors! He said he reckoned he could manage to look after his own ring. Then Edward said, "Why not let James serve for all?"

Everard, in his secret heart had hoped that the marriage might bring a partnership as a wedding present. Old Gordon was not stupid, he must realise that as a married man, and a householder, Everard would need more than his present meagre salary. He was marrying a girl of whom Mr Gordon surely approved, the daughter of a friend. Not that anyone could possibly disapprove of Diana. Nor, indeed, could anyone look at her and imagine her as a poor man's wife. No word was said on the subject, however; Mr and Mrs Gordon expressed their goodwill in a pair of majolica vases of supreme ugliness, and James contributed a handsome carving set with handles of deers' antlers.

Diana and Caroline, helped by Mrs Spicer, decorated the church with lilies and roses and mock-orange. Mrs Thorley and Deborah were to see to the flowers in the house, but Deborah gave most of her attention to something which, though flowery in appearance when completed, had a utilitarian purpose. Today, for the first time since Lavinia disappeared into the attic, the house would be unguarded and it would be full of people. There were the village women who had come up to help Jenny, and there would be the guests. Deborah had never found a use for the iron stakes she had bought to lighten the donkey's load; now they served perfectly. She wedged three of them through the bannisters at the foot of the attic stairs, and then twined them with green stuff and flowers, choosing, as far as possible, plants of a prickly kind, wild roses, blackberry brambles in full flower, heads of the decorative thistle which many people grew for winter decoration.

Everybody agreed that it was a most wonderful wedding. A good many female guests shed a few tears, daintily dabbled away with lace-edged handkerchiefs. Mrs Spicer wept for Arthur. In full regalia, and for once exerting himself, he looked and sounded so impressive that he should have been a Bishop—and now it was too late. Mrs Gordon wept because James showed no sign of settling down and giving her grandchildren. Miss Riley's tears were self-pitying. Unappreciated, unwooed, she had withered on the bough—and now it was too late. Some people cried because it was the correct thing to do at weddings.

Tim Bridges had always suspected that there would be some-

thing more like a theatrical performance—not that he had ever
seen one—than a simple ceremony; in his mind he called it a lot
of monkey business. At the crucial moment Mr Spicer enfolded
the hands that were to be joined in the end of his stole.

Outside the church there was a demonstration of what Everard
had once called feudalism. Children throwing rose petals for the
brides and their men to walk upon. Then, up at the house, a
proper wedding feast, with the last of George Thorley's champagne, a wine which did not keep indefinitely. And, of course, the
interesting inspection of the presents, each guest looking out for
his own and thinking how much better it looked than any other.

It was a wonderful wedding.

Edward Taylor made the first move towards breaking up the
merry party. He and Caroline had a train to catch. Tim was anxious to be away, too. A time for goodbyes, though each girl
avoided the finality of the word.

Diana said, "I shall come, twice a week, Mamma. Caroline,
too."

Caroline said, "We shall be away only four days, Mamma."

Deborah said, "I hate leaving you . . . But I'll come at least
once a week. I promise. That barrier I put up, Mamma, I
unhitched it and pushed it halfway down the kitchen stairs. Willy
can remove it tomorrow." It was typical of Deborah to think of
such a practical thing!

The peculiar silence that overtakes places lately fully occupied
and then left, deserted or underoccupied, a ringing hollowness
with something sinister about it, settled down on Gad's.

But at least the girls were all now reasonably safe, whatever
happened. But what could happen? The Lavinia of the story was
already married, possibly pregnant. Sudden widowhood might well
precipitate a birth. But juggle as one might there were still
months to go. And a lot of guess-work to do. Lavinia had been as
dumb about *when* as she had been about *who?*

Mrs Thorley could only judge by size. By this rough reckoning
she thought it might be August.

"Everybody said I did well." George's voice held a slight challenge.

"Darling, you did magnificently. Nobody could have done better. If I have neglected to say so, it was because I was so busy."

"I know," George said. "It was lovely, but I do feel a bit tired."

I must not tire. Nor feel deserted. I have my duty to do, and my promise to keep.

A good stiff whisky, and another and she was ready for action again.

One of the things about which Lavinia was difficult was over the business of taking a proper wash. To get the hip-bath up those stairs was palpably impossible, but as Mrs Thorley knew from her times of privation, it was quite possible to keep clean with a wash-bowl. Lavinia would dabble her hands, run the wash-cloth over her face and seemed to think that that sufficed. At first Mrs Thorley had thought that her reluctance to strip and have a proper wash was due to modesty, belated and ill-placed. So she would put the clean underclothes on the bed, the can of water by the little stand and say, "Have a good wash, Lavinia," and then go away, sometimes no farther than the landing. That Lavinia had not obeyed her—though the water had been transferred from can to slop-pail, was proved by the cake of soap lasting so long, and presently by a kind of odour—nothing to do with the commode about which Mrs Thorley was so scrupulous. Nothing to do with ordinary, healthy perspiration, either; but then how could it be? The poor girl never did anything to provoke sweat. But despite the clean clothes, the regular changing of bed-linen there was in this attic a curious scent, difficult to define, half sweetish, half rotten. Having sought any other source, some bit of food overlooked, or vase of flowers not removed in time—stocks, so sweet in themselves, were particularly offensive—Mrs Thorley decided that the scent emanated from Lavinia, and tonight—oh, the irony of it—she had a powerful bribe: a bowl of leftovers from the wedding feast.

Of that she had not counted the cost, for it was obvious that in a way she was getting off lightly; one wedding instead of three. Tonight Lavinia's evening meal consisted of several dainties, and a slice of rich fruit cake from which Mrs Thorley had thoughtfully removed the white icing. Lavinia appeared to have retreated into herself, but one never knew.

At first she had been indifferent to food, then she had shown the precarious appetite said to be a sign of mental illness; finally she had become avid and tonight Mrs Thorley had no scruples about showing her the food and saying firmly, "But you must strip and have a thorough wash first. And I shall see that you do . . ."

*

Edward thoroughly enjoyed his short honeymoon and saw nothing ominous in the question which Caroline asked on the second day:

"Edward, do you know no-one in London?"

"No. I didn't train here, you know, Sweetie; I'm an Edinburgh man."

And if he had had a hundred contemporaries and acquaintances he would not have wished to make contact with them. He had attained his heart's desire: Caroline, all to himself. He had unaccustomed leisure and money to spend. The hotel he had chosen, just off the Haymarket, was extremely comfortable, even luxurious; for two plays and one concert he had obtained the very best seats. He could afford to hire a hackney cab to jog round so that Caroline could see the sights of London; they went by river to Hampton Court and lunched under the apple trees in the garden of the ancient Mitre Inn.

Most girls would have found it an idyllic honeymoon, especially as Edward as a lover was gentle and undemanding and not altogether inexperienced. He was easily satisfied because, despite his medical knowledge, he clung to the delusion that nice girls were different. In Edinburgh he'd had a hired woman from time to time and had been left with the idea that unless you had some feeling for the woman in the bed the whole thing had no more significance than an evacuation of the bowel. Now he had his beloved Caroline and his feeling was so intense that it was enough for two.

For Caroline the four days were days of unmitigated boredom. Nothing but Edward, day and night, night and day. His dullness, his literal-mindedness laid a dead hand on every outing, every entertainment. The comedy he had chosen was innocuous, its humour largely dependent upon the misunderstandings which resulted from one character being deaf. It amused Caroline, but Edward said, "Why should deafness strike everybody so funny? Nobody would laugh because a blind man missed his way, would they?" Caroline thought: You should have married Deborah! She would enjoy such talk. I don't.

And alongside the boredom, in fact contributing to it, was the anonymity. Caroline, that popular girl, had never joined any company and not been greeted by smiles, waves of the hand. Here nobody noticed her. Her talent for amusing people, the light quip, the eloquent grimace, the mocking imitation, could not be used with only Edward for audience. Nobody even gave her a glance of disapproval—in London there were dresses far more décolleté than any she owned. She simply could not wait to get back to Baildon, even it meant the dullest committee.

They were due to go back by the morning train, but when Caroline said, "I am quite looking forward to going home," Edward, eager to please, said, "Would you like to go this evening?" He looked at his watch. "We could just about make it."

"Well, possibly Miss Humberstone may be feeling lonely."

Miss Humberstone was the treasure for whom Edward had been searching ever since his father had taken Hattie away. He was genuinely thankful that this elusive quarry—a competent cook-housekeeper—had been run to earth before his marriage, so that Caroline would have a cushioned life.

Miss Humberstone was one of that all-too-numerous tribe to which Mrs Thorley had herself once belonged, a distressed gentlewoman. She could have become a governess, but her spelling was highly idiosyncratic, her grasp on arithmetic poor; also she could not play the piano, and had forgotten any French she ever knew. She was further handicapped by the fact that she owned a few pieces of furniture and two cats to which she clung obstinately. She could cook and claimed to have some nursing experience, having done everything for her father until he died. Edward had heard of her through a patient who knew somebody who knew somebody who knew Miss Humberstone.

With two casual helpers, poor women from Scurvy Lane, one to do the laundry, one for cleaning, Miss Humberstone managed very well, and on her knees, every night, thanked God for bringing her to such a haven. She'd seen Caroline and knew that she was no threat—a butterfly creature.

Mrs Thorley, when she first took on her mixed and potentially difficult family, had tried to insist upon thought for others as a rule of life. So to poor Di, who had no honeymoon, Caroline did not elaborate upon the pleasures of hers.

"London was so hot, Di. And dusty and noisy. I'm truly glad to be home."

For the first time since he had encountered her, Everard approved of his sister-in-law. Had she come back exuberant, he would have loathed her. Such a contrast! With an extraordinary lack of consideration, Mr Gordan had not even offered Everard a day off; a day which added to the Saturday half day and all Sunday, would have made a long week-end at Bywater a feasibility—though very expensive. In fact June was the month least likely to bring Everard any leisure since James was playing cricket most of the time.

"You have made it pretty," Caroline said, glancing around the sitting room, small in size, but furnished in the latest style, mitigated slightly by Diana's innate good taste. The majolica vases, for instance, were not on display; but they were handy. When Mrs Gordon came to tea, or the whole family came to dinner, they would occupy the place of honour on the mantelshelf.

Neither Diana nor Everard knew that Caroline envied them and was thinking how happy she would have been in a house far smaller than this, in a tent, if only . . . No use thinking about it; think of something else.

"Have you been back to Gad's?"

"No. I was waiting for you and I didn't expect to see you until tomorrow."

"Shall we go tomorrow."

"We could. I have a tea-party in the afternoon, but Mrs Wedgewood comes in the morning."

Mrs Wedgewood was not quite the treasure that Miss Humberstone was, but Diana realised that she had been very fortunate to obtain even her limited services. Mrs Wedgewood had started her working life at the Mount, Lord Norton's big house. There she had learned to cook superbly. She'd married the estate carpenter, an ambitious man, and a Radical. He'd set up on his own and was finding things a bit hard. He had no objection to his wife earning a bit so long as it did not interfere with his comfort. On both market days, Wednesday and Saturday, she went to help at The Hawk in Hand; she and her skills were on call for balls, weddings dealt with by the catering firm; very occasionally she went back, in an emergency, to the Mount. But she had some spare time, and a little job in Friars' Lane, only just round the corner from the woodyard, suited her well. So well that she was happy to make, alongside the lunch, three days a week, dishes which young Mrs Spicer had merely to heat up, for supper on this day, or lunch the next.

The pony was fresh and thought, so far as he was capable of thought, that he was headed for home. So he rattled along at a good pace.

"I wonder has Deborah been," Diana said.

"She said once a week—and it is not a week yet."

"She may even be here today."

Despite their diverse characters, Diana and Deborah had paired off, and Diana thought that it might be *just* possible to ask Deborah, lightly, whether she liked being married. Deborah, so quick to understand, would know what the question meant. Nothing to do with being Mrs or proudly wearing a broad gold wedding ring, and ruling one's own household. There was another side to marriage and Diana loathed it. She loved Everard dearly, would have followed him round the world, and she knew, in theory, what marriage meant. But she'd deliberately looked away, just as she had looked away from cooking and making ends meet. The reality had simply been . . . messy, one of the most condemnatory words in her rather limited vocabulary. It had not been in accordance with the pretty night-dress—the finest cambric with tiny tucks and lace on its collar and cuffs, or with her hair, brushed smooth and made into two shining plaits, each tied with white ribbon, or with the fresh bed-linen, or indeed anything in the dainty bedroom. Diana had hated it, and then wondered if she were alone in this feeling or was it shared by all the married women in the world?

It was not a subject to discuss with Caro, who never took anything seriously, but she could have asked Deb.

With Caro one was always safe on the question of parties. Mannerly people made calls upon brides and issued invitations. Then hospitality must be returned.

"You have no need to worry," Diana said, a tinge of acid in her voice, "but I'm in rather an awkward position. Even in summer one can hardly serve a totally cold meal and nobody can play hostess *and* cook at the same time."

Caroline spared a thought for life as-it-might-have-been. Married to Freddy. A lot of happy people sitting about—on the floor if necessary—eating sausage rolls or wedges of pork pie and drinking beer if wine could not be afforded. She put the thought aside.

"Why shouldn't we give a *combined* party, Di? I have space enough. We know *almost* the same people and I'm sure our dining table could take twenty."

For the rest of the journey they discussed, happily, the form the party should take.

Deborah was not there, nor had she been. Tim regarded Deborah as a brand rescued from the burning and he had no intention of allowing her to go back. He sounded reasonable and kindly.

Deborah said, "I have a few things to fetch, Tim. Some books and sheets of music."

"There are good shops in Thetford. Buy what you want, my dear."

Deborah said, "But I promised. Mamma must be lonely, losing all three of us at once."

"She still has George. And the two girls within easy reach."

Deborah was in no state to argue against him, for if Diana had been able to ask her question: How do you like being married? Deb's answer would have surprised. Bliss undreamed of. Two healthy, untried bodies, untroubled by any physical or mental reserve, had come together and attained a shattering climax.

"No," Mrs Thorley said. "Deborah hasn't been, but I had a letter from her yesterday."

A very sensible letter, too, and one that proved that Deborah, within so short a time of her wedding, had spared some thought for Mamma. "George will now have nothing to do on Sunday afternoon. Could you change Jenny's half day and let her have Saturday instead; then George could go shopping in Baildon, or even to a matinée at the theatre. L could then have her little walk."

It was matter of indifference to Deborah whether Lavinia had a walk or not, but it was one of things Mamma worried about.

"Unfortunately, Jenny did not take kindly to the idea," Mrs Thorley said. "I quite see why. Sunday is the only day when everyone is free. I then suggested that she should have Saturday *and* Sunday, and that brought up the question of how much walking Jenny's legs could be expected to do."

"I could always have George for a week-end," Caroline said. She could foresee week-ends of such tedium that even a young brother's presence would be a relief. Edward did not have a surgery on Saturday evening, and as he once told her, very few people fell ill on Sunday—they waited until Monday when a week's work loomed ahead and a *bona fide* excuse, what they called a sustifcut, signed by Edward, would entitle them to a few shillings from one of the Friendly Societies, or from a pub club.

Diana wished that she could make the same offer, but it would entail making another bed, emptying more slops, washing more dishes. And then there was the food! George was a prodigious eater.

"I suppose it is not having seen her for five days in a row," Caroline said as they drove back to Baildon, "but I thought Mamma had changed. So much more white in her hair and her face looked thin, yet puffy at the same time."

"My hair is so like hers. I hope mine doesn't go so soon. Of course, it's this ghastly worry . . . Deb had the right idea, you know. She should have been put away, from the start. We should have insisted."

Diana thought of bag 408 wedged into the back of the little carriage alongside produce from Gad's, the last asparagus, the first new potatoes, eggs.

"It will be worse, after August or whenever it is," she said gloomily. "Babies make a lot of washing, too—things that can't wait for a week."

That was another aspect of marriage from which she had averted her thoughts. Of course everybody wanted a baby, and she was no exception; but until this moment she had thought of a baby as a pretty, living doll, ignoring the messy part. And even now she skirted it, thinking that by the time she had a baby, Everard would surely be better off. He might, at the moment, compare unfavourably, from the financial angle, with Edward Taylor and Tim Bridges, but he would achieve heights to which neither of them could aspire. She hoped very much that what she thought of as the messy side of marriage would not result, too soon, in an even messier baby.

Think of something else. Talk about the proposed party. Whom to invite; what to wear.

Just across the border, Foxton was preparing for an annual event called a Camp Meeting. *Real* Methodism had begun in a field because John Wesley, the founder of the movement, and whose intention was not to break with the Church of England but to reform it from within, had been barred from all orthodox pulpits. As a memorial to that open air meeting, Camp Meetings had been instituted. They took place after the hay was in and harvest not yet begun.

"Many of them travel miles, and sleep out," Tim explained to Deborah, who knew nothing about such gatherings. "And I always give them a good tea."

"Oh, I know the kind of thing, Tim. Food without plates."

Emma, at first distrustful of the frills and furebelows, and then dubious because the young Missus had taken more notice of the horses and outside things than of those inside the house, was totally won over when Deborah rolled up her sleeves and set to work.

"Our cook, Jenny, taught me a trick with pastry, Emma. Not the plain wooden rolling pin, a bottle filled with the coldest water you can get."

Willing to learn, too, Emma noted with satisfaction as she in turn showed Deborah a trick or two, mainly concerned with making lemonade a nutritive as well as a thirst quencher. One version which contained an oatmeal mash, just on the ferment, and a quantity of yeast, struck Deborah as not too far removed from being alcoholic, but she was wise enough to say nothing, and to herself Emma said: She'll do! and began to prepare herself for partial retirement. She had no intention of leaving Foxton, having nowhere to go, but she'd ease off gradually, leaving things in Deborah's competent hands. She'd be here and ready and willing to help with the baby which she hoped would arrive within a year.

At Gad's, though each day might seem endless, time slipped away. Furtively Mrs Thorley prepared some baby clothes. Of George's layette upon which she had lavished much time and care, only a few things remained, preserved through a mixture of sentiment and the thrift which hard times had inculcated—anything might be useful, someday. But she had kept only articles impervious to moth and now must make woollen vests and flannel binders, and diapers.

Diana and Caroline were very good; they did all the necessary shopping and came, as promised, twice a week and Caroline's offer to have George any week-end, or indeed any time, still held. It was George himself who rebelled against it. Caro had always been his favourite and his first week-end in Baildon, which included an evening visit to the theatre, had been enjoyable, the second had been very boring or something rather worse. The Friends of the Hospital had spent some money on providing little treats in the way of toys and rag books—washable—for sick children and Edward, in all innocence and goodwill, had thought it would be appropriate for a child, George, to make the presentations.

George was horrified by what he saw. It was his first encounter with that side of life. In Stonham St Paul's there was an old soldier who stumped about on a wooden leg, and always at the corner between Baildon Market and the High Street there was a blind beggar—part of the scenery. But to see children, most of them younger than himself, grey-faced, jaundice-faced, crippled or maimed, splintered, bandaged, made him feel sick. And helped to shape his attitude towards life. Afterwards he said to Caro:

"We can't help these horrible things, can we? It's not our fault, is it, Caro? And making ourselves miserable doesn't do them any good, does it?"

"No. Being miserable does nobody any good," Caroline said, and then, only then, George realised that Caro understood misery, too. She had not changed colour or been crippled or lost a limb but she had changed.

And really, Mrs Thorley reflected when George refused to spend another week-end in Baildon, it did not matter much, for he was bound for a longer stay, in another place; he was going to stay, with Deborah, at Foxton.

Tim had agreed readily to the suggestion. He regarded his young brother-in-law as spoilt, cheeky and precocious. A stay, over harvest-time, in a God-fearing household, would do him a power of good. Himself born and bred to what he regarded as the one and only faith, Tim was sufficiently aware of the fact that potential recruits were caught young.

"Of course," he said, "he can come and be welcome. Let's see, now . . . I'm free on Tuesday. We'll drive over and fetch him."

It was not the visit that Deborah had intended, but better than nothing. And to be honest nothing was all that she had been able to offer as a dullish, wettish July sped away and August came looming up. Mamma had said that she thought August . . . And if only Deborah could have gone, just for one day, on her own, she could, she felt, have done so much to help; but every attempt she had made to get to Gad's on her own had been neatly countered. So neatly that even Deborah had not seen the motive behind it.

And now, when at last she was back here at Gad's, she had hardly a moment with Mamma alone. Just time enough to notice, as Caro had done, that Mamma looked terrible. Just time enough to exchange a few hasty words; most of them used by Mamma, explaining how she was getting rid of Jenny.

"She is going to stay with Diana. I must admit that I never thought of it, but Jenny has never had a holiday in her life. It sounds incredible but she has never been in Baildon. Now she can go and have the time of her life. Even the Lammas Fair . . ."

"And you will be completely alone?"

"Yes, my dear. That is how it must be. How I wanted it to be. Not knowing *when* makes everything more difficult; but it must be soon . . . And with George going back with you today, and Jenny going with Diana tomorrow, things will be so much eased. I can manage now."

"I wish to God," Deborah said, and checked herself. It would be completely dishonest to say that she wished herself unmarried. But she did wish, vehemently, that she were free to come and go, to stand by Mamma, to help. "I wish I could be of more use."

"My dear, in taking George off my hands you are being the greatest possible help. Don't look so worried. I know exactly what to do."

Now she was completely alone in the house and could do what she must. Drag up a mattress and a pillow; two lamps, one to be lighted, one in reserve. Stoke up the stove so that water in its side boiler was always hot. Towels, scissors, fine white twine, all in neat order. And of course the whisky, now a necessity. Without it she could not sleep at all, and even with its aid, slept lightly, alert to the slightest sound. And then in the morning, only a good stiff whisky made her able to face the day, go shakily down to open the back door so that Willy could put milk from Park, or bread on the kitchen table.

She was never, she thought, drunk; but she had moments of hopefulness. Lavinia, once the child was born, *might* return to sanity. She was very young and the dumb madness was possibly the result of her condition.

"I practically stole it," Caroline said, holding out what had been a scent bottle. "Some poor woman had a . . . a very difficult confinement and Edward had to . . . to help her. He gave her some of this to ease the pain of it. So I thought . . . I hope you won't need it."

"So do I, most devoutly. It was very thoughtful of you, Caro."

August came in with sweltering heat and the attic floor, close under the tiles, was very hot, though Mrs Thorley did her best to mitigate it. Lavinia's half-casement was open, and by night so was her door, with the mattress placed just outside it. The window in the other attic had never been replaced, the door there stood wide, as did the door and window of the apple room. The ghost of old apple scents was sometimes perceptible on the landing but it was overriden by that mysterious, corrupt odour from the occupied room, though it and everything in it was as clean as human hands could make it.

Each night Mrs Thorley undressed as far as her corsets which she loosened slightly but did not remove for she would need to be active and corsets gave some support. She dared not drink enough whisky to ensure a sound sleep but she took small quantities steadily. She would lie on the borderline and review what she had done in order that life should seem ordinary.

Harvest buns, for example. Hitherto Jenny had always made them, light dough buns with currants and raisins and chopped peel. This year she asked Willy to order two dozen from the baker and bring them up each morning as soon as harvest began. Willy had thought it a bit odd that Jenny—for the first time in his memory—should go off on holiday just at this minute; on the other hand, one woman alone in the house didn't want much looking after.

She had remembered the beer, too, but this year the casks were not inside the house in the store room, but in the barn. She did not want Willy with a trayful of mugs clumping in and out of the kitchen at odd moments. Nor did she want Willy to come and sleep in, as he kindly offered to do when he realised that she would be alone in the house.

"It's very thoughtful of you, Willy; but I'm not in the least nervous." Joe Snell made the same offer and received the same answer.

In fact being alone in the house was such an enormous relief that she planned to get rid of Jenny. It would, of course, be ideal, if Jenny liked Baildon so much that she decided to stay with Diana. Otherwise she must be pensioned off. Four shillings a week? And free milk from Park?

The Felstead term commenced early in September and there was every chance that George would stay with Deborah until the end of August at least. Horses were his passion, too.

Then her thoughts would veer to the immediate present. Was everything ready? The baby would have no cradle. The one which belonged to the house, the one in which Deborah and Caroline and George had been rocked, had been lent—not given—to Willy and Katie when the myth that Katie's baby had been a bit premature had first been propagated. One couldn't ask for its return, nor, very well, go buying a new one; but a drawer served perfectly well. It was ready. Everything was ready—except, apparently the baby itself.

Mrs Thorley hoped that it would be born at night—most babies were. Harvesting had begun in what was known as Top Field, only just across a bit of garden and the moat. It would be quite possible to toss a stone from Lavinia's window into that harvest field, and in this still hot air sound carried. So if it is by day and Lavinia screams, I must close that window. Yes, I have thought of, am prepared for everything.

She had said, "Call me. Do you understand? I shall be nearby. Just call."

But it was not a call that woke her from her half-doze. It was a whimpering moan. Instantly alert and upright, Mrs Thorley took the lamp and went in.

*

The pony carriage bowled along between fields where men scythed corn and women bound and stooked sheaves and children ran about picking up stray, broken-off ears, or even a single fallen grain of corn. Harvest was harvest indeed. Men got extra money, women earned too, and the clothing for winter, in all but a drunkard's family, was thus assured. Really active or specially aggressive children could, in the course of a harvest, glean enough to provide a sack of flour.

"I wonder what we shall find today," Diana said.

"I don't know. I really am worried now, about Mamma. I would offer to stay so that she could get a proper night's rest, but I know what it would mean. Edward would want to come too, or he'd be looking in at odd hours. The *last* thing Mamma would wish."

"The last thing," Diana agreed. She had never contemplated such an offer. She was in fact enjoying having Jenny, who, after an afternoon at the Fair, a morning in the market, and an evening at the theatre had seemed at a loss for something to do, and had gladly agreed to a series of little dinner parties. The big, communal party had been a huge success, but it had, Diana felt, lacked the intimate touch. She could and would do better.

At Gad's there was nobody in the yard, even Willy was harvesting, but the pony, back again in what he still regarded as his home, stood, while bag 408 was lifted out and carried into the kitchen.

The big jug of milk stood on the kitchen table. Unusual. Ordinarily it was transferred to the cool larder.

They called, in their light, girlish voices, "Mamma! Mamma! We are here." Silence, heavy, absolute, dead.

She looked dead when they found her on the living-room settle, to which she had made her blind way. Her face, in profile against the crimson pillow, was the colour of a candle, the one visible eye sunk in a dark hollow, her mouth sagged open. On the thin cotton blue and white wrapper she wore there were irregular blotches.

They stood aghast, staring in silence until Diana said:

"Dead?" and turned to Caro for an answer. Caro, for all that she was a doctor's wife, had no more experience of death than Diana. Because of the suspicion, the near certainty, that their father, stepfather, had died of cholera, they had not been allowed to view his body. But the brownish blotches were recognisable as dried blood.

Murdered?

Crime was rare in this quiet countryside but not completely unknown and harvest-time did bring strangers in. A woman, alone,
in an isolated place and with wages money in the house, could
have been attacked and robbed.

Caroline tried to speak, but her teeth chattered so violently
that she could not bring out a word. It was left for Diana to reach
out a reluctant, fastidious hand, and touch the death's-head face.
It was warm.

Up, up, up, from the deepest depths of unconsciousness, up
through infinite layers of darkness, the entity known as Mamma
came to the surface. She opened her eyes, and closed them again
against the blinding light, sharp as a sword. Then, shielding them
with cupped hands, she opened them again and saw two of her
pretty girls, in their pretty summer muslins and their pretty
flowered hats, staring at her. And looking frightened. Her head
felt as though somebody were splitting it with an axe, her eyes
were full of gravel and her mouth full of fur, but she managed to
say. "I'm all right. It's over. They both died."

Diana and Caro shared a thought: The best thing that could
happen! Neither of them said it, however. Mrs Thorley pulled
herself into a sitting position, rubbed her grit-filled eyes, wished
she could cry, but all her tears had been shed, long ago. And now,
roused from the stupor of exhaustion, shock, and whisky, she
began to think again. There was still much to be done, and neither of these . . .

"I want Deborah," she said.

"It's Diana," George shouted. Of all the girls the one he liked
leaat, but never in his life had he been so glad to see anyone.
Diana had retained enough presence of mind to realise that the
pony carriage, though ready, would be slow, so she had called
Willy and he had harnessed up the dog-cart. Driving as though in
a race, Diana reached Foxton just as the mid-day meal was ending.

It was taken in the kitchen, for as Deb said it saved so many
steps. And Tim sat down to table in his shirt sleeves. Quite un-
knowingly, Deborah had reverted to a way of life which had ruled
at Gad's, until Mamma had taken over.

George saw only the familiar horse and cart, and Diana. Come
to deliver him. He was first to the door and then, close behind
him, Deborah.

Driving in a high dog-cart and at full speed was very different from driving in the pony carriage; Diana's hat had blown backwards, held on only by the ribbons which tied under her chin, and her usually smooth hair was ruffled. Deborah stepped forward briskly and Diana had just time to say, "Over. Both dead and Mamma is asking for you," before Tim was there, asking: What is it?

"My sister, Lavinia, is dead," Deborah said, "and Mamma is asking for me."

"You can't do anything about it." A dead girl, half a world away. "I'm sorry enough," Tim added, a shade too late, "but I can't see what you can do."

"I can *go*. I want the gig and a fresh horse. Will you harness up for me?"

"I can't see what all the flurry is about." The horse, over-driven, lathering and heaving; Diana always so prim and proper, looking as though she had been through a whirlwind, Deb ready to rush off, because news—months old at that—had just arrived.

A Deborah he did not know, somebody whose existence he had never suspected, said:

"Will you harness up, or must I?" Tim turned towards the yard. The girls had a second together.

"What happened?"

"I don't know. Mamma was in no state . . . She just said they were both dead. And asked for you."

Then there was George, his gaping valise in his hand. Diana, climbing out of the dog-cart, said, "No. I came for Deb, not for you, George."

"Then I'll walk." He wondered why he had not thought of this simple expedient before; but he knew the answer. If he ran away, Deb would be blamed as she had been for every mistake he had made during his stay in this horrible place.

Unlike the dog-cart, the gig had no seating accommodation at the back, so George sat between the girls, a great hindrance to conversation.

Deb said, "When?"

"Last night. At least I think so."

"Is Caro there?"

"Yes. Let's hope she had sense enough to make a cup of tea!"

It sounded to George as though Mamma might be ill.

"Is Mamma ill?"

"She has had some distressing news and is greatly upset," Diana said in a manner which did not encourage further conversation.

The gig was high-wheeled, built for speed, and the horse was fresh. The miles sped by. Presently Diana, having pushed back her hair and rearranged her hat, said:

"The bother is, I have a little dinner party this evening. I can't cancel it now, can I?"

"Why should you? I had a Prayer Meeting!" Something in Deb's voice informed George that she enjoyed this weekly gathering no more than he had done. He sat quietly and reviewed his hateful visit.

It had not begun badly. There'd been a Sunday School treat in one of Tim's meadows, and both Deb and Tim had told him to join in and be friendly. So he had; he'd won the sack race, the egg and spoon, and with a lump of a girl, a handicap if ever there was one, the three-legged. Then he was told to stand back and give others a chance. No word of praise!

Then he found that he was expected to work. Tim Bridges was altogether too fond of saying, "When I was your age . . ." Well, all right, George thought rebelliously, you had a horrid childhood and boyhood, but why keep harking back, and inflicting the same thing on me?

Then there were the Bible readings; every day, before breakfast, which was shockingly early, and after supper. Tim had a special Bible, divided into portions for each day of the year, and George's visit had coincided with about the worst of the Old Testament in the morning and of the New in the evening. Who cared, who could be expected to care about somebody who begat somebody who begat somebody else? And who knew or cared about Amphipolis and Apollonia, which had to be passed through before St Paul could reach Thessalonica?

So far from making a recruit, Tim had given George a distaste for anything that smacked of religion.

Deb, driving fast, knew why she had been sent for. Both dead! And what did one do with the body of a girl, supposedly on her way to, or just arrived in, India? She thought, half-resentfully: I made a sensible suggestion at the very beginning—she was mad and should have been put away. And now, though Mamma sent for me and is relying upon me, when I make the obvious, simple suggestion, she will choose something more complicated; possibly a leaden casket, presumably shipped from Bombay . . . I gave in once, but that was before I knew the whole truth. Now I do and if Mamma says anything about a decent Christian burial to me, I shall speak out.

She spoke out to George, "Look, Mamma is unwell. And she is not expecting you. You can go in and kiss her and then make yourself scarce. Find something to do."

"That," George said with dignity, "will be very easy. I shall exercise Tom Thumb. He must have missed me."

Caroline, of whom nothing much was expected, had risen to the occasion, made, not tea, but strong coffee, stirred the kitchen stove into activity, prepared a bath. And George said exactly the right thing. In later years when his success with women was notorious, he attributed it to telling them what they wanted to hear, holding up the flattering glass. But on this day his tribute was spontaneous.

"Oh, Mamma, how nice you look. How nice you smell. And you can't *think* how *glad* I am to see you again." Mrs Thorley hugged him and then Deborah. Over her mother's shoulder Deborah jerked her head at George, who said, "Excuse me, Mamma. I must see Tom Thumb."

"Why," Mrs Thorley asked of Deborah, who usually managed all things well, "did you bring him back?"

"He was prepared to walk," Deb said. "We had no choice. At least we know where he is."

Caro came in with a tray of tea; no cake. She wondered idly why it was seemly to drink when bereaved, yet almost indecent to eat. Not that this was really a bereavement. It was a relief and once Deborah had solved the immediate problem, the whole thing could be forgotten.

"What happened, Mamma?" Deb asked, taking charge of the tea-pot. Mamma was calm enough but all of a shake.

"I can't go into details. It was all so horrible." Mrs Thorley closed her sunken eyes and shuddered. "I did my best. My dears, you must believe that. I couldn't have done more if it had been one of you. And it was a beautiful baby—a boy." She knew in her heart that the continuance of her plan, culminating in Lavinia's return with the baby, would have meant months more of secrecy and connivance and apprehension; nevertheless the loss of the child grieved her. She would have to tell Deborah something of the truth, of course, because of the state of the attic. But Deb only.

The suggestion of a leaden casket shipped home from India came up inevitably, and from Diana.

"It can be done. One of my friend Barbara's cousins—he was a soldier—was brought home in that manner."

"Perhaps you know somebody who could make a leaden casket, seal it and ask no questions," Deb said. She spoke gently, almost casually, and yet with such venomous sarcasm that Diana looked at her in amazement.

"Well, no. It was just a suggestion."

"The time has come to face facts, damned unpleasant ones, too. Lavinia is supposed to be on the other side of the world. But she's up there, dead, and her baby with her."

"I know. I can face a fact, Deb, as well as anyone."

Never an unpleasant one, Deb thought.

"There is only one thing to do. Bury them. In the garden." It sounded harsh; all the worse because Deborah spoke so coolly, as though speaking of planting out wallflowers.

"And who would do that?"

"I will."

Deborah had been keeping half an eye on Mamma and saw that she was having trouble with her tea. She had made two attempts to get the cup to her lips, failed both times, and there was now as much tea in her saucer as in the cup. Deborah reached over, tipped the tea from the saucer into the slop-basin, dried the saucer and the base of the cup on her sleeve, and said, as to a child, "Try again."

Mamma had made no protest against the garden burial and Caro sat silent.

"Listen," Deb said. She had already in her mind surveyed the terrain. "It must be under the walnut tree . . . Nobody is likely to dig *there*. It's still early. I'll get hold of Willy and ask him to dig, ready for some shrubs and things which Mamma has admired in *your* gardens and which flourish in the shade. Bring them in to-morrow morning."

Let Deb do it. Through Mrs Thorley's exhausted mind a thought flitted—in olden times people like Lavinia would have been buried at a crossroads, with a stake through the heart.

Willy said, "Oh, Miss Deb, I mean Mrs Bridges, Ma'am, I wasn't looking to see you."

"I want you to do something for me, Willy."

"Anything. Anything you like to ask."

He'd adored her for years, almost as long as he could remember. Hopeless, of course, like adoring the moon, but if she had asked him to gnaw through an iron bar, he'd have done his best. As it was, in this late sultry afternoon, what she asked was easier than labour in the field. In the dense shade of the walnut tree it was comparatively cool and the soil, about six inches of it, dry and powdery.

"It needs to be deeper, Willy. Some of the new plants are deep-rooted; they must be set very deep."

So that was all right. Now for supper.

The pony carriage jogged along, the pony reluctant. He still thought of Gad's as his home.

They mentioned the catastrophe, sidling around it.

Di said, "It was the only way, really," and Caro agreed. "It is over now—or at least it will be—tomorrow. God love me, I was sorry for her . . . in a way . . . while she was alive; but what future did she have?"

What future do I have? Years and years and years of boredom, of every light remark being misunderstood, or met with flat reason. Better dead? Well, why not? She had access to Edward's dispensary.

She brooded on this for some minutes while her volatile spirit, in decline now ever since Freddy chose Susan, reached rock bottom, rested there and then bounced, began to soar upwards. The planes of her monkeyish face shifted a little, and Diana, seeing the change with a sideways glance, thought: Yes, that is all I need now, a fit of hysteria from Caro! To forestall it she said sharply:

"I don't know what there is to grin about!"

"Was I grinning? It just struck me that all you had to do to stay alive was to stay alive."

What a stupid statement! Diana flicked the pony.

"We're late already and I have things to see to. I have the Gordons this evening; I must get out their presents. And Phoebe Mayhew gave me a kind of table-centre, quite hideous, but it must be on show."

"Match-making?"

"That is rather a crude way of putting it. But I happen to know that Mrs Gordon is simply longing to see James married. And she likes Phoebe."

"She's far more likely to get that red head from the tobacconist's shop in Whiting Street."

"How do you know?"

"Edward buys his tobacco there. He believes in patronising small struggling shops." Almost unconsciously Caroline's voice mocked, imitated; serious, pedantic, well-meaning.

"And he has seen James there?"

"Oh, often."

"Well, I know nothing about that. I merely thought that a nice little dinner . . . I mean James can't very well talk exclusively to his father and mother, or to Everard whom he sees every day—and he never liked me much. It would give Phoebe a *chance*. And perhaps please Mrs Gordon."

It was essential to please Mrs Gordon. Diana, far from being dim-witted within her own sphere, had recognised the fact that Mrs Gordon was the power behind the throne and stood in the way of Everard's promotion because she was jealous. Everard was so much better looking, so much better qualified than James.

"I wish you luck," Caroline said, "but don't be disappointed. You'll be busy, and anyway, you haven't much in your garden. I'll see to the plants. For tomorrow."

"Oh, yes. Nine o'clock?"

Trust Edward to put the damper on, saying the wrong thing while doing the right one, or vice versa.

"But Sweetie, this is not the right time to move shrubs."

His mother had been a great one for the garden and had bought several things not yet common in English gardens. Neither Edward nor his father had had time to spare; Hammond, who saw to the horses, pumped water into the cistern which enabled the house in St Giles' Square to have the first proper water-flushed closet, the first proper bathroom in Baildon, did a bit of pruning from time to time. Edward knew the principles; shrubs should be transplanted in their dormant season; not in blazing August.

"Never mind. Why I want them tomorrow is for Mamma's sake. She heard this morning that Lavinia was dead—and of

course buried. And since, well, we couldn't send flowers to India,
Deb and I thought, something flowery for the garden."

"My poor dear," Edward said. He put a would-be comforting,
sustaining arm around Caroline. His memory of Lavinia was
vague; she'd never looked healthy, but she'd never seemed to ail,
never his patient. And she'd gone to India, notoriously unhealthy.
"What sad news. So young, too."

"Three months younger than I am."

As a doctor Edward knew that Death was no respecter of age,
or class, climate. Golden lads and girls all must, like chimney
sweepers, come to dust. That Edward accepted, a fact of life, but
suddenly Caroline seemed doubly precious, because so vulnerable.

"You must have had a horrible day. Have a little sherry . . .
Would you like to go back? Would your mother like to come
here? She shouldn't be alone, perhaps."

"She isn't. Deb is there."

Then everything was all right, Edward thought, and leaving
Caroline to rest, feet up, after what must have been a tiring day,
he went out to *dig*. He thought that the idea of flowering things,
planted in the garden where Lavinia had played as a child, a
charming idea and he was sorry that at first, not knowing the circumstances, he had seemed to oppose it. After all, a shrub
couldn't tell August from November; dig deep enough, and wide
enough, slip each rooted clod into wet sacking and some at least
would survive.

Diana bustled into her pretty little house and immediately
smelt cooking. A small house was undoubtedly convenient in
many ways, but doors should be kept closed. What guest wanted
to walk in and know immediately what awaited him for dinner?
She went along to the kitchen door at the end of the short passage,
closed it firmly and then turned into the dining room, which had
a communicating door with the kitchen, a fact which made serving a meal so easy that Jenny had never once mentioned her legs.

Everard was at the sideboard, a bottle of wine in one hand and
a corkscrew in the other.

"Hullo, darling. I'm rather late. Mamma greeted us with such
sad news. Lavinia is dead."

"Oh. I am sorry." The words were correct, but perfunctory;
Lavinia had made no impression on him at all and had been gone
since March.

"Mamma was quite overwhelmed. She wanted Deborah so I had to drive all the way over to Foxton to fetch her."

"You must be exhausted." Everard put down the corkscrew. "I think that in the circumstances we should not entertain, darling."

He had no faith at all in this intimate little party. There was no point in trying to please the old devil, his wife or his son. James was still friendly enough, but not in a manner that meant anything. Any real goodwill would have surfaced, in a practical manner, long before this. And no good would come of this well-meant, intimate little party. James had once confided in Everard about the tobacconist's daughter, who had made it quite clear that dalliance was not for her. "And I'd marry her like a shot, old boy, but there'd be an almighty row, and they'd hold it against Sylvia as long as they lived. Whereas, in another year or so, they'll be so anxious to hear the patter of tiny feet, they'll greet Sylvia with three rousing cheers." So why should Diana exert herself and put him to the expense of providing an expensive meal?

"Oh, I'm all right," Diana said. "A wash and a change, and I shall be as good as new."

"I was thinking of the bereavement. I'll just walk round and tell them. They'll quite understand."

"Phoebe will just about be starting now. It's eight miles. Besides, darling, it isn't as though Lavinia . . . I mean she must have been dead quite some weeks ago. And after my dreadful day, I need something cheerful."

"You may be right," Everard said, and unwillingly, he withdrew the cork. Life with his godfather had taught him about wine, and a decent red wine should breathe for an hour.

During this brief conversation the door to the kitchen had stood open and Jenny had been listening. Although she had indulged, over a long period of time, in a subtle bullying of Mrs Thorley, at heart she was fond of her, a shade fonder than she had realised. Nobody would miss Miss Lavinia much, but she was Mrs Thorley's youngest girl; quite overwhelmed, Miss Diana had said. And she'd sent for Miss Deb; *that* was understandable; if anything went wrong Miss Deb was the one Jenny would have wanted, too. But how long could she stay? Only one hasty visit since the wedding, just to fetch Master George.

Such thoughts were mere froth on the crest of a wave of emotion which had been welling up in Jenny since the first days of her so-called holiday. By that time she had exhausted what delights Baildon had to offer and had become both homesick and bored. Going to the Fair, to the theatre, to the market, looking into shop windows—all very dreary when you were by yourself. She'd tried to be friendly with Mrs Wedgewood on the days when she came, but nothing had come of that. Try to talk about cooking, the one thing they should have had in common, and the bitch reeled off a lot of outlandish names. Offer to help and you were reminded sharply that you were supposed to be on holiday. Jenny said, "I reckon I came to holidays too late in life." Mrs Wedgewood retorted that she had never had one, never expected to. Jenny positively welcomed the little dinner parties where at least she could exercise her skills. No dishes with highfaluting names, but good sound cooking.

In fact Mrs Wedgewood was suspicious of Jenny and apprehensive about her nice little job.

"I don't want to offend Deb," George said, casting a wary look at his half-sister, "but it is all rather peculiar. They don't have proper preachers, you know. Nobody like Mr Spicer. Anybody can preach."

"There is one minister and a circuit of about twelve chapels," Deb explained, "so we depend upon local preachers. Tim is one."

"I never heard him," George said, being fair. "But that man who said 'er' at the end of every other word. I don't think he was really cut out for preaching. Honestly, Deb, do you?"

"He has this unfortunate impediment," Deb said. "What made it worse was that his watch seemed to have stopped."

That was more like the old Deb. Encouraged, George elaborated; he had, like Caroline, a gift for mimicry, which for once fell flat. And then Deborah turned the tables on him and said:

"I think—er, you—er, should—er go to bed—er."

"That," George said, delighted that Deb had shown the right spirit, "is exactly how that man talked, for a whole hour!"

When he had gone, the dismissal softened by a kind of jocularity, Mrs Thorley said:

"My dear, I have not been honest with you. The truth was so awful. And I behaved in such a cowardly way. When I saw . . . Deb this is so horrible . . . I know you never liked whisky, but there is some brandy; take a little . . . Deb, at the end it was so awful, I just ran away." There were still things which could not be said, things that nobody would believe; but something must be told.

"Deb, I delivered her safely. A beautiful little boy. As you know, I had always held to the belief that once delivered she would recover her senses. And it seemed so. She said she would like some chicken broth. And I had it, ready. So I came down, it hardly took me five minutes. And in just that time, Deb, she'd smothered the poor baby, and slashed her own wrists."

"God!" Deborah looked so aghast and turned so pale that for a moment Mrs Thorley feared she might faint. And if simply hearing about it had such effect, what would the sight of it do?

"Deb, you must drink this. As medicine."

"I'm all right" Deb said, accepting the glass nonetheless. "How terrible for *you!*"

"So was my own behavior. I failed completely. It happened just after four . . . kept steeling myself to face it. To go back . . . To begin cleaning up. I had time, and I thought that if I drank enough . . . Twice got halfway up the attic stairs. I failed. I simply could not bring myself . . . I could not enter that room alone."

The question was, could she manage it now, with Deb as support? It was just possible, for she felt better. The hand which had been so shaky on the tea-pot was quite steady on the bottle. Yes, she was better now and would spare Deb the worst. She would go in first. She had told Deb part of the truth, but not the whole. Not by a long way. Nobody would believe her; they'd say like mother like daughter and think her mad too.

"She was mad, Mamma. Not responsible for what she did." With great delicacy of feeling Deborah refrained from saying things such as: I told you so. I knew it. I said so from the first. She *bit* me.

And Mrs Thorley made no mention of the ordeal which had preceded the birth. Lavinia suddenly garrulous. "They promised no pain. They promised to come for me. I was the Maiden."

In actual fact it had been a short labour, but Lavinia had resented every pang. She had cried out to the picture on the easel. "I kept faith! I never said a word! Help me. You promised!" She knelt, moaning and praying in the most blasphemous terms.

Mrs Thorley, not a woman given to fancies, was aware of another presence in the room; something evil. And once it seemed to her that face of the goat-human changed, the leering, sneering expression intensifying into one of supreme mockery. The unpleasant odour increased.

She had kept her head—then. Apart from pulling Lavinia by the arm, calling her by name, and saying, "Stop, Lavinia, stop!" she had done nothing. There was an impulse to lift her and put her on the bed, but she resisted it. Lavinia would struggle and that might hurt the baby. Also the worrying days and the long night vigils had so sapped her strength that she doubted her ability to perform the action properly.

Then Lavinia's moans and petitions changed into cries of rage. She got clumsily to her feet, seized a brush, squeezed tubes of paint, one after the other, and defaced, first the picture and then the wall-paintings. That done she became calm, lay down on the bed and submitted, like any ordinary girl, to Mrs Thorley's midwifery. Mrs Thorley said all the things that had been said to her: Bear down, dear! Go with the pain! Ah, that was a good one; it won't be long now. It was not long; a natural easy birth with no need of the opiate drops. And despite all, a perfect normal baby, better-looking, in fact, than most, not red and creased and bald as all Mrs Thorley's babies had been when she first saw them.

Lavinia said, "Thank you, Mamma," which proved that she was, as Mrs Thorley had always hoped might be the case, back in her own mind. Incredible as it might seem in the circumstances it was with a feeling of happiness that she placed the baby in his makeshift cradle. The worst was over now.

Then Lavinia said she was hungry.

"I can manage," Deborah said bravely. "You go to bed."

"I've shirked enough for one day. Will you bring the lamp? Both those . . . up there, will have burned dry. I'll bring the linen."

The first Mrs Thorley had brought to Gad's—as all daughters of decent, substantial families did—enough good linen to last a lifetime and beyond, if carefully treated. Mrs Thorley had thought about giving some of it to the girls when they married; but the linen cupboards at Foxton and in St Giles' Square were equally well supplied, so she had compromised, thinking: The Thorley linen should stay at Gad's. And for Diana she had bought new. Nothing like such quality.

Now Lavinia, not a Thorley, and always an outsider, was to go to her grave wrapped like a mummy, in such linen as money could not buy nowadays.

On the landing, Mrs Thorley weakened again. I cannot reenter that shambles and it was wrong of me to ask Deb.

She said in a weak voice. "Couldn't we just lock the door and leave it? It's no sight . . ."

"Mamma, you know what a stench one dead rat under a floor board can raise. Look, put the linen down outside the door and sit on the stairs. I may need help in getting . . . it . . . them down, but I intend to think of it, and you must, too, just a bundle of laundry."

It sounded harsh, but that was how she must think, how Mamma must think. Lavinia as Lavinia had ceased for Deborah with the discovery of those black candles, and all the rest of it, but Deborah, with uncounted generations of people close to the earth behind her, knew the healing virture of soil. It accepted the most revolting things and by some miracle transformed them. Into crops; into roses.

The heavy, blood-satiated bluebottle flies, disturbed by the light, rose lazily and buzzed.

Lavinia looked like marble, dead white in carved immobility, and the blue look which Mrs Thorley had recognised as a sign of death, irreversible, when she snatched the pillow away, had faded from the baby's face. There was a singular, almost frightening resemblance to the statue of the Virgin and Child that stood in a little niche in St Paul's church in the village. Stonham St Paul's was so small and so obscure that it had escaped the attention of those two arch-destroyers—Henry VIII and Cromwell. And the man who had made the statue had had nothing to work with except chalk, the subsoil of this area. Making the best of what he had, he worked; even Mary's fingernails on the hand which cupped the Child's head were perfectly wrought.

Willy had worked well, too. Mis Deb had asked him to dig deep, and he had done so. Through the summer dust, the dark compost of many years of fallen leaves, into the chalk. No plant would need to set its roots deeper than that.

Deb dug slightly deeper, relieved to find that below a certain level, even chalk became friable.

It would have been easier to put everything else—everything Lavinia had ever owned or touched—on to a bonfire, but, as she had once reminded Lavinia, a light at Gad's could be seen for miles, and even in the middle of the night one could not be certain that everybody was dead asleep. A man, full of harvest beer, might go stumbling out to ease his bladder, a child might wake with toothache. A fire at Gad's, in this hot dry weather, would mean only one thing, a fire in a cornfield and the age-old principle —help your neighbour because tomorrow you may need help from him—would go into action. Once the alarm was given everybody would come swarming, most to help, a few to watch. No bonfire. All the soiled clothes and bed-clothes, and the rug which had taken the brunt of the gush of life-blood, went into the chalk and was stamped down. The horrible picture, too, with others, less positive, but all tainted.

"There's nothing more we can do now," Deborah said at last. "I'll give the place a good scrub out in the morning." And splash about with some whitewash, she added to herself. Mamma—and thank God for it—had seemed to miss the significance of what Lavinia had painted. Mrs Thorley thought—and thank God for it —that Deborah had not realised the full truth.

"Share my bed," Mrs Thorley whispered, "no other is made up." The whole business had been made just that little more difficult by the need to move softly, speak low, or not at all for fear of waking George.

George, back in his own bed, had slept soundly, lulled by the knowledge that he was home, where the first thing in the morning was breakfast, at the civilised hour of eight o'clock. Nobody here was going to demand that he should rise at six and take part in feeding the horses, or say, as Mr Bridges had done, that early to bed and early to rise made a man healthy, wealthy and wise; or that one hour before breakfast was worth two after it. In that aphorism George thought there might be a grain of truth since an hour before breakfast seemed twice as long as any other hour of the day. But it cut both ways: an hour before breakfast, in bed, half awake and half asleep, was not only twice as long but twice as enjoyable.

Lolling, he surveyed the future and the possibility that early rising might be the rule at school. Hideous thought! He shuffled it off. Mamma might change her mind again. First of all he had been bound for Biddle's, which meant a very stiff examination next year. Then he was bound for Felstead—slightly easier to get into—this year. But he was all Mamma had left now; and if cajolery and cunning worked, George might possibly continue to jog down to the Rectory, learn a little and be home for lunch. A boy could only hope.

The clock, like all old things, was slow and a bit wheezy. George knew that if he jumped out of bed at the first stroke of eight he could be washed and almost dressed by the last.

Eggs, just as he liked them. Turned in the pan. It was one of the ridiculous things about Foxton that any such small preference was denounced as fanciful, the result of being spoilt. Mr Bridges like *his* eggs cooked open-eyed, so that at the touch of the knife yolk ran about and stuck to the bacon like glue. He liked his meat half-cooked, too, bloody, red juice seeping out and sullying the potatoes and peas. Nobody, in the stress of the time had noticed, but George, during his short stay at Foxton, had lost weight. The food in itself was excellent but not to George's taste. Take ham, or salt beef, both thoroughly cooked, and of the best quality, but carved with an absolute disregard for individual preferences. Mr Bridges said people should learn to take the fat with the lean— and be grateful. When George left the fat on his plate, he was rebuked for wasting good food, and when George argued that the chickens would eat it, that was called answering back. Such little episodes, too slight really to be called differences of opinion, always brought a look of pain to Deb's face, so after a day or two he did his best to avoid them.

Over breakfast, cooked exactly to his liking, George was prepared to be cheerfully garrulous, but neither Mamma nor Deb was very responsive. They weren't cross or disapproving, merely glum. Then, of course, he remembered, Lavinia was dead. They were sad. He set his wits to work to think of a way of cheering them up a little. Gifts! All women liked gifts.

"Well, I'll get on," Deb said, rising and beginning to roll up her sleeves.

Anxious to ingratiate himself, indeed, if possible to make himself appear indispensable, George asked if there were anything he could do to help.

Mamma said quickly, "Not here, dear. I have a few errands to be done in Baildon. I'll make you a list."

"I was thinking of riding there this morning. Is there anything you want, Deb?"

"I don't think . . . Yes, a jar of Fuller's hand cream."

She went out and began clanking about in the kitchen.

George said in his precociously adult way:

"Mamma, would it be possible for Deb to stay here for a week or so? I think she needs a holiday."

"A holiday? Darling, she has hardly been married two months."

"I was there less than a fortnight and I was anxious to get away. Foxton is a horrible place, and Mr Bridges is a horrible man. In fact, if I'd known how he was going to treat Deb, I wouldn't have stood there and said: I do, when Mr Spicer asked: Who giveth this woman?"

Mrs. Thorley would have said that the events of the last day or two had rendered her immune to shock, but she felt a pang. She remembered that she had never really liked Timothy Bridges.

"What do you mean, George?"

"Well, for one thing Deb is a kind of servant. There *is* a servant but she leaves all the hard work to Deb. There's a piano, but only for hymn tunes. You know that pretty hat Deb had, with the yellow roses? I asked Deb why she had taken them off. Do you know why? You can only wear plain clothes for chapel. They live in the kitchen, with the servant, and only go in the parlour when they have visitors. In all the time I was there I only got two rides on Foxy. And Deb is not going to be allowed to hunt. Mr Bridges says foxes are vermin, and he shoots them on sight. I took *Gulliver's Travels* with me to read and Mr Bridges said I ought to read *Pilgrim's Progress*, and he's the same about what Deb reads." George reeled off the list of things which had displeased him and finished off with a remark characteristic of him. "There's a text on the wall. It says, 'Christ is the Head of this house,' but it's wrong. It should read, 'Mr Bridges is Head of this house. So look out!' I hated it all, and I'm sure Deb must."

"She probably does not feel as you do, George. You see she fell in love and chose to marry Mr . . . to marry Tim."

There and then George Thorley made a decision that was to keep him a bachelor until he was fifty. Marriage was a thing to be avoided so long as possible.

And now that he was thinking on the subject, he wasn't sure about Caro, either. He'd never said anything to anybody, because really there wasn't much to tell, but it was curious . . . On the second of his week-ends there, the one which had ended with the horrid visit to the hospital, there'd been on the Saturday a party. In the middle of it he had felt the need to go to the lavatory and had gone along to the one near the surgery. That took him through a passage and there Caro and Freddy were looking at the funny pictures. They stood close together as two people looking at the same picture must do, and they were laughing. When he came back, Caro was alone, and she wasn't laughing, she was crying. He'd said, "What is the matter, Caro."

She said, "Nothing. Why?"

"You're crying."

"Only from laughing. Honestly, every time I see these pictures they seem funnier." And it was on the next day that she said being miserable did nobody any good. It now struck him that Caro, though her husband was very different, and her life far more comfortable, hadn't found married life quite all that she had hoped.

"Can you take me back this morning, Miss Di? I am all ready."

"No, we cannot," Diana said, a bit sharply. "With the two of us and the plants we shall have a full load."

Jenny sensed displeasure. Two offences. Miss Di was now Mrs Spicer. And Jenny was cutting short her holiday.

"It ain't that I ain't been happy here. But with the bereavement and all, I don't reckon Missus should be there all alone. She'll need a bit of looking after."

"Next time we go, Jenny. It is quite impossible today."

Diana was in no mood for trivialities. She hurried out, through the gateway which Edward had so thoughtfully made in the wall, and there was Caroline and the pony carriage, the rear of it looking like a greengrocer's shop.

"Well, and how did the party go?"

Ordinarily Caroline was about the last person in whom Diana would have chosen to confide, but she simply had to talk to somebody.

"It was *dreadful*. James absolutely ignored Phoebe and she hardly opened her mouth, except to put food into it. Mr Gordon talked almost exclusively to Everard, business, of course—all about something up at Lowestoft. And all Mrs Gordon could talk to me about was the food. How delicious and what was the recipe? It wasn't quite ten when Phoebe said she couldn't keep her driver waiting any longer. And you know how it is, with an unsuccessful party, once one person leaves, they all do."

"I know. What a pity. But I never actually thought that Phoebe Mayhew . . ."

"I know. You said so. And Everard said we should cancel the party altogether. I wish I had." Diana gave the innocent pony a rather sharp flick of the whip, though he was once more doing his best, headed for home, and Edward must have dug up a great weight of soil in his anxiety to please and his determination that all the things—even the dogwood—should have a chance to survive.

"And that wasn't the worst of it," Diana said. "Everard—after they had all gone—talked seriously of looking for other employment. He came to bed raging. He said decent men didn't talk business at table, and that this thing at Lowestoft was pushed on him because Mr Gordon was too ignorant to understand it and James was off to play cricket. Caro, Everard really said some terrible things—they'd always imposed upon him and now felt more free to do so because he was married and anchored down; tied to a house in Baildon. And he said he would apply for something he had had his eye on. In London . . ."

"Di, you'd hate it! I did, and I was on holiday. To live there . . . I saw streets and streets—I don't mean slums. I mean houses much narrower than yours, all squeezed together, and not a green thing in sight. Di, you must take a firm stand and refuse to go. I would. I mean that if Edward got such a crazy idea into his head, I should simply say: All right, you go but don't expect me to come with you." And God! what a release that would be!

"And then what would you do?"

"Go home. Back to Gad's, I mean."

"Don't be so silly! You're married. Mamma could be sued for harbouring you, or . . . or something called aiding and abetting."

"Is that so? Well, with me the question is not likely to arise. And you must talk Everard out of it, Di. You could say—and it's absolutely true—living in London is very expensive. So even if he earned more he wouldn't be better off." Caroline knew one of Everard's weaknesses. "Look at what we bring back from Gad's . . ."

Deborah set to work methodically. First everything out. Nothing associated with Lavinia must remain in this house. Nothing was heavy; even the chaise-longue was a light structure, much of it canework. She pushed it, the trestle-table and its stands, the easel and the wickerwork chair on to the kitchen stairs. Later she'd ask Willy to take them away and make them into kindling.

There were splotches of blood on the floor, around the place where the rug had been, and where it had soaked through. She tackled them; soda in the water and strong yellow kitchen soap. Later, when she had whitewashed the wall, she would do the whole floor.

Whitewash, often called lime-wash, was always available on any well-run farm; it was held to have purifying qualities, a guard against foot-and-mouth, glanders, swine fever, fowl pest. It had a good clean smell. She splashed it about liberally, trying not to look at what she was obliterating; some very hideous things, some beautiful. Don't look! Don't think! It is over and done with.

Funny! Last night had been enough to nauseate anyone, and she had felt sick, but had not actually been. As a matter of fact she could remember being sick only once in her life and that was long ago; something to do with mushrooms which weren't really mushrooms. She'd never fainted, either, though most girls at school had done so at one time or another and Miss Hardwicke had said that it was all nonsense. Take a deep breath and concentrate on something. Deborah now took a deep breath and concentrated on what she was doing. But the I-am-going-to-be sick and the I-am-going-to-die feeling came upon her, and she had only just time to get to the window. There she was far more indisposed than a slice of toast and a cup of coffee would have seemed to warrant, but she gulped in some fresh air, wiped her face on her rolled-up sleeve and thought: Now I know what a cold sweat is.

Back to work.

The patches of floor that she had scrubbed were drying out, but the dark marks still showed.

Deborah had read about—but never seen—blood marks which were irradicable. Wasn't there one in Holyrood Palace where Mary Queen of Scots' Italian secretary had fallen, clutching at her skirts?

I'll see about that, Deborah said to herself, attacking the dark spots with more vigour, more harsh yellow soap. They should be removed if she had to scrub down half an inch.

"Miss Deb; Mrs Bridges, Ma'am."

Willy's voice on the kitchen stairs.

In complete control of herself, and of the situation, Deborah went to the top of the stairs and across the jumble piled there looked down on Willy and said, "Good morning, Willy," in the special, friendly way she had. A way that made you free and equal and put daft ideas into your head.

"The Missus said something about you wanting something moved. Is this it?"

"Yes. I've clearing out what Miss Lavinia called her studio. We had kept it, but now she will not be coming back."

"So I understood. I'm sorry."

"Thank you, Willy." God damn all to hell! Miss Deb had only to say his name and something came over him. Something Katie had never managed. "The thing is, they have woodworm and that can spread. It could get into the rafters. I think they should be chopped up and used for kindling."

"I'll see to it."

Despite the fact that standing there, looking up, Willy Snell was the victim of one of the most romantic forms of love, he had sense enough to see that the chair was all right; basket work, and whoever heard of woodworm in a basket? Nobody wanted a board, all paint and tallow, and the couch thing was too long for any ordinary house. The chair though—just the job for Katie's mother.

Katie's mother did not think highly of Willy as a son-in-law. Not because he'd got Katie in the family way before marrying her —that was commonplace—but because Katie should have done better for herself, married a stockman, a groom, a gamekeeper, somebody with a bit more about him. So in order to forestall what he called ructions in the family Willy was committed to a long course of placatory gestures. The chair, though a bit lopsided, was more comfortable than any in his own home, but it would go across the village street to Katie's mother. Willy did not foresee that the chair would have a curious peripatetic future. Katie's mother accepted it with a pleasure she was careful to conceal, and for a day or two it was admired and envied by her neighbours. She gave it away to one of them, explaining that she couldn't rest in it, it didn't fit her, or it creaked or something; she never had a good sit-down in it. The neighbour passed it on even more hastily. She knew better than to give her real reason, which was that one evening, just at twilight, she'd seen a light in it, very similar to the will-o'-the-wisp sometimes seen over the marshes. She said the chair was too low, once you were in it it was difficult to get out of, and when something happened, like a saucepan boiling over, you needed to be on your feet in no time. With this excuse and that, all plausible, the chair moved about until it came to rest with the old soldier with the wooden leg. He said, rightly, that it was the most comfortable chair he'd ever sampled.

On this hot August morning, ear-marking the chair for Katie's mother, Willy looked up again and said:

"Miss Deb, Mrs Bridges, Ma'am, I bin giving a thought to them plants. I reckon a good barrerful of muck, maybe two, wouldn't hurt."

Deborah had already gone out and taken a look at her work. The long trench looked just as Willy had left it.

"That is a splendid idea, Willy. Leave it for a little, though. Mrs Spicer and Mrs Taylor will be here with the plants, shortly, and then you can put in the manure and help me to plant at the same time."

She was reasonably sure that neither Di nor Caro would wish to go near the spot.

She turned back to the attic. The floor showed no marks now. The wall was not entirely satisfactory. A few dark shapes showed, very vaguely, through the whitewash. But they might vanish as the wall dried. What was really needed was a second coat, but that could not be applied until the first had hardened. And she had no time. She must get back to Foxton; for she had come here in Tim's gig, pulled by his swiftest horse, and left with the heavier vehicle, the older animal, he would have just cause for complaint.

She emptied the pail of scrubbing water out of the window, pulled the half-casement close and latched it. Scrubbing brush, jar of soda, yellow soap back in the pail, and then, because the whitewash bucket was a size smaller, put that in, too.

Some instinct made her fix the chain again, turn the key in the heart-shaped padlock and put the key into the pocket of her print dress. Now, when the shrubs were planted, it would be all over.

She'd always been the strong one, the tireless one, but out on the attic landing, just as she was about to pick up the buckets, weakness, weariness, struck at the very marrow of her bones. Leaning against the wall, she knew herself incapable of lifting a cotton thread. Her mind was still active, however, and rational. It had been an ordeal, something few women were called upon to do.

There might be another reason, too. She, always as regular as the moon which controlled such things, was late this month.

I am going to have a baby!

In any other circumstances, in any other place, a most joyful thought. Too joyful, in fact, to seize upon too easily. She had explained the lateness to herself in various ways; anxiety about what was happening here at Gad's and then the small, unimportant but constant friction between Tim and George. George wasn't perfect —what boy was?—but he was anxious to please; just as Tim was anxious to criticise and rebuke.

My son is not going to be reared in that bleak, narrow-minded fashion! It'll mean a fight, long and acrimonious and all about such silly, trivial things, but I shall fight it to the last.

Gradually, as she stood there, leaning against the wall, strength flowed back. Happiness should have come with it, but did not. She had thought Tim Bridges the nicest man she had ever met, but now the inner voice asked: How many men had she met and what, really, apart from his right attitude to horses, had Tim to commend him? Look the thing squarely in the face; why shouldn't a merry tune be played upon a piano? What sort of God was it who objected to a wreath of yellow roses on a hat? Was there any particular virtue in acting as scullery-maid as well as cook? With women all about so anxious to be employed.

Diana and Caro arrived with the load of things to be planted. As Deborah had foreseen, neither of them wanted to go near the place. Everybody knew, Diana said, that Willy was dim-witted, but surely he could be trusted to plant a few shrubs. Caroline agreed with her. But Mamma was stalwart. She said:

"The things are supposedly a present to me. I must help to see them properly installed."

Once that was done, she would never go near the end of the garden again. At the moment she held the shrubs upright while Willy and Deb used the spades. She did not notice when Deborah slipped the key from her pocket and buried that, too.

Going back to the house, Mrs Thorley said:

"Deborah, you have been marvellous. Without you, I doubt if I could have managed."

"*You* are the one who has been marvellous. I mean no disrespect to my own mother . . . I hardly remember her; but I often wished that I were your real daughter. And never more so than now . . . I should like to think that I had inherited your . . ." guts was the word, the truly apt word, but Mamma disliked coarse expression ". . . strength of character."

"But you were born with it—not through me. In your own right. Deb, you just paid me a great compliment. I return it. I also wish you were my daughter. Years ago, when you were at school . . . I was always so proud of you. I had to remind myself, quite sharply, that nothing of me had gone to your making."

Now who would have suspected that behind the calm, if-I-had-only-one-apple attitude such a thought could have lurked?

"But for you, Mamma, I should never have gone to school at all. Caro and I were so wild . . . I don't know what would have happened to her; she's pretty. I should probably have married Willy!" From what deep layer of unacknowledged knowledge had that thought come?

"How absurd!"

"It's not absurd at all. If we'd got the ordinary kind of stepmother who wanted us out of the house as soon as possible."

Indoors Caro, with a vague intention of doing something that looked useful, offered to make tea. Every bone and nerve of Mrs Thorley's body was crying out for whisky, but she must wait a little. She suggested sherry. Not that sherry served the same purpose; not that she even enjoyed it any longer. She had once heard somebody say that once you took to spirits you lost your taste for wine. Deborah accepted her glass without demur and they were all sipping, as ladies should, when George walked in, and instantly looked dismayed. He had not expected to find Di and Caro here. For Mamma and Deb he had bought cheering gifts. A bottle of lavender water for Mamma and one of Eau de Cologne for Deb. All women liked scent. But he had been so reared in the tradition of treating all the girls exactly alike that now to single Deb out was impossible and his generous gesture must be delayed. If only he'd known he could have bought four small bottles instead of two large ones.

From the parcel he carried he produced the pot of hand cream. "This is what you asked me to get."

"Thank you, George. Mamma will pay you. I haven't a penny on me."

Both Diana and Caroline noted with approval that Deborah had not—as appeared at first sight—lost all pride in her appearance. That print dress was positively servant's wear, and Diana remembered how Deborah had appeared at the kitchen door at Foxton with a great smear of flour on her hair.

"And who do you think I saw on the road?" George asked, brightness returning to his face. "Jenny! Walking home, hoping for a lift. I tried . . ." he broke into laughter. "You never saw anything so funny in your life. I tried to heave her on to Tom Thumb and he just went round and round. He . . . he waltzed! I had to leave her to wait for a cart."

"I am so glad," Deb said, "that you will not be alone, Mamma."

In fact what would have been embarrassing forty-eight hours ago was now good news.

"Mamma would not have been alone in any case," George said, starting off on the path which he hoped would lead him to his goal. "I am home now."

And here, with cunning and a modicum of luck, he would stay. He sensed that Mamma had never really been in favour of Felstead—it was all Old Spicer's fault for saying that George wasn't ready for the examination for Biddle's yet. George felt that if he promised to work *much* harder this year and *hope* to be better prepared next year, Mamma could be persuaded. And he wouldn't be ready for Biddle's next year. Nor any other year. And it should not be too hard to make Mamma see that the money would be better spent on replacing Tom Thumb.

Jenny, thinking: Thass right! Thass just like you, putting plants afore people! Deciding to walk if necessary; not that it would be; on the road decent people recognised other decent people and offered lifts; had not been far wrong. Within minutes of being left by Master George, Jenny was picked up by a decent man who said he had business in Nettleton and would therefore pass by the opening of the lane that led to Gad's. In the kitchen she paused only long enough to remove her bonnet and exchange her cruel decent shoes for the old, down-trodden, shapeless ones which she kept at the bottom of the dresser. Then she presented herself.

"I'm home, Ma'am. I just had to come, hearing of your grief."

"I'm glad to see you, Jenny; but you shouldn't have cut short your holiday . . ."

Diana thought: So back to heating up what Mrs Wedgewood leaves ready, or cooking on my own! She was never at home in her kitchen. She wore a dainty, frilled muslin apron and truly tried to please Everard, but nothing ever went quite right; saucepans would boil over, she burned her fingers, and once her arm on the oven door. She always kept the doors to the kitchen closed—she and Everard would never eat in the kitchen as Deb and her husband apparently did, despite their wealth. But sometimes the smell of cooking—and that was different from the smell of the dish itself—seemed to enter with her. And there was another thing which made kitchen work so unsatisfactory. It was never done. Plan a piece of needlework or embroidery, and stitch by stitch it grew, moving towards completion. Something to show. Make a meal, however successful—and she had had successes as well as failures—and what were you left with? A sinkful of dirty dishes.

Jenny said, "I had enough holiday, Ma'am. As I said, I was sorry to hear . . . And now, what'll I cook?"

George came triumphantly into his own.

"Fish!"

He had not been commissioned to buy fish, but he'd just been trotting past Harper's when the fresh fish was being laid out on the marble slab. To George, as to most country dwellers, fresh fish was a treat; nobody hawked it around villages because it could go off, and stink by the end of the day: so apart from what market-goers brought home, fish was dried or smoked.

"I thought," George said, happily smug, "that a piece of nice fresh fish would tempt Mamma's appetite."

"Oh, George! You humbug!" Caro almost smiled. The atmosphere lightened, became more like that which George liked to have about him. And of course two minutes' thought had solved his problem for him. He knew how to give Deb her present without making what Mamma had once called invidious distinctions.

"I bought this for you, Deb. For having me to stay." The correct thing would have been to add that he had enjoyed himself, but he could not bring himself to say the words.

Back in her teasing mood, Caro said, "I had you to stay. Twice."

"I know. But you have so much, Caro. Scent, I mean. At least a half pint that Edward bought you in London. French, too. Rêve d'Amour," he explained for the benefit of those who had not seen Caroline's store.

Mention of lunch had reminded everybody of the time.

"I must get back," Deborah said.

"So must we."

"Oh, but Di! I was counting, I mean I hoped that you'd come with me and bring back the dog-cart."

"I can't. I have a tea-party this afternoon." And there would not be, as she had hoped, Jenny to cut the tiny sandwiches, carry in the tray, wash up afterwards.

Her ungeneralised grievance against things focussed for a moment upon Lavinia. Alive a nuisance, dead a nuisance; it was because Lavinia was dead that Jenny had hurried home; it was because of Lavinia that now they must wear black for at least three months. Diana agreed entirely that one could not go around saying, "My sister is dead," and wearing gay colours, but while admitting the necessity, she'd grudged it. Money ill-spent, since black was not her colour and there was nothing to be done afterwards with a black dress—except hang it up and wait for another dismal occasion. Any other coloured dress could be dyed . . . It was all very well for Mamma, with black in store, and for Caro, so fair that black became her, and who could have other new dresses, any time; and for Deborah, who plainly did not care what she wore, as the print dress bore witness. And although Diana had once hoped to—or would have relished an opportunity to—exchange a few careful words on the subject of marriage with Deb, she no longer wished to do so. What marriage meant to Deb was all too plain.

Now Deb said, "All right then. Mamma, if I may, I'll borrow Willy." What she did not want was any fuss about getting the dog-cart home. In a way, yesterday, in insisting upon having the gig, she had defied Tim; and if what she suspected was right, she would be obliged to defy him again and again. But never over small things. Strength must be reserved for real battles.

With a jolt, Mrs Thorley realised that now she was free to come and go.

"No need to borrow Willy, my dear. I'll come myself. An airing will do me good."

Would it? She felt as though the only thing in the world that would do her good at the moment was a stiff whisky and another.

To steady her shaking hands and jerking head. But the crisis was past now, and so must the indulgence be, if what her mind planned her body would perform. As it must, if George's inheritance was to be worth anything, if Gad's and Park were to survive, as they must. Life was like a string of beads, some pretty, some ugly, and now and again the string broke and all was confusion. Then you gathered the pretty ones, let the ugly ones roll away, and knotted the string. She had done it before; she must do it again, but she must stay sober.

"Do you think you're fit to drive just yet?" Deborah asked.

"I must start some time. This is going to be a busy autumn for me." The cancellation of the summer shows had meant loss of publicity which must be made up for at the sales. And the little desk by the window was piled with papers that needed attention. Amongst them was a letter from Mr van Haagen, reporting gladly that the cross between Friesian and Durham shorthorn had been, so far as one could judge in so short a time, a great success. Mrs Thorley wondered if he would come at her invitation, attend a cattle sale or two and place some fantastic bids for some of her stock. She could then make it right with him afterwards. It was worth attempting. Not that she was particularly eager to see Mr van Haagen again; there was something uncanny about the man. It was too soon yet to know about the grandchildren, but almost everything else he had foretold had come about with such a seeming inevitability that it sometimes made her wonder about predestination, a theory little to her taste.

Had the destination been any other than Foxton, George would have offered to go, keep Mamma company on the way home, perhaps be allowed to take the reins for a time. But he never wanted to see Foxton again; and one never knew what might happen. Their own horse could have gone lame and that would mean spending the night . . .

"You and Jenny will have a makeshift lunch, and we'll have your fish for supper," Mrs Thorley said.

"I'll take mine and have it in the field—my lunch, I mean."

That should please Mamma; she liked him to show interest, as she termed it, and George had no objection to being present where work was going forward; it was being expected to work, anonymously, like a labourer, that had irked him. And already a thought, benevolent if tinged with patronage, was astir in him.

Those very early, very rosy, very sweet, and juicy apples were ripe on the old trees. He'd take a big basketful, enough for all. That should please them.

Jenny said, "I can't find my bucket, nor my scrubbing brush. I know where I left them and by the look of this table and this floor they ain't been used since I went away."

George remembered Deb, cleaning up, clanking a pail, throwing things out because Lavinia wouldn't be coming back; would never need her studio any more.

"I think they could be in the attic, Jenny."

"Nip up and fetch 'em, Master George, there's a love. Your legs is younger than mine."

His legs were so young that he could take the first steep flight two at a time; the next, with its two twists, slowed him down a bit. But there, just as he had thought, were the things Deborah had used. Just near a door with a heavy padlock.

George knew of the attic floor, he'd been up from time to time to fetch apples and pears and walnuts—but not, of course lately because, however carefully stored, nothing much lasted after Christmas. In Lavinia's studio he had taken no interest; a place where she had mucked about with paints. But the fact that the door should now be padlocked was, well, a bit odd. Not that it mattered to him. He reached down to pick up the two pails, one inside in the other, and something hit him like a thunderbolt. Jenny had just said that his legs were younger . . . But they would age. Year after year would add its burden . . . Until the end . . .

One day I shall be old!

Incredible thought and instantly repudiated. I will not! I will *not* go about creaking and groaning, mumbling and muttering, supported by a stick, two sticks.

But all men must die. *Day follows day and suddenly the dark one calls, and we follow, by that road or this, into the universal silences.* A scrap picked up from the liberal education Mr Spicer offered.

All right! I know. But I intend to live until I die. And live it in my own fashion, in my own place.

George snatched up the pails and clattered down the stairs to tell Jenny that he wanted mustard, not too much, not too little, just enough on his ham sandwiches.

Mrs Thorley and Deborah drove to Foxton in a silence punctuated by trivialities. The whole affair was over and done with,
and the moment of intimacy in the garden had left them both
shy. What more could be said?

"I won't come in," Mrs Thorley said as they neared the place.
"I still have so much to do."

Harvesting was going on here. In a field close to the road, Tim
was doing one of the heaviest jobs, pitching sheaves onto a half-
laden wagon. He was at least consistent; never ask a man to do
what you were not prepared to do yourself.

Deborah waved, and he waved back; but he did not stop work.
It would have pleased all his workmen had he done so, for he set
a hard pace.

He could not fairly be said to be angry with Deborah. Half-
broken colts—and in a way he regarded her as much—did kick up
now and again. Patience and a firm hand were the answer, not
anger; but in making him hitch the gig in that sharp sudden way
and going off, for no reason that he could see, she had kicked up,
after seeming to be so amenable. So she must learn. He was not
going to run to welcome her, jump the ditch that divided the field
from the yard, unhitch the gig, hitch up the dog-cart, make himself agreeable to Mrs Thorley, offer her tea. Let Deb do it, she was
capable . . .

Quite suddenly, as he stood there, a sheaf poised on the fork, a
tiny dart pierced Tim's armour of self-confidence, self-
righteousness, his certainty that God had made man in His own
image and woman as a kind of subsidiary. Deb *was* capable. He
had a thought which should have been comforting but was not. If
he dropped dead where he stood she'd step in and take charge.
Foxton would go on as before. The only real gap he'd leave would
be at chapel! A sobering thought for one who had never been anything but sober in all his days.

The man atop the half-loaded wagon rubbed a little salt into
the little wound.

"Ah," he said. "Missus is back! She'll see to Bill's thumb."

Getting the scythes ready for the next day's reaping in another
field, Bill had nicked his thumb that morning and despite the lavish application of cobwebs, supposedly a sovereign cure, it was still
bleeding and Bill was looking a bit whitish round the root of his
nose.

Yes, Tim thought, heaving the sheaf on to the load, she's been here two months and she's endeared herself to everybody; old Emma, the men, the chapel people.

Should you not, Timothy Bridges, be glad and proud? Did you not choose well? Yes; and yes; and yes. But she'd stood in his yard and said, Will you harness up, or must I? And he could not forget it. Like the pinch of yeast that could leaven a whole batch of bread, like the teaspoonful of rennet that could turn a whole bowl of milk sour and make it into cheese, the memory of that moment was to rankle in his mind.

"It could be," Caroline said, anxious to be consolatory, "just talk. I believe all men have such fancies. Even Edward! He once told me that as soon as he qualified he thought about going to America where there's only one doctor—in the wild parts—to thousands of people. His father talked him out it; he said there was plenty of work right here. And look how he's settled down. It may be the same with Everard. Wanderlust. That's the word I wanted."

Caroline could quote the case of Edward. But in fact Freddy had been the same. Always talking about getting away, making a fresh start. Never—give the Devil his due—asking her to go with him but keeping her, between the ecstatic moments, on the knife-edge of apprehension: Will he be there? Will he come? And look how he had settled down! Look!

"I am afraid Everard is more serious in his intention," Diana said. "I don't think wanderlust takes men to London. Ambition. Everard is very ambitious, and here he has run into a cul-de-sac. But it is such a shame, just when I've got the house so nice. And all that horrid business is over and we could begin to enjoy ourselves. I don't know about you, Caro, but I do sometimes think life is rather disappointing."

"I'd say, bloody awful. Don't turn that Mamma look on me, Di. I said bloody awful and bloody awful I mean."

"I don't see what *you* have to complain about."

"No? Doddering about, befriending this, helping that, supporting the other. God knows I'm sorry for the halt, the maimed and the blind. *And* the poor! But I hate them. Di, I know it sounds terrible, but I do. I always want to cry, and I hate them for making me want to cry. Honestly, I don't see why misery should be so contagious. We all have our miseries. Why we should go about licking other people's wounds . . . ? There are times when I think I shall go quite mad and say to some fellow who's lost an arm: Congratulations; next winter you'll have only *five* chilblains!"

Half a joke, half hysteria; and with neither had Diana any fellow-feeling. She said, "Don't be so silly!" But something that Caro had said lodged in her mind. If the worst happened and Everard did get a job in horrible London and she was torn up by the roots and wounded, nobody should be asked to give her a lick. She regretted now that she had said anything to Caroline about her reluctance to move. If it came, the move, she would pretend to welcome it. She would go down, no, not down, out, with all flags flying.

George said, "Well, that was nice, wasn't it?"

"Very nice," Mrs Thorley said. But she had hardly tasted it. Within her an appetite, not for food, had raged and been with difficulty controlled. This was perhaps the worst moment. There on the chiffonier was the whisky. And George's presence was no deterrent. He had seen her drink, had even poured a drink for her, many times. She had only to reach out her arm, or say: George would you please . . . ?

And why think of it as so evil? It saw you through, didn't it? It served you well.

Yes, a good servant; but a bad master.

How about moderation? Before March, before you were under such stress, you drank a little to help you to sleep. You did not begin to drink to excess until you found yourself in such an impossible situation. Go back to that régime. You *need* a drink, just one good stiff whisky, to steady your head and your hands, especially as you have writing to do. Go on. Just one. No! I know what that would mean: another and another. And within a year you'd be useless, a hopeless alcoholic.

"Have an apple, Mamma," George said, offering the dish. "I gathered them myself. And," his voice grew pious, "I took a great basketful to the field. Everybody enjoyed them."

"I'm sure they did, darling."

What else could he report to show himself in a favourable light? Make himself seem useful and indispensable?

"Oh, and I found Jenny's scrubbing things. They were on the attic landing." With scarcely a pause his mind flitted. "Why is Lavinia's door locked, if she isn't coming back?"

That must be Deb's doing. And why had she bothered? For a second Mrs Thorley wondered if Deb knew more than she had ever mentioned.

"It is because she will never come back, dear," Mrs Thorley improvised. "It had to be cleared out and cleaned up a bit. But while it remains unused it will still be, in a way, Lavinia's room."

And used or unused, so it would remain, while the house stood.

George gave this idea the blessing of his approval.

"I think that is a very nice idea, Mamma. After all we don't need the space. And I expect Lavinia hoped to come back. I know I did, when I was at Foxton. It was a great comfort to me to think that Gad's was here and you were here and everything would be as I left it. Being homesick is a terrible thing." A seed successfully planted? His mind shifted again, and Lavinia, who had never meant anything to him, never seemed real, did for a second take on reality, a homesick girl who would never come home. "Poor Lavinia," he said. "We'll keep that room. And when I am an old man and have a son of my own I shall tell him, and tell him to tell his son—leave that room alone. After all, she didn't have a grave here."

With a jerk of the head which gave the lie to her next words, Mrs Thorley said, "No, she has no memorial."

THE HAUNTING
OF GAD'S HALL

Mrs Thorley	*Mistress of Gad's Hall*
Mr van Haagen	*A business associate of Mrs Thorley*
Diana Spicer	*Mrs Thorley's daughter*
Everard Spicer	*Diana's husband, a lawyer*
George Thorley	*Mrs Thorley's son*
Deborah Bridges	*Mrs Thorley's stepdaughter*
Tim Bridges	*Deborah's husband*
Sam Bridges	*Their son*
Caroline Taylor	*Mrs Thorley's stepdaughter*
Doctor Edward Taylor	*Caroline's husband*
Freddy Ingram	*Caroline's former beau*
Susan Walford Ingram	*Freddy's wife*
Jenny	*Housekeeper/Cook at Gad's Hall*
Bob Spender	*Present owner of Gad's Hall*
Ella Spender	*His mother*
Jill Spender	*His wife*
John Spender ⎫	
Tony Spender ⎬	*Their children*
Alice Spender ⎭	

part one

Mr van Haagen glanced about the table at Gad's and said benevolently, meaning well,

"It is not often that one has the happiness of seeing so many old faces after so few years."

What he meant was plain; it was only two years since his last visit, and he had not then seen the family together, with so many friends gathered round. Caroline, at the far end of the table, and seated next to Freddy, pulled her mobile, monkeyish face into a mask of extreme age and said, "So now we know!" He laughed; he could always be trusted to see the point. He said, "I'm ordering a wheelchair tomorrow." If she had made the same remark to Edward, her husband for five years—five centuries—he would have looked blank and then said that Mr van Haagen meant well. Nonetheless, it had been a mistake to sit next to Freddy; the mere brush of his sleeve against her arm set all the old hungers flaring. She'd never got over him. Never would.

Mrs Thorley cast a look, doting, but with something dubious, some slight reserve, at her son, in his rightful place at the head of the table. He'd always been a precocious child and physical maturity had come to him with swiftness and ease. At fifteen he was a man. He had inherited his father's height, but he'd never had a gangly, awkward stage, too sinewy for that; and he was handsome; his father's craggy good looks mitigated by her own delicately arched nose and clarity of jaw. A born charmer—and well aware of it. Too well aware of it? Sometimes she wondered had she been wrong not to insist upon his going to school, as once arranged. School was said to knock off the rough edges—but then George had never had any rough edges.

She said, "It was George's idea. When Gad's Glory scored that supreme triumph, George said we must celebrate. And since Diana," with a jerk within a jerk of her head, Mrs Thorley indicated her daughter, "was already here, it seemed a good opportunity."

"Yes, indeed. And for me most fortunate."

He was anxious to please her. Their business association had been most successful. The cross between *her* Durham Shorthorns and *his* Frisians had been a sensation in the cattle world. He had once done her a singular favour—made the rough winter crossing between Holland and Bywater and made wildly extravagant bids for some of her beasts at auction. That was the year when she had done no showing and had therefore dropped back a little. The record price he had paid—or appeared to have paid, put her back in the top class. And she repaid him fourfold. She offered to reimburse him with money, but he had, very sensibly, decided to take stock instead. Since then she had always offered him the first refusal of her best. And now lively young calves of mixed blood were established in Holland, in Germany, in France.

Mr van Haagen allowed himself a tiny, secret sigh. There had been a time, six, seven years ago, when he had seriously contemplated asking Mrs Thorley to marry him. He'd admired her greatly. She was not young, even then, but his first marriage had given him the son every man needed, so he wanted no more children. A good steady woman with a head for business, a trim figure and still pretty face, and the capacity for running a house on oiled wheels would have been just right. But of course no man of any sensitivity would propose, too soon, to a widow. So he had waited and when the time was just right, she—to put it bluntly—was not. He'd been shocked when he came over to do her that favour; hair quite white, head jerking, hands tremulous. Aged by twenty years. She had, of course, suffered another bereavement; the loss of a daughter, that girl for whom in his half-serious, half-playful fortune-telling in the cards he had seen such disaster, but had only been able to say—Beware of the dark. Actually, in the fumbling, uncertain way of the fortune-teller, he had been right. The girl had gone to India, and died, either on the journey or soon after arrival. And her mother's hair had whitened and she'd been taken by a kind of palsy. Nothing much, a jerk of the head, a tremor of the hands; but Mr van Haagen had known then—five years ago— that marriage was out of the question. For one day his nerves, so much more vulnerable than his stolid exterior would suggest, might break down and he would lean across the table and say— *Will you keep your head still!* No longer desirable as partner in bed and board, she was still astute, with him, at least, dead-honest, and still a wonderful provider, with no fuss.

Mrs Thorley had no need to fuss. Jenny was still in the kitchen —her legs, and what ailed them had always been a mystery, obligingly allowing her to do anything she wanted to do, and then drawing a line. They allowed her to cook—and she still did it superbly, but for anything other than cooking help must be enlisted from the village. And no difficulty about *that*. Jenny was related to almost everyone in Stonham St Paul's, and quite a number of people in the next village, Stonham St Peter's. She belonged to a family so intermarried, interrelated, tough, resilient, wide-branched that she could probably have produced, in a crisis, some cousin's cousin or niece from as far away as Nettleton, or Intake, or Muchanger. Two were in action this evening; Violet—not as pretty as her name—who was regular and came up from the village each morning and went back to sleep, and Ruth, older, very pretty who just happened to be home, unemployed at the moment, glad enough to earn two shillings. Recommending her, Jenny had said that Ruth knew all about waiting at table; she'd worked once at the *Hawk in Hand* in Baildon. And certainly this evening the service was going with exceptional smoothness and speed, though, to be honest, Mrs Thorley hadn't taken to Ruth at first sight; there was something pert, something bouncy, more suitable to an inn's public dining room than to a sedate little dinner party in a private house.

Mr van Haagen looked about him again and then turning to his hostess asked anxiously, "Did I say right to say old? Should I be saying well-remembered?"

"That was understood," Mrs Thorley said. "And of course, it must be at least six years since you saw all the girls together. In fact I don't think you have seen Deborah or Caroline since they were married. Diana comes every year and her husband—Everard, you may remember him—usually manages a few days. Unfortunately, this year business took him to Scotland. And Deborah's husband, I don't think you ever met him, he has a very large farm and breeds horses. He finds it difficult to get away."

And wouldn't come if he had all the time in the world! Mrs Thorley had never liked him, virtuous and worthy as he undoubtedly was; Methodist; teetotaler, drinking lemonade at his own wedding! Deborah, that good, capable, most precious girl could well have been overwhelmed, reduced, tamed. But the baby had saved her. Just at the time when one act of defiance—rushing back to Gad's to help succor and sustain, had made Tim Bridges decide that the time had come to tighten the curb, Deborah was pregnant. And Tim knew enough about breeding animals; a gravid female must not be upset; nor a female suckling. And then, just as he was ready to assert himself again, the child weaned, one of his heavy horses had trodden on his foot and broken four bones. So he had been laid up, nursed, cared for most tenderly by Deborah, but the situation which he had once, for a moment visualised, had come about. Deborah had dealt with everything, farm, stables, disabled man in her competent, capable way. He was not much missed.

Mrs Thorley, of course, could not know that Timothy Bridges' God had failed him and that he was taking refuge in a sour disillusionism. She only knew that Deborah now made regular visits, driving a rather-too-frisky horse in the high, yellow-wheeled gig. Bringing the child, a sturdy boy, saying once, in her offhand way, "Of course Tim wanted some Biblical name like Ebenezer. But I stuck out. I agreed on Samuel, it can be Sam and shouldn't cause him any embarrassment."

No doubt about it, Deb had emerged triumphant, but happy?

There were old faces, or faces well- or ill-remembered, missing from this table. Mrs Spicer, the Rector's wife, Everard's Aunt Amelia, and one of Mrs Thorley's oldest friends in this district. She'd gone plodding round, doing her duty, as always, and caught a cold which settled on her chest. Nothing that a boiled onion wouldn't remedy. Even her husband had bestirred himself for once, harried the tatterdemalion maid. Prayed. To no avail. She'd died as quietly as she had lived, and but for the efforts of a few of his parishioners, Mr Spicer could well have followed her to the grave. He was here this evening simply because it had seemed wrong not to invite him, with a good meal ready to be served. . . .

Also missing, and more missed, was Mr Walford. After years of being shackled to the bedside of a vaguely-ailing wife, he was freed by her rather sudden death, and set about making up for lost time, burning the candle at both ends. He still gave his Brewery meticulous attention for Freddy, his son-in-law, knew almost nothing of the technique, though he was splendid on the sales side. Evenings which had been so quiet and so long in the big old house, where the invalid could not bear the slightest noise, now became riotous and all too short; all-male parties often did not break up until one o'clock, two o'clock, with too much eating and drinking. A genial and generous host, a happy and appreciative guest, Mr Walford romped through his last years and was then felled by a fatal stroke.

Perhaps Mr and Mrs Gordon and their son James should not have been present at this festive board, for Gordon and Son had treated Everard abominably, using him—so much better qualified in law than either of them, as a kind of office boy, never increasing his salary or offering the partnership on which he had set his heart; so he'd gone to London in disgust. But to make a feud of it would have been awkward, for Mr Gordon was still Mrs Thorley's lawyer and had, on occasion, been helpful to her, sometimes actively and once at least through inertia. And on one of her earliest annual visits home, Diana had said she did not in the least mind meeting the Gordons; she would enjoy showing them how their miserable behaviour to Everard, so far from keeping him down, had set him up. It was both true, and untrue. Everard had joined a big firm, in the City, Upton, Binder and Smith, but a partnership still eluded him and although he earned more, living in London was unbelievably expensive. Diana would scrimp and save all the year in order to appear at Gad's in stylish new dresses; then she had a baby to show, a most exquisite little girl, and Diana knew how ardently Mrs Gordon longed for James to settle down and give her grandchildren. This year, also she had a triumph to report. No, Everard would not be coming to Gad's this year, he'd gone to Scotland on *most* important business; something to do with the administration of the Lumsley estate. He was, at this minute, staying in Lumsleydale Castle. A shrewd knock that, for when the Gordons had sent Everard on errands which involved an overnight stay he'd only had second-class hotel accommodation. Mr Gordon looked suitably impressed. But at the back of his mind something stirred; Lumsley? Lumsley? Ah, yes, a rather shady business, illegitimacy somehow involved. Nothing he'd wish to handle.

There was a new face at the table. Doctor Raven, pleasant, young, shy. Not so long ago, Mrs Thorley could remember, there'd only been old Doctor Taylor and then presently, his son, Edward. But the Hospital had grown, so that by the time Caroline married Edward—and old Doctor Taylor retired—it could afford a resident doctor. And then, thanks to Caroline's innovations, a roundabout and coconut shies and competitions, instead of the usual fund-raising methods, the Hospital could afford half another doctor. Residents came and went, but Doctor Raven seemed permanent. Half his time was his own and he had a little surgery at the upper end of Scurvy Lane. Edward was invariably kind to the newcomers, partly because he was fundamentally kind, and partly because he had himself been so lucky; he'd never had to take a paid post, or set up on his own, he'd just slipped into his father's practice. Caroline was kind to them, too. One might almost say motherly—a strange thing to say of Caroline, the least motherly of creatures. But the truth was that Caroline could assume almost any role as the fancy took her. She'd been such a flirt. And then so infatuated, so positively ill-behaved with Freddy Ingram. But he'd married Susan Walford, and after some days of crying—and a little good advice from Mrs Thorley, she'd married Edward, settled down, and never since put a foot wrong. But no child yet!

Mr van Haagen, eating ruminatively, not unlike one of his own placid animals, vaguely remembered an evening in this house when, because he could neither play the piano nor sing, and a guest should do something in return for hospitality, he had offered to read the cards for the ladies. He had exercised his art scores of times since and naturally could not remember much detail, but now, confronted with four of the five girls whose fortunes he had told that evening, certain things came back. He'd seen Miss Diana living in a big city—and she was now resident in London. Horses had loomed large in Miss Deborah's future, and behold, she had married a famous breeder of horses. For Miss Caroline he had foreseen floods and floods of tears and then a multitude of good works. His eye lingered on her as he wondered whether the tears had been shed and forgotten, or whether they were still to come. She looked merry enough now. Of them all, he thought, marriage had changed her least, and of them all she was now the most stylish, her hair looked positively French, drawn up to the top her head and then cascading in curls to the nape of her neck—a fashion said to have been introduced by the Empress Eugénie. The shift of the curls lent something coquettish as she turned her head, speaking now to Mr Ingram, now the poor old parson who seemed to be taking his widowhood more heavily than Mr van Haagen had taken his. Diana and Deborah had stuck to the demure style which had prevailed when they first put their hair up, parted in the middle, looped smoothly over the ears and then gathered into a kind of bun. The only difference was that Diana's was smooth, carved in ebony, and Deborah's was red and unruly, a curl kept breaking away to be pushed back impatiently.

Upon the fourth girl, Miss Walford then, now Mrs Ingram, Mr van Haagen's eye lingered for a moment. Not in approbation. Six or was it seven years ago . . . such a dull, quiet, dim . . . And yet the cards had said a courtship of the whirlwind. And that was true, too. In fact the cards never lied, and reading the future in them was not magic or psychic, or any of the other things which gushing ladies said; properly handled, as his grandmother had taught him, it was an exact science.

But it was not because Susan Walford had made the whirlwind marriage, as predicted, that his eye lingered. An expert, used-to-dealing-with-animals eye. Possibly those who saw her often didn't notice, but to Mr van Haagen she looked very ill. The hair on a human, like the hide of an animal, was the surest sign of health, or ill health. And Mrs Ingram's hair looked scanty, dry, without lustre. Any animal with such a stary coat . . .

Susan—once she had been Poor Susan because she also was shackled to her mother, and then she had been regarded as fortunate, marrying Freddy, so handsome and popular, sat there and asked herself—Shall I be able to see this through? So lovely, Di and Deb and Caro and I all together, I must. I must.

She could not remember when the pain first started, a silly little, niggling little, something-to-be-ignored stitch in her side. She couldn't even place it; now it was behind her ribs, and the next minute lower down. She was determined, absolutely determined not to mention it, not to be like her mother, always ailing, always demanding attention and company, a nuisance to everybody. Not me! I will not repeat that deadly pattern.

Hadn't there been a boy, somewhere far away and in a time long ago who had stood up and smiled with a fox, or was it a wolf? gnawing his vitals away? In Sparta? Very well, she would be Spartan. But sensible, too. One day, saying nothing to Papa, then alive and happy, or to Freddy, she'd driven herself into Baildon and consulted Edward, Caroline's husband. All terribly embarrassing. And futile. Edward had prodded; Does this hurt? Now if I press, do you feel anything? Or here? Here? Susan could truthfully say, No, because the pain was not to be located—and because Edward often sat at Mr Walford's overladen table, he surmised that it could be indigestion. (Susan had not then begun to look ill; in fact looked better than she had ever done in his knowledge of her.) He gave her some sound advice about diet, about tight lacing and about taking exercise—though not immediately after a meal. He made her up a bottle of bismuth mixture. He then suggested that she should go through and see Caroline. Before their respective marriages the two girls had been great friends, gay Caroline and Poor Susan. One of the things Edward admired about Caroline was that she was so tender-hearted.

"Thank you, Edward," Susan said, "but I don't want anyone to know about this," she pressed her hand to her side. "In fact you are the only person I've ever said a word to." It would have been disloyal to Mamma to explain why.

Next time Edward saw her—it was at a dance—she looked, and felt, thinner. Overdoing it? Women had no sense of proportion! Tell them not to overeat and they'd go on a starvation diet; suggest reasonable exercise and they'd walk ten miles. It was perhaps not etiquette to mix professional with social activities, but he mentioned her loss of weight and said he hoped she wasn't cutting down too drastically. She said: Oh no. Twice during that evening Edward caught sight of her, left hand pressing her side, and he made an opportunity to ask about the pain.

"Oh, better, thank you. It just comes and goes."

Edward was troubled.

The resident doctor at the Hospital at that moment was regarded as a brilliant young man, far too good for the post really, just marking time in Baildon until his father's partner retired—a crusty, pig-headed old man, impossible to work with. And of course the young man was only just qualified; Edward was conscious of the fact that his own finals were now eleven years' distant. Carefully concealing the patient's identity, Edward asked Doctor Watts' opinion. The young man was both flattered and embarrassed, for he admired Edward profoundly and knew how very thorough he was.

"It is very difficult to say without seeing her, and even then, if *you* found nothing wrong . . ."

"Nothing; heart, lungs, sound as a bell, stomach, bowels, uterus."

"An unlocated, intermittent pain. Of course," the young man said, advancing a pretty revolutionary theory, "it could be of nervous origin. Nervous headaches are now recognised."

Roughly, nervous meant nothing wrong functionally; in fact largely a thing of the imagination. But in that area Edward was very sensitive; he and his father had differed over Mrs Walford, the older man cossetting and sympathetic, Edward brisk, saying that if she abandoned bed and sofa and the role of invalid and lived a normal life she'd be all right. And then, quite unaccountably, Mrs Walford had just died. Such a thing made one a bit extra careful.

"Would you examine her?"

"Most willingly."

Nothing detectable; and the woman did not strike Doctor Watts as being the *maladie imaginaire* type; not self-assertive, not melancholic. A sensible, apparently happy young woman and inclined to make light of the pain. Still, another opinion might be desirable. Doctor Watts knew of a man, in Wimpole Street. A wonderful reputation. . . .

Getting Susan to London was less difficult than Edward had imagined. Both her father and Freddy were indulgent and thought that a day's shopping would do her good. And she would not be obliged to make the now-possible day trip by train alone because she had chosen a day when Edward Taylor had business in London.

Nothing; no explanation, no help, even from Wimpole Street.

The pain did not exist, except for her, its host, its victim.

Then her father died with dreadful suddenness and that was enough to explain further loss of weight, and pallor, and anyway everybody looked horrible in dead mourning.

Susan had a brother, Richard. Between them had been the link of shared adversity—the invalid mother who could not be left, even with the most reliable of hirelings. Richard had been more fortunate than Susan, he had gone away to school, and he spent some time getting experience in a big brewery in Burton-on-Trent. Then he'd come home and fallen in love with Diana, who had fallen in love with Everard Spicer. Richard had made some excuse to go back to Burton-on-Trent and there settled, but not married.

Could there perhaps ultimately be no heir to the Brewery; to the big, comfortable old house?

I shall have no child; nothing could live with this pain. I'm beginning to doubt if I can, myself, much longer. Give up; ask Edward for some opiate drops and swallow the whole lot in one go. . . . What, then, of Freddy? Oh he'd be all right. He'd do the decent thing and wait a year, then remarry. Not Caroline, for she was married. There had been a time when Susan had been dismally sure that Freddy would marry Caroline; they'd got themselves talked about. Susan had been the most surprised, most dizzily delighted girl in the world when Freddy had chosen her instead. Caroline had showed no sign of minding. In no time at all she'd been engaged to Edward, and ever after the life and soul, the centre of gaiety at every gathering at which she was present.

Surely this was the longest dinner party in history. How much longer could it go on? Nothing cured the pain, but sometimes a change of position mitigated it a little. Please, Mrs Thorley, dear Mrs Thorley, rise, lead the movement towards the drawing room. And please, Di, please Deb, don't suggest that we should just steal up and peep at the children, three of them now, Di's two—a most beautiful little girl, rightly called Belle, three years old; a boy not quite so engaging yet, named Melville, and best, most enviable of all, Deborah's boy, Sam; four years old and by all accounts very naughty. . . .

Once, coming downstairs after a dutiful inspection, only two of them then, Sam and Belle, angelic in sleep, Susan had said to Caroline, "Don't you sometimes wish . . . ?" And Caroline had said vehemently,

"No I do not! I see quite enough of children, what with the Hospital and the Ragged School and the various treats. And between you and me, that Sam is a devil. He'll lead poor Deb a pretty dance before he's done."

Caroline's refusal to be wistful, sentimental, yearning, had been slight comfort to Susan just then. A part explanation, too, of her charm. All things to all men; look at her now, turning one face to Freddy and quite another to Mr Spicer. It was a gift. Caroline was quite hollow, like a bell, responding to every pull of the rope. Less popular with women. Women seemed to see a little further; and if, presently they all went up to look at the children, three now, mothers, she'd say: Oh, how lucky you are. Or: How I envy you.

Mrs Thorley's thoughts centred now and again about the three grandchildren, small occupants of a great deal of space. It did indeed seem ridiculous that a house so spacious—comparatively spacious, as Gad's should suddenly seem so congested.

"Oh, for God's sake, Mamma, let's have *somebody* young,"

George said when the party was under discussion. A reasonable request. "Whom would you like?"

"The Faulkner twins," George said with revealing promptitude.

Consternation struck Mrs Thorley from varying tangents. Calf love. Part of growing up, and quite usual in boys far less mature than George; she was prepared to be tolerant of it; but she didn't want George to invite a snub. The Faulkners were very definitely County and Mrs Thorley was extremely class-conscious. County herself to begin with in Westmorland; married to a man of her own class, but a wastrel, a gambler who'd squandered her quite considerable dowry and dragged her down to the lowest depths. After he shot himself, positively the only alternative to gaol for debt, she'd known that worst kind of poverty—genteel; lost in Leicester, too proud to seek further help either from her own family or her husband's, making a very precarious living for herself and Diana and Lavinia. Then she had married George Thorley of Gad's Hall in Suffolk and become a member of another class—middle, solid respectable. All splendid chaps, as her father often said; acceptable in the hunting field—it was often their land that was ridden over; acceptable in Local Yeomanry units—they invariably had good horses. *But one did not invite them to dinner.* The real hallmark of social acceptance. Mrs Thorley, in all her years in Suffolk, had been careful, from a kind of inverted pride, had never once referred to her origins, or those of her first husband. She was a widow, with two little girls, who'd married George Thorley, with his two little girls, Deborah and Caroline, and once she had edged out the more bucolic of George's friends and captured what might be called the professional class—still middle, but better-educated, she was content. Then, in a way, when, having paid her debt to George Thorley for rescuing her from Leicester by bearing George, and was widowed again, she had broken the rigid mould by going to business—a woman on her own and a match for any man.

In George, son of a late marriage and so much indulged that behind his wish to please, his capacity to be charming, a boundless self-confidence lay. A trap to the unwary, Mrs Thorley said,

"I doubt whether Lady Faulkner would allow Chloe to come to an evening party with no other chaperone than her brother."

I never did. I was always most careful. Lenient; young men were always welcome here. But I spoke very strictly to Caroline about riding, unaccompanied, in Freddy Ingram's gig. We have our standards too!

"She would. If I asked," George said. "Lady Faulkner likes me, so does Sir John. And so they should. I saved Jonathan's life, don't forget."

It was true. On George's first day out with the South Suffolk. Hounds in full cry; everybody else too much absorbed in the chase to realise that the Faulkner boy had come to grief at a hedge with a deep ditch on the other side. George, a novice, but coached by Deborah, who had hunted for four years and who said: Don't go for the broken-down hedge, it always means heavy going on the far side. Choose your own place. I always do, and I more than make up lost time. George, choosing his own bit of the hedge, his own unslippery landing beyond, had spotted Jonathan—somebody not known to him then, just somebody who looked young at the Meet, and therefore seemed to justify George's presence. Now, face down in a narrow but deep ditch, he looked very dead indeed. George, having dismounted and hauled the boy out, hoped somebody would notice, come to his aid, know what to do. Nobody did. The hunt swept by. Well, get the water out of him. If he could. Whack, whack, whack! And if he's hurt, not merely half drowned, I'm making things worse. The water came out in spurts, followed by the remains of the boy's breakfast. And air went in, little gasps.

"Are you all right?"

"All in one piece, anyway. That bloody nag!"

"Those bloody people!"

They grinned at one another; conspirators against a world where neither horses nor people were quite up to the mark.

"What you need now is a good dose of brandy. I wonder . . ." George looked about him. Not a house in sight, and to him pretty unknown territory; the wrong side of Layer Wood. Just then a lumbering old man on a lumbering old horse, bringing up the rear, lumbered through the damaged fence and landed safely. George ran forward. Urgent, but mannerly,

"Sir. Do you happen to have a flask about you?"

"Somebody taken a toss?" the old man asked, gladly reining in. His hunting days were over; he only turned out these days just to give countenance and to indulge Old Charlie, once the best leaper in the county and still an addict, inclined to run up and down his meadow and make woeful noises if he heard the hounds.

"Never move without it." Lord Norton produced a silver-topped flask. "Serious?" God send it might not be, for if it were serious he would be compelled to get down, and these days it took a good strong heave from a good strong man to get him into the saddle at all.

"No," George said, "he's all in one piece. Thank you."

Sign of the times, Lord Norton thought, with the petulance of the old; they come out younger and younger! We shall end with babies in basket saddles! But he was not averse to a pause, an interruption, a cast-iron excuse for not being in at the kill. And Old Charlie, after a first spirited start, was feeling his years, too. Thinking of what he would say—I had to stop to succour the wounded—he wheeled Old Charlie round, saw one boy ministering to the other. Recognised the other; one of his many grand-nephews. Or godsons. He muddled them a bit these days.

"Good God! Johnny Faulkner?"

"Yes, sir."

And nothing to be proud of, distant as the relationship might be. Soaked, muddied and green-gilled. And the other boy—older of course, but nevertheless very young, so neat, competent and in control, screwing back the silver top of the flask.

"And who're you?"

"George Thorley."

"Gad's?"

"Yes."

"Remarkable woman, your mother."

"Yes, sir, she is."

Two boys and only one horse. The one standing there, waiting, meek as a lamb, was obviously a Thoroughgood, from Nettleton. It was said that the family of Thoroughgood had been breeding horses there since the Middle Ages, starting with a couple of Arabs somebody brought back from the Crusades. This one was perhaps not a prime specimen, but even so its price would be more than John Faulkner could afford. Ergo it must be young Thorley's. Well, well, well! That's where the money was, these days. Business! Venting an unacknowledged flash of discontent upon an innocent victim, his lordship looked sternly at Johnny and said, "Where's *your* horse?"

"I don't know, sir. It ran off."

"Shocking! Did nobody ever tell you? First rule after a fall. Catch your horse. Horse without a rider, danger to everybody."

"But, sir, Uncle Roger, I was in the ditch, face down."

Unplaced, the old man said, "No excuse. No excuse at all."

"Excuse me, sir, it is. He was unconscious. He'd have died if I . . ."

Lord Norton muttered something that sounded very much like: Pity you bothered! "I'll have my flask back, if you've *quite* finished."

"I see what you mean about bloody people. And he's about the bloodiest. And I'll bet you a sovereign that as soon as he's within earshot of anybody, he'll say he saved my life. Well, I shall tell them different."

"You ought to get into some dry clothes. D'you know where we are?"

"I'm a bit off beat myself. But we did cross a road back there. I'll get a lift. Look here, I've spoiled your day quite enough. You go on."

"And end up behind your uncle! No, thanks! I tell you what. You take my horse and I'll get a lift. You'll be home and dry quicker that way. Come on, Goldie. That's his name. He's very tender-mouthed, you won't jag him, will you?" One couldn't have implicit faith in a boy who'd come a cropper at such a simple fence. "Where do you live?"

"Stratton Strawless."

Not very near; never mind. "I'll drive over tomorrow and fetch him. D'you know, he doesn't even have to be tied. He'll follow a gig, like a dog."

"You're a lucky chap. I'll tell you what. Come to lunch tomorrow."

Lady Faulkner's reaction when she heard of the misadventure was very different from that of her uncle. Jonathan was her only son. Three girls and hope almost abandoned. Even of the twins Chloe was born first. Four! The name Jonathan meant *God-given*, and so he was. She never called him anything else, though to most people he was Johnny. She was delighted that George Thorley had been asked to lunch, so that she could thank him personally and perhaps make him a small present.

Sir John said: "Any boy who owns a Thoroughgood at his age doesn't need anything *you* could give him, my poor dear."

"It's the spirit of the thing that counts," Lady Faulkner said vaguely.

And of course, to one prepared for a farm boy—splendid, kind and thoughtful though he might be—George Thorley with his poise and beautiful manners was a complete surprise.

So had begun a resilient if interrupted friendship between the two boys. Johnny was at Eton and had other friends, and many relatives with whom he spent part of the holidays, but whenever he was at home he and George met, and George had been invited to two parties; one at Christmas, one to celebrate the twins' sixteenth birthday. It was, Lady Faulkner reflected with sorrow, about the only debut poor Chloe would make—unless some wealthy relative came to the rescue. But who? Of Lord Norton one naturally expected nothing.

It was at the birthday dance that George Thorley fell in love with Chloe, whom Nature had endowed with every quality to make her suitable for a first love. Her flaxen hair fell in curls, rather like a spaniel's ears on either side of a heart-shaped face, her eyes were smoky blue and set too wide apart, her mouth had the pursed, petulant shape known as rosebud. She also had the desirable trait of being completely stupid. No Faulkner was overweighted with intelligence, but as was commonly understood to be the case with twins, the wits of a normal child had been divided between the two, Jonathan getting the lion's share. Chloe's mental blankness gave her the approved innocent look, and given half a chance she should have made a good match. But unless her father decided—as he was highly unlikely to do—to sell some land, Chloe would have no chance, she'd probably marry the younger Stanton boy and and join all the other land-rich, money-poor, family-proud people of whom there were too many in Suffolk.

When George suggested inviting the Faulkner twins and Mrs Thorley had made her protest about the unlikelihood of Chloe being allowed to come, and been answered, she said,

"And if Chloe came, my dear, it would raise a problem. Mr van Haagen is always a little vague about dates, but suppose his visit did coincide with the party. We have only the one guest room."

That would of course be for Chloe Faulkner. Deborah would stay the night; she and Di would share the room they had always shared; the room once shared by Caroline and Lavinia would be given over to the children. What was known as the Little Room, perfect for one guest, had long been occupied by Jenny and it would be impossible to usurp her now, even for the one or two nights.

"We'll take that fence when we come to it," George said. "Just write and invite them. *Both*."

Quite a long time ago Deborah's husband, Timothy Bridges, had seen in George the spoilt only son, an incipient dictator. Once when George had been under his roof at Foxton, he had done his conscientious best to correct, reprove, admonish, reduce, but what could a man do in a mere ten days?

Mrs Thorley wrote; well aware of the difference between letting a boy come for a day's shooting, or to stay for a night before, or after a Hunt on this side of Layer Wood, and letting a daughter attend an evening party, stay a night. Mrs Thorley knew her world; she knew what the answer would be; glad acceptance on Johnny's part, civil regret, a previous engagement would prevent Chloe. That would be all right. Johnny could share George's room; the guest room would be free for Mr van Haagen.

She was reckoning without something which the Faulkner twins had shared more equally than they had shared their wits—a complete—and eventually ruinous—devotion to one another, and a deadly sullen obstinacy. Jonathan could not, or would not see why Chloe should miss a party. Chloe could not or would not see why she should miss one hour of Jonathan's company. Jonathan said stormily,

"You may have forgotten; I haven't. But for George I should have died in that ditch and never gone to a party again. Except, of course my funeral!"

Chloe shed a few tears and said she couldn't see why if Johnny could go to Gad's, she couldn't.

Lady Faulkner thought of the accident, of George Thorley's prompt and effective action. Suppose, just suppose, George had looked down and thought: He is not a farmer; one of us; let him drown. . . . Class was important, but there were times . . .

"They're both coming."

"What did I tell you? And I have been thinking. *If* Mr van Haagen should happen to arrive just then, he could go upstairs. In the other attic. Or of course he could share my bed with Johnny, and I'd go up. But I think he'd prefer a room to himself, don't you. He's a bit old, and Johnny snores like the devil. I did think,"

George said, in his curiously mature way, "about Johnny and me going up, but it's such a small bed and we couldn't get a bigger one round that bend. And I think the attic could be made quite comfortable."

No real reason why it should not be. The window which Deborah had, in a desperate moment, most ingeniously knocked out had been replaced long ago. The narrow bed was comfortable —Mrs Thorley had always treated her servants well.

"Leave it to me," George said.

Like every house of its period and above poverty level, Gad's was overfurnished and had things in reserve. No provident house-wife waited until a lamp, for instance, was broken and an emergency created; she had one in store. George went about like a light-hearted magpie, taking from this room and that everything he considered necessary to make the attic so comfortable that it would make up to Mr van Haagen for having to climb an extra flight of stairs, steep and twisted. The room that yielded most was the one in which the children slept. It couldn't possibly matter to Sam, aged four, Belle aged three and a half, or Melville, still in a cot, whether their washstand was mahogany, furnished with flower-painted crockery, or deal with plain white such as had served Jenny when the attic was hers. Helped by Violet—only too glad to get away from Jenny's sharp eye and strict tongue, George converted the attic into a very snug and cosy room with only its sloping roof and dormer window to show that it was, in fact, an attic. Unconsciously, George was exercising his innate ability to set a scene, and having done so he wished it to be admired. He invited Mamma to do so.

It was five years but for a month since Mrs Thorley had set foot even on the attic stairs and now she said with what George considered a regrettable lack of interest,

"I haven't time now, dear. I'm sure you have made it very nice."

He invited Diana, who at least accepted, and made nothing of the stairs. In London she lived in a horrid, most inconvenient house, built narrow and high, three floors and a basement. She looked round, observant, not very appreciative. So that's where the proper washstand went! And the quilted bed-cover. But she said, "Yes, very nice. Actually, though, the other attic is much larger."

"Didn't you know? Mamma and I agreed to keep that one locked. Always. A kind of memorial to Lavinia."

Diana's memory of that terrible, shocking, disgusting time had blurred, been silted over by her own problems. . . .

"I see," she said, and backed on to the landing and looked at the padlocked door, and was, for some unknown reason, filled with a sense of desolation. She still loved Everard; in that more fortunate than Caroline, who loved Edward so little that she had found her honeymoon boring, and unlike Deborah, who had loved Timothy, gone all Methodist, worn a print dress, worked, lived like a servant—and then suddenly rebelled. Diana loved Everard, but here on the attic landing she was conscious of a loss of faith in him. Not in him. She corrected herself quickly. In the world, where rewards were so unfair, so absolutely unpredictable. And at the same time Diana suffered a pang of self-distrust, completely alien to her; Everard might have done better if he had not married me; he could have chosen a girl with money, or influence in the right quarters. . . .

She was not prone to entertaining self-derogatory thoughts and quickly dismissed this one.

It was as well that a place was prepared for Mr van Haagen, for on the very morning of the party, there was the letter. Unless delayed by wind and weather, the cross Channel boat should be in Bywater at eight o'clock in the morning, and—since there was now a railway link between Baildon and the port, he would be in Bywater at eleven. "We must have much discussion, Madam."

Mrs Thorley said, "I think I'd better meet him. I'll pick up the fish, meet the train, and then take him to lunch at the *Hawk in Hand*. That will relieve Jenny, she has enough to do making ready for this evening. And we can have our much discussions over lunch. Diana, dear, will you see to the flowers? Deborah said she'd be here at about four."

Once upon a time—and in years actually not so long ago—the *Hawk in Hand*, like the Corn Exchange and the Cattle Market, had been all-male territory, one of those citadels which Mrs Thorley had stormed. The inn made, had always made, some provision for women—they travelled too, by coach at one time, more lately by train, but they ate in semi-private rooms. There was also, at the back, overlooking the yard and stables a place where women could await their husbands on market days. They could even drink tea while they waited. But the dining room, overlooking the Market Place, had been strictly a man's place until one drowsy, rather short staffed midday. The inn was always inadequately staffed in mid-summer. There was so much alternative employment; causal, and overpaid; pea- and fruit-picking, helping with the harvest on family farms, rushing down to Bywater to man the bathing machines, the new hostelry which called itself a hotel. Mrs Thorley, still in her widow's black then, had arrived with three men and somebody with more taste than tact had suggested segregation. The two-shilling ordinary was about to be served in the big dining room . . . perhaps the gentlemen would like to go there and talk business and perhaps the lady would like to come this way.

Deceptively ladylike, in voice, in manner, Mrs Thorley said, "But it is *my* business we propose to talk about. Ah, that corner table; just right for four."

When, years later, Lord Norton had said to George by that muddy ditch, "Remarkable woman, your mother," he had not been exaggerating. She was remarkable; she had taken what for her husband had been an expensive hobby and turned it into a profitable business. The herd, at one time subsidised by the ordinary farm, was now the subsidiser. Ordinary agriculture was in rather a poor way.

Mrs Thorley was so well-known now, so accepted in the man's world that nobody thought about it any more. She would meet Mr van Haagen, take him to lunch at the *Hawk in Hand*, pay the bill and not cause an eyelid to flicker. There had never been the slightest smear upon her reputation; devoting herself to a business as she had done—except for a little time which those with good memories recalled, when she seemed to be beaten, hadn't entered a beast for any show, or been seen herself for a time—she had married all her girls well. And when you came to think of it, it was proof of her good management that all four girls—her two, George Thorley's two—had been treated so equitably that nobody could distinguish between them. Not even her enemies, and she had some, had even found a harsher term than "unwomanly" to throw at her; she was known as a hard bargainer, but known also for her absolute integrity.

Diana derived a bitter-sweet pleasure from seeing to the flowers. Nothing grew in the narrow, sunless strip of garden behind the dismal London house, and bought flowers had very short lives. Here there was plenitude, she could be lavish.

George cut flowers, too, but furtively. A bowlful of pink roses, just in the best, half-open stage, to liven up the guest room where Chloe would sleep tonight. Trying it, in this position and that—on the dressing-table, the top of the chest of drawers, the bedside table, he was temporarily in the grip of a passion—recognised by his mother as calf love—which was capable of overruling all the elements, lurking, incipient, in his nature. He was conceited, self-assured, egoistic, exhibitionist, arrogant, cynical, ruthless: but, prowling about the guest room, he was just simple boy, bringing an offering to the shrine of a goddess.

Sex as sex—and he knew all about it—had nothing to do with his feeling for Chloe Faulkner. It would have been unthinkable, revolting. All he wanted was to adore—and to please, to pay tribute.

Presently Deborah arrived, with Sam, and she and Diana, who had not met for a year, immediately started, over tea, child talk, comparing ages, weight, teeth and of course Deborah must spend some time admiring the new baby. It was quite a while before George could decently say, "Deb, come and see what I have made of the attic."

Deborah seemed to start. "*What attic?*"

"The one I have made ready for Mr van Haagen. Next to the locked one. You remember?"

I remember and nothing, nothing, wild horses would not induce me to go near that place again.

"I didn't know," Deb said, "that Mr van Haagen was expected. . . . Should I not have said I'd stay overnight? I don't mind driving in the dark and Sam is quite good—when he's asleep."

Di said, "That wouldn't help much. Mr van Haagen couldn't very well share a bed with me, could he?"

George, watching and listening, had an odd thought: Now if Caro had said that it would have had a different flavour. A joke, with a kind of challenge in it. Said by Diana it was a plain statement.

"Dear George," Deborah said, "I don't suppose that the attic needs my approval. Sam stop it! I will not have you be so rough."

It was a pity, but it was a fact that almost since the two children—called cousins though they had no blood kinship, Deborah being a Thorley and Diana an Osborne—could crawl, there'd been a kind of antagonism. Deb's Sam was older and bigger, but Di's Belle was vicious; she bit. And because of something which had happened in the past, seeing one human being, however young, biting another, however aggressive, made Deborah feel just slightly sick.

Almost as soon as the two children had been separated, Mrs Thorley and Mr van Haagen arrived. They'd spent the afternoon down at Park Farm, where the herd was housed. And they had perfected their next move in the five-year-old game of tit-for-tat. Her idea; you couldn't really call it dishonest, just a little tricky, but extremely profitable.

Coming in with her fellow-conspirator, Mrs Thorley said, "Deb, my dear," with some feeling. No amount of time could blur her awareness of what she owed to her stepdaughter. Then she felt the teapot, poured a cup for Mr van Haagen, and one for herself, cast an unmaternal glance upon Sam who was a ruffian, and upon Belle who was a vixen, cooed over Melville, noting that the week he had already spent in the country had improved his colour. Mr van Haagen, who had eaten a hearty lunch and knew that a good dinner awaited him, made a substantial tea, saying as he took his second slice of Victoria sponge,

"I am too much eating, is it not? I am gross." He eyed his paunch with a mixture of concern and complacency. Deborah, with her lopsided smile, said,

"Shakespeare believed that well-fleshed men were the most trustworthy."

"Indeed so? The great Shakespeare?" Of formal education Mr van Haagen had none but he had somehow picked up a working knowledge of what and whom it was correct to admire. Obligingly, Deborah gave him the full quotation and he said, with delight, that he slept well, too.

The children resumed their running battle and were removed, a romp in the garden to tire them a bit, a good wash and into their sleeping attire, and the ruffian and the vixen would lie down peacefully together in the big bed, looking like angels.

"I'll leave you, George, to show Mr van Haagen to his room."

She slipped away to lie down on her bed; she had never fully recovered the energy and resilience which had been hers before the catastrophe, and the involuntary jerks, the tremors were tiring.

Carrying Mr van Haagen's bag, George led the way, past the guest room which on former visits he had occupied and on to the foot of the attic stairs. Treating the matter as lightly as he hoped Mr van Haagen would do, he explained the position. Without apologising for it. Apologies were all very well in their place, but when uncalled for were apt to give the wrong impression.

"To me," Mr van Haagen said, "where I sleep is of no importance. I can sleep anywhere. On a cattle boat. In a cowshed." He'd had a hard youth, quite unlike that of the boy now with him, privileged from the first and with a thriving business awaiting him.

"It is only the stairs," George said, "I'm afraid, sir, you'll find them a trifle steep."

"To me also steep is not an impediment." To prove it he took the stairs rather too nimbly and arrived on the attic landing slightly out of breath. I am too gross, he thought to himself; after this evening I must eat less. "Ah," he said, entering the room which George had aimed to make not only comfortable, but pleasing to the eye. "Very nice."

"And the view is wonderful. From up here you can see five church towers."

George went to the window and cast a look which he did not know was fond and yearning, to the West; towards Stratton Strawless. Somewhere, on a road between the trees, screened from him by the great sprawling mass of Layer Wood, Chloe—and Johnny, of course—would be making their way. He gave a sigh of sheer bliss.

Bliss was intensified when, some time later, Chloe appeared in the drawing room with one of his roses, cut short and pinned to the bodice of her white muslin frock. He thought it a high compliment and could not be expected to know that Chloe had added the rose because she hated the white muslin so much; it was a school-girl's dress. She had a better one, the blue taffeta she had worn at her birthday party, much lower at the neck, much fuller

in the skirt, but Lady Faulkner had decreed that it was altogether
unsuitable—as well as being very difficult to pack. "You are not
going to a ball, my dear. It would be in the worst of taste to appear overdressed."

George could not, of course, have Chloe seated, as he would
have wished, beside him at the table. All must be correct, and
married women took precedence. Still his time would come. Afterwards there would be dancing. All that was needed to bring that
about was a word to Caro: Let's dance; a word to Deb: Play a
merry tune. For so small a company the hall was big enough and
its black and white floor perfect. The old people could play cards
or just sit.

That happy dream, Chloe's hand in his, reared up, rose-
coloured, and then crashed in grey ruin.

Mamma rose and made for the door. George opened it, and as
she passed she murmured, "One glass, darling, for you and
Johnny," meaning the port wine. A quite unnecessary warning for
George grudged the time it would take him to drink one, and sit,
being amiable while his elders drank two. But this little pause in
the evening was essential; it gave the ladies time to do what was
known as titivate. Gentlemen, having drunk their port, drifted
out, if they wanted to, to a convenient bush. The decanter had
barely completed its first circuit when the door opened and there
was Caroline, white-faced.

"Edward, will you come?"

Edward, calm, schooled to face emergencies, rose, quickly, but
without haste, and as he walked to the door asked, "What is it?"

"Susan," Caroline said. She burst into tears, ran to Freddy, who
was in the act of rising, and clutched at him. "Oh, Freddy . . .
It's Susan. She's . . . she's . . . It's dreadful." Freddy steadied
her. Arm around waist, drawing her to the doorway, saying something about a faint. Doctor Raven was on his feet too, professional and cool, well aware that where Edward Taylor was, he was
of only secondary importance; thinking about the silly way
women had of tight-lacing—in which case just cutting the stay-
laces sufficed; thinking of other things, too, such as heart attacks.

"I'll go," he said, briskly authoritative, "but the fewer people
crowding round the better."

"I am thinking from the first," Mr van Haagen said, "that she
is an ill woman."

Very soon, Poor Susan was not only ill, but dead. Whatever it was that had gnawed at her had reached this evening some vital spot. She had collapsed in pain, too searing and violent to be concealed any longer, but she died in peace, in a morphia-induced coma; fortunate, insofar as one could use the word, in having two doctors in attendance.

Chloe Faulkner went—quite understandably—into a kind of hysteria. "Like a trap," she said, again and again. "She was just beside me and she fell over and screamed, just like something in a trap. Johnny, Johnny, you don't know how terrible it was. Like a trap. She was just beside me and . . ."

It was to her brother that she turned and he tried to explain, to excuse, saying that Chloe was very sensitive, poor darling, she'd never seen anything like this, the best thing to do was to get her to bed. He did not say, and to give him his due, he did not even think that such things did not happen in well-regulated households. But the implication hung in the air.

Mr van Haagen said, "For me, I am blaming the husband. With any sense of his head he should have known. The skeleton at the feast. Is that correct? She did not die in one evening, poor woman. By degrees rather and he should know. If not, who? I am saying of what I know. I have for some, many years, a wife not in good health. Of her I am very careful. Always."

Having delivered himself of this fair judgment, Mr van Haagen took himself to bed, and for what happened next he could not blame anything or anybody. And he certainly was not drunk. Before dinner two small glasses of sherry, two glasses of wine at table, one glass of port wine, interrupted. To a man of his size and experience in hard drinking, nothing at all. Nor could he claim to have suffered a shock. It was sad, of course, that death should come, so suddenly, to one so young, but the poor woman was marked for death. Years ago, he remembered, in the cards; in the cards. For Miss Walford a whirlwind courtship, marriage soon, and then nothing. No children. Her destiny was written and he had read it; but he still blamed her husband. No amount of care and precaution could have kept the poor woman alive, but she could have died, privately, in her own home, her own bed. Thus thinking, Mr van Haagen brushed his teeth, undressed, wound his watch and got into bed. To a man who led a busy life, an early night was always welcome.

The guests had all departed, practically silent. Caroline had suggested that Freddy might like to stay at Gad's, he could rest on the settle in the living room. Or he could spend the night with her and Edward in Baildon, and if necessary Edward would give him a sedative. Freddy refused both offers, though he looked shaken and stunned. It was very kind, he said, but he must get back home; he'd have a lot of things to do in the morning. Everybody knew what things. . . .

Mrs Thorley, Di and Deb huddled together in the living room and drank tea. In all innocence Deb had suggested whisky to Mamma, who looked very upset, though she had not shed a tear. Mrs Thorley replied that tea would do though she craved whisky. It was strange how, after all this time, five years, whenever she was tired, or worried she thought of whisky and how it had sustained her—and almost ruined her.

"Susan was my oldest friend," Diana said, ready to cry again.

"I know," Deb said. She had cried too. Poor Susan had not been her best friend, but she'd liked her. And to die like that made everybody seem so vulnerable. In fact one of Deborah's first actions had been to run upstairs and assure herself that Sam—and the other children, of course—were all right. Once Death got a foot in the door. What rubbish!

They talked of when they had last seen Susan.

"Not more than a fortnight ago," Mrs Thorley said. "Just before you came, Di. It was at Caro's. She seemed to be perfectly all right then. And in fact Caro, who has been more with her lately, said this evening that Susan had never said a word about feeling unwell. Of course Mrs Walford died very suddenly."

"But she'd been ailing for years. As a matter of fact, I haven't seen Susan very lately. I did think she looked a bit thin," Deb said. And her hair looked a bit dry and brittle; the result of something she used to brighten it. She'd begun to use it—yes—at that party, that doomed party, when Mr Walford broke away and left Mrs Walford with a nurse and Mrs Walford died. And Lavinia met that horrible man whom I disliked, distrusted, loathed on sight. . . .

"People don't just die of being thin," Diana said.

George, restless and discontented, said,

"I'll just pop up and see if Johnny wants anything."

Johnny had taken Chloe to bed. He seemed to be well-acquainted with his sister's hysterical turns. "What she needs is a night's sleep. She'll be right as rain in the morning."

Attention shifted, refocussed itself.

"At school, Miss Hardwicke always said that the best cure for hysteria was a smart slap across the face."

"I am inclined to agree." Mrs Thorley's comment was dry.

"I can't ever remember you slapping one of us, Mamma."

"I can't remember one of you being hysterical." Certainly when Caroline heard that Freddy Ingram was to marry Susan Walford, Caroline had gone all to pieces, but a few *verbal* slaps had sufficed.

"I once read . . ." Deborah was the great reader, "that behaviour like that comes from a wish to draw attention. She's a very pretty child, with nothing to say for herself. I mean compared with Caro. . . . So if she felt a bit neglected and then this happened . . . I rather like the boy. Sound about horses, and crazy on hunting, and he never had a proper mount. In fact I told him that if he'd like a day out with the South Norfolk, I'd lend him my Dragon."

"So you have two now," Diana said, trying, and failing to keep sour envy out of her voice. Two hunters, what opulence. And only five years ago Deborah was so down-trodden; wearing a print dress, working like a servant.

"Two of my own," Deborah said, as casually as though she were speaking of handkerchiefs, "but plenty of others handy. I school them, you see. For other people. . . . So many people don't have the patience, or the knowledge, or what you might call the knack of it. I charge, of course."

(I could make a living anywhere, any day of the year. And Tim knows it. He also knows that it would be very difficult to divorce me simply because I'm good with horses and pay regular visits to my stepmother, and very occasionally spend a night at Gad's. Go ahead, she had said, during one of their quiet but corrosive quarrels: Make a fool of yourself before the world.)

In the guest room Chloe lay in bed; Johnny sat beside her holding her hand. The white muslin dress lay on a chair, the pink rose beginning to die.

"A hot-water-bottle, if that is not too much trouble," Johnny said in answer to George's query if there was anything he could do, fetch.

"I'll get it. Shan't be a minute."

Jonathan Faulkner sat by the bed and thought what Hell being a twin was. A life-long three-legged race. And that was no flight of fancy. That he and Chloe had both suffered mumps at the same time was understandable; they'd both been at home then. But well on into his second half at Eton, when he hadn't seen Chloe for weeks, he had measles, and far away, at Stratton Strawless, Chloe went down with the same complaint, and on the same day! How explain that? Not much alike to look at, but sex explained that; tied together by something far stronger than physical resemblance, or mental ability. In nature they differed, too. He could take the sudden death of somebody known as Mrs Walford, in the middle of a party without being upset. It was a pity, and of course very sad for her husband. It had flung Chloe into one of her states, and he had done the best he could to deal with it. Now and then, when he thought about it, the future bothered him a bit. He wanted not to stay in England and always be poor, and at the same time rather grand. He dreamed of going to India. Fortunes could still be made there. He dreamed of coming home rich, say after ten years, mending not only the decrepit leaking roof of Stratton Strawless Manor, but every tenant farmer's roof; building cowsheds, draining that low-lying land called Rainwater Meadows, perhaps bringing under the cultivation that utterly opposite part of the estate, the Common, dry, sandy, riddled with rabbit holes.

It was a good dream, and not an impossible one. But whenever he thought about it, up came the question: What of Chloe? Despite what some people said, India was not very healthy or very comfortable for English women; so he couldn't very well take her. Leave her? Then his parents would marry her off to somebody like Peter Stanton, a good enough fellow in his way but quite unsuitable as a husband for somebody so delicate, so sensitive, so much in need of understanding as Chloe was.

The kitchen was still active, for successful party or ruined one, the clearing up afterwards was just the same. Jenny, her duty done, was taking her ease, drinking tea, her much-tried legs propped up on a stool. Violet was washing up at the sink and Ruth was drying.

Jenny said, "Violet, if I've told you once, I've told you a thousand times. Glasses first. Then the silver, and in a jug of hot water. They dry better. As for you, Ruth, I'd athought you'd aknown."

George said, "I want a hot-water-bottle." A curious request on such a sultry evening. The kitchen was indeed hot despite an open window, an open door, for the fire in the range had been kept in so that there should be hot water in the boiler for all this washing up.

"Somebody else took poorly, Master George?" Jenny asked with genuine concern. It could happen. She did not remember the occasion, but she'd heard tell of it; a summer fever that had wiped out half the village. That had been a hot summer, too. Inside her shrivelled skin Jenny's brittle bones shuddered.

"No, just for comfort."

"You see to it, Ruth. The kettle's only just off the boil and the bottles are there, under the dresser, right-hand side."

Jenny was old enough to remember the time before hot-water-bottles. A time when comfort was derived from bags of salt, heated in the oven, or bricks.

Ruth, gladly abandoning the dull job of wiping dishes, busied herself. George looked, a bit dismally, at the long dresser upon which some remains of the feast had been deposited, awaiting removal to the larder, awaiting, finally, Jenny's thrifty verdict; fish-pie; shepherd's pie or into the pig-pail. For one dismal moment these left-overs symbolised the whole party so carefully planned, so eagerly anticipated. He felt the need to assert himself, get back into his own skin. He said,

"You girls are late. I'll just see if there's anything I can do, and if not, I'll drive you home."

There was nothing he could do. Johnny took the bottle and tucked it in.

"Thanks. She'll be all right now, but I think . . ." He took stock of the room. "Yes, if it's all the same with you, old boy, I'll doss down in that chair. Just in case. . . ."

"Violet gets down here, don't you, Violet? I'm a bit further on, if you don't mind. Good night, Violet. See you soon. Sunday, if I don't go to Bywater. Now, Master George. Sharp left by the church and then a bit. After that it's Shanks' Pony, walk through the wood. A bit skeery, this time of night."

"Are you going to Bywater?"

"If I get a job. There ain't much around here, is there?"

"I suppose not."

With Violet sharing the seat it had been necessary to sit close, now, with Violet gone, Ruth did not move away; if anything she snuggled closer. She was, as the landlady of the *Hawk in Hand* had said, a thoroughly loose girl; not necessarily a disadvantage if a girl knew her place, but with the son of the house, and him with less sense than a cuckoo, it was instant dismissal and out you go! She was not designing or mercenary, on the contrary, inclined to be choosy. Nature had endowed her with a gift she enjoyed using —with the right person, and George Thorley was right to her eye. Like everybody else she thought him a good deal older than he was.

Initiation being bound to come sooner or later, George could have done much worse; might have spent himself and his money on some indifferent, custom-hardened hireling. As it was, the new and delirious experience healed a wound which, all unknowing, Chloe Faulkner had inflicted when she turned to her brother, not to him, for comfort and support in her distress. At that moment George had felt himself rejected, a new and most uncomfortable sensation. Now, without consciously connecting the two things, and certainly not the two girls, he was restored. He had still a long way to go before reaching the certainty that every man wanted two differing female elements in his life, a bad girl to tumble, a good girl to adore, but this evening, wrecked and then salvaged, set him on his way.

Mr van Haagen woke as though someone had shaken him by the shoulder. Ha! A child crying. There were children in the house. No! Not a child crying, at least, not now; a low voice murmuring. The mother, no doubt, comforting. Strange that sounds should carry so far. He turned, prepared to sleep again, and then was aware of a horrible smell. God in Heaven! He knew what that was, what he had done. Left his cigar to smoulder instead of stubbing it out properly. It might, indeed, have been left balanced on the edge of the ash-tray and tipped over, burning the lace mat, even scarring the bedside table. He could not imagine how he could have been so careless, except that that poor girl's death had upset him, as it had upset everybody. Hastily he lit his candle. There was the end of his cigar, properly stubbed out. There was his watch, showing the time to be a few minutes after twelve. And now that he was properly awake he realised that it was not the smell of burning, it was . . . it was . . . In none of his languages, native or acquired, could he find a word. Except evil. Similar to, different from, worse than something he remembered very vividly; a time when a dyke broke and the sea came in, and everybody was so busy mending the dyke against tomorrow's tide, and tomorrow's, that even human bodies had been left to rot, and dead cattle had been left to the crows.

Why here? In this pleasant room?

And why did he feel fear? No, more than that, terror? A paralysis that made his body rigid, and creeping inwards seemed to check his breathing, stop his heart. Death. No, because he could still see and hear . . . even speak.

Those who dabbled in such matters—Mr van Haagen never had—would have recognised his state as that of genuine trance and Mr van Haagen as a true medium between two states of being. They were few, charlatans and impostors were many . . . .

When it was over—and how long it lasted he never knew, for he did not think of looking at his watch, Mr van Haagen knew more than anybody, more than Mrs Thorley, more than Deborah about what had happened to the girl whom he had warned to beware of the dark. Who had, so they said, gone to India—a dark subcontinent—and died.

Deb was first down in the morning. Five years at Foxton had inculcated the habit of early rising and there she could refute Tim, by being first down, taking old Emma a cup of tea. Here at Gad's on her rare overnight visits, she did the same thing, giving Jenny a little surprise.

There, behind the closed door of the drawing room, Poor Susan lay, decently covered by one of the last of Deborah's mother's fine linen sheets. Poor Susan. And it was such a lovely morning. Oh dear!

Deb went into the kitchen, got the range going, put on the kettle. Remembered that there were three guests in the house. The Faulkner girl would probably expect breakfast on a tray, and China, not Indian tea. Deb went into the living room to fetch the tea-caddy. It was not until she had flung back the curtains that she saw Mr van Haagen on the settle.

It gave her a jolt. She said, "Oh!" and he woke, rubbing his eyes. But, as was his habit, instantly alert and aware. Ready with his story.

"I am unable to sleep," he said, glad that his nightshirt was long and not rucked up. "So I come down, walk a little, give myself a drink and am then overcome. You will please excuse me."

She gave him a funny look. What had happened to him last night was as clear, and in a way as real, as anything that had ever happened to him in his life. She, Deborah Thorley, Mrs Bridges, had played no small part in what he had seen—No! lived through. And just for a moment he felt that she knew that he knew. But she only said,

"You'll like a cup of tea? Mr van Haagen, there is no need to be embarrassed. I'm married. I have seen a man in his nightshirt."

Just so he had lived with her; practical, helpful, sensible, taking evil, even the ultimate evil in her stride; burying the dead, comforting the living and then going back to the horses.

After living with himself for fifty-two years, Mr van Haagen knew that he was not a man given to fancies. He was not even a religious man. Asked to describe his faith he would have said—Lutheran. His forebears had fought Catholicism, the religion of Spain, the enemy and the oppressor, for more than three hundred years; just as they had fought the sea and made the polder land. So why did he now feel a wish, recognised, suppressed, bobbing up again, to tell Mrs Thorley that her attic floor was haunted, that it needed a priest, with bell, book and candle, to perform the rite of exorcism? One reason for not doing so was pity. She had lived through something so horrible—no wonder her hair was white and her head jerky. And now, this morning, more trouble to face, a dead woman in her drawing room and presently the undertakers. . . . No, he could not possibly add to her bothers. But he did reflect, in a rather vague way, that life bore hard on the strong. Almost as though if one blow didn't floor you, there'd be another and another. She'd survived her first husband's death, and then that of her second; she'd inherited a failing business and made it prosperous; she'd lived through what he had lived through—but not in his flesh—all that took place in that locked attic. He knew it, down to the last sordid detail. But better say nothing. Go away dumb and on his next visit make some excuse for not staying in this house again.

"We were supposed to be on a kind of round trip, George. Your party last night, and then on to the Stantons'. But I doubt if she's up to it. I mean it was a shock, that poor woman falling down, screaming, practically on Chloe's feet. I think I'd better take her home and skip Muchanger. I must say, old boy, until . . . what happened . . . it was a damned good party. And that sister of yours, Mrs Bridges, is it? We got on like a house afire."

The Lumsley affair of which Everard had been sent to make a preliminary investigation was very unpleasant indeed. The first two firms approached by Lady Lumsley refused to touch it, phrasing the refusal tactfully, of course, saying that as they saw little chance of such a lawsuit being successful they could not in good conscience advise her ladyship to proceed. Upton, Binder and Smith had no such scruples; all was grist to their mill, and it was a reputation for being able to wash dirty linen in public and render it snow-white that had prompted Lady Lumsley to seek their services—after the two snubs which she recognised as such.

She was unprepared for Everard, so unmistakably a gentleman. It made things easier in a way, and at the same time more difficult. Easier because since he must be housed in the Castle and was therefore to some extent her guest, it was better that he should be presentable and at ease; more difficult because the unpleasant aspects of the case would, she felt, shock him more than they would have done an older man of coarser grain. After all, an address in Great King William Street had promised little in the way of gentility and Mr Spicer had been assigned a bedroom in the East wing; not quite servants' accommodation, but only one step above. (That of course was easily corrected. One order and Mr Spicer's luggage was transferred.)

She had, with the same thought in mind, ordered a very simple dinner, no need to confuse the poor man with too many courses. Too late to rectify *that* now, but she ordered up better wine.

They were four at table in what was called the small dining room—rather larger than a whole floor of Everard's London house. There was Lady Lumsley's aunt, Lady Cowdray, a lady of incredible age and stone-deaf, but with bright lively eyes, and his late lordship's agent, Mr MacFarlane. Both knew more than they were prepared to reveal, until they saw which way the cat jumped.

Light, dinner table conversation.

"Is this your first visit to Scotland, Mr Spicer?"

"No. When I was young, my godfather came up regularly, salmon-fishing in the Spring and for the grouse in August."

It was like excavating a ruin, Everard thought. Happy days about which it did not do to think too much. And come to think of it, there was in his own life, not quite a parallel, rather say the obverse face of the situation here.

Lady Cowdray's eyes had for some years been obliged to serve as her ears as well and she thought: Alison is clever! She'll have this young fellow eating out of her hand and breaking his neck to serve her. Mr MacFarlane brushed aside Everard's reference to past grandeur; summer visitors! and just hoped that Everard was a better lawyer than he looked.

"I understand, Mr Spicer, that talking to one's lawyer is rather like the confessional. I mean, if I'd committed murder and told you so, you'd still be obliged brief Counsel to defend me."

"That is oversimplication. It would certainly be my duty to ascertain, so far as was possible, that when you made such an admission you were sober, in your right mind, not trying to protect another person, acting under threat—things of that kind. It would not be for me to judge."

"And then?"

"I should brief Counsel. *He* could judge, to a limited extent, insofar as it would be for him to judge whether or not to accept the brief. Having done so it would be his duty to prepare the best possible case for your defence. Am I making myself clear?"

"Even if I had admitted . . . ?"

"The question is hypothetical, Lady Lumsley. I cannot recall a case where a client approached his solicitor with such an admission and then asked help in his defence. It would not be reasonable. Unless, of course, he intended by such action to show himself insane within the meaning of the act."

"I see."

Actually the opening gambit had been hypothetical. Start with murder and then when one was forced to say the word *adultery* and the word *impotent* the shock was less.

She looked very young; but the boy whose future was concerned was six, so she must have been married for close on seven years. Married, perhaps at sixteen. To a man of sixty-nine. Everard had briefed himself as well as he could, and Lord Lumsley had a two-inch obituary in *The Times*. His widow was one of those women who looked well in black. She had fox-coloured hair and amber eyes, but neither the dead-white, or rough-red complexion which as a rule went with such hair, nor the sandy eyelashes. Her skin was—well, it was a cliché—just the colour of cream, a whiteness delicately stained as though the colour of her hair had faintly drifted down. Her neck was very long and very slender, seemingly too slight to support the wealth of hair, pinned with tortoiseshell prongs, not ordinary hairpins. And her hands were beautiful, very long, very narrow, and that same cream colour.

"I have nothing to admit, Mr Spicer. Neither murder nor . . . adultery." There! She had said it.

"Your letter to Mr Upton said very little. It would be of help to me, if you would . . . give me details. Please bear in mind that I am a married man, with two children of my own." Everard was not given to leaps into imaginative understanding, but he made that one. Because he knew vaguely what she was about to be forced to say, and she looked so young and so frail. Mr Upton would have recognised and dismissed her—lecherous as a tom cat; Mr Binder would have recognised and dismissed her—mercenary as Shylock; Mr Smith *had* recognised what he called a stink and given a stink and some titles, and a very shaky case, hit or miss, a lot of publicity anyway; leave it alone. He'd been overruled.

"I will begin at the beginning. . . ."

Unlike most women she was lucid and concise.

The late Lord Lumsley had married years ago, begotten a son and a daughter. His daughter married and had a son. The heir to Lumsleydale had fought in the Crimea, survived, failed to settle down, gone to Africa, been killed in some nameless squabble.

"He died," Lady Lumsley said, "without issue. I think that is the phrase. So then my late husband married me. Wanting an heir, you see. And after two years Alastair was born. Publicly, of course, his father accepted him—no man wishes to put horns on his own head. But to me his behaviour was abominable: it had been from the moment that I told him I was pregnant. He denied, absolutely, that the child was his. He gave as his reason that he was impotent. He was *then*, but not *before*, if you understand me." Her amber eyes filled with tears. "Mr Spicer, I cannot describe what Hell my life has been for the past seven years. We went nowhere, never entertained. His age was the excuse for that and I could have borne it, but he was so unkind to Alastair. . . ." A few tears brimmed. "I was often obliged to interpose myself to prevent violence. And he put a woman of unspeakable severity in charge." Lady Lumsley's eyes dried, her voice steadied. "I dismissed her within ten minutes of hearing of his death!" There was a quiet triumph about that statement.

The lawyer in Everard stood back and said drily: A very sad story but no grounds for contesting a will.

Yet without doubt it was a strange will for a man of the world, a man of great wealth to have made. Everard had seen a copy. A single sentence. I, Alexander St Barbe Sinclair, fourth Earl of Lumsley, of Lumsleydale Castle in Inverness hereby bequeath to my daughter, Lady Dorothea Morton, everything, not in entail, of which I die possessed. It was signed and the signature had been witnessed; Ian Ross; Hector Alston.

Any lawyer would have taken the precaution of revoking former wills. Any half-literate farmer writing his own last testament would have been more specific about the extent of his possessions. Any man in his right mind would surely have appointed at least one executor.

"Have you the original, Lady Lumsley?"

An ornate, yet unformed, feminine hand; signature very shaky; witnesses obviously men who could just write their names and no more.

The lady waited for some comment and when none came—one of the first things a lawyer learned was not to be hasty—said,

"*She* wrote it, of course. He went to visit, a fortnight before his death, and had a summer cold. He came home after two days. . . . I know, Mr Spicer, that this is not a legal argument, but it supports my conviction. He was passionately attached to this place. Sinclairs have lived here since the Flood. . . . I know, I *know* that he hated me, and Alastair; he would have died happy to think we must beg our bread, but he would never have left Lumsley Castle to certain ruin, with only eight hundred acres of moorland to prop it up. Which is what this will means. . . . He *knew*. Before he took this idea into his head and ceased to talk to me, he often spoke about the little crofts that were once here. Not profitable, but self-supporting. . . . Then his grandfather made a fortune, coal I think, and could afford to evict the crofters. He spoke with regret about that. But he also said once that it took half the income from one coal-mine to keep this place watertight and he wouldn't mind if it took the whole. *And* all the rents of the properties in London. I am convinced that if this were his real will, he would have made some provision for the Castle. Imposed some condition upon Lady Dorothea, or set up a trust fund. Isn't that logical?"

"Yes. But logic is not law. Had he made former wills?"

"Mr MacFarlane says he did. When we were married. Mr Mac-Farlane made it for him."

"Mr MacFarlane?"

"Yes. You would hardly have guessed, Angus is such a silent man, but he is a fully trained lawyer. His father was agent here—before my time of course, and my husband then employed, when necessary, a firm of lawyers in Edinburgh. In some way they displeased him, and—this is Angus' story—my husband said to old Mr MacFarlane, "We have a bright boy here; we'll have him taught monkey tricks; the homegrown article is always best . . . That, the first will, was perfectly fair. Lady Dorothea was to have a street in London—the Mortons are not well-to-do."

On the far side of the room old Lady Cowdray looked at her watch and folded her knitting. She knew just when to be present and when to absent herself. Knowledge invaluable in a chaperone. By applying it skilfully, she had been able to live here, in great luxury, instead of eking out her wretched pittance in genteel poverty. In the loud, toneless voice of the very deaf she said, "Good night, Alison dear. Good night, Mr Spicer. Don't sit up too late; you've had a long journey."

Mr MacFarlane lived in great comfort in what had been built as the Dower House. Edward spared an envious glance around the big, handsome room, half living room, half office. Heavy silver inkstand on the carved, leather-topped desk, deep comfortable leather chairs, a side-table well furnished with decanters and glasses. The scent of stocks and lavender came through the open French windows. If the agent felt this his pleasant way of life was threatened, he gave no sign. He was not a talkative man, but what he said was to the point.

"Aye. His lordship came home and took to his bed. He had not a strong chest and he'd had his three-score-and-ten but we didna think he was dying. He gave me that thing that calls itself a will. Sealed and addressed to her ladyship, and he said, 'Keep it safe and give it to her the minute I'm dead.' God forgive me, I thought it was a letter. So thin."

"And why should God forgive you for obeying an order, Mr MacFarlane?"

A very curious expression crossed the healthy, honest-looking face.

"I would have done it differently. The least I could do would see that she was sitting down, and alone. As it was the shock felled her. With Lady Dorothea watching—she'd been the house the last two days."

If I had known, I would have done very *differently. Put the damned thing in the fire!*

"Was he in his right mind?"

"Difficult, Mr Spicer. I don't know how much her ladyship told you." The man was cautious. So was Everard.

"Enough to explain a possible motive."

"Aye. Well, in that regard his mind was not sound. Idée fixe. Apart from that, in itself an affliction, he was sound enough, except when he had laudanum in him."

"Laudanum?"

"Crude. He could not bear pain. He could not bear a night with a cough. A twinge of toothache, his teeth were bad, and must be expected, or a pain in the chest and he took to the laudanum as a sensible man takes to the whisky. He carried a bottle with him, and having a drink taken, he was like putty. I know." Mr MacFarlane knew. Dozens of times, dealing with the obstinate old man, he had waited for the right moment. And in his mind he was as sure as he was of his own name that Lord Lumsley had gone to his daughter's house, the cold already on him, had resorted to the black bottle with its bright label, saying "Poison," and then been putty in *her* hands. But such a surety was no argument in law.

Mr MacFarlane eyed Everard distrustfully. A Saasenach, a Londoner and a lawyer. Sent up here to tell the silly creature that she had a chance. They'd drag her name in the mud, keep up the pretence until she was penniless. And that wouldn't be long; all she owned were the jewels his lordship had given her at and soon after her marriage. And there was even an argument to be put up, in good legal terms, against her continued possession of them. What a woman owned, even what she earned, was, legally speaking, her husband's property. And that ill-made, iniquitous will was very sweeping: *everything, not in entail, of which I die possessed.*

"I told her ladyship then, that very morning, when she said she would fight it, that she stood no chance. Granted it's not a will he would have made in his right mind, condemning as it does the one thing he loved better than himself to certain ruin. It is the Castle I mean. The care he took, making his real will. But that is no argument. No more so than the laudanum."

"No. I am afraid the laudanum must be ruled out of court. . . . I suppose you don't have the earlier will."

"I have it. It is not worth the good paper it is written on."

"I'd like to see it," Everard said.

"Darling, I can't. We know now that it *is* smallpox. Raven and I must work our heads off. Of course I should wish to pay my last respects to Poor Susan; and I'm sorrier than I can say for Freddy. But I can't spare the time. And you won't be alone *there*. Your mother . . . I really am most terribly sorry, but my duty is to the living. If you get a chance to speak to Freddy, please apologise and explain."

"I will," Caroline said. "And the wreath was from us both. He'll understand. Don't worry."

So you went, wearing black, to the funeral of your best friend; the girl at whose engagement party you had been gayest of all, whose bridesmaid you had been, whose husband you had loved— and still did.

In fact Caroline had loved Freddy enough to make excuses for his choosing Poor Susan instead of herself. He'd been nothing more than a travelling salesman; a very good one, and he appeared to enjoy his job. But it offered no real security, and although he contrived to let it interfere with his social life as little as possible, there were times when he had been obliged to miss some joyous occasion. He had expensive tastes and enjoyed comfort. Caroline's dowry was a mere five hundred pounds. Marriage to Susan gave him a great deal of independence, a comfortable home, a share in —and after Mr Walford's death complete control of, a flourishing brewery. No happiness, though, no more than Caroline's face-saving marriage to Edward had brought her. She knew that every time they really looked into one another's eyes. He might seem to be laughing his head off, but the look was there.

It was there this afternoon.

"Edward asked me to tell you how deeply he sympathised,

Freddy. He intended to be present but something they hoped was chicken pox turned out to be smallpox."

"I fully understand. Tell Edward that I shall be everlastingly grateful to him for making certain that she did not die in pain."

Freddy meant that, sincerely. He'd married Susan for strictly mercenary reasons, but no man with any feeling at all could live for five years with a woman so amiable, undemanding, self-effacing, grateful for any small attention without becoming fond of her and glad that she did not die in agony.

It was a conversation which anybody could have overheard. Several did. A few—Mrs. Thorley among them—remembered a time when Freddy Ingram and Caroline Thorley had got themselves talked about. Both had settled down admirably. About the extent to which Caroline had settled down, Mrs Thorley had entertained a doubt or two. She had understood Caroline's infatuation, her despair when the engagement was announced; she had, in fact, pointed out to Caroline the face-saving action. And both Freddy and Caroline had behaved impeccably. Still . . . Caroline had never, in five years, given a party of any size without including the Ingrams. Anything she organised—and Caroline was now a great organiser—Susan and therefore Freddy must take part. Even the modest party at Gad's Hall . . . the party at which Poor Susan had died. . . . "Oh, Mamma, do ask Susan and Freddy. All of us and Susan, together for once. It will seem like old times."

There flitted through Mrs Thorley's mind a hope that Caro would not do something silly. Silly was really the worst word that could be applied to anything Caro had done in regard to Freddy —dancing four times in succession, driving alone with him. She was just capable of being silly again; widowers were as useful as bachelors as escorts to women whose husbands were very busy.

"I made a special point of giving Freddy your message, Edward. He quite understood and he said such a nice thing about you. He said he would be everlastingly grateful to you for making certain that she did not die in pain."

In his flat way, Edward said, "I just happened to be there." The poor girl was dead now, so he saw no harm in saying, "Actually I was not even surprised. She had been in pain for quite a long time."

"Oh! Why?"

"That nobody knew. She couldn't even define the site of it, and nobody could find any cause. She was exceptionally brave about it; anxious that nobody should know."

"Poor Susan! What with one thing and another, she didn't have much of a life, did she?" Caroline took a few breaths, a bite or two, a sip of the wine which Edward had thoughtfully brought up to cheer her after the ordeal of a funeral. Then she said, "I'm afraid Freddy will be lonely now. Richard came down for the funeral, but he was catching the evening train."

"Well, we'll do our best for Freddy, darling, once I've got this plague off my hands. Ask him to dinner or something. . . . Caro, would you mind . . . I feel I should just look in at that isolation shed. It is such a shambles. You know, I still regret Diana's going away. When she was there in Friars' Lane, you only had to slip through the gate in the wall and be sure of company."

It was four years since Diana had left the elegant little house in the cul-de-sac, so fortunately situated just to the rear of the house in which Edward and Caroline lived. And nobody regretted, or to an extent, resented the move, more than Diana did.

Everard, after his successful interview with Upton, Binder and Smith, had gone house-hunting. As he had feared when contemplating, backing away from and then contemplating again this critical move, rents were extortionate and his field of choice was limited since he must be within easy reach—that meant twenty, thirty minutes on a horse omnibus—of the City. He considered himself singularly fortunate to hit upon St Anne's Crescent. Some fifty years earlier a speculative builder had bought the garden of a big derelict house and there erected six most desirable residences with gas and piped water laid on and with an aspect; for, roughly completing the circle of which the Crescent formed the northermost sector, there were some trees and shrubs, the last outpost of what had once been a lovely garden.

Diana, with her capacity for forgetting or ignoring the unpleasant, did not remember the house in Leicester where Mamma had made a precarious living for herself and her two daughters by drawing designs for dresses and pottery and giving piano lessons, on a hired instrument. Had she done so Number 4, St Anne's Crescent would, despite its inconveniences, have seemed pleasant. When she made a comparison it was with Gad's, which she secretly thought of as home, or with Friars' Lane, upon which she looked, even after a year of marriage, as a kind of toy in which she played at keeping house.

St Anne's Crescent appalled her and she reflected that it had been a mistake to let Everard do the house-hunting; but she was in the early stages of pregnancy and disinclined to travel unnecessarily. Mustering her courage on arrival, she told herself that perhaps her condition was responsible for her feeling of gloom and her apprehension about the number of steps; eight up to the front door from the pavement; eight down to the back door in the area. Impossible for perambulators. Never mind, perhaps before *that* happened, the inevitable messy outcome of the messy side of marriage, she would have found something more suitable. It would not be for want of trying.

Resolutely—she was, after all, Mrs Thorley's daughter—she set about making the best of things and it was typical of her that the first room to be quite in order was the drawing room, very small when stark-empty and now overcrowded. In Diana's little Suffolk world people called upon newcomers, exercising discrimination, of course. She expected calls from her neighbours. And she was right.

Mrs Appleyard called.

So far as a group of six, mean-faced, rather pretentious little houses could be said to comprise a social unit, centring about a leader, Mrs Appleyard was that leader; the one who lived here longest, and whose husband had his own business, a double-fronted shop in the High Street, just around the corner; on one side he sold fish, on the other vegetables. She was—and rightly—conscious of having come up in the world, for Alf had started his career with a barrow, hawking fish and vegetables about the street. She had helped him to heave himself up in the world by continuing—making nothing of three pregnancies—her work in a pickle factory. And when the great moment had come and the shop in the High Street was his, she had refused to live in the room above it; so they had moved into St Anne's Crescent and been proud.

Unfair to say that Mrs Appleyard and Diana disliked one another at sight. There was no reason. Mrs Appleyard was doing the right thing, visiting a new neighbour; Diana was lonely, torn up by the roots.

But the Tower of Babel was built high, an affront to God, it was said, and when the builders were scattered, doomed to speak different languages, there were within those differing tongues, other divisions, almost as dangerous. Mrs Appleyard thought

Diana's voice and accent namby-pamby; Diana thought Mrs Appleyard's very coarse.

"You're not a Londoner, are you?"

"No. My home is in Suffolk. That is a picture of it."

Years ago when Lavinia could paint what she saw, but even then with a strange twist, she had painted Gad's hall and contrived by a trick of perspective, cunning use of light and shade, to make it look like a mansion. That was before Lavinia's pictures had always had something more wrong with them than mere exaggeration, and Gad's Hall, more impressive in paint than in actuality, had hung just to the right of the grandfather clock on the half landing, for years, passed a dozen times a day unnoticed. But, on the verge of exile, Diana had said she would like it, something of Gad's to take away with her.

"Very nice," Mrs Appleyard said, mentally discarding Diana as a neighbour. Snobbery could cut two ways. There was the namby-pamby voice, the white hands that looked as though they had never done a stroke of work, the high nose and the husband who was a solicitor.

Perversely, nobody in St Anne's Crescent felt elevated by the coming, to Number 4, of a professional man and his dainty-mannered wife. Mrs Appleyard, the greatest snob within at least a mile's radius, said that Mrs Spicer was a snob, and for the wives of men who had done marvellously; in the Post Office, on the Railway, in the Insurance business and in a printing works, that was enough.

All the silly little houses had been built on the assumption that each would have a maid of imperturbable disposition and the constitution of a donkey. Such, if they had ever existed, were now extinct; only Mrs Appleyard had a resident maid; everyone else managed with a daily woman and even they were not easily found in this area, women preferred to clean offices, early morning, late afternoon work; and they could clatter their pails in company. Diana, alone, literally alone in London and completely out of her depth, had asked Mrs Appleyard's advice about how to set about getting a maid. In Baildon, in the first year of their married life, Everard, in the grip of one of his bouts of economy fever, had been against employing permanent help who must be housed and fed as well as paid, but here, with Diana pregnant and a house

with so many stairs—both conditions for which he felt, in an obscure way, responsible, a proper servant was necessary.

When Diana, innocent of having given offence, asked Mrs
Appleyard's advice, that lady shot a glance at the hands which
Diana had taken such pains to keep nice and thought—It'd do
you no harm to do a bit of work, my fine lady! She said she would
ask around, but she had not the slightest intention of doing so.
Then she shot another glance at the picture which had put an
end to neighbourliness and said,

"Of course you had plenty of servants *there*."

Skipping, as was her habit, the time when Katie had left and
not been replaced, and her own year of managing with Mrs
Wedgewood's desultory assistance, Diana said,

"We always had a cook, and it was easy to get girls from the village." She thought of the coalshed down in the area here and
added, with unconscious wistfulness, "And there was a boy for coal
and wood and cleaning knives—that kind of thing."

She had no intention of sounding grand or of making a false
impression. That kind of behaviour was practically unknown in
the society in which she had grown up, a place where one's origins
and circumstances were known to everyone, where like mixed
with like and knew exactly where he stood. If there was an inac-
curacy in her statement it was in referring to Willy as a boy
when he was a grown man, married and a father; but he had been
the boy about the place for as long as Diana chose to remember.

"Maidservants and men servants, and cooks," Mrs Appleyard
told the neighbours. "And if you ask me she've come down in
world."

Curiously nobody wanted to rub shoulders with those who for
some reason had come down in the world, superior as they might
appear to be. Coming down, like going up, was contagious.

Diana was doomed to loneliness; she, who in her little, much-
lamented pony carriage had driven about making visits, been
recognised and welcomed everywhere within a limited range.

Everard's business associates offered little in the way of social
life. Mr Upton, a bachelor and a misogynist, lived very comfortably in his club; Mr Binder, a widower with four children, had set
up house, wisely he thought at the time, with a widowed sister,
mother of three, in a pleasant, spacious house at Mortlake. The

sister said, with truth, that she had no time for entertaining. Mr Smith led a normal—and very enviable life—he had married well —in Theobald Road, which had retained something of a country atmosphere, front gardens and trees. Diana thoroughly enjoyed the one dinner party there—experimental on the Smiths' part. The two women had got on well together, despite a slight difference in age. Both were pregnant, Mrs Smith for the fourth time, having suffered three miscarriages. She suffered a fourth within two hours of the Spicers' departure and held them to blame—at least not *them*, Diana, so likeable, so potentially companionable, interested in needlework. Inadvisably Mrs Smith had taken Diana upstairs to show her the beautiful work she had done for the benefit of the unborn, and the drawer had stuck, needed a strong tug, and that did the damage. Florence Smith never wanted to see, or hear of Diana Spicer again, a feeling of rejection which was exacerbated when in due time she heard that Diana had given birth to a little girl.

Long before that happened the question of help in the house had been solved—by Everard. Diana had done her best; one by one she had accosted the four women who worked in the Crescent and asked did they know of anyone in need of a job, whole time, part time, even two hours a day. One of them did; at least she said she thought Maggie might be able to fit it in, she'd try, poor soul, an extra shilling or two mattered to Maggie, married as she was to a terrible drinker.

Maggie—Mrs Carr—arrived and at the first sight of her Diana's hopeful heart sank; she was such a poor little thread of a woman, bone-thin, she looked as though she had never had a square meal in her life, and would be utterly incapable of heaving a scuttle of coal from the shed in the area to the drawing room. It was Diana's first encounter with Cockney toughness. For all her frail looks Mrs Carr, scuttling about like a timid hunted animal, managed in the one hour that she fit in, to do all the rough. She worked in a kind of frenzy, for this hour's job had literally been fitted in between others.

It was far from satisfactory, but at least it look care of the front steps.

Eight of them. Eight to every front door, and somebody—probably Mrs Appleyard—had decreed that they should not be merely scrubbed, but whitened, at least once, preferably twice a week. Diana was enough of a conformist to wish hers to match the rest.

THE HAUNTING OF GAD'S HALL

Deborah, who was given to such thoughts—as Diana was not—would have seen in those white steps a protest against the general grime. Diana only thought that London—at least this part of it—was filthy. Dust seeped in; lace curtains were grey and rough to the touch within a fortnight. And not clean dust either. In the High Street, in Skelton Road, almost as busy, with the Crescent making a link between the two, horses dropped their dung, which dried and was pulverised by later traffic.

Everybody else took the filth for granted. Mr Appleyard's fish and vegetables, the butcher's wares opposite, were exposed. Diana washed everything from both shops. Half an hour's shopping in the High Street made the very flounce of her petticoat grimy, and Everard, in order to keep up appearance, needed a clean shirt every day.

They'd been far better off in Baildon, but that was a thing which Diana never said. She still loved Everard. She'd chosen him, and she had had plenty of choice. One aspect of marriage, the bed part, she had never liked much, its outcome she dreaded but Everard, with his good looks, his beautiful voice, his beautiful manners had not changed. He was hers and she was his until death did them part. He'd done his best, taking a job with more promise; she'd do her best. And things, being so bad, must improve. There must be some change.

Change came; for the worse. Tap, tap on the back door. The daily woman from Number 6 who had produced Maggie.

"Thought I'd better tell you, ma'am. Maggie can't come. She's in the 'orspital. 'E always did knock her about something shameful; last night he went a bit too far. Laid her out for dead. They reckon she'll die. And a blessed deliverance."

It was Diana's first— No, strictly speaking her second encounter with the seamy side of life. Everything to do with Lavinia had been squalid, for five months, but Mamma and Deb had borne the brunt and the whole thing was best forgotten. But this was here and now. Horror!

"How shocking!"

"No more than could be expected. Bound to happen, we all said it."

Behind the shock Diana's strong self-preservative instinct sprang up.

"I suppose, Mrs . . . er . . . er Butler, you don't know anyone else?"

'Eartless bitch! Getting her name wrong, too. It wasn't Butler, it was Buckler.

"No, I don't."

Everard was very good. He carried up the coal and took down the ashes. About the front steps he did nothing, could not be expected to. They worried Diana. Everything here was so grey. Even the trees and shrubs in the little bit of garden had been so laden with dust before summer ended that their change of colour when autumn came was hardly noticeable. The only spot of colour now in the whole place was the white of the steps. In which, after four or five days, those of Number 4 made an exception, neglected; grey stone against grey stucco.

Something of Mrs Thorley, her mother, rose up in Diana. She had sense enough to know that in her condition she should not lift anything heavy; half a bucket of water would do. A pair of old gloves would not protect her hands from water, but they should save her nails from the hearthstone. So early in the morning that the grey December dawn had scarcely broken, the dainty, fastidious Miss Osborne of Gad's Hall whitened her own steps.

Even Everard noticed the gleaming whiteness. He had not shared Diana's concern about them; he said: Let them go. It's a silly habit, whitening steps that look dirty again once they're walked on. All the same, if the dear girl minded so much, and in her condition, too, something must be done. He consulted with one of the women who cleaned the office and she said that she did know a girl who was looking for a living-in place.

"That is exactly what we need."

"She ain't much to look at, but she'd be willing."

Bessie Simpson was nothing to look at; in build she was much like Mrs Carr, but whereas behind Mrs Carr's harassed, hunted expression there was a hint of a kind of starveling prettiness, Bessie's face was a disaster; she was violently cross-eyed, had prominent teeth and no chin. A great disappointment to her mother who had three quite bonny girls, who sold flowers by day and other wares by night. Mrs Simpson considered that she had made her contribution to the family good when, very early in the morning, she took a light barrow round to Covent Garden and used her experience in the selection of flowers. Ninety per cent of those who bought flowers from street vendors were men, and they

looked first at the seller, then at what she had for sale; and as Mrs
Simpson said, with cruel truth, set Bess down in Piccadilly Circus,
offering red roses at a penny a dozen and nobody would buy. So
Bess had remained at home, a slave to her tyrannical mother and
her hardly less demanding sisters. She was thirteen and rebellion
was stirring in her, she'd be better off in a living-in job with only
one mistress. Seemingly tireless, endlessly willing, and showing towards Diana that pathetic devotion which ugliness can give to
prettiness—provided the prettiness is accompanied by civility, she
was to be Diana's strength and stay. Quite apart from the work
she did she actually saved money, spurning the shops in the High
Street. "Twice the price and half as fresh," she said of what Mr
Appleyard and his fellows had to offer. Turning out of the other
end of the Crescent, trotting along Skelton Street, she searched
for a market. There must be one. She did not think in square
miles, she thought in terms of streets and their character. Behind
Skelton Street there was a warren of little streets, lined with little
houses, far humbler than the Crescent, which Bessie considered
grand. The women in them must shop somewhere. They did in a
jumbled noisy open space, called The Maypole, or simply The
Market. It had seen Maypoles in its day, and some ancient, but
still honoured law had prevented it from being built over, so the
street traders had moved in with their incredibly varied wares.
Once Diana broke one of her best tea-cups. Bessie said,

"Don't you worry about that, ma'am. I'll take one along and
match it." She came back with a cup absolutely indistinguishable
from the others.

Bessie could cook, nothing fancy of course, but considerably
better than Diana who had come to art late and unwillingly
whereas Bessie had started at the age of eight, with no praise for a
successful attempt and a clout for a failure. Not, perhaps, the
ideal way of tuition, but extremely effective.

The baby was due in April. Diana, doing everything correctly,
had consulted the doctor in the High Street who had recom-
mended a highly efficient midwife, trained and experienced; she
had served for fifteen years in the lying-in ward of St Bartholo-
mew's Hospital. The interview had emphasised to Diana the
difference between life as it had been and life as it was. In Suffolk
old Doctor Taylor had been a friend, Edward was her brother-in-
law; there she would have been fussed over. Here she was one of
many; just another pregnant woman. She had put out a wavering

signal for help, or rather assurance, saying, "I rather dread it."
And the doctor had said there was nothing to dread; natural process; she was young and healthy, in Mrs Mitchell's hands she
would be quite all right, but of course, if something did arise, he
was only just around the corner.

Mamma?

Her presence would at least have helped to establish Diana's
identity in this alien and faintly hostile place. But neither Everard
nor Diana wholeheartedly wished for her presence. She'd been
rather against the move, counselling patience, saying that Mr Gordon could not live forever, saying, in effect—Stick to what you
have, that pleasant little house, access to Edward's stables and
garden, and all that Gad's can supply. In a way they had defied
her and in her letters home Diana had made the Crescent sound
rather better than it was. One glance and Mamma's bright eyes—
the only thing about her that had not changed, would reveal
the truth—they were worse off now than they had been in Baildon in the house she had chosen for them; Everard within easy
walking distance of his office, Caroline practically next door;
friends all around.

Nevertheless Diana craved the feeling of security that Mamma
would bring with her and was actually writing a letter asking her
to come, when the need to go to the water closet—one of the real
amenities of the gimcrack house, made itself felt.

The doctor in the High Street, casual and indifferent as he was,
had been absolutely right when he said that there was nothing to
dread. No worse than the colic, the result of eating green
gooseberries. . . .

"You was lucky," Bessie said. "Girls is always easier than boys
and better early than late. And I was here to do for you. That was
lucky too."

Everard was relieved that his first-born was a girl. For his son he
would be satisfied with no education inferior to his own and
would have already been worrying about school fees. Girls were
comparatively cheap to rear and educate. He hoped for a boy, of
course, one day, when the financial outlook was brighter. How
and when such an improvement would come about he had no
clear notion; in fact there in London with a big and busy firm, he
seemed to have run into much the same blind alley as he had in

Baildon; he was clever—all the partners admitted that, here, as in Baildon; Better have a word with Spicer was the rule; he was industrious, punctilious almost to a fault, and getting nowhere.

He was always most conscious of his lack of status—and money —when he boarded the horse-bus each morning and evening. There were never enough places, people pushed and shoved and Everard must push and shove, too. Once, looking round at his fellow passengers, he thought: *Eyeless in Gaza at a mill with slaves.* All his fellow slaves, exhausted by a day's work, sank back into apathy, glad to have obtained a seat, glad of the respite. They'd known nothing else, bred to it, as he had not been.

The baby, another link in the chain, dismiss that unworthy thought! was enchanting. The star-fish of a hand, reaching out like a tendril, had caught Everard's cautious finger and hung on. When her smoky-blue eyes focussed there seemed to be recognition in them.

Illusion, self-deception, Everard told himself in his saner moments; baby apes would clutch and hold onto a twig. Any human baby's eyes would look in just that way at a shape that promised something, a lift, a jog, food.

They had discussed her name, amicably. Everard's mother, the dimmest of dim memories, had been called Belinda; Mrs Thorley was Isabel. Compromise; call the baby Belle, which meant beautiful, which she was, almost from the first. As Bessie said, "I seen early ones afore this, all the wrong colour, green, yeller, purple and none of 'em thrived. This little beauty, she'll do."

So it seemed, through April, through May, into June. Very hot this year and terribly dusty, except in the strip of back garden, facing North and shielded from the morning and afternoon sun by the high walls designed to protect neighbour from neighbour. There the dust, the filth of London, went almost slimy.

"Would you mind, Everard, if I took Belle to Gad's? I think a short stay, in the country . . . And Bessie could look after you. Until your holiday. Then you can come too. Wouldn't that be nice?"

That was the first of the annual holidays; seeing Deborah with her Sam, Caro with no child, Susan Walford the same, Phoebe Mayhew not even married. Click, click, click, a bit like shaking a kaleidoscope, the same colours and shapes, but taking a different pattern.

Except to say that London was hot in summer, dirty and over-crowded at all times, Diana did not complain. Her house sounded pleasant, she had found help of the most satisfactory kind; she always appeared to be well-dressed. When Everard came down, usually in the final week so that he could escort his family home, there seemed to be no lessening of affection between them. Yet the vertical lines on Diana's forehead were deeper every year and sometimes, caught off-guard, her face wore a look of discontent. There had been a time when Mrs Thorley had been secretly concerned about Diana's apparent friendlessness, but since Belle's birth this seemed to have improved and Diana often referred to going out to tea or entertaining in a modest way, in her own home. As a matter of fact the circle of acquaintances, centring about St Anne's Church, was of the utmost dullness. Nobody young at all; nobody under thirty except one poor down-trodden girl who in the presence of her domineering old mother dared hardly open her mouth.

Diana had never been as frivolously gay as Caro, but she had enjoyed parties, the company of her contemporaries, most of whom had admired her, consulted her about fashions, what to do with greasy or frizzy hair, or freckles. She had never been such an outright flirt as Caro, but young men as well as young women had admired her.

Outside this stuffy circle there was entertainment to be bought, theatres, concerts even balls in aid of this good cause or that. But the West End, where such delights were to be had, was a long way away. Neither Everard nor Diana would have dreamed of attending a theatre or concert, leave alone a ball, without wearing the proper clothing—conspicuous and somehow rather silly on a horse-bus. Hired cabs were expensive, and so, of course, were tickets. There was, in the vicinity of the market which Bessie had discovered, a music hall called The Maypole; but neither Diana nor Everard would have been seen dead in such a low place.

Everard could read, or work on papers he had brought home. Diana, never a serious reader, flipped over the pages of a magazine, paying most attention to articles about clothes, beauty aids and changing styles in house-furnishing. A hardly recognised boredom possessed her and she was always glad to go to bed. Glad, too, when Everard said, "I'll be along presently. Good night, darling." Then she could be asleep or pretend to be when he retired.

So *that* could be avoided. She wanted another baby—a boy—but not too soon. Later, when things got better, when Belle needed less attention. Belle had passed her third birthday when Diana became pregnant again, and was almost four when Melville was born. This time there was hardly any need to discuss the name. Everard's mother had been a Miss Melville before her marriage, so it was a family name, it went well with Spicer and had a kind of dignity about it. When his hair began to grow after the birth-fluff had rubbed off, it had a reddish tinge. Strange, since Everard was fair and Diana dark.

"Gracious," Diana said, "I hope he isn't going to be like Deb's Sam."

Sam Bridges, conceived in ecstasy, but gestated in another mood, was a very odd child indeed. He was that rarity, a nine-stone baby. Deborah had laboured from Sunday morning, through the night, through Monday and Monday night, until Tuesday at daybreak to bring him into the world. The baby clothes she had prepared were too small from the first moment. As soon as he could walk and needed shoes they were the shoes of a two-year-old. He walked, sturdily at a year, talked fluently at about the same time, and was, as soon as he was mobile, so venturesome as to be almost suicidal. In his parents' bedroom there was a tallboy, eight drawers high. That, for some reason which nobody could define, offered him a challenge. He pulled out all the drawers and climbed them, as though mounting steps; when he reached the top one, his weight and the weight of the open drawers below him tipped the balance and the whole thing came crashing down with him under it. Any ordinary child would have been killed or seriously injured. Sam emerged without a bruise or a scratch. He went into the loose-box where Tim's most famous, but worst-tempered stallion stood and emerged unscathed. "Nice horse," he said. He fell into the well in the stableyard, leaning too far over to see what was in it and why he had been told, most strictly, not to go near it. But he fell into the bucket and was pulled up, soaked, very happy. It had been an adventure and he was one who, from the first, welcomed any adventure, and if no adventure offered itself, made one. He was, unless provoked, of sunny disposition, but if angered was almost frightening to see. Such temper, his father said, not unreasonably, must be curbed. A good smack on the bottom.

"He's a baby, Tim!"

"All the more reason. Bring up a child in the way he should go."

"I will not have his spirit broken," Deborah said. "When he is old enough to be reasoned with, I shall reason with him."

"By then it will be too late."

"That remains to be seen."

What Deborah said was now law at Foxton. To the struggle for supremacy in what might have seemed an unequal battle she had brought weapons of her own, superior intelligence, a glibness with words, a rocky intransigence. Something cold and deadly.

"I know that you disapprove of hunting. I am not particularly fond of chapel, prayer meetings, camp meetings, temperance meetings. Suppose I expressed my dislike by refusing to attend. Could you drag me, by the hair, screaming? Imagine it."

Timothy Bridges imagined it and shrank away from the reality. His temper had been curbed when he was young; he never shouted; Deborah had fallen, just at the right age, into Mamma's keeping; so she did not shout either. Their disputes were never noisy. Once Tim said, again not unreasonably, that it was in *his* stable, on *his* pasture that Deborah proposed to keep her hunter.

"Not necessarily, if you object so much. Mr. Craig, I am sure, would house my horse, or my horses, at a very reasonable charge."

Which of course she could pay; her father had left her five hundred pounds. She never referred to her legacy in actual words; she had no need to say as Diana had been forced to do, wanting this or that which Everard said they could not afford, "But, darling, I will pay out of my money." Nevertheless Timothy Bridges was aware of that five hundred pounds.

And once, after a quiet dispute, he had thought things could be made right in bed. Deborah made no protest until almost the crucial moment and then she had said a terrible thing. "If you wish to commit rape, go ahead." Could any woman have chosen words more daunting?

Out of the quiet disputes a truce emerged, guarded on both sides, but workable. There had been love once, and where had it gone? Take a little ball of quick-silver, press on it, half a dozen little bright fragments scattering off in all directions, try to recapture one of them and it also broke away.

But outwardly a good marriage. It took a mother's, no, a step-mother's eye to see that though Deborah now did what she wished, went where she wished, loved her child, naughty as he was, she was not as completely happy as she deserved to be. For one thing her very smile had changed; it had once been entrancing, a bit crooked, making one dimple in her left cheek. Somewhere along the road it had vanished.

Intermittently, and—as she would have been the first to admit—without any definite reason, Mrs Thorley worried about her girls. That Diana was not truly happy in London was proved by the way in which she counted, like beads, the remaining days of her holiday: Oh dear, only four days, three days, two days left. Deborah, acquiring not a discontented look, like Diana's, but stern, and thin; it was the paring away of flesh from her strong-boned face that had made the dimple disappear. Of them all Caro gave the greatest impression of being happy, but Caro could don a mask at will and once Mrs Thorley had clapped one on her face, saying that if Caro did not get up, dance at Poor Susan's engagement party, accept the invitation to be Susan's chief bridesmaid, everybody would say she had been jilted by Freddy Ingram. But she certainly had not said: Marry Edward Taylor. In fact she had given all her girls an exceptional freedom of choice. Even Lavinia had been free to take her own fatal way. But that had all been dealt with and should be forgotten. And what good did worrying about the others do? Just an excuse for insomnia; the waking, as though somebody had shaken her by the shoulder, just as the tall clock on the landing struck three. Conduct with yourself the endless argument, ignore the anodyne of whisky; think—We all have our troubles; think, well, at least Diana took away as much as she could carry, freshly killed fowls, two dozen eggs; and Deborah who needed nothing in the material sense had gone off jauntily letting Sam hold one rein and think he was doing the driving.

So what of Caroline?

Nothing untoward, it seemed. Caroline and Edward were not the only people who felt that Freddy would be lonely. He had always been popular and now he was extremely eligible. For at least six months the hospitality proffered him was of the most sedate kind, an invitation to dinner, or to spend a quiet week-end. Mourning must be observed. Christmas eased things a little. In the week preceding it the Theatre at Baildon put on SHE STOOPS TO CONQUER, and the Saturday night's takings—cheap seat prices doubled and those of the more expensive ones trebled, were to go to some kind of charity—a fund for helping old actors and actresses. It was, as Mrs Fallowfield said, A Good Cause; so she would take a party. But even a theatre party, in a good cause, looked better with a man or two in it. Barbara, Diana's contemporary, was married, but there were three younger girls. Why not invite Mr Ingram? Freddy's presence was noticed by other mothers of daughters, and the Hospital Ball, organised by the Friends of the Hospital, was looming up. If a young widower could attend a theatre, why should he not dance—in moderation of course.

It was at the Hospital Ball that Caroline showed her first, and perhaps her only flash of discretion. Freddy still had a violent, almost a hypnotic attraction for her. It had never weakened; never would. In the past, when they were both unmarried, she had got herself talked about, but that didn't matter, because she was positive that Freddy would marry her. Instead he had married Susan and she had married Edward. She'd understood, after the first terrible days of heartbreak, and forgiven him; and for five years and some months, though their eyes occasionally communicated, and on the occasions when they danced together their bodies had acknowledged the truth that their behaviour denied, Susan had stood there, a bulwark between Caroline and the ultimate folly. Now there was nothing, except marriage vows to Edward, and Caroline knew how all too easily she would ignore them and plunge headlong.

"Thank you for asking me; but I am not dancing this evening."

"Why not?"

"You forget. I am a member of the Committee." Still the youngest, in some ways the most powerful because she represented the younger generation and her purely flippant idea of adding swings and roundabouts and coconut shies to the stereotyped Garden Fete had raised a great deal of money. At the same time, because she was young and light on her feet anything demanding much physical effort could be left to her.

"There is such a crowd," Caroline said, "that there will be three sittings for supper, and I am in charge. Unless I keep a sharp lookout the third sitting will get nothing but blancmange. . . . Who're you with, Freddy?"

"The Garrards."

"Steam-rollers! Look out for your toes!" Caroline said, and whisked away.

But they both knew that there would be another time.

Cruel fate arranged that it should be under Edward's roof. It was in February, so far an exceptionally mild and pleasant month. It was Edward himself who had suggested a little dinner party, a gesture of welcome to the latest young resident doctor at the Hospital. It was Edward who had suggested inviting Freddy, using a valid argument. Everybody else who must be invited was a bit elderly; the newcomer was young, only just qualified, he'd be a bit overawed, feel a bit out of place.

"That is something he must learn to live with, I suppose," Caroline said. She had.

"I don't want to depress him from the start. How about Freddy?"

"He could hardly be called young, dear. He's at least three older than I am."

"I know. But he can keep conversation going. He's like you in that. And we haven't seen much of him lately."

"Very well," Caroline said.

Who could have reckoned with Edward being called out? Who could have reckoned on the fog coming on and everybody—except Freddy—making for home before it grew worse?

Turned to jelly, breathless, half-swooning with desire—but she had known it before, riding, as she should not have done, alone with Freddy in his gig and risking another scolding from Mamma. Then there had been virginity to be guarded, and Freddy had understood. Now Caroline could only gasp, "Not here! Not in Edward's house."

"Where, then? When?"

Caroline, coming to it a bit late for a country girl, had learned to drive after Diana went to London, leaving behind the little pony carriage and the pony, growing fat from lack of exercise. Caroline did not know, nobody knew, or remembered, or understood why she should be timid where horses were concerned. Her own mother, the first Mrs Thorley, had been a rational, practical woman; her husband had bought a new horse, satisfactory in every respect except that he was terrified of perambulators. So Caroline's mother had had one of her practical ideas and taken the perambulator—with Caroline in it—into the stable, just to show the horse that there was nothing to fear. Confined to the limits of

his stall, faced with the dreaded thing, the horse had gone temporarily mad, kicking and rearing. Caroline's mother had backed
away, thinking in her practical fashion that she should have
pushed in an empty perambulator. But for the child in the baby
carriage the damage was done; for her the horse was always a potentially dangerous animal. She had never wanted to ride one, as
Deborah had from the start, and she had never driven until Diana
went to London. Then she had braced herself, in order to be mobile and moderately independent. She was now fully capable of
driving to Sudbury.

She had always known that what with Edward was a meaningless, dead business would be different with Freddy; and she had
been right. Caroline wept from sheer joy. For as long as she lived
she would remember that day; the heady, tremulous anticipation
as she drove through the winter countryside, with Spring just
waiting in a few swelling buds, and openly proclaiming itself in
scatters of crocuses along the drive to what was generally known
as the Brewery House.

She had, on that day, a perfectly legitimate, unquestionable errand; helping Freddy to sort out Poor Susan's clothes.

Wearing the falsest of all her false faces, Caroline had explained that Freddy couldn't be expected to do it.

"And it isn't something to be left to servants. They couldn't
distinguish between what was good jumble and what should be
given to the poor. The things have been there since last summer
and should be put to some use."

"It's a wretched job for you, darling."

"Yes. But since what you told me . . . about Poor Susan being
ill for so long before she . . . Well, you know, Edward."

Edward knew. He said,

"Don't stay too long. Get back in the light. I'd come with you
and drive you, but I really have a full day."

"I know."

There was never any time. And never actually the right time.
What they needed was a night—a thousand nights together.
There was a six-year-old thirst to be slaked. And excuses were run-
ning out. It was perfectly true to say that there was not merely
Poor Susan's wardrobe to be sorted, but her mother's as well, per-
fectly true to say that Freddy found himself suddenly obliged to

entertain some potential customers and needed somebody who could see that the luncheon table was properly set. But it was all hurried and furtive; absolutely satisfactory in itself, a gulp of water in the desert, enough to make one crave more. More. More.

"Couldn't you get to London?"

"I suppose so. But what good would that do? If I say I must visit Diana, I must visit Diana. She is the last person in the world to connive."

"One night with Diana. One with me. I know the perfect place."

There was one heart-stopping moment. Edward remembered how Poor Susan had made the excuse of shopping to go up to London and see a doctor, supposedly more knowledgeable than he was. He said,

"Caro, darling, you're not hiding anything from me, are you?"

"Hiding? What should I have to hide?"

"I just had the idea . . . Well, darling, it's almost six years and no child. . . . I don't worry. I've known plenty of babies born after ten, eleven years. I thought you might . . . Believe me, darling, there's nothing to be done—and anybody who says there is is a dangerous quack."

Caroline spared a thought: What on earth has happened to me? Everybody said I was so *soft*. I even used to take chocolate to Lavinia, and flowers. Now I am harder than nails.

"I wouldn't dream of doing anything of that kind, without consulting you, Edward. All I proposed to do was to go and stay with Di, a night, or two, and do a bit of shopping. I've never even seen Di's house."

Di's house!

One of six squashed into so small a space. Grey. Di's maid, too sinister-looking to be believed. Di's guest room, if it could be so called. And Di had always made it sound rather grand. Did Di deceive herself? Am I deceiving myself? Do we all do it? In different ways.

Aware of the discrepancy between Number 4, St Anne's Crescent as she had described it and the reality, Di was inclined to enlarge upon the social success which she and Everard were enjoying.

"You remember last summer Everard couldn't come to Gad's

because he had to go to Scotland? Apparently he did something very clever. He never talks about business, of course, but Lady Lumsley herself told me that she owed Everard more than she could ever hope to repay. She admires him very much." Dinner at Lumsley House in Piccadilly had been a most dazzling event.

"Expensive, though," Diana said ruefully. "Even Everard agreed that I must have a new dress, and we were obliged to hire a conveyance, of course."

Apparently whatever financial reward Everard's singular service had merited had gone to the firm; Everard was to paid in social recognition. Not quite as empty as it sounded though, for a fellow guest that evening, "He was Charlie Somerton, he's Lord Westward now," had remembered Everard from Eton, greeted him with pleasure, sympathised with his circumstances. "You poor chap! Until my grandfather died—and it looked as though he'd last forever—I was a wage slave, too. Stock Exchange! Frankly, I got so downhearted, I couldn't make up my mind between jumping into the Thames or emigrating." His lordship had been Everard's fag and remembered him as one who had not made inordinate demands or been as free with punishment as most were, and when later in the evening he asked Everard where he lived and Everard had described the district in general and Number 4, St Anne's Crescent with sour truth, had said, "Damn it all, we can do better than that, surely. I'll bring the mind to bear on this."

With his natural pessimism Everard said that nothing would come of it, Diana must not count any chickens. But he wronged his ex-fag in thinking that he would promptly forget. Within a few days came the news that a lease of a house in Somerton Road ended on the last day of June and if Everard liked, the house was his.

"And at *such* a low rent," Diana said. "I honestly believe that Lord Westward would have offered it rent-free but feared to hurt Everard's feelings. A bare ten pounds a year more than this. And it's huge. . . . Of course," she said, "the rates will be considerably higher in such a nice neighbourhood, and Everard will have further to travel every day. But for the children's sake alone . . ."

She had, on this occasion, the wrong audience. She could have said that Everard had done the Queen herself a service, gained entrée to Buckingham Palace and been offered a house in Carlton Terrace and Caro would have said—as she said now—"How *lovely* for you. Oh, Di, I *am* glad." But her mind was elsewhere, thinking: This time tomorrow . . .

Tomorrow started with the shopping expedition which was the excuse for this visit. They went to Hawksley's one of the earliest and certainly the best-known of the departmental stores. Its boast was that it could supply anything from a pin to an elephant and its founder had recognised the fact that most shoppers were women who enjoyed a cup of coffee in the middle of the morning, a light lunch, a cup of afternoon tea.

Caroline had plenty of money, but her shopping seemed to Diana a bit aimless, not as Diana's shopping had been since her marriage, direct and purposeful. They wandered about, staring, fingering fabrics, admiring displays. Caroline was being wildly generous—but then she always had been. "Look, Di, when you move you'll have a proper nursery with room for a rocking horse." Order the rocking horse for Melville, a doll's house for Belle, a Paisley shawl for Mamma, light as air, warm as fur. A pipe for Everard, and one for Edward. For herself and Diana something so pretty, so new-fashioned, so altogether delectable, feather boas.

At that Diana protested. "Caro, you have already spent so much. . . ."

"But for you I should have been obliged to stay in a hotel, Di." (But for you I should not have an excuse for staying one night, leave alone two. You'll never know it, my dear, prim and proper Di, but you have opened the gate of Heaven to me. And I hope to God that by the time you next come to Gad's you'll have forgotten that I stayed with you only the one night.)

A whole line of cabs waiting outside Hawksley's.

"Of course you must ride back in comfort. I dragged you out, Di. And thanks for everything." They exchanged sisterly kisses and embraces.

"Albertino's. It is in Gerrard Street."

"I know," the driver said. None of his business, but she looked young and very respectable and he had a Puritan streak in him. He couldn't help feeling a bit sorry, having two daughters of his own.

It was in Albertino's establishment, specifically designed to cater for illicit affaires that the word divorce was first mentioned.

It was feasible; a man whose wife had committed adultery could cast her off, after a somewhat tedious legal process, shaming to both.

"Edward *might*," Caroline said, her voice slow and dubious. "But it would hurt him—and he has been so kind to me. It would hurt us, too. I should be ostracised."

"Not in France, darling. I have contacts there. I've sold wine in England, surely to God I could sell it in France. I could sell my half of the brewery. Richard would be only too glad to buy me out and come home and take charge. . . . Let's do it. Let's elope."

Behind this frivolous all-for-love-and-the-world-well-lost-Caroline there were generations of sturdy people, yeomen farmers and women of the same stock; accepting what life gave, looking out, sniffing the air: There will be frost tonight, better see to the lambs! Studying the sky: No sign of rain, the corn in Top Field will hardly be worth scything. Stolid, law-abiding. Their blood in her veins could not prevent her being tempted, but it gave enough ballast to prevent a too hasty acceptance.

"That needs some thinking about."

She had always been an emotional rather than a rational creature and there seemed to her a vast difference between a clandestine affair—all right, call it adultery if you liked—which nobody knew about and which therefore hurt nobody and doing something which would hurt Edward so much, which might even deal him a mortal blow, hurt and shock Mamma, and Di and Deb, shock, if it did not hurt the little community in which she had spent her whole life. I'm bad; I know I'm bad; I'm being bad at this moment, but there *is* a difference. Divorce is an ugly word. . . .

And was there, at the very back of her mind, a tiny distrust of Freddy? Of the very quality which made him so attractive, his light-hearted attitude towards life, his disregard for convention? Give him his due, he had been, at least outwardly, a good steady husband to Poor Susan; but she had been ill and he appeared not to have noticed; and, let the fact be faced, all the time he was married he had been conducting a very secret kind of flirtation with Caroline.

As I with him. Pots shouldn't call kettles black! But look forward.

One day you will age and lose what looks you have. Women

live longer, but men age better. Could you count upon Freddy, ten, fifteen years from now?

It did indeed need thinking about. And once you began to think you rather took against Albertino's. No reason. So far as one could see it was clean. Luxurious too, but somehow it smelt wrong. Caroline had sufficient imagination to make her kind—to Lavinia, locked away in the attic, to the children at the Ragged School, the patients in the Hospital; now it turned about and demanded: Who slept in this bed last night? Who will occupy it tomorrow?

There were no public rooms at Albertino's, but room service was prompt and efficient, softly moving waiters, quietly moving trolleys which opened out into tables, food piping-hot brought along in dishes with double bottoms, filled with boiling water.

The Caroline who had always been ready with the quip said,

"This is all a bit too professional for me. I'm only an *amateur* prostitute!" That made Freddy laugh.

Hours later, she thought to herself: Not even that! For, waking very early in the morning, she lay and felt that her craving for Freddy had at last been stilled. It had smouldered like a bonfire all these years, alternately stirred a little, and then damped down. None of their comings together had been completely satisfactory until last night. Now she seriously believed that the thing had burned itself out. She was cured! She told herself that she was not only a bitch, but a fickle bitch into the bargain.

Freddy, when he woke, was surprised to find Caroline up and dressed and ready to go. In him also desire was stilled, but he had more self-knowledge, and more experience than Caroline possessed and knew that this condition was only temporary.

"Hullo, darling. What's the hurry? We're not at the Brewery House now."

"I just want to get out of this place."

"Why? What's wrong with it? It's a very nice place. And it will now proceed to provide us with a very nice breakfast."

"I don't want any."

"Are you all right?" He thought, with a mixture of complacency and tolerance, that last night had been enough to exhaust anyone. A more sensible woman would have stayed in bed till lunch time.

"I'm all right." But the glass on the ornate dressing-table had showed her a pale face, its always monkeyish look emphasised, and dark smudges under the eyes. "I must catch the nine o'clock train from Liverpool Street."

"Why? There's another at eleven."

"I know. But I absolutely promised Edward I'd be back for lunch."

Now I am lying to Freddy, too.

With a quite audible sigh, Freddy prepared to pull himself from the bed.

"Don't come," Caroline said hastily. "By the time you're dressed and have the bill paid, I shall have missed the train."

Outside Albertino's unobtrusive doorway, the porter blew a shrill whistle and a cab appeared immediately. There was nothing noticeable about early and unaccompanied departures. There were people who in the ordinary way smashed about in their own carriages—some with crests on their doors, who used anonymous hackneys when visiting Albertino's.

The train pulled in at Baildon at a quarter to twelve and Caroline was surprised, and frightened, to see Edward on the platform, scanning each carriage. Mamma! Mamma taken ill, a message sent to Di's house. Di thinking Caroline already home. And Edward, *kind* Edward, come to meet her, support her, break the news gently.

But at the sight of her, Edward hurried forward, smiling, taking her in one arm, her dressing case, and the one light parcel in the other.

"I'm such an ass," he said. "You told me Thursday, but for the life of me I couldn't remember which train. So I thought I'd better meet them all."

"Then what a good thing I came early. You would have had a wasted day."

"You look thoroughly exhausted, darling."

Exhausted how and where? Push that thought away!

"London is tiring. In Hawksley's alone I think Di and I must have walked five miles."

"You didn't buy much."

"I spent a lot. Some on things to be delivered. My dear, I have so much to tell you. . . ."

And that, at least, *was* true. Di's horrible house, Di's prospect of moving, Di's new friends, all that she had seen in the shops, all that she had bought. The rocking horse and the doll gave Edward a pang. He accepted his present graciously though it was not exactly the pipe he would have bought for himself. He admired the feather boa and the shawl meant for Mrs Thorley. Generous girl, most of what she had spent had been spent on others. All she had bought for herself was a bit of frippery.

Mrs Thorley was pleased with her gift, so pretty, so light and so warm. She was glad to hear that Diana, at the end of June, was to move from what Caroline described as a rabbit hutch of a house, for a better one in a better district. But, acutely class-conscious, as life had taught her to be, she could not avoid worrying a little about Diana's association with people of title and substance. It was an exposure to risk. No doubt Lady Lumsley, grateful to Everard, who by some legal sleight-of-hand had served her well, was grateful, and no doubt Lord Westward, offering Everard the lease of a rather grand house, was being friendly to an old school fellow. But without money, without obvious family connections, above all, without land, the way of the social climber was hard. Not that Diana was likely to be silly, not that she and Everard were not fit to mix in any society, but . . . Mrs Thorley knew the world thoroughly; in the house where she had been born, neither the family solicitor nor the family doctor would have dreamed of entering by the front door: and then, after many vicissitudes, she had almost ended in Leicester, with only one door which she was almost ashamed to open because to do so was to reveal the poor furnishing of her front room. From such indigence George Thorley had rescued her and she had settled comfortably into one section of what was called the middle class, married her three remaining daughters into it. And she knew, or thought she knew, what would one day happen to Diana. Somebody would say: Oh, from Suffolk? Then you probably know my great-uncle, Lord Norton. And to that what could Diana say except: Just by sight.

Still, let's not take too gloomy a view. Perhaps doing something clever for a titled client would advance Everard in his profession. And certainly, if Diana's house was anything like Caroline's description of it, the move could only benefit the children.

Violet opened the door.

"Ma'am, it's Ruth. Asking to see you, special."

"Oh dear. Is she *still* out of work?"

Because she had once herself been a seeker for employment,

Mrs Thorley's sympathy was ordinarily on the side of those who were out of work through no fault of their own. But Ruth Marsh did seem to be singularly unfortunate where jobs were concerned. Since that party, last summer, when Poor Susan died, Mrs Thorley had employed her twice; once at Christmas, and then to help with the spring-cleaning.

"Out *again*," Violet said in a tone which neither Mrs Thorley nor Caroline noticed, except that it implied that Ruth had been fairly recently employed.

Had Caroline not been there, Mrs Thorley would have gone out into the kitchen, prepared to tell Ruth that she had no work to offer and that really two references were as much as, rather more than, any responsible woman could provide for so casual a labourer. As it was she said, "I'll see her. No, Caro dear, don't go. I haven't heard half about your visit."

Last July, leaving for some reason the *Hawk in Hand* at Baildon and glad to earn a shilling or two, helping Jenny and Violet, waiting expertly at table, and again at Christmas, the girl had seemed to Mrs Thorley to be, or at least to look, rather pert and bouncy, but in fact her look belied her. Neither then nor at Christmas, nor during the spring-cleaning had she said a cheeky word, or refused the most distasteful job. It was the fact that she had turned up, offering to clear the drawing room after the undertaker's men had finished, that had made Mrs Thorley give her a reference, employ her over Christmas, give her another, employ her again for the spring-cleaning.

Why she had lost her most recent job was all too apparent. Pregnant. Well, nobody, however kindly, could be asked to supply a reference for a girl in that state. There flashed through Mrs Thorley's mind the horrible thought that this girl was just about as advanced on this road which had only one ending as Lavinia had been on that March morning, six years ago. But that was different. Lavinia had been sheltered, even her insanity hidden from the world. This poor girl . . .

"It's Mr George's," the poor girl said. "We went together last summer and we're being going together, off and on ever since. It's his, I swear."

Caroline had never seen Mamma, her placid, managing, unfailing stepmother, in a rage before. In fact it had been Mamma who had imposed gentle manners, self-control. . . . But now Mamma rose up in wrath, and said, "How *dare* you? Accuse a boy, only just sixteen. You've been whoring about for years, and dare to come here, brazen-faced with such a lie. Get out of my sight. Get out of my house. And I warn you. . . . You go spreading this lie about and I'll have you run out of the village. On a hurdle, and to the sound of rough music."

She had never seen that particular treatment applied to an errant woman; it must be one of the things George Thorley had told her; he'd been a great respository of old stories, sayings, customs. The rough music was the noise made by the banging on kettles and saucepans and buckets which mixed with the hoots and the jeers. Ruth was familiar with the term and blenched slightly but she stood her ground.

"I ain't a liar, Mrs Thorley, ma'am. It's God's truth I'm telling you. If you don't believe me, ask *him*."

Thank God George had gone to meet Johnny Faulkner in Baildon. They'd lunch at the *Hawk in Hand* and spend the afternoon at the theatre. Not that Mrs Thorley wouldn't have something to say to *him*. Later on.

"I should prefer to ask why you were dismissed from the *Hawk in Hand*; and from the two situations I helped you to find."

That shot went home. Ruth began to cry.

"I ain't asking much. I ain't whored about as you call it. *They* get paid. I never took a penny. A present or two now and then is all. And I wouldn't be asking now, but what else can I do? I can't get a job, like *this*, can I?" Tears and mucus smeared her face. She appeared to have no handkerchief. In silence, Caroline handed over her own. Ruth used it vigorously. "I gotta sister down at Bywater, but she ain't got a penny to rub against a key. Four shillings a week, till I'm over this. . . . Me father ain't noticed yet, when he do he'll take his belt to me."

Just then it was not so much Caroline's sense of being a fellow-sinner as pure pity for anyone in such a plight that made her lean over and whisper to Mamma, "I'd help with it." Mamma's return whisper was positively a hiss. "To give her one penny would admit obligation." Aloud, and in the most unkind way, Mrs Thorley said,

"If that is all you need possibly all the men with whom you have been intimate could contribute it between them."

Caroline was shocked. Who could imagine Mamma being so cruel. Mamma, always so kind, even to Lavinia, who, after all, but for her family would have been in exactly Ruth's position.

Caroline did not realise then what an only son could mean to his mother. Mrs Thorley seldom made much display of her feelings. She had managed to treat her own two daughters and her step-daughters with such impartiality that everybody was astounded. And if in a moment of terrible crisis she had said, "I want Deb," that was completely understandable, Deb was so practical. Mamma had been fond and just, calling them all her girls. But her relationship with George was something completely different. He was her son, and the son of his father to whom Mrs Thorley owed so much. His birth had justified George Thorley's choice of second wife, past her youth. For these things alone his mother would have loved him, but George, from the first, had possessed such charm. To say that he was the apple of his mother's eye would be a profound understatement, and to have this common, loose-living, blubbering girl . . .

The little pony carriage overtook Ruth just before the lane which led only to Gad's joined the road which ran one way to the village, one way towards Baildon. Caroline stopped and said, "Get in. I want to talk to you."

In the face of Mamma's hiss that to offer a penny was to admit an obligation, Caroline dared not offer money, but she could offer something; beginning with being a Friend of the Hospital, Caroline had, over six years, become involved in other good works. She was able to say, "I am sure I could find you work in the laundry, either at the Hospital or the Workhouse; and then . . . then, when you were . . . er . . . brought to bed a place in the lying-in place. There, I can assure you, you would have every care. My husband devotes a lot of time to the women there."

It was the only thing Caroline could think of, taking hasty leave of Mamma and hurrying the pony along in order to overtake the poor girl and offer the best solution possible.

"It's good for you to bother," Ruth said. She did not sound particularly grateful. "But then what? My name smirched forever and another bastard brat in the Workhouse. I know your mother didn't believe me but what I said was true. I've fooled about a bit, but it's his, your brother's. You always know."

Caroline imagined George's child among the Workhouse Children. Things had improved a good deal since OLIVER TWIST—compulsory reading at school, and a book which had evoked many of Caroline's facile tears—and the Baildon Board of Guardians were on the whole liberal-minded; the Workhouse Children were soundly, if dully fed, and adequately if hideously clothed, but even at the Ragged School which some of them attended, they were distinguishable by their dull look and subdued behaviour as well as their uniform. To and from school, to and from church, on the occasional walk, they walked in couples, supervised by an under matron who wore a nurse's uniform to which she was not entitled, and whose only contact with them seemed to be orders to keep in step, to close up there. In the interest of hygiene both boys and girls had their hair cropped very short. They looked like what they were—Nobody's Children, and they seemed to be aware of their unwanted state. Imagine a miniature George . . .

About the sternest thing that Edward had ever said to Caroline was that she acted without thinking. She did so now.

"Do you *want* this baby?"

"Want it? Would *you*? I mean if you was me. Even if I got the money and went to my sister. She got five of her own. To get a job I'd hev to leave it there, and what sorta life would it hev?" What indeed? Edward, though he would get up in the middle of the night to help a woman in Scurvy Lane with a difficult delivery, had often said that one of the main causes of poverty was that people had more children than they could feed. And on at least two occasions which Caroline could remember Edward had . . .

"Don't think I didn't try," Ruth said. "I was earning when this started. I could afford two shillings for female irregularities, advertised in the paper. No more use to me than old Mother Carey's brews. And they say heaving things . . . One week I got a job, sacking and heaving potatoes out of a clamp. I worked alongside men till I dropped. All no use."

"Could you walk to Baildon?"

"Of course I could. I ain't that far gone yet."

Tomorrow was Sunday, a difficult day.

"On Monday," Caroline said. "Say twelve o'clock. You know the Gateway to the Abbey ruins, those niches where statues used to stand? If you're there just at twelve, on the left-hand side one there'll be a package for you."

"That'll end it? My God? If it'll work, I'll say a prayer for you every morning and night that I live."

"And never say a word." A bit late to be cautious now.

"I swear Almighty God."

Everard never discussed business with Diana, the dear girl simply wouldn't have understood. Edward, though he could maintain professional secrecy, as he had done about Poor Susan while she was alive, was more inclined to talk to Caroline, especially when his mind was troubled. As it had been about ending a pregnancy. He'd done it twice to Caroline's knowledge; both times in very pitiable cases; one a typical Scurvy Lane case; a woman, not old, completely worn out, ten children all crowded into nine years; so anaemic, so undernourished that another pregnancy would certainly kill her. The other a woman, in better circumstances, but with a deformity which prevented her giving birth in the natural way. Two Caesarean births. Pregnant for a third time.

In both cases Edward had doubted, changed his mind, balancing the strictly ethical view against realism. Asking himself questions, and talking to Caroline, whose mind was at least lively and receptive. Miss Hardwicke, who had taught all the Gad's Hall girls, and who had thought highly of Deborah, dismissed Diana as Young Madam, despaired of Lavinia, had once thought that if Caroline would only *give her mind* to her lessons, and not be such a magpie picking up this bit of information here and another there, she might yet be regarded as educated. That had not happened, but the magpie mind, sharpened since marriage, by boredom, had made Caroline very knowledgeable.

Once before she had stolen from the dispensary which adjoined the room where Edward held his surgery. And that had been something to relieve pain, Lavinia's childbirth pains, up there in the attic at Gad's. Now she stole, well, why? To rid Ruth of her unwanted burden. To end Mamma's worry. To save some unborn child from bastardy and penury.

It took a bit of managing; the parcel in brown paper placed in the niche and then to be watched over, pretending all the while to be watching the planting out of geraniums in the beds flanking the grim old gateway. Ruth was punctual and adept, snatching the package up. Pray God it works.

Mrs Thorley had been a tigress in defending George, and she was a tigress in rebuking him.

"I always knew you were stupid—all boys are—but that you should be *so* stupid never once occurred to me. I know you think of yourself as a man, and God help us, you're big enough." A hard thing to say, for she had always been so proud of his size, his precocity. "But to go about seducing village girls . . . I'm thoroughly ashamed."

If, at that moment George had spoken the truth, looked ashamed, said that he had been the seduced rather than the seducer, the future might have been different, with Mamma scolding, but granting a kind of absolution; a very bad thing to do; and never do it again. But George said, "Silly bitch! Why did she come whining to *you*. What were you supposed to do about it?"

"Provide her with money until the child was born. And presumably make provision for the child afterwards." Mrs Thorley spoke very sharply. "Do you not realise the gravity of your offence? Did it not occur to you that a child might result? A child born out of wedlock."

"Frankly, I don't see why it should be pinned on *me*. I wasn't the first—she said so. And there've been others since." He appeared to be utterly unrepentant. "I don't say I might not help her a bit."

"Oh. With what?"

"I could sell something. My watch. Things like that." George spoke amiably, smiling even.

"All your father's," Mrs Thorley said, her irritation increasing. His father's watch, cuff-links, studs, all of the best quality.

Unperturbed, George said, "Well, why not? After the girls had their whack it was all to be mine, wasn't it?" No disputing that. What was more George Thorley, when making his will, though still feeling that he had many years ahead of him, had suffered that intimation of morality which strikes on such an occasion, and he had looked ahead, thinking: If anything should happen to me . . . He trusted his wife completely, had taken the unusual step of appointing her sole executor, but he had wanted her burdensome stewardship to be as short as possible, so had willed that George should inherit at eighteen. With a start, Mrs Thorley realised that in just two years George could sell not something, but everything if he so wished. A sobering thought indeed.

George's inborn distaste for any unpleasantness asserted itself.

"Oh, come on, Mamma, surely you and I aren't going to quarrel about a silly little thing like this. Probably all a lie anyway." He put his arm around her and dropped a light kiss on the top of her piled-up hair. And with the gesture authority quietly passed from her to him. She had always been indulgent, overindulgent, and he could wheedle almost anything out of her, but she had, in the last resort, been Mamma, the head of the family. It was no longer so.

It was curious, she thought, that two of her children, Lavinia the daughter of a bad man, George the son of a good one, should be alike in indulging in illicit sexual relationships, and alike in showing absolutely no awareness of guilt. Lavinia had never once said: I'm sorry, for all the trouble she had caused. George had shown no sign of repentance in a situation which would have made most boys of his age blush and stammer.

It must be something in *me*. But what? My first marriage was anything but satisfactory, Stephen was far from faithful, we often moved in a raffish circle, I had opportunities. I never put a foot wrong, neither then, nor when I was widowed. I had looks then, I knew a lot of people. I could have found an easier way of making a living for myself, Diana and Lavinia than by drawing designs, teaching ham-fisted children to play the piano, and finally letting the spare bedroom. I lived like a nun. And widowed a second time, I was not, in that way, completely shelved. Given the slightest encouragement, several men, including Mr van Haagen . . .

At the thought of him her eyes went involuntarily to the pretty little desk in the window embrasure.

Yes; I have a hard conscience, too! The only difference is that it operates financially, not amorously.

The thought of Mr van Haagen put an idea into her head. Over supper that evening she said, carefully casual, to George,

"My dear. I have been thinking. Would you like to go abroad? As you know, Mr van Haagen and I do a good deal of business, and of that side you at present know nothing. Mr van Haagen travels extensively. It would be almost the equivalent of the Grand Tour—except that it would not include Italy. But you would see Holland and France and Germany, and even Denmark. It would at least be experience for you."

"That would suit me well," George said. "It wouldn't interfere with the season." He meant the hunting season and the shooting of partridges and pheasants. It meant leaving Gad's, but only for a short time; it meant leaving Goldie, but Johnny Faulkner would be only too glad to exercise the horse for him.

"Yes," George said, "I'd like that."

Caroline's invaluable Mrs Humberstone said, "There's a young person asking for you, ma'am. Ruth, she said, and you'd know her."

"Yes. I do. Show her in."

What now? If the stuff hadn't worked and even Edward said nothing in this world could be one hundred per cent certain, what was Caroline to do? Give money, which Mamma had forbidden?

But Ruth came in smiling. She carried in one hand the rush basket in which servants transported their few belongings and in the other a bunch of the pale, very sweet-scented wild-flowers known as oxslips, a relative of the cowslip which would grow any-where. Oxslips were more selective and therefore rare. They grew in profusion in one part of Layer Wood but not in others; and they refused to transplanted. Years and years ago, when Deborah and Caroline had been motherless children, running wild as peo-ple said, one of their games had been making gardens, bringing things in from the wood. No transplanted oxslip had ever sur-vived.

Ruth was—thank God—her own shape again; indeed rather less curved, and rather pale.

"Are you all right, Ruth?" Hadn't she said something about heaving sacks of potatoes? Now she dropped the light rush basket as though it weighed heavy.

"Yes. And all thanks to you. I can't tell you . . . I thought you might like these. Nothing else I could think of to bring you." Ruth held out the bunch, wilting already, oxslips resented being picked as well as being transplanted, but, dying, they gave off their peculiar fragrance and Caroline remembered, on two different levels, like a layer cake, romping about the woods with Deborah, and years later turning aside, in one of those gig rides with Freddy, one of those tantalising, inconclusive . . . Oh God!

Caroline said, "Do sit down," for the girl looked as though she might drop. She had walked from Stonham St Paul's.

"I can't stop," Ruth said. "I got a job in London. Thanks to you again."

"You don't look . . . very hearty, yet. Was it bad?"

"It was quick. And it's over," Ruth said. She mustered a ghost of a smile. "I gotta catch this train. Goodbye, I'll never forget you."

Well, perhaps she had behaved in what Edward would call an

unethical way, but at least she'd helped somebody. So why sit down beside the flowers and cry? Because life was so hard—not only on poor girls like Ruth, but on fortunate ones, like herself.

"I missed Caroline by a hairsbreadth last Thursday," Mrs Bosworth said, when Edward had assured her that her ankle was not broken, merely badly sprained, and had strapped it up for her. "In fact I incurred this injury hurrying down the stairs at Hawksley's. Marble looks well, but it can be very treacherous. Such a pity. She was just saying goodbye to Diana—with whom I should have liked to exchange a word. Caroline and I could have shared a cab to the station."

A man less busy, or of more suspicious nature, might have spotted a discrepancy, but Edward simply said, "Keep it bandaged, Mrs Bosworth, and rest it as much as you can."

Mrs Bosworth was beginning to feel that the world was changing. She was old enough to remember Edward's father, dear old Doctor Taylor, never in a hurry; never brusque. He would have made much of a sprained ankle, chided her for hurrying, agreed that marble steps were treacherous, and then over a glass of sherry regaled her with a little gossip, discreet, of course, as befitted his profession, but often by omissions or elipses, very enlightening. There was none of that easy-going comfort from a visit by Edward. On this occasion he had not given Mrs Bosworth a chance to make her next remark—that it was curious that she had not seen Caroline on the five o'clock train, nor at Baildon station.

The true gossip has a nose as sensitive as a truffle hound's. Forced by her sprain into inactivity, Mrs Bosworth indulged in speculation; visited, in her affliction, by Mrs Catchpole and Mrs Garrard, she mentioned, idly, what had struck her as curious. "Lame as I was, I was obliged to hobble almost the full length of the train in order to obtain a seat and there was no sign of her. And when I mentioned having seen her outside Hawksley's, it occurred to me that Doctor Taylor was very abrupt."

"He could hardly be more abrupt than usual," Mrs Garrard said. "I much prefer Doctor Raven. We were forced to call upon him when James broke his collar bone and Doctor Taylor was too busy, for some reason, to come immediately."

Mrs Catchpole said, apropos of nothing tangible—merely the vague idea that Caroline's behaviour had been curious,

"She always was extremely flighty. I must say I endured agonies when my Simon showed a distinct partiality for her. Truly I thanked God when she turned her attention to Mr Ingram."

Mrs Garrard, who had not relinquished all hope of Freddy proposing to . . . well, Monica, or Rosa, when the year of decent mourning was expired, said,

"That came to nothing. It was probably all talk."

Mr van Haagen wrote—his English so much better when written than spoken, that he would be enchanted to have George for the summer and he assured Mrs Thorley that for George it should not be all work and no play. There would be a visit to Paris, not that pedigree stock was ever seen there, but buyers were. George would be most welcome and he should have a good time.

"God, you were born lucky," Johnny Faulkner said, when George told him what his immediate future held. Johnny, having reached the age of seventeen without showing any pronounced academic promise, had left Eton at the end of the summer half and was destined to act, for as long as his father lived, as a kind of foreman—which meant that he took all the blame, and a kind of agent, which meant that he took all the responsibility, for an estate which hadn't really shown much profit for many years.

George was aware of having advantages; two compact farms, Park with its herd and its meadows, Gad's with cornfields, very different from what Johnny would eventually inherit. But there was another difference, too. Ancestry, family connections; roots in the past. It was true that a Sir John Faulkner, a knight of some repute, had been killed in Crécy, his body brought home and laid under an impressive stone memorial in the church at Stratton Strawless. A Thorley had been there too, with his long bow, and his family, stretching their resources, had brought him home to lie with his fathers in the churchyard at Stonham St Paul's.

BUT . . . There was a difference which George had partially overcome and meant, one day, to overcome absolutely. But age—about that there was nothing to be done. Johnny and Chloe, twins, were seventeen when George was sixteen, and Chloe had, without benefit of a London season, found a husband. Prayers were sometimes answered, Lady Faulkner thought.

Of the two boys who had loved Chloe, Johnny gave more evidence of distress. No Thorley ever wore his heart on his sleeve—at least after one rebuff and George had suffered that one rebuff earlier in the year, at the Hospital Ball, a charitable affair, where various levels of society met but did not mingle. No uninformed person, looking in, could have told the sheep from the goats, but invisible lines were drawn and defended.

Fifty years later George Thorley was able to say, with proper pride, that the evening dress made for him on that occasion was still in use. At sixteen he was as tall as he would ever be, and the years neither fattened nor shrivelled him. Wearing his new outfit and extremely well-shaved . . . But not allowed to dance with Chloe Faulkner. Lady Faulkner, always so grateful because George had saved Johnny's life, always so nice to him, had taken on another aspect, had intervened, had said, while Chloe stood dumb, "Chloe's programme is full."

Warned off!

Over Chloe's engagement, marriage, presentation at Court, George Thorley bothered himself far less than Johnny did, trying to explain what being a twin meant. Saying,

"Oh, I know she'll be all right. Damned great house in Lincolnshire, damned great house in London, bagsful of the needful. But . . . well I know they say girls age earlier. I always looked on Chloe as years younger than me, to be honest, a bit dim-witted, in a nice way, needing to be looked after. I don't mind telling *you*, you're an understanding chap. I feel as though I'd had an arm lopped off."

In the first week of July, Diana and Everard moved into Somerton Road, and if only, if only they'd had a little more money, everything would have been perfect. There'd been no shortage of land, nor of labour a hundred and fifty years earlier when the present Lord Westward's great grandfather had decided that ten decent houses let to decent tenants might pay better than the strawberry field which was part of his inheritance and nothing but a nuisance. The field, within spitting distance of Hyde Park, was rented out in patches for minuscule rents, most of them never paid; the weather had been too wet, and all the strawberries had got the mildew, or it had been too dry and the strawberries had withered. Or they had been stolen. Always some excuse.

Ten houses, built in the new way, a terrace. But not pinched. Decent houses, in which, Lord Westward reflected complacently, he would have been willing to live himself if things got worse. No through traffic, Somerton Road led nowhere; like Friars' Lane in

Baildon, it was a cul-de-sac. The decent people whom that long-dead Lord Westward had visualised as living in his fine new houses were City men, riding or driving to their places of business each morning, or men retired from the Army or the Navy without having made much of a fortune. Naturally all such people would keep horses, probably a carriage. So behind all the houses and given access from one end or the other past the houses, there were stables, and above them living accommodation for grooms or coachmen. Between the houses and the Mews as such subsidiary buildings were called, there were gardens. Here, as in St Anne's Crescent, each to his own, but with a difference. Here the boundary walls were set well apart, letting the sunshine in, and to a large degree the stark boundaries were screened by ornamental trees or shrubs.

It was paradise to a young woman who regarded herself as country-bred; who had gone, taking Belle, taking Melville, taking herself, out of dusty, dirty London to breathe the fresh air at Gad's. This year there would be reason—no excuse?—for such an excursion. She would miss seeing Mamma, and Deborah and Caro and her friends—one of whom, the former Barbara Catchpole, had had a baby recently. But staying in London would save at least one new dress—the garment she had bought specially for dinner at Lady Lumsley's was not suitable for wear at Gad's, and it would save the fare. Everard, always worried about expenses, should be pleased.

Everard was not; he wanted Diana to go to Suffolk because he had received an invitation to stay in Scotland. Diana had not been included. This omission Everard explained to himself by the fact that in part his visit had to do with business; also to be considered was that Lady Lumsley had borne in mind that a woman with two small children—and no proper nurse—would find it difficult to absent herself for a fortnight. The real reason was, of course—and Everard knew it—that Diana had not quite slipped into the new milieu as he himself had done. It was not through any gaucheness of manner. Diana's manners were perfect and she had poise—of a rather static kind. It was not that she was less intelligent than those of the set in which Lady Lumsley moved, the level of intelligence there was not high. It was just, well, poor darling, she was out of her depth; she had neither the background nor the adaptability. Everard had the astonishing thought that both Caroline and Deborah would have done better, thus transplanted. Caroline, set down between two strange men at dinner, would soon have had them laughing; Deborah would have talked about horses and hunting. Diana, with her correct little answers, prim little questions was at a loss. Provincial!

Everard himself had slid back effortlessly; he could say of his humble—comparatively humble occupation, "Oh, like Old Father William, I took to the law. . . ." He could refer, caustically, to himself as a wage slave. The years he had enjoyed with his godfather, his years of luxury and privilege, calamitously ended, had left him with something indestructible and recognisable. At that first memorable dinner at Lumsley House, Diana's neighbour, for lack of anything else to say to a woman he had never seen before, asked whether she had enjoyed the latest opera at Covent Garden and Diana could only say, "I'm afraid I haven't seen it." Asked the same question by *his* neighbour, Everard said, "No. The last opera I saw was in Paris, a long time ago. Nowadays, having thrashed my way on to a horse-bus and off again, at the end of the day—I work in the City—I've had enough of people and of noise by the end of the day." Diana's answer had been correct, and sterile. Everard's different in tone.

So, when Diana said that this year there was no need to go to Gad's, Everard, to her surprise, had insisted that she should. She needed a rest after the move. He'd be in Scotland; and wouldn't her Mamma miss her now that George had gone to Holland?

Certainly the move had been exhausting, not because Diana had been obliged to lift and carry, but because there was so much contrivance to be done, all at the least possible cost. Curtains had been especially troublesome. Diana had been through this hoop before; none of her Friar's Lane curtains had fitted the mean little house in St Anne's Crescent; but shortening was easy, lengthening practically impossible. New curtains were an absolute necessity, and by the time they and a few other things had been bought her dowry would be exhausted.

They were not yet actually in the state which Everard had feared and talked about at the beginning of their marriage; they were not in debt, but the future was daunting. His fare had trebled and he had joined a club. He proposed to compensate for this extravagance by economising on luncheons at his usual chop-house and sustaining himself by taking a cup of coffee—peculiarly greenish in colour and of sinister flavour, and a sandwich. Anxious not to be seen by any member of the firm, or any clerk from the office in the act of frequenting such low places, he sometimes walked half a mile. And he was always very hungry when he returned in the evening.

Bessie worried about prices and mourned the old Maypole Market. This did not seem to be an area promising anything in the way of a market; and there was a notice at the mouth of Somerton Road, and several others, warning off street vendors. Still, she did not give up hope and scuttled about until she found Soho, cheaper and even more varied than the old Market. It was a good old trudge, especially coming back with a load, but well worth it.

Soho, as Bessie told Diana, was full of foreigners, but they understood English all right, though some would short-change you if you didn't look out. Trust me to look out.

One day on a foraging expedition, Bessie passed a young woman. They had never seen each other before, might never meet again; yet they were linked. Bessie, looking at Ruth, thought: Dressed-up tart! And Ruth, looking at Bessie, thought: That could be me! That was all.

The foreigners had brought their own religion with them and Ruth was on her way to light a candle for Caroline as she had done every week since coming to London. Lighting a candle seemed somehow more of a gesture than just saying a prayer. Ruth was not a Catholic, knew nothing of the ritual, but in her first week in London she had shared a room with a red-haired Irishwoman of dubious morals but extreme piety. The church was St Anthony's and therefore his shrine was nearest the door, and the biggest and brightest. The candles varied in size and price. One day Ruth was going to light a great fat shilling one on Caroline's behalf.

She did not know that one of the legendary qualities attributed to St Anthony was the finding of things that were lost.

Mrs Thorley said to Caroline, "Diana is coming, after all. I had rather gathered from her last letter that she would not come this year. I'm glad."

"Yes, you must miss George, Mamma."

"I miss him, naturally. I have missed you all. . . . But George is enjoying himself tremendously."

And *this* year Caroline would not go and look at Diana's children, and Deborah's one with the I-don't-care-look, which really said I-care-very-much.

Caroline was going to have a baby of her own.

What had that wretched girl said? "It's his. You always know."
Caroline knew.

There had been some days of agonising indecision. Go to Freddy and say: All right. I'll come away with you; or stay here, pretend and pretend? Deceive Edward but in doing so make him happy. And, teetering on the knife edge of decision, Caroline thought: God's teeth! I don't even *know* myself, I've slept with them both. It's imagination. It's because I feel guilty. Avoid, just for once, the hasty, impulsive action. Even the most level-headed of women didn't go rushing about saying: I'm pregnant! just because they'd missed a few days, a week, a month.

The desire for Freddy which had seemed quenched forever that morning at Albertino's had recovered, and that made the decision harder. So did the fact that if she told Edward the truth *now* sheer anger might lessen the hurt. Now and again she imagined life with Freddy, in France, which she only knew from his descriptions of it—all very lyrical. An old château on the outskirts of a whitewalled, red-roofed village, vineyards on terraced hillsides, all in hot sunshine. Married to, living with, loving Freddy, openly with no furtiveness, no guilt. Nonsense, you silly girl; you'd always feel guilty! And always just that tiny bit insecure. Pregnancy isn't a very pretty condition. . . . Once you wondered what age with Freddy would be like, think what his attitude might be when you're bulging and blotchy and useless in bed. Oh dear!

It was Edward who precipitated the decision; that and her tendency to speak before she thought.

"Darling," he said one day at breakfast, "are you all right? Is there anything on your mind?"

Irresistible! "I wouldn't say on my *mind*, exactly!"

Edward had expected the revelation of some trivial bother—so far as he knew all Caro's bothers were trivial—gaped, understood. He got up and came around the table, knelt, burrowed his face into her lap and mumbled something about this being all that was needed to make life perfect. When he lifted his head she saw the tears in his eyes, on his lower eyelids. But, typically Edward, he was himself again almost immediately, assuring her that there was nothing to be worried about; she shouldn't even feel pain, beyond a pang or two. There was this marvellous chap called Simpson who advocated an anesthetic for women in the last stages of labour. It had been resisted at first, but the Queen herself had taken advantage of it when her last child was born.

So the choice was made, and Caroline's common sense assured her that it was the right one. Sometimes she fingered, rather hesitantly, the notion that even her apparently disgraceful behaviour had been right. After all she had been married to Edward for more than five years and nothing had come of it. Perhaps, in a way, Edward's joy and pride owed something to Freddy.

Now and again bits of—well, what? You couldn't call it knowledge. Superstition, folklore, drifted back into her mind. One was reassuring; babies with two fathers, it was said, were always boys. Nobody knew or could even guess why, but in fact a glance into the history of the Workhouse Children gave some indication. By far the greater majority of the boys were illegitimate, the offspring of loose-living women. (Like me!) All but a few of the girls were the product of genuine marriages, ended by death or some other calamity.

"Naturally," the Head Matron said, "records are incomplete. We have some children who were simply abandoned." Why Mrs Taylor should be interested in the origins of the children who had fallen into the Poor Law Guardians' hands was a bit puzzling, but not to be questioned.

So the chances were that Caroline's baby would be a boy; and curiously, Edward seemed to think so too, though now and again he caught himself up in the planning of the unborn's medical training, taking over, carrying on, and said, "But of course, darling, it could be a girl. And if she's anything like her mother, she'll be adorable."

Less comfortable was an idea, no more, about inherited colouring, especially of the eyes. Somebody, who, when and where, Caroline in her light-hearted way had forgotten, had said that two light-eyed parents never produced a dark-eyed child, or vice versa. Her own eyes were greyish-bluish-greenish; Edward's clear steely grey; Freddy's brown. A brown-eyed child . . . but, thank God, Edward was unlikely to have heard this rural theory, or, if he had, paid any attention to it.

By late July, when Diana came, Caroline seemed settled, happy, the flighty quality in her outgrown. There had always been something about her young stepdaughter which Mrs Thorley had faintly distrusted, something wild, too outspoken, careless, too easily moved to tears or laughter. All that was needed now. A bit belatedly, but better late than never, Caroline had conformed.

It was about Diana, whose behaviour, speech, everything had always been so impeccable, that Mrs Thorley worried now; not because of anything Diana said or did, but the way she looked. Drawn, anxious, and—are my eyes now deluding me?—with a white hair or two. Diana! Always, in the old days, the one inclined to squander money on cosmetic preparations, the one whom other girls had consulted. And now—well, Mrs Thorley had never deceived herself, Diana wore the look—ten years too soon—which she herself had worn in Leicester.

Poor diet? That was what she had told herself, facing that face, morning after morning, angling to see, in a cracked glass, whether her hair was tidy.

Rescued by George Thorley, lifted from the weak tea and bread level, Mrs Thorley had improved in looks, plumped out, not too much, just enough, so that for a time she had defied the years—until Lavinia . . .

Mrs Thorley applied herself to the process of trying to fatten Diana a little, but ten days of good feeding did not lift the drawn look, and if it stemmed from a secret worry, plainly Diana intended to keep it secret. She deftly evaded all the openings which might have led to confidences. Quite right, too; a decent reticence was one of the bedrocks of good behaviour. But Mrs Thorley could not forget Caroline's description of Diana's first London home and the pretence which Diana had kept up. Was her new home any better? Or, horrible thought! even worse? Or, possibly so much better as to be outrageously expensive? Unlikely, Mrs Thorley thought, for Everard was the reverse of spendthrift, in fact if anything he erred on the other side. Very cautious. Indeed he would have deferred his wedding if Mrs Thorley, anxious to meet Timothy Bridges' impatience and her own, perhaps stupidly old-fashioned wish not to have Deborah married first, and not to have Deborah married in chapel, had not intervened by hiring the little house in Friars' Lane and thus speeding things along.

Deborah made two visits during Diana's stay; once for the day, and once staying overnight. Last year—was it only last year?—

when Deborah's Sam was five and Diana's Belle was four they had squabbled and fought and everybody expected trouble to break out again as soon as they met this year. But a twelve-month interval had worked wonders in Sam; in him the Thorley precocity was at work, as it had been in George, and in Deborah, whom everyone who didn't know had always taken for the eldest of the Gad's Hall girls. Sam at six was as big as most boys at ten and his attitude to Belle, who had changed very little except to become prettier, was now kindly, quite amusingly patronising. He said, "If you are a good girl, you shall have a ride on my new pony. When I get it." He shot a glance, half-assured, half-questioning, at his mother.

"You'll get it," Deborah said. "In fact, I've been writing to Mr Thoroughgood and we may collect it next week." Deborah gave her son a smile, not the one of the old days, entrancingly lopsided because it produced a dimple in one cheek, not in the other. "Now get along with you. Play ball with Belle, and don't throw too hard. Remember, she's only a girl." Holding Belle by the hand, and followed by Melville, just steady on his feet but resolutely determined not to be left out of anything, Sam went off, and Deborah thought: What a daft thing to say! Only a girl. When she'd proved, and went on proving almost every day of her life, that she—only a girl—was as good as most men, and better than many.

Most of the disputes between her and Tim had been quiet ones, wordy battles, most of which she had won by cool argument. But they had had one physical confrontation—apart from the bed thing. Both on their feet, fully dressed, and in the open; in fact in the chapel yard. Deborah and Tim had reached quite a comfortable compromise about chapel going and hunting, and Sam had been taken to chapel, as a good little born Methodist should, from an early age. But there came the Sunday morning when the preacher was the man whom George had mimicked so well, after his one miserable, curtailed visit to Foxton; the man who said er after every other word. Sam, too young to be critical but now old enough to be bored, had begun to wriggle and shuffle and then to kick the back of the pitch-pine pew just in front of him. Father on one side, Mother on the other had quelled that outlet of nervous energy, and Sam had taken refuge in saying er, loudly and distinctly, every time the preaching man said it. Worse than kicking, which could be controlled by a hand on each active young knee.

And far more embarrassing, for the poor man with the impediment which he resolutely ignored in his effort to serve his God by preaching, halted, looked confused.

Tim took his naughty boy by the arm and dragged him out and within a minute the service was disturbed again by the sound of two good hard smacks and the roar of a child affronted rather than hurt. Everybody within the claustrophobic little building— except Deborah—heard the smacks with a kind of satisfaction. Naughty children should be spanked; they had been spanked in their time, had spanked, or were prepared to spank any child of theirs. But Mrs Bridges rose, swiftly, and silently, and went out. No other sound disturbed the preacher, but he had lost the thread of his discourse and jumped from fourthly-er to finally-er.

Outside, near the tree under which Sam's paternal grandparents lay in their eternal rest, an unseemly scuffle was going on. Tim still had his hold on his son's arm and on Sam's face the marks of a heavy hard hand, back and front, were already reddening; but Sam was kicking.

"You *louts!*" Deborah said, getting between them and pushing, Tim with her left arm, Sam with her right. "I'm ashamed of you both." Released, Sam dodged behind the tree and from its shelter glared at his father, his father glared at his mother. Deborah glared at them both, seeming to divide her displeasure impartially. The first notes of the final hymn began to sound.

"Come along," Deborah said, "we don't want people staring at us." Straightening her hat, she set off at a brisk pace. Tim, like most Methodists, kept the third commandment very literally and Foxton was only a mile and a half from chapel, so they walked. For the same reason the Sunday dinner was always cold.

"I can't eat. My mouth hurts," Sam said.

"Come here and let me see."

Tim Bridges was anything but a violent or cruel man, but his hands were hard and heavy and into the two blows had gone years of frustration. The boy was already thoroughly spoiled; Deborah had seemed, from the first, to set herself against any form of correction; Sam was too young to know right from wrong; Sam's spirit must not be broken, and so forth. It had been, all unknown to himself, his wife's face, rather than his son's, which Tim had slapped that morning.

The inside of Sam's face on one side was cut and one tooth was hanging askew. It was a superficial injury and the tooth was one of the baby ones, due to fall any day. Still that did not excuse . . .

"I'll make you some bread and milk," Deborah said. Servants were supposed to do the minimum of work on Sunday; Emma, too infirm now to get to chapel, spent most of the day resting and reading, not without difficulty, what she called the Good Book. Eva, the girl brought in to help when Deborah rebelled against acting as kitchen maid, went to chapel and then spent the rest of the day with her family.

Placing the steaming bowl before Sam, Deborah said, "Take it as hot as you can, and hold it against the cut."

More spoiling! In a properly run household Sam would have had no dinner at all, possibly no supper either.

Presently Sam produced the tooth and said, "It's out."

Something was wrong. On every former occasion when he had lost a baby tooth, he'd been told to put it under his pillow and see what it had changed into by the morning. It had changed into sixpence. For the first time or two it had seemed like magic to Sam, but he soon saw through it. It was Mother! And he was beginning to suspect that it was Mother who filled the sock he hung up each Christmas Eve.

No mention of pillows or magic today. He really had offended Mother. Father he bothered less about, Father was often angry with him, though he'd never hit him before. Anyhow, I kicked back.

"I'm sorry I was naughty in chapel."

"So am I. But you're going to be sorrier, my boy. You won't have a ride on your pony for a week."

"A week!" Sam's face, slightly swollen on the more injured side, took on an almost ludicrous look of dismay. At his age a week and a year were hardly distinguishable.

"A week," Deborah said. "You were naughty to start kicking the pew and it was even worse to make fun of Mr Sturgiss."

Sharp young wits noted that no mention was made of kicking Father.

"By the time he's ten he'll be ruined for life," Tim said. "You give way to every whim and fancy. You never correct him. You interfere when I attempt to."

"You are mistaken. He is being punished for his behaviour this morning. I have banned his pony rides for a week."

That was, of course, part of the trouble. Somehow or other she always managed to be in the right, even when she was in the wrong.

Timothy Bridges was a simple, God-fearing man, little given to analysing his own motives, but he knew that married to a tractable, meek, God-fearing woman, he'd have been happy, and kindly disposed to her. Going to Gad's Hall that day and falling in love with the girl who shared his love of, feeling for, horses, had been the worst day's work he ever did. And the maddening thing was that everything had promised so well. Deborah had given every sign of being meek and tractable, and if not actually God-fearing, capable of becoming so. Then, it seemed to him, she had, by a single act of defiance, rushing off back to Gad's, against his wishes, simply because her half sister had died somewhere at the other end of the earth and Mamma needed her, radically changed.

He was a man of markedly humane nature, particularly where horses were concerned. To the proper woman he would have been kind, even slightly indulgent; he would have taken pride in his son's size and fearlessness. As it was, all had gone wrong. Love and loving-kindness had suddenly vanished and into the emptiness it had left something as sour as bile had seeped.

Listen to her now!

"Perhaps I was over severe, for I must admit that Mr Sturgiss' sermons affect me in much the same way."

"He cannot help his affliction."

"He could avoid exposing it and driving everybody mad with boredom. I can't embroider, but I don't insist upon doing it and expect everybody to admire my efforts."

Unanswerable.

Sam quickly solved the problem of no pony rides. Mother had said pony, not horse. And there were plenty of horses at Foxton; the great amber-coloured Punches which Father bred, the heavy horses; lighter ones for riding and driving, and a few old broken-down ones which Father said he had rescued. Sam went to the gate of the pasture where the big ones were, made enticing noises and soon had several to choose from. He chose the biggest, climbed the gate and scrambled on. Funny! The horse, well-fed, weighing a ton, seemed to have a very sharp backbone. And also seemed to be quite unaware of the fact that Sam, in choosing it, had done it a favour. It kept trying to brush him off as though he were a fly. Sam clung on to its mane. The horse tried to knock him off by lumbering near a tree, bruising Sam's knee and ankle, but Sam stuck on and finally steered back to the gate, where by this time an anxious little crowd had gathered.

"Now do you see about not breaking his spirit," Deborah said.

"It was downright disobedience."

"No. I said no pony."

"It was dangerous. A stallion, running with mares. He could have been killed, do you realise?"

"But he wasn't." He'd been well-bruised, and Deborah having ascertained that no bones were broken had said, "And serve you right!" But she had been at the gate, her heart in her mouth as the silly saying went; Sam so very small, the great horse, never ridden, not bred for riding.

"All right, he wasn't. God was good. But surely even you must see that this kind of thing can't go on. He's defiant, and reckless, and in the end he'll be uncontrollable. Then where shall we be?"

After a little silence, Deborah said, coolly, calculatingly,

"If you wish, not here. I think the time has come . . . Let's face it, Tim. We aren't suited; we made the mistake of thinking that because we both had a feeling for horses . . . We deluded ourselves. On no other subject do we think alike, not even over the boy. We just make each other miserable. So why go on? We have only one life, you know. Why spend it in misery that can be avoided?"

"We're married. For better or worse."

"I know. But there is such a thing as divorce."

"Do your realise what you are saying?"

"I have given the matter some thought. You can't accuse me of adultery, which would simplify matters for you. But I am quite willing to desert you."

"You must be off your head." Surely only insanity could account for an apparently decent woman using the word adultery in such a way. It was one of the words just acceptable when in the Bible, not elsewhere. As for the suggestion, it was infamous!

"No. I'm sane. And I'm serious. Think it over."

He did so and with naïve astonishment saw that the infamous suggestion was not entirely unattractive. A man should be master in his own house and here he was not, never had been after those first few happy weeks. Talk about a square peg in a round hole— the square peg could be whittled down and rounded, made to fit, but nobody yet had found a way of making a round peg fit a square hole. She'd as good as blackmailed him—I'll do all your chapel things in return for being allowed to hunt, and from that bargain she'd gone on encroaching all the time; giddy worldly tunes on the piana, regular visits to Gad's, sly little digs at non-conformity, teetotalism—all the things by which his life had been governed for as long as he could remember. Awkward about bed, too. . . . Yes, there was a good deal to be said in favour of a clean break. No shame about it. In the eyes of his fellow men, and of the law, fully in the right.

But . . . Well, visualising eventually another marriage, comfort-able as an old slipper, no conflict, no arguments, Tim thought of age. He had waited to marry, being a bit choosy, and he was now older, seven years wasted, except for Sam. He could not be sure of breeding another boy like Sam who would be well-nigh perfect, once brought under control. It could be done in a fortnight, with-out interference from Deborah.

"All right. But I keep the boy."

"Am I likely to leave him with you? He still has bruises on his face. But for me you'd probably have knocked *all* his teeth out. Oh no, if I go, Sam comes with me. And you'll never find us."

She was capable of making that kind of escape.

"It beats me what this is all about. Haven't you got a comfort-able home? Have I ever looked at another woman? Have I ever grudged you anything? Thwarted you in any way?"

"It is this everlasting atmosphere of disapproval," Deborah said. "The constant friction. You're always right, with God on your side. God is always on the side of the big battalions. I'm always wrong. I can't live in this air."

It had all begun long ago. Deborah and Caroline, motherless, running wild, picking up coarse expressions and swear words. And suddenly the introduction of a new mother—to be called Mamma—and her two perfectly behaved children. To please Mamma, to win a look or a word of approval, Deborah would have jumped into the moat. And it was the same at school; to please Miss Hardwicke, anything, anything. The desire to please, not inbred, but inculcated early, had governed her life. But there

was a limit to it. Especially when one had learned that in practically every situation one knew best, or did best.

"You may know what you're talking about—being so clever;
but I'm blowed if I do. Anyway, let's drop it."

The uneasy peace continued. Perhaps Tim grumbled less, was a
little less openly critical of Deborah's handling of Sam, and of
Sam's behaviour. Indeed, with regard to the boy he reversed his
tactics and began to woo his favour. "Like to come to market
with me today, son?" Making indulgences, allowing the boy to
hold the reins on the homeward journey when friskiness had worn
off, buying him bags of good wholesome sweets, none of your
bright-coloured rubbish; and once, on a warm day, an ice cream.

"Mother, there's a new shop in Thetford. It's called a tea-shop.
Father had tea, but I had ice cream, on a glass plate. It was wonderful. And the people were foreigners; not black like on the missionary box, but not quite white either. And they talked in a
funny way." Here Sam became a little cautious—he'd got into
trouble for imitating Mr Sturgiss, and "you wisha one-a vanilla,"
did faintly resemble that preacher.

Privately Sam believed that Father was trying to make up for
hitting him so hard. Cheap at the price, really; the tooth was
bound to fall out sooner or later, and the bruises hadn't hurt long.
They'd also served as a good excuse for not washing his face. Anyway, a boy with so many new experiences behind him, a new pony
in the offing—and a Thoroughgood at that—was far too old to
quarrel with a girl cousin.

At the mention of Sam's having a Thoroughgood the little vertical lines between Diana's eyebrows and the little down-curving
ones at each side of her mouth deepened slightly. Really life was
grossly unfair. Caroline in Hawksley's, spending money like a
drunken sailor, Deborah able to buy a thoroughbred pony for Sam
while she and Everard were so pinched, and likely to be more so.
She had urged Everard, when the move was being discussed, to
ask for a rise and he had replied, a trifle wearily, that he'd had it,
in April; ten pounds, as agreed. Against steadily rising prices the
increase went nowhere but stark economic facts remained, Upton,
Binder and Smith could easily fill his place with a man, not so
good, of course, but quite adequate and cheaper. He had repeated
what he said many times before; without money enough to

set up on your own, or some influence behind you, you were doomed from the start. But surely, Diana argued, the wonderful job he'd done on the Lumsley estate business should count for something. At that Everard looked displeased and said that there was nothing particularly clever—in the legal sense—about finding a paper which had been overlooked, put in fact into a used envelope by a man who was quite prepared to say: "Aye, I had drink taken at the time, as well as being upset in my emotions, he being like a father to me and me watching by his deathbed day and night." Little finesse was needed there; more was called for in persuading Lady Morton that she would be very unwise to contest a will, plainly dated ten days later than the one which left everything to her. Everard had—suspicious from the first—asked could he see the two men who had witnessed the will, made in *her* writing and in her house. Both had gone to Canada. Which was, as Everard said, a singular coincidence. That had made her think.

It was not an exploit of which Everard was proud and financially he had not gained a penny. Socially, he had. Apart from being so empty of pocket, he was back where he had been when his godfather had been alive. He was even about to shoot grouse again. He'd had something, a true instinct, or a layer of self-assurance, which had made him able to round the difficult corner of having no gun, no country clothes. Given the right tone of voice, the right light touch, it was perfectly acceptable to say, "I had a pair once, rather nice, Baxters, but you can't eat a gun. I can't remember now whether I sold them or pawned them in Cambridge. Anyway, since I was never in position to bail them out it comes to the same thing."

Lady Lumsley said that there must be about fifty guns in the gun room at the Castle and Everard could take his pick.

"That is all very well—and thank you. But any decent ghillie would shoot me on sight. In town clothes. . . ."

Charlie Somerton, Lord Westward now, said pop along, dear boy; order a tweed suit, better still, two, weather being what it was, and put it on his bill. God bless you, what difference did it make. "I only pay him about once in four years and I *know* he charges interest. You might as well benefit."

Diana's annual visit usually lasted a fortnight, and during it Deborah—her right to do so now unquestioned—usually came over twice. She did so this year, on the second visit staying the night because of collecting the pony.

Diana, no longer able to feel superior to Deborah, whose rough, ill-behaved little boy seemed to have reformed; nor to Caroline, so long childless, but now due to have a baby at about Christmas time, was feeling depressed; only two days left of her holiday where meals which she had not planned, of which she had not counted the cost, appeared with regularity, and where common justice did not demand, as it did in London, that she should pull her share of the load. Bessie was a blessing, a true gift from God, but Bessie could not do everything, and when she went marketing down in Soho . . . Oh, cheaper, much cheaper—but how much nicer to be able to leave the children and the house in Bessie's reliable hands and saunter out to Hawksley's oneself, place an order, have things delivered. As everybody else in Somerton Road, in the whole neighbourhood did.

Looking at the glossy pony—Sam had demanded that everybody should come and view his new acquisition—Diana said,

"Really, Deb, I sometimes wonder if you realise how lucky you are."

Me, lucky? How little you know!

There'd been one of those quiet disputes about replacing the pony which Sam had first ridden at the age of three, but it had not developed into anything much. Tim had said, "All right. Have it your own way. You always do." But all the time he'd been planning a sly trick. During the argument she had said, "I'm prepared to pay for it. The best is always cheapest in the end." And just as she was preparing to hand over the shining sovereigns, Sam had forestalled her.

"Father said he would pay. He gave me this." Sam produced what was not to him money, just a bit of paper. A cheque, signed by Timothy Bridges, good anywhere.

All the same it was an underhand trick. It made her feel silly in her own eyes. Not in those of Tom Thoroughgood, or of Sam, neither of whom cared much, or even noticed who paid, or in what form the payment was made. But not to have told her; quite possibly telling Sam to say nothing; going behind her back.

She'd always been a sensible girl and had grown into a sensible woman, and now her own sense told her that she was taking a stupid view not only of this small issue but of her whole relationship with her husband. To begin with she'd been a blind fool to marry him; she should have seen how entirely unsuited they were. When you made salad dressing you shook the oil and vinegar together and they mixed, temporarily, but in no time at all, and under no outside influence, they separated again, not through any fault in either of them, simply a law of nature. In the second place she had deceived Tim, pretending to be other than she was. He'd made no secret of his Methodism or his teetotalism, of his distaste for display. *She* had been the false one; drinking lemonade even at her own wedding!

In this self-accusatory mood she did not blame—as she often did at other times—Tim's rocky unyieldingness, his unctuousness, his lack of considerateness for her youth, her different background, even her ignorance of what kind of hat to wear in chapel. She blamed only herself.

So, out in the sunshine, surveying the pony, when Di said about being lucky, Deborah said, after a scarcely perceptible pause,

"Yes, I suppose I am." She remembered what Caroline had reported about Di's horrid little house, and Di spending a whole day shopping without buying anything. Di had kept up a brave front—but then we all do; Mamma's training perhaps. Nobody would guess how Tim and I quarrel, nobody ever guessed how much Caroline felt not having a child. . . .

And now Deb noticed—she was not so fashion-minded as Di, though she liked to be reasonably well-dressed—that this was the same dress as Di had brought to Gad's last year.

"I don't mean to insult you, Di, but I'm sure a house move must be very expensive. If fifty pounds would be any good to you, you're welcome. I've no use for it. I brought it with me to pay for the pony, Tim forestalled me and gave Sam a cheque."

Diana's eyes widened. "Are you *sure*? It's a great deal of money, Deb."

Deborah then said something that Diana was to remember. She missed, of course, half its significance, the half implied when Deborah said, "And it's not Tim's money." She noticed, and remembered the next words. "I earned it."

Not always easily, especially when a potentially good horse had been mishandled and one had to start again; but it was work she enjoyed and she was making a name for herself. Tim of course had been opposed to that, and so it had seemed unfair to use his stable, his fodder and his pasture; so, as she had once suggested, Deborah had moved the whole thing out to Mr Craig's, and Mr Craig was a man of whom no man could be jealous in *that* way; a good breeder and a good trainer in his day, he had fallen victim to what old-fashioned country people still called the joint evil, really a form of rheumatism that encroached inexorably. One stick, two sticks, presently a wheelchair.

"Well, if you are sure you can spare it. It would be a great help. If you would regard it as a loan, Deb. In Everard's profession it takes a little time to get established. . . . And of course the move *was* rather unexpected. It just happened that Lord Westward—he was Everard's fag at Eton and apparently remembered him kindly, had this house. . . ."

Sam, faithful to his word, for Belle had been good and never once resorted to biting, heaved her into the saddle and said, "Just pretend you're sitting in a chair."

Diana asked was it safe, and assured that it was, said,

"He's very like George, don't you think?"

"I suppose there's a family resemblance." Deborah's mind shifted again; once Tim had said of Sam that he bid fair to be a spitting image of George. And that implied disapproval. And after all what was so wrong with George?

Mr van Haagen had no fault to find with his own son, Pieter, now thirty years old, happily married, the father of three girls. Pieter fitted well and performed conscientiously in that corner of the business which had been assigned to him. But Mr van Haagen had never derived anything approaching as much pleasure from his son's company as he did from George Thorley's.

To George everything was new and everything was wonderful, his capacity for enjoyment, for picking up just enough of any language to get along with, seemed to be infinite. And everybody seemed to like him.

Everybody had always liked George; he'd had one little setback, his not being able to woo his first love, but though he would remember her, with sentiment, forever, he'd soon recovered; after all, he was only sixteen and she was a year older—in addition to being what was called County. It had been what was known as a non-starter from the first. Within a week of his arrival in Amsterdam he had temporarily forgotten Chloe Faulkner, who was not to be wooed, and also the girl Ruth, all too easily wooed, and was prepared to fling himself wholeheartedly into a new life. In that he could hardly have found a better guide and mentor than Mr van Haagen.

Mr van Haagen was acutely aware of the responsibility laid

upon him, and of the trust which that good woman, Mrs Thorley, had reposed in him. He must not, definitely not, allow himself to be misled by the boy's size and apparent maturity. A widow's only son. Not ignorant, no country-bred boy could be that, but innocent. I must talk to him like a father, Mr van Haagen reflected; and curiously it was easier to have such conversations with this boy than it had been with his own son. George was both quicker in understanding and less resentful of advice.

It was all, in a sense, good advice, though not particularly moral in tone. George must beware of this, beware of that, and the talks covered a wide range of subjects, starting, correctly, with alcohol. Drinking on an empty stomach was very bad; mixing too many drinks was very bad; drinking too much at any time was bad, but particularly so when talking business or playing cards. "So, fortunes have been lost," Mr van Haagen said. He was not against the frequenting of brothels, occasionally; too often was unadvisable at any time but especially for the young, and naturally one must exercise discrimination. George knew, through his association with the more sophisticated Johnny Faulkner, the definition of a brothel but he had never seen one. Such a thing did not exist —officially—in Baildon, though George's brother-in-law Edward could have named certain houses which were very little better than brothels. Discrimination must be exercised because of diseases. Like every good patriot of every country, Mr van Haagen attributed the diseases to a foreign origin; and for a Dutchman the culprit was not far to seek—it was the East Indies. "That is why," Mr van Haagen explained, "never, never a place that is cheap, and never near docks."

George was getting an extension of the liberal education begun in the Rectory at Stonham St Paul's, and enjoying himself immensely.

"Really, he is good to write so often," Mrs Thorley said, and then, looking up, realised that the letter which had arrived by the same post for Diana—Everard's writing—had given the poor girl a shock. It was . . . It reminded Mrs Thorley of the first moment after Caroline had opened Poor Susan's letter announcing her engagement . . . Except that Diana was not crying. But then she never had cried as easily as Caroline did.

"Is he . . . ill?"

Diana seemed to have difficulty in speaking; she swallowed on nothing, lifted her cup and drank. That gave Deborah time to think of the children. "Sam, go and see if your new pony likes toast. Take Belle with you."

Diana said, "Not ill. Mad."

Neither Mrs Thorley nor Deborah took the word very seriously. For one thing they had both had close contact with Lavinia when she was truly mad; for another the word was lightly used.

"He had the fortnight's holiday to which he was entitled," Diana said. "Then somebody issued a further invitation—deer stalking this time. And he wrote asking further leave. And was refused. So he wrote and gave in his notice. He says . . ." She stared at the letter with unseeing eyes, "that he is going to set up on his own."

Neither Mamma nor Deborah could really share her horror. They hadn't lived in cut-throat London, completely dependent upon one man's earnings. Inadequate, but at least sure.

"It may not be a bad thing," Deborah said.

"My dear, I often *thought* and you sometimes *said* that Everard was wasting his talent, working for other people."

"I know. I know. But if he's said it to me once he's said it a thousand times—without enough money to buy a partnership or start up on your own, or without influence, it's hopeless. And now he's done that very thing. It'll be the ruin of us all."

Mrs Thorley had always had—as her second husband had recognised—a good business head. When she was widowed and left in sole charge she had set herself a fixed goal; to so improve the prosperity of the farm and of the herd that she could pay the girls the modest dowries left them in their father's will, and hand over to George, when he was eighteen, the business in a flourishing state. She had worked hard and taken some risks. She had slipped back a little, unable to spare time or attention, during the months of Lavinia's madness, but to recoup the loss she had hit upon her plot with Mr van Haagen, and that had been extremely lucrative.

She could afford to help Everard over the difficult starting period—say two years; always assuming that he would be in a position to repay the money, if only in instalments.

Had she the right to do it? It was, after all, Thorley money, even if she had earned much of it. She couldn't have built the business from nothing. And—such a strange thing to think after all these years—Diana was not a Thorley. She had tried so hard to make no distinction between the girls, but she saw one now. Also she must ask herself, was Everard ever likely to be very successful? He had many things in his favour, good looks, a beautiful voice, beautiful manners, a good education, excellent qualifications. Why hadn't they taken him further? Was he merely unlucky? Did he lack something that was essential to success? Some defect of personality? No sense of humour.

She could remember her first sight of him, in Gad's barn at the Christmas party for the workpeople. She'd liked him well enough, he'd been most civil and helpful, but she hadn't entirely liked him; something prim and mean about his mouth; but then, that should be no drawback in his profession. But the whole thing needed more thought.

It had not taken long to think all those things. She reached over and touched Di's shoulder.

"Don't take too glum a view, my dear. It might be a turning point. And it is possible that among his—new friends, there is somebody with influence."

"Oh," Di said bitterly, "I have no doubt of that! And I know who! Alison Lumsley. I can just hear her. Promising to send him twenty clients a day because she would tell them how wonderful he is. And telling him that if he worked for himself he could take free time just when he liked. And he fool enough to believe her. By Christmas she'll have forgotten his name."

When a façade breaks there is rubble; and the better and more elaborate the façade the more rubble. Diana began to cry, and crying, she was far more pitiable than Caroline.

Deborah began to think. Of her five-hundred-pound dowry she had spent only a hundred on a half-trained and to the casual eye not very promising hunter, bought from Mr Craig. It had seemed unfair to spend Tim's money on something of which he so strongly disapproved. It had partly been her success with that animal that had started the training business.

She'd let Di have the remainder; not to help Everard to set up on his own—whatever that might entail—but to ease things for her. Over the first few fences, so to speak.

Deborah was rather given to semi-philosophical thoughts, and she thought now—Curious that Caroline who spoke without thinking should have summed Everard up on that first night and called him greedy. Later Everard had proved to be greedy and a bit idle. All the time when they'd been getting the little house in Friars' Lane ready and Deborah had been painting and whitewashing and doing a bit of impromptu cooking, he'd always turned up to eat, never to tackle a down-to-earth job. . . . Curious too, that of the three of them, Di, Caro and herself, two had made love marriages. Caro had, Deb was sure, married on what was called the rebound. Caro had been quite obviously crazy about Freddy Ingram, but at his engagement party she'd practically got herself engaged to Edward. And unless Caroline was as secretive as Di had been, as Deb was still, her marriage had really turned out best. Life was the very devil.

The Devil! Instantly Deborah thought of Lavinia, and then by transference of the shrubs which she had planted, with some help from Willy, under the walnut tree at the very end of the garden. There, under a mass of green things, shrubs and bushes which in due season flowered and were beautiful, Lavinia and her baby lay. Lavinia had killed the baby and then herself. How deep did the roots reach by this time?

"Di, don't cry about something that hasn't happened yet. We'll think up something. Mamma, I just want a word with Willy before I go."

"Good morning, Willy."

"Morning, Miss Deb, Mrs Bridges, ma'am. Anything I can do?"

"Yes. Those shrubs that we planted. Do you remember?"

I remember everything, my dearie, back to when you was, well maybe twelve and me about eighteen. Bloody silly and I always knew it. But I swear to God, if things had been a bit different, you'd look happier like than you do. More cherished.

"They need a thorough good pruning, Willy. I walked round the garden last evening and I thought they looked very overgrown."

"Maybe. Tell you the truth I ain't had all that much time on my hands. And autumn is right for pruning."

Tell you the truth I don't much fancy that end of the garden much. Tell you the truth I didn't mind that day when we worked together and you held the blasted things and I stamped them in. That was all right, that was. And for your sake I did a bit of watering, so they grew. Done a bit of pruning from time to time, too, all for *your* sake. But alone, down that end, I don't feel easy. Never have. Always felt as though I was being watched, and that ain't a nice feeling. And once . . . well, if he'd ever mentioned *that*, he'd have been a laughing stock for the rest of his life. It was one of them big foreign flowers with a fancy name. . . . It'd looked like a face, a pale face, watching.

"For most things," Deborah said, "but I read somewhere, or somebody told me, that some shrubs should be pruned as soon as they finish flowering."

"Tell you what; if you can spare the time. It'd be best if you come and show me. That'd be best."

"All right. Get me a pair of shears, too, Willy. I might as well help as stand and watch you."

One more little memory to store away. The two of them working together; the way it might have been for life if only he'd had five acres and a cow, and she hadn't been Master's daughter.

"So you see, if the going gets rough, Di, I can let you have a hundred a year for four years and never miss it. And by that time I shall have some more saved. But it is for you and the children—not for propping up a business or anything like that."

"What you gave me last night will be the greatest help, Deb dear. And I won't ask for more unless I am really driven. . . . It really is so mortifying. Seven years married and worse off, really, than at the beginning."

"It may be just the jumping-off space that Everard needs."

"I wish I dared think so. And I wish that I could earn a little. The only thing I ever did better than anybody else was embroidery."

The idea didn't drop into her mind like a seed and germinate; it sprang up, complete but for one vital detail—an outlet for such talent, but surely, in the whole of London there must be many places. One only had to look. At the thought of seeking buyers for her skill, Diana felt a little sick. That would be mortifying, too. But nobody need know. If there was anything at all to be said for London, it was there one could, if one wished, be anonymous.

Hawksley's had little trouble with the shoplifters who were a pest in many of the cheaper stores; on the whole their floorwalkers were there to help, not to guard.

"Can I help you, Madam?" Sometimes, because of the layout of the various departments, customers, especially new ones, needed a little guidance. The display case was not always in close proximity to the counter where the things were actually sold.

"No, thank you," Diana said, and went on studying the three blouses exposed in all their beauty. They—or some like them—had attracted her eye on that shopping expedition with Caro in March. Having found them, she had thought: Thank God they are still in fashion. But they were bound to be, they were so very pretty, and though extremely modest, almost, well, almost seductive. They were actually double; the inner, closer-fitting bodice made of silk or satin, and embroidered, the outer, looser blouse of sheer gauze, so that the embroidery was veiled as though by a light morning mist.

Narrowing her eyes, Diana studied the three closely. The embroidery was good enough, but she could do better. It was with a positive feeling of being in her right element again that she turned away and went down to the basement, where stuff was sold by the yard and embroidery silks were ranged like rainbows. Two of Deb's golden sovereigns were spent, happily, and Diana hoped, profitably.

One advantage of this far-too-big house was that one room could be a workroom where work did not have to be tidied away, every snippet of thread picked up as soon as it fell. One advantage of Everard's being away was that Bessie spent less time on shopping and cooking and could give more attention to the children. In three days of happy—but although she did not know it, frenzied—work, Diana had produced a blouse better than any in Hawksley's show case. White satin bodice, embroidered with wild roses and forget-me-nots, the motif repeated in the modest collar where satin and gauze met, and on the cuffs of the voluminous sleeves. It really was so beautiful that she didn't want to part with it. Some imp at the back of her mind whispered: Keep it yourself. Common sense told her that for two pounds she had bought what was necessary for the making of a pretty thing which Hawksley's could sell for ten guineas, which left, even by her simple arithmetic, eight pounds to be divided between between herself and Mr Hawksley.

This time she did need direction. "Can I help you, Madam?"

"Yes. I wish to see whoever buys for this department."

"You wish to make a complaint, Madam?" It did sometimes happen, especially with things bought ready-made. As more and more things were nowadays.

"No. I wish to see whoever buys for this department." Diana

wore her haughty look, which even her headmistress had acknowledged, and dubbed her Young Madam.

"If you will come this way, Madam."

Suddenly there was no thick mole-coloured carpet. Bare stone
stairs. Abandoned, for the floorwalker, having said, "The first door
on the right, Madam," had done his duty, Diana climbed the
stairs and was in a different world.

It was not a large room. Its one uncurtained window looked
out upon a blank wall which, because it was made of white tiles,
reflected a harsh, rather eerie light. Near the door two women,
both elderly, both wearing black sateen overalls, were sorting
things at a trestle table. Near the window two men stood, the
bigger one with both his shoulders and one extended arm draped
with strips of fur which the other, thinner, older was studying
with every evidence of disgust. There was a desk set slantwise and
at the end of it another woman, seated, pencil in hand, a note-
book before her. She was a hunchback.

As Diana took stock of the room, the thin man said, both tone
and voice unpleasant:

"Come here, Flo. What'll look all right on you ull look right on
anybody." The little hunchback stood up and went to the window
and the man who had spoken snatched two pieces of fur and
placed one on each of her misshapen shoulders. Regarding them
with no mitigation of disgust, he said, "They'll do." The move
brought Diana within his line of vision and his expression
changed. She looked like a customer—but customers never entered this part of the building; more likely a buyer of surplus
stock. For no matter how shrewdly one estimated the market, no
matter how carefully one bought, no matter what reduction of
prices was made at the end of each season, or each fashion, something was bound to be left over and must be disposed of to
humbler, less-up-to-the-minute establishments.

"'Keep you a minute," he said with as near an approach of
civility as he could attain. The further civility of offering a seat
could not be managed; there were only two chairs in the bleak
room; one was his own, his throne, the seat of power, the other
was now again occupied by the hunchback, who was writing with
extreme rapidity what was being dictated to her. The man who
had been exhibiting the furs was folding them with extreme care
and placing them in a kind of leather sack; and saying, Thank

you, Mr Burton, sir; and; Yes, August 31st; had they ever failed to keep a delivery date?

Mr Burton said, "The day you do, out!"

It was all so different from what Diana had imagined. Hawksley's was so extremely dignified that she had imagined even a department buyer to be, and the room in which he operated to have some dignity, too. And she had expected such an interview to be private, at least.

At last the fur-seller moved away, touching as he did so the lump on the hunchback and saying, "Just for luck, dearie. You don't mind?"

The woman said in the dead voice of complete resignation, "People do it all the time. Even in the street."

Mr Burton then looked at Diana and made a curious sound. Not quite Yes, in the questioning way of what do you want, what can I do for you. It was more like, Yah! A recognition of her presence, a resignation to his next job.

"Mr Burton. I have something to show you." She lovingly unfolded the paper and revealed her masterpiece. "I made it," she said, "in three days. It is better than those on sale downstairs."

That this was true did nothing very little to assuage Mr Burton's never-far-absent irritation.

"Six months out of date," he said. Abruptly, he began to punish Diana—despite her errand, by her dress and her voice one of the customer class—for his undying grudge against all customers. "It was a *fad*," he said, mouthing the word as though it were an obscenity. "Somebody had one, then everybody wanted one. I was at my wit's end . . . . Now dead as pork." That was the knife edge between demand and supply which a buyer for a place like Hawksley's constantly bestrode. A fad caught on, blazed itself out. The uncertainty of his working life accounted for Mr Burton's insomnia, his indigestion, his constantly irritable temper.

Utterly deflated, Diana folded the blouse, wrapped it in paper. She thought: Nothing I do ever prospers. And yet behind it all she saw the point. If she, if anyone with a bit of skill with the needle, could make, in three days, for two pounds something that Hawksley's sold for ten guineas . . .

She said, "Good morning, Mr Burton," and walked towards the door. One of the women, sorting, packing, unpacking at the trestle table, looked up and said out of the corner of her mouth, "Try

Preston's. Oxford Street." Before Diana could say Thank you, Mr Burton called in his querulous voice, "Wait!" Something in Diana impelled her to go on, to ignore such rudeness. In the whole of her life nobody had spoken to her like that. Not even Miss Hardwicke, at school. On the other hand . . . Diana hesitated just long enough for Mr Burton's next words to reach her and he said, "You have a good hand with the needle. Could you embroider a kimono?"

"I could embroider anything, Mr Burton, if I knew what it was. What exactly is a kimono?"

"The latest fad." Mr Burton sounded more disgusted than ever. "Connie, show . . . Miss . . . Mrs . . ."

"Osborne," Diana said.

"Osborne, a kimono," Mr Burton said.

The woman who had been kind enough to suggest Preston's in Oxford Street fumbled about and produced something so beautiful as to take one's breath away. A kind of dressing-gown or wrapper. Blue silk, embroidered on the back, on the fold-over fronts and on the wide sleeves with sprays of white flowers, a pink tinge here and there; cherry blossom? and strange, long-legged birds.

Forgetting her role, Diana said, "How beautiful."

"Pretty enough," Mr Burton agreed. Any enthusiasm he had once felt for the goods he bought was long since exhausted; saleability was the only criterion. And although the kimonos were fantastically cheap, they were rare. In the shop they would *not* be cheap.

"Could you make that kind of thing, Mrs Osborne?"

"There is far less actual needlework than in this blouse. A great deal more embroidery. Of exceptional quality, too." Diana narrowed her eyes as she had done when studying the blouses. Unexpectedly humbled in the sphere at which she had always excelled, she asked with a kind of awe, "Who did such fine work?"

"Those we have are imported from Japan. But nobody can guarantee a supply, or a date of delivery; which makes it very difficult. Well, can you or can't you?"

"Yes. But it would take me a week. What would you pay me?"

"A pound each."

By Mr Burton's standards very high pay indeed. But while the craze lasted—each one different, each one made to order, each one very special, and a week to wait . . . probably twenty-five or thirty guineas each. Selling—except of surplus stock—was not Mr

Burton's job. He bought. And although he knew and employed indirectly a great many women who lived by plying their needles, he had not yet seen any work so nearly Oriental in standard as that on the blouse which he had rejected.

"I'll see what I can do," Diana said, and went away, leaving everybody in the bleak room astonished, partly by the munificent offer—even Mr Burton himself felt that he had been slightly carried away—but even more by her casual air. She had not asked who would provide the materials upon which she would see what she could do.

Preston's in Oxford Street was far less imposing than Hawksley's though it did its best. Its front, though narrow, was glassed and polished, it had a doorman, just as attentive to a customer who came in a hired cab, or on foot. Preston's had not been able to expand as Hawksley's had done because on each side of it small, independent businesses were still surviving. But its day would come.

"The buyer. Oh, you mean Mrs Preston. She does the buying."

Mrs Preston, though tightly corsetted, bulged here and there in a comfortable-looking way; her room too was far more like a well-used sitting room than an office. Her voice was singularly akin to Bessie's, and her eyes, bright and shrewd, were not unkindly. She was drinking tea and without hesitation she told Diana to sit down and have a cup. Then she said,

"Watcha selling, dearie?"

Once again Diana unfolded the paper and displayed her handiwork.

"Far too good," Mrs Preston said. "Musta taken you a week."

"Three days."

"Once they took on . . . We had women running them up, two a day sometimes. Nothing like this, of course. Coarse and quick, while the rage lasts. You gotta catch the tide in this trade." The vagaries of fashion bore almost as hard on Mrs Preston as on Mr Burton, with a difference; she was responsible to nobody but herself.

"I ain't saying this ain't something special. Very nice indeed, but no call for such work down here."

Out of date at Hawksley's, too good for Preston's. A dead loss.

On impulse Diana said, "Mrs Preston, did you ever hear about a thing called a kimono?"

Mrs Preston drained her cup and set it down; both actions she performed noisily and would by Mamma, or Miss Hardwicke, have been rebuked.

"I heard," Mrs Preston said cautiously. It was not for her to tell anyone, let alone a complete stranger, that she had her spies in other shops, and in workrooms. "Sorta dressing-gown, ain't they? Somebody brought a few in for presents; then everybody wanted one. I b'lieve Hawksley's had a few. Never on show though. . . . And they're hard to come by. Dear as fire, too."

Almost forgetful of her disappointment over the blouse, Diana said,

"But so beautiful." She described the one she had seen. Then with a deepening of the little frown lines above her nose, she said, "And I don't see why they should be so expensive. They need not be silk. Any firm, fine cotton cloth would do. Embroidered, as you said, with coarse thread and quick stitches. I could make one in three days." She had told Mr Burton a week, but then he had not been asking for quick coarse work.

"Could you reelly?" She sounded, and was, a trifle absent-minded, for she was thinking of the women she knew who were only too glad to sew in their own homes. Preston's, unlike Hawksley's, did not make clothes to order, and so had no workroom, just a woman and an apprentice who would make minor alterations. But when something like the double blouses caught on, there were plenty of willing hands. Hands was what they were; they could copy anything, but they could not make something they had never seen. A sorta dressing-gown would mean nothing to them.

"Could you make me a model? In three days?"

"Oh yes."

"And what would you charge?"

"A pound," Diana said, daringly.

It was a lot for three days' work, but not too much for a model.

"Let's go down and pick the stuff," Mrs Preston said.

Only then did it strike Diana to wonder what Mr Burton had expected her to work with, should she accept his offer. To give Mr Burton his due it had not occurred to him to wonder, either, for he had no experience with casual, outside labour; it was just that these damned kimonos were driving him crazy.

Mrs Preston never had the slightest hesitation in supplying her outside workers with what she called stuff. She knew and they

THE HAUNTING OF GAD'S HALL

knew that if it were not brought back, absolutely clean, beautifully sewn, and on time they'd get no pay, and no further work. The taking of names and addresses was really mere formality.

"Osborne. Mrs Osborne," Diana said; and asked her address, looked at Mrs Preston with that haughty look to which her high-bridged nose was so eminently suited, and said, "Does that really matter?" And Mrs Preston immediately jumped to two erroneous conclusions; this Mrs Osborne was obviously a lady, a bit come down in the world and ashamed of her address; or she was a woman who had left her husband and did not want to be traced. Mrs Preston, whose own married life had been very unhappy—but fortunately brief—quite understood that.

In the workroom the two pieces of work went on, unevenly matched, rather like a horse and a donkey pulling the same cart, but making progress. It was relief to turn from the very fine work on real silk—bought with Deborah's money, to the coarser easier work on the sateen, a cotton fabric with a deceptively shiny surface. And then, after a spell at the coarse, quick work, it was a relief to turn to the other, slower work. On the real silk there was not one of what were called Lazy Daisies; and on the sateen there was not one petal or bird's wing of what was called raised satin stitch. And yet . . .

It was August now and the evenings were darkening, so she was working by gaslight; at the end of the third day, Mrs Preston's model ready, and Mr Burton's half completed, if you looked at the backs of both kimonos, and did not look too closely, you could hardly tell the difference. In this light—and nobody would wear a kimono in full daylight, the sateen looked like silk and the Lazy Daisy flowers almost as pretty, certainly as effective as the raised satin stitch ones.

Mrs Preston was delighted with her model, cheap fake though it was. She said she'd never seen anything quite so pretty; but she did not order another. Why should she, when there were dozens of women who, once shown what to do and provided with the materials, would do the work for ten shillings or less.

Diana's connection with Mr Burton, superficially less agreeable, was to last longer. He inspected the work with his usual expression of dissatisfaction; he fingered the blue silk. Not quite Hawksley's quality, but then the silly woman—all women were silly, hadn't given him time to tell her how to go about things.

But obviously, he approved.

"And you can make one like this in a week?"

"Oh yes." After all she made this and the other inferior article within the week; and although next week Everard would be home, so that Bessie had more shopping to do, and more cooking in the evening, so that she would have less time to devote to the children, Everard—if he stuck to his intention of setting up on his own, would be much preoccupied; and he would probably wish to dine at his Club—or with Lady Lumsley and all his other fine friends.

That was how she thought of them. In fact she had liked them as little as they, apparently, had liked her. She had not enjoyed herself at all at that first dinner party at Lumsley House; it had all been very grand, but exceptionally dull. The meal itself had lasted for at least two hours and her companion on the left seemed to think that conversation should consist of questions: Have you seen . . . ? What did you think of . . . ? Have you read . . . ? The only answer was, No; or, I'm afraid not. And that made her sound dull, too. The man on her left, older and bearing a singular resemblance to the Duke of Wellington, appeared to be rather deaf. Indeed he admitted it. Gone a bit hard of hearing, he said; 'fraid I didn't catch your name. Alison, like all the young, did tend to mumble.

"Spicer."

He cupped his ear. "Spicer," Diana repeated, a little more loudly. "Mrs Everard Spicer."

"Ah yes." The ancient, modelled-on-the-Duke man said, masticating and ruminating at the same time, "'Fraid I never knew a Spicer; but Everard . . . Yes." Possibly he took it for a hyphenated name. "Came out of India; very rich; most hospitable chap."

"I think he may been my husband's godfather."

"Ah yes." It was not a thing one could say to a pretty young woman, but godfatherdom, like charity, covered a multitude of sins. Funny how fashions—even in manners—changed; such a remark would have been perfectly acceptable, regarded as humourous, anywhere, in his youth, and even now, at this very table, there were women who would have laughed and retorted that fortunately the same could not be said of godmotherhood. But he sensed something prim and prudish about this young woman and refrained. He blamed all the changes on that dull, pompous, pious German fellow whom the Queen had chosen to marry. And really

Alison should have given him a more lively dinner companion; somebody who knew that he was deaf and had something to say. He fell back on an old standby and asked her what part of the country she came from. At the mention of Suffolk he brightened.

"Ah, then you'll know my old friend John Faulkner. Used to have the best shooting in the county; but running down, like everything else. And what can you expect? Taxes and wages going up all the time. How is he?"

He plainly expected her to know the state of Sir John's health; and all she could say was, "I don't know." It was with relief that he turned to his other neighbour, the owner of a strong penetrating voice. Diana was then left to the asker-of-questions, who had decided that a young woman who hadn't seen, hadn't heard, hadn't read, might have sporting proclivities, so he asked if she enjoyed attending race meetings.

Later, with all the ladies in the drawing room, it was worse. They did not deliberately exclude her—though nobody made any definite effort to include her. It was just that they had friends, acquaintances, and experiences in common. Somebody called Veronica had just had a fourth baby, another girl. Absolutely disastrous, because if Algie inherited Mortmain he'd gamble it away within a year. Somebody said, "It must be Hell for Veronica."

Perhaps Mrs Thorley, by the time she went to Gad's, was slightly old-fashioned about language; Deborah and Caroline, running wild, had picked up some very unsuitable words and expressions; gently but firmly eradicated. It gave Diana a mild shock to hear a lady, Mrs Murray-Miles, wearing satin and diamonds, use the word Hell like that. And the next remark shocked her even more. "Frankly, in Veronica's place, I should have felt inclined to do a swop. There're plenty of boy babies about."

"Sylvia!"

"Well, why not? A queen did it. In a warming pan. And Walter was fishing in Scotland at the time."

"Walter, anyway, is so foxed, he couldn't tell boy from girl. Up to a point."

"What point? If you ask me he never did make a clear distinction."

Well, Diana thought, I suppose it is all very funny judging by the laughter. She entertained the thought which, unknown to her, Everard had entertained earlier. Either Deborah or Caroline would have been more at ease here. Deborah would have known

which queen had, or had not, smuggled a baby—which baby?—in
a warming pan. Asked had she seen a play, been to a concert,
been to the races, Deborah would have said, God, no. I train
hunters. And then the talk would have been about hocks and
fetlocks and such things. Caroline? What she would have said or
done was quite unpredictable except for the certainty that she
would not have sat within earshot of a man, however stuffy, or old
and deaf without finding something to say, probably something
silly or giddy, but something.

Feeling out of place—yet in no way inferior, Diana had endured her first grand dinner party, and presently an end-of-the-
season garden party given by Mrs Murray-Miles. That had been
little better and she had been actually glad not to have been included in the invitation to Lumsleydale; and positively happy to
go to Gad's and be back in her own sphere, just as Everard was
happy to go to Scotland and be back in his. She had not, of
course, reckoned that Everard would be so weak-minded as to
allow himself to be persuaded to take such a risk.

Curiously—and yet typically—she had never known a second of
sexual jealousy. She had always had the capacity for turning a
blind eye, for ignoring what she always thought of as the sordid
side of life—like scrubbing steps, scouring saucepans. The idea
that Everard might be unfaithful to her had never once occurred.
Why should he be? She had never much enjoyed what she called
the messy side of marriage, nor the even messier and very painful
process that resulted from it, but she had always been acquiescent.
A good wife! Even when she had been free to gad about before
the birth of Belle, had Everard ever come home to an empty
house, no fire burning, in cold weather, or open windows in summer; had he ever not been served with some kind of meal, or been
met by a wife who whatever *her* day had been, wasn't clean, well-
dressed, welcoming? She had recognised Lady Lumsley as a per-
suader, talking Everard into taking a risk; but as a danger in another way, a temptress, a Delilah, that thought had never once
troubled her innocent, naïve, provincial mind.

Nor did it when Everard returned, bringing with him a rather
nasty-looking sack containing two brace of grouse and a great
lump of meat—a haunch of venison. She was not even suspicious
when he, always so careful about money, produced a dress length
of beautiful tartan cloth for herself and a Cairngorm brooch for
Bessie. What she *did* think, and immediately rebuked herself for

thinking, was that such a generous gesture was intended to be placatory, for she had written him a reproachful letter, saying that he was making a leap in the dark and she felt that he should have talked the matter over with her first.

Diana accepted what she took to be a peace-offering in the right spirit; she was genuinely pleased with it. Fashions, even in colours, came and went, but so long as Queen Victoria reigned, anything Scottish would be stylish.

Bessie, equally delighted with the one non-utilitarian thing she had ever owned, tackled grouse foreign to her as a peacock, with good will, and over the meal Everard explained and justified his risky decision.

"I'll tell you two things, darling. One happened in Baildon—and I was hurt at the time. There was an old farmer with some grievance against his landlord. He had no case, and I told him so, using the *simplest* possible language. He was greatly annoyed, called me a la-di-da ass and accused me of being on the landlord's side *because we talked the same*. He demanded to see Mr Gordon, pushed his way through and left the doors open. I will not repeat what he called me to Mr Gordon. Mr Gordon—and James too, when he chose, could suit their manners and their voices to their company. As a matter of fact, old Gordon in a most uncouth way, told the silly man exactly what I had been trying, patiently, to explain. And in reverse, the same thing happened last year when this Lumsley will dispute arose. Upton himself said he was sending me to Scotland to deal with it. He said, 'You talk the same lingo. They'll trust you.' "

"And they did."

"Exactly. I know I have repeatedly said—there was no need to remind me of that, Diana, that without money or influence, but there are exceptions. That evening—the post arrives there late in the afternoon, I said to Charlie, 'Exeat refused. I'm to report back to London on Monday, or else. . . .' So then we all began talking about it, and Charlie said, 'Sack them before they sack you,' and a man you haven't met, I think, Lord Romsey, said he was turning some of his property, just off the Strand, into offices and I could have three rooms on the ground floor at a peppercorn rent, if I put out a brass plate and made the place look respectable. And everybody—there was quite a crowd—said they'd let me handle their legal affairs, and direct other people to me. So you see, it isn't quite the leap in the dark that you think."

"I see. Well, darling, I just hope it will work. I didn't mean to
sound as thought I doubted your . . . your ability. I was just taken
by surprise, and a bit frightened. I was afraid that Lady Lumsley,
because you had been so successful with her, had overpersuaded
you."

"Alison? She wasn't even there. Of course she promised to help
as soon as she knew what was afoot."

The house party at Lumsleydale—the first for seven years—had
been a very riotous affair. Lady Lumsley had wasted time to make
up. There were far more men than women and so far as Everard
could make out only three married couples. Lord Romsey, was
one of the two widowers, Lord Westward one of the three bachelors and the men who had wives elsewhere all had perfectly plausible excuses for their lonely condition; one had a wife who hated
Scotland, it was too cold for her even in August; another wife
went, with the punctuality of the migration of birds, to Aix-les-
Bains to take a cure; a third had to go to Ireland, taking her children, to visit her crotchety old father who unless kept sweet by
regular visits might disinherit her, and who hated his son-in-law—
always had. Went in fact a dangerous shade of purple at the sight
of him. There were two young, moderately pretty girls, vaguely
family, a widow who was not only gay but rich, and two very
dashing women—one claimed to have shot a tiger in India, and
wore two of its claws, mounted in gold, as a brooch—whose husbands occupied positions of great power in unhealthy places. There
was also, of course, old Lady Cowdray, who could be trusted to
see that the two young girls behaved themselves, and also to know
when, and when not, her presence was desirable.

It was perhaps a typical house-party, with the exception of
Everard. Indigent young attorneys were not usually found in such
gatherings, but after all, he'd been at school with Westward, and
he'd saved dear Alison from total beggary. Also, he was a damned
good shot; and he had an admirable outspokenness. The after-
dinner amusement was gambling, and on the first evening he said
that he couldn't afford to play. "Suppose," he said, "I lost my
shirt—one of my five!" All the owners of dozens of shirts found
that amusing. The lady who had shot a tiger took careful aim at a
new target and said she'd take a side bet: if he lost his shirt she'd
stand him six.

"And if I win."

"Then we'll play a game of forfeits," she said. And that was not such an outrageous suggestion as it might have seemed; for under all the sophistication there was the childishness of the privileged and the protected. They were still capable of unself-conscious romping. They'd none of them ever been short of money, or ridden on a horse-bus or said "Sir" to any man except as a courtesy. Everard had, but in this congenial, intimate atmosphere, he could slough off all the horrid things which should never have happened to him.

Seduction was easy.

Alison, at the end of a romp, a children's game, Hide-and-Seek, for which a castle, five hundred years old and much built-on-to was most admirably adapted, said to Everard,

"Would you mind? There are a few papers that I can't make head or tail of. If you wouldn't mind. . . . They're in the library. I told them to light a fire there. Good night."

The woman who thought that Scotland was too cold for her, even in August, was not so far wrong. The days were warm, but immediately after sunset a chill came. The library, heavy curtains drawn over its mullioned windows, a pedestal table with a lamp and the papers on it, set close to the hearth, was very snug. Everard sank down into a leather chair and gave a little sigh, half satisfaction, half exhaustion. Except for the man who had once been his fag, he was the youngest man in the party, but he felt—not for the first time—that he was older than anybody else. Older both in mind and body. In body because he was unused to this physical exercise in the open air; ever since his godfather's death he'd been obliged to lead a sedentary life. He'd been obliged to take his work at Cambridge seriously, he had to qualify. In Baildon and in London he had been obliged to earn a living; so his muscles had grown flabby, whereas *they*, and that included old Romsey who was sixty and proud of it, had been riding, shooting, playing tennis, playing polo. In mind he was older too, and almost for the same reasons, he'd been obliged to fight against the world and was mature enough to see that Hide-and-Seek was a childish game, which could, when played in a building so vast, be other than childish.

The papers demanded no real attention at all. How could they? MacFarlane was qualified and shrewd. And still in charge. Asking

Everard to look them over was just Alison's nice way of making Everard feel that he was singing for his supper, as the phrase went. But all done so tactfully, so sweetly, as things should be done in civilised circles. It was like her, too, to be sure that during this pretence at work, he should lack nothing. Within arm's reach a box of cigars, two decanters, one full of port wine, one of brandy. Everard helped himself and reached for a book. . . .

Brandy on top of sherry before, red wine during, port after dinner, combined with a day's exercise in the open air and a romp, made him sleepy, and there was no reason to combat the pleasant feeling. No hurry to get to bed because there would be no hurry in the morning. No horse-bus to catch. Here, as in similar establishments, breakfast was a movable feast with every dish one could possibly desire, ranged over hot-plates, in silver-covered dishes on the vast side-board; fresh toast, coffee, or tea arrived at the touch of a bell.

Until the eighteenth century there had been no library at Lumsleydale Castle, but then it had become fashionable to instal one; and a fad which accompanied the fashion was to have one door at least made to look like a section of the book-lined shelves. Everard had not inspected this room and did not know of the door's existence. When it opened and showed a shape blocked in against a background of the palest possible golden light, Everard was not absolutely certain that he was not dreaming. It was a woman—and his dream had been mildly lascivious. As she advanced towards the area of mingled lamp and fire light, he knew who it was, and that he was wide awake.

She said, "Poor dear! I did not intend to keep you up all night."

Her gleaming hair was loose, pouring in ripples over her shoulders, and not plaited for the night. She wore a garment unlike any that Everard had ever seen before. (Lady Lumsley had been the fortunate recipient of one of the first kimonos to be sent to England—as gifts.) All women above the poverty line owned a dressing-gown, a modest garment, high at the neck, long in the sleeves, and buttoned or hooked all down the front.

Alison said, quickly, "Don't get up!" and came and sat on the arm of the chair. The kimono, held closed only by the sash, opened and revealed a leg, slender, shapely and white to halfway up the thigh. She made one of those gestures, far more enticing than the exposure, pulling the yellow silk in an apparent effort to conceal, but quite ineffective.

"Don't you think," she said, "that it is time that we went to bed?"

Back in London, face to face with Diana, indisputably a good wife, but never, let the fact be faced, a sharer of that kind of wild rapture, Everard experienced many mixed feelings; a little shame —after all his parents had been ordinary, decent, God-fearing people; a greater sense of deprivation. Like a bell in his mind tolling, Never again. Quoth the raven, "Nevermore." And alongside it all a determination to succeed; to justify himself and to give Diana everything she wanted. He'd never had a fair chance, now he had and he would make the most of it.

That autumn he was at home very little; he was running a strictly one-man business; he could not afford a clerk, cheap though they were, nor an office cleaner. He shared, with the other occupants of 19 Essex Court, a doctor, a dentist, and a publisher, the services of an ancient, bent man who cleaned the front of the building, and the communal entry and polished all the brass plates. That cost four shillings a week. The old man was willing enough to add to his duties and would have cleaned Mr Spicer's office along with the others, but Everard dared not commit himself to any such outlay—yet. Behind the locked door he did with his own hands all that was necessary in the way of cleaning. Then, as often as not, he went to his Club, partly because it pleased him to be there, partly because there, if anywhere, useful contacts should be made. He was not unaware of the irony of it.

Diana had no sense of irony; she just thought that it was a pity that at a time when she had found agreeable neighbours she was obliged to look upon them as stealers of time. She was still trying to make two embroidered kimonos a week for Mr Burton, who was thus able to please two demanding customers a week with something made to order, something very special indeed and worth every penny of the charges which crept up, stealthily week by week. He had tried to cut Diana out altogether by suggesting that the things should be made in Hawksley's own workrooms, but the woman in charge there, a battleship of a woman, a real slave driver, had said: All right, but to produce two such things a week would mean engaging four extra women.

"But this one woman, a Mrs Osborne, makes two in a week, Mrs Sheldrake."

Mrs Sheldrake said, coarsely, "Christ did miracles."

It was funny, Diana sometimes thought, that her embroidery
had always been her pride and joy, the one thing she had wanted
to do, the one thing at which she wished to excel. She had always
liked to be given time to get on with whatever piece of work she
had in hand, just as Deb had liked to be left undisturbed with a
book. But one could have a surfeit even of a likeable thing. However, being Mrs Thorley's daughter, she stuck to it until just before Christmas, when Preston's window suddenly blazed with kimonos; cotton on cotton, but very pretty, the ideal Christmas
present. After that nobody who *was* anybody wanted a kimono.

Time and life had moved on elsewhere. At Foxton, Tim
Bridges said, with right on his side, with every justification, that
he had not bought and paid for a Thoroughgood pony in order
that Sam should go hunting.

"But I keep trying to tell you . . . I shouldn't dream of it yet.
George started at fourteen and that was a bit young. I just want
Sam to come to the Meet so that he and the pony get used to the
people and the hounds."

"With the idea in mind that one day he will hunt?"

"If he takes to it."

"Over my dead body."

"Go ahead," Deborah said. "One cliché deserves another. Say
you'd rather see him dead at your feet."

Tim couldn't say it. What father could?

"You blackmailed me," he said, slow and steady. "Time and
time again. If I didn't let you hunt you wouldn't go to chapel. I
gave in. Then, over some rubbish dispute you spoke of divorce,
of all things! And I gave in again. Over this I do not intend to
give in."

"Very well."

"And what do you mean by that?"

"What I said. Very well."

Tim imagined that for once he had won; and running his mind
backwards over his married life regretted every instance when he
had given in. If only he'd taken a stronger line from the beginning things would have been very different. He cherished this illusion until the next Sunday morning, when Deborah came down to

breakfast in her riding habit, dark green, the jacket cut like a man's, modest enough—but not chapel wear.

"Aren't you coming to chapel, Mother?"

"Not this morning, my dear."

"And what am I going to say when people inquire after you?" As they would. Deborah had a way of endearing herself to the most unlikely people. Even the fact that she hunted seemed to not to be held against her as it would have been against anybody else, and once when Tim was awkwardly trying to explain and excuse this un-Methodist activity a crusty old man said, "Well, vermin gotta be kept down somehow, Mr Bridges, and you ain't supposed to shoot the creatures. It's different for you. I'm a tenant. 'F my landlord got a notion I'd shot one, I'd be out on my ear come Michaelmas."

"I can't say you are ill," Tim said.

"You can tell them I've become a free-thinker."

"What's that?" Sam asked.

"A person who doesn't go to chapel."

"Then I'd like to be one, too."

Tim reached out and boxed his son's ear. "Don't ever let me hear you say such a wicked thing again."

"And don't ever let me see you box his ear again. Children have been deafened that way. If you must hit somebody hit somebody your own size. Try me!"

"You touch my mother and I'll knock your teeth down your throat," Sam said.

Over the fireplace hung the text whose validity George Thorley had questioned: CHRIST IS THE HEAD OF THIS HOUSE.

Deb said, "That'll do, Sam." She gave him her slightly crooked smile, enchanting still, though the dimple had gone. "In any case, you can't be a free-thinker, or anything else until you are twenty-one. Run along now and wash. You have egg on your chin."

"Now you see what you have done," Tim said with suppressed violence when the boy had gone. "Always, in every way, you pull against me. You'll be the ruin of him."

"I will not see him hit for making an innocent remark. And for *you* to talk about pulling against . . . Haven't you done it to me? From the very start? I've accommodated myself to you, and you've thwarted me at every turn. Even over visiting Mamma."

"I did not consider her a good influence."

"Because you are smug, self-righteous, bigoted. She's the best woman in the world."

"So *you* think!"

"I *know*."

All through the hymns and the prayers and the long sermon, Tim thought of his problem. Sam sat there beside him, or stood beside him and sang. Perhaps less heartily than usual. And his left ear was reddened, slightly swollen. Tim felt ashamed, and then angered because such shame was forced upon him—he, so well-known for his gentle handling of horses, cracking his own son over the ear. For copying his mother. She was the one who should be punished; she was the bad influence. Without her . . .

"I'm not talking about divorce. Whom God hath joined let no man put asunder; but we could live apart. You could go back to Gad's and live with your mother and hunt four times a week if you wanted to. I'd make you an allowance. Four pounds, five, a week."

"Don't strain yourself. People get hernia that way."

"Will you be serious and listen to me? We can't go on as we are, tugging the boy between us, like two dogs at a bone. Better give up while there is something to be saved."

"Sam?"

"Yes. He stays here, he belongs here. He's my son."

"It may surprise you—but he is my son too."

"Will you stop your daft, clever talk and give me a straight answer?" He wished that it were permissible for a man of principle, a good Christian, a good Methodist to clout his wife across the face.

"The answer is, No. How could I leave him to you? I want him to have an ordinary, happy childhood and not grow up narrow-minded and twisted."

Tim remembered his wedding day; the three Gad's Hall girls in yards and yards of white satin, in lace by the lily-decorated altar. All the worldly people drinking champagne at Gad's afterwards. Just the sort of ceremony his mother would most heartily have disapproved, the sort of thing he had tried to avoid but which had been forced upon him by Mrs Thorley, that misguided woman.

"You promised to honour and obey," he said flatly.

"And love," Deb reminded him. "I must have been in love to make such rash promises."

Well, if she wouldn't go and leave the boy with him, he must exert his authority over the boy. Once before he'd struck him—blows really aimed at Deb; then he'd been penitent and tried to regain favour with his son. That hadn't worked. He'd try a different tack. He didn't believe in knocking horses about, but if one proved too frisky and unmanageable, a cut in the corn never failed to work. He'd try sending Sam to bed without supper for a week—that'd teach him who was master here.

Deb countered that by absenting herself from the supper table, and playing the piano, lively tunes; dance tunes! And, since fasting from half-past twelve dinner one day to seven o'clock breakfast the next seemed to bring no response except surliness from Sam, he suspected that Deb was smuggling food. And he was right, he caught her red-handed. Friday was the weekly Prayer Meeting evening; he left for it ostentatiously and then turned back. Deborah and Jessie, Jessie! that sound Methodist who had at first disapproved of her mistress, and then come to admire her, were preparing a supper tray; cold chicken, ham, a mound of bread and butter, cheese!

Decent men didn't quarrel with their wives in front of servants. Besides, he was speechless with rage, so he turned and walked out, went to the Prayer Meeting and in the Biblical phrase, "wrestled with God," admitting that he had done wrong in yoking himself to an unbeliever and praying for delivery from an impossible situation.

Some prayers are answered; not always straightforwardly.

George Thorley's stay with Mr van Haagen was nearing its end. He had vastly enjoyed moving about in the wider world, but he was not sorry to be going home. Gad's was in his blood, the heritage of unreckoned generations. Foreign places were fascinating, all the foreigners he had met had been kind—that is, susceptible to his charm, which seemed to be capable of overriding even the barrier of differing language. A ready smile, good looks and a strong desire to be liked went a long way.

A few days before he was due to embark, George said,

"Mr van Haagen, you have given me a most wonderful time. I've never enjoyed myself so much." The right thing to say, even if not strictly true; George enjoyed everything which was even moderately enjoyable. "And I would very much like to do something for you. And I would, if you didn't think it too silly."

"It is now two months we have been together, my dear boy, and I have yet to hear you be silly."

"At Zwolle, tomorrow you are selling some stock. Nobody knows me there. I could bid against everybody and jerk the prices up."

Mr van Haagen gave the deep, rumbling belly laugh of a fat man.

"This is your own thought?"

"Yes. It came to me in the night. I was thinking what a good time you had given me and wondering what I could do. To show gratitude. Not to repay. I can never do that."

"You are," Mr van Haagen said portentously, "your mother's son."

George grinned. "Well, so I was always led to believe."

Mr van Haagen laughed again. "No harm to tell you now. Now that you originate. It is a game which your Mamma and I have played, many years. For what she sells, I bid, by person, or agent or letter; what I sell, she does the same. By such contrivance prices go up. Two or three times perhaps, not so. Then we console each other. Not that much consolation is needed. The second bidder is happy to hear that to send the animal he wanted across the sea, with a man to attend, is not so profitable as to sell to him. At the last price he offered. You understand. It is not dishonest. It is just business. Goot business. And your Mamma thought of it. So tomorrow, you understand, to bid against a written offer would be to bid against your Mamma. Against yourself.

"And that would never do, would it?"

"It would be confusion."

"Then all I can do . . . God, it sounds so little after all you have done for me. . . . But I promise you, Mr van Haagen, any time you come to England, the best hospitality I can offer. . . ." George smiled and said, "Never again that attic for you. Though I'd done my best with it."

"So I know." The memory of that terrible night in the attic, next door to the one which was locked and most vilely haunted, wiped all the joviality from the Dutchman's face. That night had taught him something about himself—that he was the possessor of something not quite canny, some mediumistic quality which he had always denied. His ability to see something of the future and something of the past by studying certain cards selected from a pack he regarded as merely a matter of obeying certain rules, taught him by his grandmother; not unlike, he often explained, reading words on a page. Since his experience at Gad's he had been reluctant to indulge in what he had thought of, and called, his one parlour trick.

Yet now that this boy of whom he had become so fond was about to depart, he was moved by curiosity and a kind of protective feeling. Nobody could change what the cards foretold, but their authority was not absolute and there were undefined areas concerning which a warning might be given. He had warned that most unfortunate girl at Gad's to avoid the dark; unfortunately it was too late.

"If you would like, George, I will look in the cards for you. Or do you scorn such things?"

"You mean tell my fortune," George said with his charming smile. "I don't scorn such things. At Fairs or Fetes, if there's a fortune-teller, I make straight for her. One old gypsy hag told me I'd die a pauper. I thought that damned ungrateful. I'd just given her a shilling!"

"That perhaps was why when sixpence would have served." Mr van Haagen had noticed George's extreme open-handedness—and also his extraordinary luck. He seemed to attract money. They'd gone together to a casino in Paris and Mr van Haagen had been very careful and fatherly, providing George with counters to the value that could be lost without harm and telling him to stop once they were lost. George had made a great deal of money that evening—and spent it on presents for everybody.

I must not allow such thoughts to influence me, Mr van Haagen said as George went through the routine of selecting his cards.

Yet money figured prominently, even at first glance.

"You will always have money; sometimes much; sometimes little. You will disperse it, unless you mend your ways. A little more care with money, if you please."

When Mr van Haagen read the cards he treated them as though they were as fragile as dried rose-leaves, moving them into this arrangement and that with one touch of a finger-tip. The gypsy had not been quite right, though not far wrong. A great lack of money was indicated, but Death would intervene. Very sudden death at a good old age.

"You have many years. Perhaps that is why you should be careful with the money so that it lasts you many years. Also you have many friends. So many friends. I do not remember when I am seeing so many years and so many friends for one man. And goot health too. Yes, even when you are old, the same health as now you enjoy." Why then should the indication of *real* happiness be so lacking? Carefully, Mr van Haagen moved the cards again. Ah, in the heart's affairs!

He was still sticking to his grandmother's rules, and one of them was to tell the true but not the unpleasant, to tell the pleasant but not the untrue; and that of all the rules was the most difficult. After a pause, he said, "With you where the heart is and the marriage is, they do not lie side by side. But," Mr van Haagen looked up, an expression of surprise on his wide face, "that you know already, is it not? Yes, a lesson bygone, but with less such confusion. Confusion will be, but take it gently, gently. It will pass. . . . Now, marriage at good age and of children one. A boy."

No particular joy in that relationship either, but there was nothing unusual about that; Mr van Haagen had his Pieter, he respected him for his solid qualities, his business acumen, but outside business they had nothing in common.

"I think that is all."

"Well, thanks, Mr van Haagen. The best I've had yet."

And what more could a man ask, Mr van Haagen asked himself, gathering the cards together, than long life, splendid health, great popularity? So why feel sad? Why feel that this delightful boy deserved more and better?

George was home; so glad to be home that if Mrs Thorley had not had his letters saying how much he was enjoying himself, she could have suspected him of being homesick. All the way from Baildon station, where she had met him in the gig, he'd kept saying that everything looked the same, rather he had been away twenty years instead of two months.

The table in the living room was littered with things, unwrapped just enough to show their contents. Gifts for everyone.

"And last, but not least, Mamma, *you*," George said, producing with pride a pair of diamond earrings.

"They're real," he said.

"But how could you possibly afford . . . ?"

"I *knew* you'd ask that! Well, I could. I won a lot of money in a place called a casino; that was in Paris; but I bought those in Amsterdam. Amsterdam is the place for diamonds—something to do with South Africa. Do you like them?"

"Of course. They're lovely. Thank you, George."

"With my love," he said, and bent to give her another kiss. But her head jerked and the kiss landed on her ear.

"Put them on," George said. And her head jerked again and her hands were unsteady. George realised that something had changed.

"Is something worrying you, Mamma?"

"My dear, yes. I didn't want to greet you with miserable news, but it's Deb. She just went away, nobody knows where. She just went away. She sent me a letter, saying she was doing so, but she didn't say where she was going. Then Mr Bridges came storming down, accusing me of harbouring her. Most fortunately I had her letter, and Jenny and Violet and Willy could all swear they had not seen her. But he was *most* unpleasant, indeed very rude. Not that that matters. I never liked him from the first and his opinion of me . . . It is Deb. Homeless, out of touch, lost. She was the best of them all. . . . George, it's all over and done with but *I* was once cast on my own resources—as Deb must be now. And it was horrible. Honestly, when I think of Deb and Sam adrift in the world, it really is more than I can bear—and I've borne a lot, one way and another."

"We'll find her," George said. "And anywhere Deb went, she'd be all right. I mean . . . she is so sensible; she wouldn't just have gone off unless she knew where. Did she say why?"

"Nothing specific. Just that life had become intolerable and that she was leaving for Sam's sake. And that she would write."

"I can't say I blame her. He's an impossible man. Had she any money?"

"She had her dowry—five hundred pounds; except for fifty. That she gave to Diana. But she may not dare to touch it. To transfer money might reveal her whereabouts. I know—nobody better—how sensible Deb is, but, George, she knows nothing of the world. She's never even seen a big city."

"I don't think she would go to a city. She'll be somewhere where there are horses. Did she and Sam take their horses?"

"No. According to Mr Bridges, they all went in the gig to Thetford. Deb had some shopping and Sam was to get his hair cut and they were to meet at four o'clock, at the minister's house. And there was a letter—addressed to Mr Bridges, telling him. Really, if he hadn't been so violent and blamed me for it all I should have felt quite sorry for the man. It must have been a terrible shock. But I'm even more sorry for Deborah; she must have been desperate to do such a thing."

The one earring which Mrs Thorley had managed to hook in twinkled and shimmered, emphasising the shaking of her head.

Not the homecoming which George had anticipated. He felt both uneasy and resentful. He hated to see anybody unhappy and would go to almost any length to relieve their distress, but when there was nothing one could do . . . Then impatience and self-preservation took over.

"They'll be all right, Mamma. You mustn't be upset. I tell you what. Tomorrow I'll ride over and talk to that man—Craig, I think that was the name. Deborah hired a meadow and some stabling from him. He might know something. We'll find her, don't you fret. Now, how about a welcome-home drink? What would you like?"

"Whisky," Mrs Thorley said, giving in. Whisky had served her well in the past, enabling her to endure the unendurable; then for everybody's sake—but mainly George's—she had renounced it, pulled herself up from the crutch that it offered, been sober, attended to business. Now for some reason it seemed to matter less. George was older, he could manage. And the whole business about Deb had been such a blow because in a way it mirrored a part of her own life; a woman alone, anonymous, fighting the world with nothing much to fight with. This was something different from Lavinia's more tragic and dramatic story; never once had Mrs Thorley been able to put herself into Lavinia's place. Into Deborah's she could slip all too easily and Deborah was not so well-equipped; she'd seen nothing of the world. And was so good. Clever, yes; resourceful, yes; dependable, yes; but completely unsophisticated.

"Well," George said, "at least we know now that Deb didn't act on the spur of the moment. I saw Craig; he knew nothing except that Deb had paid him to the end of the year and said she wouldn't train any more hunters. He thought she was going to have

THE HAUNTING OF GAD'S HALL

another baby. So she tied that up neatly. Then I went to the bank at Thetford. They were far more cagey but I ferreted out the fact that Mrs Bridges' account there was dead. And that, I may tell you, took a bit of doing. I had to pretend I was French and that Deb owed me ten pounds. It's a curious thing," George said, "but it was the same everywhere Mr van Haagen and I went, foreigners get preferential treatment. If I'd gone in and asked outright, said I was her brother, they'd have chucked me out. As it was—and believe me, Mamma, I was *very* French—I finally got what I wanted to know. Deb took her money. So she didn't go unprepared, and she isn't starving—yet."

"That is some comfort. It was very clever of you, George."

"Oh, George, how clever of you. Just what I wanted. Everything about me is getting so ugly now, except my hands." Caroline slipped on the bracelets, smooth oblong plaques of jet linked together, making a white hand look even whiter. "Lovely, how sweet of you. Now sit down and tell me everything. I've been so dull."

Pregnancy, however much coddled, was a loathesome state. Caroline had always known that she wasn't actually pretty, but she had been presentable. Now she was not. Even her face was swollen. As for her ankles . . . She'd tried to joke about it. "What's that new complaint, Edward? Something to do with elephants."

"Elephantiasis."

"That's it. It's happening to me."

"Darling, I think there has been only one case of it known in England. A certain amount of oedema is quite common in pregnancy."

"You say that when I begin to grow a trunk," Caroline said. And that was the last joke she made so far as Edward could remember. She'd just lain back, eschewed all company, obeyed all the rules, and grown fat and full, like a vegetable marrow. There'd been none of the quips and none of the self-will. When the question of engaging a proper nurse arose, Caroline said, "I think Miss Humberstone should pick the person. If *we* did and chose somebody Miss Humberstone didn't like there'd be trouble. I'll leave it entirely to her. And to you."

The dullness of which she now complained to George was largely self-inflicted. Female company had never pleased Caroline much and now she hated it; all women, young and old, seemed to think that pregnancy was the beginning and end of all things; and they were capable of congratulating her in one breath and in the next launching out into some horrifying tale of what they, or someone known to them, had suffered. As for men, who would want to see a man when one's face was blown up like a balloon? Edward had now achieved his aim of having Caro to himself, except for Mrs Thorley, who paid at least one visit a week, and Doctor Awkwright, who dropped in with fair frequency.

George, to whom superficial gallantry came easily, assured Caro that she didn't look a bit ugly; on the contrary, very pretty. Then he gave a lively account of his visit to Mr van Haagen. He spoke with special enthusiasm about Paris, happily oblivious to the fact that the mention of France lacerated Caro's feelings; for Freddy had adhered to his plan and was now living there. And with a little more ruthlessness, a little more guts, she might have been with him.

"And what do you think about Deb?" George asked. He assumed that Caro knew.

"What about her?"

"Oh God!" Perhaps there were things that women in Caroline's condition should not be told. "I thought Mamma . . ."

"Unless Mamma has business to do, she comes to see me on Sunday. *What* about Deb? Is she ill? Hurt?"

It was all right then. Mamma had only received Deb's letter last Monday, and would doubtless have shared the information with Caro tomorrow.

"Far from it! She's done what she should have done years ago. Run away from Tim Bridges."

"Deb? Who with?"

Curiously that aspect of the business had not occurred either to Mrs Thorley or to George.

"She took Sam, of course."

"Where did she go?"

"That nobody knows. That is what Mamma is so worried about. But she's all right, I'm sure. She has some money, and before that is gone we'll know where she is and can send her some."

Apparently there were some things that pregnant women should not be told, for Caro was beginning to cry.

"Oh, for God's sake, Caro, don't *you* start. It's nothing to cry about. Wherever Deb is she's better off—and so is the boy—

than living with that horrid man. I stayed there, you know, and I'd have run away the first day except that he'd have blamed Deb."

Caroline was not crying, directly, about Deb; she was crying for herself. Deb had done exactly what she should have done, given a mite more strength of character. Now, through fumbling and indecision, she was stuck here for life.

Edward always knew; he said, "Darling, you have been crying. What about?"

"Only silly little things. First I was touched because George brought me these. Not many boys of his age, on their first trip abroad, would have been so thoughtful. And then he told me something which upset me a little. Deborah has run away."

"To Gad's?" In Edward's experience most women who left their husbands—and many had the soundest of reasons—went home to their parents.

"No. She's just disappeared. Gone away, leaving no trace."

"That is practically impossible," Edward said. In fact, in all his experience, which though limited in scope had great variety, of all the women who had left their husbands, because of a black eye or the man's infidelity, or a mere fit of temper, only one had failed to be traced—until four years later when her body had been found, buried in a field. Tim Bridges had not, Edward thought, blacked Deborah's eye, or been unfaithful, or killed her. He was a very dull dog, but fundamentally a good chap. And Deborah was a good sensible girl; if she'd flung off in a fit of temper, she'd soon realise the impossibility of her position and come back, willing to forgive and to be forgiven.

"You simply must not worry about such a trivial thing," Edward said. "Wherever Deborah is, she's all right. And I bet she'll be home within a week."

"My name is Willoughby; Mrs Willoughby," Deborah said, "and if you wish for a deposit, here it is." For the first time in her life she was free—her own woman—and although Mamma, back at Gad's, had thought of Deborah as unsophisticated because she had never seen London or any other great city, such a thought had underestimated Deborah's reading and the fact that she could read, not only a printed page, but a map. It was, after all, Deborah who when Lavinia was pregnant and mad and needed some cover story to save them all suggested Killapore as a possible destination in India. Deborah, though she had travelled so little, knew more than most people of her kind about the outer world. Some of what she read might be rightly denounced by Tim as rubbish, but even in rubbish there was sometimes a grain of information, and from less rubbishy books, *Rambles South of the Thames, A Visit to Glastonbury, Norman Churches Still Unspoiled*, and works of a similar nature, Deborah's magpie mind had accumulated a number of facts which were of use to her when it came to choosing a destination of her own.

She did not wish to live in a big town; and in a small village any new arrival would be conspicuous. A place about the size of Baildon would be ideal. It must possess, or be within easy reach of a good Grammar School, for Sam must be educated and she would not be able to afford boarding school fees. Preferably it would not be in hunting country, for a certain section of the hunting fraternity had, like County families, interconnections, and she might be recognised.

She needed, she thought, a hiding place for about nine years. Sam, properly schooled and handled, should by the age of sixteen have enough strength of character to stand up to Tim, or anybody else; and he would have had a peaceful childhood, untroubled by parental dissension. She was certain that she had taken the right course and this certainty bore her up through several disappointments in finding a suitable place and the prospect of being poor for a long time— But better a dinner of herbs where love is than a stalled ox and hatred withal. There she had Biblical authority.

Now she had found a small, isolated, self-contained town in a Shropshire valley. It was called Abbey Norton and offered houses for sale or for rent because its population was falling. Some young people had been drawn away to the industrial Midlands, some had emigrated in search of wider, more tractable fields. The house she finally settled upon stood about a mile outside the little town and was cheaply rented for its size because it was delapidated. It had a neglected garden, a piece of small rough pasture, a stable and a pigsty. Sam should have a pony.

Here Deborah set about weaving the kind of story around herself and Sam just as she had once woven a story about Lavinia. She was Mrs Willoughby. Memory threw up the name which had been her own mother's maiden name; she was a widow.

"And you have his birth certificate?" the Headmaster of the Grammar School asked.

"I am afraid not. Sam was born in India. He remembers nothing about it," she added hastily. "We came home when he was a baby. I intended to go back, but then my husband died—suddenly."

Fundamentally, Deborah detested lies, and paradoxically, told them very convincingly because she looked and sounded so honest. "We have lived with various relatives. But I thought the time had come to set up house on our own." Perfectly understandable —the boy was old enough to be company for her now.

"He has had previous schooling?"

"Only such as I could provide. He reads quite fluently, and can do simple arithmetic."

The Headmaster had before this encountered boys brought up —and sometimes taught—by their mothers; they were usually namby-pamby cry babies, spoiled and ignorant.

"We'll have him in, and I'll set him a test or two."

Sam had entered into the whole thing with the enthusiasm of a seven-year-old given a part to play. Life without Father was very enjoyable—though he missed his pony and did not eat so well as he had at Foxton. Mother had explained everything; make one slip and he'd be back at Foxton, with Father, and without her, before he could blink, and that was not a pleasant prospect. Children apparently belonged to their fathers.

Sam was far from namby-pamby; he'd been taught to say "Sir" when addressing an elder man; he read fluently, could add and subtract. Very satisfactory; he could start on Monday.

Deborah whitewashed the kitchen at the Stone House, and thought that there was a strange affinity between herself and whitewash. She had done the whitewashing at Diana's first home in Friars' Lane in Baildon; she had whitewashed the attic at Gad's, blotting out the terrible paintings which Lavinia had done on the walls. Now she was whitewashing for herself and Sam.

She'd bought the minimum of furniture—all secondhand; two people needed only two beds, two chairs and one table; but two people who had absconded without luggage needed clothing for the coming winter; needed crockery, and cooking utensils. She'd paid a year's rent, £26, and term's fees, £10—but that included a midday dinner, in advance. She'd bought a pig, and six fowls, and a pony, a rather sorry little creature, which perked up surprisingly when better fed and required only to jog a mile and back in a day.

All these things cost money, and well before Christmas, Deborah was assessing her capacity to *earn*. It was very limited. In a larger and more flourishing, and more socially ambitious community than the one she had chosen she could have given children a few elementary lessons; she could, as Mrs Thorley had done in her time, have taught some girls to play a few tunes on the piano. Had the need to avoid anything horsy not compelled her to settle in a place where horses were used for use, not for pleasure, she could have used her one inborn gift and schooled hunters. As it was she could not even fall back upon that last resort of a woman without means—needlework. Nobody could deny that she was handy, she could drive a nail straight, plant things, deal with harness; but that small thing, the needle, was defeat from the start.

One evening, late in the year now with everything practical that could be done, over and done with, and Sam doing his homework at the kitchen table, Deborah was struck by a feeling of deprivation. No book. She had always been a prodigious reader, at school where Miss Hardwicke had given her, in the last year, the run of her small library; then at Gad's where books could be obtained from the circulating library in Baildon, or even bought; then at Foxton where books from the Thetford circulating library had been denounced as rubbish. Abbey Norton had no library, no bookshop even; it was in fact a very backward community.

The fire glowed in the range, the lamp cast a good light and Deborah would have been glad to read anything, even one of Tim's dismal books, the *Guide for Local Preachers*, or *St Paul's Steps Retraced*.

Quite suddenly the need to read became, like the making of the chicken house fox-proof and all the other things which had occupied her, something to be done by herself. Make your own book! Tell yourself a story. Deborah said, "Sam, have you an empty writing book?"

Ordinarily it was Mother who ended the evening sessions by making cocoa and saying, "Time for bed." On this evening Sam waited, and waited, and finally said,

"Shall I make the cocoa?"

"That would be kind," Deborah said, without looking up.

Sam made the cocoa and placing the cup on the table, said,

"That's a very long letter."

"It's not exactly a letter. It's something . . . else."

Deborah wrote regularly to Mamma, and there was no need to make her letters sound cheerful; they exuded happiness. She had been very cautious about her new name and her address; she preferred nobody but Mamma to know; if Di or Caro wanted to write to her they could do so through Mamma—not that either of them was much of a letter writer. Mrs Thorley had told George that Deb had found a home, placed Sam in school, and reported every other scrap of news as it came along, and George showed no curiosity. So long as Deb was all right and Mamma not worried he was content. He allowed Mamma to send on Deb's present from Holland, a gold brooch in the form of a fox head, and he occasionally said, "Send her my love," or "Tell her we're solidly behind her if it comes to needing money."

He had positively enjoyed a face-to-face encounter with Tim Bridges in, of all places, the yard behind the *Hawk in Hand*. A planned encounter since places where spiritous liquors were sold were sinks of iniquity in Mr Bridges' eyes.

"I've been waiting for you to come out," Tim said. "George, *where is Deb?*"

"I don't know."

"You must. Look here, George, you're old enough to understand. She's my wife. Sam is my son. I want them back."

Rather gleefully George repeated something which had been said to him in the past when he made some inordinate demand,

"Then I'm afraid want will be your master. I don't know where Deb is. And if I did, I wouldn't tell you."

George stood there, confident, handsome, saucy, elegant, smooth-speaking, the epitome of everything which Gad's represented and distrusted.

"You're a liar."

"No man calls me a liar," George said, still smoothly, but hotly. The high romantic days, when a man whose word was questioned called the questioner out to a duel, were long over, but George squared up and said,

"You take that back."

"You're a liar."

The innyard had seen many fights in the past, and would see others, but the present innkeeper disapproved of people resorting to fisticuffs on his premises. It got a place a bad name, and his usual method with squabblers was rough and ready. Take them both by the scruff of the neck and chuck 'em into the Market Square. He was a huge man, six foot three inches in height and he weighed eighteen stones, all bone and muscle, no flabby flesh. In his day he'd gone twelve rounds against Irish Paddy, the most notable bruiser of the time. He was light and swift on his feet, and before any blow was struck, had interposed his bulk, saying,

"Gentlemen!" For the two preparing to hit one another were not drunken drovers. One looked like a Methody minister—and that was shrewd of the landlord, for Timothy Bridges wore his sober chapel-going suit when he went to market; and the other—God help us—was young Mr Thorley, very young Mr Thorley, but already a known customer and generous. But they were not going to be allowed to fight in *his* yard, however respectable they were. So he put himself between and said that if they had a difference of opinion it should be settled privately.

"I take it you don't want to make a raree show for ostlers and drovers."

Neither did, so that was the end of that.

Then Tim tried Mrs Thorley again, and again rebuffed, though she was magnanimous enough to tell him that she had heard from Deb and that she was well and happy, he tried a despicable trick.

"That Mr Bridges," Jenny said, "waylaid me in the yard and said he'd give me a sovereign to do a bit of spying for him. Amongst your letters, ma'am. I told him . . ." Jenny's face turned poppy red. There were expressions one could use to a man who had offered such an insult, but they were not fit for Mrs Thorley's ears. "I said no," Jenny finished on a weaker note.

There were people who said that all new-born babies looked exactly alike; and it was true that one could not tell anything from hair colouring, for if they had hair at birth it rubbed off, and the eyes of the new-born were always a slatey blue, but there was always, just a brief time—which might be outgrown, when the baby, boy or girl, looked like a very old version of its father. Mrs Thorley had noticed it with all her children, and looking at Caroline's little boy for the first time, she thought—Freddy Ingram! The ears particularly, set rather high and pointed, like a faun's.

God send, she thought, that nobody else would notice, or that the resemblance would vanish. Above all, God grant that Edward would never see.

This new anxiety threw her into such a jerky state that Nurse Rose, who had allowed the child's grandmother to hold it, hastily took it back.

Caroline's baby was born on Christmas Day, and everybody had made sure that there should be as little pain as possible. Nurse Rose rather disapproved of methods she regarded as new-fangled, but she could not argue against *two* doctors. Doctor Awkwright had been involved too. And Nurse Rose, though hired and installed a fortnight before the event, had not come into full power until it occurred.

Miss Humberstone had chosen Nurse Rose as the one, of all the applicants, she could live with; a woman of very similar background, though Nurse Rose, unhampered by family ties, had been able to train for what, if not quite a profession, was a specialised job. Caroline, who partly from tact and partly from lethargy had allowed Miss Humberstone to do the choosing, had taken against Nurse Rose at first sight. Too much like Miss Hardwicke, who had on occasions criticised Caroline severely. But after all, what could one ask of a nurse for one's child except that she should be exceptionally clean, willing and conscientious, and that she should be able to get along with Miss Humberstone, about whom the activities and the splendid organisation of the St Giles' Square house centred?

Caroline came out of the anaesthetic haze to hear Edward saying,

"Darling, we have a little boy. Perfect in every way." Most fathers took for granted that their children would be perfect, but Edward, like every doctor, had seen the freaks which two ordinary parents could produce, and had had some bad moments. To Doctor Awkwright, who had once mentioned the sex of the unborn, Edward had said, "What do I care? So long as it has its arms and legs in the right place; and its head, of course."

One glance was enough. Caroline knew what Edward must never know. And though she was not yet fully herself, had, as usual, the word ready.

"How old he looks! Edward, he looks just like your father!"

Edward, who had not considered his son's looks, agreed and made for once a light-hearted remark,

"He'll grow younger every day!"

After an interval devoted to admiration of the baby, Caroline said, "Where is Mamma? I thought she was here."

"She was, darling. . . . Until it was all over. Then she went home."

In one tiny corner of his professional mind, Edward was concerned about his mother-in-law. He liked her and admired her. That jerk of the head—a thing of long-standing, and non-progressive, could be dismissed as nervous tic akin to a twitching cheek or a blinking eye. There was also the pleasant-sounding term, "A benign tremor," but Mrs Thorley's extreme shakiness, after it was all over, after she'd seen the baby sound and safe, smacked more of the irreversible paralysis agitans. He had not seen much of her lately, and when she arrived to be with Caro during the birth, he had been too much agitated himself to notice anyone else's condition. But *after* . . . he had noticed and was a little worried. He soon forgot that though in the joy of presenting Caro with a set of cameo trinkets, brooch, necklet and earrings.

The abrupt cessation of orders from Mr Burton which followed the gay display in Preston's windows early in December dismayed Diana for a short time, but she did not despair. Some other fashion would come along in the New Year, and she had established herself with the irritable little man as a good worker and one who was punctual. In the meantime she had leisure to cultivate the acquaintance of her new neighbours, so much more to her taste than those in St Anne's Crescent, or than Everard's fine friends. Nobody in the cul-de-sac called Somerton Road was very rich, or very grand; and on the whole they were people who had come down in the world, rather than scrambled up. Here poor Lavinia's idealised painting of Gad's Hall and Diana's pointing it out—My old home—roused no rancour at all. It and Diana's nice manners could be matched, or outmatched, often in a nostalgic manner. Almost every woman with any pretensions to gentility could draw and paint with fair adequacy, and even some men did not despise the art: This is the bungalow in Simla, where we spent the hot weather; This is Cape Coast Castle, just at sunset; not very polished perhaps, but the sun goes down fast in the tropics; This is my old home, painted by my aunt Augusta.

Everybody in Somerton Road had a resident maid—a few had two, but even two was a come-down after India, after life aboard ship, or in the Army. Dinner parties were rare, tea-parties frequent. Only two of the houses were occupied by young couples and only one of them, the Cressets, had children. That family employed a proper nurse who proved amenable to her mistress' suggestion that little Belle Spicer should sometimes accompany her charges on walks in the Park. Young Mrs Cresset could not imagine how Diana managed with only Bessie as maid-of-all-work. But she did not despise Diana for her apparent penury, because if her husband's tea-import business failed to pick up, and fairly soon, she might be in the same position. The upper-middle-class solidarity in Somerton Road was as viable as the lower-middle-class solidarity of St Anne's Crescent, and much easier to deal with.

Just before Christmas, Lady Lumsley decided to give a children's party. Not, as she explained, just Hunt the Slipper and similar games, followed by tea and buns. She proposed to hire a conjurer of international repute who would entrance the children and entertain a few dull adults who did not exactly fit in on other occasions. It would slide into another kind of party, sherry for those mothers who had accompanied their children, and for such fathers as came to collect their families. A piece of hospitality aimed mainly at what Lady Lumsley called The Dullies. And into that category Everard's wife, so prim and provincial, slid all too easily.

About Diana as Everard's wife, Alison Lumsley had no conscience pangs at all, and had the woman shown a spark of liveliness, she would have included her, gladly, in the gay round. But Diana had failed the test. So, bringing her daughter, Belle, "and friend," Diana was invited to a party intended to wipe off a lot of Dullies; women who took the business of motherhood seriously, following the Queen's example, a few elderly people who had reverted to the early bedtime and the tastes in amusement of childhood. Belle's only friend in London, in the world, was the elder of the two Cresset boys, so Diana asked him, and Mrs Cresset felt more than rewarded for her kindness over the walks in the Park.

What existed, during that autumn and winter, between Lady Lumsley and Everard could hardly be described as a love affair; there was no fondness in it on either side, merely a mutual attraction which needed physical contact to fan it into appetite. Meetings were easy enough to arrange; they met at her house, in the houses of a few people who liked Everard, but time alone together was difficult to find since Everard was married and must be in his office all day. (Not busy in his office—in fact the lack of business was alarming, but it made it all the more necessary that he should always be there to deal with what little there was to be done.)

Everard's brass plate, like the doctor's, attracted some chance clients, mainly of the humbler kind. He drew up a few wills, did some conveyancing of property, appeared in magistrates courts on behalf of a few people who had a defence to put forward, and money to pay; but it was all small stuff. That euphoric moment in Lumsleydale Castle, when everybody had said that he *must* set up on his own, and everybody promised him *volumes* of support, seemed to have been a bud which died before it flowered. And joining Brinkley's Club had been equally disappointing. No single bit of business had emerged from that pleasant place—so far.

Had he and Diana still been living at St Anne's Crescent, the Club would have served another purpose; he could then have said that business demanded that he sleep in the West End occasionally; but Somerton Road was the West End, practically fifteen minutes' walk away from Brinkley's. Still, after its fashion, the Club served. He could say, "I shan't be in to dinner, darling. Something may be looming, and I'll have a bite at the Club." Then—and such occasions were always arranged beforehand—he and Alison were free to be together.

It was all extremely unsatisfactory; everything was unsatisfactory. At home penny-pinching and a wife who never was much of a one for bed, now definitely feared another pregnancy: Two takes us all our time to provide for; three would be ruin. Until things improve.

It cost Diana a great deal to make such an outright statement; she had always been one to evade real issues. Engaged to be married, she had set about embroidering—not learning to cook. Practicality had been forced upon her and she hated every aspect of it. She hated the penny-pinching, too; worried—not about the rent, she still had some of the money Deb had given her, some of what she had earned—but for the future. Belle's education did not present much of a problem, little schools for girls were plentiful and cheap; but there was Melville. Everard said he must go to Eton— had even put his name on the waiting list; but first he must either have a tutor or go to a preparatory school. It was all very worrying, and life would have been unbearable but for the little round of tea-parties in Somerton Road and the friendliness of her neighbours. And, of course, Bessie, who trudging down to Soho could make sixpence go as far as a shilling. And the hope that some new fad would come in with the New Year and that Mr Burton would employ her again.

But this is not what I wanted, or expected when I fell in love with Everard. This is not as it *should* be. We've all, except Caro, gone wrong. Lavinia—better not think of her, and yet the picture was a reminder—Deb run away, me in this mess.

Miss Hardwicke had never insisted upon what was called copperplate writing, up strokes thin, downstrokes thick. A waste of time, she called it, what she demanded was legible writing, something as easy to read as print. By the end of February, Deborah had filled three notebooks with this easy-as-print writing and the tale that she had set out to write for herself was told. It was a strange mixture, an amalgam of what she knew and what she imagined, and what she had read. She knew, better than most, what was involved in keeping a living body hidden away, a deadly secret, yet needing food and sanitary arrangements, and exercise; what she imagined was a different and far less domestic background, and what she had read had provided her with a background and a motive. France, during the Revolution. . . . The hidden person an aristocrat who had endeared herself to an innkeeper of great determination and resource—Mamma to the life. The story had a tragic ending, most of the stories which Deb had enjoyed reading ended unhappily, and the story of Lavinia, the one story she knew at first hand, had been unhappy in the extreme. The innkeeper had a task even harder than Mamma's had been, for he could not leave his inn to underlings as Mamma had left her herd to Joe Snell; and he had no collaborators, as Mamma had had in Di and Deb and Caro; also he was subject, as Mamma had never been, to searches. Ordinarily the door of the hidden room was concealed by a cupboard, its shelves piled with bed linen. It was mounted on rollers, made by the man himself—given the motive and the tools, Deb could have rigged up a contrivance —but once, in a very tense scene, a search was made when the linen cupboard was out of place and the hidden door in full view. Then the innkeeper had to rely on his wits and said quickly that the revolutionary soldiers who were still searching for La Marquise, opened that door at their peril because behind it there was a man dying of smallpox. That sent them clattering down the stairs!

When she started to write herself a story because she had no new book to read, Deborah had not visualized it as a book, printed and bound, but at the end she read it through and realised that it was a tale that she would have enjoyed reading; it deserved a wider audience. Like most readers she had taken note of titles and of authors, but not of publishers and the only book available to her was the one she bought to enliven her train journey on the day she ran away. That was published by Hammond and Curtis, a firm who had an office in Regent Street. But they—or rather he, for there was not and never had been a Mr Curtis, he was a myth, and existed only as a cover for Mr Hammond when he, a kind man, was forced to be unkind. The firm had moved to 24 Essex Court, just across the hallway from Everard's office. The rent was less and it was better-situated; trades, professions and businesses were inclined to occupy certain areas. The Post Office had been alerted to the change of address of Hammond and Curtis and in due time Deborah's three notebooks, neatly packed, reached Mr Hammond, who, having nothing much to do that morning, began to read with the professional suspicion and scepticism proper to publishers. . . .

Presently he felt a regret that there was no partner, no Mr Curtis to share the excitement of this new discovery—new in exactly the right way; there had been enough of cloying sentiment, tastes were changing. But not yet quite to the point where everything in THE HIDDEN ROOM, by D. Willoughby, would be accepted by the circulating libraries, the foremost consideration in the publishing trade. It would not do to come under the ban of Mr Mudie's circulating library, or of Mr Smith's stalls at railway station; but with just a few adjustments THE HIDDEN ROOM was a potential winner. There had been plenty of books about the French Revolution, but every one had taken a stance, pro, or anti a political situation. THE HIDDEN ROOM avoided such imponderables and told, simply and clearly, the story of two people, involved in one incident.

Mr Hammond went out to lunch, brooding over the title. Did THE HIDDEN ROOM give a little too much away? In his mind he fingered possible alternatives and settled on SECRET. Back in his office, he wrote and his clerk copied—one should have a record of such things—a letter to D. Willoughby, whom Mr Hammond assumed to be a man, partly because the drinking scenes were so explicit—and must, with a few other things, such as the mentioning of the emptying of chamber pots, be cut. Women writers did mention drunken orgies, but none, in Mr Hammond's experience, had ever given an exact description of man being drunk and sick on his own boots.

The Brontes, of course, had all taken pseudonymous, male-sounding names, and so had many other writers, and yet Mr Hammond was surprised when confronted by Deborah who had come, at his invitation, to discuss a few changes in her very promising book. *His* very promising book, as Mr Hammond had thought of it until this moment of meeting. He was shaken; all that stuff about chamber pots, and vomit on boots! How could he possibly discuss, with a woman? And yet it was this woman who had written the little pieces which might offend Mr Mudie and Mr Smith. He fell back on Mr Curtis, his partner, who refused manuscripts with the utmost ruthlessness, and cut pay down to the bone and did all the other things which allowed Mr Hammond to preserve his kindly, genial, sympathetic façade. And so far as Mr Hammond remembered, nobody had ever questioned Mr Curtis' verdict. Until now, when D. Willoughby said,

"He's wrong. I am a reader and it always irks me when quite important things are slurred over. What people live on, for instance. Income, or earned money—that kind of thing."

"You may be the exception, Mrs Willoughby. Most people read to escape from reality."

"Oh." Deborah pondered that for a second. "Even so, Mr Hammond, the escape is more *thorough* if the world into which one escapes is made to *seem* real."

Mr Hammond, having survived the slight shock of finding that D. Willoughby was female, and having sidled around the bits to which Mr Curtis was said to have objected, could now study his new author without embarrassment. Like everybody else he thought her older than she actually was; early thirties. Very well-dressed. Deborah, when she dressed herself on that last morning at Foxton, had donned a dress and basqued jacket of good broadcloth, stuff that would wear and weather well. For working in the house and garden at Abbey Norton she had bought the cheapest, shoddiest clothes. Obviously a lady, Mr Hammond concluded, composed, even slightly authoritative in manner. So how did she know exactly how men behaved when they were drunk? He ventured to ask, in an indirect way,

"That scene," he said, "where everybody, even the landlord, be-
comes so intoxicated is very real indeed."

"So it should be. It happened, but of course with different people."

For there had been a time which Deborah could remember, before her father married Mamma, when her father and those who
were then his friends had drunk themselves silly and some had
been sick. From the half landing where the grandfather clock
stood, a curious child could see it all.

And possibly those incidents had inculcated her love of horses,
waiting patiently, intelligent enough to take a drunken master
home.

"Yes," Mr Hammond said, "there is the ring of truth there.
And of course . . . on the other matters to which Mr Curtis took
objection."

Deborah said, "But when a person is incarcerated he or she
must still perform natural functions. That is what I mean about
slurring over things. Any reader must *know*."

"I agree with you," Mr Hammond said. "But Mr Curtis does
not." Mr Curtis, that myth, represented Mr Mudie and Mr
Smith. "With the slightest adjustment, Mrs Willoughby, this
could be a very successful novel indeed. Mr Curtis was so taken
with it—on the whole—that he suggested a down payment of fifty
pounds, and twenty pounds for each subsequent impression."

Had Deborah been on her own, carefree, foot-free, she would
have reverted to the language of her youth and said: To Hell with
Mr Curtis. Had she known a little more about the trade upon
which she had embarked she would have said: Very well, I'll try a
less timorous publisher. As it was she had Sam to think of, and
the long years ahead; and she knew no other publisher. And after
all, fifty pounds was no negligible sum, just for some words written in these notebooks.

"All right," she said, giving in with ill grace.

"And you will make the . . . the amendments?"

"No. Mr Curtis can do that, since he is so fussy. I still think
he's wrong. You may tell him so and ask him to reconsider."

Mr Curtis was going to have a good deal of reconsidering to do
for D. Willoughby had impressed Mr Hammond. He had had a
good deal to do with she-novelists as they were called; some were

very feminine and fluttery, some conceited and arrogant; all
rapacious, even those who claimed to be writing for pin money.
Whatever he offered—and thirty pounds down was more usual
than fifty, they tried to extract a little more, and he invariably
said that he would consult Mr Curtis, who as invariably upheld
his decision. There was about this young woman something forthright, and unyielding, which he recognised as integrity.

Like everybody who struck what looked like gold, he was anxious to find out how deep was the vein.

"And have you further books in mind, Mrs Willoughby?"

There again she was different. Most she-novelists, given such a
lead, would have begun to talk about the absolutely marvellous
idea already crystallising in their minds. D. Willoughby looked
thoughtful for a moment and then turned upon him one of the
most entrancing smiles he had ever seen and said,

"I sincerely hope so. Writing a book is the next best thing to
reading one."

Since completing THE HIDDEN ROOM—now to be called SE-
CRET, Deborah had found that the evening hours hung heavily.
She would willingly have helped Sam with his homework—but it
was mainly in Latin, of which she had no knowledge at all. It was
still too early to work in the garden; she mended in her inept but
thorough way anything that needed mending. Everything in the
sparsely furnished kitchen was as clean as it could be, and between the substantial tea which greeted Sam when he came home
and the cup of cocoa just before bedtime there was an aching
void. Yes, she would certainly write another story.

She would have liked, on this visit to London, to have visited
Diana, but thought it inadvisable. For one thing she felt that she
had let Diana down, promising her financial help whenever it was
needed and then running away with only a limited amount of
money to keep Sam and herself for nine years. Also Diana was
married to Everard, who was a lawyer, and the law was all on the
side of Tim, a husband wronged indeed.

Better not; better go straight home, close the hen house against
the ravages of foxes, which in this unhuntable region were an everlasting menace, feed the pig.

Calling upon Mr Hammond, Deborah had been within a few
feet of Everard. She was so single-minded that in looking for

Hammond and Curtis on a brass plate she had not noticed Everard Spicer's.

Being, on her return to the station, fifty pounds better off than she had been earlier in the day—and with the promise of more to come, she allowed herself the indulgence of buying two books. Richness indeed! Yet, in the jolting train, there came between her and the printed page a kind of film, shadowy and vague with another story, one of her own making, advancing, retreating and then coming forward again, more clearly. Two main characters, both admirable in their way, but irrevocably divided in opinion. Against what background could they be placed? The answer came, clear as a bell; the Civil War in England; one of the ill-matched pair would be for the King, one for Parliament; each working away like a mole, and a child, Sam, torn between them. By the time that the train reached the end of the line, five miles short of Abbey Norton, Deborah had her story and was ready to begin again. Through the February dusk, lingering, with its promise of Spring and primroses, she walked happily, gulping down the fresh air. London, she realised now that she had time to think about it, was a horrible place, crowded, noisy, smelly and full of decrepit old cab-horses, kept going only by the whip, and donkeys even more pitiable than the one whose load she had once attempted to lighten by buying up a lot of heavy things.

Nothing to be done about it. Nobody was rich enough to save them all.

London was horrible; Caro had found it so, even on her honeymoon; and there was Diana doomed to live in it forever. It just didn't bear thinking about, and things which could not be thought about must be resolutely ignored. She had agreed with Mr Hammond that most people read to escape from reality; now she admitted to herself that some people wrote for the same reason.

Diana had no such escape. Ever since Christmas she had haunted Hawksley's, looking for something in the embroidery line which she could produce, imitate, quickly and cheaply. There was nothing, no fads.

She made a dress for Mrs Cresset, but naturally she could not charge for that because Mrs Cresset's nurse now took both Belle and Melville on little walks. Wearing gloves to protect her hands, she worked in the garden, but she was, for a country-bred girl, singularly ignorant about plants, and it was not until the old sailor, he who had painted Cape Coast Castle at sunset, and had never had an inch of ground to till until he retired to Somerton Road, pointed it out that she knew the difference between the true rose bush and the suckers. She worried perpetually about money. The rent, the rates, the full bill. Everard admitted frankly that self-employment took a long time to show a profit and that he was earning only just enough to keep the office going. In the past he had always been rather haughty about what Diana referred to as *her* money, been against her spending it, warned her that five hundred pounds would not last forever. Now he had changed and when she produced some money did not even ask how she had come by it. He simply said, "Thank God!" and a second later, "I'll make it up to you, darling, one day." Even as he said it he asked himself when that day would be. Security was like the horizon, it receded as one moved towards it. Sometimes it seemed as though everything he had ever done had been a mistake; moving from Baildon, moving from St Anne's Crescent, setting up on his own. Sometimes he felt like one of those wretched men who tramped about the streets between two boards advertising a new play, a new restaurant, a new shop; but both his boards read FAILURE!

There were brief intermissions, now and again in Alison's bed, now and again at Brinkley's. But such pleasant times became more and more divorced from reality, further and further removed from the bread-and-butter business of ordinary life. The feeling which he had at first enjoyed and revelled in, of being amongst his own kind again, faded. March was a particularly bleak and hostile month. Alison and her gay crowd had gone to the South of France; Brinkley's was being redecorated, given over to men with scaffolding and ladders and paint pots. The East wind blew relentlessly, sometimes with flurries of sleet. The ancient crooked man who had cleaned the hallway and kept the brass plates bright came croaking, came voiceless, did not come at all—he'd died of pneumonia in Bermondsey Hospital—and the younger, but less active man who took his place jerked up the charge; five shillings a week from each tenant now. Imagine, just imagine being in a position where one shilling a week mattered so much.

Everard's mood was sometimes suicidal but his nature was not. He was too self-confident, despite all rebuffs, too self-preservative to do himself any damage. Years ago Caroline had summed him up in one word. Greedy. She'd referred only to the matter of food, but her judgement had not been far wrong; Everard was greedy; he wanted money, security, sexual satisfaction, social recognition, all so far, except for Alison, elusive; things just brushed with the tips of his fingers, never yet grasped. But in a blind, obscure way, even at his most desperate, that little nugget of self-assurance stood steady. One day . . .

Mrs Thorley avoided, so far as she could, any close contact with Caroline. She knew that she was being inconsistent, for she had done her best, stretched every available resource to its limits and beyond in order to protect Lavinia. But the two cases were not comparable. Lavinia had been caught in a web of evil, had practised black magic; and she was mad, been possessed, and if her own last words could be believed, impregnated by the Devil.

This was different. Caroline was not a demented, deluded young girl; she was a grown woman, with a devoted husband whom she had betrayed. Of her three sons-in-law, Edward was the only one of whom Mrs Thorley had fully approved, and the thought that Caroline could have done such a thing to such a good man filled her with disgust.

And sometimes, because she was an extremely rational woman, Mrs Thorley was disgusted by her own disgust. She told herself that Caroline could have had a good reason; a sterile marriage for five years? Perhaps that was the explanation, in which case . . . But somehow she could never fully accept it, and when she saw Edward fawning over the baby, her skin seemed not to fit and the shakiness which she did her best to conceal took over. Mrs Thorley did not think in terms of placard-bearing men, she just thought how sad life was. The four little girls, two her own, two George Thorley's, all always treated as her own; and gone such different ways, all regrettable. Lavinia mad, possessed of the Devil and lying under the walnut tree; Diana poor, in London; Deborah absconded, and Caroline, obviously an adultress. But thank God the baby, filling out, had lost that early resemblance to Freddy Ingram. Only those high-set, rather pointed ears . . .

I notice such things because I breed cattle.

I notice.

But to what end? There would be no point in scolding Caroline now. And in any case what right had she even to think so critically? So far as men were concerned her own record was clean, but some of her business dealings with Mr van Haagen were of dubious probity; and she drank more than she should. All that Spring she visited St Giles' Square as rarely as possible and stayed only briefly. One day Caroline remarked upon this change of habit and Mrs Thorley said, "I don't like the way Edward looks at me—as though I were a patient. When I need a doctor, I'll send for him." The words came out more tartly than she realised. There was truth in them. Lately she had been aware of Edward eyeing her now and again, almost furtively, with speculation and curiosity. Then the tremor and the jerkiness increased. Like most other people she credited doctors with some extra perception and wondered whether he knew what ailed her. She was always almost ostentatiously abstemious in his house. One tiny sherry, please, Edward.

Caroline repeated this scrap of conversation, making, as usual, a joke of it: "Mamma says you look at her cross-eyed or something."

"I am interested," Edward admitted. He had no intention of worrying Caro. He had dismissed the idea of paralysis agitans because that was a permanent state, whereas his mother-in-law's condition was variable; even the jerking of her head followed no regular pattern; he'd run into her once in the Market Place, talking to a man, a cattle dealer by the look of him, but with manners enough to stand aside a little and wait. On that occasion Mrs Thorley had seemed as steady as a rock, and Edward attributed the whisky odour to the man. "I think her tremour is of nervous origin," Edward said. "After all, she is no longer young and she's had a hard life. If you ask me it's time she sat back a bit and let young George pull his weight a bit more."

There had been no need to tell Caro to sit back. Being pregnant, and then feeding the baby for three months, had provided an excellent excuse for shuffling off all the dull aspects of the good works which had accumulated ever since she became engaged to Edward. Nobody wished her to resign from any committee, for although many women didn't like her much, all the men did and everybody acknowledged her talent for raising funds. The Friends of the Hospital Committee had always met in Mrs Bosworth's house—now they met at Caro's because Mrs Taylor could not possibly be expected to exert herself yet; nor could she be expected to visit the Hospital, the Ragged School, or the Work-house. But her ideas, her knowledge of what would attract people, and money were still invaluable.

Caroline was too soft-hearted to be a bad mother, too careless to be a good one. Not that it mattered. Nurse Rose enjoyed being omniscient in the nursery, just as Miss Humberstone enjoyed being omnipotent in the household. Caroline had travelled through her vale of tears; her shallow nature had betrayed her over Freddy Ingram. Over him she had not been a butterfly, but it was over now; Freddy somewhere in France was very different from Freddy within reach and any guilt Caroline felt over Noel's parentage—born on Christmas Day, the baby's name was forecho-sen—was easily cancelled out by Edward's joy in the child. Ed-ward said that Noel grew more and more like his mother every day; and it was true that Freddy's colouring had not been trans-mitted; Noel's eyes were like Caroline's, bluish green, and his hair was fair. Dominant strains, thought Edward, who had read Mendel; Noel like George, like Sam Bridges, was a Thorley.

In that year there was a spell of weather in May quite as hot as August, and in the squalid, overcrowded rookeries of Soho, and other areas of London, there were outbreaks of cholera, but what Bessie couldn't see she did not fear, though in a way she shopped more carefully, avoiding shops and stalls too near an open drain or those which seemed to have changed hands overnight. She always shopped early in the morning, leaving Madam to deal with the breakfast, all prepared, as far as possible, overnight. She was al-ways back in time to do the steps and the brass, and the washing up. Then a resuscitating cup of tea and she was ready to wash, clean, cook, to perform all the duties which in better-off house-holds took two, even three women. On this morning she came in, sweating and panting partly because of the effect the weather had on herself, but, more urgent, the effect it had on meat. Unless parboiled, or thoroughly doused with vinegar, meat could go off in the course of the day.

Diana, who usually at this hour was upstairs, making beds, doing a little light dusting, was in the kitchen, leaning against the sink and looking like death. The horrible idea that the sickness, so prevalent in what Bessie called the poor parts, had actually encroached into this most respectable neighbourhood and struck the mistress of whom she had the most genuine affection made

Bessie's small world rock. She dropped the two heavy baskets just inside the kitchen door and ran forward.

"Oh, ma'am, are you ill?"

Diana just managed to shake her head.

Everard, unable to afford a proper lunch, must have a good breakfast; growing children needed a good breakfast, too. She had *just*, only just, managed.

Something, age-old, very female, took possession of the kitchen, no words needed. Until Bessie said, almost as an accusation,

"You've gone and fallen for another."

"I am afraid so." Really it was an appalling situation. It was difficult enough to manage as it was. That horrible Dutchman, pretending to tell fortunes, had said, three children, life in a city, just enough money. Diana, with her capacity for disregarding the unpleasant, had been curt and disbelieving, had dismissed the whole thing from her mind.

"You want it?"

"No. Not just now. It is extremely . . . inconvenient."

"Well, you don't have to, you know, ma'am. You just say. Where I come from, there's doses; clear you out in a blink. Cost a shilling."

Could squalor, the sordid part of life which Diana had so sedulously avoided, go deeper? To this I am reduced. I could— and curiously this was the first time she had thought of it—I could have married Richard Walford, lived in that big old house, lived in luxury, had a dozen children. It was only a fleeting thought to be sternly dismissed.

"Would it . . . Would it do me any damage, Bessie?"

"Lor' bless you, ma'am, no. No more'n a dose of salts."

Bessie knew; she had lived among prostitutes, would have been one herself had she been a little less positively ugly.

"Very well," Diana said after a pause. "Take a shilling from the jar."

"I'll take fourpence, too. I got fourpence left over from the shopping. Then I can ride. Be quicker like that. You go and have a lay down and forget all about it."

There was a certain amount of comfort to be derived from Bessie's point-blank, commonsense attitude, but not enough to prevent the rising tide of nausea.

"There're the children," Diana said feebly.

"Miss Belle's big enough and old enough to look after herself

and her brother for one morning," Bessie said harshly. Surely to
God! Getting on for six! What hadn't Bessie been doing at that
age, with the threat of Dad's belt always looming?

What Bessie brought back was essentially the same thing that
Caroline had filched from the surgery in order to help Ruth, and
in a way, Mamma and George. Diana had some scruples about
swallowing it; she was an extremely conventional, orthodox young
woman, and apart from conniving with Mamma to keep Lavinia's
shame hidden, she had never said or done anything which lessened her self-esteem. She had worked for pay, which was lowering,
but not shameful. This was, in a way which she would have found
difficult to put into words, but felt very deeply. Something in her
was outraged when at last she raised the glass, tilted it, gulped;
and when the desired effect was brought about, some virtue, some
fortitude seemed to go with the cleansing flow. She'd never been
an easy crier—unlike Caroline; she'd been, in her own way, tough.
She'd faced scrubbing steps in St Anne's Crescent, embroidering
until she was almost blind, living from hand to mouth, being
snubbed by Everard's fine friends, and done all this with dignity
and self-control. So far as she could order her life, it had been orderly—never once, for instance, had she failed to wash her hair on
Friday. Now, helped by Bessie out of what Bessie called a muddle,
something within her collapsed. She cried for the slightest reason,
or for no reason at all.

Even Everard, preoccupied with his own apparent failure, and
knowing nothing of the pregnancy or its termination, was
alarmed. She had not been cut out for or by life trained to be the
wife of a poor man, but within her limits she had always operated
well, always been spruce, tidy, agreeable, a loving wife, a loving
mother. Now for some unknown reason, she had changed, and
one night she gave him a real fright.

He woke from deep sleep and slowly realised that somebody
was moving about in the room; and that Diana was not in bed beside him. He said, "Di!" There was no answer. With some agitation he reached out and lighted the candle. The wavering,
strengthening light showed her standing, in a curiously rigid posture, midway between the foot of the bed and the wardrobe.

"Di, what is it? If you want to go across . . ." That was the
euphemistic term for the water closet, adjoining the bathroom on
the other side of the landing.

Diana said, "I don't know."

"Darling, surely you know better than to go stumbling about in the dark. Here, take this candle."

Diana had never before shown the slightest sign of having been influenced by her schooling; now she turned about and confounded Everard by saying, " 'How far that little candle throws his beams! So shines a good deed in a naughty world.' That, my dear, is a quotation. But don't ask me to explain it. I never could, you know. I could never explain anything, even to Deb or to Everard, or Mamma. It's a very lonely life when you come to think of it."

She stood staring into space, talking to herself.

Everard hopped out of bed, took her by the arm, steered her back towards bed. "Di," he said, "wake up. You're dreaming. I'm here. I'm Everard."

Diana said, "Really. I apologise for any seeming discourtesy, but I did not recognise you immediately. I admit that my sight is not what it was. Quite possibly my memory is failing, too."

He got her back to bed and in the morning she remembered nothing of it. He was quite prepared to talk about it. He said,

"You gave me a fine fright last night."

"How?"

He was cautious. "Getting up and trying to go across in the dark."

"That I am sure I never did. You must have been dreaming."

It was again the day for Bessie to go marketing, and Diana's day for making breakfast, which by this time she could do quite adequately. But she was short of temper. She said to her beloved son, "If you can't eat your egg properly, I shall take it away from you." Melville thereupon burst into tears and Diana cried too.

In his office Everard held his pen poised; Dear Mrs Thorley, after all these years, sounded rather formal, especially when one was about to ask a favour, but Dear Mamma sounded too familiar. Better be on the safe side.

"I have," Mrs Thorley said, "a letter from Everard. He says that London is unusually hot for the time of year and that Diana seems to be a bit under the weather. He wants me to write and invite her to come now."

"Well, why not?"

"No reason at all," Mrs Thorley said. "I just wanted you to know."

For in tiny ways authority had moved over to George, ever since that evening when she had attempted to scold him over his behaviour with Ruth. His talent for enjoying himself, and making others enjoy themselves, was already well-developed; he would seize on any excuse for a party and he liked to have overnight guests; nobody to whom the fondest mother could possibly take exception, and to George's credit it must be said that he was just as charming and attentive to quite old people as to his near contemporaries. The elderly guests were mostly men connected with the Cattle Shows, the Cattle Sales. "Poor old Bennett," George would say, "he'd be far more comfortable here than at the *Hawk in Hand,* and we ought to provide him with a little company." It grieved and puzzled George that Mr van Haagen never took advantage of Gad's hospitality.

Lady Faulkner, once Chloe was safely married, had allowed the sun of her approval to shine upon George again; and Johnny Faulkner was inclined, Mrs Thorley thought, to exploit George and Gad's. Johnny and *his* friends, who rapidly became George's, too, used Gad's as a base from which to shoot, hunt, attend point-to-point meetings and, finally, the races at Newmarket. The Faulkners' place at Stratton Strawless was a bit off the map, and for all their grandeur the Faulkners were pretty hard up. And as George said, "We can afford to entertain a bit." It was true; business was booming. And although in the past, some well-meaning people had warned Mrs Thorley of the danger of spoiling an only son, it was difficult to find any real fault with his behaviour. She had never seen him the worse for drink, for instance (And if it happened, what could I say?). Johnny Faulkner was a year older than George and some of his friends were older than he was. They did get drunk occasionally. George gambled a bit, but never to any great extent, and he was almost invariably lucky. He was not overattentive to the business, but then, why should he be, when she was there to take care of it? One was only young once; let him make the most of it.

"I just wanted you to know," Mrs Thorley said, "in case you had planned anything."

"I never do. Things just happen to me."

Something had happened to Diana; Mrs Thorley saw that in the moment of meeting the train. Everard had simply said that Diana was a bit under the weather, but the poor girl looked ill, pale and thin. She'd had the best figure of them all; where had the pretty curves gone? And she had always been so fastidious, so well turned out. Last summer, Mrs Thorley remembered, Diana's composure had cracked and she'd cried after reading the letter that told her that Everard had decided—without consulting her—to set up on his own. But she had recovered, and letters had been cheerful; all about her nice new house; her nice new neighbours.

Well, let's hope that there's nothing wrong that a good long holiday in the country can't cure. And here I am, shaking like a leaf. Any little thing upsets me nowadays; and I can't take a drink until I get home.

These days she drank a very peculiar mixture, happened upon by sheer accident. Knowing that she would be cut off from supplies for a whole day because she had to attend the newly founded Cattle Breeders' Association, she had prepared herself and poured some whisky into what she thought was an empty bottle of eau de Cologne which happened not to be quite empty. The brew had been quite effective, and ever since she had carried one of the eau de Cologne bottles, in its half nest of wickerwork with her in the gig, but she must resort to it now.

During the drive from Baildon to Gad's, head jerking, hands unsteady, Mrs Thorley came to the conclusion that she worried too much and too easily, for Diana seemed all right. She expressed interest in Caro and her baby, for whom she had made a garment, beautifully smocked. She talked about Deborah and said she blamed Tim. Anybody who couldn't get on with Deb couldn't get on with anybody, Di said, and Mamma agreed. About her own state of health she was reserved, defensive. "I did not feel too well for a day or two. But I was singularly fortunate; one of neighbours employs a nurse, a very nice, willing woman. She took charge."

Di sounded all right, but she looked all wrong.

The children, Mrs Thorley noticed, were extremely well-behaved. Mrs Cresset's nurse stood no nonsense and had a firm belief in the virtue of a good smack on the bottom.

"And what of Deborah, Mamma? You never did give me her address."

"That was her wish, Diana. But she sounds very well and happy. She seems to have found some way of earning money. She did not say in what manner."

"Something to do with horses, no doubt."

"Possibly."

In fact for all who had the time and the inclination to read, Deb's way of making money was plain and certain.

Mr Hammond, who knew his job, had discarded the title THE HIDDEN ROOM as being too revealing, too naïve; but the essence of the title, he had used, pictorially; a locked door with Heaven knew what secrets behind it. The picture chimed perfectly with the new title, SECRET, and the book sold as hot cakes were said to do. Mr Mudie wanted it, Mr Smith wanted it, countless people who bought instead of borrowing books wanted it. It was one of the lucky books, people went about saying: You simply *must* read it! When the mythical Mr Curtis had made his cuts, the book passed one of the tests of the times: Would you like your young sister, your daughter, to read this book? The answer was a resounding Yes! With the valuable addition that men could enjoy it too. It was not pious, or too much concerned with domesticity. It also had the appeal of being almost classless. The lady hidden was an aristocrat, the innkeeper was a man of the middle kind, and there were servants and drovers, even rough soldiers, sympathetically treated, not stock figures, real people. Something for everybody, suspense, romance, solid worth. Twenty pounds for each subsequent impression, Mr Hammond had said, but to Deborah the words had been virtually meaningless since she did not know what an impression was. To her a book was a book; but there was twenty pounds at the end of May—forty in June, sixty in July.

In a curious way Deb never regarded the money as real; to her it was akin to the fairy gold which turned into crumpled leaves when handled. She disposed of her pig on the tit-for-tat basis common in this area; a man came and took away the pig, killed it, allowing her a good joint for roasting and some sausages, and presently she was to have from this or another pig a side of bacon and a ham. She bought another pig. In her fowl run she had some home-reared pullets which would lay in November, and the first fowls she bought; they would be eaten one by one. The garden provided her with potatoes and greenstuff. Even with her rent and rates and Sam's fees paid, she was fully solvent without Mr Hammond's payments.

There were many things she could have done with the money: furnished a comfortable sitting room, bought new clothes, but the kitchen was comfortable and she seemed to have lost her taste for finery. She could look back with a wry smile at the resentment she had felt when Tim told her to take the yellow rose wreath off her hat. The one indulgence she allowed herself concerned books; there was a lending library in Shrewsbury which supplied books by post to people who lived in small towns or the country, so she was no longer starved for reading matter; but without being conscious of conceit, she thought her own book, A HOUSE DIVIDED, more entertaining, and wrote in it diligently. It was completed by August, and once again Mr Hammond regretted that he had no one with whom to share his jubilation. D. Willoughby was that rare bird indeed—a writer capable of taking a hint. No cuts were necessary here. And yet, when he had finished reading and rejoicing over what he recognised as saleability, he was left with a faint unease. The dissension between the Puritan husband and the Royalist wife was just a little too well-portrayed. No open quarrel, no shouting, no blows, just the steady divergence of opinion, eroding what had been a good marriage; it bore some resemblance to the situation which existed between Mr Hammond and his own wife, though in their case no such great issue as a Civil War was involved; it was just that after a few halcyon months they seemed not to agree about anything. It was all here, with a good deal of what Mr Hammond called top-dressing, costume stuff, the ebb and flow of war, man and wife intriguing against one another; and a strangely ironic ending: the son of the marriage—loved by both parents, and the real subject of the dispute—being sent off with money and three good horses to join the Parliamentarian forces, and entrusted, at the same time, with his mother's last trinket, to sell for the King; and the boy riding away to join neither party, intending to buy a ship and turn pirate. Old enough to choose for himself.

It has everything, Mr Hammond thought before sitting down to offer D. Willoughby slightly better terms; down payment the same, but twenty-five pounds for each subsequent impression.

At Gad's, Diana seemed to improve in health; her flesh plumped out, her hair regained some of its lustre, but she had what Mrs Thorley called mental lapses. They went to see Caroline and the baby, and Di presented the smocked dress. Caroline thanked her.

"It is such beautiful work, Di. But then you were always so good with a needle."

"It isn't easy, you know. Take a week, it goes nowhere. Wednesday lunch time is the halfway line, so you must be finished and ready to start on the next. It is difficult, by lamplight, to tell a certain blue from purple, so one lays them out in daylight, and then one forgets. Old men forget and we shall be forgot."

Mamma and Caro exchanged a look, concerned, bewildered.

"Yes," Diana said in that same reasonable, aimable way. "I talk too much. It is confusing for you. I apologise."

Just then Miss Humberstone came in with the tea-tray and Diana seemed to recover from whatever it was. She talked with animation and apparent pleasure about her new house, her new neighbours. They were both left with the impression that they had misunderstood, or, looking at Noel and the dress he was to wear, had missed some vital connecting link.

Two, or perhaps three nights later Mrs Thorley was wrenched away from that comforting thought. She had taken her nightly dose and was drifting into sleep when she was aroused by a noise on the landing. George, she thought with as much anger as she could ever bring to bear upon him. He'd said he would be late and she had told him to come in quietly because of the children. And yet, she realised as her mind cleared, that the noise on the landing was not George's kind of noise. When George came in noisily he took two stairs at a time and tended to hum or whistle.

She relit her candle and holding it went to the door and knew a moment of sheer terror. Something in white, fumbling along in the dark and crying. Lavinia? No, of course not; what rubbish. Diana.

She took her daughter by the arm, noting as Everard had done the unyielding rigidity. She steered her into her own room and said, "My dear, what is it?"

"I don't know. It's lost. Why should you interfere and add to my misery?"

"Darling, I'm your mother. You're dreaming; sleep-walking."

"Why should you accost me? I have nothing valuable."

Caroline at her worst had never wept so copiously or so heartbrokenly.

"Diana, you must wake up! Look at me. I'm your mother."

"I suppose that makes a difference, but I have forgotten what it is. I don't see so well and my memory is failing, too. All a very great pity."

"Lie down," Mrs Thorley said. She pushed Di into the warm bed. "And stop crying. You have nothing to cry about. Whatever it is we'll talk about it in the morning. Sleep now. Sleep. That's right. Let everything go, darling. Sleep."

Diana changed from rigidity to flaccidity and slept. Donning her warm winter dressing-gown, and leaving the door open in case one of the children should cry out in the night, Mrs Thorley lay down alongside, outside the bed, but under the eiderdown. An uneasy, troubled night.

In the morning George, who sought popularity, even with mere children, took Belle and Melville to Baildon to savour the delights of ice cream, and that gave Mrs Thorley an opportunity to talk to Diana. She was less easily deceived than Everard had been and far more persistent.

"I am willing to believe that you remember nothing about it. But surely to goodness you must have wondered why you woke up in my bed, not your own."

"Now I come to think of it, of course I should, but Mel was calling me. I went straight to him, still half asleep. Are you quite sure, Mamma, that you didn't dream it all?"

"I am absolutely positive. My dear, something must be troubling you. It would be far better to bring it into the open and talk about it and see what can be done. Is it money?"

"We still have to be careful; almost tiresomely so. But we are not in want. And Everard's business must improve."

"Is your sight worrying you?"

"My eyesight? No, why do you ask that?"

"Because at Caro's the other day you mentioned a difficulty in distinguishing between two colours. And last night you said you did not see so well as you did. Possibly you need spectacles."

Mrs Thorley for no reason except that she was a good mother had always been concerned about eyesight, considering that Diana might overstrain hers with too much very fine work—so different from plain sewing, and doing her best to prevent Deborah from reading in bed, lying down, so that the candlelight barely illuminated the page.

There the forgotten things and everyday memory did interlock

briefly. Sometimes, working against time on the kimonos, Diana
had, at the end of a long session, been aware of strain on her eyes.

"Oh no," she said. "I see perfectly. I try to avoid too much
close work by lamplight."

Baffled on that trail, Mrs Thorley, like a good, indefatigable
hound, cast about and tried another.

"When you were sleep-walking . . ." That seemed the best way
of putting it, ". . . you seemed to be afraid that you were being
accosted."

"Oh that," Diana said, almost brightly, as though relieved by
the change of subject. "Everybody fears it, if obliged to go out
alone, in certain streets. This you will hardly believe, but quite
recently my maid, Bessie, was in a shortcut, called Brewers' Lane,
and a little girl, Bessie thought her no more than six, came from
an opening and drove one of those iron hoops straight at her, almost knocking her down. And in the resultant confusion the little
girl snatched Bessie's reticule." Diana allowed herself a grim
smile. "Bessie grew up in a poor part of London and carries her reticule purely for show, stuffed with rubbish. Her purse she carried
on a string round her neck."

In her day, during the bad times, Mrs Thorley had lived in
areas where such things had been a daily occurrence, so she was
not unduly shocked and she was not diverted—if that were
Diana's intention. She charged again.

"Last night," she said, "you also talked about your memory
failing."

"It was never good. As you know, Mamma. At school we were
always set pieces from Shakespeare or *Paradise Lost* to learn. I
never could; that is why Miss Hardwicke despised me so much."

A most unsatisfactory conversation. Well, all she could do was
ply Diana with the best of food, see that she rested as much as
possible, and enjoyed her holiday. That included the offer to drive
her about to see old school friends. Barbara Catchpole, for instance, now married with a little girl somewhat older than Melville and a new baby; wouldn't that be a nice thing to do on a
sunny June afternoon?

"I don't particularly want to," Diana said. "And to be truthful,
mothers with new babies are very boring. Every time I see one I
want to cry."

Mrs Thorley missed the significance of that remark. But she
was alerted by something that Diana said a few days later.

"Mamma, if it would not cause you any great inconvenience, I would like to stay a little longer. London is still very hot and Bessie looks after Everard quite adequately. Also he has his Club."

"My dear, you know, you are welcome to stay as long as you like. This is your home."

Was the whole thing another wrecked marriage? Was Diana, both in her ordinary, waking state and during her mental lapses, really running away from a partnership which had become unworkable? Mrs Thorley's own first marriage had been, by ordinary standards, quite unworkable, but she had held on to it; like a bull dog. To the end; the bitter end, when Stephen had shot himself, leaving her cut off, alone with two little girls, Diana and Lavinia; cast adrift in an alien, hostile world.

I never ran away from any situation, she thought proudly, and then her inner, honest mind said: Except through whisky!

Undeniable, she admitted, with just that slight shrug of the shoulders with which, when on a rare occasion she had been outbidden, she had turned away from a sale.

Somehow the thought of Stephen, dead, buried long ago, stayed with her throughout the day. He'd fathered Lavinia, who had been demented and suicidal; and Diana, who seemed to have taken a melancholy turn which might lead . . . No, the idea must not be entertained; something must be done. Much against her wish Mrs Thorley decided to consult Edward. And that decision put her in a quandary; stay sober and face Edward all of a-twitch? Drink enough to steady herself and go in smelling like a distillery, for though the whisky and the eau de Cologne was a deceptive mixture, the whisky scent lasted longer. Well, what of it? she asked herself half-angrily. She wanted Edward's help about Diana, not his verdict on her own behaviour. She was in no way responsible to him, and she preferred to be thought a whisky drinker than a poor shaky old woman.

In order to make her visit look professional she used the surgery entry, and arriving deliberately late, had not long to wait.

Edward listened with attention and sympathy and a growing sense of hopelessness. Really there was very little to go on; a scrap of slightly disjointed talk in Caroline's drawing room, and what sounded like a bit of sleep-walking and a crying fit in the middle of the night. And even with much clearer evidence of mental disturbance there was so little one could do except prescribe a mild sedative, advise a change of air and scene, and the latter palliative

Diana was already having. If there were any specific worry it might be removed, or alleviated.

"Is it just possible," he asked gently, "that you are worrying overmuch?" She was quite steady, but the scent of eau de Cologne had suffered its usual defeat and Edward was reasonably sure that what ailed his mother-in-law, most admirable woman, was not a nervous tic, or a benign tremor, or the dreaded paralysis agitans. She was an alcoholic! There was no condemnation in Edward's conclusion; poor woman, she'd had a hard life, taking on a man's job.

"It may seem so," Mrs Thorley said, speaking with crispness. "But . . . Edward, I have never spoken of this and I am sure that you will regard it as confidential. My first husband, Diana's father, fell into profound melancholy when things went wrong with him, and committed suicide while still in his thirties."

"Oh." He felt even sorrier for her. And then being only human was momentarily glad that Caroline's father had been hearty jovial George Thorley. Contradicting this reflection, he said,

"One must not pay too much attention to such things, you know. At the same time . . . You say when things went wrong with him. Has anything gone wrong with Diana?"

"I can only say that if it has she has not confided in me. Her new house sounds to be a great improvement on her former one and she has nice neighbours, now."

"Do you think she would confide in Caro—if they had a day alone together?"

Mrs Thorley considered and then said, "I think not. All my girls were friendly with one another, but from the first they paired off according to age. If Di was inclined to talk to anyone it would be Deb. And she is out of reach." That was a slightly misleading statement, for Caroline and Lavinia had never been a pair; Lavinia had had no real contact with anyone, until she fell in with those wicked people.

"All the same, we'll give Caro a chance, I think. She has a way with her, you know." Mrs Thorley knew—but it was a way that worked much better with men than with women. "And at the same time I will test Di's eyes."

"She denies that there is anything wrong with them."

"We'll make a game of it. I'll pretend I have some new eye-testing process, I'll test Di's and Caro's and then they can test mine.

It may be at the root of the trouble. A hidden fear of needing spectacles. Most women regard them as disfiguring. And of course any preoccupation is inclined to affect one's memory in other spheres. . . . I'm sure you have no cause for worry."

By this time the smell of whisky was quite strong in the little surgery and Edward longed to add that whisky never cured anything, but he hardly dared. Still, he realised that his mother-in-law was caught in a vicious circle, she drank to cure the shakes, and drinking provoked more shakiness.

Quite abruptly he changed his plans for Noel's future. From the moment when he knew that he had a son he had visualised him as a doctor, taking over the practice which had been in the family for five generations. Now he decided that a surgeon had an easier life with far fewer problems. A surgeon asked himself one question: to operate or not to operate, and if he operated as skilfully as he could, his job was done; the patient recovered or died. Nobody came to a surgeon seeking advice on nervous conditions and mental states or even social problems. And the status of surgeons was rising steadily. In the time of Edward's great-grandfather surgery was despised, not even regarded as a profession; but times had changed, and with the coming of a proper anaesthetic, like chloroform, the age of painless surgery was beginning, operations, hitherto unimaginable would be possible. Noel should be a surgeon.

If eye tests were anything to go by, Diana had nothing to worry about on that score; her sight was fully as good as Caroline's and rather better—unless the girls had bungled things—than Edward's own; he seemed to be the one who might presently need spectacles for reading. And Caro, though warned in advance to try to find out if anything were worrying Diana, drew a blank.

"Naturally," Diana said, "I am not so well-placed as you are, but then Edward was established when you married him. Everard has his way to make. But I have no doubt he will do it."

Their day together did produce something of significance which neither of them recognised.

"As you know," Caroline said, "I never was much of reader, but people who do like books, like them; so this year, when the question of the White Elephant Stall for Friends of the Hospital was being discussed, I suggested having a few books on it; secondhand but not raggy. At sixpence each they sold very well, but old Miss

Riley—do you remember her? She was a great friend of Mrs Spicer, Everard's aunt; definitely senile now and can't tell Easter from Whitsun; she sent this book, a week late. So it was here and one evening, having nothing better to do, I looked into it. It is very odd, in a way it's exactly what we all went through with poor Lavinia."

"You always thought: Poor Lavinia, and used to smuggle her chocolate," Diana said. "I never did. I thought she was a disgrace, and I only undertook to take stuff to the laundry in order to help Mamma."

"The poor man in this book, trying to keep somebody hidden in a secret room, hadn't even that much help," Caro said. "Of course it's all about long ago when things were different. And yet there is a likeness. . . . And it is a good title, don't you think? Secret. That was what it was, for all of us, until she died, wasn't it?"

"I suppose so. And it was horrid. For myself I wouldn't want to read a book that reminded me of it."

As the eldest of the four when they were all girls together, oh, such happy days, the happy, happy days when we were young! Diana had acquired a kind of ascendancy, and a shadow of it remained; nothing to do with position or possessions. (Caro had seen Diana's horrid little house, slept in her cupboard of a spare room. Don't think of that. Bear in mind that Diana would never in a thousand years cuckold Everard, self-absorbed and unsuccessful as he was, as Caroline had cuckolded Edward, quite the best man in the world.)

Yet Caro was aware of the edge of disapproval in Diana's voice and hastily changed the subject.

Diana's holiday, begun in May and extended, with Everard's full approval, into June, just impinged upon the best time for the Newmarket races. By that time George had tired of his role of fond uncle and in his mind applied epithets to the children—little horrors, little beasts—which he was tactful enough not to use in the company of a fond grandmother and a doting mother. Di had never been his favourite of the girls, but by God he felt a bit sorry for her condemned to their company day and night. A day off the chain would, he thought, do her the world of good. Mamma agreed, so he said,

"Di, come with me to the races tomorrow."

"That is very kind of you, George. But, thank you, No."

Too terribly prim and proper, George thought. He disliked having his well-meant gestures rejected.

"Why not? I assure you, Di, a great many ladies attend race meetings nowadays and enjoy themselves very much."

"I shouldn't. Too many people."

George glanced at Mamma, whose head moved, whether in a warning signal or the jerk which came and went he did not know. Since it accorded better with his own inclination he took it as a negation and said no more.

Next day luck was definitely good, in every way; he'd backed two rank outsiders who simply strolled home; and he came back to Gad's by himself, so there was no witness to a most embarrassing and distressing scene.

Gad's though prosperous was not yet one of those places where one simply dismounted and left one's horse to somebody else's care. But Willy always left a full bucket and a full manger, and rubbing down could wait until the morning. So it was still the last of the lingering dusk when George opened the back door and saw something, white, a figure, moving about in the kitchen.

He had the unshakable nerve of somebody who had never been frightened and whose imagination had a limited scope. He did not think, as in a similar situation Mrs Thorley had thought— Lavinia! for he knew nothing about Lavinia except that she had gone to India, years ago, and died there. And that on the attic floor there was a locked room which had been her studio and was her memorial—his own suggestion—because she had no grave in England. So a white-clad figure roused no superstitious feeling in him. He said,

"What are you doing, fumbling about in the dark?" At the same time he lit the candle which awaited his entry and could narrow down the inquiry which could have applied to any one of the four women in the house.

"Di! What are you doing, fumbling about in the dark?"

"What right have to speak to me in that tone of voice? I know you *employ* me, but civility costs nothing. However, since you ask, I will tell you. I have lost something. I no longer see very well and my memory is going and I need help."

George had somewhere heard about people who walked in their sleep and performed incredible feats such as climbing out of windows and scrambling over roofs, things they could not have done while awake. But did sleep-walkers go about with their eyes open?

He'd never bothered to ask. Di's eyes were wide open. And although what she said had no meaning, sounded daft, that part of his nature which was kindly and gallant made him say,

"What have you lost, Di? Tell me, and I'll help you look."

"I don't know. I can no longer remember. What I *do* know is that if this goes on much longer I shall not see to thread a needle. Of *course* money is important," she said, as though somebody had said that it was not. "But what is the use of it when you have lost everything else? And can't see? Or remember?" She began to cry. George walked towards her and took her by the upper arm and was conscious as both Everard and Mrs Thorley had been of the rigidity. But he pushed her towards the rocking chair in which Jenny spent her leisure time and said,

"There, have a good cry. I'll make a cup of tea."

By all but country standards it was still early; the kettle at the back of the stove soon boiled. George, moving a bit clumsily about, in familiar surroundings, but with an unfamiliar purpose, got together what was needed, at the same time keeping an eye on Diana, who sat stiffly in the chair, crying and letting the tears run down unstaunched so that the front and the lap of her white nightdress turned grey with the dampness. Hers was not the posture of one having a good cry which would bring relief.

He carried the steaming cup towards her and said awkwardly,

"Here, Di. Drink this and try to pull yourself together."

"I daren't. It's poison! Oh, I know all the arguments. It may not damage me physically. What about my mind?"

George knew several lurid tales of husbands who had poisoned their wives, or wives who had poisoned their husbands. Di *had* looked very ill when she arrived at Gad's, and had postponed her return to London. It seemed completely absurd to suspect that stiff, self-righteous Everard of the slightest misdoing; but then, weren't they just the ones who got away with murder? And didn't it look a bit sinister that Everard had not shared Di's holiday either last year, or this? Last year perhaps he couldn't help it, but this year he was his own master.

"It's a cup of tea, Di. I just made it. It'll do you good."

She stopped crying as suddenly as she had begun and reached for the cup and saucer.

"Thank you. It is very kind. As a matter of fact Mr Burton has just informed me that he has no further work for me. I must not allow my dismay to show. I shall walk through Hawksley's as though I owned it."

She drank her tea and George drank his. His good luck had been properly celebrated with champagne, a drink that always left him thirsty.

He was completely bewildered; not even sure if she were asleep or awake. His instincts were kindly, his nature impatient.

"Look here, Di, I don't know what you're talking about. Don't go rambling on. Tell me what's the matter and I'll see what I can do."

"I don't know. I lose things. And I forget and I can't see very well."

"What do you mean talking about poison?"

"Oh, it undoubtedly *was*. I was extremely indisposed for several days. That was why . . . But there you are; my memory is not reliable."

The cup of tea having failed, all George could think of was bed.

"Come along, Di. Let's get to bed. You'll feel better in the morning." He'd feel better, too, when he'd had a talk with Mamma.

In fact he felt rather worse for it was almost impossible to associate Diana calmly supervising her children's breakfast, eating her own, with the distracted, rambling creature of the previous evening.

"Honestly, George, I know little more than you do. Except that Edward has assured me that Diana's sight is perfectly good, and that in a whole day, alone with Caroline, she had mentioned no trouble or problem."

"Last night, just for a moment, she seemed to think that somebody had tried to poison her. Do you think that Everard could possibly . . . ?"

"No, I do not. And for a very simple reason. Men who intend to poison their wives don't—after one abortive attempt—send them home to recuperate. It wouldn't make sense."

George allowed himself to laugh at his own absurdity.

"Mamma, you are my absolutely favourite woman. The only logical woman I know."

"And your experience is so wide?" She said that lightly, but almost instantly reverted to seriousness. "All the same, we cannot blind ourselves to the fact that something—something which she will not admit, even to herself, is wrong with Di. I've tried to talk to her, so has Caro. Nothing useful emerged. Apparently *you* got no sense out of her last night."

"Wait a bit. Of course, I see your reasoning about poison—that was silly of me, but last night she talked about work; about a Mr Burton having no more work for her and walking out of Hawksley's as though she owned it . . . I couldn't make head or tail of it but it was something she felt deeply. Does it make sense to you?"

"Perhaps." In her good days Mrs Thorley had had no need to walk through Hawksley's as though she owned it; she had more than owned it, being a customer with ready money in her hand.

In the good days that she remembered Hawksley's had employed a few sedate women, all in black, all wearing black satin aprons, in some departments, and it had also had dressmaking and millinery rooms. Was it possible that Diana had sought employment there, perhaps overstrained her eyes by too much close work; perhaps lost something, or forgotten something, made a mistake in matching two colours, and been given what was vulgarly called the sack? Diana, so proud, so fastidious, so good with her needle. Mrs Thorley could imagine the shock and humiliation. Quite enough to upset her mind.

"It is possible, my dear, that you were given some kind of clue. I shall think about it. I'm sure she'd be better if whatever it is were brought into the open."

"If it's anything to do with money, we could help her, couldn't we?" In George's simple philosophy the very word work implied penury. He'd never really worked, not even during his lessons with old Mr Spicer, and where the farm and the herd were concerned he did exactly what suited him to do; showing off, being charming, leaving all the real work to Mamma.

"I offered help a year ago, but Deborah had forestalled me . . . But then of course Deborah's own circumstances changed."

It was rather like a mist on an autumn morning, slowly clearing, allowing glimpses of solid shapes to emerge.

"I shouldn't like any sister of mine to be short of money," George said. And despite everything Mrs Thorley felt a small glow of satisfaction. She had made, out of discordant elements, a family. And in a way held it together.

Knowing how secretive Diana could be, Mrs Thorley made a direct attack, but speaking as casually as though mentioning the weather.

"'What work exactly did you do for Mr Burton at Hawksley's, my dear?"

For a second or two Mrs Thorley felt that she had made yet another wrong step. Diana looked as though someone had struck her a heavy blow—from behind. Then she said violently,

"Who told you? I never told anyone. I never even used my own name. Even Everard didn't know. Sometimes I had to work late and he'd ask what I was doing. Not really interested. And I'd say making something for the children, or embroidering a cushion. Something like that. . . . *Who told you?* Who could possibly *know?*"

Better not bring George into this.

"When you walk in your sleep, you talk, too. I am sure it must have been a very painful experience for you. And I am sure it would be better to talk about it—when you are awake. Come along, tell me everything."

"Mamma, you cannot imagine and I cannot possibly describe the utter humiliation. Taking money from Deb was bad enough, but I did it. I was so sure that once Everard was started on his own, I could repay. And in the meantime—it all takes so long—I thought I should *do* something. So I tried, and I failed. Even Mr Burton said he'd never seen embroidery like mine. But there is no longer a demand for it. . . . And since we are having such a frank talk, I may as well tell you. . . . I very much doubt whether Everard's fine friends have stood by him as they should. He does not discuss business with me, but I should have known. If any one of them had entrusted him with a real piece of legal work he'd have come home so uplifted. He never has. They're all false, but he can't see it. I knew from the start. Hateful people. And there is poor Everard, so deluded. He considers it a privilege to belong to Brinkley's Club; at ten guineas a year! Sometimes I *despair.*"

"That is the one thing you must never do, Diana. I can't remember who said it, or if I read it, but it is true. Despair is the ultimate sin. And I don't mean that in a religious way; I mean that once you despair you're done for. And your situation is not so hopeless, my dear." She had been in worse herself, but harking back was a futile exercise. "We must take a good cool look and consider what we can do. Anything but despair, my dear."

Yes; take a drink, take to chicanery, tell lies, cheat—all active, living things, whereas despair was dead. The thought of death linked with what George had said about poisoning. Self-inflicted? In a moment of despair? Ignore that for the moment; concentrate upon the general situation. Take marriage first. Diana had certainly made a love-match, but Mrs Thorley knew from her own experience that that was no guarantee of a happy marriage. Avoiding the use of the word love, she said,

"You and Everard get along well together, do you not?"

With some fervour in her voice, and deliberately ignoring that part of marriage which she did not find enjoyable, Diana said,

"Oh yes! We never quarrel. Of course I see less of him now and he is often preoccupied. But as you know it was his idea that I should take my holiday early—and indeed it was he who suggested prolonging it. As I was only too glad to do."

So far, so good.

"And you have two adorable children."

Perhaps a slight exaggeration; Belle was extremely pretty and could be engaging when she chose, but she had a wilful, spiteful streak and Mel was querulous, inclined to start every sentence with "I want," or "I don't want," and roaring loudly if his will were crossed.

"Yes. But to be honest, London is not a good place for children. I wish with all my heart that we had stayed in Baildon. That move was a mistake, I knew it at the time; and every subsequent one has been worse."

That was an extreme statement, coming from Diana, never a girl to face unpleasant truths; the girl who had prepared herself for marriage by making dainty tablecloths. But then Deborah, so far more sensible, who had set about learning to cook, had fared worse. And look at Caroline!

Still it seemed to Mrs Thorley's practical mind that there was nothing much about Diana's dilemma that a steady two pounds a week couldn't alleviate. About that she must talk to George, for although she had been left in complete control until George attained the age of eighteen—still a year to go—she had never regarded herself as more than a trustee.

"We'll see what can be done," she said. Then she remembered

that one thing had not been mentioned. "Diana, when you feel out of sorts and depressed, do you buy any patent medicines?"

Could that horrible, but effective brew be called by that name? And how did Mamma know? When I wander in my mind how *much* do I say?

"What makes you ask that?"

"In one of your somnambulist states you used the word poison."

"No more than that?" All Diana's defences were up; for if Mamma *knew* about that there would be certain disapproval. Mamma might in many ways be unconventional but she was a monument of moral rectitude.

"Just the one word," said Mrs Thorley, who in fact had not heard it.

"Then perhaps I was talking about some fish. Bessie goes some distance to shop because ours is an expensive area. In the hot weather . . . Nobody else was affected, I was poisoned. Hideously indisposed for two days. . . ."

"Why, of course we can manage it," George said. "What's two pounds a week?"

About what most working men earned in a fortnight; exactly the amount that Diana had earned, sewing herself blind during a period of employment which, fortunately for her, had been brief. Almost three times as much as Mrs Thorley had managed to scratch together in Leicester, piano lessons at sixpence a time, designs for dresses, designs for china, letting the spare room.

"I can make that much any afternoon at the races, or in an evening with cards," George said.

"It would be most unwise to look upon such entertainments as a source of income, George," Mrs Thorley said, not too sternly, for George's generosity and good will were disarming. And in fact George was anxious to help Diana, poor girl, and to please Mamma because he wanted Mamma's approval for what he meant to undertake in the coming autumn—amateur steeplechasing. It was not in her power to stop him taking up this pursuit, but if she protested and grumbled life at Gad's would not be very happy, and misery anywhere, but particularly at home, was one thing that George wished to avoid. Mrs Thorley recognised in her son many of the qualities of his father, the open-handedness, the

424   THE HAUNTING OF GAD'S HALL

generosity of spirit which had made him accept Diana and Lavinia
as his own—an action which she had reciprocated by accepting
Deborah and Caroline as her own. Then there was George, their
own. She'd often said in the early days that if she had only one
apple she would divide it fairly amongst the girls. Quartering a
thing was dead-easy; once George was born such strict material
impartiality had failed her. If she had but one apple, half would
be George's, the other half fairly quartered.

"It may not be for long, George. Just until Everard finds his
feet."

Everard was about to find his feet in a most unexpected way.

It was August, Brinkley's and indeed all the fashionable part of
London was deserted. But Everard had worked out the economics
of belonging to a club; a glass of sherry—really good sherry—was
threepence a glass cheaper there than in any ordinary public
drinking place and twopence a glass cheaper than a much inferior
beverage at home. That was one slight bonus which the ten-
guinea subscription conferred.

Di was back home, seemingly fully restored in health and saying rather smugly that Mamma had promised her two pounds a
week to help out for a time. Alison was lost to him—that was
nothing new; every one of their encounters had left him with the
feeling of never more, a feeling which had served to keep a sharp
edge on appetite, since every parting seemed to be the last, every
reunion seemed to be the first. But now she had gone forever,
married to a self-exiled Hungarian, Prince Rakoczy, who had chosen to live in the South of France, where he had built himself a
kind of fairy-tale palace overlooking the Mediterranean midway
between Nice and Monaco. She'd had her fling, Everard Spicer
only one of her many lovers, and the idea of being a Princess appealed to her. Also, as she explained to Everard, even the will
which he had so fortunately *discovered* amongst Mr MacFarlane's
muddled papers did not make *her* very rich. That grim, uncomfortable castle at Lumsleydale, with its eight hundred unprofitable
acres, all entailed, must be kept up, out of the rents derived from
the other Lumsley property. Lumsley House in Piccadilly was also
very expensive to maintain. "But, darling, I shall miss you, quite
terribly."

"I shall miss you, too," Everard said, with great truth.

But it was not of Alison nor of Diana that he was thinking as he sat, drinking his subsidised sherry on that August evening. He was thinking, very glumly, about his failure in life. Frustrated in Baildon, frustrated with Binder, Upton and Smith, and now frustrated when out on his own. *Why?* He knew that he was a very good lawyer, but Goddamn it, how could you be a good lawyer with no practice? It was like asking a chef to show his skill with nothing to cook.

The stranger approached with the curiously light and quiet step that went, incongruously, with bulk and weight. Making straight for him. That was the worst of the Club in the off season; only the dregs remained, lonely men who just wanted somebody to talk to.

Like me? No! I don't want anybody to talk to, or anybody to talk to me.

"Mr Spicer?"

"Yes," Everard said in the manner which so many people found discouraging. There was less than half an inch of sherry left in his glass. One gulp and then he could say he must be going.

"Lord Westward said I might find you here."

Instantly Everard was all attention and he said, "Yes" again, but with a different intonation.

"My name's Crawford. Not that that'll mean anything to you."

"That rather depends." Everard produced his most charming smile and manner. "Mr Ralph Crawford? Then of course I have heard of you. How do you do. May I offer you a drink?" Everard wondered about saying *sir*; a term of courtesy used by any man to any other man obviously his superior in rank, or his senior in age. Oddly enough, between equals it was used as a challenge: Sir, you are a liar! Mr Crawford was perhaps a trifle young to relish being called sir by Everard.

"Thank you. Not sherry," Mr Crawford said. "Livery stuff. I'll have whisky."

Mr Crawford was not exactly a gentleman; he was a very astute businessman. Everard recognised his name because he had figured largely in some of the many inquiries which had taken place following the Mutiny in India. The East India Company, which had begun just over two hundred and fifty years earlier as a mere combination of merchants for purposes of trade, had grown into a powerful oligarchy which ruled all but the few remaining native states of India, raising its own army, waging its own wars, and employing a vast number of administrators. It had, in its time, been self-critical, Robert Clive and Warren Hastings, both servants of the Company, had been obliged to defend themselves against charges of misrule and extortion. Now the whole future of India, how and by whom it should be ruled, was under discussion. Ralph Crawford, who had gone out as a servant of the Company when he was sixteen, had spent twenty-four years in India, built up his own business and prospered by *strictly legitimate means*, which could not always be said of similarly successful men, had attained some fame as a kind of specialist on the subject. He was knowledgeable, honest, seemed to be open-minded, and was capable of making a pithy retort to criticism. Amongst other things he owned jute mills near Calcutta, and when a member of the House of Lords, noted for his humanitarian leanings, made a remark, well-intentioned, but ill-informed about wages and conditions in such places, Mr Crawford had said, "My Lord, I'll make you a fair offer. Let you and me go and work, as ordinary workmen in a Manchester cotton mill, and then go alongside and work the same way in any one of my jute mills and then you decide which you like best." The challenge, though not accepted, gained him the nickname of Honest Offer Crawford.

And it was an honest offer which on this glowering August evening he made to Everard. There was, he said, a lot of reshuffling to be done in India, and that means a lot of legal business. There'll be a need for well-qualified, honest men. And they're scarce." He gave Everard one of his straight honest-offer looks and said, "Let's admit it—apart from the Army, the best in the world, they proved that in the Crimea, India has been ill-served on the professional side. All too often, and I speak from experience, we've had lawyers and doctors who'd failed in some way, or done something they'd be unfrocked for if they'd stayed in England. But there you are, in areas as big as England and Wales put together, a bad doctor is better than no doctor, a bad lawyer better than none. That's got to be altered."

He talked and Everard listened. Cautious, as was his way.

"Yes," Honest Offer Crawford said, "you have a wife and two children. You must talk it over. Bear in mind that India is safe now. The Mutiny was just a boil that was bound to burst. It burst and it's over and done with. Maybe the climate isn't healthy for the young. Personally, I think a bit too much has been made of that. People who can't afford to send their children home as they call it, keep them there and a surprising number survive. In any case, if you decide to accept, you could well afford to send your wife into the hills during the hot weather, and your children home to be educated. Give it a week," Mr Crawford said. In his opinion that was a fair offer; caution, up to a point, was a virtue, but any man who needed more than a week in order to decide a vital issue wasn't worth bothering about.

Diana recoiled from the idea of going to India, just as she had recoiled from coming to London, and from the idea of Everard setting up on his own. One couldn't possibly say it, but the fact was that every move that so far Everard had made had been in the wrong direction.

"It needs thinking over," she said. Everard agreed, but she knew, just by the look of him, that the offer had restored his self-esteem and that he would take it. She also knew that if she could produce any good argument against going herself, with Belle and Melville, she would use it.

Only two doors away was Mrs Pembroke, who had spent many years in India and had painted the bungalow in Simla, where she had spent the hot weather. Mrs Pembroke was dead against it.

"There were certain advantages," she admitted, "but they were dearly bought. I do not wish to discourage you, but the filth . . . I soon learned not to go near my kitchen. This you may find hard to believe, but it is the truth. Before I had learned better, I did visit my kitchen—they're set slightly apart—and there was my cook boy straining soup through one of Algie's old socks! That and a few other things with which I will not disgust you taught me to avoid the kitchen. In order to eat enough to keep oneself alive it was necessary to turn a blind eye. That I eventually managed. One can shut one's mind, to a certain extent . . ."

"My chief concern is the children," Diana said, using her old trick of ignoring the unpleasant.

"I had three," Mrs Pembroke said. "They all died."

She could have been speaking about plants which had failed to take root and flourish. It was an old grief, healed over, but under the scar enough feeling was left to make her advise very strongly that even if Mrs Spicer felt impelled to accompany her husband, she should not take the children with her. "It is a matter of hygiene," she said. She had often wondered how it was that people thought and spoke nostalgically of the scent of the East, meaning spices and jasmin; the scent she remembered most clearly was that of human ordure. But naturally she would not say that to young Mrs Spicer.

Mr Crawford had said that it was a thing to talk over, yet after the first opening of the subject, four days passed without further mention. Diana said it was something that must be thought over, and both she and Everard were thinking. Everard had in fact gone rather farther and talked to Mr Hammond of Hammond and Curtis and learned with delight and relief that the publisher was not only willing but eager to take over his lease. Hammond and Curtis needed more office space, for just as there was the law of diminishing returns, so there was what could only be called the snowballing effect. Several writers with well-known names had noted what Hammond and Curtis had done for D. Willoughby, an absolute newcomer; what might not so progressive a firm do for them?

There was a curious superstition about pork: it was supposed to be more liable than any other meat to go off in hot weather, so there was a rough-and-ready rule about not buying it when there was not an R in the month. What was regarded as uneatable during the last week of August was perfectly all right during the first week of September, and Bessie was glad, for pork was the cheapest of meats.

The dish was presented attractively; a mound of well-mashed potatoes, with the three chops—one for the mistress, two for the master, propped against it and the whole edifice surrounded by apple sauce. Everard helped Diana, then himself. He'd taken and enjoyed several mouthfuls before he realised that she had not lifted knife or fork and was just sitting there, stiff and staring.

"Di."

"I didn't know," she said. "Everything has been so different. So wrong! What seest thou in the dark backward and abysm of time? I always thought that such a silly question. Now I know. You do not, of course, and everybody will say—Another broken marriage! What a doomed family. Quite untrue. And if you are so very deaf you should get an ear trumpet! I was brought up not to shout. But I can. Listen then. Mine is not a broken marriage. We just did not have enough money. That is the nub of the matter. In ordinary circumstances I should have welcomed another baby, but that was impossible. And it is quite possible—as I have proved—to love somebody without all this bed and baby business. And scrubbing steps! What I am trying to say is that I cannot think. Think! Think! As though I hadn't enough to think about with my eyesight failing and my memory going? Yes, I suppose I shall end, blind and idiotic, in some place that Deb said Lavinia should go to. All a very great pity."

There was nothing that Everard could do except coax her upstairs and into bed. Out of the jumble one thing had been made absolutely plain to him: she was not a woman who could be safely taken to India—and he was now absolutely determined to go there; to cast off all the failures and begin again.

"Not here," George said. "I mean not in this house, as a permanency. The children would drive us all mad; and Di is so fussy, always plumping up cushions and emptying ash-trays. Besides, did you know—I only heard the other day—the Chinese write in pictures and their picture-word for unhappiness is two women under the same roof? It wouldn't work, Mamma. And, if as she says she is sure of six pounds a week, she is no longer in *need*. Baildon would be ideal for her. That little . . ." Mind your language! ". . . Belle is just about ready for Miss Hardwicke's, and Mel . . . well, if Everard fails again, Mel can go to the Grammar School—or share lessons with Caro's Noel, or something. Yes, Baildon would be best. Of course she's welcome to come here, but not to stay forever. It wouldn't suit anybody."

"I think you are right. I must go house-hunting again."

"Why you? Di can do her own house-hunting, I should think."

"Of course. I shall just make a few preliminary inquiries. I suppose it is too much to hope that there would again be a house vacant in Friars' Lane. It would be so nice for the girls to be next door to each other again. Poor Di seemed so out of touch with everybody else when last she stayed here."

"It'll be different now that she has a steady income." George's view of money was very variable; he always exaggerated his gains and minimised his losses; if a bet or a game won him six pounds he felt rich and justified in spending ten; the loss of the same amount was a mere flea-bite. Still . . . "Everard must have got himself a substantial job at last, to be able to spare her so much."

"I believe all posts in India are highly paid because of the unhealthy climate. Everard should insure his life."

George took the chance to twist the conversation.

"I'll insure mine, Mamma, before I start riding point-to-points. I'll do it for some fantastic sum, so that if I break my neck you'll never have to lift a finger again."

Her head jerked several times in rapid succession. "Don't joke about such things, George, please."

"Don't count on, though. My neck's good for another sixty years. Old van Haagen made me a cast-iron promise."

For some time after her return to Baildon—and by some stupendous coincidence to Friars' Lane, in the house immediately opposite the one she had formerly occupied—Diana suffered recurrent pangs of guilt because she felt so extremely happy. Without Everard! Anybody would think she hadn't loved him! Sometimes she would deliberately induce a feeling of the kind of melancholy which she *ought* to be feeling, by standing at the window of her present house and looking across at the one in which she had begun her married life; sometimes the feeling would take her unawares, generally at the sight of something associated with Everard; the shabby old chair which he bought cheaply when they moved to Somerton Road and he had room for a study; the few clothes which he had left behind and of which she could not bring herself to dispose. At such moments she felt genuinely bereft. The rest of the time she felt happy and free and secure and would salve the guilt by saying how much she missed him, how she felt almost widowed, how worried she was about him.

In fact it was far easier now to be in love with Everard, almost in the old way, when they were just engaged, than it had been to love him when he was present, needing to be fed, inclined to be glum, and sharing her bed.

The house she now occupied, though at the front the mirror-image of its neighbours, had been enlarged by an extension on the garden side, a ground-floor room that could have been designed for children, and a bathroom above it. And for all the sentiment that Diana might feel about Everard's old chair it had no place in her dainty drawing room, it was relegated to the children's room.

Bessie, who naturally had come with her adored mistress, made no secret of her happiness. Far less work in this more manageable house, the High Street barely round the corner and the wonderful market, better even than Soho, twice a week. The prices never ceased to astonish Bessie; nor did the placid, law-abiding atmosphere. No need here to walk warily, or carry your money in a purse on a string around your neck. And here, in this happy place, a lot of things were free; Madam and her sister, Mrs Taylor, often drove out to their old home and came back laden with vegetables, with eggs and cream. And Madam's brother, quite the most beautiful young man Bessie had ever seen, looked in from time to time, always with gifts; two pheasants, their heads tied together; partridges; a hare. Bessie, though inexperienced in such matters, never faltered. If indeed somebody had come to Friars' Lane with a dead lion and said it was edible meat, Bessie would have dealt with it.

With Diana so happily settled, and Caroline settled, if not quite so happily, and George, so far from breaking his neck riding triumphantly and winning several prizes, Mrs Thorley, rather like a clucking old hen rounding up her chicks, often thought of Deborah, not her daughter. But, after George, the son who must take precedence in her affection, the best beloved.

She wrote: "Deb dear, if ever you have the slightest need of money, do let me know. I was prepared to help Diana, but she is well-placed now and needs no assistance. . . ."

Deb wrote back a very grateful letter, but denied that she needed help. "In fact, dearest Mamma, I seem to have hit upon a curious way of making money. If ever you or George or anybody should need some, just let me know."

It was probably, Mrs Thorley thought, something to do with horses.

There were times, well-known to Mr Hammond, when a new book by the same author knocked the former one into oblivion. It was not so with D. Willoughby. Everybody who read A HOUSE DIVIDED—and that meant everybody who could read, wanted to read, or reread SECRET. Both books were selling in America—not in pirated editions; and there were translations. A good story, as Mr Hammond had always known, was a good story the world over. And of all the authors he had ever dealt with D. Willoughby was the least troublesome. She never came to London, demanding to be entertained or feted; she never interfered; once the manuscript was in his hands, it was his. In return he respected her privacy and hoped with great fervour that the two books might not prove to be just a flash in the pan. Oh no. Almost as

soon as A House Divided was under way, D. Willoughby wrote
that she was busy with A Woman Alone. To a large extent this
was Mrs Thorley's story, suitably disguised; the woman in the
story had not been left alone to deal with a cattle herd in Suffolk,
but with a sheep range in the Cotswolds, and with a family far
more bothersome than that at Gad's had ever been.

Because she could lose herself so thoroughly in the book she
was writing or reading Deborah was seldom aware of being lonely.
She shied away from what social contact was offered by the few
people who from a sense of duty or from curiosity did call upon
her. The standards of social behaviour in the little town were not
high and nobody was particularly eager to cultivate the acquaintance of a woman so poor that she had not even the pretence of a parlour and who wore a print dress like a servant's, attended neither church nor chapel, was in fact rather queer.

Presently there was one person in Abbey Norton who could
have told people—except for a code of behaviour every whit as
strict as a priest's, that Mrs Willoughby was not at all poor, and
that was the manager of the bank. He had a sincere regard for
money in a curiously abstract way, he liked it to be used to advantage, deployed, used to make more money, and when Mrs
Willoughby's account stood at just under two thousand pounds,
dead money, idle money, to an extent wasted money, he became
quite perturbed. Face to face—at his own request, with this queer
client who had once had so little and then suddenly had so much,
he adopted a benevolent, fatherly attitude, directed, not at the
young woman herself, but at that accumulating money.

"Forgive me for speaking personally, Mrs Willoughby, but I understand that you are a widow? Then you have no husband to advise you."

"I understand about money. At least—what did Mr Micawber
say? 'Annual income twenty pounds, expenditure nineteen six, result happiness. Annual income twenty pounds, expenditure twenty
pounds and sixpence, result misery.' "

"Mr Micawber is your financial adviser?"

His queer customer disconcerted him by bursting into hearty
laughter.

"No, a man in a book, who did not take his own advice. I did,
it was so sound."

But already her mind was fitting this delicious conversation into
A Woman Alone. What a lovely bit of light relief. She was so

preoccupied that she gave the earnest man the minimum of attention as he talked about the virtue of investment, the magic of five
per cent. At the end of it she said, "Well, thank you. It was kind
of you to bother. But I think I'll leave it. It's safe where it is. And
I may have more." She gave him her sudden, entrancing smile
and hurried home to incorporate this nugget of real life into her
story.

What she missed most of all were horses. Never mind. In her
imagination she owned them, rode them, went hunting, enjoyed
that intoxicating moment when the horse, trained over false
fences, rising inch by inch, gathered itself together and took a real
fence, a real ditch. In each of her books she managed to introduce
a number of horses and at least one hunting scene.

Sam did not lack for company; he made friends easily, and even
when she was obliged to be parsimonious in other ways Deborah
provided lavish teas. The empty rooms at Stone House were also
an attraction, lending themselves to a number of games imprac-
ticable in a well-furnished home. Sam's choice of a favourite
friend, a real bosom pal, was surprising, unless one took seriously
the attraction of opposites. Sam was big for his age, inclined to be
noisy, intelligent enough but far from studious; Robbie Duff was
small, frail-looking, bespectacled and very studious indeed. His father had a small-holding—Deb judged it not to be very prosperous—rather more than a mile further out from Abbey Norton
than Stone House was, and he had no pony. He had little spare
time either, for his father shared Tim Bridges' belief that the
young should make themselves useful. It was a red-letter day in
Sam's life when Duff could be spared to spend a Saturday afternoon with him and partake of one of Deborah's substantial teas.
And yet those visits were very quiet and dull, with no wild romps
in the empty part of the house. After tea, out came the homework, followed, if time allowed, by some kind of paper game, or
dominoes. It was a curious friendship, but Deborah approved of
it. Duff—the use of Christian names was discouraged at the
Grammar School—had, Deborah thought good influence on Sam,
bringing out his better side, a kind of paternalism that had no
smack of patronage about it.

Like most Thorleys, Sam grew fast and as he outgrew his
clothes he invariably suggested handing them on to Duff.
"They're very poor, you know."

Duff fell into the habit of calling for Sam on the way into

school, and Deborah fell into the habit of giving Duff a supplementary breakfast.

"Plenty of time," Sam said, "if we ride and tie." That meant that Duff rode the pony most of the time and Sam ran alongside.

When Deborah began to earn money and was almost certain of earning more, she wanted Sam to have some better mount than the one only just saved from the knacker's yard and she suggested buying Sam a new, bigger, more lively pony and giving the old one to Duff. Then all Sam's mixed heritage came together for once and he said,

"I don't think it would do. Mr Duff wouldn't feed him properly, unless he could drag a plough. No, let poor old Merry live his last days in peace in the paddock."

It could have been Tim speaking; or herself.

Is this real, or am I dreaming again? Diana asked herself when Mrs Gordon, invited to a dainty tea, broke down and wept. Diana had always suspected Mrs Gordon as the power behind the scenes which had prevented Everard being taken into partnership with Gordon and Son and thus being the cause of the London exile and all the misery. Mrs Gordon had always been jealous on her son's behalf, thinking the world of James, and she had looked forward to telling Mrs Gordon that at last Everard had attained his proper level. But before she could bring the conversation round in a proper polite fashion, Mrs Gordon, that iron woman, was crying.

"When I think of all the opportunities . . . and then to decide on that *dreadful* girl. I suppose you knew. Everybody knew except me."

Diana remembered an evening, years and years before, when, in the house just across the way, she had tried to please Mr and Mrs Gordon by inviting them and James and Phoebe Mayhew, a most suitable match, and Caro had said that nothing would result because James was infatuated with a girl in a tobacconist's shop. The evening had, in fact, been a disaster. And it was so long ago that Diana could truthfully say,

"At least James has not made a *hasty* decision."

"He was waiting for me to die," Mrs Gordon said. "James knew I should *never* agree. Never accept her, and he knew that my husband has always been guided by me. Now, because I didn't die, even pneumonia couldn't kill me. But I think this will! All that dreadful red hair—dyed, of course. And seeing one's son make such a fool of himself, picking up other men's leavings! Forgive me, such a coarse thing to say, but it is true!"

Mrs Gordon had chosen the wrong confidante. By breaking down and behaving in such an extraordinary way she had robbed Diana of her triumph, which would have been to tell Mrs Gordon how extremely well Everard was doing in India, where, in his own words, a really qualified lawyer was as important, and perhaps slightly more powerful, than a judge was in England. Diana felt no pity; in fact during the whole of life the only person for whom she had felt pity was herself. Naturally she behaved correctly, fetched a clean dry handkerchief when Mrs Gordon's had reached saturation point, emptied the neglected cup of tea into the slop basin and poured a fresh one and made all the correct little remarks—Don't fret too much; Things may turn out better than you think. . . .

As Noel grew out of little babyhood to toddler, it sometimes seemed extraordinary to Caroline that his likeness to Freddy should pass unnoticed. It showed particularly when he was pleased or displeased. When he smiled—and he was a ready smiler—his upper lip lifted so that there was a crease, like a half-moon under his nose; when he was displeased and had what Nurse Rose called a fit of the sulks, his lower lip protruded. Nurse Rose warned him about making ugly faces. "One day when you have an ugly face on you, the wind will change and you'll have that ugly face forever."

Caroline discounted the fact that Freddy had made a far less deep impression upon other people than he had upon her. To most people he was now only a name. And the terrible thing—or perhaps the happy thing—was that even in her memory he was fading, might have faded altogether except for Noel.

Nobody brought up by Mrs Thorley was likely to become a religious maniac. But there was in Caroline the kind of impulsiveness which in other circumstances might have made her when Freddy married Poor Susan fling herself into a convent, and regret the action immediately.

Every decent person attended Morning Service on Sunday morning, and the Taylors were no exception. In the rather clinical, middle-of-the-road church of St Mary's, Caroline's petition was fervent enough to stand out.

"Oh God. I owe Edward a baby. Please give me a baby. I don't deserve anything, but Edward does."

Whatever the power was that ordered such things was kind, and when Noel was two and a half, Caroline was pregnant again.

"I do hope it will be a girl," Caro said to Diana. "Edward would absolutely dote on a girl."

"He dotes on Noel," Diana said.

"I know. But this would be different."

What there had once been of jealousy between them, Caroline envying Diana because she had married for love, Diana envying Caroline because she was comparatively rich, had died down. A small spark shot up at that moment, as Diana remembered how Everard had never doted on Belle or on Melville; never greeted either pregnancy of hers with any positive joy. Considerate, of course. . . . But he would certainly not have welcomed a third child; that little lost one, thing, thing. So one must think. Even now.

George reached his eighteenth birthday and now was, since the will of a dead man could override the ordinary law, master of Gad's and Park, and the herd and all the business that went with it. Mrs Thorley had attained her aim, that when she handed over to George everything should be more prosperous and more promising than it had been when she took charge. There it all lay, in the neat handwriting which had so much impressed George's father: pedigrees, accounts, bank statements, and milk yields and stud fees and a list of business contacts; the summing up in labelled files and notebooks of twelve years' hard labour.

On the eve of his birthday she said, "Well, my dear, here it all is. From tomorrow all responsibility will be yours."

Blank dismay showed on George's face. The notebooks, the files —worse than being back having lessons from old Spicer.

"Mamma, what *do* you mean?

"It was your father's express wish that I should have full charge until you were eighteen and then hand over to you."

"I can't do it. I just can't do it, Mamma."

She knew that as well as he did, had thought about it a great deal and planned this move in order to shock him into a realisation of his responsibility.

"Then who will?"

"Well, I thought . . . I mean I hoped . . . You. I mean you do it so well. . . . So much experience. Everybody says you're the most knowledgeable. . . ."

"When your father died," Mrs Thorley said, "I barely knew a cow from a bull. I was obliged to learn, by trial and error. And I had no one to whom to turn—if one excepts Joe Snell. I shall always be available should *you* need help or advice."

God! She sounded serious.

"I know," he said miserably, "that perhaps I haven't been as much help in some ways as I should have been. . . . But you said yourself that we're only young once."

"That is true. But nobody can stay young forever."

"Eighteen isn't all that old."

"It is the age at which your father, presumably, considered that you would be old enough to be responsible."

He'd never before known her to sound so cold and remote. On very rare occasions—such as that affair over that wretched girl—she'd been angry, but never distant. George's comfortable little world rocked on its foundations.

He had a certain talent for diplomacy.

"You wouldn't know what to do with yourself, Mamma. This whole thing has been your life for so long. And you're far too young to think of retiring."

Nobody, in fact, knew exactly how old Mamma was. Her hair was quite white—but it had been so for a long time; her general appearance was frail and she sometimes—not always—had a tremour, but she was extremely active, both physically and mentally, and by the rough-and-ready reckoning that a woman's childbearing years were over at forty she couldn't be more than fifty-eight—allow for gestation—nearly fifty-nine.

"I think I could contrive to amuse myself, my dear." She was determined to make him *see*. "I should like to visit Deb, for one thing."

Thwarted, George fell back on the rocky obstinacy which he had inherited from both his parents.

"Then I shall have to hire a bookkeeper," and to give emphasis to the statement pushed all the notebooks and files into a clutter at the end of the table.

Mrs Thorley said, "An *honest* fellow would cost you twenty-five shillings a week. And even then you would have to exercise supervision. And since we are now talking frankly, I may as well say that you could not afford it—if I cared to exercise *my* legal rights.

Your father, when he made his will, enormously overestimated his resources. At the end of my stewardship, I was to retire with five hundred pounds a year."

She had not the slightest intention of claiming it, but it was her intention to bring home to George—before she died—that his present way of life was untenable. Hunting twice a week during the season, riding in point-to-point races, some of them at a fair distance away, playing golf, playing cricket. Nothing reprehensible, but nothing conducive to good business. He simply had to be brought to his senses, and she was doing it—as she had always done everything—in the way that seemed to her best.

When, just before the nightly whisky served her—and for a long time now she had attempted to ration herself, just enough to stay steady, just enough to provoke sleep—she blamed, in her mind, that chance encounter with Johnny Faulkner for George's failure to attend to business as he should. Johnny Faulkner and many of his friends, God knew, were poor enough, but very few of them had ever done a day's honest work. They shuffled, much as Mrs Thorley's first husband had shuffled, on the wavering border line between affluence and indigence. There were overdrafts, mortgages, expectations. Mrs Thorley knew it all. She also knew that George had no part in that kind of life; George's inheritance, built up by her, a new bee working inside an old almost ruined hive, cell by cell, had solid worth, but definite limitations. Which George *must* realise.

However, her perhaps belated attempt to make him realise was not outstandingly successful. George had other weapons in his armoury.

"This has spoiled my birthday. And I was so looking forward to it."

It was to be one of those purely male gatherings, not dissimilar from those from which Mrs Thorley had successfully weaned George's father during the first year of their marriage, except that dinner was a properly served meal and the card-playing and the horse-play came later, and the noise—plenty of it—had a different quality, since none of George's friends had rustic voices, or became unduly aggressive even when slightly drunk. Most of them were young men whom George had met through Johnny, but there were others, any kind of sport was a great lower of barriers between classes—after all, good old George himself was not

THE HAUNTING OF GAD'S HALL 439

County by a long chalk, but he was a damned good sport! A similar tolerance was extended to James Gordon and Richard Walford and Simon Catchpole and a few others who, in addition to
being non-County, were getting rather old, being in their late
twenties, but James Gordon was still the best golfer in three counties, Richard Walford beside being a brewer had a wonderful
wine cellar, and Simon Catchpole, having taking to training race-
horses, was a useful man to know. In fact it was only when it
came to the question—Would you like him to marry your sister?
that the question of family and background obtruded much.

Mrs Thorley, when George gave his own parties, merely received them in the drawing room and made cordial conversation
while the sherry was drunk. They were all extremely polite to her;
she had acquired quite a formidable reputation, and newcomers
to Gad's were invariably surprised by her appearance and her
manner. So dignified, so feminine, so utterly different from what
one would expect of a she-cattle-breeder and a hard bargainer.

When on the eve of his birthday, George said plaintively that
Mamma had spoiled his birthday, she relented inwardly but said
briskly,

"Nonsense! I was merely trying to draw your attention to the
fact that you must now assume some responsibility. After all I am
not going to live forever. Nobody does!"

George looked even more appalled than he had done when
faced with the notebooks and the files.

"Mamma, what should I do?"

He was her son, her well-beloved, her justification for making a
marriage of convenience, and it hurt her to strike him another
blow.

"It is to be hoped," she said, "that you will marry. Not yet of
course. And that is another thing I must speak to you about—and
then we will have done with this dismal conversation. You must
set your sights on a target within reach. You understand me? If
you give your attention to business, there will be no need to marry
for money, but, my dearest, there are certain rules in this harsh
world, and we must learn to live with them."

When, as a child, he had fallen and bumped his head or grazed
his knee she'd said: There, a kiss will make it better. Now she had
dealt him two blows which no motherly kiss could ease.

"I know that," George said. He gave her a rather wry, half-conspiratorial smile. "No need to worry about *that!* As for these," he indicated the books and files, "I promise you, I will pay all that side more attention. But you must help me. Eh?"

"Of course."

"Then we're friends again. Good."

She knew again that little sense of failure. And for a second a flash of resentment against George's father for having made his will as he had. No doubt, she thought, he believed that a half-baked boy could run the business as well as *he* had done; sliding downhill fast when I took it in hand, the herd an expensive hobby and no proper accounts kept. Gross overoptimism was his trouble; five hundred pounds' dowry for each of the girls, five hundred pounds a year allowance for me when George came of age. Where did he think it was all coming from?

God send that George would develop more sense. God send she could keep going until he did.

And now, despite the fact that she had braced herself for this little confrontation with a good dose of the eau-de-Cologne-tinctured whisky, she was all of a shake once more and needed another.

"I'll drink to your birthday now, George. Give me a very unladylike whisky."

The adjective was one of their private little jokes. Once George had told her—having surprised her, glass in hand—that whisky was no drink for ladies and she had retorted that old age must have its privileges.

Pouring for them both, George thought what an excellent thing it was—and how rare—to have a mother with whom one could drink companionably; a mother who could deal with all the dull part of earning a living, a mother whom one could so easily coerce. As he had coerced Mamma into agreeing to the form his birthday party should take; she had made a tentative suggestion that it should be a small, family affair, with Diana and Caro and Everard and an old friend or two. Easily argued down; too old . . . after all, it was *his* party, wasn't it?

So tomorrow evening she would stand, looking singularly like a Dresden figurine with her piled-up white hair and delicate features, and she would be gracious to his guests and then disappear.

"You know, you are my ideal woman, Mamma. There was some truth in it, but not the whole. He had another ideal, made in the image of Chloe Faulkner, for whom he had once—when young and silly—gathered a bunch of pink roses and who probably could not add two to two and make four. This clash of idealism, combined with the limitation of choice which George had understood after one rebuff, was to keep him single for thirty years.

Letters from and to India were usually carried by the shorter, overland route, as it was called, though it involved a journey across the Indian Ocean, up the Gulf of Suez to Suez itself; then overland, by swift camels, to Port Said; ship again to Marseilles, by train across France, by packet boat across the Channel and so to England. It was a long process, but if correspondents were determined to keep in touch with each other—as Diana was, as Everard was, and wrote and despatched a letter faithfully once a week, contact was regular and the exchange, though stale, was welcome. Not a broken marriage, Diana told herself, sealing up her letters, all faithful accounts of the children's progress, the weather in England, little bits of news like James Gordon marrying such an unsuitable person; Caroline having another baby—a girl, which was just right. Parish pump news. In return Everard sent her rather carefully edited accounts of his experiences, his progress and above all, his health.

Caro once said, cruelly, "Di, by this time he's either cured or dead." And Edward said, "Warburg's Drops! Do tell him, Diana, that unadulterated quinine would be better. And however hot the weather he must wear flannel next to his skin."

Diana was always careful to mention each of Everard's letters and to make great display of everything he sent in the way of presents: a necklace of moonstones for Belle, some carved animals—really far too good to be used as toys for Melville, a silk shawl for herself, and for the house an exquisite Indian rug which warranted a special tea-party. To talk about money outside the family would have been extremely vulgar, but to Mamma and to Caro she could confide that Everard's salary had been increased and the allowance he made her with it. To outsiders she merely said that Everard had gained promotion.

She was not fully aware of the fact that she was following a deliberate policy of giving evidence that hers was not a broken marriage, but as happy, comfortable day, followed happy comfortable day, Everard as a person receded in her mind, became my husband who is in India. "Our Father which art in Heaven," as Caro remarked irreverently to Edward, adding that there had always been a good deal of the spinster in Di and that it showed now in her house. Too finicketty, too many little lace mats and antimacassers and knickknacks. And Edward admitted that Di's house contained only one comfortable chair, and that was in the children's play room, and that to smoke a pipe, or even a cigarette in such surroundings would be unthinkable.

Naturally Everard had holidays, long week-ends, sick leave, but home leave was due only every five years; necessarily a long leave because so much of it must be spent in travelling. The possibility of cutting a canal through the Suez isthmus was being discussed, but not yet as more than a project. Since letters were so slow, mention of this long leave which would bring Everard home was made early and immediately Diana fell to worrying. Five years was five years. They'd meet as strangers, and what would he find? Her looking glass gave her one answer. The happy, comfortable years, with ease of mind after so much anxiety, had made her fat, at least—as usual her mind sidled around any disagreeable fact—plump, and that made her look middle-aged. Worse still, just at the temples some white hairs showed amongst the glossy black. Nothing to be surprised about, Mamma's hair had turned white; not quite so soon, but surely prematurely.

Diana had not changed in appearance overnight, nor had she in any sense, since that frightful time when she'd taken Bessie's dose and been so ill, let herself go, and indeed even now her thickening figure was well corsetted, her hair given an egg shampoo and vinegar rinse once every two weeks, her skin creamed nightly and her hands well-tended. She was vain—always had been. As a girl, amongst girls, she had been considered a model of what a girl should be, in order to secure a husband. But she had never been, like Caroline, a flirt. She'd fallen in love, married, disliked some aspects of married life, but borne up, doing her best. For the last five years she had regained her position among her contemporaries, or women slightly older; a woman with a dainty, well-kept house, pleasant little tea-parties, pleasant afternoons at whist. In five years not the slightest breath of scandal had ever blown upon her.

The notion that five years in a hostile climate might have affected Everard, too, and that he might not be as she when she chose to remember him, did remember him, never once occurred to her. In her mind she had idealised the absent Everard, and she imagined that he had done the same; so she must slim down, apply a little dye to those white hairs—and get that ruined chair upholstered; and find—where was it—the solid ash-tray into which Everard knocked the ashes of his pipe. She made other preparations, Belle and Melville must recognise their father, photographs were a help. And deep, deep down, below all other thoughts was the memory of the bed thing which had so disgusted her fastidious nature, and the possibility of its resulting in something even worse. She was a very good, very devoted mother, but as she had once said to Caro, "We have retrogressed since hens."

And then it all came to nothing. Everard wrote, abjectly apologetic; he'd had another attack of malaria and his doctor had advised him not to make the journey, even by the sea route, around the Cape, which could be rough, and a constitution already debilitated by fever should not be exposed to sea-sickness. The overland route was at the moment even more dangerous, there was plague rampant in Suez; so Everard's doctor had advised a three months' convalescence in the hills and then a kind of working holiday, a combination of business and pleasure in Killapore, where there was still a chance of shooting a tiger. Everard's doctor, not a very good physician, had long ago learned the trick of telling patients what they wished to hear.

Without any conscious intention of being a humbug, Diana behaved as convention demanded: Isn't it terrible? So disappointing. I am thoroughly miserable—who wouldn't be? But in her heart she was relieved, a little ashamed of being relieved, and as over Lady Lumsley completely unsuspicious.

"I want Deb," Mrs Thorley said, and that was the first thing, coherent and clearly enunciated, that she had said since she had what Edward—hastily summoned—called a stroke. Stroke was the right word, one fell stroke.

Friday had seemed the best time for George to do, as he said, better at all that side of the business, and for almost five years Friday night had been devoted to the record-keeping and to future plans. George was shaping up wonderfully—as she had always known he would, given time, and it was with a feeling of satisfaction that she said, "You finish off, George. I feel rather tired." Violet, whose duty it was to present early morning tea, came down and said that Ma'am was asleep still. "Let her sleep," George commanded, "but tiptoe up and peep in now and again."

He tiptoed along himself and peeped in before riding off to the races at Newmarket. Mamma was still asleep, actually snoring slightly. Well, a good sleep never did anyone any harm.

George was back at nine o'clock—early for him, and although he had had a few drinks he was quite sober, and once he was over the first shock he thought that Edward's manner had been unnecessarily reproachful—as though George had deliberately absented himself, out roistering while his mother was dying.

"There's nothing that I, or anyone else, can do," Edward said. "But I didn't like to leave her alone with servants."

It was a plain statement of fact but Edward's manner made it sound like a rebuke.

Violet had obediently tiptoed and peeped until four o'clock in the afternoon, then Jenny decided to make one more tray of tea.

"Take it up and this time go a bit noisy. *Wake* her up. It ain't natural to sleep all day like that."

Violet made noise enough. In fact when closer inspection showed her that something was badly wrong, she dropped the whole tea-tray, backed away from the wreckage and galloped downstairs.

"Jenny, oh, Jenny! She ain't asleep. Her eye's open. But she ain't awake neither. She didn't know me."

"I'll see for myself."

Jenny's legs, which for twenty years had served as an excuse for not doing anything she did not wish to do, while conveniently allowing her to do what she did wish to do, had been less accommodating of late. She no longer went down to the village on Sunday afternoons and she faced the painful task of descending, and the even more painful one of ascending, stairs only once a day. Now she hauled herself up, took one look at Mrs Thorley and knew the worst. Apopletic stroke, similar to the one that had carried off her own grandfather, and a number of other people. All men, curiously enough. In all her years, and although they could not be exactly reckoned, they covered a considerable period of time, Jenny had never known, or heard of a woman having apopletic stroke.

She did not go down again, but shouted to Violet to send Willy for the doctor and mind he got Doctor Edward, nobody else.

Then Jenny remembered that her grandfather, though paralysed down one side and speechless, could hear and with his one good hand would lash about with his stick if what he heard displeased him, went close to Mrs Thorley and said,

"You've had a slight turn, ma'am, but you're all right. I'm here and Doctor Edward is coming. Could you drink a cup of tea if I held it for you?"

Edward came and confirmed Jenny's diagnosis; and he, too, seemed to understand that people struck down in this way were not so insensible as they might appear to be. He spoke cheerfully.

"You've had a slight stroke. Just take things quietly. We'll have you all right in no time." She mouthed at him. God forgive him for using the word slight; it was a massive stroke. Everybody knew the cause now, but nobody knew a cure.

Then Edward deeply offended Jenny. Outside, out of Mrs Thorley's hearing, he said, "She'll need a nurse. I'll send one."

"What for? What could a nurse do that I couldn't do as well or better?"

"I was thinking of your lameness, Jenny."

There again was a recognised ailment, a wearing away of the smooth tissue which made joints move, smoothly, like well-oiled wheels; but nobody knew how to prevent the erosion, or how to restore the worn tissue.

"I'm lame, I know," Jenny said, "but if it come to looking after Ma'am I'll do it, if I hev to go on my hands and knees. We don't want no nurse."

Now, after two days of incomprehensible mumblings, Mamma said, quite clearly, "I want Deb."

"Where, Mamma? Tell me where to find her."

"Secret, darling. Secret."

"I know. I promise, I won't say a word. Just tell me where."

She had moments of clarity, and then everything would blur. In a clear moment she wanted Deb, because Deb, in another crisis, had been her strength and stay. Diana and Caroline, both good girls, but Diana couldn't face—in fact broke down when faced with—anything distasteful; and Caroline cried and cried.

In this, her final extremity, for some reason which she knew was no reason, she wanted Deb. If only to say goodbye. Frantically she tried to tell George where Deb was living and the name she had taken, but the effort defeated its own purpose; nothing but mumbling and moaning emerged.

George, subscribing to the general pretence that this was just a passing affliction, said gently,

"Never mind, Mamma. You can tell me when you are better and I'll have her here the same day." A curious expression, fond yet mocking, almost teasing, lighted and for a second rejuvenated her sunken face; it was as though she saw through the game, knew that she would never be better. Would see no tomorrow.

No clue to Deb's whereabouts could be found amongst Mrs Thorley's personal papers. After Deb had communicated her fixed address and her new name, she had always sent unheaded letters, and Mamma, with perhaps excessive caution, had always destroyed the post-marked envelopes. Her own letters to Deb she always posted herself.

Anything left behind by the dead has a pathos of its own, and George, grown man as he was now, wept unashamedly when he opened a drawer and found what Mamma had saved for sentiment's sake, all the letters he had sent when he was abroad, a few from Diana, a few from Deb. Caro, living so near, had had no need to write. There were photographs, too, one of Sam misled him for a second, the pictured face so closely resembled his own. Mamma had not kept all the girls' letters and from those of Deb's which she had chosen to preserve no useful information could be gained. They sounded lively and happy, but were just the sort of chit-chat about domestic affairs—I have just made fourteen pounds of plum jam. Sam actually won a prize this year; it was for Scripture, and no wonder, though at his school they call it divinity —not unconnected, I feel, with the divine right of headmasters!

On the very morning of the funeral a letter arrived addressed to Mrs Thorley and George very nearly didn't open it, for Deb too was being very cautious, as though suspecting the possible existence of an enemy in the camp, and addressed her letters to Mamma in the characterless block capitals much in use by half-educated people or by those who distrusted the legibility of their own scribble. However, he did open it, mainly because, in his sorrow, he had promised himself to attend more closely to business than ever before—a kind of tribute to Mamma's memory. And there was a letter from Deb. Her real hand-writing was unmistakable. And so was the post mark. Abbey Norton.

He still had time before all the melancholy pageantry of a

proper funeral began to sit down at the pretty little desk in the bow window and write to Deb.

In Abbey Norton there were two families bearing the name of Bridges. The postman, a sensible man, took the letter to the respectable family first. Mrs Bridges, the corn-chandler's wife, opened it and was bewildered. Her mother had been dead for fifteen years and she had no loving brother called George. So she resealed the letter with a brush of white of egg and next day handed it back to the postman who, conscientious and indefatigable, carried it on to the house of an ignorant family, to which, so far as he could remember, he had never before delivered a letter. Abbey Norton, like every other place, had its rough quarter—to do the distasteful, but necessary work in the shambles, men had to be rough. To the slaughterman's wife a letter meant nothing, except as some paper useful for kindling a fire.

Dearest Mamma, Deb wrote; No letter from you this week. I do most sincerely hope that you are well. If not do tell George to let me know. I would come at once, despite the risk, not that there would be much for me. T certainly wouldn't want me back and Sam is safe. I must tell you about Sam. . . .

As Caroline had once realised, Deborah was interested in abstract generalisations. So her letter went on to mention heredity and to say that Sam's farming blood had triumphed and that he had chosen to spend his holiday helping his best friend on the best friend's father's rather miserable little farm. "Really no more than a small-holding, but for Sam it will be a useful experience . . . if after all he takes to farming."

"But I *did* write," George protested. "On the very morning of the funeral. And the letter did not come back."

Diana said, "Of course there is a possibility that Deb may not be using her right name." Touting for work, she had not used hers; it was Mrs Osborne, not Mrs Spicer, who had haunted Hawksley's, and made that seemingly fatal suggestion to Mrs Preston in Oxford Street. She had reverted to her maiden name and Deborah might well have done the same.

"Try Thorley," Di said.

There was no Thorley at all in Abbey Norton nor indeed any name remotely resembling it.

Another week and no letter from Gad's. Mamma must be ill. That she should be dead was inconceivable; indeed even to those who had seen the coffin lowered the fact still seemed inconceivable; Mamma had always been there, never interfering, but always ready to help, to listen and advise. There'd been no lingering illness to prepare them for the loss; Mamma was a bit shaky at times, that was all.

Dear George—Deb wrote—Is Mamma ill? I said I would come and I will. I could leave Sam easily and I'm better at that kind of thing than Di and Caro. Please let me know, if only a line. In case she hasn't told you and is still preserving my secret, here I am known as Mrs Willoughby, and I live in Stone House.

George was still in that state when seeing something funny or interesting he'd think, I must tell Mamma that and then remember! He derived a certain comfort from sitting down and writing to Deb, telling her what had happened and how he felt about it. Some innate delicacy forbade that he should tell Deb that Mamma's last words concerned her. He could, however, write with truth that Mamma had suffered no pain, had simply had a stroke on Saturday and died on Sunday without ever regaining full consciousness. He also gave details of how he had tried to reach Deb.

Deb, not a facile crier, cried when she read George's letter. There was a tinge of remorse in her grief. If she had been a bit more compliant, a little less concerned for Sam, rather less—let's face it—anxious to get away from Tim and Foxton, she would have been within reach, visiting regularly, enjoying the company of the woman she loved and admired. She'd always intended to go back—one day; acting as though time were inexhaustible, and now it was too late.

Sam came in. Ostensibly he was spending his midsummer holiday with Duff and he usually slept there, but he came back, hungry, to be fed now and again, and to pick up a clean shirt. This happened to be one of those days, and Sam, who had never seen his mother cry, asked what was the matter.

"My mother died. You remember Grandmamma, Sam?"

He didn't really. Multitudinous new experiences had overlain childish memories. But he must not lie. So he compromised with,

"Not very well. She was rather old, wasn't she?"

"Not old enough to die."

Sam considered that. Quite young people died. A master at school, a kind man with a terrible cough; and a boy, younger than Sam who had fallen down, with an injured knee during a football game. He'd been taken to Shewsbury Hospital, had his leg off, since it wouldn't heal, and died.

"All the dead," Sam said, "are safe in the arms of Jesus."

There was really nothing very extraordinary about that simple, well-meant statement. The vast majority of decent people believed in a life beyond the grave, in rewards in Heaven, punishments in Hell. They truly believed that a dead child had been called away, untimely, to join a choir of angels.

It was, Deb supposed, a simple and beautiful faith, one that poor human people clutched to themselves for comfort in moments like these. But it had ugly offshoots; look at the Inquisition! Look at extreme Puritanism.

Now, too sad to put up any argument, she said, "It would be nice to think so. I expect you are hungry."

She produced a large meat patty and Sam said,

"Would you mind if I took it along with me? There's enough for four. Mrs Duff hasn't much time to cook—or much to cook with, to be honest."

To Sam, who had fallen so entirely under Robbie Duff's influence, honesty in minor matters was very important. Sam knew that every time he answered to the name of Willoughby, or wrote it on an exercise, he was living a lie, and Duff had once told him that every lie any man told was one extra nail on Christ's Cross.

Deb said, "Oh, take it and welcome. There's a fruit cake, too."

Wrapping them, and the clean shirt, she looked at her son and recognised once again the force of heredity. Sam's extreme resemblance to George had faded away and now, deeply tanned by work out-of-doors, he was very plainly Tim's son.

Tim's son. Capable of saying safe in the arms of Jesus, thus disposing of a dead woman, and then walking off, leaving a living one alone with her grief.

Well, there had been some warning signs which she had ignored.

Once she had said—"Come along, boys, surely you have done enough homework now. Knock off and have supper."

Duff said, "I must work hard, Mrs Willoughby. My mother has
set her heart on my becoming a minister."

She'd missed that. She had regarded Duff as a good influence.
She had hardly noticed the dropping away of Sam's other friends,
the noisy, hearty ones who regarded homework as an imposition.
Nor had she been disturbed when Sam said, "We can put Duff
up for the night, can't we? There's a meeting he wants to go to.
And he wants me to go with him." She'd been completely
confident that any meeting patronised by Duff wouldn't be cock-
fighting, or dog-fighting, both sports which though coming under
general disapprobation in the wider world were still rampant in
places like this. Far more likely a lantern lecture, a missionary
meeting, something to do with school.

She'd been very careless and she could not offer, to herself, the
excuse that she had also been busy, though that would have been
true enough. A book a year for Mr Hammond and some exercises
known as keeping in the public eye, which, since she refused to do
it in person, she must do in print; stories and articles for magazines and for the annual, beautifully produced Albums which
made such excellent Christmas presents. Then there were alterations and additions. Libraries liked long books, reading matter for
ten days or a fortnight; foreign publishers who had translation
charges to meet suggested cuts. Magazines which published seriali-
sations demanded rearrangements, so that each instalment ended
with a crisis or a situation which left the reader avid for the next.
With her inborn thoroughness and her grafted-on desire to please,
Deborah had complied.

But she had neglected Sam, thinking it enough that he should
be well-fed, well-clothed, healthy and happy and, under Duff's
influence, getting on well at school. It was not enough. Man did
not live on bread alone; he needed some spiritual compass, and
having none herself she had none to offer; merely a few rules of
behaviour, chaff when compared with genuine religious belief, the
sort of thing that could dismiss death—Safe in the arms of Jesus.

Sam, like many new converts, was full of proselyting zeal.

"If you'd just *come*, Mother, with an open mind, I'm sure that
Mr Sturgiss would convince you and bring you to the mercy seat."

Trying to conceal the revulsion that this kind of talk roused in
her, Deb said,

"My dear boy, I've been to many Revivalist meetings."

This was the time of year for them; those who had harvests to gather had gathered them in, yet the weather was still mild and the roads open. People faced long dull evenings and a rousing Revivalist meeting was a form of entertainment.

One must not decry, of course. At any Revivalist meeting some good was undoubtedly done, and as Goldsmith had said, long ago —Fools who came to scoff remained to pray. Were they fools, or were they fooled? Victims of the mass hysteria which men with the gift of the gab and complete conviction could whip up. . . .

It was the language, particularly the phrase "washed in the blood of the lamb," which Deb had found hard to swallow. Just as she had found, at the other end of the religious spectrum, the concentration upon the Crucifixion revolting. It had all happened a long time ago, but there was something in her which, had she been present, would have made her say to the Roman with the lash: Hit me!

Blood, sacrifices; the theme ran straight from the children who were given by their parents to the fires of Moloch to Tim, who couldn't drink a glass of wine at his own wedding, nor allow his wife to wear a rose-trimmed hat when she went to chapel.

The chapel at Abbey Norton was slightly larger than the one Tim's mother had built at Foxton, but it was crowded out. And hot. The packed bodies and the oil-lamps and presently the mounting excitement made the atmosphere almost intolerable; in fact not so unlike the Hell which Mr Sturgiss described so vividly. He was indeed a very powerful speaker, a born orator; he believed in what he was saying; he gestured, his eyes flashed. He would, Deborah thought, have made a splendid actor or a real Radical rabble-rouser.

She was here, just to prove to Sam that she wasn't prejudiced or against him in any way. That was necessary, because the future was concerned. She sat there, obliging, willing as always to do her best, but critical, but sceptical. And she saw a miracle happen.

By this time, although she had avoided as far as possible all social contacts, had lived almost a hermit's life, she knew, by sight, some of the familiar characters in the little town. One was known as Cripply Charlie; born so, a heavy broad torso poised upon useless legs, a freak. He could not use crutches because even crutches needed some propelling from legs; so Cripply Charlie got about on his hands, protected by stout leather pads. Sometimes he begged outright, sometimes he sold matches.

"Come," Mr Sturgiss shouted. "Come to the mercy seat and

though your sins be as scarlet they shall be white as snow. Come, just throw yourselves into the loving arms, anxious, longing to receive you." Then suddenly his all-embracing gaze focussed. "You can walk, Brother. Trust in the Lord. Get up and walk."

There was no denying it. Everybody saw it happen. Cripply Charlie did get up and he did walk on legs no bigger than those of a new-born baby's. There were shouts of "Hallelujah" and "Praise the Lord."

"It *was* a miracle, wasn't it?" Sam demanded.

"It seemed so. But, my dear, it raises as many problems as it solves. Why should the poor man have been born so and been obliged to wait forty years? And suppose Mr Sturgiss had decided to end his mission in Shrewsbuy? What then? To be quite honest, Sam, I think the whole thing is beyond our understanding. We just don't know."

"Those who believe, know. We *know* that our Redeemer liveth."

It could have been Tim speaking; in those early days of their marriage, when they could allow themselves the luxury of argument because in bed all was made right.

In a flash of irritation, she said,

"Oh, Sam, *must* you talk like a tract?"

He gave her a glance of deep reproach. And she reproached herself. It was a phase, he'd grow out of it. It was born in him, it was bound to come out. It should not be allowed to come between them.

Until Duff had become the centre of his life, Deb and Sam had lived in exceptional accord, both refugees, both enjoying their new freedom, living in happy-go-lucky fashion. She had eventually been obliged to take him into her confidence about the books—one could not go on vaguely writing "something else" forever, but she had made him promise not to tell—again using Tim as the bogey-man. To speak about her book, Deb said, might lead to their whereabouts being discovered.

Sam's memory of his father had blurred over with the years; he recalled certain incidents—the slapping of the face outside the chapel—somehow connected with the present of a wonderful new pony. A general atmosphere of strictness; a boxing of the ears across the breakfast table. And then the running away, which had fooled Father and seemed, at the time, like a game. Now it assumed a different appearance. To Sam's newly awakened conscience it seemed that possibly Father could have been right, and that, by inference, meant that Mother was wrong. And that thought opened a little gulf, a chilling, too; that atmosphere of disapproval in which Deb had once said she could not live.

It was all the more baffling for Sam in that there was so little to attack. In almost every sense Mother was irreproachable. She worked hard, in the house, in the garden, in her writing; she did not drink, have anything to do with men, use bad language, dress gaudily; her faults were all negative: she refused to attend chapel, or any meeting connected with it, and she had a curious, disconcerting attitude. Towards Cripply Charlie, for instance.

Cripply Charlie was back where he had been before the miracle, heaving himself about on his padded hands, his undeveloped legs again useless.

Deb has an explanation.

"Once, years ago, I saw a hypnotist at the theatre. He had positively staid old gentlemen turning cartwheels, or barking like dogs."

Sam had an explanation.

"While he had faith, he could walk. He lost it and reverted to being a cripple."

Both mild statements; but poles apart.

In Baildon Miss Hardwicke's Academy for Young Ladies was still in existence, though Miss Hardwicke had died, as she had often expressed a wish to do, in harness. The numbers of pupils, both boarders and day girls, had been declining steadily for a decade. There were a number of reasons, mainly the lessening of prosperity in agriculture and all the trades dependent upon it; but, in a sense, the Academy had been self-defeating, in that it had produced a generation of young women who considered themselves capable of instructing their daughters if not their sons. Miss Hardwicke's successor saw a method of survival—take little boys up to the age, say, of eight. Until then they were relatively harmless, practically sexless, though they could only be accepted as day boys.

Both Diana and Caroline were, in theory, qualified to give such elementary lessons as Deb had given Sam, but they'd both been rather poor scholars and shrank from the task. Besides they could both afford to pay somebody else to perform it.

Noel Taylor, escorted by his cousin Belle, began to trot round to the Academy—the word Female had been discreetly dropped when he was five. And he made singularly little progress. He knew his letters, parrot fashion, but had difficulty in assembling them, even on his illustrated bricks, into such simple words as DOG, CAT, HAT, BUN, BAT. He eventually mastered his tables, but the simplest multiplication or addition seemed to be beyond him. Edward tried, with matches, with marbles, even with sweets.

"Now look, Noel, here are six aniseed balls. If you take two away, how many are left?"

"One; two; three; four."

"Quite right! Now try to do it in your head. I mean without looking. There are six and I take three away. How many left?"

"I don't know. I can't see."

Apart from this—even Edward hesitated to call it stupidity—Noel was altogether satisfactory and delightful; good-looking, gay-tempered, kind, rather tough. One of his baby teeth failed to fall out on time and developed a small abscess which gave him tooth-ache. And while Edward was deciding between a proper extraction with forceps and that age-old trick of tying a piece of cotton around the offending tooth, attaching it to a doorknob, holding the end and saying, Shut the door, Noel removed the offending molar himself, using a pair of scissors.

"I just dug it out. It was hurting me."

A surgeon in the making.

The little girl, rather more than two years younger than Noel, had been christened Daphne, because just at the time flower names for girls had become fashionable: Rose; Lily; Daisy; Marguerite, even Pansy.

When Caroline saw her two children together she thought how unfortunate it was—even allowing for everything—that Daphne should be so much the less attractive. Caroline knew that she had never been pretty in the approved way, but she had always had *something*. What she had had, and what Freddy had had, had combined to make Noel something quite exceptional. Daphne, oh, poor little girl, was dead-plain. She had straight brown hair which defied all Nurse Rose's attempts with alum water, curl-papers, and finally hot tongs to make it conform. Put a curl into it and within an hour there it was, like a sweep's brush, straight and intractable. Unlike the child herself; even Nurse Rose, whose standards were high, said that Daphne was a very good little girl.

Most fathers were inclined to dote upon their daughters, at

least for a time, treating them more or less as dolls; but Edward tended to concentrate upon his son, who *must* learn; who must carry on the family tradition. Edward was a just man and kind but what energy, and what time he had left, after a full working day, tended to channel towards Noel. Until one evening when Daphne said,

"I know, Papa. Eight. Take twelve from twenty and it is eight."

"How did you know?"

"I have been looking and listening, Papa. I can do it. *I did it.*"

The three little words rang out in the comfortable, lamplit, firelit gloom and nobody recognised their doomful quality.

Edward said, "That's a clever girl! What else can you do?" A single correct subtraction could have been a mere shot in the dark.

"Everything Noel can." Caro noted that a smug expression did not improve a plain face. But Edward's attention had been arrested. Over supper that evening he said that he thought Daphne should go to school.

"I don't think they take them until they are five."

"Miss Pakefield would take a baboon if *I* asked her," Edward said. It was probably true, for Edward, guessing her financial difficulties, was moderate in his charges and had once given her some splendid, if stringent advice about drains.

Miss Lark, who taught the under-sevens, gave a secret groan when informed that Noel Taylor's little sister would be joining her class. If a boy could be so backward and dull, how much worse would the girl be? Discovering that Daphne was not at all dull, Miss Lark tried to use the fact to her own advantage.

"Unless you make more effort, Noel, Daphne will pass you."

It worked the other way. When Noel was tired of this mild threat, he thought, Let her! and ceased to make any effort at all. Yet one could not really be angry with him; everybody was agreed on that; he was so beautiful, so like a young fawn and he had such an unusual smile.

Imperceptibly Edward's concentration passed to his daughter. Caro hardly noticed the change, partly because it was so gradual, and partly because she was so engrossed in appearing to do good works while avoiding anything unpleasant.

"I think," she said, trying the idea out on Edward, "that the Hospital Ball this year should be a Fancy Dress Ball."

Edward knew, everybody knew, that Caro's ideas were not to be lightly dismissed. Years ago she had suggested, it seemed frivolously, that the sedate Garden Party in aid of Friends of the Hospital funds should include swings and roundabouts and coconuts shies, and the Friends' income had quadrupled.

"It'd be so cheap, for one thing," Caroline explained. "Anybody can rig up a fancy costume out of a little muslin or sateen. And it would help to break down, well the stuffiness; the who can dance with whom. You know what I mean."

Edward knew. All people of good will, County or otherwise, felt bound to patronise the Hospital Ball, but there were the invisible barriers.

"What is more," Caroline said, pursuing her unconsciously egalitarian course, "we could alter the supper arrangements. Pair people off. Lady Norton is certain to come as Britannia and it would do her good to take supper with a Jolly Jack Tar."

"It might work. In fact with you behind it, darling, it can hardly fail to. What role would you assume?"

After the slightest pause Caroline said,

"I think Old Mother Hubbard."

Old Mother Hubbard went to her cupboard, to get her poor dog a bone; When she got there, the cupboard was bare, and so the poor dog had none.

In a crude way it described her own plight. She had everything: a kind, loving, indulgent husband who had never for a second doubted her fidelity; a most comfortable home; a secure place in the social hierarchy; two children, one beautiful and charming, one apparently very clever. But her emotional cupboard was empty and the poor dog—her one overriding passion—though often apparently dead of inanition, still showed sporadic signs of life, a gnawing at her vitals. The poor dog, denied the bone, would turn and rend other things.

At Foxton, Tim Bridges had suffered a deprivation, dissimilar in kind, but not so different in effect. Caroline, in weak moments, grieved over Freddy Ingram, her own lack of strength of character which had made her choose the easy way. Tim grieved only over the loss of his son. And over the scandal which attached itself to a broken marriage—however innocent one partner might be.

He'd decided early that after the way Deb had behaved, he did not want her back. She'd been, after those first blissful two

months, argumentative, sarcastic and—strange thing to think—
too capable. He would have been resigned to the dirty trick she
had played him, but for the fact that she had taken Sam. If he
had succeeded in tracing her he would have said, bluntly, Give me
the boy and go your own way. As it was, she had vanished entirely, and the boy with her, and after a while when he ran about
like a headless chicken, he settled down to wait. The mills of God
ground slowly, but they ground extremely small, and Tim had
complete belief in his God who dealt justly in the end, after sub-
jecting true believers to tests and trials such as this— Look at the
story of Job.

Everybody said that Mr Bridges had held up wonderfully.

He would, of course, have been justified in divorcing her, but
the thing was unthinkable. Whom God hath joined, let no man
put asunder. And twenty divorces, in the circumstances, would
not give what he wanted—his son back, and all his, with no sub-
versive influence at work, pulling the other way.

There was the Book of Job. There were other encouraging bits
of the Bible. I have been young and now I am old, but I have
never seen the righteous forsaken. . . .

Gradually, over the years, Tim Bridges, a most practical man,
built up a fantasy, based on some extent upon the Parable of the
Prodigal Son. Deb's little dowry could not support two people for
long, the way prices were rising and her only other source of income—breaking in horses by kindness, not violence and then
training some of them to jump, was obviously lost to her: he'd
have heard.

So he waited.

Now and again he woke in the night. (For some reason which
he did not examine, the fantasy dealt with night, with Deb and
Sam, in rags, footsore and hungry, coming to seek his charity.)
The noise, whatever it was, a bough creaking, a window rattling,
always woke him to hope, which, disappointed, never ran downwards into despair. He had faith. He could wait. It was all in
God's hands. By some quirk of the mind, although he *knew* otherwise, he still thought of Sam as a child.

When the mills of God began to grind their first produce was a
letter. It bore a London post mark and was not addressed in
Deborah's clear neat hand. Inside, however, was an enclosure. A
bit brusque, but not unfriendly.

Dear Tim: I think the time has come to consider Sam's future.

I have come, reluctantly, to the conclusion that he would, after all, be happier with you. Some time ago he became an ardent Methodist and we no longer live in accord. He is fifteen and seems to know his own mind. He would like to return to Foxton, and since that is the most *sensible* of his several plans, I felt bound to agree. I do *not* propose to accompany him. Any letter addressed to me, c/o Hammond and Curtis, Exeter Square, will be forwarded, but we are not living there.

She had not been reduced to rags or hunger; she had been driven to appeal. Her intention had been to allow Sam to grow up, to the age of sixteen, and then let him choose. She had then not reckoned with all that fairy gold mounting up in the bank. And certainly she had not reckoned on Robbie Duff's influence; or of a headstrong boy, completely out of hand, proposing the most outrageous plans for his own future.

"It is called United Missions, Mother. It works among the poor in London. And they welcome young recruits because the young appeal to the young.

"Now I am exercised in my mind, Mother. Duff's mother is absolutely set on his being a minister, so he must have more education and his parents will miss his help. Ought I to go and work there?"

There were organisations for providing sailors with something other than drinking places and brothels when they were ashore; and for offering non-alcoholic refreshments at railway stations. There were, in fact, innumerable good causes. All admirable; that was part of the trouble; nothing Deb could really oppose. She had in the end been driven to say: Look Sam, it's time for us to sit down and have a serious talk.

The letter to Tim was the result of that talk; and proof of her failure. All the subterfuge and the effort, quite wasted. Sam for his own sake must go home.

Nemesis!

But now she could go home too. She had in writing, Tim's writing: I want nothing to do with you; I never want to see you again; but I shall welcome the boy home.

And that left her free to go back to her own country; back to Gad's.

Sam said, "Ever since I saw the light this living under a false name has worried me."

"You were in no way to blame, Sam. It was my idea and it did not work. I tried and I failed. But that does not matter. If you are *quite* sure. All I ever wanted was your happiness."

"I know; and I appreciate it," Sam said gently. Then with a change of voice and manner, "But you know, Mother, happiness must not be the sole object of one's life."

She did not wish to provoke another pious lecture, so she did not say that she intended to be as happy as she could. Returning to Gad's would not be unmitigated happiness, she knew; it would not be the same without Mamma; but there would be Di and Caro and George, friends, the familiar countryside, the well-known streets in Baildon—and of course, horses.

Stone House had never really been much more than a camping place; all she had done was to keep it in decent repair and buy more comfortable beds and chairs, better lamps than those she had started with. These she did not propose to cart half across England, and Sam had often spoken of the Duffs' poverty. At the moment she did not feel very warmly towards that family, but common justice made her see that Sam had an inborn fanatic streak and if he had not taken to Methodism he might have chosen something worse, so she sent a tactfully worded message to Mrs Duff, saying that there were certain things she must leave behind and it would spare her a great deal of trouble if Mrs Duff would take any or all of them off her hands.

George had extended the heartiest of welcomes; she could come when she liked, stay as long as she wished. Gad's needed a woman about the place. He added, for kindliness came easily to him and despite the passage of years his memory of Foxton and its master were still vivid, "Make sure the boy knows what he's letting himself in for."

Deb had made sure; it seemed to her that Sam would slide back into his natural environment as a fish, momentarily stranded, would slip back into water.

Sam's first pony, Merry, had finally succumbed to old age, his second, Benjy, made the journey to Gad's in comfortable fashion, in a horse box, specially chartered. The Railway did transport animals of every kind, but trains moved quickly, and since cattle trucks were always attached to the rear end of trains where every movement was exaggerated, casualties were frequent.

"It would seem silly to send Benjy to Foxton where there are so many horses," Deborah said in her sensible way. "And probably one of your cousins can ride him."

Sense indeed rather than sentiment was the keynote of their final arrangements. Sam had an adequate wardrobe which needed a proper trunk, shaped not unlike a Noah's Ark. Rather ostentatiously, he printed labels for it, his correct name: S. Bridges. Deborah had only hand luggage. She had sent a box of books on the footboard of the horse box, and she owned few clothes. There had seemed to be no call for them. But it would be different in future; she must not be a disgrace to her family or her friends; and by ordinary standards she was now quite rich.

Robbie Duff was the only person in or around Abbey Norton who had been told the truth and his lips were sealed because his parents would have been horrified to learn that all these years he had been friendly with the son of a woman, had enjoyed vast hospitality from a woman who was living apart from her husband. It was unheard of.

"I shall miss you, Sam." Was it true, or just a trick of Duff's glasses, that Duff's eyes had tears in them?

"You need not," Sam said. "There'll always be a warm welcome for you at Foxton—I gave you the address. And if you *do* go to work at the United Missions, let me know and I'll take the first train. . . ."

Deborah said, at the moment of parting, "You know, my dear, where to find me, if ever you want me."

"We're not saying goodbye, Mother. Foxton is less than twenty miles from Gad's."

She'd thought the very same thing, on her wedding day; she'd said to Mamma, left in the most awful predicament, "I shall come every week." And that, because of Tim, had not been possible.

"You may not find it possible, Sam. Above all, don't insist. Don't quarrel." Almost as an afterthought, she added, "Don't forget me."

"As though I could," Sam said. But already he had done with the past; was pressing eagerly towards the future. Lost to her; the product, after all, of a broken marriage; a boy who, for the time being, had had enough of Mother and was looking forward eagerly to reunion with his father.

George met the train and advancing along the platform thought, with pity and admiration, Poor Deb! She has been putting a brave face on it all this time, pretending she'd found some way of earning money.

The grey broadcloth dress and jacket in which Deb had run away had served her well, perhaps a little too well, for it had made it seem silly to replace it; it was so good and so seldom worn. But it had aged. George couldn't have said, exactly, what changes fashion had undergone in the last few years, but he could distinguish between a well-dressed woman and a shabby one, and Deb, in the late sunshine of a June afternoon, looked shabby. Never mind, he'd soon put that right! His financial position at the moment was a bit tricky for bad luck, both in business and pleasure, had dogged him since Mamma's death, but something would turn up.

He greeted her with enthusiasm, dodging under the brim of the rather battered-looking old hat to kiss her cheek, which was hard and thin. Funny! Both Diana, who was not a Thorley, and Caroline, who was, were exchanging their youthful curves for others, more pronounced.

His conviction that she was poor was confirmed when she said that this one valise was all her luggage.

"I sent my box ahead, with the pony. Did they arrive?"

"Yesterday. All safe and well."

Light as the small valise was, it must be handed to a porter. Porters were very poorly paid and depended largely upon their tips. Twopence would have been adequate, sixpence generous; failing to find a sixpence amongst the small change in his pocket, George bestowed a shilling, which evoked not only thanks, automatic, but blessings.

"Oh, George, let me drive, please. It's so long. . . ."

"He's new, and a bit of a handful; but all right. But make it lively. I've got a bit of a party waiting."

"Di and Caro?"

"No. You can see them tomorrow. Just a few fellows, back from the races. It was fixed, Deb, before you settled your day."

"Oh dear. Have I spoiled something for you? George, you shouldn't have missed anything on my account. I could have hired . . . And I'm not dressed for a party. I'll just slip in and go to bed."

"It isn't that kind of a party. Just men. At least . . . Do you remember Chloe Faulkner?"

"Vaguely. Years ago. Wasn't it the year Poor Susan died? And then she married; was it . . . ? Yes, Lord Mildenhall. And then, wasn't there a divorce?"

"That bit of information seems to have spread to every corner of the globe." George's voice was bitter. "Nobody knows how that old brute behaved to her—and to Johnny."

"Oh. In what way?"

"Jealous! They're twins. There was always a close bond between them, and the cure for that was that they mustn't meet, weren't supposed even to write to each other. They did, of course, meet on the sly. London mostly, Oxford sometimes. So then he had her *watched*. Can you imagine anything more despicable?"

"Is seeing one's own brother, in defiance of one's husband's orders, grounds for divorce?"

"Of course not. But given a judge who didn't understand the situation, an old, powerful man absolutely set on divorce, and a few bribes . . . They made it look as though Chloe had gone completely off the rails. Meeting Johnny was believed to be a cover for . . . for other activities. Connived at by Johnny, of course."

"How grossly unfair!"

"I hoped you'd think so. Nobody else does. In fact you'd think from the way people have behaved that the poor girl had small-pox *and* leprosy and . . . anything else you care to name. Simply unbelievable."

The whole thing was unbelievable. Sir John and Lady Faulkner could not, of course, refuse to give a destitute and disgraced daughter a home; but when they went out they did not take her with them, and when they entertained, which was rarely, she was banished. In common with most other people they believed that if Johnny had if not actually connived, he had encouraged Chloe in her wild career; parents and son were hardly on speaking terms, and old Lord Norton, who had willed three thousand pounds to each of his godsons, disinherited Johnny and let the fact be known. Lady Faulkner wailed, "Now look what you have done between you!"

George was not really surprised that Di should be censorious; she'd always been what he called stuffy; he was surprised and disappointed when Caro took upon herself to point out that running around with a divorcée did his own matrimonial prospects no good.

"God help us, Caro. I am not running round with her! She never comes to Gad's or the races or anywhere else without Johnny."

"You must have been reading the papers!"

That was just another case of speaking-without-thinking, of letting the ready tongue, grown sharper over the years, run away with her. But when George took in the implication of the quip, he was deeply offended. Caro ceased to be his favourite sister.

"So *you* won't feel everlastingly contaminated by sharing a meal with somebody who's been divorced?"

"It'd be a bit idiotic of me, wouldn't it? Tim could have divorced me had he felt so inclined."

There was sense in that statement; Deb had always been the sensible one. Not perhaps as amusing, or as easily indulgent as Caro; but sensible. The one Mamma had asked for on her deathbed.

"One thing," George said, with warmth, "nobody is going to treat you like that, Deb. And while I have a roof and a crust, we'll share it."

Turning skilfully into the lane that led to Gad's, Deb said,

"As a matter of fact, George, I'm rather rich. I seem to have earned a great deal of money and spent very little."

And the manager of the bank at Abbey Norton had at last had his way and persuaded his eccentric client, Mrs Willoughby, that money in a deposit account, upon which interest was paid, was every bit as safe and readily available as money lying, doing nothing, in a current account.

It isn't that kind of a party, George had said. And it was not. It could not exactly be called rowdy, George apparently had enough sense not to go in for roughs and toughs; but the only two women present were Chloe Faulkner, still called Lady Mildenhall, whose reputation was irretrievably lost, and James Gordon's wife, who had never had a reputation to lose. It was less the company than the state of the house which gave Deb a mild shock. She'd never been as pernicketty as Diana, but . . . To see Mamma's beloved piano all rings where wet glasses had been set down . . . the chintz covers soiled and rumpled, the velvet ones greasy, a curtain hanging lopsidedly, and dust everywhere.

The meal was bad, too. Not perhaps to men who had spent the afternoon at the races and had drunk well; not perhaps to Chloe, who had never in her life set a table and was thankful to be accepted at any table, not to Millicent Gordon, who had probably never before her marriage seen a properly set table, but to Deb, reared by Mamma . . . Oh dear! Plenty of food, but ill-prepared and slapped down just anyhow. Oh dear! George certainly did need a woman about his house. Now and again, with this thought in mind, Deb glanced at Chloe, upon whom neither years nor tribulations seemed to have made any visible effect; she was as pretty, in a pink-and-white, doll-like, vapid way, as ever. Deb could remember her, very virginal in white muslin at George's doomed party, and now, though dressed for the races in russet bombazine, she looked just as virginal. Every boy's ideal—and every old man's! The contrast between her and Millicent Gordon seemed almost contrived. Mrs Gordon had commented upon her future daughter-in-law's red hair. It was very red, and there was a lot of it, puffed and piled high. Not unattractive—but purple was not her colour. Still, she was animated and friendly and completely unpretentious. "Any of you boys," she said in one of the silences that occur at any party, "want a decent Havana without going broke, me Dad's just had a delivery and tomorrow's my day at the shop."

"Milly," James said—and he said it with pride, "only married me on condition that every Saturday should be Dad's day."

"Thass true. But what else could I do? He's such a helpless old b . . . bumbler." Plainly a word substitution! Deb was capable of liking Milly and at the same time wondering about Mrs Gordon's feelings and at the same time thinking about how the housekeeping standards had declined, what could be done about *that*? And how were Sam and his father getting along?

Tim's sense recognised that Sam was now fifteen, yet, because he had not seen him grow from stage to stage, he still thought of him as a child—the young boy whom Deb had stolen from him. Or, conversely, bred of the Prodigal Son fantasy, he'd thought of him as lean and hungry, in rags, glad of a welcome and a meal. Neither mental picture had prepared him for Sam. Nor, though she had tried, had Deborah fully prepared Sam for Tim. She had said that Sam's father was rich, bred horses, lived very comfortably, but such facts had glanced off Sam's awareness. He'd never known a Methodist who was not poor. And rightly so; nobody with any conscience at all had any right to be rich in a world where so many good causes were in desperate straits. Sam knew—through Robbie Duff—of a woman who took in washing and who regularly gave the pay for one household's wash to help missionaries. And the Duffs themselves, very poor, put pennies into boxes with various labels.

Under the text which still declared that Christ was the Head of This House—a sentiment of which Sam fully approved—arguments, quite as bitter and all the worse for being well-founded, were presently to break out. And Tim, who had done his best to convert Deborah and train up his son in the way he should go, found himself subjected to a conversion campaign, against which he had no defence except sense. Sam, who had cut his proselyting teeth on Mother—and failed, was now prepared to tackle Father. . . .

Deb tackled Gad's. It was nobody's fault; Jenny had simply taken to her bed and Violet said,

"She still eat hearty. I spend half my time going up and down with trays and such. I had to let the house go a bit. Master didn't mind. 'S'matter of fact when Jenny took to her bed—it was Ma'am's death *and* the funeral, she would go, that finished her off—I did say to the Master I'd need a bit more help. But he said all right for a bit. *He* been satisfied."

Violet gave Deb an antagonistic look and that part of Deb which was still oversensitive to disapproval hastened to apologise.

"I am not criticising, Violet. Just feeling my way about. I didn't know that you were single-handed with Jenny to care for."

Well, you know now! So don't talk to me about spring-cleaning; I only got one pair of hands.

So much could be said without words.

"I'll get Willy to help, with the curtains at least."

"And Willy ain't as spry as he was," Violet said ominously.

"Why? What has happened to Willy?"

"Got older. We all do. And some get cantankerous, too. Thass Jenny, knocking now. Got a clock in her head, she hev. 'Leven o'clock and she's wanting her broth. Minute late and bang, bang, bang. Excuse me, ma'am."

Willy—older, of course—silly of her not to have expected that, proved to be spry enough when called once again into service for his idol. His lack of spryness had been defensive; if Violet had had her way she'd have had him in the house all day, even washing up most likely. He was only too happy to help Deb to spring-clean the drawing room, and as he worked he talked. Everything, he said, had started to fall to pieces when Mrs Thorley died.

"And no blame to the Master. He did try. He steadied down considerable; didn't seem like the same man. He just lost heart what with one thing and another. First the foot-and-mouth, then cows slipping calves all over the place. Apart from the loss, that sorta thing get a herd a bad name. Ask me, he went back to the giddy life to stop hisself from brooding." Willy had the feeling, which he could not explain, leave alone justify, that things would look up now that Miss Deb was back. He repeated that he was glad to see her back; and volunteered to polish the piano. "Man's hands stronger'n a lady's," he said. In fact his sharp, loving eye noted that Miss Deb's hands didn't look as though they'd been cossetted much. And her old print dress was no better than a servant's. Whatever had happened to her—and it was all a bit of a mystery, things hadn't gone easy for her. Once again Willy thought: Oh if only he'd had five acres and a cow and she hadn't been the Old Master's daughter. For *her* he would have washed dishes at a sink.

"I have no doubt at all," Di said, "that George will twist *this* to his advantage and say that if we can be friendly to Deb we could ask Chloe Faulkner to tea. I for one do not intend to." In effect she was warning Caro, who was inclined to be, despite her sharp tongue, rather too easy-going.

"Even George can hardly think the two cases the same. Deb isn't divorced."

"She could have been. If Tim Bridges had been as spiteful as Lord Mildenhall. Hers is, after all, a broken marriage."

Di's was not. She was in fact enjoying all the benefits without any of the drawbacks of the matrimonial state. She was Mrs Spicer, she had two adorable children, she had a comfortable allowance. In a prominent position in her pretty drawing room stood a silver-framed photograph of Everard, standing by the body of a huge tiger which he had shot. She drew everybody's attention to it as diligently as she had once drawn attention to poor Lavinia's painting of Gad's Hall. And her attitude was not false. Everard in this guise *was* admirable, and preferable. . . . He wrote regularly, sent presents. Di was capable of ignoring the fact that the regular letters became shorter and less informative, degenerating into the I-hope-you-are-all-well,-I-am category. Now and again he referred to his health, and then she would worry, too, and invite everybody to worry with her. By no means a broken marriage!

Mrs Thorley had achieved her aim of imposing solidarity upon her girls and both Di and Caro were unfeignedly glad to see Deb and sorry to see her looking thin and shabby. But that could soon be remedied. A little money from both of them, and Diana's skill with the needle . . . And then, in a short time Deb made these kindly thoughts sound ridiculous by saying that she had a pony to give away. Belle and Noel already shared one, and Daphne, who must do everything that Noel did—and do it rather better—was clamouring for one of her own.

"It's a very nice pony, called Benjy. It seemed silly to send it to Foxton. And I couldn't put it on the market."

They both thought, How typical of Deb!

Then she said, "Has either of you been to Gad's lately?"

"I simply couldn't bear it, after Mamma . . ." Caro had not lost her gift for crying easily. "It didn't seem the same."

"And besides, one never knew lately whom one might meet there," Di said.

"It was in a fine mess, I assure you. Violet has been working under difficulties, I admit; but she's just taken soiled table linen and crammed it into drawer. There are wine stains which I doubt whether even the Hand Laundry can remove."

All the young women, reared by Mamma, knew what a heinous thing Violet had done. They were drawn together by a memory of Mamma putting salt on any stain, then stretching the soiled piece of cloth over a basin and pouring a kettleful of hot water through it.

"Do you intend to stay with George?" Di asked, thinking what a good thing it would be.

"Until I get the place straightened out. After that, I don't know. I did wonder, this morning, about taking Park."

"It would cost a small fortune to make it habitable," Di said.

"I have some money. And it would be an unobtrusive way of helping George."

"But, my dear girl, I shouldn't dream of selling Park. Or anything else—except livestock. I shall pull round. Of course you can *have* Park; do what you like with it. And if you are so flush of money, you can lend me a bit—at five per cent."

"I'll do that. And set the five per cent against rent." She laughed suddenly. "Isn't it an odd world? Do you realise, George, that if Tim cared to exercise his legal rights, he could claim every penny I've earned? I don't think he *would*; but he *could*."

"Damned unfair! How much could you lend me?"

"How much do you need?" Some deep instinct warned her to be cautious. Better not let George have too much, too easily. On the other hand the thought of using some of the money which had never seemed quite real to her on bolstering up Gad's was curiously satisfying.

"What could you spare? Without robbing yourself? I'm not trying to sponge, Deb. I had bad luck with the herd."

"I know. Willy told me."

"And I have a few debts."

"Would a thousand help?"

"God! It'd be a life-raft. But could you lend that and still mend up Park? Deb, I don't want to sound nosy, but how did you come by so much money?"

"Quite honestly." Well, sooner or later, she supposed, people would have to know. And why not? Why this curious reluctance to come into the open? It was nothing to be ashamed of, was it? "I wrote some books," she said in a gruff, offhand way.

"God! Did you really? Well, I always knew you were clever." Silent, upon the air, hung the words: But not as clever as that!

George was all in favour of Deb setting up her own home—though naturally, had her circumstances been otherwise, she would have been welcome at Gad's. He appreciated the better order of the household, he liked a clean tablecloth. But in a way Deb's coming had interrupted a regime which had been jogging along quite comfortably. George knew that Violet was a bit of a slut, making Jenny an excuse for things left undone, or done badly, but it had been only a temporary arrangement. Once he'd pulled round he intended to make better provision for poor old Jenny, hire more help, get things cleared up.

And marry Chloe?

Upon this subject his mind, his whole nature suffered such savage divisions that he underwent the mental equivalent of being torn apart by wild horses. He had fallen in love with her romantically and wholeheartedly, and the thing should have ended there. But she'd come back, just as pretty, so that every time he saw her the old dream woke and walked in beauty; and she was now within his reach. Sir John and Lady Faulkner would be only too glad to get her, disgraced and discarded, off their hands.

But what sort of wife would she make? A girl in love with her twin brother, whose first marriage had wrecked on that rock. George knew that Johnny's attitude towards Chloe was purely protective, because she was only half-witted; the subtle, mischievous hints about an unnatural relationship, which had been the inevitable result of the divorce court proceedings, carried no weight with George Thorley. He knew Johnny too well. Johnny said,

"That old devil had two things against her, poor child. She was fond of me, and she didn't give him the baby he expected."

Would she do better with George Thorley? There was Gad's to think of. A boy could fall in love without regard to such practicalities and what remained of the boy might be moved now and again, but the man who had grown up around the boy must think.

So George thought and wavered and time moved on. Deb left off fussing about Gad's and renovated Park, madly excited to find that several miserable little rooms, their lath and plaster walls demolished, revealed beams as old as and similar to those in the barn at Gad's.

"Honestly, George, I believe the Vikings came ashore and built their houses as they built their ships, but upside down as it were."

At a time when everybody was boarding over, papering over any old beam, Deb was exposing hers and glorying in them. She had also bought two Thoroughgood hunters, a spanking gig and a horse to draw it; two riding habits, two silk dresses and four hats.

Now she said, "I think it would be nice, George, to have a family Christmas party here—if the girls agree; and make it my housewarming, too."

"I'm fully in favour." There had been no purely family party at

Gad's since Mamma died. Her memory was too closely associated with the place and everybody would have felt that it was not the same. Nor, try as she might, could Deb build up, in Park, quite the right atmosphere. The family entity had broken, and although the four children enjoyed themselves unreservedly, the grown-ups were aware of change and loss and absences. As Caroline said later to Edward, "I think *all* anniversaries are a mistake."

Still, there was the Meet on Boxing Day to look forward to. Whatever the weather the South Suffolk met at Baildon, outside the *Hawk in Hand,* on Boxing Day. The hounds ran about and were petted by onlookers, especially by children, enjoying for a brief hour the domestic, human contact which all foxhounds secretly craved. And the landlord of the inn, with his henchmen, dispensed punch, steaming-hot and very faintly flavoured with rum. There was always a cap-round, and this year, due to Caroline's mechanisations, it was to be in aid of the Friends of the Hospital. Also, this year, Noel would be there, mounted on his pony, and Melville on the one that had been Sam's. Just part of the parade.

All I wanted for Sam that day; had Tim only been a little less stubborn . . .

"See you tomorrow," everybody said. Though the sky threatened snow and George said, casting an inherited weatherwise eye at the sky, "It won't be much of a turnout tomorrow, Deb, if there's a fall."

"We must go, for Caro's sake. Call for me, eh?"

A few flakes fell indecisively as George walked home. It was still early, Deb's party had died under its own inanition and the threat of the weather. Was there anything more depressing than the tag end of Christmas Day? He was not going home to an empty house; Jenny's room was lighted and from it came the sounds of seasonable revelry; since Jenny could no longer get to the village, half the village, it seemed, must come to her.

George was closing his front door when he heard the thud of hoofs. One of his bachelor friends come over to share a Christmas evening drink. Happily, he pulled the door wide. A thicker flurry of snow momentarily obscured his view. The rider came on, reined in at the very doorstep in a most unhorsemanlike way, and Johnny Faulkner fell, rather than dismounted, from the saddle.

Johnny Faulkner; about the last person George expected to see;

there was always a big family gathering at Stratton Strawless for Christmas.

"George! Had to come, George."

George's first thought was: Drunk. Johnny did sometimes take the glass too many; but in the light of the hall lamp, George saw that Johnny looked more upset than drunk. He was not dressed for riding, wore no overcoat or hat. And he was crying! George had never before seen a man cry and had not, since childhood, cried himself. He was appalled.

It was likely that Johnny had had another blazing row with his parents—probably about whether Chloe should be admitted to the family circle. But there had been blazing rows before and Johnny had been hotly angry, not tearful.

Violet had her faults, but her good points, too; she had remembered to mend the fire and to light the lamps, so that the living room was welcoming. George pushed Johnny on to the settle, poured some brandy and said, "Here, drink this. That'll pull you together."

Johnny's teeth chattered on the glass; tears and drips of water from his soaked hair dripped into it, on to it.

First things first.

"Shan't be a second," George said. He galloped upstairs, two at a time, snatched his warm woollen dressing-gown and a towel. He even spared a thought for the horse, ridden hard for quite a distance and then left out in the snow. He ran along to the door of Jenny's room and shouted,

"Is there a man in there? Go round to the front, take Mr Faulkner's horse to the stable and chuck a rug over it." Then because it was quicker he thundered down the back stairs, through the kitchen littered with the debris of the hospitality that Violet had extended to all-comers, and so into the living room by the rear door.

"Shuck those wet clothes," he said. On the side nearer the fire Johnny's clothes were already beginning to steam. George had a sharp, sudden memory of another time, a long time ago, when he'd been concerned about Johnny's being soaked. That had really been the start of it all, a sincere, happy friendship with Johnny, and for Chloe a love which was more imaginative than real.

Johnny had managed to empty his glass and the brandy had helped. He was no longer crying and the violent shuddering was

easing. George replenished Johnny's glass and poured a measure
for himself. He was to need it!

"Chloe's dead," Johnny said.

"Dead! Good God! What happened?"

"I knew you'd understand. I had to come, George. I knew at
least you wouldn't say, Oh what a pity, oh what a dreadful accident, and we mustn't spoil the children's Christmas. When they
know as well as I do she killed herself and they drove her to it. I
just couldn't bear. The humbug. I just couldn't stand it. I'll tell
you. . . . It was like this. They've been putting out their tenta-
cles, trying to get the poor darling decently disposed of, and somewhere in the wilds of Yorkshire there's an old great-aunt by marriage or some such, going blind; she wanted somebody to lead her
about and read to her. I did protest. George, I made a stand. I
pointed out—poor darling, she could just read, about like a child
of four. No use. They wanted Chloe out before Christmas. All
those prim-faced, snotty-nosed little brats might be contaminated!
And my sisters and their husbands, all so smug and noble, acting
as though she was an open sewer. Anyhow, she said she'd rather go
than stay, and can you wonder? So I took her as far as York and
saw her safely on to the little branch-line train. . . . I swear,
George, she seemed all right then. But she opened the door and
stepped out, down a fifty-foot embankment." Johnny's composure
broke. "She must have looked like a broken doll. . . . And *they*
call it an accident! They're delighted."

George felt a flick of remorse. If he'd been a shade less cautious,
followed his heart and let his head have no say, this might not
have happened. He would have known that in Chloe's life he
would never be first, he could have arranged for her to see Johnny
as often as she wanted to.

But that was no way to think! George had never found it easy
to accept blame, even from himself.

"I am damned sorry, Johnny."

"I knew you would be. You liked her, too."

"Yes, I—liked her."

"I blame myself entirely. If I hadn't worked like a slave and just
for pocket-money, I could have set her up, somewhere snug and
away from them all. Waiting for dead men's shoes, George, my
boy; very unprofitous occupation!"

When Johnny began to jumble his words, sometimes most

amusingly, it was a sign of imminent intoxication. Well, why not? What other comfort could he offer?

"I'm not going back," Johnny said. "That'll give 'em something to think about. Let 'em explain that away. What a pity! What a sad accident!!"

"You mustn't talk like that, Johnny. What'd happen to Stratton Strawless?"

"Rosa's boy can have it and I wish him joy with it. I'm off to Canada."

"That's nonsense, Johnny."

"I'd like to see somebody try to stop me. . . ."

Deb did a bit of desultory clearing up in the big room, went into the kitchen and made a pot of tea and carried it into the little room where she worked. All in all the family party had not been a good idea. Sam was missing. She had not abandoned him, he had abandoned her and no doubt he was happy, in his own way at Foxton. One could only hope so. But there had, in addition to the general, rather sad feeling of change, a few of those— well, you could only call them unfortunate remarks which could only be made in close family circles. The worst of all perhaps, Edward's earnest, and professional opinion that the best cure for Everard's multifarious small ailments would be a real holiday in England.

"He goes up into the hills," Diana said. She sounded defensive.

"I know. But it is not the same. If it were why should there be the more or less general rule of home leave after five years? You should insist, Di."

Caro said, "How would you like it if I insisted that you came home punctually for supper?" Caro asked.

"I do try," Edward said, humbly.

"Papa always does his best," Daphne said. "Miss Pakefield says my papa is the best man she knows."

"Well, Honey, perhaps she doesn't know very many."

"Miss Pakefield says it's a pity Noel isn't more like Papa."

"And that is enough of the Gospel according to Miss Pakefield for one day," Caroline said, with quite an edge to her voice. She found it extraordinarily easy to be irritated by her daughter, the child she had actually *prayed* for. Plain, solid, stolid and boring, altogether too much like Edward.

Well, it was over now. Deb dipped her pen, wrote *Chapter Five* and underlined it, and was soon lost to the world. She was brought back by a growl from her great dog, a present from George when she moved into her own house. "He's a proper guard dog—Walker still breeds a few. And he'll be company for you."

"It's all right, Walker. It's only Sally."

Sally was Joe Snell's youngest daughter; delighted to find a place within a few yards of her own home. She'd had permission to sleep out on Christmas night, but probably the snow had prevented some other members of the family from getting home, so Sally had come back.

Walker did not believe that. He put up his hackles and moved to the door.

"All right then. Go see for yourself," Deb said. She opened the door of the little room and Walker went bounding across the now dimly lighted space to guard, if necessary to defend the front door, which opened directly into the big room. When the door opened and his sense of smell caught up with his sense of hearing, Walker was all fawning apology. Deb said,

"George! Come back for a nightcap?" But before he spoke she knew that something was wrong.

"Deb, it's too awful. I don't know what to do."

Old Mr Gordon had been Coroner for many years but he had at last handed over the thankless job, and James had, naturally, been appointed to succeed him. So to the horror of it all was added a touch of absolute unreality; James was sir; George was Mr Thorley; Johnny was the deceased.

"Mr Thorley, can you tell us exactly what happened?"

"No, sir. It was too sudden. I was showing him—the deceased —my new gun. It was a Christmas present. It is a new model, one with which neither of us was familiar, but I had tried it out, earlier in the day, so I knew more about it. . . . So I said: No, not that way. Here give it to me. And as it changed hands, it went off and . . ."

The story was a concocted one—never had Deborah's skill been better employed; but the emotion was genuine. Everybody recognised that. And that a loaded shot-gun should be thus casually handled struck nobody as strange. Similarly lethal weapons stood about in almost every farmhouse kitchen, and the first thing a country child learned was not to touch.

As Deborah had said, a story to be acceptable must be simple and plausible, with a grain of truth in it.

What had actually happened was far more dramatic. Johnny, mad with grief and a bit a drunk, bent on going to Canada, had spotted the gun, snatched it up and threatened George with it. And one grappling hand must have moved the safety catch, another touched the trigger. "Deb, it took him just under the chin. But it could have been me. And I wish to God it had been."

Death by misadventure sounded a bit better than plain accidental death, though they both meant much the same thing. The foreman of the jury gave that as his verdict, and said, "Sir, if allowable, we'd like to say two things. Loaded guns shouldn't be played about with. And we all felt for Mr Thorley." They all felt —but in a remote way, for the dead man's parents. But they came from the other side of Southbury; they weren't local as Mr Thorley was, well-known and well-liked, popular as he was to be to the end.

The earth kept on turning on its axis, night and day, day and night, Spring, Summer, Autumn, Winter; Spring again. The peripheral elements of the once close-knit family over which Mrs Thorley had once brooded so carefully span off and were absorbed into the wider world and were by the years engulfed. Only George left any kind of memory behind him—and that a bitter one.

Sam left no trace. He stayed at Foxton for three years arguing with Tim. Sam said, "The truth is, you care more about horses than you do about people. Think about all the poor people in London. Think of the lepers in Africa."

"I do. I subscribe. I can't save them all. Nobody could. Nobody ever will. And let me tell you, all this Radical talk is damaging the Methodist cause."

"Not as much as apathy. You think your duty's done if you live a sober life and support the chapel."

"So it is."

"Didn't Christ say—sell all that thou hast and give to the poor? And you won't even give fifty pounds to Duff's soup kitchens! All right, I shall ask my Uncle George."

"You'll need to pick your moment, son; from what I hear most of the time he hasn't got fifty pence." Sam thought, but did not say, that he would ask Mother. By common consent, Deborah was never mentioned in house. Some perverse streak in Tim made him more resentful against her now than ever before—she'd taken away a good sensible boy, promising Methodist material, and sent back a daft tub-thumper.

Deb gave Sam what he asked for without a quibble and George, flush at the moment, donated two pounds. Sam thought he might as well take the money to Duff personally, fell under Duff's spell again and stayed, busy and happy in the slums of Bethnal Green until he died of typhus.

Deborah left no trace, except insofar as her constant loans to George kept Gad's intact, and that Melville Spicer owed his education—Eton and Trinity—to her. Her career as a writer proved to be meteoric; as suddenly as everyone had wanted to read D. Willoughby, they ceased to do so; for no specific reason that Mr Hammond could name, except mounting competition; a new meteor every six months. He remained kindly, and aware of the debt he owed her, but his terms dwindled to twenty pounds down and ten for any subsequent impression. A sum he knew he would never have to pay.

Everybody had always regarded Deborah as the eldest of the Gad's Hall girls, so it seemed fitting that she should die first. She died as unobtrusively as she had lived—all things considered. "Just a simple cold, Sally. I'll have a day in bed. And a boiled onion." Three days and several boiled onions later, Sally suggested sending for the doctor.

"He couldn't do anything. I would like to see Willy, though." Her voice was now a croak and a full breath was hard and painful to draw.

Willy came, just as he was, smelling of stables and horses, and almost speechless with distress.

"Willy, if I don't get the better of this, you'll find my will in my writing table, the long drawer in the middle." She had made her will as soon as she received Robbie Duff's letter informing her of Sam's death. She'd thought then—The trouble is, George can't be entirely trusted; he *means* well, but he'd sell my horses, if he found himself in a tight corner. And he had a fatal way of getting into tight corners.

". . . so, if it isn't too much to ask, Willy, look after them all, and pay yourself for the work. When the money runs out, or you get past it, send for the knacker and have them killed *here*. I don't want them sold. I don't want them to go to the yard."

She was not without assets, even now. George had borrowed, paid back, borrowed again. He was honest, after his fashion, and would realise that Park and its meadow were rightly hers until he had repaid every loan, and although both Caro and Diana thought her home bleakly furnished, she had a few valuable things. A pair of superb Chinese lacquer cabinets, several Persian rugs, her writing table, some silver.

It was torture for her to speak, torture for Willy to listen. When he spoke he sounded just as hoarse and choked up as she did.

"You know me. You can trust me, Miss Deb."

"I always did, Willy."

"Yes. We allus . . . got along all right."

He tried—and failed—to reckon the span of years.

"But you'll get the better of this . . ."

"Perhaps. If not, well, you know, Willy."

"I'll see to it."

She said, "Thank you, Willy," and held out her hand. Afterwards when he could think better, Willy reckoned that he'd loved her for thirty years; and they parted with the kind of handshake that men use to seal a bargain.

"Forty-four does seem so young to die," Caroline said, weeping bitterly.

Diana agreed, but felt bound to add dutifully that Everard had died at an even younger age. She had taken so easily to widowhood that convention demanded some extra show of grief as a form of appeasement to some undefined kind of guilt. Even the silver frame around the picture of Everard and his tiger was replaced by a black velvet one. After a time Caro, who was fundamentally kind, said, "Really, Di does carry this to extremes; you can't even mention the weather but she'll drag Everard into it and say that he liked or loathed this kind of day. It's morbid."

The only aspect of her widowed state about which Diana was reticent was the financial one. In India Everard been successful, earned, by English standards, large sums of money; made her a useful allowance. But his provisions for the future were completely inadequate; hardly anything saved and only a miserably small life-insurance. But for Deb's generosity Melville could not have continued at Eton or hoped to go to Cambridge. But, of course, one could always say that Everard had been cut off in his prime. One could always say that one could just manage, and proceed to do, remembering that odious Mr van Haagen who, years ago, had read in her cards that she would never have much money. One curious quirk of fortune befell her which Mr van Haagen had not foreseen and that was the marriage of Belle to Richard Walford. Old enough to be her father, everybody said with truth. Indeed, except for the arrival of Everard Spicer in Baildon, and Diana's falling in love with him, Richard might well have been the father of Diana's children. As it was, middle-aged, well-to-do, a confirmed bachelor, Richard, across a crowded concert room, had seen Diana's daughter, so like her mother, and felt his blood run hot again. And this time nobody should be given time to intervene. "Pressing his suit with a red-hot iron," was Caro's comment on that whirlwind courtship.

Edward continued to enjoy, in a way, the company of the butterfly he had caged, but by stages too small to be measured he had transferred his attention and his hopes to Daphne, his daughter. All hope of making anything out of Noel had faded. He was idle, just about literate and no more; at the Academy Miss Pakefield had regretted that he was not more like his father; at the Grammar School to which he was presently transferred, he was frequently subject to the cane—not as often, however, as his behaviour warranted. He had such charm, such an engaging manner. Really, the exasperated and conscientious Headmaster thought; it is like beating a roe deer because it is not an ox.

Edward was even more realistic. Bitterly disappointed in his son, he said, "The only future I can see for him is a salesman. He could sell hot soup in Hell." Eventually, using his influence, Edward found a place for his son, selling medical supplies and equipment; quite respectable, and in a way worthy. Edward himself had always tried to keep up to date, but there were, he knew, doctors in outlying places who still used wooden stethoscopes, and if they had ever used chloroform had splashed it on lumps of cotton wadding in an uncontrolled, dangerous way.

Cheerfully, jauntily, Noel set out on his rounds. He wasn't selling hot soup in Hell. He was selling, not only new instruments, new ways of packaging pills and potions, but himself, Noel Taylor. In almost no time at all he had his own business. Doing well.

For Daphne the path was far less easy. She had always been clever; she had always known what she wanted to do. "I want to be a doctor, like you, Papa."

"Honey, you can't."

"Why not?"

Why not? Could you say to an earnest, studious girl, fired by a worthy ambition—Because you are a girl? Such an answer, unfair in any case, was rendered more so when Edward thought of his stepmother-in-law who had defied all the rules about what a woman could or could not do, braved the Corn Exchange and cattle markets and Cattle Shows, made a success, without—and this was a vital point—without ever sacrificing her femininity. Even when she drank whisky.

"I see no reason why not," Edward said. "But a lot of other people will. However, we can but try."

So he committed himself to the long, uphill, discouraging struggle. But a well-rewarded one.

When George Thorley was forty he married, because after all a man must have a son to succeed him. He chose well, a pretty, plump girl, one of the many who had been trotted out for his approval. Her father was a hearty, coarse cattle dealer who had prospered and could afford, without robbing his son, to dower his daughter with two thousand pounds, upon which he was determined George should never lay a finger. He liked him, most people did, but he did not regard him as financially sound; too many ups and downs had occurred since that game old girl, Mrs Thorley, died. So Amelia was to have the interest on the money, which should ensure her of moderate comfort whatever happened.

Since Amelia was eighteen and George over forty—and living a remarkably dangerous life, hunting and steeplechasing, always, however getting off lightly, his nose broken once and his collar bone twice, it was odds on that Amelia would live longer. So when she was a widow the whole sum was to be hers. In the unlikely, unthinkable event of her dying first, the money was to revert to her father, or her brother. Amelia's mother, with whom every major action was discussed, ventured a protest.

"What about 'Melia's children?"

"They'll be his. He can do the providing. Steady him down a bit to be responsible."

Nothing steadied down George Thorley, least of all his devoted, admiring wife, who thought—as her father did—that George had shown her great honour in choosing her.

The marriage was happy enough. Amelia had none of the out-of-this-world fairy quality of his first lost love, none of the style or wit of his mother, but she was a good audience, and a good housekeeper. She would probably have proved to be a good mother too, but she died in childbed.

George's son did not admire, emulate, or even like his father, and George found it hard to be fond of the stolid, solemn boy, so plodding, so penny-pinching, so *dull*.

Many people—growing fewer as the years went on, did remember George Thorley for his generosity, his lavish hospitality, his infectious high spirits, above all for his sportsmanship; he rode —and won—his last race when he was seventy-one and hunted until he broke his neck, surely the most suitable death and the one he would have chosen. But to his son he was an extravagant, irresponsible show-off who had damned near ruined Gad's and left behind a pile of debts, all of which were paid. By the son who never had a good word to say about him.

part two

Bob and I and our two boys, John and Tony, lived happily enough through our first dark winter at Gad's. I say happily enough, which is a qualified statement, because the family never seemed complete without Alice. Heap the fire, draw the curtains, set the table and listen to the wind howling and think—They're all in, thank God, and immediately I remembered that Alice was not with us. She was safe enough, happy enough and in good health; but she was with her grandmother, in Baildon, not here, part of the family, as she should have been.

Bob, busy with the perfecting of his design for his sugar-lifting machine, thought, or chose to think, that Alice was with his mother to be company for her, and I did not dream of telling him the truth. Poor man, he had enough to contend with, the flaccid left arm and leg, the still unreliable speech that his accident had inflicted upon him. It would have been cruel as well as ridiculous to say Alice was scared to death of something in this house.

John had known—actually before I did—that Alice was scared to go upstairs alone, even in broad daylight; but he was only eleven and completely engrossed in school and what were called extra-mural activities. He'd probably forgotten. I remembered; and I knew, because I had experienced it, that something *was* slightly wrong with the attic floor. I'd felt it in October when I was storing apples; something that I can only describe as despair, ultimate hopelessness. Not fear. Alice, not yet nine, could hardly have felt despair, that feeling of the utter futility of everything, so in her case it had been fear. She had confided in her grandmother, who from the first had sensed something wrong in the apparently ideal, welcoming, and extremely cheap house. Ella, my mother-in-law, had called it Evil, had understood Alice better than I did, and whisked her away.

I would have avoided, had it been possible, that attic floor, but it was impossible. I was trying to make—making—a precarious living for us all, by selling what Gad's produced, and the stored apples and pears were an asset. I had to mount that last, twisting stairway, brace myself, shut my mind, concentrate upon what I was doing. Is this apple spotted? Has this pear rotted inwardly?

Quick, be quick; put anything however defective into one basket, the sound, saleable fruit into the other and hurry down, for this is dangerous ground.

Who coined the phrase, Something nasty in the woodshed? It had passed into common usage; a kind of joke. Well, with me it was something wrong with the attic floor in the house that had been our life-raft.

Whatever it was seemed to be contained there, that is for me; the rest of the house was all right.

It was coming round to Christmas again and I began to wonder whether Ella and Alice could be coaxed into spending it with us. Ella was always such a stickler for family get-togethers at Christmas—it was in fact her insistence that I and the children should spend Christmas with her in Baildon instead of, as I had planned, with Bob in Santa Barbara which had saved us from being involved in the bomb outrage which had crippled Bob.

Ella's response to my suggestion was an unequivocal No.

"I'm sorry, Jill. Naturally I want us to be together at Christmas, but not in that house! Quite apart from my own feelings, it would be most unwise for Alice ever to enter it again. It would revive all her fears and set her back. You must come here."

I said—and I knew that it sounded fatuous,

"But Mr Thorley has promised me a turkey."

"And what is to prevent your bringing it here?"

Nothing that I could think of on the spur of the moment. John would grouse, I knew; he'd never really fitted into Ella's small elegant house. In order to help to pay for Bob's expensive treatment at a place called Everton, Ella had gallantly sold her valuable china, but a great deal remained, the worthless things, but pretty and cherished. A growing boy, all feet and elbows, was not at ease in such surroundings and sometimes the very effort to be careful made him seem clumsier than usual. And Tony, emerging from the toddler stage, was just naturally clumsy.

I had no choice, however.

Ella said, when I had conceded,

"I don't think you realised how near Alice was to a complete nervous breakdown. As I have said before, Bob is incapable of believing anything that can't be measured on a slide rule. And you— frankly I don't think you are very different in some respects. Had you been you would never have gone to live in that horrible house."

I remembered how, after one visit of inspection, on a summer afternoon she had denounced it; and then confounded me by offering to sell her pretty doll's house, add her resources to our meagre ones and set up house with us somewhere else.

"It hasn't served us too badly," I said. I thought of all I wrenched out of Gad's garden, of the infinite kindness shown us by the former owner, George Thorley. I also thought about Ella, so staunch in our time of trouble, and how curious it was to be able to admire, esteem, like, even love a person, and yet find hardly an inch of common ground.

Ella said, "Did you ever see the drawings which Alice produced when she was living at Gad's?"

"Her Art Teacher once told me that her style had changed. And then recovered. But, no, I never saw any that could be called —peculiar."

"Well, I did. Towards the end of each term, drawings not wanted for the Open Day are brought home. Alice brought some of hers. I burned them. They were *so* horrible."

"In what way?"

As so often happened in my mother-in-law's presence, I felt rebuked, without any words. No doubt during that brief period when Alice lived at Gad's she had made drawings under my very eye, but God! I'd had other things to think of at the time. And when her Art Teacher had used the word *Macabre* and spoken of imps and hobgoblins, I'd called it a phase. And after Alice had gone to stay with Ella, I'd had a message, saying that I had been right, the phase had ended and Alice was now drawing in her old, promising way. End-of-term, Open Day, exhibitions had confirmed this.

Now I felt that I had been very much remiss, having to ask Ella in what way my own daughter's drawings had been, for a short time, so horrible, so macabre.

"It is very difficult to explain," Ella said. "As you know she paints flowers quite beautifully, but many of those she did at that time had horrid, leering faces in their centres. There were other things, too; distortions—a goat with four horns, for example. . . . Very *nasty!*"

There again one could not quite dismiss Ella's judgement, for she had once told me that she was sure of Elsie, her maid, because she gave her her twice-daily insulin injection, a task I should have shrunk from. There was more in Ella than met the eye. Behind the prettiness—which lasted to the end—the devotion to Bridge, to the Ladies' Luncheon Club and the Flower arrangers, there was rock. I knew. I had now and again butted my silly head against it, and I had leaned against it when the rest of the world rocked under me.

It is strange to think that in a way the Baildon Ladies' Luncheon Club should ever have affected me. I never joined it; I had no time, I had no hat—they still wore hats on occasion! And, on the whole, I dislike being talked to. If somebody has written a book called TWENTY YEARS IN TIMBUCTOO, and one can buy it in paperback, does it further inform one to listen to a repetition?

However, one evening in May—another five months of Alice lost to us—the telephone rang. The telephone was really a luxury which we could not afford, but it suited my customers to be able to ring up and know what I had to offer this week, and Bob's invention involved many calls, too. The telephone stood on his worktable and it was rather clever of Ella to have chosen supper time, when he would not be near it, and I, being more agile, would reach it first. She sounded excited, but of course in a controlled way; except when she cried, which she did easily, Ella was always controlled.

"Jill! Our lecturer at luncheon today was a medium. Mrs Catherwood. Have you ever heard of her?"

"No. Should I have done?"

"Perhaps not. But she is very famous. And I think *completely* sincere. As you know, we cannot afford high fees." Some of Ella's talk was like that; there was a certain logic, but you had to work it out. In this case it meant that she considered Mrs Catherwood sincere because she was unmercenary enough to come and lecture Baildon Ladies' Luncheon Club for five guineas, plus expenses.

I said, "Yes?"

"Well, as you know, dear, I am inclined to be sceptical in these matters, but she was very convincing. *And* since she is staying with Mrs Gordon overnight and a few of us went on to tea there, I seized the opportunity of talking to her about your house. She was immensely interested and would like to see it."

"You mean in a professional capacity?"

"Yes. But, dear, Bob must not know that. You know how he would jeer. You must just say that she is a person who is interested in old houses."

"He might believe that—though there are quite a number about. But what does she intend to *do*, Ella? Hold a séance? Go into a trance? I mean even Bob might notice if she did."

"Dear, you are completely out of date. Nothing like that. Mrs Catherwood is extra-sensitive, but unlike most of us she can *interpret* what she feels."

I thought of what I had felt that October afternoon outside the attic, which had been locked for so many years and which George Thorley had broken open at my request. Let her interpret *that*, I thought.

"All right. When?"

"Well, if entirely convenient to you, tomorrow morning. She has another speaking engagement in Bywater in the afternoon. She drives herself. May I tell her, then, about half-past ten?"

Little knowing what I was letting myself in for, I said yes. I then offered Ella's explanation of Mrs Catherwood to Bob, who accepted it placidly.

Maybe I was out of date. To me the word "medium" called up a woman, fairly old, rather fat and dressed in black, so Mrs Catherwood was a surprise to me. At most thirty-five, very slim, almost, not quite pretty. She wore a very smart trouser suit of a pleasing shade of green, just right with her hair, auburn and close-cropped. You had to be very close to her to see what was different: her eyes. They were greenish and the pupils were mere pinpoints. I thought instantly: Drugs! Not that I knew all that much about them either.

Drugged or not, she drove well; and she had a good car to drive. A Jansen, very enviable!

I had been looking out for her, and though I did not say, Mrs Catherwood, I presume, I did understand in a flash how Stanley felt when he made that famous remark to Livingstone.

"It was very good of you to let me come, Mrs Spender," she said, as soon as we had greeted each other. "I'm always anxious to learn."

Learn what, I wondered.

She entered the house briskly; she might have been come to read a meter. Halfway across the hall she paused and seemed to sniff the air, as I had done when I first entered this house. But I was sniffing for evidence of damp and decay. What was her quarry? She gave a tiny nod of satisfaction, looked at the stairs, hesitated and asked,

"You have another stairway?"

I led her into the kitchen and indicated the back stairs.

"Thank you. Do you mind if I go alone? Some concentration is demanded."

"Help yourself," I said. "Would you like coffee—afterwards?"

She said rather cryptically, "Thanks. I may need it."

She was gone a long time. The coffee was ready, and when the clock on the landing struck eleven I poured a cup and took it through to Bob, who came out of his trance—work-induced—just long enough to thank me. I then went back and began making preparations for lunch, peeling potatoes and mincing cold meat for a shepherd's pie.

When she did appear, Mrs Catherwood looked paler and was wiping her palms on her handkerchief.

Tony had come in for milk and biscuits and was still there. He was now so fully mobile, able to open doors and mount stairs, that I was used to his appearances and disappearances, and to his presence. I lifted the coffee pot and ushered Mrs Catherwood into the living room, where I had the cups and the biscuits ready. She'd lost all her briskness and sat down on the sunny window seat as though exhausted. I thought I saw her shiver.

She said, "*Pas devant l'enfant.*"

Tony said, loud and clear, "Isn't she *ugly?*"

She said, "It *is* contagious!" and I said,

"Have another biscuit, Tony, and then go and feed the hens. The crusts are on the dresser."

"You must be careful of *him*, too, Mrs Spencer. He may be sensitive, too. Your daughter certainly is; and your mother-in-law." She drank some coffee and shivered. This time I was sure.

"Would you like a whisky?" I recalled how I had felt after my experience on the attic floor, and how I had thought about how helpful a good whisky would be. I had not taken it, and so far as I knew the half bottle most carefully and tactfully brought by Ella on the day when she came to lunch—and took Alice away—was still there on the top shelf of the larder.

"No, thank you. That is another thing I must warn you of. Amongst all the many impressions, there is a distinct tang of alcoholism. Compulsive drinking. Until this place is purged, nobody should drink in this house."

That, at least, was original, something Ella could hardly have primed her with. I must admit that in my mind I still half suspected some kind of collusion; Ella saying that she sensed something dreadful and that Alice was afraid, and Mrs Catherwood latching on to it; something else to write about, something else to go hawking round to Ladies' Luncheons.

"Alcoholism is not much of a risk here," I said. "My husband's condition allows him to drink hardly at all. And I'm hardly likely . . . if only because of the cost."

"I know. But circumstances change." From one of her jacket pockets she produced one of those very expensive cigarette cases with a lighter in the lid.

"I'm sorry," I said. "I have some, somewhere."

"Never mind. Have one of these. . . . Now, I have no wish to alarm you, only to help, if I can. And you must not dismiss this as nonsense, Mrs Spender. I am not a novice. I have on more than one occasion helped in police investigations—some of a grisly nature, but physical. This is different, more elemental. I fully realise that what I am about to say may sound ridiculous, but it is there in that attic; devil worship, demoniac possession, ritual slaughter and suicide, that final act of despair. An elemental took over and is still there, evil and unappeased. Hungering for new victims."

She smoked, frowning, for several seconds. Then, in a more composed manner she went on,

"I have a feeling that you think that I am merely repeating—with some elaboration—what your mother-in-law told me. That is not so. She told me that she had felt something evil, she used the expression, "almost overcome," so that she hurried away. She also said that your daughter was always afraid in this house, and began to draw in a style different from her own. I was interested and decided to expose myself. I am not a crank. After all, people vary in their ability to bear pain; hearing varies, so does sight. I just happen to be super-sensitive to something, call it atmosphere if you like; and I assure you I know more about that attic, indeed about the whole house, than your mother-in-law could possibly know. I very much doubt if what I know can ever be checked; it all happened a long time ago. But the subject, the victim, was young— and a creative artist. Such people are extremely vulnerable. I don't suppose that it has ever occurred to you, but think how many creative people go mad, commit suicide or become debauched in some way. The old adage said that Satan found work for idle hands to do. He may. I don't know. I do know that he prefers to use busy ones, creative ones. Who wants to recruit a lot of lay-abouts? I see that my use of the word Satan embarrasses you, Mrs Spender. Why?"

"I wasn't aware that I was embarrassed. If I seem so, it may be because, well, I think it too personal. Like . . . like calling a destructive hurricane Emily."

For the first time she looked at me with something approaching approval.

"We'll stick to abstractions then. Evil came into this house, innocently invited, by a young girl, an artist. It affected what I gather was a hitherto happy family. It destroyed her. It could destroy again. That is why I say that your daughter should not come home—and that the little boy is at risk—until the place is exorcised."

"Oh, come! That is too mediaeval."

"Evil—and Good are timeless, Mrs Spender."

"Besides, if one can believe all one hears, exorcism can do more harm than good."

"True. The ritual may be improperly performed. Or again it may be performed by somebody who is not strong enough to bear the confrontation. Remember, your mother-in-law spoke of being almost overcome. And even for me, veteran that I am, it was a disagreeable experience. As, I think, it once was for you."

Now how could she know that? I had never breathed a word to anyone about that October afternoon.

I suppose I gaped. Then I hastened to defend myself—not always a wise thing to do.

"I happened to be feeling low, both in mind and body. My back was aching, I'd been overworking; prospects were not too good. And I had a very personal problem."

"I know. *You* left an imprint there, too. But consider; suppose at that moment the Dev . . . the Force of Evil, I mean . . . had presented itself, wearing a very attractive disguise, offering comfort and security, and you had been a weak character. What then?"

"Complete chaos."

"There you are. You were strong enough to resist. I would hazard a guess that you had a strongly religious background, as a child."

"You would be right."

"Well." She looked at her watch. "I have an engagement. I've done what I could, and I do beg you to think seriously about it."

"I will."

She gave me a kind of grin. "Your mother-in-law, who, incidentally, is extremely fond of you said you were incorrigibly stubborn. Try not to be for the sake of the children."

We went out together to the front of the house, where her car stood. A race horse of a car. I thought of my poor, ailing old station wagon.

She caught that in a flash and said, "Window-dressing! I'm most anxious that people shouldn't think I'm *selling* whatever gift I have. Why should I? My father left me a fortune. Easily disposed of with things as they are. But window-dressing comes naturally to me. I was born a Hawksley!"

I knew the world-famous store; I had even been inside it, once. In the good days when Bob was managing a beet-sugar factory at Scunwick, and doing well. But with his ambitions unsatisfied, so he'd joined the brain-drain, and come back a wreck.

Mrs Catherwood stuck out her hand.

"I don't need to tell you to be brave—you are that. Be sensible, though, and hopeful. Much awaits you!"

This was one of the moments when I was aware of a lack. In the old days Bob and I could discuss anything; we often argued—no holds barred. Now I had to be very careful. One of the many doctors who had helped to put him together again had warned me that he must not be subject to any kind of stress. Not that Bob, even now, would worry about living in a haunted house; as his mother said, he would jeer; but he would be annoyed with her and with me, and with Mrs Catherwood. He'd call us a gaggle of silly, superstitious old women. And anger, after all, is a form of stress. Also he was quite capable of saying that if Alice had gone to Baildon because of such rank tomfoolery, she'd better come home at once and learn some sense. That just would not do. Offhand as I may have seemed to Mrs Catherwood, incorrigibly stubborn as I might appear to my mother-in-law, I knew that there was something wrong on that attic floor. I wanted to talk about it. I may give the impression of being strong and brave, etc, etc, but I am not. Actually I'm weak-minded; on almost every subject under the sun I dwell in a halfway house. Even when I appear to be brave it is often because I'm scared not to be.

I said, "Tony, you were very rude to that visitor." He was only three, but manners must be inculcated early. And perhaps . . . Oh, let's swallow the whole dose, I thought; believe that she had actually met Evil head on, believe that it was, as she called it, contagious, and the child had seen more than I had. "It is rude to call people ugly."

"But she was. Just like Mr Thorley's dog. The cross one."

I knew which one he meant. The Thorleys had no children. I think that if they had had, George with his strong sense of tradition would have put up more of a fight against his wife's dislike of Gad's and her determination to have a modern house. But they had no children, so they lavished a lot of affection on their dogs. By that I do not mean that people who have children and love them cannot love their dogs, too. But there was something a little extravagant about Mrs Thorley's poodle, which had bows on its head, and regular beauty-parlour appointments, and could distinguish between plaice and haddock. George's cross dog was the most unfriendly, unrewarding animal I ever met. A real rogue with far more than the first allowed bite on his scoreboard. He tolerated his master, bullied two amiable spaniels and snarled at everybody.

I said, "Darling, how could that nice lady look like Mr Thorley's cross dog?"

"She did. She looked like Mr Thorley's cross dog. Like this."

My three-year-old wrinkled his little snub nose, drew back his upper lip, snarled. And then laughed.

"So I said she was ugly. And she was."

"But it was rude to say so."

"Must I say I'm sorry?"

"You can't. She's gone away."

"I'm glad. She looked just like Mr Thorley's cross dog. . . ."

Ella rang that evening, again as we were just sitting down to supper.

"Well?"

"She came," I said. "And she agrees with you."

There was a small silence, and then Ella said,

"Then, my dear, something must be done about it."

"What?"

"My offer still stands. You know, I was so against that house from the first. Sell it. I'll sell mine and we'll find somewhere where we can all live together. Not in each other's pockets, but together. I believe the Old Rectory at Muchanger is for sale."

I could hear my own weak voice.

"But, Ella, it is such a good garden. And I've worked so hard."

So I had; I'd weathered the winter with cabbages in the open, lettuces under cloches. I'd grown new potatoes in the mended-up greenhouse and had them for sale at Easter. And now, at the end of almost of a year at Gad's, I should have within a month all the produce of the old asparagus bed, and, if bloom promised anything, masses of strawberries.

Must I forgo it all? Move away? Begin all over again. Just because of something, still not truly defined, in one small part of this house.

And there were other things to think of. George Thorley had only sold Gad's to us because he feared compulsory purchase, or squatters. Most of the furniture in the place belonged there; stuff he'd taken away and stored in the loft down at Park, and so gladly given—or lent us—on permanent loan, as with museums. We couldn't take that away with us.

"And besides," I said, "Bob is so happy here. No, Ella. It is most kind, and I do appreciate it. But I think we must stick it out."

"You're being unfair to Alice."

"I know." And probably to Tony too. There must be some reason why a perfectly normal young woman, not pretty, but far from ugly, should seem to him to resemble a snarling dog. God! What a muddle.

My first-born appeared in the doorway carrying a bowl of soup with exaggerated care. He said in what he considered a tactfully low voice,

"I thought you'd better have this before it was cold."

I managed a smile of thanks as Ella said,

"Jill, *do* think about it."

"I will. I'm grateful, Ella. Good night."

John said, "I knew it was a female. How they do natter! Now Terry and I can say all we have to say in half a minute flat."

"That's sex discrimination, dear boy. You'll end in jail!"

I'd seldom felt less like cracking a joke, however mild.

I'd washed up and was just putting things back on the dresser when George Thorley walked in. He often did. The machine upon whose design Bob was working owed a great deal to George's practical suggestions and they enjoyed talking about it. Often, too often, he'd bring gifts, stuff from his dairy, toys for Tony—that I found pathetic in a man who should have had children of his own, some contribution towards whatever John's latest hobby was. There never was a more generous man.

"It's such a nice evening," he said, "and this brute needed a walk." The cross dog, inaptly named in puppyhood, Chum, had defeated his own purpose in life; he'd been bred as a guard dog, but a dog so congenitally ferocious as to attack everybody, postmen, legitimate callers, regular workpeople, is no guard at all, and Chum spent most of his time in a wire enclosure, big enough for an elephant. Even on his walks he had to be on a lead, the end of which George now attached to the dresser leg, as usual. As usual I offered a bowl of water, ungraciously received.

"Nobody ever got himself lumbered with such a beast," George said. "I ought to have him put down, but I can't bring myself to it."

I said, "I think Bob went back to his workroom. Do go through."

I believe Catholics, absolved, are exhorted to avoid the occasion for sin, and George Thorley and I, without a word spoken, had done just that. There'd been just that one flash between us, a communication between eyes, no more, and after that absolute caution.

This evening he said, "It's you I want to have a word with."

My heart gave a painful little jump and I thought—He's heard from that engineering firm in Peterborough. They're not going to take Bob's machine after all, and I shall have to break the news, which will just about finish him. It had been the idea that despite his handicaps, he could still be useful, productive—and eventually earning—that had kept Bob going. It had allowed him to ignore the fact that physically he had not improved quite as much as the optimists had predicted.

It was not that at all.

When we were seated, opposite each other by the kitchen table, George said,

"I've been a bit worried about you. Doris went to her Ladies' Luncheon thing, yesterday, and then on to tea with the chosen few and then to Bridge somewhere. So I didn't hear until break-fast time this morning, and then it was market day. I came as soon as I could. . . . Did that bloody-daft woman come here and bother you?"

"Mrs Catherwood came this morning."

"And scared you? I was afraid of that. Look, you mustn't take any notice. Doris never liked Gad's; she'd say anything to decry it —it was too inconvenient to run without more help than was available; it was isolated, it was draughty. I don't have to be mealy-mouthed with you, do I? It's a well-known fact, no animal breeds in an unfavourable environment. . . . So I gave in; moved down to Park, built her that pink boot-box and hoped—with what result, you know." I knew; at our first meeting he had mentioned his childlessness in a surprisingly resigned way. "I suppose we all have to justify ourselves, and of course Doris joined in that gab-ble, saying the place was haunted and all that rot. I don't often allow myself to get irked by Doris's goings on, but this morning I was damned annoyed. She shouldn't have done that. . . . There's some excuse for your mother-in-law, she's old and entitled to her fancies, and the daft creature, I suppose, makes a living out of quackery. Doris shouldn't have joined in."

Bob once said of me that in conservative company I turned bright red, in the company of those with socialist views, dark blue; he said I had an anti-chameleon complex. It went to work now.

"I'm not so sure," I said. And suddenly there I was, pouring it all out: Ella's experience, my own, all about Alice and Mrs Catherwood, who certainly was not a quack out to make a living. I cracked up entirely. I actually cried. George got up and came round the table and held me and made soothing sounds. Just what I needed, of course, strong supporting arms and a solid shoulder to cry on.

Absolutely disgusting!

Finally I pulled myself together sufficiently to say, "Go and talk to Bob. I'm all right. I shall manage. It was just . . . everything piled up."

"I know."

He did understand; he went to see Bob, having given me a final assurance that everything would be all right.

I was too utterly exhausted even to wonder how.

My grandmother—Mrs Catherwood had guessed, or sensed, rightly, about my childhood background—had often said that self-pity was the most destructive emotion. All afflictions, she held, were put upon us either by God, and therefore to be accepted with patience and humility, or brought upon us by our own foolishness, and therefore to be accepted with patience and humility and a determination to do better in future. So self-pity was despicable. I knew that and was indulging in it nonetheless. It seemed to me that from the moment Bob had decided to take that very inviting post in Santa Barbara, I'd been forced to pretend. I was against his going, but must pretend to be agreeable; pretend I didn't mind our separation; and when we were reunited, thanks to America, I had to pretend that he was getting better every day, pretend that I believed him capable of earning a living. . . . Finding Gad's had seemed such a stroke of luck, a roomy, solid, watertight house, a garden that could be made productive. And look how that had turned out—the biggest fraud of all. Now didn't know what to do, or what to think.

I said to myself: Snap out of it! Go tend your garden!

It was still light; the lingering end of a hot dry day. A good many things needed water. And water was handy. I had only to open the movable part of the chestnut fencing—Ella's gift to prevent Tony falling into the moat—and dip up bucketsful. Bob said that once he had his present job off his hands he'd rig up some less primitive way of irrigation.

I dipped water and sloshed and my back began to ache; a reminder of my moment of despair outside that attic door when I'd seen myself hopelessly disabled . . . That was back in October, and this was May, and here I was, still going strong, except for moments like this. I tried to cheer myself up; strawberries already formed; little pods on the peas, an abundance of asparagus, potatoes doing well. . . .

I closed the gateway in the fencing and turned and there was George Thorley, huge in the glimmering dusk.

He said, "If I've told you once I've told you a dozen times . . . You have only to say and I'll send a man up. But that's not what I came to say. I've been raking in my mind. I was so inattentive,

your husband thought I had market-day hangover. But I was putting bits and pieces together in my mind and I'm certain—so far
as anybody can be about the long ago, that your Mrs Cather-
whoever had it wrong. You remember, I told you once that Gad's
had gone straight from father to son? It was a byword. Thorleys
didn't breed girls—except once. I never knew my rascally old
grandfather, and my father hated him because he damned near
ruined the place, but he talked about him sometimes. *He* did
have some sisters, at least two sisters and two half sisters—my
great-grandmother had two of her own, so that makes four, and
then, years younger, my grandfather. And adding this and that, all
the girls are accounted for. So far as I can put it together there
never was a girl here who fits in with that load of rubbish. According to my father, all his aunts made decent marriages. . . . My
father never knew them; my grandfather lived to a good age, and
my father couldn't marry till he was out of the way. But one of
them lived down at Park—the old house—for a bit. I believe she
wrote a few books. One of them married the doctor at Baildon.
Another married a solicitor. And the other, the youngest, I think,
went to India and died young. So you see there couldn't have been
anything like the goings-on that crank described, could there?"

I could see that he was desperately anxious to reassure me, so
did not say what I thought, which was the goings-on might have
occurred at some much earlier time, before the byword of Thorleys only breeding boys had become established.

I said, "Yes. That sounds reasonable. And of course Mrs
Catherwood's story was rather extreme. I was silly to let it upset
me."

"If you ask me, you're in state where you could get upset over a
broken plate. I've been thinking about that, too. In future I'm
going send a man up every day for a couple of hours, whether you
like it or not."

The gable end which contained the attics jutted out over the
garden. Without thinking I looked out and saw something move
behind the bars of the window. Vague, pale grey, a face, but not
human. So now, I thought, you're beginning to *see* things. I
looked away, screwed my eyes shut, then looked back. It was still
there.

"Look!"

"My damned dog!" George said. "He must have chewed
through his lead."

He was right. Chum, having freed himself and found no other exit open to him, had galloped upstairs, and up and up. And Mrs Catherwood must have left *that* door open.

On Saturday I went into Baildon, taking some of cloche-grown stuff, and some flowering sprays from the shrubs which grew under the walnut tree, and some eggs. I did some shopping and then went to Ella's, with a dozen of the eggs and the very choicest of the sprays. Alice greeted me with the news that Gran was having a day in bed, but would like to see me.

Ella, though not far short of seventy—she was cagey about her age—had, for as long I had known her, enjoyed very good health, despite, or perhaps because of her fragile, Dresden china appearance. Nobody expected her to make any physical exertion or venture forth in bad weather.

Her bedroom—and never forget that when we were homeless, she had given it over to Bob and me because it was the largest in the house—was all pink and white and blue, except for a great bunch of dark red carnations, sent, I knew, by Ella's long-standing, absolutely platonic Boy Friend, Colonel Murray-Smith. Ella looked very pretty, but pale.

"It's nothing," she said. "I think I overdid things. Tuesday was a very busy day—as you know. On Wednesday I went to a Coffee Morning in aid of Oxfam. On Thursday there was a meeting of the Flower Club about the June display in St Mary's. Yesterday I felt quite exhausted. So today I thought I'd be lazy."

"Have you had the doctor?"

"My dear, what could he do? I'm beginning to suffer from a very common complaint. Anno Domini. For which, so far, nobody has found a cure. I must resign myself."

Something inside me fell away as I imagined Anno Domini catching up and devouring Ella. I admired her, I was grateful to her, I loved without liking her, which sounds a contradiction of terms, but can be fact.

Almost instantly there was an example of what annoyed me about her. I'd given my flowering boughs to Alice and said, "Put them in water," and now Alice came in with the vase, carrying it with that same care as John had shown, bringing me my cooling soup.

Ella said, "Thank you, darling. Is the vase quite dry?"

"Yes, Gran. I wiped it. Shall I put it on the dressing-table?"

To this trivial problem Ella gave concentrated attention and then said,

"I think not. On the chest-of-drawers."

It was probably this meticulous attention to detail which had transmitted itself to Bob and made him such a good engineer. It should not have grated on my nerves, but it did.

When Alice had gone, Ella said,

"Well, have you thought about it?"

"I have indeed. All the time."

"So has Mrs Catherwood. In fact I had a letter from her this morning."

Ella's mail, brought to her bedside, was not just scattered, helter-skelter; it was in a neat pile, under a very pretty paper-weight, on her bedside table. Before I could move to reach it, Ella leaned over, slid the wanted letter out neatly. It had been neatly opened, too. None of this hasty ripping-open-with-the-thumb.

"She says that she was extremely perturbed, and having thought it over, sees the only solution in exorcism. Of course you know what that is."

"In a vague way. I mean I've read about it."

"Well, I intend to consult Canon Lauder—with your permission, of course."

"Oh, I'd agree to anything, so long as it didn't make things worse . . . Or upset Bob. I managed to pass Mrs Catherwood over as a woman interested in old houses. Bob didn't even see her. But a religious ritual . . . that might be more difficult. Bob would get angry, and anger is bad for him."

"I think we may rely upon Canon Lauder to be tactful. The point is, my dear . . . I cannot be expected to last forever. When I go, sooner or later, Elsie will be obliged to go into a geriatric place where she can be given her injections. And where would that leave Alice? With no home but that horrible house to which you are so stubbornly attached and in which she lived in complete terror."

That was indeed a cogent question, but I let it go. I was overcome for a moment, by the prospect of life without Ella. In my limited firmament she had been a fixed star for so long. She remembered birthdays and any other kind of anniversary. . . . She was brave and she was good. Pernicketty, conventional, a bit snobbish, she could be exasperating, particularly to anyone like me, but she'd leave a terrible gap. So of course I said, in the wrong tone of voice.

"Oh, for Heaven's sake, Ella, don't talk about dying."

One's perspective changes with age; when I was eighteen and my grandmother nearing eighty, I was sad, I felt bereaved, but she seemed—and had seemed to me for a long time—so old. It had seemed natural that she should die. And of course, while I haunted that hospital in Miami where Bob lay in a deathlike coma, I'd been prepared for the worst every moment. This was somehow different.

"I merely mentioned the fact that I am only mortal, dear, and that we have Alice's future to consider."

"I know. I promise you, I will. And I'll come in tomorrow and bring Bob."

"That would be very nice."

Downstairs I said to Elsie that I thought a visit from Doctor Taylor might do no harm. Elsie's face set like concrete.

"Mrs Spender want the doctor she'll say so. Mrs Spender say she don't want him, I go by what she say."

"Of course." But outside I looked at my watch. Just on eleven. I might catch him. His house, with surgery attached, was only on the other side of the square. Going towards it, needing to distract my mind, I thought what a triumph of mind over matter, his being called Doctor Taylor represented. His grandmother had run Elizabeth Garrett Anderson pretty close in the race to force the recognition of women as doctors. She had qualified; then she married, a man named Bennett, and was known, during her lifetime, as Doctor Taylor Bennett. But the people of Baildon didn't take kindly to the name. They'd known her father, possibly even her grandfather. To them the name Taylor was practically synonymous with the word doctor; so her son was Doctor Taylor, the Bennett dropped into obscurity.

Her grandson, the current Doctor Taylor, was a thin, rather harrassed-looking man who I had met briefly as a fellow member of the Parent-Teacher Association. Doubting whether he would remember me, I said,

"I'm Mrs Spender."

"I know. What is it?" What did I want, bursting in on him,

just as he was arranging papers and preparing to close his surgery and start a round of urgent house calls?

"My mother-in-law, Mrs Spender," I pointed towards Ella's house, "doesn't seem well. But she didn't want to bother you, so I thought . . ."

"You'd do the bothering?" For a second his worried face changed contour and took on a mischievous monkeyish look, almost immediately banished. "I didn't mean that, Mrs Spender. It's no bother. Is she in pain?"

"I don't think so. No. At least she didn't say. She said she was tired and having a day in bed. But I thought she looked pale. So I wondered . . ."

"There is nothing I can do. Except of course relieve pain, should it occur. She has a valvular lesion, of long standing. She has lived with it for years and been very sensible; and if she is now resting and not in pain . . . There is nothing I can do. But . . ." He scribbled a note on one of his papers. "I'll try to look in, later in the day. . . ."

He was a busy, an overworked man; hurried meals and disturbed nights showed in his face and his manner. I was not old yet, but I could just remember more leisurely days. On his paper-cluttered desk the telephone gave its raucous call. He snatched the receiver up and said, "Speaking! . . . Yes! . . . Yes! . . . No! On no account! I'll come right away."

Next morning I drove Bob in to see his mother. John, who had always been a sensible, reliable boy, was now quite capable of seeing that Tony came to no damage; and of switching on the oven at a given time.

Ella was up and dressed, and looked pink and white again. Perhaps, I thought, she was always pale behind the discreet make-up and her appearance had alarmed me yesterday because I was seeing her with a bare clean face.

"A most curious thing happened yesterday evening," she said. "Doctor Taylor dropped in for a glass of sherry. Most unusual for him; he is such an unsocial man. Very different from his father."

I was glad that he had been discreet enough to make his visit seem casual. He may have been a trifle out of line in telling me what ailed her, but perhaps he was issuing a warning.

Was Canon Lauder's visit that morning similarly contrived?

He'd never seen Bob or me, for he'd come to St Mary's after we moved to Gad's. I knew that Ella liked him and did not deplore, as some people did, his mild attempt to shift St Mary's towards a higher form of Anglicanism. Ella said she thought Matins and Evensong sounded nicer than Morning and Evening Service and she approved of the proliferation of candles. Also, of course, he played Bridge.

I suspected that she had talked to him on the telephone the previous evening, for he subjected Bob and me—especially me— to very close scrutiny. His rosy, well-fleshed face gave him an appearance of benevolence contradicted by his eyes, a cold grey in colour, rather small, very shrewd. Did he see in me a rather hysterical woman who had been listening to some old wives' tales? And worrying her mother-in-law.

Alice came back just in time to say Goodbye to us. She had attended Matins, but had stayed to help arrange the Lady Chapel for some meeting to be held in the afternoon.

"Gran, your flowers looked lovely."

Ella said, rather hastily, to me, "I sent the carnations, dear. They were so very *red!*"

The year moved on, into a hay-scented June. A busy season for most people. George Thorley had been as good as his word and every morning a very amiable, very idle young man whom at first sight I had mistaken for a girl—not only on account of the long beautiful hair, but with beads, with several bracelets—came up, dipped some buckets of water, planted main-crop potatoes, runner beans, tomatoes. I gathered strawberries and cut asparagus, and lettuces and radishes, and rushed them down to the Women's Institute shop and the private customers I had acquired. I was glad of the help, limited as it was, and thoroughly grateful to George Thorley, who was very busy too, with haymaking and with Agricultural Shows.

I tried to see Ella every day instead of two or three times a week, and just at this season I could do so without seeming to be watching over her; there was always something I could take from the garden. I noticed that she was cutting down on her activities slightly; playing Bridge less often in the evening, handing over some of her little offices.

"I feel, dear, that it is time for younger people to take over. I don't mean you, of course, you have your hands full, but your Mrs

Thorley, for example, no children and every labour-saving device known to man. I've suggested that she should take my place in the Flower Club.

"That should please her."

All the same it was sad. Flower arranging may sound trivial, but it gave the arrangers aesthetic satisfaction, and their exhibits, as well as raising money for many a good cause, had brought beauty into a world from which it seemed to be receding every day.

"I refused another job, too," Ella said with a little laugh. "Canon Lauder asked me to organise the provision of new kneelers for St Mary's. Various designs, but all on blue grounds to give a look of uniformity. Guess whom I foisted that on to?"

"I have no idea."

"Fred Murray-Smith! I don't expect you knew that he is a devoted embroiderer."

"Wonders will never cease." Hard-bitten old ex-Indian Army officer, living in a strictly run buff and brown house, kept in meticulous condition by his ex-batman, even more hard-bitten. Towards the end of our stay with Ella—just before we found Gad's —Bob and I had dined and eaten curry so hot that it almost blew our heads off.

For at least a month, even between ourselves, Ella and I did not mention Gad's. There were times, during that busy season, when I forgot for hours on end that I lived in a haunted house. Such work-induced amnesia never lasted long, however. I would become aware of Alice's absence; I'd look at Tony and wonder.

It was Ella who broke the silence. I remember the rich ripe scent of the basket of strawberries I had brought her and which stood between us as she said,

"This business of *exorcism* is very complicated, Jill. Canon Lauder has been *most* kind, *most* sympathetic, but there are difficulties. Apparently the Anglican Church has abandoned the ritual and even the Roman Catholics have become very wary. I suppose rightly so. With them it seems, it is no longer sufficient to ask permission from a Bishop—a priest must be specialist . . . Not unlike getting a driving licence. But I *think* we may now be on the right track at last."

She reached out and took from her pretty little davenport, a letter. Holding it well away—most people, normally sighted all their lives, become long-sighted as age creeps on—she read it again and said,

"It all sounds very pompous and legal. First you must be investigated to make sure that there is nothing frivolous or anything pertaining to undesirable publicity. I am fully prepared to say what I know. I shall shield Alice, of course, though it will be necessary to refer to her. And I took the precaution of getting a written statement from Mrs Catherwood. That was *totally* disregarded. However, I shall bring it up again when Father . . . really, how badly people write! It could be Jessop or Joseph, Jessop, I think. When he comes to make his preliminary investigations. And you will co-operate?"

"Of course. But it is going to be difficult with Bob." *He* mustn't be upset; *she* mustn't be upset, *thou, we, they* mustn't be upset; only *I*. *I* could be upset. And was.

Ella said, "I am not altogether sure whether this policy of concealment is wise. I know he would jeer, but we could bear that."

"He would get angry, Ella. There's that place on the side of his head where the exposed vein shows; it swells when he is angry."

And he was so often angered now.

"My God," he said, "if only I could get about, I'd ginger them up. Lot of lazy slobs. Here we are, June! They were interested last October; they wanted modifications, I made them. They deferred, they discussed, they keep me informed. I've worked like a slave, and what have they done? Sweet . . . damn all! June . . . and they haven't . . . even made a proto . . . type. I'll sell it . . . to the . . . Germans."

The vein swelled, and as always when he was angry his speech deteriorated. I hastened to soothe.

"Would it hasten matters if you went to Peterborough?"

"No! Fine impression . . . I should make. Shambling, stuttering. . . . They'd think . . . I couldn't design . . . . a corkscrew."

Poor Bob. He'd been so marvellously confident and optimistic; hardened doctors had remarked upon what an asset his attitude was. Now because he was progressing more slowly—or not at all, and his brain-child had been, not rejected, but subject to delays, probably inevitable ones, something seemed to have seeped away. Apart from lightning flashes of temper, he'd had such a sunny nature; now it was souring. Not towards me, however. After that outburst he said,

"My poor girl. I've mucked up your life. And . . . I meant . . . so well."

I said, "Don't talk rot, darling. I'm fine. So are you. This hitch is probably due to a little jam in, I quote—Those devious and uncertain waterways known as the usual channels. It'll get unjammed and you'll make a million."

But that night, in the big old four-poster, on permanent loan from George Thorley, I woke, as though somebody had shaken me by the shoulder. And something inside my head said: *It could be that the house is having an effect on him!* The grandfather clock, also a loan, struck three.

Beside me Bob stirred and turned clumsily; with one side weak the movement was difficult.

I asked, softly, "Are you awake?"

"Yes. For a long time. Thinking. Darling . . . you should . . . quit. Divorce me. You'd . . . be all right then. One-parent family. Everybody'd be . . . bending over . . . backwards to help you. And me . . . home for derelicts."

Pretend again! I said,

"If that's the best thought you can come up with in the middle of the night I don't think you're very inventive."

"Maybe I'm not. . . . Been thinking that . . . too. Maybe they've . . . detected . . . some flaw that had . . . escaped me."

That, coming from Bob Spender who *always* knew best, was a shattering statement. The idea that the house was affecting him lodged more firmly in my mind. It was despair, rather than terror, that I had felt outside that attic door. I longed at that moment to talk to Bob about it, tell him everything—except of course about my feeling for George Thorley, and offer Gad's as an explanation for his despondency; but somehow I couldn't do it. All I could do was give him a near-maternal kiss and assure him that everything would be all right.

However, in the morning I rang up George.

"I know you're busy with hay and the Shows, but if you could spare half an hour. Bob is getting a bit downhearted."

"Funnily enough, I was coming up this evening. I wondered if he'd like to come to the South Suffolk next Thursday. It's at Southbury this year, so he wouldn't have a tiring drive. I suppose you wouldn't care to come too?"

I excused myself.

And then, by one of those curious chances which Life does occasionally throw up, Father Jessop chose that very day to make his preliminary visit of investigation.

So far everything to do with this side of the affair had been conducted by Ella, who had also, incidentally, begun to correspond
regularly with Mrs Catherwood.

"He will drive himself," Ella said. "It is no great distance. His
headquarters are in Essex. I shall give him coffee—or sherry—and
tell him all I know, and I shall try again to draw his attention to
Mrs Catherwood's statement. He will then visit you. And, my
dear, I shall *pray* for a happy outcome."

I should have to give him lunch, but at this time of year it was
easy; salad stuff with hard-boiled eggs.

In appearance Father Jessop was exactly what I had expected,
priestly garb, thin ascetic face; but his manner was disconcerting.
A bit like a police officer sent to question someone of whom the
authorities entertained the deepest suspicion—tax evasion, drug
smuggling, murder. This impression was emphasised by the fact
that, having shot questions at me, he wrote—in shorthand—my
answers in a little book. And by another thing: he never permit-
ted me to say much; he always cut me short, quite courteously,
but firmly. "Yes, we shall come to that later." Or "If you would
just answer the question, Mrs Spender."

One of the questions was: Had there been any sign of polter-
geistic activity? I could only say, No. So far as I could tell nothing
had been moved by any supernatural agency; nobody had been hit
on the head by a flying saucepan.

Any visible or aural manifestations? I could only say that Alice
had heard bumps, that I had asked her, when next she heard a
bump, to call me. She never had.

Patiently and meticulously he discounted this, eliminated that,
and reduced the whole thing to what Ella had felt, what I had
felt, what Alice had felt—and to him feelings were not evidence.

He then came up with an ingenious explanation.

"Prior to your coming here, Mrs Spender, you lived with your
mother-in-law. Did it ever occur to you that she was opposed to
your move?"

"No. I should have said that exact opposite. She had been
obliged to give up her bedroom. . . . And three children, however
well-behaved, were a disruption in that neat house. I think she
welcomed the move, until she came to see this house and felt
. . ."

"Yes. I know." He flipped some pages of the little book backwards.

"You saw no significance in the alternatives which she suggested?"

"You mean . . . Buying another house which we could share. Certainly, since that would have entailed great sacrifice on her part, I considered it evidence of her sincerity of feeling concerning this house."

"Which she was not invited to share?"

"Good . . . Heavens, no! Why should she be? She has a perfectly good house of her own. Near the shops, near all her friends. . . ." My voice tailed off. Now he seemed not to be suspecting, but accusing me.

"Friends grow fewer with the years, Mrs Spender; and can never be a full substitute for family."

I said, "Are you trying to tell me . . ." My voice sounded too loud, angry almost. "I mean you are implying that my mother-in-law *wished* to share a house with us?"

"It would be a natural desire. And a feasible explanation."

"That I *cannot* accept. The consequent implication is quite unthinkable. I've known my mother-in-law for a long time. She is *absolutely* honest. I've never known her to tell a lie; she's far too . . . honourable."

"I am not suggesting otherwise. But we must allow for the subconscious, which often dictates in an extraordinary fashion."

"Then we'll allow for it. Let us postulate," good word, I thought, "that Ella—my mother-in-law, wished to share a roof—but not a kitchen with me, and came and saw that Gad's was not suitable; so she went upstairs and her subconscious took over and translated her dislike of the house into a conviction that it was evil."

"Stranger things have been known."

"But that does not account for *me*, Father Jessop. Or for Alice. Or Mrs Catherwood."

"The subconscious is an area peculiarly susceptible to auto-suggestion."

We were reaching that point of abstract discussion in which some priests were trained. How many angels could sit on the point of a needle?

I said, "Would you like to go up to the attic floor?"

"There is no necessity. But if it would help in any way, of course."

"Then may I offer you lunch?"

"That would be very kind. I do not eat meat in any form."

I was gently fatiguing as the French say, the salad, when Tony came in. He had been, for the last five or six days, the proud owner of a rather battered, third-hand tricycle which *his* subconscious mind was busy translating into a car. He made all the appropriate noises, low gear, middle gear, top gear, hooter. A stick tied to the handlebar was the gear lever. It kept him happy for hours on end. But he had an in-built clock of appetite and came in saying he was hungry. I gave him a quick wash—he had an infinite capacity for getting dirty. Then Father Jessop came down, having experienced—I could tell at a glance—absolutely nothing.

But—and it is a fact, I think, nobody brought up on the Bible ever gets completely away. "Out of the mouths of babes and sucklings," it says.

Tony said to me, "Mummy, may I whisper?"

Manners had been drilled into me so thoroughly that I said to Father Jessop, "Do excuse us."

"Mr Thorley's cross dog," Tony said in a whisper calculated to split an ear-drum. He gave me a conniving look, wrinkling his nose and his upper lip; a joke. Shared. "Don't let him kiss me, will you?"

I said, "Of course not. Would you like to take your plate and make a picnic?" He scuttled away. Father Jessop, eating salad with the impersonal air of a car taking in fuel, seemed not to notice this small exchange of words which to me were meaningful. Finally I said, "That *was* relevant, you know. Tony is too young to pretend. Even *you* can hardly regard *him* as the victim of mass hysteria."

"Is there, in fact, an ill-natured dog?"

"Yes." I told him about it.

"And your little boy sees few strangers? Then the association is obvious. Any person unfamiliar to him takes on the semblance of hostility."

"Casuistry," I said, "is an art."

"You intend that as a reproach? Or are you using the word loosely? It means concerning one's conscience. To the best of my ability I have conducted this inquiry in a conscientious manner.

The outcome, of course, is not for me to decide—that will be for my superiors. Believe me, that you dislike me, and all that I represent, has no bearing on the matter. None at all. I shall report, impartially."

Yes, go away; dismiss Ella as a cunning old woman, telling lies; me as a dupe; Mrs Catherwood as a fraud, Alice as a silly little girl. . . . Tony as a child living too insulated a life.

"You are wrong in imagining that I dislike you—or what you represent. It is simply that I cannot share your clinical approach."

"No. I fully understand. You need sympathy. I will risk a very personal remark, Mrs Spender. I think you may *require* sympathy with problems quite disconnected with your attic floor."

Nudging middle age, mother of three, I blushed as though I were twelve.

We took leave of one another civilly, he assuring me that I should be hearing from his superior, and I thanking him—for what? He was an appalling driver; his mini stalled twice and then went off down the drive in a series of bucking leaps. I telephoned Ella.

"He's gone. I don't think he's going to *do* anything."

"Nor do I. I thought his manner very casual and very inquisitive. I fail to see how my age, or whether I have ten children or one had any bearing on the point in question. . . ." She still sounded ruffled. "Never mind, dear. I still have another string to my bow. I'll tell you about it when I see you. When will that be?"

"Tomorrow." Ever since I had learned that she was, if not actually ailing, in rather a frail state of health, I'd tried to look in, if only for a moment, every time I went into Baildon. On this Friday morning I was keyed up to note any sign of that loneliness which Father Jessop had apparently detected in one short visit. And naturally, I found them. Tiny things.

"When I relinquished my active part in the Flower Club," Ella said, "I said that of course, all the committee meetings could be held here, as in the past. This is so central. But your Mrs Thorley thinks otherwise. For those who drive—and the majority do—her house is more central. Or so she says."

"I suppose Mrs Gordon will give you a blow-by-blow account of all the meetings." Mrs Gordon, a friend of long standing and not long widowed, could always be relied upon to make up a four for Bridge, or share a little outing.

"Oh, didn't I tell you? She's gone to visit her daughter who married an American. If she likes California, she may stay there. I told her it was insane at her age, but it was like talking to that chair."

Even the Boy Friend, dear old Fred Murray-Smith, did not escape criticism.

"He has those kneelers for St Mary's on the brain. He has a team of embroideresses—some living at quite a distance—and he regiments them like soldiers. Last time I saw him he told me how many miles he had driven in one week, delivering materials, collecting finished pieces and encouraging laggards."

I thought: Yes; Father Jessop was perceptive, though perhaps wrong in his conclusions.

Ella then abruptly changed the subject.

"If, as we both think, Father Jessop proves to be unhelpful, I shall appeal to Mrs Catherwood. Not only is she more sympathetic, but she has infinitely more experience."

There was no real reason why I should feel dismayed. Mrs Catherwood had herself spoken of the necessity of the ritual of exorcism being *properly* conducted. I could rely upon her to be careful. Would she be orthodox? And that was a strange question for me to put to myself; I had as a rule so little use for orthodoxy. Still, I did hope at that moment that Father Jessop's superior would take Gad's seriously and send a priest—or two; I had a vague idea that where some things were concerned they were coupled—like old-world hunting hounds.

Nothing happened for an extraordinarily long time. I made some futile, forlorn little attempts to alleviate Ella's loneliness. The tropical weather continued, and for Bob's birthday I suggested having a party in the garden. John said he could rig up all that was needed for a barbecue. He'd seen one at some Youth Club outing and was sure he could improve upon it. I was reasonably certain that even Fred Murray-Smith would approve of an impromptu, out-in-the-open meal; I'd ask the Thorleys, too, and maybe drop a little hint about Ella and the Flower Club; I'd tell John to invite, not only Terry but any other friend who had a bicycle, and Alice could do the same.

Ella said, "It is very kind of you, dear, but I hardly think I should fit in."

"I thought of it because, this way, you need not come into the house." By this time we had been there more than a year and she had come only twice; on her first visit of inspection when she talked of evil and haunting, and begged me not to go there, and later, one brief luncheon, after which she had taken Alice away. Never again; and not now, even in the garden. "I think I am getting a little old for such things, dear."

"What about you, Alice? It is Daddy's birthday."

"I might," Alice said, but as I left she came with me to the door.

"Mum. I can't. You see Elsie keeps going off."

"What do you mean?"

"Funny turns. Only two nights ago she had one. I *thought* I could smell gas, so I went along. One jet was full on, but either she hadn't lighted it or it had blown out, the kitchen door was open. And there was Elsie, absolutely purple—and unconscious. Like being asleep. You know."

"And what did you do?"

"I turned the gas off. And telephoned Doctor Taylor."

"Good girl! And then what?"

"Elsie had to have some sugar, at least glucose. You see, if you're diabetic you either have too much or too little. Elsie knows and keeps some sugar lumps handy, but sometimes she isn't quick enough. Then she goes off. And it upsets Gran. So I don't think I ought to leave them, even for Daddy's birthday."

Alice was right; but the whole setup was wrong. Too much responsibility, too soon.

In the end Bob's birthday was celebrated in two places and in very different ways. I could not deny John his barbecue nor let Ella and Alice be left out. I took Bob and Tony and a fully prepared meal along to St Giles Square and John and twenty of his friends had a barbecue you could smell a mile off.

On the way home, Tony asleep on the back seat, Bob said,

"Jill, we have to face facts. You may not have noticed, but Elsie has got to the end of the road. I've been working it out; she must be eighty. And I doubt whether Mother could boil an egg—and she's too old to learn now. It may . . . sound . . . silly, but she . . . never had to, so she never did. It would be like . . . you or me . . . in old age . . . having to learn . . . to play the piano. God knows . . . you have enough to carry and I shouldn't say this . . . but I must. . . . She'll never find another Elsie. I think . . . we should . . . offer her a home. I know . . . I'm a bloody nui-

sance. . . . But she is my mother . . . and so fussy. She'd be . . .
happier with us . . . if you . . . could bear it."

"Look, darling . . . To begin with you are *no* nuisance. Let's
get that straight to start with. There isn't a more independent
man in the world. And I would most gladly offer Ella a home and
I'd cook. But she wouldn't come. For a reason you would never
understand—not in a million years."

"Tell me. At least give me a chance to understand."

"All right. But not just now. Never the time and the place, as
somebody said. By the smell of it the boys have set the whole
house on fire."

Two corners to negotiate and both leading to inclines. Unless I
were careful with the worn gears on the old car, I'd be bucking
along or stalled, as bad as Father Jessop. And in the lane I had to
be careful, so many boys on bicycles . . . Some of them shouted,
"Good night." They had not set the house on fire. John and
Terry, who was staying the night, hauled Tony off to bed. He was
more than my ricketty back could manage at the end of a long
day.

I went into the kitchen and made a pot of tea. Then in the living room, I said,

"Now I will tell you all, and please, Bob, don't interrupt
me. Above all, don't laugh."

I had—as usual—been wrong. Bob listened as it all came pouring out and he did not even *look* mocking. Just profoundly concerned and pitying. I didn't cry, as I had done when telling the
same tale to George Thorley. I did my best to sound phlegmatic.
At the end I said,

"So you see, darling, the position I'm in."

Bob heaved himself up and stumbled over to where I sat on the
settle. He sat down beside me and put his good arm, his right,
around me, holding me close.

"You poor, silly girl. Keeping it all to yourself. Why didn't you
tell me? Don't you know that bottling things up is bad for you?"

"We, Ella and I, thought you'd jibe. Ella said you couldn't believe anything you couldn't measure with a slide rule."

Then he did laugh. "Just because I don't go to church! In any
case my belief or lack of it doesn't affect the existence of anything. I might not believe that this is Saturday—but it'd still be
Saturday for most people."

Once he had commiserated with me on being left with only half a man, which was true, in a physical sense. He had a flaccid leg and arm, his speech was sometimes hesitant but what was left of Bob Spender was worth half a dozen other men.

"Something must be done about this. To start with I'm going up to that attic myself, first thing tomorrow morning."

"The stairs are very difficult."

"I'll go up on my hands and knees and come down on what I was once chided for calling my bum."

He was up there for a long time. I interrupted my baking three times to go to the foot of the attic stairs and shout, "Are you all right?" His third answer was irritable. "Of course I am."

Tony was with me in the kitchen, diligently clearing out the bowl in which I'd mixed the ingredients for a chocolate sponge. When, at last, Bob came through from the living room, Tony dropped the spoon and bolted. Mr Thorley's cross dog again?

Bob, tired by the unusual exertion, dropped down on a chair. I produced coffee and the mid-morning cigarettes.

"I've been flaking off whitewash. . . . Somebody . . . to say the least . . . highly peculiar . . . painted a wall up there. Then somebody smeared black paint, or . . . tar, and . . . then . . . somebody whitewashed. The face I managed to uncover was . . . devilish. I think perhaps your Mrs Catherwood had something there."

"Did you *feel* anything?"

"Curiosity. A kind of disgust."

"No despondency?"

"No more than usual. But that's not to say that other people didn't. Even *I* admit that feelings are things that can't be measured on a slide rule."

It was wonderful to be able to talk about it.

Father Jessop wrote me a letter which could have come from a lawyer; rejecting a dubious case. He did indeed use the word. The case had been subjected to the most careful consideration and was not deemed suitable for such extreme measures as exorcism. So that was that.

During that week another letter came, too; from the Peterborough firm who had been interested in Bob's invention; they finally surfaced with the news that they had been in negotiation with their German counterparts who were willing to make it a joint production. They were now anxious to take an option, £2,000 down (non-returnable). Patent rights must be established, prototypes made, etc, etc.

"There you are, darling," I said. "I told you you'd make a million."

"Well, at least it is launched. But before I dance in the street I shall need to know that some ironmonger in Wuppentaal or a blacksmith in Hockwold hasn't forestalled us. . . . Still, even now, two thousand is not to be sneezed at. I must sound out George Thorley. The original idea was his. I only put it on paper."

Orthodox approaches having failed us, Ella appealed to Mrs Catherwood, who responded gallantly. Yes, she did know a priest, Father Lomax, who was extremely interested in the occult. She would get in touch with him on our behalf before she herself went off to America on a prolonged lecture tour. Father Lomax was currently without a parish, being one of those who could not accept the change from Latin to English Mass.

"All the better," Ella said, surprising me again, for she had always seemed to me a very middle-of-the-road Anglican who had accepted Canon Lauder's small changes on purely aesthetic grounds. And she was totally ignorant of Latin.

But in fact, Ella was changing, even in looks. Maybe that pretty beige-blonde hair had always been the result of regular visits to the hairdresser's; it was now fading, growing duller and greyer, and no longer cut and curled, let to grow and turned up at the back of her head into a surprisingly tiny bun. Oddly, her eyes had faded, too, from bright cornflower to periwinkle blue. Age and circumstance were catching up on her at last. The cherished look had vanished.

Changes in the house, too. Less clutter, and more dust.

"I have put my few silver ornaments away, dear. Elsie has all she can manage now with the cooking. And even so I am worried about her. I feel that she needs more *expert* care than I can give. The injections are no longer *entirely* effective. But I simply cannot consign her to Sunset Court, can I? Not after sixty years."

Paternalism had become, within my time, a dirty word, but the thing itself was not without virtue.

Mrs Catherwood wrote to me, a hurried cryptic scribble. "Sure you're doing the right thing. Hope all goes well. Have alternative host ready. See Mark 12:5."

Father Lomax might have no parish, but he seemed to be extremely occupied. It was September before he wrote to say that, if convenient, he would like to come on the 18th—a Saturday—and stay the night. He would take no food until after the ceremony, and anyone intending to participate should abstain from food after Saturday lunch time.

Food had become my bugbear—not the preparing and the cooking, but the organising. I was now trying to feed two separate households, and just at my busiest season. Doctor Taylor had finally insisted upon removing Elsie; not to the Old People's Home, of which both she and Ella had such a dread, but to the Hospital, where she could be observed and tested, and if not cured, at least relieved. That left Ella, genuinely helpless where food was concerned, and Alice, who was at school all day. Alice did at least get a dinner at school, and although she, being faddy, often made derogatory remarks about school food, John spoke well of it. Smashing grub, he called it. There was some wonderful comestible known as Meat Loaf, which I tried—without much success—to produce myself; there were beefburgers and chips; fish fingers and chips. All the same, he was always ready for his supper, and it was my desire, my intention, that Alice should also have some sort of meal in the evening. And what about Ella, during the day?

The answer might appear to be that she should go out for a meal; but that was difficult. Baildon boasted three public eating places. There was the *Hawk in Hand*; "Under New Management," it always was; it served a business man's lunch; a bar snack and a proper luncheon in the newly decorated (it was always being newly decorated) restaurant. There was also a place with a pretty shady reputation, known as *Round the Clock*, and one of those ever-so-dainty tea-shops, tea, coffee, biscuits and scones. A luncheon in the restaurant of the *Hawk in Hand* might have served, but it was terribly expensive. Ella tried it once and said, "It was extremely nice, and of course all the waiters knew me, from the Ladies' Luncheon Club. But I only had one dish, nothing to drink, and it was over two pounds. Two pounds ten, or as you would say two-fifty. I simply cannot afford . . . Not, my dear, that I want to bother you with my financial problems. But since Arden and Somers went into liquidation, my income has been even more reduced. Jill dear, you must *not* worry about me. Whatever Bob says, I *can* boil an egg. And I do. I fully realise that Alice is growing, but they say a boiled egg with whole-meal bread and butter is quite as nourishing as steak."

Outside the boiled egg area she was genuinely incapable. She did not even know that an oven should be hot before meat is put in. Of potatoes—"I just went to answer the phone and they boiled dry, quite ruining my saucepan." Of apples—"There are some apples that simply will not cook. I stewed some for two hours and they just got harder and harder." She'd cooked eating apples, of course.

In September the hot, dry, and but-for-the-moat ruinous summer, ended in torrential rains and days as dark as November. Through the rain and the mire I flogged to and fro, with produce to sell, and food that could either be heated up by Alice, who could at least distinguish between the switches of the oven and the grill, or eaten cold.

Just before Father Lomax's letter came, I said,

"Honestly, Ella, I know how you feel, but apart from that top floor Gad's is all right. If you liked I'd make the drawing room into a bedroom for you. Alice could sleep there with you—or I would. It'd be so much easier—for you." That day she'd washed and ironed some handkerchiefs; they couldn't go to the laundry because she never got the right ones back; she'd left the iron, still switched on, on the ironing board and damned nearly caused a fire.

"Dear, I know. It would easier for all of us. But until something is done, I cannot enter that house. And it is absurd to say that whatever it is is contained on the attic floor. Alice was terrified everywhere—and affected in other ways. As you well know."

I tried an alternative—in my mind. We'd come back to the pretty little house. I'd make everybody a good breakfast; leave something for Ella's lunch; drive Bob back to his worktable, tend my garden, collect my produce, let Tony work off his energies on the tricycle, which was now more like a car than ever since George Thorley had found somewhere one of those old-fashioned horns with a bulb. Then I could do the whole thing in reverse, go back to St Giles' Square, make supper for us all.

Double journeys for my poor old car, already on its last legs, more muddling about for Bob—now busy on a new project which often occupied his after-supper hours. And John would most strenuously object.

For me, Father Lomax's letter came just in time.

He came, on an ink-black evening, though it was barely six o'clock. He was driving Mrs Catherwood's Jansen and emerged from it like a grub from a chrysalis; such a small man and so thin, so frail-looking that when he began to haul a quite oversized bag from the car, I ignored my aching back and said, "I'll take it."

"Thank you."

"Would you like to see your room straightaway?"

"Thank you."

Possibly he weighed seven stones, certainly not more, and his head, almost completely bald, looked too big for his body. His eyes were remarkable; that warm green-brown that for some reason is called hazel, with whites as clear as a child's, though what remained of his hair was quite grey. Eyes any girl might have envied, but their expression was disconcerting; even when he looked straight at me he seemed not to be seeing me.

I'd made Alice's room as nice as I could, even to a bowl of my very best chrysanthemums, the kind that fetched 9p each at the W.I.

I said, "The bathroom is next door." I'd made that nice, too, and threatened John with unspeakable things if he entered it for what he called "a quick swill," which meant that blobs of soap-froth, the size of a 10p piece, bore evidence that he had washed, though the towel said otherwise.

Father Lomax said, "Thank you," again.

"I know you said no food, but I could make tea, or coffee. . . ."

"No, thank you. I shall do very well." Aiming his glance at something deep inside my head, or far behind it, he said, "I understand that neither you nor your husband is a member of *any* religious community."

"That is so."

"Were you baptised?"

"I was born Methodist; they call it christening. My husband was baptised—Church of England." Ella, so very correct, would have seen to that. He should have been confirmed, too, but by the age of seventeen he'd lost faith. Probably I was the only one who knew why, probably I was the only one who knew that Bob, up to age of sixteen, had had faith until he saw his father die of cancer. He'd only spoken to me about it once, saying briefly, "I prayed. Not that he should live, I knew by that time that death was inevitable, but I did pray, with all my heart, that he shouldn't *suffer*. He was the kindest man that ever lived; he just happened to be impervious to morphia. They gave him enough to kill a regiment, but he died in screaming agony. . . . I gave up then and went over to St Augustine; if God is benevolent He is not omnipotent; if He is omnipotent, he is not benevolent. So I quit."

"But not confirmed?"

For the sake of politeness, I said, "I'm afraid not," instead of a plain "No."

"Will there be present any person in a state of grace?"

The only person I had asked to come was George Thorley, who was to bring his dog, and if by being in a state of grace meant coming straight from Holy Communion, the answer must again be: No. George was strictly a Christmas and Easter communicant, Sunday being his busiest day since only one of his workmen would work on Sunday, despite the overtime pay, and cows must be milked and fed as usual. Doris went regularly to church, but she had no part in this. George had decided against telling her—much to my relief. "She does so love to talk," he said, "within two days half Suffolk would have heard a highly coloured tale."

"A pity, but never mind," Father Lomax said.

Since we were now talking about tomorrow, I said tentatively, and feeling rather foolish, that Mrs Catherwood had suggested an alternative host and that I had asked Mr Thorley to bring his very unlovable dog.

I think Father Lomax, as well as abstaining—and asking us to abstain from food, had imposed, if not silence, at least the minimum of speech upon himself.

"Not strictly essential; but harmless," he said.

Just then Tony yelled up the back stairs,

"Mummy! Mumm*ee*. I want my supper."

Something within Father Lomax sprang to instant attention.

"A child?"

"Yes. My youngest."

"How old?"

"Just over three and a half."

"Baptised?"

"I'm afraid not."

"Good. Baptism is a form of exorcism. With your permission I will baptise him before I undertake the other task."

With that he turned away, dismissing me. He threw open his big suitcase and I caught just a glimpse of a huge crucifix, silver and ivory, beautiful, if a crucifix can ever be said to be beautiful; personally I shrink from them, as I would shrink from models of the rack, the thumb-screw, or the Iron Maiden of mediaeval times. Below there were some folds of gorgeous-coloured stuff.

Both Bob and George, in their differing ways, had been very tolerant and indulgent about the whole thing. Bob had at least admitted that feelings could not be measured on a slide rule; and he had been worried about conditions in Ella's house since Elsie had been taken away. If anything could persuade her—and Alice —to come to Gad's and share family life, he was, he said, prepared to stand on his head. George was more guarded, partly because it all reflected upon his beloved Gad's; he called it a lot of mumbo-jumbo; but if it would ease my mind he was willing to go along with it. As for the dog, he had an inbuilt devil, one more couldn't hurt him.

Once, in the happy days at Scunwick, I had attended—wishing to be friendly—a Catholic baptism of a child, the daughter of a friend of mine. She and her husband were absolutely decent characters, and as the ceremony proceeded, in essence a purging of a three-week-old child from original sin, I stood there in my church-going hat and thought: What utter rubbish! What an implied insult to that little baby, who could not yet have entertained even a sinful thought.

And now, there I was, years later, committed.

Bob said, "Well, it can't do Tony any harm. He'll probably think it's a game. Having started on this, we might as well go the whole thing."

I had taken the precaution of getting John out of the house. He was old enough to be inquisitive, so he'd gone off, happily enough, to spend a week-end with Terry.

Except for the absence of godparents, Tony certainly had as splendid a christening as any prince. I'd warned him beforehand to stand still, not to talk, but such behests were unnecessary. Father Lomax, in full panoply, was awesome even to my eyes. His outer robe was white and stiff with embroidery in gold and silver thread; his stole was purple, with gold fringe. Everything else was equally sumptuous; he had come well-prepared; all he needed from me was a small table, he said. I thought wildly—Just the one thing we don't own! Then I remembered that John and Terry had spent a blissful wet Saturday at what they called carpentry. The result of their work was in John's room.

"Where?" I asked. "Where would you want it?"

"In the infested place."

I hauled it up; it was heavier than it looked, and at the turn in the stairs I was awkward, or it was awkward; my back gave its preliminary protest. Like a voice saying: Unless you watch it, I'm going to give you Hell.

And now I had to go into the attic itself, not skirting by, as was my habit. The feeling that emanated from the place, utter hopelessness, hit me again—and this time with a sense of inexplicable guilt.

In a flash I saw how wrong I had been. Listening to Ella; taking notice of Alice's feelings, misconstruing my own. And being led, simply by being weak, into dabbling with something better left alone.

Then all that was resistant and sceptical in me asked, Why? What would be better left alone—if there is nothing here, *what is to be left alone?* Argue your way out of that!

It took Father Lomax a very few minutes to transform that clumsy table into an altar; a blue cloth, like his robe heavily and richly embroidered; candles in silver holders, a small, beautifully chased silver bowl; a censer, a bejewelled bauble, its chains dangling.

I had another thought.

For so many hundreds of years people had complained about the outward grandeur of the church, asking how it fitted in with the teaching of a humble carpenter from Nazareth. I saw why. The worldly grandeur of princes, kings, emperors had to be matched, outmatched. Authority must be seen to be authoritative. An Emperor must hold the Pope's stirrup.

"Send the child to me," Father Lomax said. "I will deal with the rest later."

I said, humbly, "Do you wish me to be present?"

"Better not."

So I went downstairs and found Tony and said,

"Now remember what I told you. Just stand still and do whatever you're asked to do. And then . . ." I opened the fridge and showed him the covered bowl of ice cream, homemade, in the freezing compartment. "You can come down and help yourself."

"Two helps?"

"As much as you like."

Very soon after our coming to Gad's, in fact as soon as Alice had mentioned bumps in the night, I had put that crooked flight of stairs out of bounds, saying I doubted its safety. So Tony was entranced to be allowed to scramble up them.

I stayed just long enough to hear that this service was to be in Latin. At the Scunwick baptism we had been given a folder, Latin on one page, English, for the benefit of the ignorant, on the other. So standing on the landing and listening would not enlighten me much. I went down and found that George Thorley had arrived, very formal-looking in a dark suit.

Since the evening when Chum had bitten through his leather leash he had taken his walks on a chain, no thicker or heavier than a bicycle chain, but very strong. It had a catch which fastened to his collar, and at the end a similar catch; this, passed round the dresser leg and snapped into one link in the chain, bigger than the others, tethered him securely. He greeted me with his usual snarl, though over the months I'd done my best to ingratiate myself with him, I'd even tried bribery with biscuits and bones. All to no avail, and yet, at this moment I felt that my suggestion of *using* him had been callous, a bit too light-heartedly suggested—and as light-heartedly accepted by George; one devil more couldn't hurt him. It was unlikely that a dog would feel what I had felt, despair and the complete futility of everything; but who knew? Also, would what Mrs Catherwood called an elemental be content with a dog as dwelling?

Bob said, "Don't look so worried, darling. If what's going on will just satisfy Mother and get her here, we're doing the right thing."

"I'm thinking about the dog."

"Then don't," George said. "If he hadn't had this appointment with the Devil this morning, I'd damned well have shot him on Friday. He bit *me!*"

The ultimate offence! George had gone through the gamut of excuses. Chum was young, he'd learn; he was too much inbred; he was nervous; somebody had been frightened just by the sight of him, and dogs could smell fear; somebody else had been too bold and tried to stroke him. I'd heard the lot. Now Chum had over-stepped the mark.

"Where?"

"I think we won't go into that," he grinned. "He ruined a damn good pair of breeches."

"Did he break the skin?" Bob asked. "If so you should have an injection."

"What for? Rabies? If you ask me, we're all pretty mad as it is."

I said, "No, seriously, George. I think they now give tetanus in-jections for dog bites."

"Load of old rubbish. If his teeth weren't clean to start with, they were when they'd been through all that good whip-cord."

Before there could be any further argument, Tony clattered down the back stairs.

"The lady says she is ready now. But you must wait outside. *I* can go in. *I* have something to do." He was bursting with self-im-portance, and his eyes were just like Ella's when she was feeling emotional, wide black pupils with just a rim of blue.

Bob went towards the front stairs with shallower treads and a sturdy banister. I knew he hated to be watched, even making that comparatively easy ascent, the flight to the attic would be more exacting, so George and I waited.

"Is it true about the dog? Or did you say that just to make me feel less guilty?"

"It's true. I can show you my breeches. I'd taken the brute for his run, then I fetched his food, put it down, and was just at the gate of his enclosure. He came at me from *behind*." He sounded genuinely aggrieved. Then with a complete change of manner, he said, "Jill, if this . . . performance doesn't satisfy the old lady or make you feel happier, we'll think of something else. Maybe I could get possession of Park Old House again; I did a good job making that into two. In any case, of course you could have your money back."

"That's mighty noble of you, George. But . . . well, I like this house. Apart from that one place."

"I know. Well, let's hope a drop or two of holy water will work."

"You don't believe a word of it, do you?"

"Do *you?*"

"I truly don't know. I'm doing this for Alice—and Ella. . . . I think we could go now."

Sometimes, not always, there'd been a faint foul stench near that attic. I had not been aware of it when I went up earlier with Tony for his lonely baptism; but now it was very strong, indefinable but nauseating. I thought: Whatever it is, it *knows* and is mustering its forces.

And Father Lomax was mustering his. Even his voice had changed. What few words he had said to me had been spoken in a low, ordinarily civil voice; and what little I had overheard of the beginning of baptism rite had been gentle. Even an unknown language has its cadences.

He said, in English, "Come no further!" And that was an order. So Bob and George and I halted on the landing. Three people not in a state of grace; mere witnesses. I *had* cricked my back and knew that I must lean against somebody, or something, or drop. On one side of me was Bob leaning on his stick; not to be leaned upon for obvious physical reasons; on the other side stood George, sound as rock, but not to be leaned upon for other reasons. So I leaned against the wall and had but a limited view. I could hear though; and I heard Father Lomax's voice take on, not merely authority but absolute aggression. He held the beautiful crucifix high, and with his free hand scattered water from the beautiful bowl. And my son waved the smouldering censer as though he were sixteen years old and had been doing it since he was ten. . . .

And then there was the most awful noise, a crash, as though the roof had fallen in. I disgraced myself by fainting, a thing I had never done before in my life.

I came to on the settle in the living room. Bob's big chair had been pulled close and he sat in it. He was rubbing my hands. George Thorley was on his knees, propping up my head with one arm and trying to make me drink brandy. They both looked pale and extremely concerned. Father Lomax sat slumped in a chair, completely exhausted. (I discovered later that he had fasted for forty-eight hours.)

Tony wasn't there. Fear seized me.

"Where's Tony?"

"In the kitchen. Eating a chicken drumstick and ice cream simultaneously," George said. "Try a sip of this now."

Bob's sound hand tightened on mine.

"My God," he said, "you gave us a scare."

I whispered, "Offer Father Lomax a drink." I was too slack-minded to wonder then where the brandy had come from. Actually I'd been out long enough for George to take my car and rush down to Park.

Father Lomax accepted, only stipulating that he should have a little water with his brandy.

George said, "Well, I must now go hunt my damned dog. He can't have gone far, lumbered as he was."

I understood that when, feeling better, and remembering my obligations, I went into the kitchen.

The huge dresser there was, literally, part of the house; it formed the greater part of the wall between the kitchen and the living room. Its back was the wall, its front supported on two stout legs, at least four inches in diameter. The one to which the dog's chain had been attached had been literally ripped away, so that now the whole thing sagged.

I'd never had anything really worthy of that dresser, just ordinary, utilitarian household crockery, but I'd been fond of the things I had, and now all were smashed. Out of the unsightly mess I salvaged only two things, a saucer and my wooden pepper mill. If only I'd had sense enough to set the table beforehand!

Now we had no choice but to follow Tony's example and eat our cold chicken without bothering about plates.

I have never seen a few mouthfuls of food work such a transformation on anybody as Father Lomax's few bites did.

"Food tastes much better, eaten like this," he said cheerfully, munching away. "Though of course I regret the reason." He eyed the pile of broken shards. "I was negligent. I should have warned Mr Thorley of the force which no chain can hold. Tennyson was in error in imputing the strength of ten only to the pure in heart."

"Where *did* the cross dog go?" Tony sounded rather apprehensive.

"Uncle George will take care of him," Bob said. "You don't have to worry. Nor do you." He shifted his glance to me. "If Ella now decides that this is a fit place to live in we shall have china galore."

"She should so decide," Father Lomax said, speaking as though it were a matter of choice between two colours. "It *was* a very strong infestation, but it is ended now. Yes, you may be assured of that."

I said, "Tony, go and see if there are any of the red apples down, you know which ones."

When he had gone I asked what to me seemed a vital question.

"If somebody shoots that dog, what happens then?"

He turned his luminous eyes on me.

"You have an inquiring mind and *some* belief. I cannot answer you exactly. Deprived of a habitation, the evil may dissipate itself. It was concentrated here; I gave it a destination. As you did, just now, to that dear child. It is perhaps an oversimplication . . . but if you had said, Go away, the response might have been less immediate, less willing, less directed, even, perhaps, negative." He rubbed his high, domed forehead. "It is a little difficult to explain without sounding puerile; and there are so many variables. Each case is different. This, for instance, would have been easier for me had I had the support of positive believers—even a member of the Salvation Army." That was said half-jocularly, and I managed what I feared was a rather pallid smile.

Almost immediately he said he must be going; he had to drive back to London and he was not yet thoroughly familiar with Mrs Catherwood's car. He parted from us with solemnity, wishing us better health and more happiness and bidding us remember that Tony was now a child of God. He said, "Peace be with you, and upon this house."

Tony came in with some of the red apples.

"Oh, has she gone? I wanted to give her some. I rubbed them shiny. She was a very nice lady."

Ella's house, which had once smelt of potpourri and lavender water and other pleasant things, absolutely stank. I'd made a beef-steak pie which simply needed to be heated through. She'd put it in a roaring-hot oven before she went to church and left it to burn. Returning to the stench, and some black charcoal in a pyrex, she'd taken it out, put it in the sink and turned the cold tap on it. "It made a noise like the shot of a gun," she said, mildly surprised. "I've been hunting around for a replacement. I seem not to have one exactly the right size or shape." She looked quite distraught, wild wisps of hair all adrift, a smear of dust on her forehead and a fair-sized burn on her right hand. I was truly happy to be able to say what I had come to say; but first . . . "Where is Alice?"

"Gone to borrow half a loaf. Since I ruined the lunch we had to eat bread and cheese. There is not enough now for supper and breakfast. I'm afraid I am not a good provider."

I said, "Ella, I want you to come to Gad's and make a test. A very nice old priest called Father Lomax purged the place this morning, and judging by one result, he did it most effectively. If you think it's all right now, I'd like you to stay . . . Apart from everything else," I gave myself high marks for tact, "it'd be such a help to me. Tony is now far too much for Bob to manage, and when I take him around with me, he is a nuisance. I have to lock him in the car at each stop while I unload, and even so he tampers with the dashboard."

Ella began to cry and then Alice came in, carrying what looked like a whole loaf in a plastic bag.

She turned on me like a young tigress.

"Have you made her cry over that pyrex dish? She couldn't help it. It was my fault. And I was going to buy a new one first thing tomorrow."

Ella's tears, as I knew, came and went in unpredictable fashion. They stopped now and she said, "Alice! That is no way to speak to your mother! Apologise immediately!"

Alice said, "Sorry, Mum," but with a glare that was anything but apologetic.

"If you will go upstairs, Alice, and look in the bottom of my wardrobe, you will find a little blue overnight bag which I keep packed ready for emergencies. Pack a similar one for yourself— including whatever you may want for school tomorrow."

"Why? Where are we going?"

"To Gad's."

Alice looked horrified. "Oh no! Gran, please, please, not that. I know it has all been awful since Elsie went, but I have tried. I'll try harder. I won't forget things. I will learn to cook. . . ." Hysteria, threatened.

Ella said—her Rock-of-Gibraltar quality well to the fore,

"Alice! Come here, dear. How long have you known me?"

Checked, Alice said, "Why, Gran—well, as long as I can remember. All my life."

"And in that time have I ever done or said anything to make you consider me untrustworthy? No. Then trust me now and go and do what I asked."

When Alice had gone, I said,

"How much does she know?"

"Nothing; except, of course, that she was frightened at home and I said I understood and brought her here, where she ceased to be frightened. We never discussed the matter; she is far too young."

I spared a moment to consider Alice. More guilt.

"She never even *told* me that she was frightened. I think John knew. . . ."

"She knew that you were very busy, dear. She's a considerate child. Or she might have feared that you would laugh—she's very sensitive, too. But if the absolute evil which I sensed on that first day has been . . . overcome and if you really want me . . ."

I said, "Ella, you aren't all I want! Of my pitiable collection of goods, I now have one saucer and a pepper mill."

"Why? What happened?"

"It was part of the procedure. I'll explain, later. In the meantime, if you could lend me a few things, cups, plates . . ."

"But, dear, I told you, when you moved to Gad's and went to buy a teapot, I had at least three unused. I have masses of things, in the cupboard under the stairs. Nothing of value of course or they would not be there. Now, let me think. In the old days the laundry used to come and go in a hamper. I think I could find it."

She found it; she opened the cupboard, Ali Baba's cave. I took only essentials, aware that I should have to lift the hamper into my car and that I had already broken my back once that day. However, when I lifted it I felt no pain at all.

Alice remained withdrawn—some people would have called it sulky—during the drive. Ella chattered quite gaily, mainly about the beauty of the golden September afternoon. Both she and I addressed Alice occasionally and drew monosyllabic replies. I was anxious to get home and the experiment made.

John was there, with Terry. Terry's mother, though very hospitable, was a haphazard housekeeper and believed that boys could forage for themselves on Sunday evenings, so we often had Terry's company at Sunday supper. The boys, directed by Bob, had already made a good temporary repair to the dresser, and were promising to make a new leg in the woodwork class during the next week. They had also cleared away the mess. They carried the hamper in and would have started redecorating the dresser, but Ella said, with truth, that everything needed to be washed first. "You'll see to that, won't you dear," she said to Alice. "You wash, the boys can dry." The sight of the new—and if worthless, rather beautiful teapot inspired Bob to say he'd make tea. Ella gave me a beckoning glance. In the living room, she said,

"Now. I propose to go up and test the feeling of the place."

I then remembered that she had an unsound heart, so I said I'd go first. Not that I was really a good test subject; I'd never felt what *she* claimed to have felt, and what Mrs Catherwood and Father Lomax had confirmed. I'd simply felt despair, and now and again been conscious of a faint, foul stench.

That, at least, was not there this afternoon; the attic floor smelt of apples, eaten long ago, and the incense. I went right into the attic itself and stood, almost inviting despair and despondency. I could very well have felt, if nothing so extreme, a certain *dismay* at the prospect before me. There was the question of fitting Ella in, both physically and psychologically; which rooms should be hers, so absolutely hers that she would have her own place, while being one of the family. Alice was hostile to the move —to me? And I'd seen the boys exchange glances, mocking, but not lacking in significance when told to dry crockery. Bossy grandmother!

I knew all these things in my mind, but I did not feel them. What I felt was joy at being all together again, the surety that whatever cropped up, I could cope . . . and my back was strong again.

Then I noticed a curious thing. Bob had tried to understand, to investigate, had flaked off some whitewash and found what even he described as a nasty face. All I could see in the space where the whitewash had been removed was a beautiful garden poppy, pink, with black stamens.

I went down and Ella was waiting at the foot of the twisty stairs.

"I think, it's all right," I said. I added, sounding very urgent, "If you feel . . . anything in the least hostile, call me. I'll wait here."

I watched her as far as the first bend of the stairs; I saw a particular pathos about her ankles and what showed of her calves. They'd always been slender, no doubt, now they looked shrunken, an effect accentuated by the shoes she wore; the type known as court, with high, rather waisted heels.

She was gone rather a long time. I went on to the stairs and called, "Are you all right?" "Yes. Just looking at something." From below there were calls, "Tea's made! Tea up!" I yelled back, "Coming! Just a minute."

Ella came down. She looked radiant.

"Not a flicker," she said. "And I've had such a wonderful idea. I do hope that you and Bob will approve."

Afternoon tea as an institution had ceased to be regarded at Gad's. Bob or I made a pot if we felt like it and drank it in the kitchen. Our real tea was high tea or, as we called it, supper, a solid meal, with tea to drink, taken at six, or thereabouts. Such an arrangement fitted in with working habits—as working people learned long ago. How this would suit Ella was one of things which might have worried me when I stood in the attic. Bob had shown a nice sense of situation by having tea brought into the sitting room, and at the same time murmuring to me that he had switched on the oven. John and Terry accepted a cup of tea and a biscuit as they would have accepted anything for the stomach, and went off. Alice somehow managed to give the impression of a grand lady doing a bit of slumming. Only Tony protested. Brought in from his tricycle by calls about tea, he said, "Is this all?"

"It would make a delightful apartment," Ella said. Two attics thrown into one would be quite a spacious drawing room; the third would be my bedroom, with a part of the landing—all waste space now—made into a bathroom."

"What about those fiendish stairs?" Bob asked, forestalling me.

Once again Ella surprised me.

"I thought about them. Possibly the person who planned them had some reason for giving them a double twist, but a new staircase, rising towards the *other* end of the landing, could be straight and far less steep. If I had a pencil . . ."

I provided a ball-point and some paper and she scribbled. Bob watched and said, "Quite feasible." I don't suppose that even he had guessed that part of his talent was derived from his mother. He sounded surprised.

"Here," Ella said, pointing, "I should have a tiny kitchenette so that I could make tea, or coffee, or boil myself an egg. I have no doubt that it would all be very costly, but I have a house to sell. . . . I think I could afford to instal full central heating, which would be to the advantage of us all, and even, if the planning people agreed, alter those dormer windows into French ones, opening on to a balcony, with a few plants in pots. That is all I need, nowadays, especially as my windows would overlook your garden."

Alice's, the only dissentient voice in the atmosphere that all was for the best, asked, "What about *me?*" Ella and I began to speak simultaneously. A bit of jumble, assurances that Alice was home —would always be welcome in Ella's apartment, should have a bicycle. . . .

The jumble was interrupted and ended by the sound of a shot, very clear in the still afternoon air.

When everybody spoke as Gad's being up and Park being down, they were being literal. Gad's stood higher, surrounded by George Thorley's arable fields; beyond them the ground rose into what, in rather flat East Anglia, was called hill, meaning slight rise. Its summit and its inclines comprised a farm, devoted mainly to sheep. Its owner was a man of marked melancholy nature to whom the long drought had been a great trial. Another few days without rain, he'd frequently said, and he'd shoot himself. He threatened the same thing indirectly when he had his rate demand, his income tax form to fill in, when his car broke down, "Might as well shoot yourself and have done with it." Bob and George Thorley said that potential suicides never made such threats, and were inclined to joke about it, varying the formula sometimes into—I'll shoot *you.*

The drought had broken; it was Sunday when even the tax gatherers cease to trouble and the rate demanders take their rest, and yet somehow that one single shot sounded ominous, coming as it did from that direction. We'd never heard a shot from Top Farm before, and had, indeed, no evidence that Mr Sutton even owned a gun. And what, but himself, could he shoot? On his sheep-nibbled land a rabbit would have found it hard to exist.

I said, "Bob, do you think . . . ?"

The special kind of communication that had enabled us to stay in close touch when Bob was speechless, and when his speech was greatly impaired, worked again.

"He could have, poor bastard, and probably made a balls-up of it. We'd better go see."

Ella's face and Alice's face registered identical expressions. What language! With ladies present, too!

"I'll go," I said.

"You will drive me, Honey; and stop when I tell you to. You've had enough today without a lot of rawhead and bloody bones."

I gave a few instructions about beds and sheets and pillows, and going through the kitchen, switched the oven to a lower heat. Then we got into the car and I drove. A short distance, but uphill. Well away from Mr Sutton's house Bob said, "Stop here." It may have been my fancy but he seemed to me to walk better, stumping away with his stick, using it as a motive power rather than a support.

Mr Sutton came out of his house and gesticulated. I relaxed. No need for me to brace up and help to get an ineffectual suicide into Baildon, to the Hospital.

They came towards me. I still thought Bob was walking better, and I remembered the optimistic doctor who had said improvement would come, even if it seemed slow.

I wound down the window and could hear Mr Sutton speaking with more than his usual grievance against life in general.

". . . off the place for weeks on end," he said, "and never at week-ends, people out with their curs. Then today I just go down to Muchanger, sick-visiting. Get asked to stay for dinner and come back to bloody massacre."

"How much damage?"

"Remains to be seen. Had to shoot the thing first, then call the vet. Save what we can, but the damage may not be all on the surface. Fright like that could make ewes abort. Good afternoon, Mrs Spender. Nice of you and your husband to look in, see what happened. No sight for anyone, I can tell you. Dog was mad. Always was. I've said to Mr Thorley twenty times if once—If I couldn't get a better dog than that, I'd shoot myself."

I said, "I'm very sorry indeed." I was sorry. Sheep are such defenceless things. *And the most generally accepted official sacrifices!* Even Christ—the Lamb of God!

"One thing though," Mr Sutton said, "I always insured the flock. Well, must get back and do a bit of first aid till the vet comes."

Bob came round to the driver's side of the car and said,

"Move over, Honey. I'd like to *try*."

"Well, if you feel like it." I was pleased; a little dubious.

"I do. And where better than on a road where there's no traffic?"

He was wrong; on that short bit of unfrequented lane we met George Thorley in his Landrover. He had his gun propped beside him.

"Too late," Bob shouted as we drew level. The two vehicles slid past each other, and both drivers backed, very expertly in the narrow lane. Bob explained what had happened and George said,

"Thank God! I was so damned afraid it might be a child. . . . I've been on the hunt ever since. All the villages, Layer Wood. I never thought of poor old Sutton. . . ."

Hooting, the vet came up behind George, who just had time to shout,

"Can you give me some supper? I've had nothing since . . . I'll just see if I can lend a hand. See you!"

Hoping for the company of Ella and Alice, more or less expecting Terry, I'd made a huge casserole, rich with the mushrooms which had just begun to whiten one of George's meadows. I had also a dish of what in high places is called Pommes Lyonnais, simple to make, tasty. Followed by baked apples and cream, this was a good meal, whether one called it supper or high tea. Alice seemed to have resigned herself; Ella was happy, full of talk about her plans. George and Bob had a lively argument about insurance.

That little whining wind which makes indoors on an autumn evening seem to be so extra-valuable sprang up; and now I could look around with satisfaction. All is safely gathered in—at least for the time being. . . .